STARCHILD

A Science-Fiction Romance Adventure Novel

JIM G. STYLES

ARPress
45 Dan Road Suite 5
Canton MA 02021
Hotline: 1(888) 821-0229
Fax: 1(508) 545-7580

Ordering Information:

Quantity sales. Special discounts are available on quantity purchases by corporations, associations, and others. For details, contact the publisher at the address above.

Printed in the United States of America.

ISBN-13:   Softcover   979-8-89356-832-5

                eBook   979-8-89356-833-2

Library of Congress Control Number: 2024908961

In loving memory, and appreciation, of my Parents,
Blanche Rosemary Styles,
&
Reverend James Styles,
Who believed in my work
before anyone else.

And to Kate Johnson, who has taken up where they left off,
Helping me the rest of the way.

StarChild

7

My destiny brings me to the moon Fewer
snakes are there than by the Nile,
fewer insects and fewer people.
I will go with Ed or go alone.

The year 2000 was once tomorrow,
And yesterday I came from the cave
To talk with Socrates about love
and harmony. It seem long ago
that the moon was something to wish on:
now it's an object to walk upon
and the man in the moon shines no more,
having been upstaged by the woman who
makes the Cosmos her theater.

And moonbeams are shafts of silver air.

—Moon Song #7
by
Ms. Joanne Seltzer (Appearing
here with permission from the
author)

II

DEDICATION & ACKNOWLEDGEMENTS

This book is dedicated to several very special people without whose constant help, support, and encouragement this work would not have been possible; or at least not as good, or as rewarding to write.

And at the top of this list is, of course, the good Lord Jesus whose loving hand I could feel guiding, directing, and inspiring me while writing he is following pages—the first person I wish to thank here for all His help, love, and support. For what you like in <u>StarChild</u>, PRAISE HIM: for what you don't like, BLAME ME!

However, on a more Earthly plane, there are also my former wife and still good friend, Judy, and my parents, James and Rosemary Styles. As it is I owe all three so very much for all their support—the many forms it all took during the writing of this book—including how they put up with all my various moods as I struggled, labored, and worried over <u>StarChild</u>.

Thank you all so very much. I can never repay all of you for everything that you've all done for me in my life. Thank you!!

Yet there are others as well out there who I also wish to remember here for all their kind thoughts and support. Good and dear friends (past and present) such as Ms. Mitzi Phillips, Ms. Joy Apperson, Lewis & Gloria Palmer, Ms. Jeri Flick,

Mr. Boyd K. Jackson, Joanne Seltzer, Loni K. Anderson, Jeanne Jensen, Robin Bianco, Ms. Elissa Malcohn, and Ms. Harriet "Deedee" Rex. And while I might have lost contact with some of these very dear people, I nevertheless remember them all with fond memories, wishing to remember them as well here.

And while I have this unique opportunity I also want to acknowledge the inspirational music of Deborah ("Blondie") Harry and "Oldies 101.1 FM" in Spokane, Washington. They likewise played a large part in the creation and expansion of the StarChild universe in my mind's eye, offering me much needed encouragement alongside the good people at "1-800-4-PRAYER" (the "National Prayer Center") who helped bolster my spirits during trying times indeed.

And last, but NOT least I also owe a big vote of thanks to professors Judy Adams and Alan Lamb of N.I.C. ("North Idaho College") for all their invaluable assistance and advice. Taking time from their busy schedules each of them advised me on important particulars appearing in StarChild while likewise giving me fresh, new ideas and insight which greatly improved this book.

Professor Adams was very helpful with the scientific/technical aspects of StarChild while Professor Lamb and I shared some rather interesting talks concerning the realities of actual historical matriarchate societies as I created here the "Tammyite Matriarchate"—supporting and encouraging me above and beyond anything I could have hoped for when originally contacting him for help.

And on an interesting side note I'd also like to thank Norman Lear for his excellent TV series, "All That Glitters", that planted the seed years before it took root. My favourite of all the great TV Series' he created and I love. I just wish I could find "All That Glitters" on DVD.

So, to all the above, I want to say, "thank you", expressing to all of the above my sincerest appreciation. I hope each and every one of you enjoys StarChild.

And this holds equally true for each and every one of you out there in the so-called 'real' world reading this …

StarChild is dedicated to all of you as well, your support likewise appreciated.

—Yours in Christ,
Mr. Jim G. Styles

INTRODUCTION

For those curious-minded individuals reading this who might wonder, my main purpose in writing <u>StarChild</u> was to create a positive portrayal of a matriarchate culture/civilization—the society in <u>StarChild</u> a kinder, gentler matriarchy in which the men are treated with both tenderness, respect, and nobility by the women; the women nevertheless remaining in control.

In <u>StarChild</u> women are portrayed as strong yet gentle, aggressive yet sensitive, and both decisive and self-assured while also loving and deeply spiritual. Throughout the following pages they are portrayed as resourceful, intelligent, and courageous as well as chivalrous and compassionate in their treatment of men.

And for their part the men in <u>StarChild</u> are likewise portrayed as both gentle, loving, nurturing, supportive, and devoted to the needs of others as well as both intelligent and self-confident possessing both great inner strength and courage. Even though they renounced long ago all claims to domination, the control of others, they all the same don't allow themselves to be neither abused, insulted, and/nor mistreated.

So while I freely admit that there might be a couple of women and men on the following pages who happen to be obvious exceptions to the above rule of thumb, I include them here only as an example of what the men and women in

<u>StarChild</u> are *not* about. The object here wasn't to portray women as more masculine or men as more feminine: my aim here to extol instead those virtues both already possess, qualities in each that often go sadly ignored within our own present culture/society, while also taking into account those obvious properties already recognized in each.

Then again <u>StarChild</u> is more than just a story depicting some future matriarchate culture/society in the early 30th century; dealing as well as it does with the far past—how male dominated societies first got their start to begin with. In <u>StarChild</u> I put forth a possible answer to what I, personally, consider a very real and obvious anthropological mystery---a purely fictional answer of course ... many believing *in fact* that Human society was, originally, matriarchal in nature.

Yet, even so, my primary reason for writing <u>StarChild</u>, my devotion to creating a positive portrayal of a matriarchate civilization in <u>StarChild</u>, stems quite simply from my deep and abiding love, respect, and admiration of women. In fact it is no exaggeration on my part when I claim to believe in the intrinsic superiority of the female of the species, some of my reasons for believing in female superiority listed on the following pages:

Others.... well ...:

Which is why it should come as no surprise to anyone concerned I view the matriarchate system as depicted in <u>StarChild</u> as making more sense; being more in keeping with what's both natural and beneficial in life, than what we know and have today.

However, be that as it may, I also enjoy being a man, appreciating my own gender, believing as well that men also deserve respect, fair play, and justice in life. In my opinion the superior administrative ability of one doesn't imply in any way that the other deserves (in any way, whatsoever) to be treated with cruelty, disrespect, or contempt.

In short, those who hold power by virtue of their superior ability, their superior qualifications, duty-bound to treat those under their rule with both kindness, sensitivity, and thoughtful behavior.

"With greater privilege comes greater responsibility" is a moral imperative reflected quite clearly in <u>StarChild</u>, I myself believing as well in both "The Code of Feminine Chivalry" as well as all the other social, political, sexual, and moral principles upon which the "Tammyite Matriarchate" in <u>StarChild</u> is based, considering myself as I do as much a devout "Tammyite" as anyone else depicted on the following pages.

So having said all the above I guess another good reason I had for writing <u>StarChild</u> are all the negative portrayals out there of matriarchal/matriarchate societies in both literature, television, the movies and other forms of popular entertainment today.

Throughout the vast majority of fictional material dealing with his particular subject such societies/civilizations are usually portrayed in a very poor light indeed... both sexes badly drawn... the matriarchate cultures therein likewise portrayed as lacking any true spirituality or compassion.

All too often in such fictional entertainment the women are portrayed mostly as cruel, sadistic, androphobes while the men are continually typecast in either one of two ways (depending mostly on the gender of the author in question)—as either perpetually abused non-entities with no sense of self-worth whatsoever, or as perverted monsters who deserve to be stomped into the ground for no other reason than being men and therefore evil.

Soooo…. for those individuals out there who might accuse me of making the "Tammyite Matriarchate" (named after its founder in StarChild) sound a tad too Utopian in nature, that's why I did so. After all the bad publicity matriarchies have received in the past I decided that it was high time indeed they received as well some positive treatment.

In fact I'll go you all even one further, freely admitting right here and now that StarChild is just as much a love-story/romance novel as it is science-fiction—this to be especially noticed in Part One of StarChild: *"Of Women and Men"*.

However, for those of you who prefer a more science-fiction/adventure story, don't worry: Part Two of StarChild just the thing for you. And for those of you who also prefer well-developed characters, poignant Human drama, and more than just a little mystery as well then StarChild is right for you, too. So now that I've had my not-so-little say here, I guess it's high time I get on with the main event … the main reason we're all here … StarChild!!

—Jim G. Styles

Prologue (Part One)

"SCARLETT'S FEVER"

(Wednesday, October 27th, 2038, AD)

And so this day's world comes to an end,
The devil's last victory now at hand,
The ashes of victims a constant blight,
While the stench of evil now fills the night …
    And those few of us left don't seem to care,
    That death-camp winter now chills the air.

Nowhere to run,
Nowhere to hide,
As freedom and justice,
Are all swept aside …
    Scarlet men now taking the lead,
    Their sinful ways spreading like weeds.

Yet even now hope's on the way,
Goodness and mercy having their say,
God finally coming to set us all free,
Passing along His final decree …
    Promoting Woman to rule over man,
    Leading the way with a much sweeter hand!

****

Death, damnation, darkness, cold. Cries of despair, hopelessness, and the constant stench of evil. The culmination of all the Human soul dreads; the fever of plague, pestilence, and famine holding the entire world in their cruel, sadistic, grip.

Calamity without end in sight, waves washing now over nearly every land, the waters cleansing now the poor Earth of all its suffering; the "Lion's Roar" crushing now their very progenitors under the awesome sound of their mighty bellow...

Patriarchate rule now passing into oblivion...

And as that horrid state of Human affairs reaches its ultimate climax, a future quite different just around the corner, the master architect of all this mayhem cries out his ultimate blasphemy, the end of all his pernicious scheming now in sight:

"I am the Lord thy God!", that vile creature of all time did vent all his burning rage...

"I am the Lord thy God!!", that fearsome dragon declared yet a second time still, high hopes dashed against the Risen Rock quickly approaching...

"I AM the Lord thy God!!!", that author of all heinous evil cried now a third time yet, summoning at last with his foul declaration the only one greater than he:

"NO!!! You are NOT the Lord God Almighty!!!", a supreme voice even mightier than his denounced him from behind—a sudden light flooding the dim, dark, chamber in which that father of all lies did rant and rage:

"But I Am that I Am! I am the Creator of all that you covet. I am the Alpha and Omega, the Lord Judge of all who oppose My Holy Will: And for this day's work I pass final judgment on both you and all mankind. From this day forward the rule of man is over, the rule of Woman begins eternal!"

"DAMN YOU NAZARENE!" that serpent of old turned at last, facing his archrival—a glorious figure in the whitest robes of absolute splendor, a golden crown resting upon His noble brow.

No time left to protest the Risen Lamb's just decision, choosing to flee instead that scene of shattered fortune, that wicked monster made a quite hasty retreat, leaving in the wake of such humiliating defeat that pathetic creature of mere flesh and blood he possessed up to now for so very long.

And as Colonel Philippe "Sanguinary" Scarlett looked around him, left now on his very own... abandoned now by both God and devil... he gazed, aghast, beyond that grand balcony across the dark-again chamber in which he now knelt, bowed and beaten.

Gazing out over that land he once ruled with bloody hand, a fallen tyrant forsaken, he watched with horror that mighty wall of ocean sweep away with a thunderous roar both he and his once terrible empire—a mountain of water relegating all such as he to the hoary pages of herstory past.

Prologue (Part Two)

"TEARS OF SORROW"

(Thursday, September 4th, 2910, AD)

Quite aware of what might be waiting for them back at the colony, troubled by what she might be forced to do once back there, Raechal realized she couldn't risk taking the small child sitting next to her back to "Paradise".

Under no circumstances could she take back there the young boy sitting at her side, riding "shot-gun" as it were in the front passenger seat of the jeep in which mother and son raced across an alien landscape far removed from that which they first came from.

No… this was something she had to do on her own!

With this in mind, she threw at once her arm out in front of him, slamming her foot down… hard… on the brake pedal below her. The racing jeep coming to an abrupt stop, the forward momentum of both their bodies were held in check only by their seat belts snapping them roughly back into their original positions.

A sudden, violent, jolt.

"It's all right sweetheart", she tried to comfort him, the immediate shock of their sudden, brutal stop having set the young child to crying.

"Why did you do that, Mommy??" he whimpered through his tears, a plaintive sound. Mingling with the thick dust floating on the blue/green air they left muddy streaks running down his face, the pale yellow/brown dust of the dirt trail they traveled beginning now to settle:

"That hurt!!" he whined yet again, rubbing himself where his seat belt dug deep into his tender stomach.

"We have to talk, Rodney", Raechal began to explain in a soft, yet serious voice. It was a tone reserved for those special occasions on which she needed to discuss something with him, something sure to upset the seven-year-old boy still rubbing his flat belly in absolute confusion.

"About what??", he asked… slowly… a definite trace of dread creeping into his already unsteady voice.

"I have to go back to the colony and try to stop them from doing something really bad", she continued, getting out now of the jeep. Rodney watched his mother with wide-eyed, childish trepidation make her way to the jeep's rear, removing a large canvas backpack from in back of his seat. Although he knew intellectually what was coming his young mind refused on a more emotional, basic level to accept it.

"Mommy has to go back there and do something really, really important. But she also doesn't want anything bad to happen to you", Raechal added, placing the heavy canvas bag down to the edge of the meager road—a dirt trail leading back to the one and only 'home' either of them knew, or had left in life:

"So I'm going to leave you here until I've done what I have to do there. Then, when I'm finished, I'll come right back right away for you".

"*Noooo*, Mommy. Don't", Rodney moaned in utter despair, in deepest misery, recovering at last from his initial shock just enough to finally speak up:

"I want to go back with you!!"

"I know, sweetie," Raechal assured him, fighting all the while her own overwhelming desire to burst out weeping: "You must believe me when I tell you that I really, *really* don't want to leave you here, but I'm *soooo very* afraid that something really, really bad will happen to you there if you go back to Paradise with me. And you mean more to me than anything else in the whole world".

"No, Mommy!!", Rodney insisted through renewed tears, crying again uncontrollably.

"I know, honey, but you can't!", Raechal pleaded for his understanding, tears making their way down her face as well: "If you come back with me there you might die. And it would kill Mommy inside if anything bad ever happened to you".

Too stunned by all taking place around him to make but a single move, Rodney remained quite still—motionless—as his mother unbuckled through her tears his seat belt, lifting him out of the jeep…

"There's enough food in the pack to last you for tonight's diner and tomorrow's breakfast if you eat only half of what's in there each time. I should be back no later than early morning, just after both suns come up, although I hope to be back for you by sundown tonight.

"However, if I don't return for you by then, or by noon when the suns are directly above you, I'm afraid that you'll have to walk back to Paradise on your own".

It was only then it sank into every fiber and sinew of his very being, his very essence, every emotional and mental level at his disposal, that his mother was indeed serious…

Convinced like an arctic chill cutting through his very soul his mother was serious, Rodney began right there and then to struggle about in Raechal's arms, howling and thrashing about like an enraged bobcat—Raechal setting him down on the ground, giving him a gentle but firm shake, unable to subdue her son with mere words alone.

Never before in her life had she ever shaken him!

Getting through to him in the end Rodney fell silent instead, abandoning both his verbal and physical protests, standing in front of her… immobile… his face crumpled up in an expression of hurt surprise.

Nor did he even take any notice of Raechal's loving arms wrapped now tightly around him. Giving him one last hug before leaving him all to himself, her arms wrapped tight about his small, pathetic form her son just stared, empty-eyed, over her shoulder.

Feeling completely abandoned inside, convinced now all was indeed lost to him, including her, he was at a total loss for how to respond— his wide, blank, expressionless eyes staring out into empty space as Raechal held on with all her might to her only child, afraid to ever let go.

In the end it took every ounce of willpower she possessed to finally let go… let go of her young son's rigid, unresponsive body.

Backing slowly away from him with heavy heart it tore her up inside to see his almost catatonic expression, realizing this was how they'd remember their last, precious, moment together. Sure now she'd never see her son again, what began as a growing suspicion became now an unshakeable conviction, a bitter faith she could no longer renounce.

Convinced now she was rushing headlong towards her own demise Raechal couldn't help, but wish she could leave him with more than just some miserable backpack full of food alongside feelings of both desolation, and abandonment.

Realizing that loving him now meant having to leave him behind like some deserted puppy abandoned by the roadside, she still couldn't help but hate herself for doing so, looking upon the forlorn expression he now wore on his small, pitiable face.

Turning swiftly away from him in one quick move least she lose her wavering resolve Raechal climbed back instead into the nearby jeep. Gunning its engine as she did so wave after wave of unreality swept over her as she sped away, the distance between mother and son growing ever greater.

And feeling inside "uncomfortably numb" it wasn't for several moments what she did, no matter how necessary, came crashing down on her like a ton of bricks.

"Please forgive me, Rodney", she wept over and over again, her body wracked with jagged, hysterical, sobs:

"Mommy is so very, very sorry!!!"

****

The jeep taking his mother away from him passed at last out of sight, leaving only a trail of dust in its wake, by the time Rodney's mind began functioning yet again through that haze of disbelief holding him in its icy grip.

Despite her insistent reassurances she'd return for him he knew for a fact she was going back to "Paradise" to die.

Overcome yet again with an overwhelming sense of utter panic, he began at last to chase after her quickly as his small, young, legs could carry him—crying out as well in a desperate, pitiful voice for his mother to come back for him.

It wasn't long after traveling only a couple dozen yards, or so he realized just as quickly there was no hope of his mother ever coming back… *ever*…

XII

stopping dead in his tracks once understanding he'd never catch up with her on foot.

Nor was it long after this sad realization it occurred to him as well it would soon be night. The afternoon suns already beginning their slow decent in the far west Rodney trudged slowly back to the spot where his mother just discarded both him and the backpack.

Having no desire at all to stumble around in the coming dark, Rodney sat himself down instead next to the heavy nylon sack in question. Searching its contents he looked for the battery-powered camping light he saw his mother pack away there just that very same morning.

Wanting it for the light it would provide it would suffice in lieu of a campfire when night soon claimed the entire land. Heat wasn't a real concern given the nights there were quite warm enough. And while there were no dangerous animals, no fleshly predators prowling about this new moon-world he now lived on... no mindless beasts-of-prey to ward off with its bright light... he still felt better with it on.

Not that he'd have really minded much if there were such alien carnivores skulking about those lush, verdant forests beyond that otherwise tranquil meadow his mother just left him by. At that moment dying was all-in-all preferable to how he felt right then and there:

Nor was that the first time Rodney, even though just seven years old, entertained serious thoughts of death, serious thoughts of suicide itself. Knowing quite well what the immediate future held in store for him the only problem was that *they* wouldn't consider at all letting him die:

At least not yet!!

Sitting still by the dusty trailway as midnight made its eventual approach, sitting cross-legged next to the small lamp of before, the only other source of illumination present was the massive world around which Rodney's new home orbited. A grand, Jupiter-like gas-giant it was surrounded as well by bright gold rings that seemed to almost reach out and touch the earth-like moon on which Rodney now found himself.

Found him now sitting there all alone, abandoned.

Casting ethereal shadows across the surrounding landscape, a rosy-hued glow almost phosphorescent in its quality, the impressive red/yellow/orange planet above filled indeed the entire night sky with awesome splendor.

A sight Rodney used to enjoy very much gazing at all he could manage now contemplating its swirling, cloud-covered surface was a dull sorrow. A fatalistic resignation to his inevitable fate, it was more adult than childlike in its emotional quality.

No need to tell him he was all alone now, everyone he ever loved in life taken from him now in brutal fashion. Ripped away from him in the most violent manner possible he fell asleep only when no longer able to keep his eyes open, his growing fatigue proving too much to do otherwise.

****

Sleeping late into the morning despite the golden-white glare of twin suns against his closed eyelids the only reason he woke up at long last was a terrible pain in his lower abdomen.

Stirring at last from his exhausted slumber with an urgent need to empty his bladder it proved quite painful indeed. So much so it was all he could do to manage just a couple of steps before having to relieve the unbearable pressure building within, finishing only after what seemed like an eternity of just standing there.

Once done it was only then he noticed as well his hunger pangs, gathering up both the backpack and camp-light from the night before. Carrying each a fair distance down the road the very idea of eating so close to where he just 'did his business' grossed Rodney out to the max.

Not really wanting to eat, too hungry all-the-same to deny that painful emptiness now gnawing away at him, he sat himself down at last in the short, stubby grass growing all about. Eating whatever he could find rooting around in the backpack his mother left him he washed down his morning meal with swigs of warm fruit juice from a small plastic jug he found there as well.

Not that he really paid any serious attention to what he ate however, his every thought was focused instead on the absolute dread he felt even thinking of his eventual return to 'Paradise'—the colony his people established on this accursed world only two years earlier.

All the same though there was still no denying young Rodney would, even so, still go back.

Despite the sure horror waiting his arrival there, feeling all the same no real choice in the matter, it still remained the only home he knew. The only home left him since his people made their long journey there from Earth. The very thought of his cozy room back in that very same living unit he shared once with his parents filled him with a definite sense of security…

Albeit a false one!!!

Completely focused as he was on all those fearful images he knew awaited him upon his return, young Rodney paid little-to-no attention at all to the food he likewise put in his waiting mouth.

Eating in fact only to quell the all-consuming hunger dwelling in the pit of his empty stomach it wasn't until later he took notice at last notice of his mid-morning meal; a peanut butter, chocolate chip, and honey sandwich held in trembling hands.

His all-time favorite made just the way he liked it he did no more at first than just savor the sweet taste, finding there yet another like it in the nearby sack.

However, as he ate the last one, it occurred to him in just as sudden a flash this wasn't just the last of his all-time favorite sandwiches there, but the last one his mother would ever make for him *ever again*.

Raechal Roderick no longer 'out there' to make him another just like it that sweet treat held now so secure in shaking hands symbolized for him his entire family forever lost.

No longer hungry realizing this young Rodney nevertheless made himself eat that last bit of sandwich his mother prepared him with such simple love. Not finishing it would be in his young mind's eye a betrayal of her very memory, tears streaming down now ruddy cheeks!

And so it was he just sat there under the noonday suns, eating through his tears…

Eating…
Crying…
Feeling **helpless**…
Feeling **hopeless**…
Feeling **dammed**…
Feeling **cursed!!!**

CURSED!!!!

Part 1

"OF WOMEN AND MEN"

Tuesday, February 12th, 2915 AD
To
Friday, February 15th, 2915 AD

**"The more things change,
The more they stay the same".**

—Anonymous

****

**"For the Lord has created a new thing in the earth—
A woman shall encompass a man".**

—Jeremiah 31:22 (*NKJV* Bible)

****

"I've always depended on the Kindness of Women".

—Jim G. Styles

****

**"Q: Why are men no longer allowed positions of authority in human
civilization?
A: Because Earth has only one continent left...
AND WE'RE DARNED IF WE'RE GOING TO LOSE THAT ONE, TOO!!".**

**—Ancient Matriarchate Riddle
(Early 22nd century??)**

A Quote from *The New Matriarchate:*

"No one must allow themselves to ever forget the obvious truth that both sexes will ALWAYS and FOREVER need one another in so many ways reaching far beyond mere procreation, the genetic wellbeing of the species. The social, cultural, emotional, and even spiritual health and stability of the entire Human race must also to be considered.

"No matter which gender played the dominant or passive role in Human society, each always needed the other for positive counterbalance.

"Even in the past, when gender roles defied the natural order of things, men still needed the positive influence of their female counterparts in order to provide both emotional continuity and an essential sense of spiritual completion—two halves of a united whole without which there can be no true Humanity.

"So now that the natural order has finally been restored, women once again in control of Human civilization, they will likewise forever need men. Need them not to just sire their children, but also to love, cherish, hold close, and share with all forms of Human intimacy.

"Now that men have accepted once-and-for-all that theirs isn't to rule, but to follow women will still need them all-the-same as an emotional outlet upon which to lavish both love and tenderness—partners in life with which they can share all their innermost feelings: their laughter and tears, love and compassion, anger and joy, problems and successes.

"And by that very same token this likewise means that, from now on, men will always need still women as a central part of their very lives.

"Not only will they now need women to take charge, provide for their needs in life, protect them, and be the mothers of their children, but also for the expression of their previously ignored nurturing abilities in Human society:

"Such abilities as to render emotional support, comfort, love, gentility, tenderness, and sympathy while likewise sharing with others their innermost selves in a non-dominating fashion free from any selfish desire to manipulate.

"Furthermore, in addition to all the above, women will also continue to play as before a major role when it comes to men's feelings of self-confidence, self-esteem, and self-worth.

"Therefore it will be of vital importance that women continue to nurture such feelings within men while remaining as well the leaders, protectors, and providers in their female/male relationships they were always meant to be— *destined to be!* —as the stronger sex".

—The Rt. Reverend Tammy E. Garfield.
THE NEW MATRIARCHATE
—2056 AD—

CHAPTER 1

"A SAPHIRA FAMILY PORTRAIT"

(Tuesday, February 12th, 2915, AD)

That day began like any other for Commodore Jenniboni Kaye Saphira, her husband Andrei, and the rest of their close-knit family unit since moving to Demeter just a little over one year ago—none having any idea how that fateful day would set in motion a series of events altering not only their lives, but the entire course of Human herstory.

Nor did they have any way of knowing all this as the alarm clock in the Saphira mistress bedroom ripped loose back then with its usual, irksome, early morning buzz—this followed right away by Andrei's weary arm reaching out from under the bedcovers.

Cutting off the shrill sound in mid whine, his open palm connected sharply with the de-activation pad on top of the annoying device.

Muttering beneath his breath, mumbling to himself how much he hated that darn thing, he gently went about disentangling himself from his sleeping wife's tender embrace.

Sitting up instead on the edge of their bed, bare feet sinking into cool, deep blue shag carpeting, he heard Jenniboni murmur something unintelligible from right behind him, the weary woman rejoining as well the waking worlds in her own good time.

Reaching up Andrei turned on as well the nearby lamp on the nightstand right next to their bed, its soft white light driving away at once the surrounding darkness just as Jenniboni asked in a groggy, but clear voice the time.

"Its 07:00 hours, love", he informed her straightaway, glancing briefly at the close-by clock's bold, red display panel.

"Very well, then. In that case I guess I better start getting ready for my meeting later this morning with Stasha", she sighed, propping herself up on one elbow, watching her husband stand up.

Getting out of their bed, stretching stiffened muscles, Andrei held his arms out to either side, arching his back replete with a little groan.

Smiling to herself at sight of his naked body as he made his way over to the closet across the way, Jenniboni always enjoyed watching his exquisite form rise each morning from their bed.

Savoring the view of his firm, young body she constantly looked upon doing so as her own special, private little early-morning pick-me-up. Having a lithe, trim, well-toned physique Andrei's fluid movements and graceful figure always put her in mind of a professional dancer.

Not really much of a surprise taking into consideration how much he loved to dance, having taken classes during his old High school days when they first met. Had they never married Jenniboni could easily imagine him having a quite promising career in the performing arts.

Given his dark, handsome features he would have been a natural.

Thick, straight, luxurious raven black hair, dusky olive-complexioned skin, and a strong, square jaw line all spoke well of his ancient Latin American ancestry; a pair of the of the most brilliant blue eyes Jenniboni ever saw bearing as well loud witness to his paternal Gaelic forbears.

Right from the very get-go Jenniboni took great pleasure in showing Andrei off on the dance floor, his incredibly good looks and excellent dance skills something she took great pride in—the meticulously kept moustache and goatee he sported an added bonus contributing likewise to his already rugged good looks.

Lending him a devil-may-care pirate-of-the-open-seas quality right out of some ancient, by-gone era long past in the distant annals of pre-matriarchate herstory, he could have easily been a public heartthrob... a star of stage and screen... had he only chosen that particular path in life.

Then again he could have just as easily made a successful *"go of it"* as a professional singer/musician, possessing as he did a beautiful singing voice; a deep, rich baritone Jenniboni always found *"charmingly masculine"*.

Having sung in both his high school glee club as well as the church choir, Jenniboni always managed to cajole her multi-faceted husband into singing and playing as well whenever they hosted either a large gathering, or just had a few friends over to visit.

It was at times like these that their guests would more often than not request their favourite songs only to listen entranced, enraptured as he happily obliged each and every one of them to the best of his considerable ability.

Nor did it take all that much persuasion... *not really*... to encourage him into performing. Enjoying down deep the occasional opportunity to *"strut his stuff"* Andrei was also a gifted virtuoso on the guitar.

Not that he ever came across as either pushy or arrogant when it came to the display of his many talents. A bit of a show-off at times, but nice about it he was even modest in fact when it came to his willingness to perform, always waiting to be asked first.

All-in-all Jenniboni considered it a pity that, given her busy schedule as of late, they didn't have many a recent opportunity to entertain.

Even so that didn't prevent Andrei from indulging his periodical appetite for the limelight when with just the immediate family, all three of their children adoring it whenever their father sang them to sleep each and every night, preferring as they did Andrei's music to some *"dumb old bedtime story"*.

Always keeping his guitar at the ready it sat in the corner of the mistress-bedroom like some faithful puppy sitting there in eager anticipation of its owner's return home—resting next to the very chair in which Andrei now sat, putting on both a pair of black trousers and white cotton shirt, leaving his top two shirt buttons undone to his chest just the way Jenniboni preferred.

Yet even while his superb physique and many exceptional talents were in Jenniboni's own considered opinion a definite plus, she had to confess they'd all be worthless without his quick wit and superior intelligence rounding out an already impressive package.

No matter what else it would be a misery for sure living one's every day in the company of a life-partner who couldn't hold up their end in any sort of meaningful conversation; someone unable to participate worth a darn in a knowledgeable exchange of ideas, keeping you intellectually stimulated.

Right from the very get-go Jenniboni was quite impressed with both Andrei's mature bearing and superior intelligence, both leading even so to a minor misunderstanding rectified easily enough once discovered.

Remembering it as though just yesterday their initial meeting had been eleven years ago, Jenniboni at the time a uniformed law enforcement officer in the *"Commonwealth Civilian Protection Force"*.

A fledgling *Protector* for only a year when answering a burglary call at the home of Andrei's parents she was but a young rookie all of 21 years old, graduating first in her class from the C.C.P.F. Officer's Training Academy. And with Andrei's mother, Ms. Joannah-Ruth Sollos, being a very rich and powerful businesswoman known throughout the entire System, the stolen items in question were without surprise of an extremely rare and valuable nature.

Yet even though the case proved more complex than originally anticipated Jenniboni managed to wrap it all up within just three weeks' time, apprehend all those responsible, the resulting publicity putting her *Protectorate* career on the immediate fast track. And an already ambitious woman to begin with, young Jenniboni K. Saphira used the resulting publicity to fuel even further her quick and steady climb through the ranks.

Nor was that all she came away with from that particular case, the investigation also resulting in the first time she ever laid eyes on the young man destined to be her future spouse.

However, while aware from the very start that Andrei was a tad younger than she, this mattered not, the custom being to wed younger men.

What she didn't know was just how much younger the future Mr. Saphira really was. For while he was still in High school when they first met she originally assumed from both his mature bearing, and superior intelligence, Andrei was at least 18 years old.

Heck, he was even in the graduating class of 2904 for Gosh's sake!!

And graduating with honours as scheduled Valedictorian it remained just as fresh in her memory how precious Andrei looked standing there behind the podium, delivering his valedictory speech before the school's entire auditorium.

Resplendent in both his grand graduation gown and cap, quite proud of how he handled himself so skillfully before all those present… a born orator indeed… Jenniboni's smile was as wide as those of his parents, sitting there next to them in the front row of the audience.

No more proud though than Andrei, insisting as he did on introducing her to all his classmates. She even wore her full-dress crimson and gold Protectorate uniform Andrei begged her to wear for that very special occasion complete with its majestic high-peaked cap and floor-length deep-forest green cape with its glistening gold trim.

Just as he hoped from the very start all the other boys likewise present were just as properly… duly… impressed with her. Not having believed him at first when Andrei told them he was dating the beautiful, dashing policewoman now in their midst's Jenniboni found the entire incident rather endearing in its own child-like innocence.

Nor did she prove able to resist a quite similar urge to take a whole slew of pictures she kept tucked away even still, stored away in a private photo album kept as well with other treasured keepsakes. All of them valued momentos she'd often sneak a look at them whenever quite alone.

Yet even so it wasn't until later she learned Andrei's true age. Not until after their fifth, or sixth date out on the town. Nor was it he who told her but his mother instead. Taking Jenniboni aside to ascertain if she was aware she was in fact dating a sixteen-year-old boy, Joannah-Ruth wasted no time doing so when learning the young Protector was in fact courting her son.

Already hopelessly in love with one-another both proved just lucky enough both Joannah-Ruth and Colm Harold Sollos were likewise willing to accept her sincerest guarantee she would uphold their son's honour, having gotten to know Jenniboni well during her previous investigation—Jenniboni popping "the question" four months later, asking Andrei's hand in marriage.

Yet even while a man could marry on his own at the age of eighteen, requiring parental consent if only seventeen, he was still prohibited by Commonwealth law to wed any earlier—the young couple getting married only two weeks after his 17th birthday, doing so in the very cathedral where Andrei sung in the choir every Sunday since early childhood.

Turning out a quite lavish affair, his parents pulling out all the stops for their only child's most special day, the young couple took their marriage vows before all their friends and relations—the mid-morning sun, streaming through the towering stained-glass windows, casting a brilliant kaleidoscope of every colour possible all about the crystal cathedral's vast interior.

While true Jenniboni never set out to marry on purpose someone quite that young she saw all-the-same both the wisdom, the benefits behind the customary practice of taking a younger man to wed—Andrei looking exceedingly handsome in his custom-made, three-piece white wedding suit—Jenniboni wearing in accordance with Protectorate tradition her formal, full-dress crimson and gold uniform.

Of course one of the most common justifications cited more often than not for doing so was that younger husbands are more easily handled, less difficult to condition to married life. Not to mention how it was likewise refreshing as well as even invigorating to come home after a hard day's work to a virile, perky, and energetic young thing.

To Jenniboni's way of thinking the best excuse for marrying young was that younger husbands helped women retain their own feelings of both youth and even vitality.

Or put another way still, it was both physically as well as spiritually rejuvenating having a younger man to both wed and bed. And while Jenniboni herself was confessedly just 32 years old even a woman her age could feel tired, worn out at times.

Especially when she was an aspiring and ambitious overachiever already at a level of power, fame, and prestige only dreamt of by other women, her sights focused firmly upon even broader horizons somewhere down life's road.

****

Buttoning his shirt cuffs before putting on his black leather dress-belt, Andrei noticed Jenniboni watching him from the corner of his eye—the dreamy smile on her full, luscious lips telling him that, whatever her thoughts might be at that particular moment, they were most surely the pleasant sort—those warm recollections one couldn't help, but savor whenever coming to mind.

And from the definite way she was gazing in his direction Andrei felt it reasonable as well to assume they were all centered around-and-about him. Nor was that a case of ego by any stretch of the imagination, Andrei simply able to recognize that familiar look in his loving wife's eyes.

Running his belt through the loops on the waistband of his pants, fastening the polished bronze buckle completing his ensemble, he returned her smile with one of his own.

"I hate to intrude but I think you better be taking your shower now, put on your uniform, while I take care of the children and get breakfast ready. Either that or you won't make your meeting on time".

"I suppose you're right", Jenniboni agreed with a wee sigh, reluctant.

Hesitant to forsake that silent reverie occupying her every thought, deciding all-the-same Andrei was right, she swung her legs over the far side of the bed they shared as husband and wife, sitting with her back to him.

"Are you still planning to visit my father at the Shelter today?", she asked after a moments silence, running her fingers through full, long, wavy honey

5

blonde hair.

"Yes".

"Excellent. In that case be sure to give him my love and please remember to check and see if the package we sent him arrived safely".

Ah, yes… the mysterious package.

Assuring his wife he'd see without fail to both there was little chance at all Andrei would forget, his curiosity working double overtime ever since she first asked him to mail it, refusing at the very same time to discuss its actual contents.

"Don't worry, love", he promised: "I'll see to everything".

****

The mistress bedroom opened into a long hallway, plainly decorated in the same blue shag carpeting and plain white walls found throughout the rest of their penthouse apartment—Andrei having hung a row of tri-dee photos of family events on either side of the narrow passageway in hopes of alleviating the monotony.

Having done likewise throughout other areas of their new home these included a grand portrait of Jenniboni over the head of their bed as well as a large family portrait proudly displayed just above the living/dining-room couch.

Pausing halfway down the hall Andrei gently knocked on one of two opposing doors across the way from one another.

After waiting a couple of minutes, no answer forthcoming, he slowly pressed down on the door handle, taking care not to make too much noise entering the still, quiet room beyond.

Making his way across the room to a small, single-sized bed… a tiny form curled up under a brightly coloured blanket… Andrei reached down, drawing back gently the festive bed sheets from atop of the little boy sleeping beneath in sweet repose.

Curled up in a tiny ball, thumb in mouth, his blue pajamas with the floppy-eared puppies embroidered on them, he looked even younger than his mere four years—a tender, paternal, smile lighting up Andrei's face seeing how wee, vulnerable, and even angelic he looked.

Lightly stroking his son's sandy blonde hair with paternal affection the sleepy child murmured, large innocent eyes lazily opening.

"Hmmm?", he peered up at his father, curious.

"Time to rise and shine, Tommy", Andrei gently announced, tousling affectionately the young boy's hair while doing so:

"Time to get dressed and ready for breakfast and school".

"Okay, Daddy. Sure thing".

"That's a good boy", Andrei beamed, turning towards a nearby closet alongside a series of toy-laden shelves.

Returning with a light sky-blue shirt, charcoal grey pants, and a pair of sneakers in hand he arranged neatly each item atop of Tommy's bedspread, removing after that a pair of freshly laundered briefs and rolled-up socks from a small dresser bureau situated against the far wall.

Once having taken care of all that Andrei then set about tidying up the childish mess scattered all about the unkempt room, exotic animal posters on each wall seeming to watch, Tommy all the while taking off his pj's.

Collecting together the discarded toys and dirty laundry strewn about the floor Andrei sighed, grinning all the while:

"Honestly, son, I wish you and Tammy would remember to put away your things in their proper places".

With that Andrei placed each errant plaything in either the rainbow-coloured toy chest to the dresser's right, or upon their assigned shelves—soiled clothes going straight away into a laundry hamper left of the little boy's dresser bureau.

"Sure, Daddy", Tommy promised, watching his father go about his daily chores with wide, clear, expressive dark brown eyes he clearly inherited from Jenniboni.

"So how are you doing with your clothes?" Andrei soon asked after just a brief pause, glancing casually over his shoulder in Tommy's general direction.

Perched on the edge of his bed the little boy just stared sheepishly at his feet, a trace of embarrassment on his face, looking up at his father in a silent plea for help.

Having managed for the most part to put on the rest of his clothes he'd evidently run into a bit of a snag when it came to his socks, having stopped once they'd reached his heels.

Andrei grinned at the comical way in which they dangled from Tommy's feet, made even more humorous by how they swung about, the little boy swaying his feet back and forth in a slow, circular, pattern.

For some inexplicable reason Andrei could never quite fathom Tommy often had trouble getting them all the way on, finally helping him pull the pesky items all the way up before slipping his shoes on.

Bracing the boy's feet against his thighs, kneeling in front of his son by this time, Andrei then proceeded to tie Tommy's shoelaces.

"Not so tight Daddy" he complained with a little whine.

"Sorry", Andrei apologized, undoing them once more:

"Now pay close attention to how Daddy does this", Andrei then instructed him, smiling before tying them yet again…

"After all you're getting to be a big boy now and it's just about time you learned how to do this for yourself".

Explaining ever so slowly each step with great care… careful exactitude… he couldn't help being amused by the serious expression on Tommy's face, watching his father's fingers with rapt attention, not wanting to miss a single detail.

Once done Andrei gave the tops of the little boy's shoes a little tap each with the tip of his finger.

"There, all done", he proclaimed, reaching up afterwards to redo Tommy's shirt, the top button inserted by mistake through the opening meant instead for the one below.

"Good", he smiled once satisfied his son was ready at last for the long day ahead. Making sure he brushed his hair before sending him out to the living/dining-room, he told Tommy he could watch a little 3-DV until breakfast was ready.

Crossing after that the hall beyond to repeat the same early morning ritual with the younger of his two daughters, Andrei was pleasantly surprised to discover Tammy already wearing an off-yellow velveteen dress she selected all on her own.

Still though, while proving herself more adept in the art of dressing herself than her brother, she still insisted Andrei comb her hair back into a ponytail. She even handed him a pale peach ribbon of her own choosing to tie it back with:

"Because it goes so good with my dress", she informed him, a lively twinkle dancing about in those sparkling blue eyes she inherited so clearly from her father.

Positioning himself on the edge of her bed to brush out her long, flowing, chestnut hair Andrei soon found himself caught up in a veritable hurricane of words as Tammy chattered away a mile a minute.

Detailing each and every one of her plans for the day ahead with bubbly enthusiasm she was without doubt more of a live wire than her brother. Although fraternal twins born only moments apart, Tammy was definitely the greater ball of energy among the two, Tommy more laid-back... sedate... in character.

So, as Andrei went about styling his daughter's hair as per her request, he smiled wearily, trying the best he could to keep up his end of the conversation.

It wasn't until after arranging the pale coloured hair ribbon according to her instructions he finally sent her out to the family room to join her brother, gently breathing a soft sigh of good-natured relief when finally alone.

CHAPTER 2

"THE HEDONIST"

Pleased with the results she achieved in the application of her cosmetics Naomi gave her reflection yet another conceited little smile full of smug satisfaction.

"Quite smashing", she congratulated herself:

"Stunning as usual", she complimented her mirror image, blowing herself a jocular little kiss in absolute high spirits—bright green eyes, flaming red hair glistening in the light pulled back in a youthful ponytail, and a full, sensuous, Rubenesque figure quite desirable.

Giving her preparations a complete and thorough once-over for what seemed like the millionth time in a row she wanted to make sure everything was just so for her overnight trip to Chiron City, all the while taking careful note of the time.

Not wanting to miss the shuttle scheduled for planet-side in just a little while there were times she had to admit it would be more practical in the long run to just use her base apartment on Demeter rather than living chiefly aboard StarChild.

Heaven only knew her base quarters were certainly more spacious, more luxurious, than these aboard ship—choosing nevertheless to live mostly onboard StarChild, holding her planet-side residence in reserve for entertaining, whether it be hosting parties or more "intimate" affairs.

And, if she were successful, tonight would hopefully be one of the latter.

Yes, indeed! It would certainly be more convenient to simply stay on the base during her off-duty periods like the greater majority of the crew.

Yet, even while mindful of this, Naomi still preferred spending the majority of her time aboard StarChild—her best reason for this being that, as Chief Engineer, she hoped to be close at hand should any problems arise as the newly constructed starship went through all his pre-departure checks and re-checks.

Having no family commitments to speak of she was free to choose where she lived, her only responsibility in life being the vessel around her. An arrangement which suited Naomi just fine… thank you so very much!!

However, while her sense of responsibility might have played one important part in why she always remained so close at hand, love played an even more crucial one. No exaggeration on anyone's part to say that her feelings towards StarChild were more maternal than anything else she loved this splendid ship she served aboard so proudly, so devotedly, as if her only child.

Present throughout his entire construction Naomi looked upon how she labored so heavily upon his growth and development as comparable to how a woman's body and soul labored so heavily upon the growth and development of her child right from conception onward.

Yet, even so, there still comes a time when even the most conscientious parent has to take every now and then a well-deserved respite from their offspring. No matter how much one might love their children, and care for them, there still remains the need to explore and indulge from-time-to-time other aspects of their existence.

And so it was with Naomi, her main interests in life reading technical manuals, working aboard ship, throwing raucous parties, and pursuing members of the opposite sex whenever her busy schedule allowed. A veritable genius in every sense of the word with an equally astounding libido, one could quite easily describe Naomi Leonora Marlowe as a unique blend of intellectual fulfillment and sexual frustration.

And although her intellectual endeavors occupied the greater majority of her free time she still entertained hopes of temporarily abandoning the disciplined left hemisphere of her brain to gratify the more hedonistic impulses of the right.

Fancying herself as being both a connoisseur of good food, fine liquor, and quality men she was always on the look-out for all three. However, while she experienced little difficulty in procuring the good food and liquor, her concept of good men was another matter entirely—"good" in the case of men referring to their performance in the boudoir.

More often than not it left her quite baffled trying to determine what the problem could be. Fully aware of all those positive attributes working in her favor from a winning personality to stunning good looks, Naomi's lack of success in wooing prospective bed partners left her quite perplexed…

What could it be?

After all she was strong, intelligent, witty, confident, and very aggressive.

Willing to chase after whatever she desired with unbridled gusto she furthermore just so happened to be a very attractive Rubenesque women blessed with long, fiery, silky red hair, sparkling green eyes, rosy cheeks, and a round, cherubic, face more than just easy on the eyes.

Nor could she find any fault in her lovemaking, showing those who willingly succumbed to her sensual delights and magniloquent encouragements both tenderness and gentility. Always sensitive to the desires of her current partner at each given point, Naomi always saw to it that a truly memorable and satisfying time was had by both parties involved.

So from whence did the problem arise? With whom did the fault ultimately rest?

Unable to see the proverbial forest for the trees she just couldn't understand that, in a society where men were expected to remain pure and chaste until after marriage, they weren't about to chance it all on Naomi's selfish brand of casual fling. The peril of other women, the marrying kind, looking down upon them as "damaged goods" was too great a hazard to risk.

Simply put the social stigma they'd endure would be considerably more severe than that which a woman might encounter in the same situation. While she might possibly find herself on the receiving end of a few disapproving glances the man's life could, in all likelihood, be ruined for a long time to come.

For Naomi the weaker sex was merely there to slake whatever carnal yearnings she might experience when not pursuing other more career-oriented goals in life. She had no desire whatsoever for a permanent commitment or family of her own, the men around her realizing this in no uncertain terms.

Yet even so she very rarely ever grew despondent or discouraged when it came to such setbacks. Basically a good-humored individual who enjoyed the pleasure of the chase almost as much as the capture, Naomi remained able to accept rejection without any ill temperament on her part. Although invariably doing her best to cajole and sway perspective conquests into submission, she never became ugly or hostile in defeat....

Winning or losing, she still enjoyed playing the game.

And tonight the game should prove especially interesting, two other StarChild officers joining her for the upcoming 'festivities'. Accompanying her on this particular outing would be none other than StarChild's esteemed Chief of Security, Lt. Cmdr. Frances Straker, along with Naomi's Assistant Chief of Engineering, Lt. Gloria Greensley.

In fact the hunt should prove especially amusing this time around, having arranged a little surprise for Gloria later that very same day. Something the young Lieutenant should find most stimulating when considering her past, or lack thereof.

While Naomi and Frances had already cruised nearly every 'hot spot' the outer system had to offer this would be Lt. Greensley's first time on the prowl as it were. A most fitting way in Naomi's opinion to begin with a big bang their bachelor voyage to the very stars beyond.

At the very least she hoped that her plans for her timid and inexperienced assistant would end by building up the young woman's confidence, something Naomi felt she so desperately lacked. At that particular moment Naomi had no way of knowing her scheme would not only have its desired effect, but leave StarChild's Chief Engineer deeply chagrined in the bargain.

So as she finished applying the final subtle touches to her make-up, taking care that her hair and uniform were likewise in perfect array, Naomi once again glanced at the time. Assured that all was going according to schedule she bestowed upon her mirror image yet another contented, self-centered smile before snatching her purse up from a nearby table.

Casually draping it over her shoulder she then exited her quarters to see if her two traveling companions were similarly all revved up and ready for their approaching adventure in Chiron City.

CHAPTER 3

"J.J."

Gently closing the door to Tammy's bedroom behind him, Andrei continued on his way down the remainder of the hall to the opposite end from the mistress bedroom.

It was there he passed by the main entrance to their apartment just to his immediate right, the small kitchen where Andrei prepared his family's meals every day off to the left—its serving counter separating it from the large living/dining-room area comprising the heftiest portion of their home.

Meanwhile, positioned off to the near left of the hallway entrance one or two meters beyond the kitchen counter, there was a splendid polished dark oak dining set. Intricately carved table and chairs lent a definite touch of elegance to where the family ate their meals while the section of the living area frequently referred to as the "family room" rested directly ahead in the far right-hand corner of the living/dining area.

Consisting of a long, plush, verdant green couch, two easy chairs of the same colour, and a silver chrome coffee table complete with a crystal blue glass surface, there was also a large 3-DV cube pressed up against the far wall between the couch and chairs.

A device Andrei scornfully dubbed a "boob cube", it was this inane appliance in his opinion that held Tammy and Tommy's rapt attention so firmly in its grasp as he approached their location, watching some three-dimensional animated children's program playing within its transparent exterior.

From the disinterested cursory glance their father gave it the show seemed to revolve around some C.C.P.F. Protector as she went about solving some crime or another in the asteroid belt between Earth and Mars:

Probably, by the sounds of things, the large mining asteroid of Ceres.

Taking note mostly of the high volume they had it set at Andrei ordered them however to turn it down without delay least they disturb their older sister, the door to her bedroom situated next to the couch on which they sat.

Respecting his elder daughter's privacy Andrei awaited her permission to enter the room beyond, waiting patiently upon her threshold after knocking on her door.

"Whose there?" came the prompt reply from within.

"It's your father, J.J.… May I come in?"

"Sure", she granted in a chipper voice full of lively good cheer.

Making his way into the inner sanctum on the other side of the door Andrei found his older daughter seated at the vanity table next to her bed across the room from him. Brushing out long golden hair glistening in the light from above she watched both their reflections in the large mirror in front of her with keen interest.

Already dressed for the school day ahead she wore an ankle length red dress, ruffles about the neck and wrists, with a pair of black suede shoes reaching almost to her calves completing her ensemble.

"Good morning, Father. How may I help you", she greeted him in a mature, congenial fashion. Still turned away from him as Andrei shut the door, glancing out the large bay window running along the wall on the other side of J.J.'s bed, Andrei smiled while observing the base beyond.

It was a paternal smile taking a certain amount of pride in his daughter's impeccable, gracious good manners and mature bearing. No wonder most others erroneously assumed young Jenniboni Jr. was in fact older than her seven years.

"No need to trouble yourself, dear. It's nothing of any great importance", he shrugged. Then, turning to the right, he made his way through the doorway to her small private bathroom off to the side: "I just wanted to be sure that your dirty laundry was all gathered up in your hamper as I plan to do all the wash this afternoon".

"Don't worry, Sir. It's all taken care of ", came J.J.'s swift assurance. True to her word all was present and accounted for.

Unlike her two younger siblings J.J. was a quite responsible young gentlewoman. She always kept her room spotless, made sure that all her chores were done, and took care of all her homework on time, excelling in her scholastic endeavors.

Andrei didn't even need check, doing so out of a sense of fatherly duty and a desire to feel needed. Although naturally proud of his daughter's mature and responsible ways, it nonetheless stung him a bit at times to feel that she didn't really need him.

Finding himself trapped between a rock and a hard place, Andrei felt he owed it to her to acknowledge her responsible nature, wishing all the same from time to time she'd come to him for help… no matter how trivial the problem… more often than she did.

Sometimes it hurt to feel so excluded.

Yet, be that as it may, it was in recognition of J.J.'s ability to conduct herself so well he and her mother allowed her this particular bedroom after moving to the Project StarChild Base. Not only was it farthest from theirs, but it was also the only other besides the mistress bedroom with its own private adjoining washroom…

All in honour of her desire for privacy.

Proving herself so responsible, so dependable even earned J.J. her mother's permission for the fantasy pet she always yearned for since toddlerhood—a white ferret answering to the name of "Ricky" J.J. kept in a cage on her work desk.

Nor was that all…

Just right of the vanity table at which she now sat her parents even trusted her with her very own PC complete with limited access to the Stellar-Wide Net, taking great pains beforehand to make sure that every possible childproof block was firmly in place. Not allowing any access to any inappropriate web sites it likewise sat upon her desk right alongside Ricky's cage.

Returning from the bathroom, Andrei stood behind her chair as she applied the lip-gloss her mother permitted her to use in lieu of lipstick. Looking down at her reflection in the mirror before them he then asked her what she wanted for breakfast.

"I believe I'll have the same as Mother", she requested… casually… placing the tube of lip-gloss in her hand back down atop of the vanity table before her.

"Sorry, Sweetie", Andrei grinned ruefully, "but I'm afraid that's quite out of the question".

Each morning Jenniboni Sr. started her day without fail with two glazed donuts and a steaming cup of strong black coffee.

"But why?"

"Because it's one thing for a grown woman to eat whatever she wants, but it's another thing entirely for a child", he patiently explained: "You're still a growing girl and need a well-balanced diet".

"Oh, Father;", J.J. exclaimed in that imperious tone of voice brimming with annoyed impatience all children employ when feeling their parents aren't treating them like the mature adults they 'know' themselves to be.

While her reaction brought a smile to Andrei's lips it was-all-the same a bittersweet expression. Sweet because it proved beyond any doubt that, no matter how mature and responsible she behaved, no matter what she might think, she was still a little child who still needed her father. Bitter because, in spite of all that, it also indicated another problem giving him from time-to-time serious pause for concern.

It wasn't so much what she'd said that troubled him, nor the childish way in which she said it. Having behaved the same way when he'd been her age this didn't bother him in the least.

Not at all!!

What actually worried him was that, while most girls her age were able to enjoy their childhood and live for the day, J.J. seemed so determined to be an adult, so anxious to grow up all at once, she in all honesty didn't appear at all to want to be a child.

Not that she didn't like to have fun, enjoying watching 3-DV with her family, playing games with the twins, and participating in the occasional family outing.

Yet while she didn't refuse the company of her parents and siblings she *did* seem to avoid the companionship of other children. When it came to socializing with those her own age she appeared for all intents and purposes unable to relate to others in her own peer group.

Almost seeming to scorn their company she apparently preferred the company of adults, having little to no friends her own age since moving to Demeter.

In J.J. he could already observe the same wonderful feminine qualities that her mother possessed in such abundance, qualities that had drawn him to Jenniboni Sr. in the first place. She had her mother's assertiveness, determination, self-confidence, and superior intelligence alongside her mother's similar compassion, sensitivity, sense of duty, and her gallant and chivalrous attitude towards the weaker sex.

Nevertheless he oftentimes noticed J.J. trying too hard, struggling to be someone she wasn't yet meant to be. And compounding the problem in Andrei's eyes was the further realization his wife - while sensitive to her husband's feelings of concern, was also of the opinion the real problem lay with Andrei being an only child - lacking much previous experience with the raising of little girls...

Especially since girls matured faster than boys.

Maybe she was right he thought to himself.

Still, though...

"Don't 'Oh Father' me", Andrei finally chuckled at last: "You know very well your mother would be furious if I served you coffee and donuts for breakfast.

"Who knows", he teased, "she might even decide to trade me in for a newer model".

"Oh, Father, don't be so silly", J.J. giggled, amused by such a preposterous concept.

"Well, then, why don't you just humor your silly old Dad and tell me instead what else you might like for breakfast".

"How about some scrambled eggs, sausages, toast, orange juice, and strawberry jam", she suggested in a serious, dignified manner following a minute's deep concentration.

"Very good", came Andrei's pleased response: "That's a very mature and responsible choice".

The obvious pleasure that she derived from this simple compliment made him feel much better inside, lovingly placing his hands upon her shoulders to give her a tender, gentle kiss on the top of her head.

Grateful that, unlike many children her age, she didn't pull away or grow annoyed at such displays of parental affection Andrei was relieved that, although J.J. wanted to be an adult so badly, at least her concept of adulthood didn't preclude such simple yet important elements in life as love, affection, and other such simple expressions of tenderness.

Wishing at that moment to convey to her how truly proud of her he was, wanting to let her know right then and there just how much he really loved her,

Andrei decided to pay her the ultimate compliment he knew she'd take immediately to heart.

Aware how much J.J. deeply admired her mother, desiring nothing less than to follow in Jenniboni's footsteps… exploring someday fascinating new worlds in command of her very own starship… he likewise had no doubt she'd make all of her dreams come true, sure within his heart of hearts she'd grow up someday to be a truly remarkable woman of whom he'd be quite proud.

And in the end what father could ask for more??

"With every minute that passes you remind me more and more of your mother. You're getting to be like her more and more with each passing day", he told her in a voice full of tender devotion.

Visibly pleased by his words, able to see this from her reflection in the mirror, J.J.'s entire face lit up, her beautiful dark brown eyes brimming with both pride and satisfaction.

"Thank you, Father. And I love you, too", she beamed with obvious gratitude.

CHAPTER 4

"THE WARRIOR"

The fact Lt. Cmdr. Frances Straker's quarters were situated smack-dab right next to Naomi's on deck S-4 would explain how they came to be such good friends… at least in part… such close proximity leading more often-than-not to feelings of either amiability or animosity.

Or, at the very least, a sense of ambivalence.

It was just fortunate a firm and lasting friendship had developed between the two StarChild department chiefs despite their myriad differences and continual disagreements:

Perhaps a part of the reason for this was due to the many positive traits they more or less shared in common. Each woman was confident, aggressive, and highly intelligent receiving the respect and fidelity of those serving under her command. Both were strong leaders, fair and just in their dealings with others, even though **Naomi** was less respectful at times of higher authority, proper protocol.

Likewise each could be considered in her own right a champion of lost causes, a crusader with a deep and abiding passion for justice, honour, loyalty, and fair play. And while Frances came across more often than not as both humorless and emotionless—often to the point of seeming dour—she was actually gifted with a sly, dry, subtle wit counterbalancing Naomi's rather boisterous and outgoing joviality quite nicely.

Yet in spite of all this even the most devoted friendship could be sorely tested at times, Frances' original inclination having been to refuse Naomi's invitation when asked to join her on Demeter. The only reason for her sudden change of mind came when Naomi either innocently, or inadvertently let slip she invited Lt. Gloria Greensley along on this particular "man hunt".

Something her good friend and colleague never did before, convinced Naomi was hatching some devious scheme resulting in possible humiliation and even heartbreak, Frances decided it might be best to accompany them, providing any possible damage control proving necessary. Her suspicions were only further aroused when Naomi grew evasive, asked why she invited Lt. Greensley to join them in the very first place.

It was no secret to anyone she'd been pushing her introverted deputy quite relentlessly to come out of her shell more, be less withdrawn, and take a more active part in social gatherings:

Especially those in which the opposite sex was involved.

Unfortunately Lt. Gloria J. Greensley appeared to lack the ability to tell her immediate superior to shove off and mind her own business, an event Frances wished very much to be there for should it ever occur.

Naomi might be her best friend, but that didn't mean Frances condoned her constant pushiness, her frequent tactlessness.

Not by a long shot!!

Had it not been for her deep desire to provide Gloria moral support Frances would have never agreed to join Naomi on yet another one of her little sexual safaris to begin with, planning to inform her she'd no longer accompany her on these little expeditions. Simply put Frances didn't care much for her companion's perpetual objectifying of men, how she'd try to take undue advantage of them at nearly every turn.

Viewing such behavior as grossly inappropriate… disrespectful… what began as mild disapproval on Frances' part soon blossomed into full-fledged repugnance. Naomi's lascivious conduct growing even more blatant during recent outings she'd come to the conclusion the only way to preserve their friendship was to distance herself from Naomi on these particular occasions.

Of course this wasn't to say that Frances herself didn't delight in more innocent displays of physical affection. Yet deriving much pleasure from tender kisses, loving embraces, gentle caresses, and simple cuddling she drew the line however at using men for the base gratification of her own carnal desires only to toss them aside like so much refuse afterwards.

Being a devout believer in the "Code of Feminine Chivalry", the principal doctrine upon which all society's gender relations were based, such callous treatment of the opposite sex went against her very grain, her innermost self.

Then again her attitudes towards men could be traced as well to yet another key source besides "The Code", Rolan Straker having always been a major influence in his daughter's life.

Finding himself a widower upon his wife's death in an explosion at the experimental hydrocarbon research facility for which she worked, Rolan did his best to see that Frances wanted for nothing.

Being a single father, raising a child all on his own on the Saturnine moon of Titan no easy feat by any stretch of the imagination, he did all-the-same an admirable job caring for his little girl without benefit of female support and/or protection.

Showering her with all the love, attention, and encouragement in life a parent could he gave Frances an intimate and unique perspective on men and their particular problems faced in stellar society. Gaining from her father a deep appreciation for his gender Frances discovered herself able to relate with men on an intellectual, emotional, and personal level Naomi found more often than not so problematic. And as a result of all this Frances was understandably very protective of him as well, growing up as "the woman of the house".

As a very handsome, desirable man Roland Straker naturally attracted his own fair share of female admirers. And heaven only help the ones who became too forward, or aggressive in their advances—facing under such circumstances the considerable wrath of his only daughter.

Yet, try as hard as she might, Frances proved unable in the end to save Rolan from his ultimate fate, devastated when he passed away from a lingering illness gradually draining all the life out of him. While her mother's death remained only a shadowy recollection in the back of her mind Frances would never forget the suffering she endured sitting Shiva for her father, saying Kaddish in his memory.

Shalom, Papa!

Nor was it long after this Frances transferred all her feelings of protectiveness onto men in general, helping to explain her chosen profession, her desire to protect the weak and defenseless, and why she often proved herself more popular with the male of the species than Naomi. Having no grand illusions whatsoever in the matter of appearance, Frances realized that it had nothing to do with her physical charms—her sharp, strict, angular facial features and hollow cheeks falling short of classical beauty by a country mile.

Even the manner in which she wore her hair could hardly be considered inviting to gaze upon—pitch-black hair pulled so tightly back in a restrictive bun so severe it looked quite painful indeed. Less than appealing attributes that were only emphasized by her deceptively lean build and remarkable height.

Standing almost half a foot taller than the average woman at an impressive six feet, eight inches Frances possessed a rakishly thin appearance that only belied her true physical strength. An unintentional deception on her part often leading others to the false conclusion she was likewise weak in body, many detractors would erroneously assume that she was an easy mark.

Going solely on the evidence of their eyes some belligerent individuals would, on rare occasions, even try to provoke her into some sort of physical confrontation. Only then did such misguided souls inevitably discover the folly of their ways. A formidable, even deadly fighter well versed in every form of combat imaginable Frances Straker was someone not to trifle with, or take lightly.

One look upon her face alone was warning enough that she wasn't a woman to be tangled with unless willing to suffer the consequences. The grim set of her thin, pale, lips and the smoldering ferocity in her eyes spoke volumes of the fearsome warrior she was.

Nevertheless Frances still had about her a certain undeniable charm and appeal, an amazing transformation taking place whenever she smiled, her severe countenance softening into something softer, more congenial. And it was this aspect of her personality she decided to take advantage of this particular trip planet-side once sure Lt. Greensley didn't suffer any traumatic experience at the hands of her immediate superior.

Once satisfied Gloria wasn't going to end up hurt by any Machiavellian plotting on Naomi's part Frances planned to take her leave of the latter's company, spending the remainder of her stay planet-side in the company of a singularity handsome, charming young laddie she knew well and often enjoyed stepping out on the town with. Never let it be said Lt. Cmdr. Frances Miriam Straker didn't appreciate the rare opportunity to take a well-earned break from her duties aboard ship.

So while she didn't share Naomi's particular obsession with her appearance Frances all the same desired to look her best, inspecting the functional yet stylish casual dress uniform she wore in the mirror hanging above her narrow set of dresser drawers.

And once satisfied with her attire she then reached up, freeing her hair from its tightly packed confines with a little shake of her head before putting on her make-up. Today was a day to look less imposing and more approachable, time for the dedicated warrior and fighter to literally let her hair down and indulge her gentler nature, her tender side.

Letting her long, wavy, hair cascade down and around her shoulders and back, she held it in place with an antique tortoise shell barrette handed down from mother to daughter since time immemorial. Having received numerous compliments from the many male admirers she'd courted over the years on the silky softness of her hair it always pleased her when they'd ask to run their fingers through it, more often than not granting them her permission to do so.

However, other than for a light shade of pink lipstick and an equally subdued blush, she didn't bother much with cosmetics. Pale skin and gaunt features alongside coal dark eyes and raven black hair bestowed upon her a disturbingly vampire-like quality whenever she wore dark or bright make-up. So, quickly taking care of that last task, Frances was in the midst of storing away her toiletries when she heard the doorbell to her quarters softly chime in back of her.

"Enter", she automatically called out in a crisp, clear voice.

"Great. I see you're already ready", Naomi observed upon entering the room, a cheerful grin plastered all over her face.

"Almost", Frances replied. "Just need one more thing."

Saying that she turned to the triangular table dominating the sitting-room area of her quarters, removing from its gleaming white surface a twin to the same compact, standard-issue green and gold S.E.A. purse Naomi likewise sported, hung over her shoulder. Double-checking its contents to make sure nothing crucial was missing from within Frances listened to Naomi's claim they were so far making good time.

"Let's just hope Gloria's also ready to go", she finished.

"So she's still coming along?", Frances grumbled in a dour tone, hoping the young woman somehow summoned up the courage to back out at the last moment.

"Of course", Naomi confirmed, somewhat startled out of her complaisant frame of mind, Frances closing her purse with a clearly annoyed snap.

"After all the hard work she's logged in on all the pre-departure diagnostics I figured she could use a little R and R. You know how it is", Naomi grinned rather nervously, confused by Frances' unanticipated attitude, her smile beginning to falter mid-stride.

"Yes, I know how it is", Frances responded sourly. Barely able to disguise the utter contempt in her voice she arranged her purse over her shoulder with an angry jerk. Actually liking Lt. Greensley from what little contact they'd had with one another there was no longer any doubt poor Gloria was being set up for something she was, in all probability, not ready for.

"Yes, I know."

Chapter 5

"KISSES GOOD-BYE"

Placing the children's' breakfast before them upon the large, polished oak dining-room table Andrei could hear as well the sound of Jenniboni's approaching footsteps. Coming from down the hall her cheerful proclamation that "…something sure smells wonderful out there…" likewise echoed along the passageway.

"Your breakfast is almost ready", Andrei returned her salutation with one of his own just as she appeared from down the hall in her smartly pressed, casual-dress 'Star Exploration Administration' uniform.

"I'll heat up your coffee and donuts right away. Be back in a jiffy", he assured her, turning back towards the kitchen. Taking her rightful place at the table's head Jenniboni found herself lost in a delighted chorus of "Hi, Mommy", from the twins and a dignified, proper, yet enthusiastic "Good morning, Mother", from J.J..

Returning from the other room, neatly arranging his wife's first meal of the day before her, Andrei couldn't help but sneak an adoring glance in her direction before collecting his own early morning repast from the kitchen counter by the stove. It never failed to take his breath away how dashing, powerful, and sexy Jenniboni looked in her uniform. Form fitting enough to please the eye while not too revealing, gathered as well about her waist with a stylish gold belt, the fit of her one-piece dark green jumpsuit complimented quite nicely her full, sensuous, hour-glass figure.

To be perfectly honest it brought to Andrei memories of her old casual-dress Protectorate uniform, only green where the other had been red, light brown tan knee-high boots replacing her former highly polished black footwear. Only the royal gold turtleneck sweater worn beneath this outer garment alongside the bright yellow armbands, each adorned with a dark green fempacem, remained the same.

All-in-all he had to confess her present attire possessed a distinctly warmer, friendlier aura about it—one certain improvement being that this outfit didn't come equipped with those silver-tinted, mirror-paneled sunglasses that came with the other. Not only did they hide those lovely, soulful, dark brown eyes of hers they were also quite intimidating to boot. So much so Andrei would insist Jenniboni take them off least J.J. catch sight of her wearing them whenever returning home from work back on Earth.

Only four years ago and the sight of her mother wearing those oppressive spectacles with their blank, coldly reflective surfaces would always set their three-year-old daughter back then to crying, almost hysterical with fear.

Nevertheless Andrei remained of the firm conviction women just looked so naturally wonderful in uniform, so resplendent with power and authority. And Jenniboni was, without doubt, one of those fortunate women whose natural feminine qualities of courage, strength, power, and leadership were only further enhanced by the wearing of such.

Not that she wasn't already an achingly beautiful woman to begin with, blessed with both a voluptuous figure and an angelic face. Along with a cute button nose, olive complexion, and exquisitely large, gorgeous, dark brown eyes she was also graced with finely sculptured cheekbones and a strong jaw line granting her a proud, regal bearing.

And as a final crowning touch of glory her already divine looks were topped off by a full head of long, wavy, honey-blonde hair—a splendiferous golden crown cascading down and about her shoulders like a sun-dappled waterfall.

Tearing himself away from his loving reverie just long enough to gather up his own breakfast from the nearby kitchen, only then did he take his customary place at the other end of the family table from his wife.

Too busy each morning to partake of a regular, solid meal he nevertheless enjoyed sharing this special time together with his loved-ones, indulging in a quick, but nutritious liquid repast. Conversing among themselves while consuming the superb meal he prepared them, the entire family engaged in one of those casual sorts of everyday discussions that families have participated in for countless ages.

Probably one of Andrei's favorite times of the day he listened contentedly as the twins chattered on, speculating upon what might occur in school that day while recounting amusing anecdotes concerning the childish antics of classmates the day before—Jenniboni likewise asking Andrei to wash a couple of her personal items she'd left for him in their laundry hamper by hand instead of using the sonic wash—J.J.'s turn following that to tell her mother of the homework assignment she and her father worked on the night before for herstory class.

Dealing with the colonization of the outer System over the last two hundred years, Jenniboni told her that she genuinely looked forward to reading it. Andrei, although never doing the children's' homework for them, always remained ready to lend a helping hand whenever needed, inspecting their assignments for errors while likewise making sure they were always ready on time.

Finishing his breakfast drink Andrei noticed soon thereafter both twins beginning to fidget about in their seats at the very same moment J.J. asked if she could be excused.

Observing that all three children had cleaned their plates he told them all to go, get their jackets for school just as they began raising their voices in boisterous disagreement over some infantile matter, or another—the sort of insignificant subject matter small children find themselves more often than not arguing over.

Having not heard their father's command the two youngsters continued bickering, their voices rapidly escalating as they began to shove one-another back and forth in their chairs.

Their unruliness ground to an immediate halt soon enough though, doing so when Jenniboni leaned forward, cutting them off with two abrupt, attention-grabbing snaps of her long, graceful fingers in both their unsuspecting faces.

Taught from infancy to recognize this as an implicit directive to cease all untoward behavior they both froze in their seats like statues, immobile and erect, staring at their mother with wide, expectant eyes.

Having their undivided attention Jenniboni instructed them then in a firm, brisk, no nonsense voice brooking no contrariety:

"You heard your father: You shall now get up from your seats, push them in, and go about gathering up your jackets and school supplies. After that you shall then report back here by the front door before your father takes you to school.

*"**No running**!*

"And in future both of you better listen to your father, do as he says without my having to step in and take charge! Have I made myself understood?

"Tommy? Tammy?"

"Yes, Ma'am", they both replied, dutifully, knowing better than to do otherwise.

"Excellent", Jenniboni addressed them then in a softer voice, confident her point was made to the satisfaction of all those present: "In that case you'll thank your father for the outstanding meal he made before each of you do as I've instructed".

"Yes, Ma'am" they did again as told, doing so in a most subdued fashion.

Only then did Jenniboni turn her attention towards J.J., smiling warmly, answering her previous question:

"Yes dear, you may be excused: Go get your program wafers and ei-pad for school".

With that the young girl thanked her mother with an equally warm smile, thanking as well Andrei for breakfast before heading to her room. Alone for a moment with his wife Andrei rose as well to his own two feet, walking around the table with a leisurely gait to where she sat—her eyes closed in a relaxed, peaceful expression sipping daintily her coffee.

Reaching her side, placing a soft kiss upon her tender cheek, he expressed all the while his gratitude for how she handled so well each twin.

"You're absolutely welcome, Sweet-pea", she assured him, smiling between sips as he went about clearing dirty dishes from the family table:

"Just a matter of getting their undivided attention", she declared with a wry grin.

"Well, you certainly did that", Andrei chuckled, taking dirty tableware into the nearby kitchen.

Arranging all with care in the kitchen sink he then made his way back to the living/dining area, making his way over to the highly polished bronze coat rack standing near the door to their apartment.

Removing his favorite slick black leather jacket from one of its protruding hooks, he then inspected with care each and every pocket, making quite sure that all he needed for the long day ahead was all present and accounted for. When satisfied at last that nothing important was missing he was in the process of slipping it on over his shoulders just as Jenniboni placed gently her cup back down on its saucer.

With a mischievous little smile dancing at the corners of her full, sensuous lips she raised her hand, once again snapping her fingers in that same authoritative manner as before.

"Andrei! Come here. You've forgotten something important", she commanded sharply, using that same forbidding tone employed only moments ago chastising both Tommy and Tammy. Even with their backs to one-another, well-removed from each other's line of sight, Andrei had no trouble at all discerning his wife's true intent, her actual mood, beneath all her feigned bluster and angry posturing.

Knowing her so well there was no mistaking the subtle mirth in her otherwise stern, imposing tone most others would have missed. And choosing to play along for the sheer fun of it he tried to assume the same timorous, submissive demeanor as both twins, having all-the-same a difficult time trying to suppress an amused chuckle of his very own:

"Yes, Ma'am? I humbly apologize if I have displeased you in some way and I beg your forgiveness. What's the matter? What have I done?"

Jenniboni's lips curled upwards even more so at the plaintive sound of her husband's mock groveling. Struggling to keep her voice full of intimidating displeasure, gradually failing to do so from moment to moment, she pressed on all the same...

"Well, you have displeased me. You were about to leave before I could give you something!!"

"And what might that be, dearest?" he asked, having an increasingly difficult time maintaining straight face.

"Just this;" Jenniboni proclaimed.

Swiftly rising from her chair, forsaking every pretense at anger, she swung about to face him instead, wearing a smile that literally radiated both love and affection. Stepping quickly towards him, gathering him up in her arms, she held him ever so close in a strong yet tender embrace.

"Ahhh, I see what you mean", Andrei sighed, his pleasure evident.

Caressing broad shoulders he readily succumbed to her persuasive and irresistible charms, melting straightaway in her arms. Closing his eyes, his face tilted up towards hers, Jenniboni's warm, soft lips pressed now against his, her rose-scented perfume filled as well his senses with its delicious fragrance.

Heightening the already heady sensation brought about by the passionate touch of her loving mouth, a shudder of sensual delight set him all atremble when, parting her lips ever so slightly, she ran as well the tip of her tongue along the inside of his mouth. Weak in the knees with burning desire he almost cried out "*No Fair*" when she drew her face back from his, severing contact.

"Please don't stop now;" he moaned with intense longing.

"I'm sorry, sweetness'; she whispered throatily: "I guess I got a little carried away".

"I nearly got *very* carried away", he laughed weakly, gazing upwards into her beautiful, fawn-like eyes.

"I'll make it up to you. I promise", Jenniboni assured him, a soft smile full of gentle apology: "Consider that a down-payment on the near future".

Once separated from their loving embrace time began marching on yet again. Continuing its steady flow, no longer oblivious to its forward march, Andrei realized soon enough it was time to take all three children to school, his legs still somewhat shaky after withdrawing from her loving embrace.

"Come along, everyone", Andrei called out, all three children swiftly appearing before him as he removed his car keys from the outer right-hand pocket of his jacket. Lining them up for a little inspection, making sure each and every one had all they needed for the long day ahead, he then instructed them to say good-bye their mother once satisfied all was in perfect order.

J.J. didn't hesitate whatsoever to approach her as Jenniboni crouched down, receiving a kiss on the cheek although… at the very same time… the twins appeared quite reluctant to approach her, their mother's firm rebuke still fresh in their young memories. Neither of them either paused, or wavered any further though when they saw Jenniboni stretch her arms out to them in a gesture of loving welcome, a beatific smile upon her face.

Forgetting at once her earlier admonishments they delayed no longer, rushing without restraint over to their mother in eager anticipation. Wrapping her arms around each in a snug embrace Jenniboni lifted the both of them high up off the floor, planting a firm kiss on the cheek. Giggling in unison as their mother placed them back down they, too, said their good-byes as Andrei swung open the front door leading to both the small foyer and elevator beyond.

Watching them with a full heart go about their day Jenniboni gave all four of her little family a big smile and loving wave promptly returned as the door between them shut with a gentle click.

Chapter 6

"THE UNAWARE"

It was with an undeniable sense of self-pity, no enthusiasm whatsoever, Gloria went about preparing for her trip to Chiron City—the planet Demeter below.

Cursing under her breath her misfortune alone in the privacy of her shipboard quarters, she finished brushing her hair. Arranging her dark rimmed glasses with the relatively thin, light lenses back in place she felt a definite sinking sensation in the pit of her stomach upon noticing the time, realizing Lt. Cmdr.'s Marlowe and Straker would be coming for her shortly.

When invited at first to join them on shore-leave Gloria's first understandable response was to feel both quite honoured, and even flattered, to say the very least. Having for a long time admired in her immediate superior all those feminine attributes she considered sadly lacking in herself: Naomi's assertiveness, aggressiveness, strength and the way she seemed to always be in control of any given situation in addition to her clearly feminine good looks never ceased to inspire Gloria's imagination.

It wasn't until dwelling upon her 'idol's' invitation a little further it dawned on her with painful clarity what was most likely in store. Especially when, later on, she was instructed to look her best for the upcoming event. Convinced Naomi was trying her hand at a little matchmaking, Gloria couldn't help but feel like some dumb lamb to the slaughter.

Staring mournfully at her own reflection in the mirror before her, it once again occurred to her she wouldn't be in this whole mess if she'd only returned to the base instead of electing to stay onboard ship. Preferring the lonely solitude of some remote area aboard StarChild where she could lose herself in her work, Gloria considered it doubly ironic—bitterly so—that it was during one of those periods of voluntary isolation Naomi caught up to her.

Starting out with a few much-appreciated compliments on her work performance, Naomi soon followed that by asking if she'd care to join her and Lt. Cmdr. Straker planet-side to "see-the-sights". And accepting this most unanticipated offer with such unbridled effervescence at just being asked Gloria couldn't bring herself to back out at this late date, positive her superior would no doubt see through any flimsy excuse that she might concoct.

The very memory of how she leapt upon Naomi's invitation with the same unfettered joy a starving dog might show a scrap of raw meat was humiliating enough without having to endure the silent scorn… the possible ridicule… she feared Naomi might feel towards her should she likewise bow out now. With this worry first and foremost in her mind Gloria chose in the end to just resign herself to whatever sad fate might be in store for her—hoping in quiet desperation all would, in the final scheme of things, turn out for the best.

The problem wasn't that she didn't like men, or secretly covet one all for herself.

Quite the contrary!

Nothing further from the truth, still waters running deep indeed, the only real issue here was her lack of any real experience with the opposite sex. That and her equal lack of confidence needed in order to actively pursue one.

Down deep maybe that's why she still chose to join Naomi on this particular little excursion no matter her obvious trepidations. Someone to do for her what she didn't have the 'guts' to do for herself, a go-between to handle all the messy little particulars and preliminaries involved beforehand…

Someone to do Gloria's "dirty-work" for her ahead of time.

Experiencing yet another all-too-familiar pang of self-contempt, near loathing at the mere sight of her very own reflection, it was with yet another strong hint of self-pity Gloria considered her lack of confidence only justified.

"You're definitely not much of a catch, that's for sure", she scowled at herself in the mirror, not only ignoring all she had going for her, but actually turning the positive likewise into the negative.

Beautiful, sparkling brown-green eyes looking in her opinion both mundane and even insipid, the rich luster of her dark sable-brown hair was likewise judged unfairly as being 'dull and mousy'.

Even her pleasant, wholesome features and sweet, innocent face went unnoticed in her long search for the power and authority she considered absent.

Yet even while totally aware of the reasons for her low self-esteem, Gloria couldn't likewise imagine how anyone could ever hold her accountable. Not when obsessing on the constant, negative re-enforcement she endured throughout the entire length and breadth of her oh-so-young life.

From an early age onward Gloria could recall all at once the cruel taunts measured out by childhood peers in response to her boyishly short hair, masculine attire, and her passive, shy, and retiring demeanor—this torment growing steadily worse during her painfully recent teen years. While the other girls grew taller, filling out in all the right places, she remained not only several inches shorter than the average woman, but even a couple less than the average man:

A prime target for those who can only feel better about themselves by making others feel just as bad.

Nor did the boys help bolster her dwindling, already eroded, ego any.

Passing her by in their preference for the taller, stronger, and more outgoing girls they often treated her as though she never existed, a complete and total non-entity. Her face still burned with shame remembering one especially awful spring day back on Mars sitting by the large picture windows in the school library, daydreaming when she should have been working instead on the computer console situated before her.

Looking out at the green campus grounds beyond just as a group of the most handsome, popular boys in school came strolling by she was able to spy among them none other than Trevor Hanson. Even though Gloria knew there was no conceivable way he'd ever be interested in her, there was still nothing she could do about the schoolgirl crush she had on him.

Boys like that only went out with the really popular girls.

And captivated to the exclusion of all else by sight of Trevor walking by in his blue gym shorts and white T-shirt with the navy school letters on it, Gloria was taken by complete surprise when snuck up on from behind. Given the clear direction of her intense stare, her lustful young thoughts written for all to see all over her love-smitten face, the object of Gloria's adolescent desire was painfully obvious to everyone present.

Trevor's passing form was forgotten at once however at the sound of a cold, mocking voice cutting rudely through her awareness like a double-edged sword.

"Forget it, Greensley," the voice taunted her with scornful glee: "Trevor only goes out with real women. He'd never be interested in a miserable, creepy little hermaphrodite like you. So you can stare at his ass all you want 'cause you'll never get a piece of it."

Looking up from her seat to see a tall girl with dark auburn hair and ice-chip blue eyes staring down at her Gloria found herself confronted by Constance Turner herself. Not only Captain of the school basketball team, the most popular girl in school, Constance and Trevor were also going steady, Trevor wearing proudly about his neck her class-ring on a gold chain.

Nor did it take long to dawn on her that the girl standing over her wasn't the only one laughing, everyone else in the room likewise sharing a laugh at her expense. Her face turning a bright red Gloria could feel hot, stinging tears welling up, Constance still standing above her, arms folded across her chest, wearing an expression of amused contempt.

Mortified at the very thought of crying in front of everyone there, leaping from her chair, Gloria fled instead that scene of such utter humiliation... loud laughter ringing in her ears... before the tears finally burst forth freely from within.

From that day onwards she never returned to the scene of her embarrassment. Carrying a porta-comp with her at all times, she worked on her assignments in the lonely seclusion of the school basement instead.

Thinking only later about the whole affair she realized it wouldn't have been so bad had Constance flown into a jealous rage, beating Gloria senseless when observing her innocent ogling of Trevor's firm, supple form. At least such a clear display of violent emotion would have given everyone there the impression Constance saw Gloria as an actual threat, a "real" woman having a chance with the object of her desire, instead of having to endure such scornful ridicule.

Such degradation it was this which hurt more than anything else, more than any physical attack ever could, leaving her feeling inside so utterly worthless.

Then again the main contributor to the vast majority of her past trials, tribulations, and miseries in life had to be laid without a doubt at the feet of her Uncle Les, the original source of all her childhood sufferings.

Like Lt. Cmdr. Frances Miriam Straker before her, Gloria was likewise raised by a single male guardian. However, unlike the late, lamented Mr. Rolan Straker, Mas. Lester Peterson was, to Gloria's great misfortune, nothing at all like the first—Uncle Less a man renowned for neither his compassion nor his sensitivity …

Born and raised in the small Martian farming town of 'Telis-Ville', both Gloria's parents died one night in a transport accident when their only daughter was just three years old—this misfortune compounded even further upon finding herself left in the sole custody of her only living relative, her father's older brother, Uncle Les.

Over the centuries elderly Martian bachelors had come to be stereotyped as bitter, reserved, strict, and even oppressive as though living in perpetual mourning for their lost youth and wasted opportunities, taking out both with a vengeance on those young and wise enough not to fall into the same sorry trap.

And with Uncle Les living up happily to this ugly stereotype his total lack of experience with, or understanding of, little girls… his total indifference… made matters only that much worse.

End result?

Uncle Les went about doing his darndest to turn her into a "him", raising Gloria as one would a boy. Her short hair, passive demeanor, and even the masculine style and cut of her clothes back then, all the final result of her uncle's odiferous influence.

Finding both release and a certain amount of solace from her dismal existence in her studies, however, Gloria soon discovered a real aptitude for all things of a technical and mechanical nature—physical escape from her surroundings coming likewise into view learning of "Project StarChild"—the newly formed "Star Exploration Administration" seeking women of exceptional ability to crew the Commonwealth's first starship.

Motivated as never before in her young life with a goal worth any sacrifice, Gloria saw at long last a light appear at the end of that dark, bleak tunnel which was her life, applying for admission to the S.E.A.'s Officer's Training Academy.

Dearly hoping but never actually expecting to be selected, she couldn't believe her incredibly good fortune when accepted at the tender age of seventeen. Especially when given her previous track record with both good luck and the fates—further delight in store when awarded both the rank of Lieutenant alongside her position of Assistant Chief Engineer.

Nor did she care if her new rank and position were based more on her technical genius rather than age or experience, viewing the last three years of her young life as her best ever, the youngest commissioned officer aboard Humanity's very first starship at the impressive young age of only twenty.

Finally an active, vital, contributing part of something truly significant she discovered a new sense of self-worth slowly, but surely blossoming forth from within. Being with others who honestly respected her and appreciated her abilities, showing her both friendship and acceptance, Gloria found herself gradually distancing herself from the old world of before, moving towards new worlds and possibilities.

Yet even granted this newly discovered positive re-enforcement in her life, Gloria still found herself feeling both awkward and anxious in certain social situations, especially those in which the opposite sex was involved. Wanting desperately as she did to finally take that particular plunge in life... men still remaining uncharted waters... the influence of past experience still had a firm grip on her very soul she had yet to completely shake off.

So much so in fact as to elicit from her a self-depreciating frown at the very sight of her own reflection, her mirror image returning the favour with an equally disgusted frown all its own. The only thing she could find to admire there was the green and gold S.E.A. uniform they both wore in common. It's clear, smart design and impressive green and gold armbands displaying with pride the emblem of all Womankind never ceased to inspire in her a clear sense of awe.

Lost in thought Gloria nearly jumped out of her skin, jolted back to reality by the sound of the door chime to her quarters announcing the arrival of her two traveling companions. Certain that it was they, she grabbed in haste her purse from atop the nearby bed, calling out in as cheerful a voice she could possibly muster:

"All ready!"

Chapter 7

"THE CALL'

Left now all to herself in the quiet solitude of her apartment, the rest of her family going about their daily routines elsewhere, Jenniboni checked her watch only to discover she had an extra half-hour before her meeting. Still feeling a little peckish after breakfast she decided then and there to fill in those few remaining gaps with yet another hot, steaming cup of her husband's excellent rich, dark, brew:

"No question about it. He sure makes one darn good cup of coffee", she smiled to herself… content… making her way into the neighbouring kitchen.

Then again he was an excellent cook and homemaker in general, knowing as she did men twice Andrei's age who didn't measure up at all in the kitchen like he did. No doubt about it, none in the least, she was indeed a lucky woman in possession of a wonderful husband, three beautiful children, and an exciting career.

Thinking nevertheless how fortunate she was to have such a family Jenniboni experienced all-the-same a twinge of guilt thinking how little time she spent with them as of late.

Certainly less than she used to.

Leaving the kitchen once having poured herself another cup of coffee, thinking further on the matter, she opted for a few minutes of silent meditation in front of the large living/dining room's window-walls.

Meeting up together in one of the living/dining room's four corners, comprising two of the room's four walls, they stretched all the way from the kitchen along the first wall, and along the second wall from where the 3-DV cube sat in the rooms opposite corner—this northwestern exposure Jenniboni's favorite feature of their penthouse apartment, providing as it did a spectacular view of the "Project StarChild" base on which she and her happy family lived.

From this vantage point she could gaze out and down at nearly half the base, their living unit resting atop one of the four tall apartment complexes containing quarters for all base residents—all four located in the exact center of the base, allowing those living there a clear view of a considerable segment of their daily surroundings.

Situated just below the highest section of that protective dome covering the entire StarChild community, directly beneath the 'dome orb' high above, they were the tallest structures to be found anywhere there, offering a truly remarkable view of what lay beyond.

In the foreground, off to the immediate left, Jenniboni could observe quite readily a full half of one of the other nearby high-rise complexes, its glistening silver chrome exterior glistening, sparkling in the light from above.

Having the same appearance as its three sisters it soared upward like a brilliant shard of ice while, in direct contrast to the cold, arctic facades of all four high-rises, a vast greenbelt of woman-made parklands lay directly below.

Encircling the massive, tapered residential buildings pathways of a smooth black material meandered throughout the realistic leafy syntha-trees and rich dark green artificial grass like ribbons of jade—low-lying Japanese bridges spanning likewise the small crystal blue ponds scattered here and there throughout the park.

From her current vantage point Jenniboni could even make out a few people looking almost like insects from where she stood on high... base personnel walking about along the shiny black pathways below... some women down there strolling along with their men, others making their lonely way to work.

And in the far distance, on the park's other side, there were several structures of various sizes and shapes, each surrounded by its own syntha-lawn connected to the others by the same winding obsidian walkways.

Without question the largest of these was the Base Administration Building—a sprawling, low-lying collection of cubes, spheres, and cylinders melded together to form one harmonious whole—beyond which there existed at the very edge of the base one of the two shuttle ports servicing the entire compound.

The port from where Jenniboni would take her private shuttle up to StarChild himself.

But until then she planned for the moment to enjoy the bright 'sunny' day outside, a sight courtesy of the luminous "dome orb", a light fixture simulating day and night embedded in the uppermost center of the base dome itself,.

Programmed for twelve hours of each it would glow at its stellar brightest a brilliant golden white, turning the dome's interior a brilliant sky-blue during daylight hours while during its nocturnal phase it took on a lunar glow like a full moon back on Earth, the dome becoming at that point completely transparent.

It was then, during this period of simulated night, that the brilliant stars above and the frozen, lifeless grey surface of Demeter beyond... totally devoid of any form of atmosphere whatsoever... would be visible.

Jenniboni's preferred time even moreso than the daylight hours she would stand at night before the magnificent window walls of her apartment home, meditating. Looking out at the base below and the stars beyond she would contemplate what lay outside of Womankind's solar-system in silent speculation. Watching the shuttles arrive and depart for their various destinations the children, also enjoying the night view, often stood next to her to see what might be out there.

And of all three J.J. enjoyed especially this opportunity to share time here with her mother stargazing, sharing philosophical conversations speculating what might be out there in the vastness of deep space. Jenniboni always smiled, impressed, hearing her older daughter compare the stars above to diamonds scattered across a field of black velvet.

Sometimes Andrei would even bring them a little unanticipated, but always appreciated after-dinner snack and/or beverage like cookies and/or hot cocoa. Serving it to them while they stood there he'd quietly depart afterwards, leaving mother and daughter alone to their cosmic discourses.

It was at these Jenniboni got the distinct impression Andrei preferred looking out the windows during the day-time hours, observing him taking advantage of the view mostly then. She couldn't help but wonder if this was because he missed living back on Earth, the dome reminding him at such times of the blue skies of home.

If anything the Project StarChild base had about it a certain tranquil, Zen haiku quality not unlike a Japanese garden, or a futuristic Buddhist monastery.

The women responsible for both its design and final construction clearly took into consideration the effects of aesthetics on the long-term mental and emotional well-being of permanent inhabitants. Hidden from view in the subterranean levels beneath the idyllic scenery directly below were the more functional technical and mechanical aspects that kept the base running smoothly—life support, storage, power generators, mechanized transport, and freight facilities—kept otherwise out of sight.

****

Jenniboni had just finished her second cup of coffee as a mechanical trilling interrupted her silent contemplations.

Quickly setting her empty cup down on the dining room table she hurried over to the source of this rather insistent sound, a V-phone mounted on the wall partition between kitchen door and the hallway leading to the mistress bedroom.

Activating the insistent device's com-screen the warbling sound it made was replaced immediately by Admiral Sellers' jowly face. Wearing a grave business-like expression she stared at her with an expectant look. Noting the mood her superior was in, recognizing that look from their years of long association, Jenniboni greeted the other woman in as official a tone of voice as possible.

"Good morning, Admiral".

"Commodore…"

"How may I be of service?"

"I need to see you in my office, immediately!"

"I was about to attend a meeting with my second-in-command, Commander Nikarov, aboard StarChild in less than half an hour".

"I'm afraid that will have to wait for now. We have a serious matter to discuss", the senior officer addressing her told her in a no-nonsense tone of voice allowing no further contradiction.

"May I enquire as to what the problem might be?".

"You may, Commodore", Admiral Sellers came back at her with a grim little smile: "but, I don't intend to discuss the matter with you over the phone".

"Serious indeed."

"Believe me, it is", the Admiral assured her in that same no-nonsense voice as before: "Serious enough for the Prime Arch Matri herself to make a special trip all the way out here from Earth on her own private cruiser'.".

"The Supreme Mother is coming here?" Jenniboni asked, a note of concern creeping into her voice. Anything this major couldn't be good. It was safe to assume that the P.A.M. wasn't traveling all this way merely to wish them 'bon voyage' and say her farewells.

"Correct."

"I'll be right over."

Chapter 8

"THE ADMIRER"

The building lift reached the end of its long, leisurely descent from the penthouse apartment above, dropping off all three children and their father on one of the underground parking levels directly under their high-rise.

Stepping off the lift first the twins chattered amiably amongst themselves, their voices echoing off of the light tan brown perma-plasti walls, while Andrei and J.J. brought up the rear, listening to how the sound of their footsteps likewise bounced off of the hard plastic/metal compound.

Except for the four family members present the entire level was uninhabited save for the parked vehicles stored there, the sounds they made the only disturbances in the otherwise deafening silence surrounding them on all sides.

Although the vast parking compound was well-lit by bright overhead lighting tubes running everywhere throughout the entire level, their glow banishing any and all shadows... any otherwise dark spaces... Andrei still didn't care much for the apartment complex's parking facilities.

It always struck him as more than a bit cold down there, impersonal, and even somewhat intimidating.

At least they didn't have to go far before reaching Andrei's little chrome-blue sports car, complete with its set of vanity license plates simply reading "ANDREI", nestled between two other vehicles.

Sitting in a long row of vehicles... a wide assortment of types, colours, and sizes... the sleek, sexy, little two-door was a 10th wedding anniversary gift from Jenniboni about three months ago, just two weeks after his 27th birthday. As it was he already had something special in mind for her 33rd birthday, on the 5th of August, planning to spring it on her during the next local Commonwealth Day celebration in Chiron City.

When she first presented him with his shiny new dream machine she told him it was for being so brave and devoted, leaving all his family and friends back on Earth without any word of complaint, only to move out to the very edge of the entire System.

Not really having though much choice in the matter, his duty as her husband being to follow wherever she led, Andrei was all-the-same deeply touched by both the sentiment and her generosity of spirit. Jenniboni even allowed him to pick it out for himself, her only stipulation being that it must be roomy enough for the entire family, having as well enough trunk space for groceries.

While not appearing to do so from the outside Andrei's final choice actually met with all her requirements, Jenniboni apparently pleased with his choice since she clearly bought it for him. No longer did he need her permission to use her car to do the shopping, take the children to school, or run other errands.

Unlocking the passenger side door first, pulling the front seat foreword, he instructed the twins to climb in back before letting J.J. take her rightful place as the eldest daughter in front. Of course it went without saying that, had Jenniboni been present, it would have been her place as his wife to drive while he rode up front at her side.

Pulling out of the parking area into the complex series of warren-like auto-tubes connecting the many different sections of the base, Andrei drove along until reaching the wide thoroughfare that would take them directly into Chiron City. And blocking his entry into the tunnel beyond were two horizontal blue-grey metal bars, a sentry booth to the left of the accessway.

A checkpoint guard sitting within Andrei slowed to a stop some thirty meters away. Not having long though to wait for clearance the young woman on duty within was reading an electronic information pad, a broad smile leaping to her face when looking up in Andrei's direction.

Placing the ei-pad down on the small counter to her side, picking up a clipboard instead, she wasted no time getting up, Andrei rolling down the window on his side just as the young Ensign in her S.E.A. uniform made it half-way to the car—sauntering along with a light, breezy, carefree gait.

No sooner had he lowered the driver-side window though, J.J. leaned over to her father, giggling: "Here comes your girlfriend".

"Hush", Andrei hissed, mortified: "Don't say anything to embarrass me; please, dear".

Although painfully obvious to both the junior officer now approaching had a definite crush on Andrei the object of her affections had no problem with this. At least not as long as the young gentlewoman in question didn't try to take any undue liberties with him. And having given him no reason to worry so far, always behaving herself and treating him with the obvious respect a proper laddie should be, he found her polite attentions rather sweet...

Even flattering.

"Don't worry, Father. I won't say anything", J.J. grinned only a few seconds before the smiling young guard leaned over, looking in the driver's side window at both Andrei and the Saphira children.

"Good morning, Mr. Saphira", she greeted him with obvious enthusiasm, possessing both a warm smile and a lively twinkle in her eye: "And how is everyone doing on this fine day?"

"Very kind of you to ask", Andrei returned her greeting with a warm smile of his own: "We're all doing quite well, Ensign Zeppner. Thank you for asking. I'm just on my way to the city to take the children to school and pay a visit to my father-in-law at the Chiron City's Men's Shelter".

"And how are you doing today this wonderful morning?", she then asked J.J., leaning a little further into the car to give the young girl seated at her father's side a friendly smile full of sincere interest.

"Oh... I'm all right", J.J. grinned, barely able to suppress the giggles welling up inside her.

Although the congenial young checkpoint guard didn't seem to take any notice, Andrei could detect without fail the suppressed laughter in his daughter's voice just barely under control. Closing his eyes he prayed in silence to the Good Lord above his daughter wouldn't do, or say anything to cause him any further embarrassment, giving rise to any awkward situations.

Nevertheless he still managed to reach as well into the left breast pocket of his leather jacket for the Base Resident I.D. he carried always on his person and, noting this out of the corner of her eye, Ens. Zeppner stopped him at once:

"That won't be necessary, Sir. I know who you all are", she assured him sweetly.

"Thank you Ensign", Andrei smiled appreciatively: "That's very kind of you, I'm sure".

"Not at all. Think nothing of it. My pleasure," the young officer swiftly assured him, trying to sound as businesslike as possible despite the obvious feeling written all over her face. Pulling her head and shoulders out of the car window she then made a little check mark beside Andrei's name on the list of base residents coming and going, using the computerized clipboard she'd been holding all that time.

"I'll just open the gate so you can be on your way", she announced, leaning over yet again, taking one last lingering look at that object of her unrequited love:

"I've no wish to detain you any longer".

"Once more, thank you", Andrei smiled almost with pity, starting to feel sorrier than anything else for the moonstruck young woman hardly out of her teens.

"No trouble at all", she assured him, another heart-felt smile: "Have a good day".

Then, almost as an afterthought, she added: "And please be sure to give my best to the Commodore".

"I promise to remember for sure to do that very same thing", Andrei guaranteed her: "And you be sure to have a good day, too, Ensign".

"Why, thank you, Sir", Ms. Zeppner beamed with obvious delight before returning once more to her little booth.

By the time she reached her post Andrei had already rolled up his window, starting up the engine yet again. No sooner had the motor come to life the good ensign pushed the button on the console beside her chair to draw back the gate, the two thick bars retracting into the tunnel's side.

Yes, indeed…

He'd be sure to tell his wife of the ensign's good wishes and fond regards Andrei reflected, giving the young gentlewoman in question a friendly little wave good-bye as he put the car in forward. Little did the love-smitten young officer know he'd already informed Jenniboni all about the checkpoint guard and her oh, so obvious feelings for him.

Sure that no one would attempt any improprieties with the husband of the second most powerful person on the base, having complete faith in Andrei's ability to handle such situations, she even found the whole matter quite amusing…

Even endearing.

Maybe so. On the other hand however Andrei couldn't help, but feel a certain sense of undeniable pity for his hapless young admirer.

Once well on their way though J.J. finally gave vent at last to the torrent of laughter she'd been holding back until now, all the while mimicking the infatuated ensign:

"'Have a gooooood day and please be sure to give my best to the Commodore'".

With that the twins in back squealed in approval with gales of laughter all their own, sharing their sister's hilarity with her. Peals of laughter ringing in Andrei's ears, getting under his skin right away, grating on his very nerves:

"That will be enough from all three of you", he was quick to admonish them: "Don't be so cruel".

Then, giving J.J. a pointed look, he added: "Besides, that could very well be you someday".

"Don't be silly, Father. I'm not going to be some dumb old security guard sitting in some stupid little booth somewhere when I grow up. I'm going to command my own starship someday, just like Mother", she proclaimed in a haughty voice dripping with smug superiority.

"Don't be such a little snob", Andrei reprimanded her, sharply, doing nothing to hide his disapproval:

"Besides, that's not what I was referring to", he added with a little sideways glance, diverting his attention from the road ahead just long enough to give her a wry little grin.

Taking J.J. a moment to figure out what he was driving at her eyes bugged out in complete and utter disbelief once she did:

"Oh, Father—really!" she exclaimed, shocked and confounded.

"Well, in that case, maybe it would be best if we just dropped the entire subject. Agreed?" he suggested with a sly smile full of merry amusement.

"Yes, Father", J.J. relented, returning his smile with a broad grin and wee little giggle of her own.

****

It was some twenty minutes, or so before they started up the gradual incline leading to the surface, up from the tunnel they traveled so far onto the streets of Chiron City. Making their way down broad avenues and by-ways lined with quaint little shops and office buildings, passing by City Hall, they traveled a wide thoroughfare lined on both sides by tall artificial pine trees towards the children's school.

Standing in the center of a large expanse of syntha-grass it was a sprawling, low-rise, off-white building constructed of the same durable plastic/metal compound used on the base. Parking the car in front of the main entrance, relieved they weren't late after all, Andrei could still make out the active forms of happy children buzzing about a playset in the school's front lawn, a group of attentive teachers keeping a close eye on them.

Escorting the twins to their classroom, trusting J.J. to make it safely without assistance to hers once inside the building, Andrei exchanged then a few pleasantries with Tommy and Tammy's teacher… a ginger-haired laddie in his early 30's, Mas. Claude Jenkins, whom the twins absolutely adored… before heading out to see his father-in-law.

Chapter 9

"RAOUL"

Traffic was light as Andrei made his way across town. Making good time he turned into the parking lot for the Chiron branch of the Commonwealth Men's Shelter. Luckily there were few other cars present, allowing him to park as close as possible to the side-gate entrance—black wrought iron bars set against sparkling, high white walls surrounding the entire complex—an imposing sign posted there declaring in large, bold letters:

"NO WOMEN OVER 18 ALLOWED PAST THIS POINT"

Regrettable as this meant Jenniboni couldn't visit her father on shelter grounds, Andrei could understand nonetheless the underlying reason behind this particular decree. Originally founded just before the 'Ahnteekahn Civil War' as a means of protecting those few remaining men at the time it eventually evolved into a sanctuary for those very rare battered and abused men in society alongside those in need of temporary shelter until able to secure more permanent lodgings elsewhere—Jenniboni's father, Raoul, falling under this secondary category.

Still though it must be said in their high honour the women of the Tammyite Matriarchate very rarely, if ever, abused their men.

Walking alongside the pristine, sparkling white wall towards the glistening gateway ahead Andrei spotted an elderly man with wavy silver hair positioned just inside the gate ahead. Reading an ei-pad mystery novel, a lawn table resting at his side upon which sat a clear mug of either coffee or tea, Andrei recognized him at once—one of the shelter residents.

Assigned on a rotational basis various tasks in aid of the shelter's upkeep the older laddie ahead always seemed to draw sentry duty. All-in-all a rather cushy job, his single responsibility was to admit only those allowed on shelter grounds,

"Hello, Vince", Andrei called out, the other man returning Andrei's salutation. Peering up from whatever he was reading, Vince returned Andrei's greeting with a smile of his own. Setting the small, flat, flexible ei-pad down beside his mug of "who-knows-what" he got up from his chair, making his way over to both Andrei and the wrought iron gate between them.

"I gather you're here to see Raoul?" Vince asked in a congenial voice by way of welcome.

"Yes, indeed. Is he up in his rooms?"

"Quite. As a matter of fact he just finished up with kitchen duty and is waiting for you up in his apartment right now as we speak. Would you like me to let him know that you're here?" asked the elder laddie present.

With that he patted with the palm of his hand a black leather protective holster hanging from his belt, a portable V-phone within.

"Sure thing. Thanks", Andrei agreed as Vince unlocked the gate between them with a tiny jingle of the security programmed computer keys kept secure on his person. Crossing the threshold into the shelter grounds the actual shelter itself consisted of a pale bluish white building with a functional cubist design standing some six storeys in height.

Complete with reflective mirror-paneled chrome windows all in the name of sweet privacy the shelter compound boasted as well a lush, green syntha-grass lawn extending all the way to the tall alabaster-like walls. Encircling likewise the entire property all this greenery included artificial weeping willow trees strategically placed, practically indistinguishable from the real thing, providing shade for dark brown park benches arranged beneath.

Protecting them from the bright "day-time" light of the city's dome-orb high above, there was even a swing/slide set and small sandbox set up nearby for whatever children might live there with their fathers. Casually taking all this in Andrei could make out no youngsters playing there, noticing nevertheless two men sitting under the nearest weeping willow, two toddlers and a little baby with them.

Both men appeared to be just a little older than Andrei, one cradling the small infant baby in his arms, feeding it formula, while his companion leaned forward, playing with two little girls wearing pale daisy yellow summer frocks.

Sitting together on a pink and white checkered blanket spread out on the ground, a plentiful assortment of toys arrayed about them, the second laddie was trying to keep them entertained the best he could with one of those many playthings gathered about.

"Recently widowered fathers", he speculated to himself with more than just a small trace of sincere pity, reaching by then the end of the walkway leading up a short flight of steps into the sanctuary's interior. While counting his blessing the rest of the time as well it was times like these that drove home most for Andrei how lucky... truly fortunate... he was to have a loving wife, three beautiful children, and a roof of his own over his head.

Stepping through a set of double doors comprised of the same reflective paneling as the shelter's windows, he found himself in a small lobby decorated in festive colours, a panoramic mural painted upon the walls. Painted by both the adult residents and their children, the love and skill that must have gone into its composition never ceased to amaze and impress Andrei whenever seeing it.

Approaching the reception desk ahead to sign the guest register he was greeted by another shelter resident, engaging the young man stationed behind the counter in casual conversation before taking a nearby lift up to his father-in-law's flat.

****

No sooner had the elevator doors parted on the fourth floor than Andrei was met by Raoul. Already waiting there to greet him in that deep, rich, resonant voice of his, he led Andrei down the hallway to his private quarters:

"Would you care for some coffee, dear boy?", Raoul offered, closing his front door behind them.

Sure he'd find another place soon, his late wife having left him in her will financially secure, he turned down Jenniboni and Andrei's original offer to come live until then with them. Claiming to value his independence too much Raoul simply didn't want to be a burden, realizing they didn't really have the extra room, not wishing to impose.

"I'm afraid the coffee maker has suffered some sort of nervous breakdown, or some such thing, as it appears to have gone on the fritz. Regrettably this means I'm only able to offer instant".

Unable to abide the beverage himself, preferring tea, Raoul kept it on hand nevertheless for those times his son-in-law visited, Andrei feeling the same way about the latter.

"No problem. That will be quite fine, thank you", Andrei assured him.

Removing his jacket, he could hear Raoul likewise moving about in the kitchen....

"Would you like some assistance?"

"No need, dear boy", came the reply from across the breakfast counter separating the small kitchenette from his apartment living room: "Please have a seat".

Laying his jacket down on the couch at the far side of the room, preparing to take a seat, Andrei's attention was captured at once by the sight of a large silver-grey envelope replete with navy blue security stripes. Sitting on the coffee table directly before him that mysterious package Jenniboni was so very closemouthed about, refusing to reveal any of its tantalizing secrets. There, right between two dark blue racing stripes, was Raoul's address clearly written in her own bold, distinct handwriting.

No mistaking it at all for anyone else's.

44

Controlling though his burning curiosity he refused to give in to the overwhelming temptation now smoldering within to take just one little, teensy-weensy peek inside. Despite his natural, innate curiosity he had no desire, no wish to violate his father-in-law's privacy.

Returning from the kitchen, carrying a tray replete with two cups and a plate of assorted cookies, Raoul couldn't help grinning, Andrei's all-consuming curiosity easily visible.

"I see you've noticed the letter Jenny sent", he teased with gentle good humor, the only person alive who could actually get away with referring to Jenniboni as "Jenny".

So absorbed with his curiosity Andrei didn't even hear Raoul's soft approach. Totally ignorant of his return until hearing Raoul's voice from across the coffee table a scant meter away, Andrei's head snapped upwards in Raoul's direction. Visibly jolted out of his quiet reverie, his face turned a bright red.

"No need for embarrassment, son", the older man smiled in perfect understanding. Placing the tray down on the table between them, he did so right beside the object of Andrei's obvious obsession.

Raoul handed him his cup.

"Well... I must admit being curious ever since Jenniboni asked me to first mail it for her", Andrei confessed with sheepish hesitation, afraid of appearing too nosey as Raoul took a seat in the well-padded armchair across the way. With a cup of tea in hand he settled back, crossing his legs in a relaxed posture, as Andrei plucked up a chocolate wafer cookie from the plate. Dunking it in his cup of coffee it was then he heard Raoul tell him in a quite casual manner he could take a look inside if he so desired.

"Are you sure?"

"Absolutely", Raoul asserted with a wry grin: "Besides, you're going to find out sooner or later anyway".

Trying not to appear overly anxious Andrei slowly placed his coffee cup back down on the tray, picking up the envelope instead. Slipping its contents carefully out of their silver-gray container he found himself scanning what were clearly legal documents. Eyes growing wider as he turned each page faster than the one before Andrei could hardly contain his surprise when reaching the last page.

"These are Jenniboni's official Guardian Fem papers for you, all signed," he exclaimed in a startled voice. Voluntarily responsible for the physical and legal protection of a single, divorced, or widowered male relative should the need for such ever arise a 'Guardian Fem' was usually the man's nearest living female relative who—by her own choice—took those responsibilities upon herself.

At least that is until a man chose to wed, his Guardian Fem signing then her legal obligations over to his future wife.

"Soooo ... you're getting married again. I had no idea. Congratulations," Andrei finally spoke up with a sly grin, having recovered from his initial surprise.

"Jenny didn't have any clue either until I sprang the news on her just a couple of weeks ago".

"That time you asked her out to lunch alone?".

"Precisely dear boy. Needless to say she was rather startled as well. I'm sorry to have left you out of the loop for so long but I thought it best to tell her first, for obvious reasons, before telling anyone else", Raoul explained, giving the legal documents still in Andrei's hand a pointed look.

"No need to apologize. I understand completely. So who's the lucky gentlewoman? Did Jenniboni meet her at your meeting?", Andrei rushed, asking in a hurried voice, eager in his natural excitement for more details.

"Well, in the first place her name is Rebecca Illingworth. She's a deputy prosecutor with the Chiron Ministry of Justice and no, Jenny didn't get a chance to meet her. Becky and I felt it best to wait until we were sure of where our relationship was going before telling anyone. She didn't even propose until only a few days before my lunch with Jenny:

"Besides", Raoul added with an amused little smile of his own: "I thought it would be best to break the news to her alone, father to daughter, first. Wouldn't do to just show up with Becky and announce right from the start: 'Oh; by the way Sweetheart, I'm getting married. Here, meet your new Step-Mother'".

"I see your point", Andrei laughed. "Noooo… Jenniboni wouldn't care for that at all".

"Precisely what I thought", Raoul agreed, wholeheartedly: "Don't worry, though. You'll get a chance to meet her soon enough. Jenny and I have arranged for all four of us to get together and have a night out on the town after she returns from Alpha-Centauri".

"This is fantastic", Andrei beamed, absolutely delighted; "even though I have to confess to being rather overwhelmed by all of this.

"Nevertheless I guess it should come as no big surprise that you'd end up marrying someone in law enforcement again", he added in a wry tone of voice, having to admit it was strange to think of Raoul as no longer being a "Saphira".

All the same, though, 'Raoul Illingworth' definitely had a nice ring to it.

"Of all the people in all the worlds throughout the System, you're the last one I would have expected to drop such a bombshell out of the clear blue like this", Andrei confided with an amused little shake of his head.

"And why might that be?" Raoul asked with good-natured reproach: "As they say 'just because there's some snow on the roof doesn't mean that there is no fire in the furnace anymore'…

"Then again I have to admit that there's no longer any snow up there either. Not anymore", he concluded with a broad grin, running the palm of his hand lightly across his bald scalp.

"No, no, that's not what I meant", Andrei rushed to assure the older man, afraid he'd actually offended him: "It's just that, after eight years ago, I was always of the impression that you never wanted to get married again".

It didn't come as any surprise whatsoever to Andrei that Raoul would easily attract the attentions of the opposite sex with both his youthful, well-toned physique and his noble, aquiline, and aristocratic facial features.

And there was likewise something many women found sexy about men like Raoul, so unabashedly bald and yet confident in their appearance—both men quite aware how, whenever out on the town for a bite to eat or do some shopping, there were just as many women giving Raoul the same lingering, desirous glances as would look at Andrei....

Even women Andrei's age would stare appreciatively at his father-in-law from across crowded rooms.

"No need to fear", Raoul assured Andrei with a paternal smile:

"I understand fully your surprise and sympathize. Yes, eight years ago was indeed a pivotal time in my life: As *you* are clearly aware, dear boy", he concurred with a knowing wink.

"I'll admit that, when my beloved Elissa was so suddenly taken from me, I was convinced my life was over. I was convinced beyond a shadow of doubt that I'd never be happy with another woman ever again.

"Until I met Becky that is.

"I'm certain that Elissa would approve of both Becky and our plans to marry. In fact, to be quite candid, I have little doubt Elissa would be disappointed in me that I have waited this long to find someone else".

Andrei had to agree with his father-in-law's assessment the late Ms. Saphira would have indeed been upset with her husband for having taken so long to get over her death, catching likewise the actual meaning behind Raoul's use of the words "as *you* are clearly aware".

Unable to miss the significance of how he'd stressed the pronoun "*you*", along with that conspiratorial little wink he just gave him, the passing away of Commissioner Elissa M. Saphira marked as well a major turning point in the relationship between those two men now talking, getting along so well.

It wasn't always this way.

In fact it was no lie to say that, during the first two years of Andrei's marriage to Jenniboni, the two men couldn't stand one another in the least, their earlier relationship a purely antagonistic one. While Andrei's new mother-in-law clearly adored her daughter's new, young groom it was equally apparent his father-in-law didn't.

Right from the wedding reception onwards Andrei knew exactly what his new in-laws thought of him. He'd always remember overhearing by accident a private conversation between mother and daughter at the reception, recalling how Elissa told Jenniboni how fortunate she was.

Referring to Andrei by such positive and enthusiastic adjectives as "sweet", "wonderful", and "exceedingly handsome" he smiled at the memory of how his new mother-in-law called him a "sweet, charming, and endearing young Laddie"—instructing her daughter to always love, cherish, protect, and be good to him, treasuring him always with both tenderness and understanding.

On a less pleasant note however Andrei could also remember, while still at the reception, asking Raoul what he should now call him. Right from the very start he'd been nervous around his new father-in-law, not knowing how to act in his company. Nor did it help matters any when the senior male Saphira gave him a harsh, cold stare informing him in a frosty voice: "I'd prefer it if you call me 'Mr. Saphira'" before turning on his heal, walking away, leaving behind in the wake of his words a shocked Andrei too stunned to speak.

From the very beginning Raoul viewed his new son-in-law as a shallow, superficial, spoiled rich little pretty boy. And in return Andrei considered Raoul a cold, hard tyrannical autocrat.

It wasn't until two years later, after Elissa had her fatal heart attack working in her beloved garden, the relationship between both men began taking a turn for the better. Elissa always loved working in the soil in her back yard, the love she put into it showing in its beautiful symmetry and, during those first two years of his marriage to Jenniboni, Andrei would seek refuge from Raoul's frigid hostility there with Elissa whenever visiting his in-laws.

Realizing that horticulture wasn't really her son-in-law's cup of tea the elderly matriarch still enjoyed his bubbly, cheerful, and devoted company alongside his youthful enthusiasm and sharp, enquiring mind. Often complimenting him on his intelligent inquiries into her gardening activities she proclaimed him a "bright young thing"—an obvious term of endearment Andrei would always treasure and cherish along with her very memory.

Given the all-too-brief time that he had with which to share her company, Andrei was at least grateful for the time that he did have in which to know her better. He would always and forever remember his mother-in-law as a warm, caring, and remarkable gentlewoman—able to see in her where his wife had likewise acquired her exact same wonderful, chivalrous, feminine qualities.

Still regretting her dying so soon after just getting to know her really better, it was only then the thaw in his relationship with Raoul occurred some two weeks after the funeral. It was then Jenniboni asked him the day before to help her father with some packing, too occupied with a case at work to help herself.

Dutifully obeying her he dreaded nevertheless doing so, Raoul selling the large estate upon which he and Elissa lived together for most of their married life.

Arriving at his father-in-law's front door he was greeted by Raoul with his same, usual icy contempt right from the very get-go before even letting him in. It wasn't until a couple of hours later he witnessed his father-in-law's cold Prussian-like exterior shatter into little pieces, right in the middle of packing away a series of framed tri-dee photo's.

Coming across one of him with Elissa at their wedding he stared at it for what seemed like an eternity, his face frozen in an anguished expression of true inner turmoil—torment—before doing something Andrei never saw him do before. Tears slowly, silently crept down Raoul's cheeks before he began to openly sob and tremble. Staggering over to a nearby couch, collapsing into it straight away, he buried his face in his hands, weeping openly over his loss.

Andrei's surprise was fleeting but his concern remained, rushing as he did to the older man's side. Sitting beside him, forgetting all about their stormy relationship, he put a sympathetic arm around the other, holding him close.

Comforting Raoul in a soothing voice he ended up crying himself, part of him over the grieving man's pain and part for the loss he likewise felt over his mother-in-law's death. From that day onward their relationship took an immediate change for the better, the false impressions each had of the other were finally dispelled. From that point on their relationship grew much better, a deep and true friendship progressing even further into that of father and son.

"I'm likewise sure Elissa would approve", Andrei agreed with a gentle smile:

"And, on that note, I likewise want to assure you both Jenniboni and I wish both you and Becky all the happiness, love, and good-luck in the System", he added, putting the Guardian Fem release forms back in their envelope, placing them back where he first saw them.

Reaching once more over to the tray for his coffee cup it came as no surprise to learn Jenniboni offered not only to give him away at the wedding, standing in as the *'Mother of the Groom'*, but even offered to pay for the entire event. Frankly, Andrei would have been somewhat disappointed in her were she to have done otherwise.

Settling back into the couch, cup and cookie in hand, he couldn't fail but notice the somewhat hesitant look on Raoul's face, clearly trying to work up his courage to ask something important.

"Go ahead", Andrei grinned: "I can see you have something serious in mind you want to ask me".

"Well it's like this, dear boy. Jenny and I were discussing the actual particulars of the wedding and she suggested that I talk to you, sure you'd be the best choice", Raoul hemmed and hawed, beating around the bush …

"Now I realize that it would be a major inconvenience, and I'll understand perfectly if you tell me…"

"I can't tell you anything unless you ask me first", Andrei cut him off with an amused chuckle.

"Yes. Of course", Raoul grinned at his own foolish reluctance:

"Well, what I'm trying to ask in my bumbling, round-about way is if you'd be willing to assist me in planning the wedding as well as consent to being my 'Servant of Honour' during the actual ceremony?"

"Absolutely", Andrei accepted. Always a romantic at heart, his pure delight was evident in both the expression he wore on his face and in his eyes.

****

For the rest of their visit together they went over various bridegroom catalogues Raoul purchased on ei-pad, going over various selections, planning nearly every detail of both wedding and reception they could think of. And during their strategy session Raoul likewise brought out several pictures of his intended, showing them to Andrei with obvious pride, delivering all-the-while a glowing report detailing all his bride-to-be's positive attributes.

Having to admit Ms. Illingworth was indeed an attractive woman, attractive gentlewomen naturally gravitating towards Raoul, Andrei found himself even more impressed with Raoul's precise description of both her character and personality.

Truly looking forward to meeting this remarkable sounding gentlewoman, also quite absorbed with their planning session, neither paid any attention to the time. At least not until Raoul, looking up from a catalogue to discover Andrei's cup empty, asked if he'd care for yet another.

"Only if it's no trouble".

"None at all, dear boy", Raoul assured him with a smile, getting up to collect both their empty cups, making his way into the kitchen.

"And, while you're taking care of that, I guess I better check the answering machine at home", Andrei mused out loud. Doing so on a routine basis whenever away from home, he sometimes found there an item requiring his prompt attention.

"Of course, of course: Be my guest. You know where the V-phone is", Raoul's voice came back at him from the kitchen as Andrei made his way over to the kitchen counter between them, the small VP sitting there to one side. Typing in his eleven-digit number instantly through the use of Raoul's automatic 'friends-and-family' dialing attachment, this was followed by the access code for his message service itself.

Once done he found only two messages awaiting him at the other end.

The first was simply a short communiqué from Jas Stevens, Andrei's best friend on the base since moving to Demeter. Informing him he purchased the groceries Andrei asked him to pick up 'if at all convenient', he asked Andrei as well if he wanted him to bring them around later that afternoon.

It was the second recorded message that, without fail, grabbed his immediate attention:

Watching intently a handsome middle-aged Asian woman with high cheekbones and youthful voice tell him about trouble at the children's school Andrei recognized her as none other than Ms. Li-Wong: The Principal at the children's school he knew her well from such gatherings as P.T.A. meetings and school assemblies,

Concerned to learn J.J. got herself into some sort of difficulty what really confused, and even troubled him was how her Principal refused to divulge what actually transpired. All throughout her crisp, business-like message Ms. Li-Wong gave him no specifics, only telling him there was trouble.

"I'm sorry Raoul, but I'm afraid I'll have to take a rain check on the coffee", Andrei apologized, grabbing his black leather jacket off of his father-in-law's couch: "I'm afraid there's been some trouble at J.J.'s school. I need to get over there, quick", he added, making a hasty dash instead for Raoul's front door.

"No need to explain, dear boy", Raoul assured him with obvious, sincere concern: "I understand fully and pray all turns out for the best".

Chapter 10

"THE MESSAGE"

Although enjoying most of the time a leisurely stroll through the base greenbelt Jenniboni's mind was wrapped this time too tightly around the Admiral's cryptic call to take much notice of her immediate surroundings. Many were the times she and Andrei would meander about arm-in-arm taking a leisurely, romantic stroll beneath the night stars shining through the dome above—the dome-orb high up providing during its night cycle a fair replica of a full moon back on Earth.

However, for the moment being, romance was the last thing on her mind.

Hurrying instead along both black pathways and over small, picturesque bridges all that occupied her thoughts for now were the Base Administration Building ahead, the Admiral's curt summons, and the impending arrival of the Prime Arch Matri herself.

Arriving on her private cruiser no less!

Those base personnel passing Jenniboni by, glancing casually in her direction, had no way of knowing her inner turmoil. With the cool, collected and dignified aura she exuded for all to see, head held both proud and high, she hid her innermost worry well.

'I don't like this one little bit! Not one, single bit', she thought to herself over and over again in complete, absolute silence. Walking along at a quickened, rapid pace she could see her final destination just ahead around a bend in the path, a tall flagpole to the walkway's left directly in front of the administration complex…

Casting her eyes further upwards Jenniboni could also make out the flag of the entire Commonwealth, all Womankind, at full mast. Disappointed there was no breeze to set it fluttering majestically in its full glory for all to see it hung there instead limp and lifeless. All she could make out were its green, gold, and pink colours alongside a slight curve of its gold fempacem, its majority hidden in folds of cloth:

Originally a blending of two earlier emblems already popular as far back as the late 20th century, one element comprising the fempacem was the Venus symbol adopted by the ancient feminist movement back during the early 1970's.

The second, located within the first, was created originally by an ex-British naval officer, an expert in British semaphore, back in the early to mid-1950's.

Already famous world-over only a decade later, it was simply referred to back then as a "Peace Sign"—an emblem often raised high during protest marches staged by the rebellious and disenfranchised "counter-culture" way back then during those chaotic days in ancient herstory.

It wasn't until the latter 21st century that—combined—they officially became the fempacem, the banner under which the Rt. Rev. Tammy E. Garfield and her "Sisterhood" united Humanity, creating the "Tammyite Matriarchate", the Commonwealth of all Womankind.

Since then the fempacem had come to represent over 800 years of lasting peace, prosperity, and true justice… over eight centuries of "Commonwealth"… during which time the Human race continually flourished. Colonizing the rest of its home System Womankind thrived on most every planet, moon, and many other celestial bodies scattered throughout Earth's solar-system.

And from this day onwards it would likewise be the emblem under which Womankind's expanding civilization reached for the stars, taking its rightful place alongside whatever awaited it out there in the endless reaches of deep space.

Given such lofty and idealistic thoughts, mindful of the significant role she was likewise destined to play in the forefront of said expansion, Jenniboni couldn't help the superstitious feeling it was some personal warning from on high that fempacem on the flag ahead was so hidden.

****

Entering the Admiral's outer office with all due haste she approached quickly the secretary's "L"-shaped desk across the room, doing so with a purposeful stride. Behind it, working busily, Admiral Seller's personal secretary looked up from the computer at which he sat to ask how he might be of any assistance.

'Good Lord', she mused to herself with a wry little grin, struck at once by his tender youth: 'She keeps hiring them younger and younger'.

"Yes", Jenniboni answered the young laddie sitting at the desk before her:

"Would you please inform Admiral Sellers Commodore Saphira is here to see her".

"Yes, Ma'am", he replied smartly. Tapping the small button on the side of the earpiece he wore, part of the delicate speaker unit arranged upon his head, he then announced Jenniboni's arrival into the slender mouthpiece curved forward to just an inch from his mouth.

After but a moment's silence, his head cocked over to one side like a puzzled puppy, he finally looked up in Jenniboni's direction, informing her the Admiral would see her in just a few minutes. Hearing this Jenniboni couldn't help but feel somewhat annoyed, summoned so abruptly only to be kept waiting.

No point however in taking it out on the young man now sitting in front of her, gushing on in an enthusiastic, effervescent voice how very honoured he was to make her acquaintance. Claiming to have seen her every appearance on all the many 3-DV news broadcasts and interviews she'd been featured on he rattled on excitedly.

"Thank you", she smiled sweetly, having gotten semi-used at last to her recently acquired celebrity status over the last two years. As commanding officer of Womankind's first starship she garnished more often than not the popularity usually reserved for major entertainment bigwigs and certain notable media hotshots.

And witnessing the awkward expression appearing now on the painfully young secretary's face sitting on the other side of his desk there was no doubt at all in Jenniboni's mind what the shy young man wanted, working up the courage to make his desire known...

"I really hate to be a pest", he slowly began in a voice full of hesitant trepidation; "but I was hoping you wouldn't mind giving me your autograph:

"Only if it's no trouble, though," he rushed to add.

"Of course not", Jenniboni granted with yet another sweet smile: "No trouble at all".

"Thank you, Commodore", he literally shone with delight. Ecstatic, quickly handing her both a pen and small steno pad, he wore a look of eager anticipation.

"And who should I make this out to?"

"Albert, Ma'am", he cheerfully informed her: "Albert Granger:"

"To Albert Granger—With Love and Best Wishes ALWAYS,—Commodore Jenniboni Saphira", she wrote with a bold, dramatic, flair.

Handing the small writing pad back to him his eyes lit up upon reading what she'd written, thanking her profusely for what seemed like an eternity. Although starting to get used to the idea of having 'fans' such fawning attention still made her a trifle self-conscious—Jenniboni deciding right then and there to change the subject, asking Albert how long he'd been working for Admiral Sellers.

"Just a few days now", he informed her, clearly excited just to be there:

"Just moved up from the secretarial pool".

Well, at least that explained why she'd never seen him before now.

"Your very young, Albert", she found herself remarking out loud before able to stop herself. Fully aware of her superior's pension for pretty young office help he was definitely a handsome young laddie to say the very least.

"I'm nineteen", he announced, a triumphant gleam of personal satisfaction in his eyes: "Just graduated from secretarial school three months ago. Graduated top five in my class".

"Very impressive", Jenniboni complimented. Noting the obvious pride brimming over in his voice his sense of achievement was easy enough to understand. Not much more than just a boy and here he was working for the most powerful woman on the entire base, sitting at her right hand as it were. Quite heady stuff for such an innocent young man of such tender years.

"Well, Albert, I'm sure you'll do a wonderful job for the Admiral", Jenniboni confided in a warm, reassuring, voice: "After all I'm sure that she wouldn't have chosen you for such an important position if you weren't eminently qualified".

"Thank you, Ma'am", he practically glowed with certifiable joy, quite flattered by her undivided attention, her kind words.

Often irked by how most people treated office secretaries more like office furniture most of the officers and other base personnel dropping by would pause only long enough to tell him what they wanted before leaving, promptly dismissing him from their minds after doing so....

No casual conversation in the meantime…

No real Human contact…

To them he was nothing more than a stick of furniture…

Not so here, though. Here was the most popular, dashing, and debonair member of Project StarChild taking time out of her busy schedule, talking to him as though he were an actual Human being. Like the rest of the general public it was Commodore Jenniboni Saphira he thought of most when thinking of Project StarChild.

As the brave, courageous, and oh so beautiful commander of the Commonwealth's first voyage to the stars, it was she who garnished the greatest amount of media attention, the public spotlight.

That very same beautiful, larger-than-life media giant spending now her valuable time talking to a mere nobody like him.

Now that's class, he reflected within—sheer class. He'd be dining on this for a long time to come, no doubt about it. That was for sure.

Witnessing however the sudden flash of immediate regret, the disappointment in Albert's eyes, the reason was made clear soon enough, the young laddie now addressing Jenniboni in a more official capacity. Completely enthralled by both her continued presence and charming company he felt an unmistakable stab of resentment, hearing the Admiral announce right then and there over his headset she was ready now to see her.

"It has been a very real pleasure talking to you, Albert", Jenniboni comforted him with one last angelic smile, softening the personal blow he so clearly felt: "I've thoroughly enjoyed our delightful conversation together. I assure you".

"Thank you, Ma'am", he answered her in a breathless voice full of deepest respect and admiration: "It was a real honour and privilege to have met you, Ma'am".

Watching Jenniboni enter the Admiral's inner office, the automatic doors sliding shut behind her, Albert sighed, blissful, once more getting back to work.

****

Admiral Sellers rose from behind her desk, hand extended in greeting, once the doors shut firmly behind Jenniboni. Well within her fifth decade, a somewhat handsome woman of sturdy build, the base commander for Project StarChild came complete with a jowly, bull-dog face and long platinum-silver hair held back in place by a golden hair clamp both stylish yet functional in design.

Standing at only an inch shorter than Jenniboni she nevertheless stood at a full six feet, two inches in height, the average norm for any woman of that day and age. And often coming across as a blend of both businesswoman and professional dignitary this was only to be anticipated, her primary duty being of both an administrative and diplomatic nature.

Occasionally having to play hostess to visiting V.I.P.'s Jenniboni figured the Admiral would have her work cut out for her this time. Can't get any more V.I.P.-ish than the Supreme Mother herself. Dispensing quickly with the usual words of welcome it was then Melissa Sellers proceeded at once over to the well-situated wet bar situated against the sidewall just left of her desk.

"Would you care for something to drink? I'm having scotch and soda on the rocks myself ", she offered in as casual sounding a voice she could possibly muster under the given circumstances. Friends for many years now Melissa knew already from their long association her friend and subordinate was likewise allergic to alcohol in all its myriad forms. Having once been Jenniboni's commanding officer in the Protectorate it was for this reason more than anything else Melissa always kept on hand an ample supply of various non-alcoholic beverages.

"I'll have an orange juice and soda-water with ice", Jenniboni informed her, hearing soon after the familiar tinkling sound of ice against glass. Knowing Melissa equally well from over the years she also knew the only time her superior ever drank this early in the day was when she was extremely agitated, depressed, or had some bad news to discuss.

News of an unusually disturbing nature.

The pending arrival of the Supreme Mother would easily explain her anxiety, leaving only bad news.

Handing Jenniboni her drink, Melissa sat down once again behind her desk without uttering a single word. Taking a sip instead from her glass she just stared off into space wearing a deep frown of consternation. Wishing that her dear old friend and superior would just come out with whatever was on her mind, not caring at all for the silent tension permeating the room all about them, Jenniboni realized as well her immediate superior couldn't be rushed into revealing whatever it was that bothered her.

Melissa, the type who needed time to work her way up to discussing what

56

bothered her, was impossible to rush before ready.

However, while Jenniboni respected this about her immediate superior, she still didn't care much for the awkward, uncomfortable silence which fell upon them both. Only then did Jenniboni mention in a casual voice meeting the Admiral's new secretary, deciding to fill the void with a little idle chitchat instead.

At least until Melissa revealed at last their reason for being there.

"Oh, Albert", Melissa mumbled almost absent-mindedly, taking another small, almost exploratory sip from the fair-sized crystal glass held in her right hand:

"He's quite darling. A real peach. Isn't he?"

"Quite", Jenniboni agreed, taking a seat on the other side of Melissa's desk:

"I just hope your husband doesn't get jealous", she gently teased.

"Charlie? Not at all", the Admiral chortled with a dismissive little wave of her hand: "He's fully aware I like to look, but never touch".

It wasn't until after yet another brief moment's silence, marred only by the soft rattle of the ice in each of their drinks, Jenniboni inquired concerning what happened to her last secretary:

"Oh, Zack? I'm afraid he ended up getting married", Melissa sighed with a good-natured grin:

"Lose more than one good secretary that way. Crying shame they have to leave the work force when they do. Maybe I should hire only ugly ones from now on", she continued in a more playful vein: "Only problem there is they don't add much to the overall positive decor of the office, or go far in impressing visitors that much. No fun there".

Deciding not to respond, Jenniboni tasted instead her drink when hearing the older gentlewoman clear her throat at long last. Doing so in a most decisive manner the younger woman realized the older was ready at long last to discuss the subject of their meeting, Jenniboni looking up expectantly from her own drink in hand.

"Well, Commodore, I'm sure you must be wondering why I've summoned you here", Melissa proceeded now in a more official manner.

"Yes, I have to admit the question has crossed my mind".

"Yes, indeed", the Admiral smiled with grim humor: "I'm sure it has.

"Well, Commodore: The truth of the matter is the P.A.M. wishes to discuss some important new particulars concerning your mission with you, in person, the details of which I'm not allowed to discuss here.

"Yet even so we both agree there are at least a couple of crucial additional details you need to know about, straight away, in order to better prepare for your mission before she arrives—the first item on the immediate agenda being that of your new departure date".

"A *new* departure date?" Jenniboni cut in, confused.

"Yes, I'm afraid so: This February, the 15th, at 15:00 hours to be exact."

"*This* Friday?! But that's only three days away! Our departure is scheduled for two weeks' time", Jenniboni protested in vein: "We haven't even received the needed components from Earth yet for the new teleportation units".

"Unfortunately, I'm afraid you'll just have to leave without them".

"I'm afraid I don't understand. Why?"

"And that's the second matter we need to discuss", Melissa declared with grim resolve and a solemn, steely expression. Taking yet another sip from her now half-empty glass, getting down to brass tacks without any further delay, she cut at last to the very heart of the matter:

"On Wednesday, January 2nd, of this year one of our S.E.A. observatories here on Demeter received a telecommunications signal from the Alpha Centauri system. Or, to be more precise, the Earth-like moon our unwomaned scout probes discovered orbiting the gas giant—'AB-1.5'—back in the year 2907. Until now the Supreme Mother had sworn me to absolute secrecy".

"I'm afraid I still don't understand", Jenniboni confessed, her voice full of reluctant trepidation: "I distinctly remember the probes revealed no signs whatsoever of an active, sentient civilization in the vicinity. Only what appeared to be the ruins of two ancient cities exposed to the elements near the moon's equator".

"True. And our scouts wouldn't have detected anything else. At least not in the year 2907", Melissa nodded mysteriously in total agreement.

"All right, then. What is it you're not telling me?" Jenniboni demanded in a wary, suspicious tone not sure if she really wanted to hear the answer: "I can tell you're holding back even more. I can tell already it must be bad".

Having a sinking sensation it had to be quite unpleasant to say the very least she knew all the same she had to hear it, needed to hear it, regardless the ultimate outcome.

"You have a talent for understatement. Commodore", the Admiral agreed, sourly, reaching for the desk top P.C. situated to her immediate right. Switching it on, turning it slowly about, its screen faced now Jenniboni's direction.

"Yes, I'd say it's bad. And since I can think of no easy way to break news of such a magnitude to you beforehand, I might as well just show you the actual message itself without any further to-do".

Leaning forward in her chair to get a closer, more detailed look... eyes narrowed... she noted straightaway certain significant segments of the message were missing, faded, and/or undecipherable. Nevertheless there still remained enough to rapidly feed Jenniboni's already growing sense of apprehension:

"BEGIN TRANSMISSION.
"THIS TRANSMISSION IS BEING SENT BY THE
RESIDENTS OF PARADISE COLONY, FOUNDED TWO
YEARS AGO AFTER DEPARTING SPACE STATION
HAWKINGS IN ORBIT OF EARTH IN THE
YEAR 2035, AFTER TRAVELING FOR ... (Undecipherable) ...
ON A SET TRAJE ... (Undecipherable) ... **LATER.**

**"SINCE ARRIVING AN UNKNOWN ALIEN FORCE HAS
TAKEN CONTROL OF** ... (Undecipherable) ... **SITUATION
HAS ONLY GOTTEN WORSE, REACHING LETHAL
CONDITIONS WITH** ...
(Undecipherable) ... **FEAR THAT THESE** ... (Undecipherable) ...
ANYONE WHO TRIES TO SETTLE ... (Undecipherable).**

**"THEREFORE WE INSIST THAT ANYONE SEEING THIS
WARNING STAY AWAY FROM THIS PLANET. DO NOT
APPROACH** ... (Undecipherable) ... **PLANET ORBITS A RED GAS
GIANT 50 TIMES THE** ... (Undecipherable) ... **LARGE SATURNIAN
RINGS. OURS IS THE FIFTH OF EIGHTEEN MOONS
ORBITING THE** ... (Undecipherable) ...

**"ENTIRE COLONY DEAD. ONLY A HANDFUL OF SURVIVORS
LEFT. CHANCES
OF SURVIVAL SLIM TO** ... (Undecipherable) ...
"—END TRANSMISSION—"

"I find this very hard to believe. Why hasn't anyone ever heard of this before?", Jenniboni asked, incredulous, taking a brief moment's pause to sort out and gather her many thoughts.

"Simply put the P.A.M. wanted to keep this entire matter a secret until she could consult with both her Council of Advisors, the Supreme Council of Matriarchs, and the various branches of government in closed session, before taking any further action".

"That's not what I'm referring to. What I mean is why has such a mission to Alpha Centauri back in the early 21st century never appeared in any of the herstory books. Such an event would naturally rank right up there with such herstorical events like the first moon landing almost a thousand years ago".

"Two reasons come to mind quite readily", the Admiral explained, patiently, holding up two fingers:

"One quite possible reason for this could be this might have been some private venture sponsored back then by some clearly wealthy non-government agency, or organization. Even as far back as the early 21st century private enterprise was beginning to take a steadily more active role in extra-terrestrial travel, exploration, and research.

"Given the specific events and the heightened emotions during that period in Earth's herstory it isn't beyond the realm of possibility some elite, private group of wealthy and powerful individuals came to the conclusion the Human race was doomed to total annihilation. Don't forget this was the most chaotic, violent, and confusing time human herstory ever saw. No surprise then some wealthy and influential individuals back then could see the obvious writing on the wall, deciding to flee instead to some other fresh, new world on which to start all over again".

Having suggested this Melissa took a slight pause, letting Jenniboni process what she just said before picking up where she just left off:

"Secondly, and also to be considered, is the fact that most herstorical records from that particular period are, as you must know, rather sketchy at best. Current events back then were occurring at such a fast and furious pace they defied complete and accurate coverage. Given the conventional methods of documentation existing back then it's also relevant to keep in mind that, in those days back when Ahnteekah was still known as 'Antarctica', our ancestors on the continent weren't exactly kept up to speed on everything going on across the rest of the world.

"Don't forget that our foremothers back then were, themselves, nothing but remote, out of the way colonists from every other continent now gone, isolated by both their geographical location and the once harsh climate", the Admiral concluded. Giving the other woman a pointed look she paused yet again, giving her subordinate time to collect her thoughts.

"All right. Accepted", Jenniboni conceded: "but, that still doesn't explain why we're being asked to move up our launch time so soon".

"I'm afraid once more I'm not at liberty to explain why you have to leave so soon", Melissa apologized. Noticing the somewhat skeptical expression Jenniboni was wearing she spoke up quickly enough, hoping to dispel any doubts Jenniboni might have concerning her veracity, her sincerity:

"I assure you I'm being completely honest and aboveboard with you. Not only has the P.A.M. sworn me to secrecy concerning the whole matter, but she's also made any further releases of information on a purely need-to-know basis. All I've been authorized to discuss with you is the advancement of your departure date and the actual message itself. The Supreme Mother realized you'd need to know about both in order to better prepare your ship and crew for a potentially dangerous situation in time for your new schedule.

"Otherwise she wants to wait until she arrives here in person to discuss the matter further with us all. You're not allowed to discuss any of this with anyone except your senior officers and command staff.

"No one else, *absolutely no one,* is to know. Have I made myself perfectly clear?"

"Perfectly, Jenniboni dutifully assured her.

"Good", Melissa smiled at long last: "I had a pretty good idea that were the case".

"So when will the Prime Arch Matri be arriving?"

"Her private cruiser will be entering standard synchronous orbit over Demeter early tomorrow evening at 18:00 hours", Melissa informed her:

"At 20:00 hours you, your senior officers, and whatever escorts you might wish to bring along are invited to attend a dinner party aboard her cruiser to be followed by a private, high-level meeting. In attendance will be your senior officers, ourselves, and the Prime Arch Matri herself while the men-folk will be well taken care of in Stellar One's Hall of Audiences".

"Well, that sounds all pretty straight forward enough. Is that everything?"

"Yes, I'm afraid so. I'm sorry I can't tell you anything more".

"No need to apologize", Jenniboni assured her with an understanding smile:

"I appreciate your difficult position and sympathize. And on that note I'd say it's about high time I get down to the business at hand, preparing for our new departure date".

Taking leave of her superior officer Jenniboni rose from her chair, placing her half empty glass gently down upon Melissa's desk.

Chapter 11

"THE SET-UP"

The bar which Naomi chose for their first port of call was adrrinking establishment, both poorly and strangely lit, aptly named "The Dark Room". And upon her arrival alongside her two companions Frances Straker's initial reaction to ther new surroundings wasm to say the very least, and unenthusiastic one:

"Why in Heaven's name did you bring us here?" she demanded, contemptuous, giving Naomi a disgusted, puzzled, sideways glance: "This place has all the charm and atmosphere of the ninth circle of Hell, or walking through the shadow of the Valley of Death".

"Well, in that case you've got nothing to worry about", Naomi snickered; "as you're probably the biggest, badest mother in this whole darn shootin' match".

"Humph", Frances snorted as they made their way over to a secluded, out of the way, corner table off to the far right: "And you still haven't answered my last question. What in blazes are we doing here?"

"Don't worry", Naomi grinned, acting mysterious: "All will be revealed in good time. In the meantime may I suggest that we just kick back and have a few drinks".

No sooner though had all three women taken their seats Frances found herself momentarily perplexed, seeing what appeared to be a headless specter wearing a white suit gliding with a purposeful stride towards their table.

Approaching them from out of the surrounding darkness the phantasmal figure in white reminded Frances of ancient Greek myths involving the ghostly Hall of Lost Souls, its formal attire glowing with a neon flair thanks to the black lighting shining down from above. Able finally to discern its face once the mysterious phantom got closer however she saw it was just a young server in uniform, his waiter's outfit designed to look like a white, three-piece bridegroom's wedding suit.

Stopping at their table, wasting no time introducing himself as Jason, their waiter for the day, he pulled straightaway from his jacket's outer left pocket an ei-pad, ready to take their orders. Once having typed in their requests, he asked if there was anything further they might like.

With that Naomi raised her hand, motioning him closer with her forefinger to discretely whisper something private in his ear. Leaning over to hear whatever it was she wished to say over the intrusive background music playing in the distance, it was only a little under a minute before he straightened up once more:

"Don't worry. I'll take care of it", he promised, telling her further '*it*' would take twenty or so minutes.

"No problem. That'll be fine", Naomi assured the young man, all sweetness and smiles, removing a five-krodit note from within her purse:

"Here, this is for all your trouble", she told him with almost grandiose largess, handing him the money just before he turned to leave.

"Thank you, Ma'am", Jason smiled, grateful, addressing after that all three S.E.A. officers present: "And please enjoy your stay, Gentlewomen: I'll be back shortly with your drinks".

Finding herself alone again with just her two shipmates, Frances immediately shot Naomi a significant look:

"All right: What are you up to?" Having already a pretty good idea what '*it*' was, she still wanted confirmation from the horse's mouth.

"All in good time", StarChild's Chief Engineer promised with yet another coy grin. With a sly twinkle playing about in her emerald eyes she gave Gloria both a contemplative look and smile, filling her young assistant with yet another certain hint of immediate foreboding.

Returning a few minutes later conveying a tiny black tray with four drinks resting atop of it, Jason set correctly each beverage before each particular woman who ordered it. Priding himself on his ability to always remember which customer ordered what, he placed an extra glass in front of an empty fourth chair situated as well at their table:

"He'll be here in a few minutes", the laddie serving them informed Naomi afterwards. Leaving once more all three gentlewomen to themselves Gloria grew more anxious still, Frances beginning however to fume. Leaning over to Naomi, Frances demanded an answer to her previous question in no uncertain terms:

"All right. That's it. Spill it NOW!" she hissed forcefully.

"Sure", Naomi grinned once more, a proverbial Cheshire cat, her voice full of smug self-satisfaction: "Why not? The secret's half-way out of the bag anyway."

Then, turning to Gloria: "I thought you might enjoy meeting an acquaintance of mine. A most delightful and charming young laddie whose company I'm sure you'll enjoy immensely".

The butterflies already fluttering about in the pit of Gloria's stomach transformed all-of-a-sudden into bats, all being just as she feared.

And it only got worse, the bats tuning now into condors, with Naomi's very next words:

"I've even arranged for the both of you to go on a little blind date together. An all-night date if the two of you like each other. And I'm sure you'll like him", Naomi insinuated, giving Gloria a lascivious wink. Starting to squirm about in her seat, discomforted, she felt a warm flush of embarrassment turn her cheeks apple red.

Grabbing the soft drink before her, taking a long draft from it in hopes of settling her queasy stomach, she discovered herself wishing she ordered something stronger. Trying to speak Gloria was horrified to find her larynx took it seemed a little impromptu vacation all of its own, leaving her stranded high and dry with no speaking voice.

And noticing the young woman's emotional turmoil Frances handed Gloria her own drink, a gin and tonic.

"Here, take a sip of this", Frances gently instructed her: "It will help settle your nerves".

Instead of just sipping it though the smaller woman took a large hit from Frances' glass. Doing so Gloria's nose crinkled up with distaste, mouth puckered, shaking her head.

"Yes, I realize the taste takes some getting used to", Frances sympathized with an understanding smile: "but I assure you it does at least help when taken in moderation". Saying this she then looked towards Naomi, casting another decidedly hostile, disapproving glance the other woman's way:

"I don't think this is such a good idea", Frances glared angrily in Naomi's direction: "Blind dates can be quite stressful affairs putting a lot of pressure on both parties".

Especially when one of the parties in question was totally inexperienced in matters of the heart, Frances mused to herself once having spoken. Her feelings of pity for Gloria matched only by the anger she felt right about then towards Naomi, she viewed the casualness with which Naomi just ambushed her young subordinate as bordering on the callous.

"Don't worry", Naomi tried to placate Frances, attempting as well to reassure the timid Gloria: "This guy's perfect: Nothing to worry about. I promise."

Giving Gloria another quick glance to see for herself just how well she was holding up, Frances was glad to see she finally managed to regain at least some of her composure. While clearly still nervous she'd at least managed to calm down. Observing Gloria polished off almost all her entire gin and tonic Frances had to admit Naomi could surely drive one to drink.

No doubt about it!

"I agree with Lt. Cmdr. Straker", Gloria spoke up at last on her own behalf, the alcohol in her system beginning to take its desired effect: "Maybe this isn't such a good idea after all".

"Hey", Naomi raised her hands in a comical little gesture of surrender: "All I'm suggesting is you spend the day with the young laddie in question. A purely innocent little date. And if you still don't want to continue with the date by the time evening rolls around I'm sure the young laddie himself will understand".

"Well …" Gloria slowly relented, still somewhat uncertain: "I guess that sounds only fair". No matter how lacking she might have been in any personal, first-hand experience courting the weaker sex Gloria still knew enough to realize a proper gentlewoman didn't go about standing laddies up.

Aware of how truly persuasive her immediate superior could be she had no doubt her "date" was likewise coerced against his will into this little get-together, both of them victims of Naomi's plotting and planning. Looking at it in such a light it occurred to her it would be unfair, and even cruel to the young man in question to add the humiliation of being stood-up to already being pressured into going out with her.

Gloria just hoped he wasn't too terribly disappointed, too disillusioned with what he ended up with upon meeting her.

"So would you care to divulge the name of the young laddie with who you fixed Ms. Greensley up with", Frances asked with ill-concealed sarcasm: "After all I think it's only fair she have at least some idea what to call him besides 'hey you'".

"Actually I believe you already know him, my dear Chief of Security", Naomi grinned, playful: "Care to guess his identity?"

"Stop trying to be cute all the time and just cut to the chase", Frances snapped, beginning to reach the end of her already considerable patience.

"You're no fun", Naomi pouted childishly, announcing the young laddie's identity right thereafter: "Well, if you really must know, his name just so happens to be none other than 'Master Frank Weller'."

Saying this as though it should mean something significant to everyone present, doing so with a self-satisfied smirk, Gloria had no idea whatsoever of whom she was referring to. However, by the look on Frances' face, it was clearly another story, a broad smile of approval spreading from her lips to include right thereafter her entire face.

"So did I do good or what?" Naomi asked, smug, noticing at once Frances' reaction. Refusing however to dignify her question with even the briefest of answers, Frances chose to address Gloria instead:

"You have nothing to worry about, believe me", she promised in a most comforting voice: "I know Frank quite well and you can rest assured he is a very sweet, charming, intelligent, and gracious young man. A true laddie in every sense of the word. I'm sure the two of you will get along quite famously and have a wonderful time together".

When it appeared Naomi was about to start giggling hearing this Frances shot her such a dirty look she suppressed *at once* any more urge to laugh, unable to mistake that fiery anger burning in those large, dark eyes for anything else.

Frances Straker's expression softened though when hearing Gloria, having once more just cleared her throat, speak up again:

"Excuse me, Lt. Cmdr. Straker? I was wondering if you wouldn't mind giving me a little advice. As you well know I've never been out on a date before and I'm rather nervous about how to act and behave:

"I mean… well… how do I treat him exactly?"

Although the other woman's words helped her feel somewhat better, soothing somewhat her troubled mind, she still had a couple of nagging doubts.

Respecting the courage it must have taken for her to admit this out loud, especially in front of Naomi, the fact Gloria turned to her instead for advice on matters of the heart wasn't lost either on Frances' part.

Touched, and even flattered by the inexperienced young officer's evident confidence in her, Frances smiled at her with tender sympathy before continuing any further:

"To begin with I wouldn't give this advice to just anyone—especially the likes of our 'dear' Ms. Marlowe here—but in your case I think it would be best to just be yourself. I know it might sound a bit trite, but I'm sure that if you just relax, be yourself, and remember treat him like a laddie… be a proper gentlewoman… all will turn out for the best".

"Do you mean like how you're supposed to hold doors open for them and hold chairs out for them?", Gloria asked in pure innocence.

"Well, that's part of it", Frances agreed with gentle amusement:

"However, what I'm actually referring to is how, while the woman is supposed to take charge in such relationships… be in control… she nevertheless needs to take the man's feelings and needs as well into consideration. It isn't just a one-way street, just you and not him. You have to treat him with respect, kindness, and sensitivity, never forgetting to be considerate of him.

"No need to fret. I'm sure you'll do just fine", Frances added, placing a comforting hand on Gloria's when noticing her troubled frown.

"And don't forget to be sure that you have enough money in your purse to show him a good time. After all the last thing you want to do is look cheap", Naomi chimed in cheerfully with her two centi's worth. Unable to restrain what she considered her fun-loving, 'playful' nature she grinned rather lewdly, adding right thereafter:

"And if you *do* get nervous just remember to picture him naked. After all that's what they say to do when giving speeches in front of large audiences".

Retribution for that particular little piece of advice was swift in coming, Naomi's grin turning just as quickly to an expression of sheer agony:

"Jeepers H. Crispey!!! WHAT the SANGUINARY HECK was THAT for??" she cried out in absolute pain.

"You know very well what that was for", Frances growled, furious: "That's for all your constant, flippant, cutesy little remarks!!".

Gloria couldn't help but laugh at the sight of Naomi reaching down to rub her aching shin, especially after that crack about picturing her date naked. Served her right. Not only had it made her quite nervous all over again, but it likewise embarrassed her in the extreme.

"And you *still* haven't answered my original question", Frances persisted, still clearly perturbed.

"Which was?" Naomi groaned through tears of pain inching their way down round, cherubic cheeks.

"What are we doing in this 'Gosh' forsaken place?" Frances reiterated yet again, grumbling with frustration.

"We're here to meet Frank of course", Naomi enlightened her in a 'sometimes-you-can-be-so-dense' tone of voice, looking up after having checked her aching leg for any clear damage: "He's a waiter here now".

"Since when?" Frances wasted no time, quite astonished: "I thought he was waiting tables at the Glitter Path Lounge".

"He was until a week ago", the rubenesque red head made sure to not to leave any detail out least she anger any further her already irate companion: "But he decided to come work here after learning from a friend already here they paid waiters more, not to mention increased medical benefits and a better dental plan".

"They must offer all that just to get anyone to work here", Frances commented in a most sour tone.

"I can't see what you have against this place" Naomi countered: "The drinks are actually quite excellent here and I kind of like the decor. It has a sort of clean, cool, streamlined high-tech retro alienesque feel about it. Perfect setting for crewmembers of Womankind's first interstellar vessel to congregate if you ask me".

"I'll tell you one thing: If StarChild's interior looked anything like this place I would have surely thought twice about serving aboard him", Frances stated, quite emphatic: "Besides, how did you find out Frank was working here?"

"Oh, that", Naomi sighed with a casual little wave of her hand: "Well, when I met him over a week ago at the Glitter Path to arrange this little date he told me he'd be working here by now".

Not paying much attention now to the two senior officers talking among each other Gloria caught sight instead of yet another glowing specter approaching from out of the continual gloom, the perpetual darkness all around and beyond. Another waiter in yet another one of those formal three-piece white suits replete with its almost preternatural aura…

Looking up in his direction once reaching their table Naomi announced quite merrily with a bright smile of clear recognition: "Well, here he is now. The man of the hour. Speak of the Devil and in he walks".

In keeping with proper etiquette all three gentlewomen stood up upon the young laddie's arrival—Naomi taking care as well of the formal introductions following her rather discourteous, ungentlewomanly quip comparing him to the Devil. Enjoying indeed playing the part of matchmaker she proceeded in a rather loud, grandiose voice:

"Lieutenant Gloria Greensley, may I introduce to you Master Frank Weller: Frank; this is Gloria, whom I've likewise told you much about".

Dumbstruck, unable to believe her incredibly good luck, Gloria could only stare in open amazement at the golden-haired Adonis standing so temptingly close. Never before in her life had she felt such an immediate and intense longing for another person coursing… pulsating… throughout every fiber and sinew of her very being, her very spiritual and physical essence.

"This is MY date?? He's absolutely drop-dead gorgeous," she almost cried out loud in sheer, all-encompassing delight. Nor was it just his exquisite body, or his curly light blonde hair and handsome features that captivated so her imagination, enflamed her passion.

There was also that angelic smile full of kindly grace, tender compassion that fit so well his angular features—his strong jaw line and the well-trimmed van-dyke beard complimenting so well that intelligent sparkle in those gentle, soulful, dark brown puppy-dog eyes likewise full of lively humor.

Convinced she'd surely fallen into the jam pot this time, Gloria had to at least give Naomi credit where credit was due:

She sure knows how to pick 'em!

Chapter 12

"STRANDED"

Heading back across the city to the children's school, pleased with the excellent time he was making, Andrei suddenly noticed some sort of commotion up ahead. Unable at first to clearly determine what actually took place, obstructing as it did the even flow of traffic along the main thoroughfare, it became apparent soon enough the closer he got.

Slowing his approach almost to a crawl just to be on the safe side he was finally able to make out a large transport vehicle stalled at an odd angle. Reaching nearly from one side of the road to the other it looked as though it almost jackknifed across the entire street.

Probably having occurred during an attempt to avoid something in its direct path Andrei watched lazy tendrils of thick, white steam slowly curl upward from under the lorry's front compartment.

In the meanwhile however its much larger rear freight section, seemingly none the worse for damage, was angled backwards at a sharp degree in Andrei's direction, two C.C.P.F. patrol cars parked alongside it. Their red, green, and blue roof lights flashed around and about in their usual, urgent fashion four women stood nearby the open driver's side door to the large transport vehicle in question.

One, clearly the driver, was dressed in dark slacks, jacket, and white blouse while the other three women wore the crimson and gold Protectorate uniforms so intimately familiar to Andrei's searching eyes. Clearly taking down for their official report the first woman's eyewitness account concerning what just happened there were even more law enforcement vehicles present… even more Protectors… cordoning off traffic both there as-well-as on the other side of that nearby wreck.

Complete with a series of red detour signs and roadblocks positioned between Andrei and those red-clad policewomen ahead, their blinking white lights forming arrows pointing left, Andrei slowed down even further, a fourth uniformed Protector signaling all oncoming traffic to divert course in the same direction.

Doing so in a decidedly authoritative manner her tired, haggard face looked especially stern beneath its heavily etched worry lines.

"Darn", he swore angrily to no one in particular, slapping the edge of the steering wheel with his open palm:

"I definitely don't need this", he muttered under his breath as the uniformed woman directing traffic motioned him to turn left along with others onto a smaller one-way street.

Worrying how long this unexpected delay would keep him from his daughter's side he just couldn't bear the idea of J.J. waiting all alone in Ms. Li-Wong's office wondering where her father was. No matter how mature, how independent she liked to imagine herself he realized with a father's keen sense of awareness just how vulnerable, even scared, she no doubt felt at that very moment no matter what brave face she might be wearing.

Unfamiliar with this particular part of Chiron City, its numerous side streets, he switched on the small information screen included in the dashboard to his right, ordering up a directional guidance map for the immediate area.

Studying the streets depicted as yellow lines against a dark green background, his car depicted by a bright red dot moving slowly along one such line, he discovered soon enough four other one-way streets directly ahead cutting across the one he was now traveling. And although the first three all lead the wrong way the fourth, as good fortune would have it, promised to take him right to the school's front entrance by way of yet another right turn several blocks further on.

Feeling much better now about his chances of soon being there at his daughter's side Andrei's spirits began climbing once more, falling hard quickly enough again turning right onto a secluded two-lane avenue. Encountering a jagged pothole that seemed to appear as if out of nowhere the sudden, violent jolt resulting from the immediate impact sent a shooting pain up Andrei's tailbone… throughout his entire spine… almost causing him to lose control of the wheel.

As it was he managed to travel only a hundred meters further before the engine started acting up, a red warning indicator flashing now on the dashboard in front of him. Forming the words "FUEL CELLS" Andrei knew he was in trouble even before the sleek little blue sports car began as well to stall.

Sputtering along… stop, start, stop, start… it finally gave up its feeble attempts, surrendering instead to inertia some 150 meters beyond its initial encounter with that crater now behind it. Managing to pull over to the right-hand curb before it gave up the ghost once and for all, Andrei came to a complete stop in front of a small Laundromat.

Eyes squeezed tightly shut in angry frustration he pounded clenched fists against the steering wheel. Swearing in his ancestral Spanish, his despair soared at the very thought of poor J.J. wondering what was keeping him.

Opening his eyes once more to get a better look at his immediate surroundings, he noticed an odd establishment right across the street from the small Laundromat he was now stalled in front of. Possessing no windows, only a single mirror-paneled door set in a blank white exterior, what struck him especially ominous was the establishment's name written over its single entranceway in large, pitch black, block letters.

Simply called *"THE DARK ROOM"* Andrei couldn't explain even to himself why that simple, albeit strange name gave him such an almost instinctive pause for concern.

"You're being foolish, irrational", he admonished himself with an annoyed hiss, disgusted over such paranoid flights of fancy.

Turning instead his attention from that source of disquiet to examine likewise the other buildings lining both sides of the mostly empty street it wasn't difficult to tell right off the bat what purpose they served by way of their endless identical rows of large, flexi-metal rolling doors—private storage facilities rented more often than not on a monthly, or even annual basis.

No wonder the street around him was so deserted, indicating he was near Chiron's storage/warehouse district smack-dab right on its outer rim. No fool by any stretch of the imagination there was no need to remind Andrei such places could be rather rough. Not a safe place for an unescorted laddie all on his very own without the benefit of female protection.

No question about it.

Taking at least a wee bit of comfort in the relative safety of his car, doors securely locked, he decided even so to waste no time calling for help, confident the Vehicle Rescue Service would have no difficulty finding him.

However, reaching into the inside pocket of his leather jacket, he felt a sudden rush of shocked dismay, finding the little portable V-phone he always kept there missing instead.

"Sanguinary Heck", he swore yet again under his breath, remembering only then he left the darned contraption back on his bedside nightstand. Wishing he could kick himself for such foolish absent-mindedness, he could remember now changing the small PVP's rechargeable solar batteries only the night before.

Planning at the time to return it to its customary resting place at once he'd been distracted from doing so however by Tommy's clear, plaintive voice calling out in the middle of the night for a drink of water. And by the time he took care of that, returning soon after from his son's nearby room, the infernal device completely slipped Andrei's already weary mind.

With an angry growl rumbling at the back of his throat, getting now out of the car, he slammed the door shut behind him. Muttering yet another ugly expletive in Spanish he set out instead to find a public VP to call for both a tow as well as contact J.J.'s principal.

Hoping to explain the delay and, if possible, talk to J.J. himself he wanted to reassure her everything would be all-right, that he'd be there for her as soon as humanly possible. Finding at least some sweet relief at sight of the small laundromat only a few meters away Andrei was certain they'd have what he was in search of.

As Andrei anticipated all along the place was just as shabby looking inside, as run down as its exterior. Even those denizens occupying space there looked no better, spotting straightaway a couple of tired, haggard-looking old men sitting on a bench between two rows of washing machines.

Situated against the wall directly ahead of him both seemed oblivious to the world around them, their noses stuck in a couple of ei-magazines, sitting there slump-shouldered, looking beaten down by life. At least the female attendant situated behind the service counter to Andrei's immediate right proved more lively—a rotund, elderly matron asking with both a friendly smile and warm welcome how she might be of service.

Removing a one-krodit note from his wallet, requesting both change and the use of their public VP, Andrei's heart sank at once to the bottom of his feet learning their only V-phone in the entire place was, by sheer dumb luck, out of order.

"The service repairwoman is due in a couple of hours" she explained:

"You're quite welcome to wait until then", she offered with an apologetic little smile, handing him his coinage from the till.

"I'm afraid I can't wait that long", Andrei explained his situation, describing his dilemma with a wan little smile all his own. His tale of honest misfortune clearly touching the slightly frumpy woman's heart she looked down at him with evident sympathy written all over her craggy features.

Nor was that all, a certain amount of guilt and trepidation likewise visible alongside her obvious pity realizing that, with the exception of her next suggestion, she had nothing more to offer the distraught young laddie standing in front of her:

"I hesitate to even suggest it, but I know for certain that, should you prove interested, the bar across the street has a working V-phone available to the public", she suggested slowly, reluctantly, glancing across the street.

Following the direction in which she looked, her gaze wandering beyond the large plasti-glass windows next to them, Andrei noticed at once that same establishment with that same forbidding name—*"THE DARK ROOM"*— giving him such an unpleasant start, such an overwhelming sense of foreboding, just moments ago:

"Unfortunately I'm afraid I can't leave here as I've been left here all on my own to run things. Otherwise I'd gladly serve as your escort", the attendant's expression of concern only deepened as she added:

"So in light of this, I highly recommend you wait here instead until the VP repairwoman finally arrives. I promise to do my best to make your stay as comfortable and pleasant as possible under the circumstances".

"That's all right", Andrei smiled, quite touched by her sincere and obvious concern; "but, I'm afraid that I can't wait.

"Don't worry, though, as I understand perfectly", he added in hopes of easing the poor woman's clearly troubled conscience: "You've been very kind as it is, I assure you, and I'm sure that I'll be fine on my own".

Upon saying his final good-bye's Andrei paused only for a brief moment after leaving the Laundromat, a multitude of conflicting thoughts and emotions running through him before crossing the street. Considerations such as how Jenniboni would disapprove of his going into such a place and whether or not they would even let him in there without female supervision, female protection, all coming to mind.

In the end though it was thoughts of J.J. waiting desperately for her father, needing him by her side at that very same moment, which made Andrei's final decision for him. Thinking only of his little girl all by herself, both frightened and worried, he crossed the narrow avenue before him—boldly entering the lioness' den, head held high in proud defiance of his own inner turmoil.

Chapter 13

"MASTER FRANK WELLER"

When Naomi first approached him, requesting he go out with the shy, starry-eyed young gentlewoman now standing before him, Frank at first turned her down flat. Having though no qualms or hang-ups about being seen in the company of a woman both younger and shorter than himself, neither had been his reason for doing so.

Nor was it her outward appearance, any lack of comeliness on her part…

Quite the contrary!!

Right from the very beginning Frank had to confess the young starship engineer was quite attractive the very moment Naomi first showed him a picture when arranging this little meeting.

With a pleasant, open, honest face and a sweet smile almost child-like in its innocence he found her quite appealing indeed. Only three years younger than Frank himself she seemed to come across as even more so.

One probable reason for this being likewise the fact that, standing at a mere 5'6" tall, she was almost three inches shorter than he.

No…

None of these differences between Lt. Gloria Greensley and the average woman inspired at first Frank's initial response to Naomi's request he go out with her. Truth be told Lt. Greensley didn't even enter the equation, the plain and simple truth being that, all said and done, Frank didn't care at all for the great Naomi Marlowe, or her base attitude towards men.

And having just cause for his animosity, he felt he owed her no favors…

None in the very least!

While having been courted by many gentlewomen during his relatively brief young past there were only two with whom Frank succumbed to 'the temptations of the flesh'. Certainly not something he was proud of at least the first woman he allowed to bed him without the benefit of holy matrimony had been serious in her intentions, neither party involved holding the other accountable for the reasons they finally parted ways.

Then along came Naomi at that particularly vulnerable period in his young life and, believing her to be likewise serious, he surrendered at once to her persuasive charms. Readily acknowledging the part that he played in the compromising of his own virtue, it nevertheless hurt to discover later the woman with whom he shared so much of himself saw him as no more special than any of the other men she ever knew or, worse still, those she was yet to know.

Nor did the realization he was foolish expecting Naomi to change her evil ways just for him, that doing little to ease much the bitterness he still felt toward her…

The resentment.

So it should come as no surprise to anyone at all Frank saw himself as owing Naomi absolutely nothing. Now had it been Frances Straker who asked instead there would have been no question *at all* about saying yes.

In his opinion Frances was the perfect Gentlewoman with a capital "G"!

Having gone out with her on previous occasions Frank knew her to be in fact a truly gallant, take-charge kind of woman always respectful, polite, considerate, and well-mannered possessing as well great charm and charisma. Never did she try taking advantage of him or compromise in any way his virtue, his social standing.

Needless to say he would go out with her at any given time were she to only ask again.

However, by that very same token, he fully understood her expressed desire not to become seriously involved with someone at this particular point in her life, too honourable to indulge in casual affairs of the heart, trifling with the affections of those laddies she would court.

No…

What finally changed his mind about going out on the town with Gloria was instead something Naomi said, realizing Frank was resolute in his refusal to go out with her, steadfast in his convictions. It was then Naomi reverted to what Frank considered true form, resorting to threats to get her way, responding with a crafty smile replete with calculated cunning:

"That's all right, Frank. No need to worry. I'll just ask Lucien if he'd like to go out with her", she announced, casually.

LUCIEN!: Frank's former roommate was someone who, having no sense of self-respect or propriety whatsoever, played musical beds with both great alacrity and élan. Then again his predilection to sleep around wasn't what had earned him Frank's utter contempt so much as his cold, cynical stereotyping of the opposite sex and the many cruel forms it would take.

A cold, cruel, and heartless parasite he would use his physical charms to take women for all they were worth only to toss them aside once having taken them for everything he possibly could. Sexually manipulating them to get whatever he wanted only to chew them up and spit them out afterwards Lucien was, in Frank's opinion, nothing more than a vicious whore.

Seared forever into his memory Frank would never forget that fateful night some two years ago. Bringing their already volatile relationship to a tumultuous end it occurred right after one of their few, rare double dates together with two gentlewomen Frank met waiting tables the evening before.

The date itself went reasonably well for the most part even though, right from the very start, Lucien was playing his usual cute little-boy games. Dropping not-so-subtle hints willy-nilly he made it clear to one-and-all he was ready, willing, and available for anything. All the same though his escort for the evening didn't seem to really mind…

At least not too terribly much:

The real trouble didn't occur until later, after their dates had seen both Frank and Lucien safely back to their place at the end of their time together. Proving themselves completely proper in their conduct and deportment, quite courteous while together, neither woman tried to coerce or force their way into the ladies' apartment uninvited.

Not that Lucien would have minded in the least had they done so.

And it was just about then, just as Frank finished thanking his date for a wonderful evening, Lucien insisted their two gentlewoman callers come in and stay for a little "night cap" as he put it.

Frank's worry beginning to mount, knowing quite well what his roommate was getting at with that particular little euphemism, things went quickly downhill from there on out when the two gentlewomen in question proved themselves unwilling to do so. Not wanting to compromise the reputations of either their dates it was then Lucien wasted no time making it known he didn't give a sanguinary heck about either his reputation or good name, confessing even further he wanted them to stay the night.

It was only then, when both women still insisted against such impropriety, Lucien finally blew up, exclaiming in a loud voice full of indignant surprise:

"But you're women. You're supposed to want it any way you can get it. What's wrong? don't you like men??"

Too shocked, stunned, and even horrified to say or do much of anything other than close his eyes, Frank groaned in absolute dismay. Feeling his stomach do sick, nervous somersaults turning in absolute revulsion the two insulted gentlewomen simply excused themselves, politely but firmly, never to be heard from again.

Having truly enjoyed his date's charming company Frank regretted all which happened, unable to blame her in the very least for being both offended, even scared off, after Lucien's irreprehensible behavior. It was right then and there Frank realized that, to save his own good name and reputation, he'd have to sever at once all ties with Lucian Malloy

Was it not Shakespeare who said, "He who steals my purse steals trash, he who steals my good name steals all"? To that very day Frank was still appalled to think there remained, even now, some women out there convinced he was cut from the same cloth as his loathsome former roommate.

However, before dissolving their already unsatisfactory boarding arrangement, Frank planned first to make the most of this one, last opportunity to tell Lucien as plainly as possible what exactly he thought of him in the privacy of their apartment, behind closed doors, once their dates had left.

Wasting no time whatsoever in doing so, it wasn't long before their heated verbal exchange quickly escalated into physical blows when Lucien, operating under the mistaken impression he could take his roommate in a plain, old-fashioned fistfight, threw the first punch. Immediately proving him wrong however Frank then proceeded to beat the living daylights out of the other man, tossing him headlong out of their apartment.

Quickly locking the door between them Frank then made a complete and thorough search of their entire premises, gathering up all of his former roommate's belongings only to fling them out their seventh story window to the ground below. It was less than a week later Lucien tried sue Frank for wrongful expulsion from his former place of residence.

Yet, what with his odious reputation already preceding him wherever he went, Lucien had a difficult time just finding legal counsel willing to represent him.

Nor did it really matter, Lucien more often than not delinquent in living up to his financial responsibilities. In the end the judge in charge of the case made a swift ruling in Frank's favor when it came out during the trial it was mostly Frank who paid the rent for both of them. Not only that but she also fined Lucien the cost of the other man's legal debts incurred throughout the trial along with all the back rent he owed him.

Therefore it was with equal amounts of both dread and revulsion Frank shuddered at the very idea of the innocent young girl standing now before him, naive in such ways of the System, being delivered into the clutches of that horrid, gold-digging woman-eater.

After listening to Naomi's description of Gloria Greensley Frank was of the unshakeable conviction it would be a great tragedy indeed if she came away believing Lucien typical of the male gender. Although pretty sure Naomi's threats were only a bluff to gain his cooperation Frank remained nevertheless unwilling to take such a chance with a young psyche as tender and fragile as Lt. Greensley's. No doubt about it. He'd never be able to forgive himself in the least should anything unfortunate happen to her.

Frank's blood ran cold yet again at the very thought of what might have happened in such a case were Lucien to try and force himself upon her, painful images flashing through his mind with lightening rapidity. Under any normal circumstances any average woman would be able to swiftly overcome any man should be so bold as to actually try and physically force himself upon her:

Gloria however???

And even if his former roommate didn't try to take any physical advantage of her Frank knew from previous encounters Lucien had other ways as well to rip further the poor woman's untried heart to absolute shreds.

Fortunately men like Lucien Malloy were an extreme rarity in society. Another reason Frank felt it would prove doubly sad if the young gentlewoman in question ended up being scared off of men by such a miserable !#@&!!, giving his whole wonderful sex a black eye in the bargain.

Altruism aside however he had yet another reason for likewise consenting to this little get-together with Naomi's shy and retiring young assistant: Simple curiosity!

Rather intrigued by what he already learned about her so far Frank felt it only fair to further avail himself of this opportunity to meet her.

As a matter of fact there remained only one further concern still worrying him, his previous agreement with Naomi to make their outing together an all-night "affair". Agreeing to do so only because he remained hopeful the timid, young gentlewoman now facing him wouldn't press him for that kind of 'intimate tryst' her immediate superior preferred, Frank found himself praying even so she wouldn't end up proving him wrong.

What if she felt compelled by some tragic inner need to prove herself, attempting something they'd both deeply regret for a very long time.

He only hoped Gloria would prove herself strong enough to resist the pressure Frank was sure she no doubt felt, an inner turmoil thanks to Naomi and her incessant badgering! Otherwise Frank didn't quite know how he'd handle such a situation should things get out of hand. Above all else he hoped to avoid any possible eventuality where she might end up feeling both hurt and rejected.

So, as all three gentlewomen from StarChild rose from their seats at his arrival, it was with a certain amount of trepidation Frank proceeded any further:

"Hello, Gloria: I'm so very pleased to be making at long last your acquaintance".

Chapter 14

"DARKNESS"

The bar before him had no windows, only that mirror paneled door set in a blank white front... its name directly above in large, solid black letters... leaving Andrei no hint at all concerning what might be lurking in wait for him once inside.

After only the briefest hesitation he hesitated yet again once inside, this time trying to catch his bearings the very moment he found himself within that new, surreal establishment. Taking a little while for his eyes to adjust to the sudden, overwhelming darkness surrounding him now on every side it left him feeling momentarily off-balance.

However, when finally able to make out his immediate surroundings in the dim light shining from above, he wasted no time approaching the long counter bar opposite him. Situated on the far side of this uninviting establishment, standing behind the broad counter with its gleaming, well-tended, coal-black surface was either the proprietress of this place, or one of her staff.

Approaching her, leaning over the counter's flat surface between them in hopes of being heard over the raucous music from overhead speakers, he asked in a loud voice if she would be kind enough to possibly help him. Looking up from the glass she was polishing with such an intense gaze the bartender gave him a dubious, sour glance:

"No unescorted men allowed in here!" she was quick to glare at him once having recovered from the initial surprise seeing a laddie of such obviously impeccable class and breeding standing there in her particular place of employ.

"I understand", Andrei assured her, a note of desperation creeping at last into his voice: "And I promise you I wouldn't have dared intrude if it weren't indeed a dire emergency".

Upon saying this Andrei continued thereafter to explain even further all about his car braking down, how his little girl was in trouble at school... no doubt waiting anxiously upon his arrival as soon as humanly possible... and how he already tried the aforementioned Laundromat first.

Listening to the young father's impassioned plea on behalf of his daughter, her own obvious plight, the harsh appearing bartender's facial expression visibly softened, her stern countenance soon more sympathetic.

"All right, Sir", she relented upon hearing his sad story; "but I'm afraid that, once you've finished with the VP, you'll have to wait outside for your ride".

"Yes, of course", he practically gushed with sweet-sounding relief: "I'll make it as quick as possible and then leave right away. I promise."

"That should be fine, then", she smiled in reply; quite amused, even touched, by his sudden, youthful effervescence:

"The public VP is over there", she then informed him, pointing off into the distance off to his right: "Just go that way down to the beginning of the hall leading to the public rest rooms. You can't miss it. It's just this side of the entrance to the hallway".

"Thank you", Andrei smiled brightly, turning at once in the direction she indicated just as she returned as well to polishing that glassware still in hand until glistening, sparkling to her satisfaction in the dim light from above.

Continuing on in the direction he'd been told to go Andrei scrutinized now his new surroundings with wary eyes, attempting all the while to keep up a carefree appearance in direct defiance of those negative feelings they gave rise to. From what he could so far tell there didn't seem to be all that many customers present.

Hard to tell though as the place sure lived up to its name:

It was indeed dark!!!

Even the lighting was dark, utilizing more black lights than regular. Casting likewise strange double shadows all about, they lent the building's interior a truly bizarre glow. Glancing casually downwards Andrei could even observe how the ultra-violet lighting from on high made his white shirt literally radiate with an eerie, otherworldly luminescence.

Truth be told the entire bar had a quite jarring effect on him. Caring very little for the unknown proprietress' choice in décor he appreciated least of all the peculiar manner in which it served to only accentuate the surrounding darkness, magnifying its disquieting effect upon his nerves. Extremely uninviting the walls within sight were all a stark, pitch black—the carpeting a similar dark charcoal grey.

Andrei could only assume the same held true for the rest of this strange downtown tavern's perplexing interior.

As for the furniture arranged all about each and every tabletop seemed to be constructed of some transparency supported by a silver chrome framework, the same holding true for all the chairs. Neatly arranged four to a table each seat was padded with shiny black leather held together by a framework of glistening chrome.

In the meantime there were also scattered throughout the dark room a series of round pillar supports reaching from floor to ceiling. Covered with small, highly polished mirror tiles they likewise reflected what scant light there was in every possible direction. As though he were lost in some endless cavern morbid walls and strange lighting effects gave the entire place the appearance of being much larger than it could actually be.

Feeling more than just a wee bit anxious and alone, making his way over to the public VP, the cumulative effects of this particular environment inspired within Andrei's very heart and soul an irrational, almost child-like fear of the dark.

A dread he'd never experienced before, a feeling totally foreign to his very being, the ironic thing was that, all things said and done, Andrei actually enjoyed the dark. Lying in bed, listening to his wife sleeping next to him with her gentle, rhythmic breathing he truly felt warm and secure during those nighttime hours, wrapped securely about in the comforting stillness and intimate safety.

And by that very same token he appreciated as well other such dimly lit rooms. Fondly recalling the swanky restaurant Jenniboni took him to for his 27th birthday just this last November the darkness there likewise possessed as it did a truly intimate, romantic atmosphere. Decorated in a plush pink, gold, and white motif there were even fine Irish linen tablecloths shipped all the way from Eire City just off the shores of Continental Earth.

Partaking there in a sumptuous meal by the soft, seductive glow of gently flickering candlelight he and Jenniboni later danced close to one-another in each other's tender, loving embrace to the sound of equally gentle music drifting lightly upon the air.

There the shadows were soothing, adding to the romantic ambiance of their surroundings, enhancing the intimate atmosphere all about them:

Not so here!!

Here the darkness was cold, hostile and even inhuman in its alien quality, the colour and style of the furnishings all around him only adding to the lack of any warmth and humanity whatsoever. Nor did the disembodied voices talking and laughing somewhere out there help alleviate any his growing sense of alienation.

Serving up a quite sinister, and even surreal climate to the already oppressive, claustrophobic atmosphere engulfing him Andrei had no idea who or what might be lying in wait for him out there. All he could hope for was that who, or what might be out there wouldn't notice him.

Little did he realize that, had at least two of those unseen denizens of that darkness beyond noticed him, the traumatic experience Andrei was about to suffer might have never occurred.

Chapter 15

"LADDIES AND GENTLEWOMEN"

"Hello, Gloria: I'm so very pleased to be making at long last your acquaintance. Naomi's told me all about you."

Saying this Frank could readily detect a fleeting expression of worry flash across young Gloria's face.

"Don't worry, it was all good I can assure you", he added quickly with a gentle smile: "As-a-matter of fact I've been looking forward to meeting you for quite some time now."

Noting the look of definite relief in her eyes, a subsequent smile appeared now at each corner of her mouth. Ever so slight… unsure… but still there nonetheless.

About to take a seat in the empty chair across the table from Gloria's position Frank was stopped however from doing so, Frances speaking up from right next to him:

"Here, Frank, please take my chair instead", she insisted, proceeding without any further delay to hold it out for him.

Thanking her straightaway Frank couldn't help but notice Frances likewise placed him right next to Gloria herself, claiming right after that the empty fourth chair on her own behalf. Doing so she them picked up the extra drink Jason, their waiter from before, brought earlier to their table:

"Here. I believe this was meant for you", she continued, handing it straight away to their new arrival.

"Why, thank you", Frank smiled, appreciative.

"I ordered it for you!", Naomi jumped in hastily in a somewhat ingratiating manner, cutting Frances off before Frances herself had a chance to say anything further: "I remembered it was your favorite".

The smile on Frank's lips switched just as quickly from one of genuine warmth to one of frosty politeness, turning now his full attention towards the other woman directly across the table from him, responding to her claim in a truly icy tone of voice:

"How nice of you to remember: Very kind of you I'm sure!"

Totally confused, Gloria couldn't fathom Frank's open resentment of her immediate superior, believing them to be such good friends. The sudden transformation in the handsome young laddie sitting next to her was remarkable, a pleasant summer's breeze flash freezing into a bitter arctic wind cutting one to the very bone, no advance warning.

None at all!

At the same time though it was evident from the broad grin she wore Frances understood completely, quite enjoying the sight of one of Naomi's former 'conquests' giving her instead the cold shoulder. And trying on her part to shrug off Frank's slight with a little nonchalant smile, the hurt dismay in Naomi's eyes was just as obvious.

And then there was the young Laddie himself:

Noting his date's look of confounded surprise, and even a trace of nervous apprehension, Frank regretted at once exposing Gloria to such a display, letting his feelings for Naomi spillover into what was supposed to be Gloria's big day out. With this in mind, attempting at once to rectify the situation, he immediately donned his most winning smile and, lifting his glass high in a toast, proclaimed in a cheerful voice:

"L' Chayim!"

No sooner had he done so, placing his drink back down on the transparent tabletop before him, he turned at once to Gloria, giving her his complete and undivided attention:

"I understand from Naomi you're Assistant Chief Engineer aboard StarChild. Must be a truly fascinating and rewarding experience", Frank insisted, the sincerity of his interest evident in both his tone of voice and the look of fascination he gave her.

"I like to think so", Gloria spoke up with renewed certainty, finally dealing with a familiar subject she felt secure with.

"Great! In that case, if you don't mind, I'd really like to hear all about it. It must be exciting working onboard the Matriarchate's very first starship preparing for its bachelor voyage".

It didn't take much encouragement at all on Frank's part to get the otherwise shy, uncertain young gentlewoman he was out with to open up when it came to both her career and how she found her new life in the S.E.A..

Leaning forward in his seat Frank, for his part, listened to what Gloria had to say with rapt, wide-eyed attention, wearing an expression of respectful admiration. While true he asked at first about her profession as a simple means of putting her at ease, an effort to build up her confidence, it was just as true he was sincerely fascinated by the subject at hand. Yearning to hear more, the look of devoted interest he bestowed upon his young date was an honest display of emotion, not just a polite show feigned for her sake only:

"Personally, I think it's really impressive that someone so young holds such a position of authority", Frank confessed, sensing a lull in the conversation once Gloria finished speaking:

"You must be both very intelligent and gifted to be entrusted with such awesome responsibilities":

Hearing this Gloria blushed, a smile of genuine pleasure spreading from ear-to-ear. Finding her reaction quite endearing, Frank swiftly continued in the same honest and appreciative tone:

"And on that note, I also want to add that that uniform looks wonderful on you. Quite becoming! You certainly wear it well, looking both very noble and dashing in it. Not to mention quite attractive as well".

Blushing even more so upon hearing this, modestly lowering her eyes, the smile she wore not only remained, but actually grew even wider. Enjoying immensely his sincere attentions and complimentary words, eating it all up with a truly ravenous appetite such honest, heartfelt praise was a new experience Gloria found quite intoxicating to say the very least.

Especially when coming from an attractive, attentive young member of the opposite sex.

Yet even though she didn't want it to ever end she still couldn't help but feel it unfair to the kind laddie hanging on her every word, using him merely to bolster her own ego. In the end it struck her only proper to give him the chance to tell her something about himself, to share something with her about his own life:

"And I think that's enough about me. What about you?", Gloria asked with wide-eyed interest of her own, just as curious about the handsome, charming young man next to her as he apparently was about her.

Pausing a moment to consider where to begin, a trifle uncertain, Frank was under no illusion that a career comprised mostly of waiting on tables could ever compare to what she did. Or to what she would soon be doing. Serving drinks couldn't by any stretch of the imagination ever hold a candle to a life traveling among the very stars themselves.

So with this in mind Frank glossed briefly over his job as a waiter, limiting himself to just a few humorous anecdotes of past job-related experiences.

Concentrating instead on mostly those various interests and hobbies he was the most passionate about he began instead by discussing with her such subjects as music, literature, and the arts. Revealing how much he loved to paint, sculpt and sketch he also told her of his deep and abiding love of the great mistresses in those fields.

Performing a veritable juggling act with his different subjects at the very same time he spoke, Frank would alternately switch from one to another whenever he felt Gloria might be growing disinterested. Grateful for the look of rapt attention she gave him it appeared he was succeeding in maintaining her interest. Gloria especially came to life at his mention of music, sharing eagerly her own preferences in hopes of discovering even further common interests:

"In that case maybe you'd like to take me to an outdoor concert", he suggested slowly, hesitant, with a certain amount of hopeful anticipation:

"There's one in the Prime Park scheduled for just a couple of hours from now".

"Sure! Sounds great", Gloria agreed straightaway, not needing to think twice about it:

"But how will we get there? We all came here in Lt. Cmdr. Marlowe's car", she added quickly with a hint of concern.

"Don't worry. Mine's out back in the employee parking lot", Frank assured her: "We can even use it to take you back to the base later on".

"I'm afraid that wouldn't be possible", Frances informed him with a hint of regret, "but no unauthorized civilians are allowed on the base without both prior notification and authorization".

"No problem", Naomi announced full of cheerful, boisterous generosity: "I can just pick you up at Frank's apartment at 08:30 hours tomorrow!"

Frances shot her friend yet another angry glance, irked by the other woman's cocky assurance their date would inevitably end with Gloria and Frank under the sheets together.

The young couple in question having likewise picked up on Naomi's true meaning Frances thought it a terrible shame poor Gloria lacked the basic courage to tell off her immediate superior in no uncertain terms. After all it was her duty as Frank's escort for the day to uphold Frank's honour in the face of such implications.

Under any other circumstances with any other woman Frank would also have every right to be both offended, and even angry had his date failed so to defend his reputation. This time however all he could feel was a sinking sense of pity—even sympathy—for Gloria, realizing the difficult position she was in. Nevertheless he refused to let Naomi get away with such an impropriety Scott-free, employing that same icy tone when addressing her before:

"I'm sure we both appreciate your offer to serve as Gloria's chauffeur. So *very* generous of you I'm sure!"

Picking up on Frank's anger at long last Gloria finally took a stand of sorts, slowly getting up from her chair:

"Maybe we should be leaving now", she suggested, rather uneasy, able to sense already trouble brewing on the near horizon.

Following her lead Frank likewise got up from the table.

"I'm really sorry you have to be leaving so soon", he heard Naomi remark immediately thereafter: "Please don't go quite yet. I was hoping we could all get caught up on current events."

"Such as?" Frank enquired, cautious, somewhat reluctant to suffer much further her company.

"Well; for starters I was wondering how you're enjoying your new position here so far, if you were finding it as satisfying working here as much as you did at the Glitter Path. And I'm also naturally curious as to how your painting and sculpting is going these days, what new projects you've been up to recently".

"Oh, everything's going pretty well", Frank gave her a more genuine, friendly, smile this time around:

"I've even completed a couple of new works since we last spoke", he added, relaxing his guard. Frank's smile froze quickly in its present position though, hearing Naomi's next question:

"And I was likewise curious as to whether or not you're currently seeing anyone new on a regular basis now", she asked, her otherwise casual demeanor belied only by what seemed to be a desirous gleam in her eye, an expectant look on her face. A seemingly innocent question on the surface Frank nevertheless felt his cheeks flush, shamed and angry at the very same time. Conscious of the real reason behind her query the almost hungry expression Naomi now wore backed up only further his initial suspicions.

He couldn't blame Gloria for not picking up on the other woman's hidden meaning although, from the very way her jaw was clenched in absolute rage, it was clear to see Frances had. This more than anything else drove home for him in no uncertain terms why he held Naomi in such disdain.

Just because they once shared a base, physical relationship that one and only time some two years ago… admittedly a major mistake to begin with… that didn't give her the right expecting him to continue gratifying her carnal desires without showing any consideration for his feelings at all. Especially after he made it painfully clear how he wanted a commitment, one including marriage, before continuing with the type of physical intimacy she seemed to still lust after.

Willing to recognize her right to choose whether, or not she wanted to make such a commitment in life he likewise—*by 'Gosh'!*—expected her to respect as well his own feelings in the matter! And having likewise reached the limit of what she'd tolerate in the matter of Naomi's disrespectful conduct, her deportment towards the weaker sex, Frances for her part burned in silent fury.

Wishing now she'd worn a pair of heavy-duty, steel-toed boots with which to deliver Naomi another good, resounding kick in the shins… do some real damage this time around StarChild's chief engineer wouldn't soon forget… Frances chose instead to verbally blast Naomi into little pieces right then and there.

However, before able to rip into her errant shipmate with that sharp edge of her tongue she was beaten to the punch, Frank leaning over the table in Naomi's direction, his full weight resting on clenched fists:

"Personally, Lt. Cmdr., as far as I'm concerned that is none of your darn business!", he informed her in a steely, determined voice full of bitter resentment, glaring at her straight in the eye: "Furthermore I find it extremely inappropriate, even disgraceful, for a 'decent' gentlewoman to ask a proper young laddie such a highly indiscreet question when 'out on the town' with another gentlewoman!"

Ashen faced with shock Naomi literally shrank back in her chair in response to the vehemence in Frank's voice, not to mention the smoldering outrage in his eyes. Truly astonished and deeply embarrassed she felt all of a sudden rather small inside, quickly apologizing without a single moment's delay.

Never before had she been addressed in such a manner in exactly that way. Although the angry young laddie standing before her was some ten years her junior Naomi felt not unlike some small child on the receiving end of a definite dressing-down by either a parent, teacher, or some other senior authority figure.

While having been criticized by irate laddies in the past none managed to drive their message home quite so effectively as right now. Seeing at last true contrition in her eyes, able to hear the sincere regret in her voice as she apologized, Frank's mood somewhat softened, seeing at last what appeared to be honest remorse:

"I accept your apology, Naomi", he managed, somewhat mollified.

Nevertheless there still remained a certain, awkward tension in the air thick enough to slice: "But I believe that Gloria wishes to leave so I guess we should be on our way now", Frank continued, increasingly uncomfortable with the present situation:

"Please; no need to get up" he added immediately thereafter, noting both Frances and Naomi preparing to stand: "Good-day, Gentlewomen", he finally bid them farewell, bestowing upon each a simple smile and small nod of the head.

Observing Naomi's shamefaced expression just as Gloria set out to escort him elsewhere, he was nonetheless amused to note the subtle look of approval Frances likewise granted him. Nor did Frank miss the puzzled, even mystified glance his young date cast surreptitiously in his direction while opening the door for him. Clearly hesitant to question him on the matter he could nevertheless see in Gloria's expression a clear hint of admiration for the way he just handled her immediate superior.

****

Stepping out into the street beyond Frank allowed himself a momentary pause, blinking repeatedly as his eyes once again acclimated themselves to the "light-of-day" from above.

Made little difference to his way of thinking that the "sun" up on high was merely a city dome-orb, or that the crystal blue skies were just a blister-shaped encasement protecting the city's carefully maintained environment below— protecting its denizens from exposure to the cold, inhospitable, airless surface of the dark, frigid, world beyond.

None of that mattered in the least, unable to think of anything now but how very glad he was to be free at last from the gloomy confines of his new workplace. Silently reveling in his present change of surroundings Gloria waited without complaint for Frank to acclimate himself once more to the sparkling brilliance of Chiron City during its regulated, pre-programmed, daylight period.

Only when apparent he finally did so did she offered him her arm, hand resting on hip, as Frank likewise slipped his hand around the bend in her proffered elbow, letting Gloria lead him along at a leisurely pace. Making their way down the street, arm-in-arm, he offered directions at the same time how to find his car.

Turning down the clean, narrow alleyway beside the bar leading to the parking lot in back, Gloria suggested taking him to a nice little close-by restaurant she knew before the actual concert itself. Both hungry and tired from being on his feet all morning Frank readily agreed without any need of further encouragement, coming up right then upon a quite clearly expensive luxury sports car.

Pointing it out to her as being his, Gloria's astonished delight was evident in both voice and face, drawing nearer with eager reverence the dazzling red vehicle with its sleek design. Sensing her obvious desire to examine it more intimately, closer up, Frank let go of her elbow.

"Oh, my", she whispered, awestruck: "A model X-7 Lembarchini!"

Listening to her list aloud to herself all its various accessories, watching her circle it over and over with the same ravenous desire he saw in Naomi just moments ago, a broad grin leapt at once to his lips seeing the consummate engineer and technician within her come at last to the forefront.

It was then Frank began to get his first hint what she must be like in her native element aboard StarChild although, even as she rattled off a running inventory of all the car's basic features and added luxury extra's, he saw likewise in her eyes the question he feared most. While true Frank accepted tokens of affection from female admirers, the fine machine his young escort was drooling over right now infront of him no exception, it was just as true he was painfully honest with each and every one.

Making it clear to one and all his gratitude would not include slipping between the sheets with them, their offerings were likewise returned with the same frosty treatment he showed Naomi if learning their gifts were meant indeed to be sexual bribes. Nor was that all, similar arctic blasts in store as well for any woman foolish enough to propose making him their "master", a term for the last few centuries having now only two meanings.

Used most often as the title appearing before a single man's name, as opposed to "Mister" for married men, the second—more disreputable—use of the word referred to a kept man providing sexual favors without the protection, legitimacy, respectability, and/or any of those other benefits coming with marriage.

Wanting nothing more-or-less than to be a "Mister", not a "Master", the only proposals Frank was interested in were those of Holy Matrimony. And while most women understood this concerning the little trinkets he might receive from others, there were still those few who reacted with shocked outrage, jumping to the wrong conclusion.

To some it didn't matter the car with which Gloria was so taken with was nothing more than a 23rd birthday present from a kindly old gentlewoman, their relationship more akin to that of mother and son. A wealthy old spinster who liked to be seen out on the town with Frank, it was a purely platonic relationship beginning just a little over a year ago soon after first waiting on her at the Glitter Path.

Too discreet to go about discussing her identity with just anyone she was a wealthy, powerful and very lonely businesswoman of substantial means wanting nothing more than to make up in life for having no children of her own. Doting on Frank like a favorite son she'd been a regular customer at his former place of employ, striking up a sincere friendship with him after having gotten to know him better during frequent visits.

Feeling quite awkward at first accepting such an extravagant gift, he initially refused to do so. It wasn't until she quite literally begged him that he relented, assuring him there were no strings attached other than the simple joy it would give her doing for him this "one little thing".

Nevertheless there remained those few who'd accuse Frank, even after hearing all this, of being no better than Lucian Malloy, accepting even under such innocent circumstances such gifts. And not knowing if Gloria might be in fact one of these he wanted to avoid any misunderstandings, hoping she wouldn't ask the obvious question already forming there in her eyes:

'How could a mere waiter even hope to ever, ever afford such a fine and expensive item?' Seeing as this was her first time out with a man it pained him to think of this innocent girl with untried heart leaping to the wrong conclusion, scared off of all men altogether.

Feeling as though walking on eggshells, wanting to avoid any possible misunderstanding, Frank proceeded at once to remove instead his car keys from the right breast pocket of his white, three-piece suit vest. Thinking quickly in hopes of deflecting any awkward situation, a playful smile dancing at the corners of his mouth, he held said keys out to her between thumb and forefinger:

"Hey, there: How'd you like to drive it while we're out on the town together?", he called out in a loud voice to the clearly star-struck young gentlewoman, jingling his keys back and forth in a beckoning fashion.

"Are you serious?", Gloria squealed with absolute delight like some little child receiving an unexpected gift always hoped for—an expression of both disbelief and sheer joy spreading rapidly from her bright, eager eyes to every corner of her face.

"No joke!" he insisted, grinning himself from ear-to-ear, pleased at her response:

"I'm not teasing", he assured her even further: "I really mean it".

Needing no further encouragement she ran instead to within arm's length, holding out a trembling, tentative hand… palm up… giving him all the while a look of both wide-eyed hope and uncertain expectation. Taking her outstretched hand in both of his Frank passed the keys over to her waiting fingers, gazing for a moment deeply into her eyes.

Withdrawing at last his hands from hers she stared down for a few seconds at the glistening metallic strips resting there. Sparkling in the light from far above she clutched them tightly in her fist, overcome with deep emotion, misty-eyed. Momentarily forgetting herself, throwing caution to the wind, Gloria followed this by flinging her arms at once around Frank's neck, pressing her lips to his cheek in a grateful kiss.

Pulling quickly back from him remembering where she was, blushing as she did so, she then ran over to the driver's side of Frank's car, climbing in as quickly as possible least he change his mind:

"Come on: Let's get going", she called out after him in the highest of high spirits. Complying at once with her boisterous request, Frank climbed into the front passenger side likewise all smiles:

"I've always dreamt of driving a car like this with all the windows down, the wind in my hair, while listening to some real powerful music", Gloria confided, rolling down all the side windows once they both were completely settled in.

"And so you shall, dear gentlewoman!" Frank laughed merrily, his date's buoyant spirits becoming his as well:

"And I have just the thing for you", he offered, taking an audio-wafer from a collection situated in a small compartment embedded between their seats:

"How about a little 'Alan Hooper'?", he suggested, slipping his offering into the player located in the very center of the dashboard just right of the steering wheel. Doing so a loud, powerful, rhythmic beat was accompanied as well by an equally strident, yet compelling woman's voice filling their ears from the speaker units both in front and back.

"Perfect!" Gloria giggled, backing the car out of its assigned parking space, whisking them off at once to lunch.

Chapter 16

"DEFENDING THE LADDIE'S HONOUR"

Neither spoke to the other as each finished her drink in somber silence, each held captive by private thoughts and dark reflections. Frances ordered another gin and tonic—with a lime twist, of course! —while Naomi proceeded to consume not only the drink she'd ordered herself, but the remains as well of both Gloria and Frank's remaining beverages.

Simply pouring the different containers into one glass she was too torn up inside, distraught, to give a sanguinary darn about how her concoction would actually taste. In the end it was Frances who finally broke the silence between them, speaking to her companion in a voice full of stern disapproval, obvious reproach:

"Well, I hope you've finally learned your lesson at last", she grumbled with ill-hidden contempt. Too upset to manage a single word Naomi just nodded in mute agreement. Making Frank angry was the very last thing on her mind, the very last thing she wanted to do.

Of the honest opinion she was just being cute, even amusing, she still thought so even after Frances gave her what she now realized was a well-deserved kick under the table. Never was it her intention to offend either young person who just left:

Especially Frank!

The plain and simple truth was that Naomi deeply regretted for a while now the past which developed between them, longing ever since for a way to repair the rift between them. Wishing in all honesty she could make that commitment he both wanted, and even deserved, Naomi found it all the same impossible to do so.

Ever since then she searched diligently for a way to communicate her sincere regret over the whole miserable affair but, no matter what she tried, he remained always so cold, aloof, and immovable. Even this little date she arranged was such an attempt on her part, truly believing Gloria would be as good for him as he'd be for her.

She only hoped her junior officer had more success with him than she, coming now to the sad conclusion it was simply best to just back off and leave him alone. Unaware before this of how deeply she hurt him Naomi never realized until that very moment just how really, truly intense Frank's animosity towards her really ran in its depth, breadth, and even height.

Meanwhile, able to see at last some honest remorse in Naomi's eyes—the pained, penitent, expression on her face—Frances felt her anger towards the other woman begin to soften, dissipating at long last.

"I have to admit you did a good thing here today in at least bringing those two together", she confessed, feeling now more generous in her attitude:

"I admit I had my doubts in the beginning when you first sprang on us the reason for coming here but, when hearing it was Frank you fixed Lt. Greensley up with, I began thinking more about it, realizing they might end up being good for each other after all.

"Well done".

Ending with that, Frances gave then Naomi's hand both a friendly pat and compassionate squeeze.

"Thanks", Naomi sighed, managing just barely a weak smile. Although truly grateful to the tall, thin, severe-looking woman next to her for both her continued friendship and comforting words they nevertheless served to increase further her sense of guilt, remembering how she so cruelly maneuvered poor Frank into this little rendezvous.

Certain Frances would be livid should she ever learn of her hidden Machiavellian machinations, fearing it might result in a permanent dissolution of their friendship, that was one dirty little secret Naomi promised herself never to reveal. Given already her present state of mind Naomi just couldn't bear the idea of losing yet another friend still.

"You know what", it was Naomi's turn, throwing in her own two centi's worth after yet another silent pause: "I'm starting to think you were right all along about this place not being so hot after all. How about we just finish up here, pay the bill, and head out for greener pastures?"

"Sure thing. Absolutely", Frances agreed straightaway, understanding completely. Unwilling to leave her friend alone in her current, fragile emotional state she decided against her original plan to simply ditch Naomi in favour of the young laddie she planned to take out later that afternoon. Promising to make it up to him in the near future, she was just as sure Shotoku would likewise forgive her once hearing why:

"When the waiter comes back we can ask for the bill and head out".

"No need to wait. We can just pay up at the counter bar", Naomi offered this time in a somewhat firmer tone, tilting her head backwards at a sharp angle, swiftly pouring the last of her drink down her throat.

Setting the now empty container back down on the transparent table with a loud clank of dura-glass against dura-glass, she pulled yet another multi-hued five-krodit note from her purse, slipping it under her now-empty container. Rising slowly from her leather and chrome seat Frances followed suit, polishing off as well what remained of her gin and tonic.

"And, since you've taken care of the tip, I'll pay for the drinks", Frances offered, likewise standing up.

"Sure", Naomi muttered in reply: "Thanks".

****

Andrei just finished with his call to J.J.'s school, Ms. Li-Wong proving herself quite understanding, and was about to place a call through to the nearest Vehicle Rescue Center when detecting a source of movement out of the corner of his eye.

Turning to his right it was then he observed two women emerge from one of the washrooms near the far end of the well-lit hallway. Situated next to where he stood it was the only section of that dark and foreboding environment bright enough to see what was actually going on. Drawing closer to where he stood just outside the narrow passageway, Andrei realized soon enough there wasn't enough room for both approaching gentlewomen to pass him by.

At least not with him standing right there in front of the bar's public V-phone.

Leaning up close against the wall beside the phone mounted between them, back firmly pressed up against the black wall now behind him, he allowed both approaching women ample room in which to get by.

Watching their gradual approach from around the protruding VP next to him the woman in the lead had long, straight, lanky dusty-hued blonde hair that looked absolutely greasy in its presently unwashed, unkempt condition. Her otherwise bright blue eyes bloodshot, her puffy eyelids drooping and sagging at the corners, what drew Andrei's attention to her most were the glaring features of a habitual drunkard ravished by years of substance abuse.

Staggering her way closer to him with a noticeable swaying motion her sallow cheeks also appeared puffy, even jaundiced, in the otherwise generous light from above. The flesh hanging from them like melted wax, the effects of prolonged alcohol abuse were painfully evident upon her every feature. Pretty sure she had to be in her late 3O's she all the same looked much older, more haggard than she should have, the ravages of continual heavy drink having taken their toll as well upon what must have been once a quite appealing physique.

Given the unwashed and disheveled state of the pink pantsuit she wore Andrei felt it equally safe to assume she'd likewise been out on an all-night bender, wearing the same wretched clothes as the day before. It was only then the sad thought occurred to Andrei that, if not for her obvious problem with liquor, its subsequent effects upon her physical appearance, she might have been rather attractive if not for her slovenly attire.

Meanwhile the other woman trailing close behind the oily drunk wore a pair of stylish navy blue jeans and a dura-denim jacket appearing in a better state of repair than that of her clearly intoxicated friend. With long, curly brown hair reaching well down past her shoulders she was also slightly taller and

93

thinner than the first 'gentlewoman' leading the way. Able now to get a closer look Andrei noticed likewise she didn't exhibit the same advanced telltale signs of perpetual substance abuse. While true her eyes also appeared somewhat red and puffy Andrei concluded that, in her case, this was merely a sign of fatigue.

For a moment there it seemed they'd pass him by, paying Andrei no heed at all. At least that was until the dirty blonde in the lead turned her attention towards the VP at his side.

"Excuse me, laddie, but are you using the phone?", she asked, slurring her words in a slow, hesitant voice; her moist, weepy eyes finally focused now on Andrei's very person:

"Yes, I'm afraid so", Andrei informed her:

"I need to make an urgent call", he explained apologetically.

"I hope there's nothing wrong. Anything we can do to help?", she offered in an overly solicitous manner giving Andrei a brief pause for concern, a shiver passing straight through him.

"That's very kind of you", he smiled courteously, uncertain he could readily imagine any situation in which he'd desire this particular woman's assistance: "However, I'm sure that the Vehicle Rescue Center will be able to help".

"Problem with your car?" she then enquired in a strange tone of voice he found not at all trustworthy, unable all-the-same to explain why.

"I'm afraid so", he continued against his better judgement with a weary little sigh, every cell of his body suddenly warning him he should be leaving instead: "I think it has something to do with the fuel cells, but unfortunately I don't know that much about that sort of thing".

"Well, that's perfectly understandable", she declared with a trace of smarminess, if not outright condescension: "After all an attractive young laddie such as yourself shouldn't have to worry about such things. That's women's work!"

"That's very kind of you to say", Andrei forced himself to remain polite, a hint of scorn appearing in his voice neither woman seemed to pick up on. Wishing this insufferable sot would just go away he decided to switch tactics, try another ploy:

"And on that note I'm afraid I must be going about making my call now so I can get back to my wife", he added: "She's already ordered for us so I should be getting back to our table as quickly as possible and let her know when the Vehicle Rescue people will be here".

"Oh", she mumbled, a momentary flash of uneasiness crossing the pink-clad woman's face. Quickly replaced however by an expression of dumb animal cunning she all the same pressed on, undaunted:

"In that case maybe she'd like to join the three of us for a drink".

Realizing with an overwhelming sense of utter dismay his bluff was just called Andrei sighed yet again, holding up his left hand so she couldn't miss the gold wedding band there:

"Look, I really am married", he pressed on in a deceptively calm voice, wiggling his ring finger back and forth just inches from her face: "So even if I wanted to join you for a drink, I'm afraid she wouldn't approve. So please let me just make my call and leave".

"Hey honey, I'm sure she wouldn't mind sharing the wealth", the greasy drunk responded with a lascivious sneer, transforming Andrei's annoyance into a stab of fear when she leaned forward, placing her left hand flat up against the wall next to his head.

Effectively boxing him in, her arm on one side and the VP protruding from the wall on the other, she pressed her body in even closer over him in a threatening fashion. Maybe a couple of inches shorter than Jenniboni that still made her some five inches taller than he.

Nevertheless Andrei hid his fear well, proceeding forth with both steely determination and firm resolve: "Now look here, 'Ms. Whoever-you-are': My little girl is in trouble at school, and I have an urgent appointment to keep with her principal so I must be going now".

Attempting to duck under her arm to freedom the woman before him nevertheless anticipated this move on Andrei's part. Sliding her left hand further down the black wall behind him, she prevented the beleaguered young father's escape:

"Don't worry hon. I'm sure she's being taken good care of. Must say though she's really lucky to have such a handsome, good-looking daddy", she added in a sickeningly sweet voice:

"Reeeeeally lucky!"

A wave of unreality swept through every avenue of Andrei's consciousness, his anger bubbling and rising at long last to the surface. Totally unable to believe what was happening never before was he so detained against his will by any previous "admirer", never treated so discourteously in his entire life.

Even the most ardent flirt always accepted "No!" for an answer. And with gracious good manners one might add!

"Let me pass right now!", he demanded at once, snapping angrily.

"No need to get so huffy", the odious 'Ms. Whoever-you-are' protested: "I'm just trying to be friendly. I just thought that the three of us could have a little fun. That's all".

"I'm not interested in that kind of 'fun'", Andrei retorted hotly: "Especially with the likes of you!!"

For a split second the intoxicated smile on the sleazy bar hag's face vanished, soon to reappear. However, in that brief instant of discomposure, Andrei was chilled to the bone seeing in her eyes the inner cruelty, the almost lunatic rage, dwelling at the very core of her personality.

Tempted at first to slap her face in hopes of either dissuading her from further sexual harassment, or at least startle her long enough to make good his escape, he now realized with a sinking sense of despair what might affect his release with any normal woman would most likely get him killed by this monster.

With growing horror it quickly dawned on him that, in addition to being atypical of the female gender, she was in all probability quite unbalanced as well. Coming to the swift conclusion further displays of anger wouldn't help his cause any, he once again switched tactics in desperate hopes an appeal to sympathy might do the trick.

Therefore it was with a look of pitiable entreaty that Andrei finally gazed up into her eyes:

"Please let me go. I'm terribly sorry if I have offended you, but please find it within your heart to forgive me", he pleaded: "I can't understand why you would want a man who doesn't want to be with you when I'm sure there must be so many out there who would no doubt enjoy the pleasure of your company".

"The only reason you don't want to be with me is because you don't know how gooooood I can make you feel", she drawled with a wicked giggle. Sneering right at him her right hand reached with evil intent upwards between his legs.

Lashing out at her before she could make actual contact with his manhood Andrei's right hand struck out at her with a quick movement born of pure, reflexive outrage. Bringing his open palm down sharply on the inside of her wrist he slapped it away from him with a loud, violent snap before her offending appendage could make actual, physical contact:

"Keep your stinking hands off of me *YOU FILFTHY SLATTERN*!!!" he snarled, all fierceness, burning with rage. Upon hearing all this the "Filthy Slattern's" friend in the blue denim outfit begin to likewise giggle.

Andrei's head snapping about in her direction, having until then forgotten she was even there, demanded in an equally outraged voice full of justified indignation:

"And what kind of woman are you?? How can you just stand there and let this monster treat me like this?? Have you no sense of decency. Or didn't they teach you 'The Code' in school??" he insisted, enraged.

At this the black-haired woman stopped giggling at once, her face turning scarlet with shame. Yet, instead of coming to Andrei's rescue, she did nothing but stare sheepishly at the dark grey carpeting directly beneath her. Seeing no relief from his torment being offered up from her direction his eyes flashed with smoldering fury:

"You're no gentlewoman!!" he spat at her in utter, absolute, contempt: "You're nothing but a miserable, contemptible, pathetic coward!!"

However, his attention quickly drawn back to the sweaty woman in the grubby pink pantsuit, she pressed herself up even closer to him, her face only inches from his. Able now to smell the rank, acrid perspiration emanating from her unwashed person, feeling as well the swampy warmth of her fetid, booze-soaked, breath against his face, he felt his gorge beginning to rise.

Struggling not to throw up, filled with both revulsion and even horror, he turned at once his face away from her. Pressing his left cheek up against the wall behind him as hard as he could, eyes squeezed tightly shut, his only desire right then was to simply melt away into the wall behind him. Struggling with all his might he tried to drive what was taking place from his conscious awareness:

"I like fire in a man's eyes. Very impressive. You know what else I like?" she whispered in his ear in a vain, useless attempt to sound alluring.

Not waiting long to answer her own question his grubby abuser proceeded right then and there to fill both Andrei's very mind and ears with such precise, graphic verbal depictions of such perverted, foul-minded, and depraved sexual acts... each more monstrous than the last... they were without doubt beyond the ability of any sane mind to even conceive much less tolerate.

Each twisted and barbarous image literally tore into Andrei's very being, raping his very soul, his face growing paler and paler with fathomless loathing, measureless disgust. Quite ashen with shock his skin crawled as though a multitude of squirming, writhing, insects were buried underneath his entire body. Trembling anew, blood boiling, he felt as though infected by some virulent strain attacking every cell in his body.

In a very real sense it truly was a disease. Working its way through every fiber and sinew of Andrei's entire being it was a disease of the very spirit with which his attacker now infected him, carried on the back of each and every obscenity.

The slimy, sleazy, whispers she uttered plus her warm, swampy breath against his face were like some foul contagion driving Andrei to tears of both impotent rage and humiliation filling him with an overwhelming urge to scour his entire body with the strongest disinfectant—the most abrasive cleansing pad available—just to purify himself of the wretched sensations this evil woman's vocabulary inspired.

Inspiring within him such feelings of endless humiliation, degradation, and despoilment Andrei truly felt it better to die rather than continue living in such a miserable condition as this. The weight of feeling so soiled and sullied inside felt like bricks of offal being piled on his head in such liberal doses as to beggar the imagination.

Feeling through and through like nothing but filth himself, feeling so all the way through to the very core of his most inner being, Andrei refused to give vent to those tears welling up right then from the very depths of his soul. Unwilling to give his verbal rapist the satisfaction it was then there rose up alongside that degradation a burning hate, an anger the likes of which Andrei never knew before:

How dare this she-devil treat him in such a fashion?!

Why should he be forced to endure this foul abuse and assault??

Hands clenched tightly into fists of rage, driven beyond all limits of Human endurance for the first time in his life, it was also then Andrei prepared to strike out at her, make her pay for every single perversity she just inflicted upon him.

Cognizant of his assailant's superior strength he nevertheless braced himself to do battle for both his honour and very worth as a Human being, a part of Womankind likewise created in the Almighty's own image. No longer did it matter if she killed him for doing so.

"Leave me alone or else I'll..." Andrei growled menacingly through clenched teeth, tears of humiliation running down his cheeks.

"Or else what, little man?" she laughed, full of derisive scorn, pressing on with a yet another taunting little cackle: "So, boy, what 'cha gonna do to me?"

Spared in the end from needing to lash out in his own defense it was then, without missing a heartbeat, Andrei heard all-of-a-sudden the blessed intrusion of yet another feminine voice snarl its way into his awareness. Full of moral outrage it sounded to him like some avenging angel from on high come to his rescue:

"More to the point you should be asking ME what I'M going to do to you!!!"

****

Standing at the dark counter bar Frances took the change the bartender handed her from the till, slipping it in her purse. Re-adjusting its carrying strap once more over her shoulder, she felt an immediate tapping on her shoulder after doing so.

Turning about it was Naomi pointing towards something ominous 'going down' in the direction of that brightly-lit hallway leading to the restrooms beyond.

At first Frances proved unable to determine what exactly it was they were looking at, the rest of the bar still too dark to reveal any telltale particulars. All she could see at first were the shadowy silhouettes of three distinct individuals, one further back in the hallway partially obscuring the light in back of them—the music from above likewise preventing whatever voices there were from being heard.

Not that it mattered, though. Years of rigorous and exhaustive training had honed her senses to acute precision, alerting Frances to the immediate presence of certain trouble nearby:

"I definitely don't like the looks of whatever's going down over there", she announced in a crisp, taut, voice:

"Let's go".

Not waiting for Naomi's reply she headed out anyway, sure the other would follow. Drawing closer to the incident in progress Frances was able at last to make out what was actually taking place through the thick gloom all around her. The magnitude of what was happening sinking in her blood ran icy cold with utter fury, moving in on target of her newfound outrage with the purposeful stride of some dark, sleek panther closing in for the kill.

And able as well to see now what was going on Naomi could likewise see trouble on the immediate horizon ahead—avoiding it the very last thing on her mind. However, even while planning to follow Frances' predictable lead, equally offended by the sight before her, Naomi's anger—her righteous indignation—explained only part of her complete willingness to charge so readily into battle.

Redemption was another. Not so much in anyone else's opinion than her own, a chance to redeem herself in view of recent misdeeds.

Coming into position behind that shorter woman in her disheveled pink pantsuit Frances could see with heartbreaking clarity the obvious horror, humiliation, and revulsion present there on the face of the young laddie involved. Eyes screwed tightly shut, face turned towards the wall behind him, the trauma so evident on the tortured man's face inspired an even greater rage in Frances hearing his abuser now ask in a contemptuous voice:

"So, boy, what 'cha gonna do to me?"

"More to the point you should be asking ME what I'M going to do to you!!!", Frances snarled in venomous reply, speaking up with no less contempt in the victimized laddie's place. Provoking by this an immediate response from 'Ms. Whoever-you-are' the other woman swung about, clearly annoyed by this sudden intrusion.

The young laddie's reaction just as swift his eyes flashed wide open, his head whipping about. Gazing straight upward into Frances' burning eyes the immediate look of desperate hope, the silent, pitiable look of entreaty he gave her, moved Frances herself almost to the point of tears.

Gazing upwards into the pale, somewhat gaunt face of that new arrival made even paler by her clearly violent emotions, Andrei realized for a fact now his deliverance was likewise at hand. And alongside that came as well a slight twinge of worry, catching sight of that look of pure, unadulterated hate his new champion bestowed now upon his molester, the latter still standing between them.

Even more so than the burning rage there in his feminine messiah's ebony eyes, what really captured Andrei's attention was the green and gold S.E.A. uniform she wore. For a brief, crazy moment Andrei actually thought Jenniboni responsible for sending her to save him now from his present ordeal.

Not that it mattered whether it was his wife, or God Himself who'd sent her his way. At that moment, no matter which, that tall, thin woman with her stark features and severe countenance was nonetheless the most beautiful sight Andrei ever witnessed in his entire life.

Meanwhile the nasty drunk standing still between them gave Frances a look of both scornful derision and outright defiance Her understanding too dulled after years of continual substance abuse she didn't realize the honest extent of the clear, immediate danger she was now in.

Anyone else in full possession of their complete faculties would have noticed right from the very start the obvious tell-tale warning signs staring them now straight in the face. The dramatic way in which Frances' nostrils flared, her coal-black eyes narrowed into angry cat-like slits, the way her thin, pale lips were pressed together so tight were all clear warning signs easy to see.

Blissfully ignoring these obvious warning signs however Andrei's attacker continued on instead in a highly belligerent manner, doing so one might add at her own peril:

"This is between the laddie and me so get out of here while you can", she finally countered with a cantankerous sneer, momentarily confused by this sudden intrusion.

"Not anymore", Frances shot back, her inner rage just barely suppressed behind a self-imposed mask of deadly calm: "So it's ***you*** who can get out of here, right now, before you end up experiencing such pain the likes of which you've never imagined!".

"Just who the 'darn heck' do you think you are??", the vulgar woman in the rank, grubby pink outfit demanded in a rough, coarse frog voice.

"More to the point just who the 'darn heck' do you think *you* are!?!", Frances countered, glowering down at her in fiery repose, giving at the same time Andrei a meaningful glance. Instructing him with a silent, subtle sideways motion of her head to vacate the premises Andrei had no need to be told twice, making at once a move towards the far exit.

Yet before he could take even a single step 'Ms. Whoever-you-are' stopped him. Quickly extending her left arm she slammed him back into the wall behind him with naked, merciless force:

"I didn't say you could leave yet honey, did I?" she giggled, a cruel smirk now appearing.

"How *dare* you treat a laddie like that?!!", Frances let out with an angry roar, pouncing now on her hapless target like as mother tiger defending her young. Completely taken by surprise her dull-witted opponent had barely any idea what was happening, Frances grabbing her by the very same arm with which she just assaulted Andrei, spinning her roughly about.

And equally startled by his rescuer's quick reflexes Andrei jumped to the side just in the nick-of-time, StarChild's outraged Security Chief in her oh-so-familiar green and gold uniform slamming his former assailant... face-first... into the wall next to him, doing so with a quite loud, painful thud:

"Now you've gone and done it", Frances snapped, pressing herself up against the other woman's back, almost coiled about her like some deadly serpent: "Now you're going to pay like you've never paid before".

Backing her promise up with just a tiny sample of what she was truly capable of, Frances then wrenched her captive's arm even further up along her back. Crying out in complete agony, tears of pain beginning to trickle down her face, the other woman ripped loose with a truly astounding stream of obscenities.

"Didn't anyone ever teach you not to use such profanity in the presence of polite company?" Frances enquired, her snide tone brimming with absolute disgust:

"I ought to rip you apart right here and now!"

Finally recovering at last from her initial shock over this sudden, drastic turn of events the denim-clad brunette stepped at long last foreword to render her beleaguered comrade some much-needed assistance. Never getting though the chance to do so it was Naomi's turn to move in, thwarting her attempts in mid-stride. Blocking swiftly her path the other StarChild officer proceeded at once to warn her off in a soft, but challenging voice:

"You'd be wise to stay out of all this, try nothing, or else matters could turn out just as badly for you, too".

Until Naomi stepped forth Andrei was too focused in on what was going on right in front of him between Frances and the miserable sot he christened "Ms. Whoever-you-are" to even notice the other S.E.A. officer present:

'So I have *two* rescuers!' Andrei mused to himself; sure all the same Frances could handle both provocateurs all on her very own. Still though he found it a comfort knowing the playing field was now even odds. And calculating her chances against the solidly built red-head now blocking her way, the denim-clad woman Andrei called a 'pathetic coward' came to the quick conclusion they weren't at all good.

Although somewhat taller than StarChild's Chief Engineer she was hardly as well built as the woman now blocking her way in her crisply tailored green and gold uniform. And from the vehement look in Naomi's brilliant, emerald eyes her opponent realized she'd be risking as well her own wellbeing were she to even dare try and intervene on behalf of her grubby friend.

And being the coward Andrei deduced her to be right from the very beginning, she moved nary a muscle. In the end it was Andrei himself who intervened on his assailant's behalf.

Witnessing the naked rage burning out of control in Frances' coal black eyes he really feared the possibility of real violence, dire injury, taking place. It wasn't that he no longer harbored any deep resentment towards his newly cornered attacker, still loathing her down deep with every fiber and sinew of his very being.

Nor did he fear for Frances' safety in the matter, having no doubt she was clearly the superior force here. Simply put he just couldn't bear the idea of being responsible for still more suffering yet even if the person to suffer so richly deserved it. Having had more than enough unpleasantries for one day, he was simply unable to handle the idea of even more on his account:

"Please, Ma'am, no more", Andrei begged his outraged messiah, his voice full of obvious concern: "She's drunk. I just want it all to end. Please just make her go away and leave me alone: Please?!"

"This is your lucky day", Frances informed 'Ms. Whoever-You-Are' with a sardonic grin: "You should be grateful to the young laddie here for being so forgiving. He just saved you from a most unhappy fate.

"Therefore I'm going to let you go this time with just a warning. If I ever— *EVER*—catch you abusing anyone ever again I will, so help me, *destroy* you. Do we have an understanding?

"Yes!", 'Ms. Whoever-you-are' just managed to gasp through her clear, obvious pain.

"Very good. However, first, you're going to apologize to the young laddie for being such a crude, vulgar, abusive '*witch*'. Understood?"

Once again the woman in pink gave her captor a positive reply, proceeding then to apologize in a tortured voice full of undeniable fear.

"Splendid. Quite good", Frances responded in a cool, pseudo-friendly tone of voice doing very little to mask her true feelings: "Now I'm going to let you go so you'd better not try anything foolish. Wanting to is understandable. Doing so however would be extremely foolhardy on your part. Have I made myself perfectly clear?"

For a third time yet the other woman answered in the affirmative, Frances slowly stepping back, releasing her prisoner from her painful confinement. Free at last from Frances' steely grip she gradually turned about, her plans to strike back evident in the look of hateful defiance she gave her former captor.

"I wouldn't if I were you", Naomi cautioned her with a wicked grin all her own, still keeping the vulgar drunk's denim-clad friend at bay: "I've seen my associate here squash opponent's superior to you under her thumb like nothing but little bugs".

Just when it seemed 'Ms. Whoever-you-are' was about to open her filthy mouth in pugnacious reply, it was now Frances' turn to cut her off:

"Don't say a thing!", she did so in deadly earnest, doing so in a firm, commanding voice full of forbidding authority: "Not one single word. Just shut up and get the sanguinary heck out of here".

Whether it was Naomi's words that finally got through to her, or the angry gleam in Frances' hostile eyes the result was the same. With dawning awareness it finally occurred to 'Ms. Whoever-you-Are's' booze-addled brain her very existence was still in jeopardy, moving away as quickly as possible, her cowardly cohort following close behind.

Chapter 17

"AT THE OFFICE"

'Not good', Darren reflected in perfect silence, glancing up from all the work on his desk, hearing the auto-doors across the room swoosh open.

Entering her outer office with a determined stride Darren could tell from that worried frown on Commodore Saphira's troubled face all was not well. This assumption was only confirmed further when, forgoing the usual pleasantries (like asking how his day was going), Jenniboni continued instead her rapid pace for the door to her own, private inner office.

Although he'd seen her distracted on previous occasions Darren never before saw her quite so anxious. Something must really be amiss. Something major! Along with her thoughtful and considerate manners the one thing he always enjoyed about being her private, confidential secretary was her basically open and easy-going nature:

"Cup of coffee with an ice-cube in it!", Jenniboni demanded, sounding brisk, taut voiced, passing by his desk.

'Yes indeed' Darren grinned within, full of wry humor: 'Definitely not one of those days it paid to get out of bed'. Making it a career point to commit his boss's little peculiarities and preferences to memory, he already knew she requested an ice-cube in her coffee only if in too much of a hurry elsewhere for it to cool down on its own:

'Oh well', he sighed, leaping up from his workstation, abandoning everything else in sight, trailing dutifully behind her. Crossing the threshold into her own inner office Jenniboni made her way over to the large, simulated oak desk at the room's far side, the door sliding shut behind her.

Meanwhile the older laddie with distinguished features still in back of her turned instead toward the right-hand side of the room. There a coffee machine sat atop of a small, squat cabinet pushed up against a wall made of the same syntha-wood material as Jenniboni's desk.

Much like the Admiral's workplace in its decor the only discernible difference was the noticeable absence of a fully stocked wet bar. A caffeine addict instead, Jenniboni had just the coffee maker, a small cabinet amply supplied with all the makings for her favorite beverage, and a well-maintained mini-refrigeration unit brimming with both soft drinks and ice cubes.

As for the remaining wall space corresponding to where Melissa Sellers kept her impressive array of fermented spirits, it was occupied completely by a just-as-grand series of walnut bookshelves. Heavily laden with a varied assortment of books, nick-knacks, and other similar memorabilia these included several tri-dee photos of family and friends interspersed among other items.

"How are you coming along with the daily updates?" Jenniboni inquired, crisply, assuming her rightful place in the plush seat behind her large, imposing office desk.

"Almost completed, Ma'am", Darren hastened to assure her. Busy preparing a fresh pot of coffee he always saw to it she never had to suffer a stale cup:

"I already have them on ei-pad for your inspection and am now correlating them with the reports from last week".

"Excellent", Jenniboni responded at last in a more pleasant voice, all the while bestowing upon him a pleased smile. Really a quite skilled and accomplished assistant who carried out the performance of his many varied duties with diligence, devotion, and great care she felt a certain twinge of guilt for having spoken so sharply to him just moments before.

Let the Admiral keep her pretty boys, Jenniboni preferring the experience and wisdom that came with age. Which wasn't to say that Darren wasn't also quite handsome: wavy silver hair and distinguished character lines adding only extra depth of personality to his already rugged good looks.

All-in-all Jenniboni had to admit it was true what they said about men retaining their sexual desirability longer than women, some even improving with age. Not that she ever considered being unfaithful to her husband, knowing a good thing when she had it....

Still though, as Melissa would be quick to point out, "no harm in just looking". All things being equal she guessed it only fair God might grant men this one tiny advantage over women, having deemed it only fitting to bless women with so many more over them.

Activating a small panel to the side of the desktop computer at her right, she then asked how long it would be before her coffee was at last ready:

"Coming right up", Darren answered straight away as Jenniboni heard the unmistakable sound of an ice-cube being dropped into her cup, followed soon after by the audible tinkling of a spoon stirring it about along with the rest of the contents therein—this accompanied by the soft hum of her office VP emerging from the desk before her, summoned forth at her command.

"Excellent", she smiled yet again in his direction, the VP completing its ascent, positioned to her left next to a picture of Andrei and the children: "Once that's taken care of I want you to go back to your desk, finish correlating those reports. How close are you to finishing?"

"Just a few more minutes to go", he informed her, approaching with cup and saucer in hand. Standing on the other side of her desk he leaned forward, placing her drink before her. Acknowledging his offering with both a nod and "thank you", she immediately returned to the subject at hand:

"All rightie, then: By the time I leave here I want those reports ready for me to take up to StarChild on ei-pad. Unfortunately that will leave you only ten minutes, or, so. Any problem?"

"No, Ma'am".

"Fine, then", Jenniboni continued even further, her otherwise pleasant demeanor taking on now a more serious tone. Instructing him not to allow anyone from then on free passage to her office, her voice took on an especially sober quality when including Darren as well in her directive.

****

Left alone to her own devices Jenniboni picked up the silver spoon resting on the saucer next to her cup. Darren, having excused himself, gave her his solemn promise he'd carry out her instructions to the letter.

Stirring her coffee, the spoon producing a gentle tinkling sound within, she leaned back in her plush black leather chair. Lifting both cup and saucer towards her once the ice had completely melted she stared intently at the VP directly before her. Partaking of the beverage in hand with shallow, delicate sips Jenniboni organized her thoughts, contemplating how to word the call she was about to make.

Putting the cup down once deciding what to say, Jenniboni then jabbed with the tip of her finger a button on the VP's left side. Employing a bit more force than necessary a direct link to her ship above was immediately established, the youthful features of one of her junior communications officers on StarChild's bridge appearing without delay on the screen before her:

"This is the 'S.E.A.S.S. StarChild'", Ensign Rosetta Noble announced in a crisp, clear, professional voice: "Noble here".

"This is Commodore Saphira, Ensign. Please locate Commander Nikarov and patch me through to her on a secure line".

"Yes Ma'am: Understood".

It was only after the briefest of delays the answer came back that Jenniboni's First Officer was in her office on deck B-5. Accompanied by a momentary flicker appearing on the screen before her, this was followed straight away by the attentive image of StarChild's second-in-command looking back at her:

"Yes, Commodore", the other woman greeted her with a trace of curiosity.

"Are you alone, Commander?"

"Yes Ma'am?!" Commander Nikarov assured her C.O., a hint of concern creeping now likewise into her voice, spreading as well to the rest of her face.

"Good", Jenniboni sighed with clear relief: "In that case I want you to arrange an emergency meeting aboard ship, all Department Heads in attendance in the senior officer's briefing room. I want this meeting to be kept both private and confidential. Don't tell them anything except that their attendance is mandatory. Understood?"

"Yes, Ma'am", Ms. Nikarov was quick to reply: "Unfortunately it might take a while to set it up since many of them are on shore-leave planet-side on Demeter".

"Understood", Jenniboni granted: "I'm fully aware of the situation. Therefore you'd better arrange the meeting for 19:00 hours tonight. Call them right now on their PVP's right after this transmission is terminated".

"Yes, Ma'am. I'll see to it right away", StarChild's X.O. guaranteed her commanding officer, all StarChild personnel required to carry on their person at all times private V-phones in case of emergency.

'Well, I'd definitely call this an emergency situation', Jenniboni mused before hearing her X.O. speak up again:

"However, in the meantime, can you tell me what's going on?"

"Afraid not old friend", Jenniboni apologized this time around in a somewhat more cordial, familiar voice: "All I can say is that I'll be leaving here momentarily and plan to arrive aboard ship within the hour. I'll explain everything then... shortly... in your office".

Remembering how Admiral Sellers refused to discuss the matter in any great detail over even the securest of comm. channels Jenniboni likewise decided it wise to follow that very same, prudent course of action.

"Understood", the other woman now replied in a rather tight voice, clearly irked despite her obvious understanding.

Smiling, Jenniboni found herself momentarily amused by the involuntary twitch she observed in the vertical scar running down the entire right side of Cmdr. Stasha Nikarov's face, disappearing only in part beneath the eye patch where her right eye used to be. A definite sign that she wasn't all too happy being kept out of the loop even for the briefest of moments:

"Is that all, then?"

"Yes. At least for now", Jenniboni confirmed: "I'll meet you in your office aboard ship in just a little while".

"Very good, then: I'll be waiting for you here: Over".

"Over and out", Jenniboni concluded, severing at once the comm. link with her ship, switching off as well her desktop VP.

Leaning back once more in her chair, taking another small sip of coffee, her vision wandered to the nearby 3-D photograph of her family sitting there in its simple yet attractive gold frame. Catching sight of it, realizing she had one more call to make, Jenniboni put her cup back down. Placing a call through to their base apartment, already aware no one would be home, it wasn't until after a few seconds of dark, blank screen the answering machine finally kicked in.

Confronted with the previously recorded smiling faces of both Andrei and herself cheerfully asking callers to leave a message after both the beep and flash, Jenniboni did as she was told:

"Hi, Dear: Just thought I'd leave you a brief message since I'm sure you're still at Dad's. Hope you had a good time together. Unfortunately I'm afraid I have to take care of some unfinished business aboard ship that'll probably take some time. So I'm afraid I won't be home until at least 22:00 hours. Sorry", she apologized, continuing further with a wan little smile:

"Don't worry as I'll get something to eat aboard ship So you won't have to go to all the bother of keeping something warm for me until I get home. Even so I'm sure it won't be as good as your cooking", Jenniboni added.

Laughing lightly as she did so Jenniboni brought her call to a final conclusion:

"Either way I hope you and my father had a good time together and that all is well with both you and the children. Be sure to give them all an extra kiss for me tonight when you tuck them into bed as I probably won't be home in time to do so myself. I love you. Good-bye".

Pausing just long enough to blow her husband an affectionate kiss over the screen directly before her Jenniboni terminated her call. Activating the internal mechanism within her office desk right thereafter, the upright VP slid slowly back into its storage area likewise within.

Gulping down the last of her coffee as her VP completed its final descent Jenniboni left her inner office, picking up from Darren the requested daily reports and other correlated material on ei-pad. Stopping at his desk only long enough to ascertain that all was in perfect order, complimenting him on his usual job-well-done, she then headed off her 'merry' way.

Chapter 18

"A PERFECT GENTLEWOMAN'

Once confident the young laddie's assailant had disappeared for sure into the city beyond, Frances wasted no time turning her full attention back towards Andrei himself. Waiting whatever might befall him next, too deeply in shock to budge from the spot he seemed glued to, Frances had no difficulty spotting the obvious emotional distress on his face and in the way his trim, lithe body trembled as if chilled to the very bone.

Her harsh, strict countenance visibly softening at sight of this her body shifted likewise from combat mode, assuming a more relaxed, caring posture before slowly trying to approach him any further. Having previous experience with victims of criminal violence and abuse during her days in the Protectorate she could readily detect the immediate danger signs of possible, emotional withdrawal.

Knowing she was treading here on shaky ground Frances continued even so to gradually approach him, cautious as to not spook him any further with any sudden movements. Reaching out slowly, placing her hands gently on Andrei's shoulders, she found it reassuring he didn't try to jerk away, or strike out even though he still flinched slightly at her touch.

Good sign.

With this to encourage her even further Frances then spoke to him in a soft, soothing voice not unlike a well-modulated, verbal caress:

"Everything is all right now, Sir. You have nothing to fear anymore. The danger has passed. It's time for you to start dealing with what just happened. However, before you do, you'll need to trust me. Do you understand?"

"Yes", he nodded, his body growing a slight bit less tremulous.

"Very good! Now I want you to close your eyes and take a deep breath. Let it flow all through you and fill your lungs. Feel all the pain and fear leave your body". Carefully gauging Andrei's every response it appeared at first he was reluctant to comply with her gently voiced instructions, hesitant to surrender himself over to anyone else's control.

Perfectly understandable in light of the traumatic experience he just endured Frances repeated with stern sympathy this same procedure several more times until able to observe both his face and body relax further—calm down even moreso—observing some clear, obvious cessation of their continued trembling.

Only then, when sure Andrei was making some sort of satisfactory emotional response, did she tell him he could once more open his eyes. While Frances knew it would require a much greater amount of time and effort on his part to affect a complete and total recovery his initial progress right here and now was nevertheless encouraging:

"All right. You're doing very well", she continued in that very same mellow, tranquil vein as before: "Now I want you to look me straight in the eye and tell me your name".

"My name is Andrei", he told her in a soft whisper, his head tilted back, looking up at his rescuer with those sparkling, brilliant, oh-so clear blue eyes of his. Striking an instantaneous cord with both Frances and Naomi they scrutinized even further the shaken but still handsome laddie they just rescued from a most dire fate, Naomi standing behind her to Frances' immediate right.

From almost the very get-go both S.E.A. officers and gentlewomen recognized somewhat the young man in their company without having ever made his formal acquaintance.

"Very good", Frances encouraged him even further, a subtle note of audible curiosity slowly seeping now into her voice: "Now can you tell me your full name?"

"Yes, of course", he spoke up louder with a hint of returning confidence: "My name is 'Mister Andrei Saphira'".

"Whew!" Naomi whistled directly in Frances Straker's unsuspecting ear:

"The Commodore's husband!"

"Hush!" Frances cautioned her startled companion. Doing so with an urgent hiss she wanted nothing to intrude on her carefully orchestrated attempts to further calm down the still distraught young laddie standing before them. Even so Frances had to confess a similar amount of sheer surprise meeting her commanding officer's husband in such sordid surroundings under such extraordinary circumstances.

Able now to see why she recognized him while never having actually met him before both women saw him before at his wife's side during various 3-DV news interviews, not having paid much attention to the comely young man sometimes at her side:

"Yes", Andrei spoke again, also with a touch of recognition: "You're from StarChild, aren't you? You serve under my wife?"

"That's right", Frances beamed, pleased to see her 'patient' starting to interact with his surroundings without having to be coaxed any further. Able to hear as well the life returning to his voice, she could see alongside that a newly reborn twinkle of restored spirit in his eyes.

Average height for a member of his sex, standing a full 5 feet, 8 inches tall, he was still a complete foot shorter than Frances, forcing her to look down at him at a sharp angle to judge better his facial expressions given their close proximity.

"I'm Lt. Cmdr. Frances Miriam Straker, Chief of Security aboard StarChild, and this is Lt. Cmdr. Naomi Leonora Marlowe, our Chief Engineer".

"At your service, Sir", Naomi nodded; a gentle, kindly wisp of a smile appearing at the corners of her mouth. Instead of telling her friend to be quiet this time however, Frances just smiled with warm approval at her words.

"I'm very pleased to meet the both of you", Andrei guaranteed each gentlewoman standing before him; "and I am eternally grateful to both of you for your kind intervention on my humble behalf".

"On the contrary, dear Sir, it is we who are pleased to have been able to render assistance", Frances assured him without delay:

"I must confess however a certain amount of confusion meeting someone such as yourself here of all places", France added on a somewhat more hesitant note, unsure if she was prying into private matters without due reason.

Now Andrei's turn to feel somewhat awkward, embarrassed, he answered her, explaining all the day's events leading up to his present situation. However, when reaching those events approaching the subject of his molestation, Frances picked up at once on the note of agitation worming its way back into his voice. Concerned for his emotional well-being she gently reassured him it wasn't necessary to continue.

Relieved at being spared the burden of reliving what just transpired Andrei paid immediate heed to her advice, letting the whole subject drop as he felt Frances slip her arm around his shoulder in a most comforting manner:

"I think the first thing we need to do is get you out of this horrid place", she advised yet further: "I'm sure Naomi will have your car up-and-running again, good as new, in no time".

Taking quick comfort in how Frances already took such complete charge in such a decisive, no-nonsense fashion he had to confess it likewise felt just as good having her arm around him, helping him feel both secure and protected. Which is why, when Naomi promised him she could fix absolutely anything of a mechanical nature, Andrei immediately took her words to heart, believing her without question:

"I'd appreciate anything you could do for me and am likewise grateful for all each of you have already done", he assured both women with a warm smile, expressing his heartfelt thanks for all each S.E.A. officer continued to do on his behalf. Unfortunately the next voice he heard speak out of the darkness, as if in sudden reply, was that of neither Frances, nor Naomi:

"Good! Get him out of here", Andrei heard the bartender from before exclaim in a loud, bold voice as all three of them passed by the counter bar: "I knew there'd be trouble the moment he came in here!"

Keeping her arm around him as she gently led him away, Naomi following close behind, Frances could feel Andrei wince at the other woman's angry tone:

"You're darn right there was trouble:" she hissed in furious reply: "And it's all your fault! Where was your Enforcer?"

"She's on her break period right now", came the bartender's now peevish response.

"Then *you* should have served as his escort", Frances wasted no time in coming back at her: "It was your responsibility as the only female employee present to ensure his safety!!"

"I couldn't", the object of Frances Straker's fiery ire continued to protest: "I had to take care of all the other customers".

"Of course", Frances sneered in utter contempt, her voice dripping with bitter sarcasm, looking all about her at the near empty establishment:

"It's real busy in here, isn't it?"

* * * *

Leaving behind him the oppressive gloom of his former surroundings Andrei's left hand sped upward from his side, shielding his defenseless eyes from the sudden light now all around him. And observing this from the corner of her eye Frances turned. Looking down at him she asked in a voice full of honest concern how he was doing, if he were feeling better.

"Yes, thank you", he assured her, clearly moved by her sincere devotion to his continued well-being: "You've both been very kind as is. To be perfectly honest I don't know how I'll ever be able to repay you for all you've already done".

"No need to even try", Frances answered him with firm resolve:

"Don't even bother yourself with such thoughts. I'm just glad we were there for you when you needed us most", she added as Naomi walked out in front of them.

Pointing across the street at Andrei's car she asked if it were indeed his. And when he answered in the affirmative it was then Naomi complimented him as well on owning such a fine vehicle:

"Impressive", she added with an engineer's respect and appreciation for quality design:

"Very nice", Naomi continued, asking Andrei for the keys.

Handing them back straight away once having popped the hood she proceeded with a surgeon's keen eye to examine the engine beneath. Leaning forward for an up-even-closer look-see, Andrei waited on her diagnosis with bated breath. Seeming to him like an eternity's wait Naomi explained but a moment later the difficulty at hand, revealing what the problem was:

"Ah, yes. There it is", she announced in a purely analytical fashion, maintaining a purely clinical air about her: "It would seem that the hydrogen container in one of your fuel cells ruptured, allowing the compressed gas within to vent at high velocity until there wasn't enough left to react with the oxygen in the other compartment".

Pointing further at a hair-line fracture in one of the cell's cylinders before them her finger wandered even further downward, coming to a complete rest just above what appeared to be a piece of loose tubing dangling about in mid-air. Nor did the bad news stop there:

"Likewise it would appear one of the connectors to your back-up cells was jarred free at the same time, preventing it from kicking in when the main unit was damaged", Naomi sallied forth with the same expert professionalism as before.

"So what can we do?" Andrei demanded, sounding a trifle plaintive. Intellectually aware he wasn't at fault for any of those events having transpired so far this didn't help ease any his overwhelming sense of guilt. Not when dwelling on troubled thoughts of a scared, forlorn J.J. sitting in Ms. Li-Wong's office waiting even now in quiet desperation on her father's arrival:

"No need to fret!" Naomi was swift to assure him in a soothing voice: "I have a friend nearby who both owns and runs a well-stocked vehicle repair center. I'm sure she'll help me get your car over there and let me use all the tools and necessary parts I'll need to get it up-and-running in perfect order:

"And while I'm taking care of that Frances can give you a lift to the school in my car in back of the bar". Upon mention of the bar now behind him Frances could feel at once Andrei's body stiffen, a sudden look of fearful apprehension coming to light.

"Don't worry, Mr. Saphira", Frances comforted: "I'll make sure nothing further happens to you".

"Please call me Andrei", he invited, embarrassed somewhat by his renewed timidity: "I apologize for behaving so foolishly and can assure you that I am not usually so skittish as a rule. I usually handle myself quite better than this. Pretty embarrassing actually".

"You have nothing whatsoever to feel either ashamed, or foolish about", Frances contradicted him with solemn determination: "After what you've been through you have every right in all the worlds to feel uncertain. What happened to you was monstrous beyond belief!!"

"I appreciate your saying so", Andrei managed gain another smile:

"And I'm also grateful to you as well for helping with my car", he added in Naomi's direction: "So how much do you think it'll cost to repair it?"

"Well… let me see: What with parts and labor I figure it will cost, oh let me see… oh… absolutely nothing!" Naomi quoted likewise with a cheery grin full of good humor.

"NO! No way!! I can't let you do that!" the recipient of her sincere generosity objected most strenuously: "At least let me pay you for the parts involved".

"Sorry, but that's my price", Naomi insisted, still smiling from ear-to-ear:

"Not one centi more or less. Just getting the opportunity to tinker about under the hood of such a fine machine as magnificent as this is reward enough".

"Please", Andrei practically begged, feeling quite small inside, not able to repay these two wonderful women for all the kindnesses they'd already shown him so selflessly: "It's the least I can do: At least something for your friend at the repair center for the use of all her tools and parts".

"NO!!" Naomi insisted, emphatic, remembering with awful clarity how shabbily she treated Frank that very morning: "It's the least '*I*' can do!" she added yet once more.

At a complete loss as to how he should interpret Naomi's rather cryptic claim Andrei was totally baffled as to how Naomi owed him anything. All he knew for certain was there had to be some hidden meaning behind her otherwise carefully chosen words. Frances on the other hand gave her companion a proud look of quiet recognition, understanding right away who and what the other woman was referring to.

"To be perfectly honest with you my friend at the repair center owes me several favors. So I'll just tell her to consider this merely part of the outstanding payment she already owes. As-a-matter-of-fact I'll let you in on a little secret" Naomi confided with a conspiratorial little wink, noting the expression of self-reproach Andrei still wore:

"Truth be told the simple fact of the matter is that I have people all over this little burg who owe me, *big time!:*

"So my dear laddie, may I further suggest you and Frances simply head out now and leave the rest to me. And if the two of you are still at the school after I've taken care of everything here I'll just leave your car out front for you while Frances and I head out from there".

"Capital idea!", Frances agreed enthusiastically: "In that case we'll be on our way and leave Andrei's car in your capable hands".

****

Seated at Frances' side as she drove him to J.J.'s school Andrei found himself in higher spirits the further away they got from that scene of his recent trauma. Although somewhat jumpy when Frances led him down the alley beside the bar, guiding him towards Naomi's car in the back parking lot, he felt much better after climbing into the front passenger seat. With Frances at his side, all the doors securely locked, he was overjoyed at the very thought of being reunited soon with his elder daughter.

Even so however Andrei still remained unable to help the furtive glances he cast from side-to-side every now-and-then in both the alleyway and customer parking lot. With the comforting presence of Frances' protective arm still about him he continued to still feel silly for being so jumpy, so very anxious despite his champion's reassurances he had no cause for further embarrassment.

Having always been so confident in his ability to handle whatever life might throw his way, Andrei's reaction to what happened back in *"THE DARK ROOM"* left him almost as shaken as the actual event itself. Which is why he resolved to do his best to put it all behind him, get on with his life regardless of those feelings of anger, degradation, and violation still churning around and about within the very core of his being.

Quite appreciative of Frances' constant attention as they made their way along street-after-street, approaching the school ahead, she enquired after what he considered pretty common-day matters—how he found life on the base, how the children were doing, and other basic aspects of his life as a homemaker.

Doing her utmost to engage him in casual conversation, she appeared truly interested in what he had to say no matter how mundane the subject matter.

113

Although Andrei remained aware of the psychological motivations behind her inquiries, he still appreciated her attempt to keep his mind occupied with non-threatening everyday matters. Not allowing him any time to dwell on how he was so shamefully abused and mistreated, it was a simple continuation of those deep breaths she had him take right after the event in question.

All the same though her display of genuine interest in what he had to say gave rise to those simple feelings of both warmth and importance as a Human being he so desperately needed at that particular moment. Regardless her initial motives maybe it was just the obvious sincerity of her interest Andrei found so especially gratifying.

Under Frances' tender administrations Andrei soon found himself slowly but surely regaining both his mental and emotional feet beneath him, finally discovering enough renewed inner confidence to initiate conversation without any help from others. Questioning now with eager interest this noble woman sitting next to him, asking her for a change all about her life and interests, Andrei yearned very much to learn more about her.

While probably not beautiful by popular standards there was still a certain sensual appeal about Lt. Cmdr. Frances Straker he found quite captivating indeed. Clearly in possession of certain physical attributes and qualities that captured his attention her graceful moves, physical strength, piercing gaze, dark expressive eyes, and long, wavy, beautiful black hair flowing down and about her comely shoulders were not to be overlooked in any way, shape and or form.

Then again there was likewise no doubt in Andrei's opinion that the real attraction about her was her ability to converse with him, treat him like an equal, and make him feel as though he counted for something in her eyes.

It was this talent, combined with her naturally chivalrous treatment of him, that left no room for doubt in Andrei's heart-of-hearts there had to be many, many others of his gender out there who likewise found just being near this woman both an incredibly compelling and intoxicating experience.

And as she willingly answered his questions, revealing her innermost self to him with such effortless confidence, such simple ease, Andrei's admiration for her grew only that much greater, sure as he was she could have her pick of any man she so desired.

While Frances Straker's interest in historical battles, combat strategy, and athletic competition came as no surprise given her apparent choice of occupation he nevertheless found intriguing her similar passion for such esoteric subjects as philosophy, comparative religions, and her love of both classical music and art.

A deeply spiritual person with a likewise creative bent of mind able to appreciate the creativity of others, a blend of both the practical warrior and sentimental romantic, she revealed also to him a fervent interest in both ancient literature and poetry, further disclosures involving her childhood likewise fascinated him.

Born on Titan's ethane-rich surface in the experimental refinery town of New Kimberly, raised by a single father in the poorest, roughest sector of that community, Frances' story of childhood difficulty moved him deeply. Listening to her describe that environment with neither a trace of bitterness, or self-pity when discussing the hardships she encountered back then it was like taking a guided tour of an existence he'd never known before.

Living on the shores of one of its naturally occurring ethane lakes scattered across Titan's surface—Lake Ontario—it was a world further removed from that one of sheltered wealth, luxury, and privilege Andrei grew up in than could be measured by the actual physical distance separating Saturn's largest moon from Earth itself.

Absolutely bewitched with the pleasure of her conversational skills Andrei actually experienced a noticeable twinge of regret when Frances soon announced their arrival, pulling up in front of the school. And remembering why they were here in the first place he was overcome at once by a keen sense of guilt over this fleeting moment of selfish weakness.

Expressing yet again his humblest thanks for all the gentle kindnesses she'd shown him that day, it was then Frances asked if he'd further like her to wait for him just in case he didn't feel up to the long drive back to the Project StarChild base afterwards. Sorely tempted to accept her magnanimous offer, wanting to talk further, he nevertheless resisted the compelling urge to do so, reluctantly assuring her that such wouldn't be necessary.

Believing he'd already monopolized enough of her precious time as it was Andrei came likewise to the conclusion it was high time to once more take charge of his own life.

Even so however Andrei's hand nevertheless hesitated when reaching for the door handle alongside him. Realizing he had still one last request to make before likewise on his way it was a request giving rise to feelings of both timidity and even unease. Especially after all both Frances and Naomi had already done for him:

"I really hate asking you this, but I was wondering if you would mind doing me just one more favor", he ventured slowly.

"Not at all!" Frances granted without any delay, or reservation whatsoever.

"Well, I really hate to impose on your generosity any further than I have, but I'd really appreciate it if neither you nor Lt. Cmdr. Marlowe mention any of what happened today to my wife.

"I'd much rather keep this our little secret just between the three of us",
Andrei struggled in a hesitant voice full of obvious reserve.

The quizzical smile Frances wore up to then evaporated quickly enough into a sour frown of consternation. Hearing what it was the handsome laddie next to her actually wanted she wondered as to the possible reason for his request, picking up on his renewed anxiety.

Dreading the possibility of some dark secret being the motivation behind his petition it pained her no end thinking she might have rescued the poor man beside her from one vile abuser only to surrender him up into the waiting hands of yet another.

Could it be Andrei's evident concern stemmed from his wife's possible reaction to the knowledge of what had taken place that day, the very real possibility she might actually turn violent herself? Did he fear for either his own safety and/or that of his children, worried she might somehow blame him for what transpired today, taking out her anger on her family instead?

Among the many things Frances always respected concerning Jenniboni Saphira, both as a commanding officer and a genuine person in her own right, was how there was a warm, compassionate, and caring Human being within the cool, efficient, and dedicated starship commander.

Understanding that some crewwomen saw their erstwhile C.O. as cold and aloof, Frances was able to see the whole woman behind the relentless perfectionist Commodore Saphira mostly came across as. Undoubtedly because, in many ways, Frances also had that habit of projecting one face to the general public while being quite different in her private, personal relationships.

Yet be that as it may Andrei's request left her wondering if there was some darker aspect to Jenniboni Saphira's very nature, something maybe even cruel, leading Andrei to worry for his very safety and physical well-being. Albeit an excellent judge of character Frances had to confess even she couldn't know all there was when dealing with the deep, dark recesses of the Human soul kept hidden from all but a very select and intimate few.

Could she have honestly misjudged the Commodore so badly?

It broke her heart to think of this remarkable young man so close by being so mistreated on a regular basis by someone with whom he should be able to rely upon for love, tenderness, and protection…

Not pain, fear, and oppression.

Noting Frances' expression of troubled concern Andrei mistook it however for silent disapproval over keeping secrets from a superior officer, the trouble which might ensue should his wife discover her duplicity in this whole affair…

A very personal, family related affair at that!

"I can understand and sympathize with your reluctance, hoping you don't think any-the-less of me for asking", he blurted out in a hurried voice, unable to bear the idea of his 'deliverer' ever thinking less of him:

"It's just that, with everything else my wife already has on her plate, I just don't want her worrying about me as well. What with all she's got on her mind concerning the weeks ahead I want her to feel able to devote all her time and energy to any problems that might arise during the performance of her duties without the added stress of worrying as well about those she leaves behind".

"No need to worry any further. I understand completely", Frances quickly assured him, her frown turning just as surely into a smile of sheer admiration:

"And I promise your secret will remain perfectly safe with both Naomi and myself. I respect your wishes in the matter and won't mention anything to the Commodore about our chance encounter today".

"Thank you", Andrei sighed with visible relief.

"And if you'll pardon me for being so bold my dear laddie, I must honestly say that you are truly a most remarkable and impressive young man with a lot of moxie. A lot tougher I dare say than you give yourself credit for".

Hearing this Andrei just couldn't believe his ears. This fantastic woman whom he already held in such high esteem actually saw in him someone equally worthy of that very same sincere admiration and utmost respect. Considering the circumstances under which they just met Andrei could see her feeling an understandable sense of compassion, and even pity for him. Never though could he ever imagine she'd ever feel the same for him as he felt so deeply for her:

Wanting to thank her with more than mere words he stroked lightly away from her face a few stray strands of raven black hair, placing upon her cheek a gentle, tender kiss full of all his loving appreciation. In response Frances reached down between them and, bringing the back of his hand up to her face, gave him an equally pure and chaste kiss replete with both honest respect, appreciation, and even a hint of unanticipated affection beginning to develop.

The soft touch of her lips sent a thrill of both pleasure, and even a trace of unexpected passion throughout Andrei's entire body that, although manifesting itself in physical form, was more spiritual in both flavor and essence.

"And now, dear Sir, I think you should be getting to your daughter. I've no doubt that she's wondering where you are", Frances advised with a tender, beatific smile, gently lowering Andrei's hand least innocent stirrings turn into something that should remain unexplored.

"Of course", he agreed at once, the very mention of J.J. inspiring within Andrei yet another surge of remorse over how long he remained already absent from her side:

"You're quite right!"

Yet, stepping out of the car he first paused, turning yet again his attention back to Frances:

"If you're not here when I'm finished inside I hope we'll someday have the further opportunity to see one-another yet again. Under less traumatic circumstances of course", he added with a slight smile, unsure as to how she might respond, a little tremulous in his uncertainty least she consider him most un-laddie-like. Realizing Andrei's suggestion was intended to be a purely innocent one, Frances expressed readily a similar wish, accepting on the provision Jenniboni must first approve.

Truly appreciative of her gentlewomanly propriety, too madly in love with his wife to even dream of any indecent behavior with another, he agreed straight away to her terms without any vacillation, or hesitation whatsoever. It was then, upon saying their final farewells, Andrei decided in all certainty to discuss the question of meeting further his rescuer with Jenniboni, finally closing the car's passenger-side door behind him.

Then again, making his way up the wide pathway to the school's main entrance, it dawned on him this might also require telling Jenniboni how he came to know StarChild's venerable Chief of Security in the first place… the real reason she stepped at first into his life… feeling also that, as a married man, it would prove best to meet with Frances only when in Jenniboni's company.

While having no qualms at all with such a chaperoned arrangement, he nevertheless decided it might prove better to wait until Jenniboni's return from Alpha Centauri before hazarding any likely discussion of today's events.

Then again Andrei couldn't help, but wonder if he'd ever prove able to really speak aloud what actually happened to him back in that twisted bar.

Chapter 19

"STARCHILD"

"This is the private transport shuttle, 'Saphira II', to S.E.A. starship, StarChild, requesting permission to commence with docking", the shuttle pilot for Jenniboni's personal transport announced in an official tone:

"I'm transporting Commodore Saphira: Over".

"This is the S.E.A.S.S. StarChild", Ensign Noble acknowledged with the same crisp professionalism, the shuttle carrying the first two women making likewise its slow but steady approach:

"You have clearance to dock: Over".

"Thank you, StarChild. Over and out", the shuttle pilot finished, disconnecting her comm. link with the starship now appearing on their foreword-viewing screen:

"Well there he is, Commodore. Truly impressive. I never get tired of seeing him", the young pilot then addressed the senior officer standing behind her, both S.E.A. personnel gazing with appreciative awe at the approaching vessel before them.

"I know what you mean", Jenniboni agreed with a proud smile, brimming with personal satisfaction the other woman couldn't see from her position:

'And he's all mine!', she then thought to herself with a definite sense of personal accomplishment, watching the only other 'man' in her life draw even closer. Having the distinct impression the starship ahead was actually beckoning her forth with seductive promises of endless adventure and excitement the likes of which she never knew before, it appeared even StarChild's gleaming white titanium-alloy hull radiated a veritable life and vitality all of its own:

A healthy glow full of vim and vigor, virtually chomping at the bit, he seemed truly impatient to be put through his paces and be on his merry way.

'All in good time, dear boy: You'll be getting your chance soon enough', Jenniboni smiled once again to herself in complete silence. An exquisitely designed vessel—an elegant, graceful bird born to soar throughout the cosmos—StarChild's smaller foreword section was joined to the larger aft portion by a long, slender, yet sturdily constructed neck—the name "**S.E.A.S.S. StarChild**" printed in bold letters along both its port and starboard sides—a regal fempacem proudly displayed before and after its name close to the ship's decoratively-hued running lights.

Likewise his foreword section was triangular in shape possessing a straight, noble 'beak' and two broad, graceful, winglets swept both upwards and drawn back to finely tapered ends. Curved outwards on either side of the ship's eagle-like 'head', his larger aft section extended outwards as well on either side to form two giant, massive wings tilted down and frontward, each proud appendage ending in a deadly stinger-like laser cannon.

Able to target any possible hostiles both coming and going such formidable weapons, capable as well of the simultaneous rapid-fire discharge of matter/anti-matter torpedoes, were likewise arranged with exacting precision along each wing's fore and aft edges. Although praying such awesome weapons wouldn't prove necessary, Jenniboni was nevertheless grateful for their continued presence—*just in case!!*

And in addition to that each of the massive aft-section's wings also grew denser the closer they approached one-another to form StarChild's main body, rising upwards to form several straight-edged levels angled both foreword towards the base of his neck as well as sideways. Facing both port and starboard, each drawn as well slightly back from the one directly below it, they formed a series of tiers sheltered beneath the extended rim of StarChild's broad, flat, spine.

Centered in the rear of that broad, flat platform positioned just before StarChild's rear-most engines there was also a large domed structure shaped not unlike a brilliant, glistening water droplet containing the larger aft section's four uppermost levels. And directly below that, serving as its base on the ship's broad back below, was StarChild's only actual landing bay, its large hangar bay doors parting already to allow Jenniboni complete access aboard her ship.

Opening wide to welcome onboard his commanding officer, StarChild offered her shuttle even further guidance all-the-way in, a series of both green and red runway lights arranged in a straight line all the way from his hangar bay entrance to the base of his graceful neck.

Similar lights were located also at the base of a sleek tail fin arched both forewords and high above the aforementioned 'tear-drop' dome. Situated close to the powerful engines positioned in back of the ship it was this metal tower in connection with StarChild's graceful beak that would pry open before them that "gateway" into that other reality known as "Ultra Space"—an alternate realm of existence in which StarChild would travel in record time the majority of his journey throughout those vast areas of uncharted space well beyond Womankind's home System.

Harnessing incredible energies of a potentially destructive nature to do so the collection of lights at the tower's base, arranged on either side of it, were there for the exclusive purpose of warning away any errant vessel foolish enough to stray too close. Meant to inform others when StarChild was preparing to launch himself forward into that cosmic breach at 'full steam ahead' others knew exactly what to expect depending on what colour each light would be at any given moment—also made aware by whether or not it was flashing or constant in its continual glow.

And putting all this together StarChild was in Jenniboni's adoring eyes a unique blend of both straight, practical lines and fluid curves—a poetic work of art that exuded both power, style, and a certain raw sensuality all of his very own. Naturally biased in her honest opinion of Humanity's first faster-than-light starship she truly believed him to be the most impressive example of Womankind's technical skill and genius existing today.

Enraptured by the very sight of him growing ever closer and closer on the viewing screen before her, Jenniboni came close to even resenting the ponderous dry dock situated squarely above her supreme pride and joy. Situated near the center of that celestial triangle formed by the dwarf planets Pluto, Persephone, and Demeter both starship and space station above were anchored at their present spatial location by the natural gravitational pull of each planet tugging on each artificial body in three different directions.

Made possible by way of their constant trinary orbital arrangement this was done to conserve on energy that would otherwise be required maintaining a stationary orbit above any single world, preventing as well any unwanted drift from their present positions. And just as StarChild was of a graceful, avionic, design conceived for soaring among the stars the dry dock above was rather reminiscent of a fat, bloated spider replete with eight leggy magnetic clamps holding Jenniboni's ship firmly in its clutches.

Comprised of two globular spheres, one much larger than the other, it even possessed two mandible-like protrusions thrust outwards from that smaller section's free end serving as twin hangar bays for lesser craft. Nevertheless Jenniboni didn't resent too much that voluminous station's intrusiveness, fully aware her sleek, proud starship would soon be emancipated from his temporary confinement, free to roam at long last the vast beyond.

Both ship and station aside however, Jenniboni could likewise make out from her steadily improving vantage point a superior number of almost gnat-like objects buzzing around and about StarChild's virtually radiant outer hull.

Occasionally lighting upon his surface only to float away after a short while with nearly fluid, flowing choreographed moves these were in fact workwomen from the station above in either self-propelled environmental work suits, or small, cramped one-woman repair pods—work vehicles performing last-minute routine maintenance checks prior to StarChild's originally scheduled departure date.

'They're definitely going to have their work cut out for them to get everything ready in time for Friday afternoon', Jenniboni mused, the shuttle pilot seated before her bringing the Saphira II in even closer to their final destination. The dry-dock loomed right above while, directly ahead and below, StarChild's hangar deck waited for them replete with runway lights leading the way in.

Hovering only fifty meters, or so above her ship at a dead stop, Jenniboni was even able to make out at such close range an occasional shadow pass by in the ribbons of soft light streaming forth from the many well-proportioned viewing portals on each deck—crewwomen going about either their various duty assignments, or just moving about in the privacy of their own quarters.

Once more on the move after just a few minutes' pause, having waited until the hangar doors parted full way, Jenniboni experienced as well a slight shudder passing through her shuttle, crossing over the hangar bay threshold.

Although invisible one could always detect their passage through an air-seal by the slight resistance it offered up, designed as they were as a containment field for any section of any spacecraft routinely exposed to the lethal vacuum of endless space. Preventing the escape of precious air while allowing at the exact same time solid matter to pass through, one was still subtly made aware of their continual presence.

****

Handling their arrival with expert aplomb her private pilot brought Jenniboni's shuttle in for a perfect three-point touch-down with nary a jolt, the 'Saphira II's' landing pads making exact contact in synchronous alignment with the landing target and launch tracks in the hangar bay's precise center. And seeing Jenniboni exit her shuttle for the nearest anti-gravity lift terminal several nearby crewwomen all at once snapped to attention, no delay whatsoever, as she quickly passed them by:

"As you were!", she commanded without breaking her determined stride, miraculously transforming them yet again from rigid statues back into mobile Human beings.

Riding the small craft elevator in the hangar bay's rear port-side corner down to deck S-6 one level below the large, flat platform deposited her soon in StarChild's 'drone and small craft storage bay'. Spotting directly ahead of her an available ag-pod terminal off to the near right she quickly made her way over to it.

"Maccs, deck B-.5: Commander Nikarov's office", Jenniboni demanded in a crisp, clear voice once the pod's auto-doors slid shut in back of her.

"Yes, Ma'am", a dutiful masculine voice replied from a discreetly placed comm. unit situated directly above her: "And may I say that it is indeed a pleasure to welcome you back onboard, Ma'am".

"You may", Jenniboni granted with a wee little smile, all the while cognizant of just who... or 'what'... she was actually conversing with back-and-forth: "And it's likewise a pleasure to be back onboard, hearing your voice as well".

"Why thank you, Ma'am", Maccs responded with clearly sincere appreciation, the ag-pod meanwhile making its way with rapid progress through the various lift-tubes interconnected throughout the entire ship. Sounding in tone and voice like nothing more than an ordinary man in his approximate 3O's 'Maccs', or 'M.A.C.C.S.', stood quite literally for 'Multi- Analytical

Cybercerebral Centracomp System'—a semi-organic centralized computer control system governing all of StarChild's endlessly complex functions with both nano-instantaneous reflexes and results.

It was this synthetic artificial intelligence—or 'A.I.'—that served as both StarChild's very heart and soul as well as his brain. Programmed with a congenial personality unique to himself and no other, Maccs was truly StarChild himself, each inseparable and indistinguishable one from the other.

Eternally joined for better or for worse his main control center, or 'brain' was housed on deck B-5 right across the corridor from both Jenniboni and Cmdr. Nikarov's neighbouring offices. And mindful of all this Jenniboni mused that such would make the actual, full name of that 'other man' in her life 'Master Maccs StarChild', an errant little reflection completely out of left field tickling her fancy.

"Did I say something amusing, Ma'am", the object of her humorous thoughts asked straightaway, hearing Jenniboni begin to giggle.

"No, Maccs", she stifled her involuntary display of humour least, even in this most private of settings, she dared appear undignified aboard her own command—changing the subject without pause least the curious ship question her any further in the matter.

At times a little too pushy for his own good Maccs could be something of a royal buttinski, a regular 'Chatty Charlie' doll, pursuing any topic that might capture his interest with bulldogged determination. Quite talkative he could go off without warning on a lengthy tangent about practically anything under the sun, any subject grabbing his immediate attention, his enthusiasm sometimes difficult to manage unless handled with a firm hand.

Admittedly a bit trying at times he definitely took a little getting used to. Considering the simple fact men weren't allowed aboard active-duty starships, Jenniboni found it rather strange when Maccs was first brought on-line.

It didn't take her all that long though to see the almost poetic logic in using a male voice for her ship's central interactive A.I. command control system, getting used at last to hearing a young laddie's voice aboard ship. Helping to distinguish his voice from those of her exclusively female crew over StarChild's countless audio-communiqué units scattered throughout his interior, it also made sense when given the fact it was standard practice to refer to all manner of vessel and craft by such masculine pronouns as 'he', 'him', and 'his'.

Then again there was also the distinctly masculine role Maccs played aboard StarChild—that primary function of men in general—tending house and taking excellent care of their families, seeing to the constant needs of their wives and children. And so it was with Maccs, his main function being to take care of both the continued smooth operating procedures involved in managing her ship's many onboard systems alongside serving both Jenniboni and her crew; seeing as well to their many, varied wants and desires.

Nor did it end there, Jenniboni viewing as well the equally masculine tone and timbre of Maccs' voice as serving yet another purpose altogether. Albeit an unofficial one much more personal, more emotional to be sure, he also helped both Jenniboni and her crew remember those they'd leave behind, venturing out into the endless reaches of the deep unknown. No matter how far they might journey, or how long they might be absent from home and family, Maccs would hopefully help them feel just a little bit less alone, a little closer to those loved ones waiting for them back in the Commonwealth …

Maybe *that* was the real reason StarChild's chief programmer and design engineer decided to endow Maccs with his particular voice and masculine personality when first she dreamt him up.

And so it was Jenniboni passed the time of day chatting with him while traveling along the lengthy interior of his midsection—or 'neck'—connecting the thirteen 'S' decks comprising StarChild's aft section to the foreword section's seven 'B' decks …

At least that was until he informed her they finally reached her requested destination. And true to his continually faultless, efficient programming Maccs dropped Jenniboni off on level B-5 at the ag-pod terminal closest her X.O.'s shipboard office.

Chapter 20

"ANGRY FLASHBACK"

Hurrying down empty hallways in a desperate rush to be at his daughter's side, Andrei could hear as well behind closed classroom doors the muffled voices of both students and their teachers going about their daily lessons. And having been there before he had no trouble finding his way to the principal's office.

Making his way with all due haste to the building's very core it was there he reached the school's administrative complex, accessible through a wide pair of frosted, sliding glass doors set in a highly polished brass doorframe. Entering a sizable front lobby full of busy secretaries going about their daily routines both at and away from their individual desks, Andrei quickly introduced himself at the receptionist's station

Explaining why he was there to the diligent young laddie on duty he was ushered soon enough through an office door just a little way off to his right, both J.J. and her principal waiting for him on the other side.

****

Getting up at once from behind her desk across the room Ms. Mai Li-Wong was a quite attractive, medium-aged Asian gentlewoman in her late forties possessing both high cheekbones, refined features, and a noble bearing.

Wearing a pleasant smile she got up from behind her desk, approaching the clearly worn and weary young father before her with hand held out in welcome:

"Thank you for coming, Mr. Saphira, and I regret all the trouble you had getting here"; Ms. Li-Wong offered Andrei her commiserations, J.J. unaware her father just entered the room until that very moment: "I apologize for the inconvenience and am sorry we have to meet under such circumstances. I always regret having to call parents down to the school due to situations like

124

this".

Turning around only then in her chair, realizing it was her father who indeed just entered the room, J.J. gave him a look full of expectant hope and absolute relief as he likewise stepped forward. Grasping the school administrator's outstretched hand he rested likewise his other hand on his little girl's shoulder, giving it a gentle, reassuring squeeze.

Taking care of the usual introductory social amenities he took a seat in the empty chair to J.J.'s immediate right, her principal insisting he make himself perfectly comfortable.

"And may I reiterate I'm indeed sorry you had such problems getting here", Ms. Li-Wong apologized yet again: "I regret having to summon you down here on such short notice and hope all turned out well".

"No need to worry. All's been taken care of in a most satisfactory manner", Andrei was quick to assure her, remaining quite congenial, seeing no further need to elaborate:

"Thank you though for your concern".

Leaning back in her chair, back once more behind her desk, Mai Li-Wong wasted no time expressing her sincere relief to hear so before finally cutting to the chase:

"And with that in mind I have as well no wish to impose further upon your valuable time any more than is quite necessary. I'm sure you're no doubt very busy so I'll therefore get right to the heart of the matter".

"Yes, of course", Andrei agreed, all smiles: "And I appreciate your thoughtfulness".

"Well, the problem is that Jenniboni Jr. here managed to get herself in a little scrape with another girl in her class out on the playground during morning break", Ms. Li-Wong calmly explained:

"Now while I admit that this does occur from time-to-time we still feel it is best for the child in question to be given a 'time-out' to reflect as it were on the inappropriateness of their behavior.

"Therefore we feel that it would be best young Jenniboni here be sent home with you for the remainder of the school day".

"I see your point", Andrei nodded, directing then his stern gaze towards the anxious little girl squirming in her seat next to him:

"And as for you young gentlewoman, haven't your mother and I repeatedly told you about not getting into fights. Frankly, I'm surprised at you", he gently chastised her, the look of tender disappointment in her father's eyes hurting more than anything else.

"But you don't understand, Daddy!", she leapt at once to her own immediate defense: "I just had to hit her!"

"You're right", Andrei agreed in the same soft, disapproving manner: "I'm afraid I really don't understand. Maybe you better explain in greater detail".

Wondering if it might be easier on J.J. if perhaps she were to explain in her stead, it was then Ms. Li-Wong took it upon herself to further elaborate:

"Well Mr. Saphira, it would seem that your daughter here saw another girl hitting her little brother, immediately taking it upon herself to defend the young boy from his sister. Now while this is perfectly understandable the problem I still have with this, however, is that…”

Unfortunately the rest of Mai's carefully chosen words were now falling on deaf ears, Andrei now clutched in the firm stranglehold of an uncontrollable flashback. The tale of that other girl striking her brother hitting much too close for comfort, a juxtaposition of those characters in Ms. Li- Wong's narrative took place now in his tortured mind's eye.

Visualizing the boy's sister now in the guise of his recent assailant, Andrei himself acted out the sad role of the little boy in question, J.J. assuming quite naturally the part of Frances Straker. And finding himself increasingly unable to control recent memories Andrei's righteous anger began increasing by both leaps and bounds:

'Why should my daughter be persecuted for merely defending the defenseless?' he fumed away in utter silence, feeding on purpose his own inner hate, his feelings of victimization:

'Should either that boy, or myself have just allowed ourselves to be abused without anyone coming to our rescue?', he then asked himself, the volatile rage welling up within him joined now by feelings of both shame and resentment.

And having once asked himself all this the only sincere, honest answer he could give himself was a fiery protest of 'NO:'

NO!!

Momentarily overwhelmed by fresh memories of that vile degradation, torment, and verbal abuse he endured just that very day Andrei leapt up quite unexpectedly from his chair. Doing so in passionate response, the dam within burst forth at last:

"NO!" he almost yelled in absolute fury, leaning over Mai's desk, resting his full weight there upon clenched fists:

"I don't see why my daughter should be persecuted or discriminated against for simply doing the right thing. Does your school actually condone the physical abuse of its male students? Don't you even teach 'the Code' in this institution?" he continued in a scathing tone of voice: "As far as I can remember it was mandatory reading for children of all ages when I was growing up!"

Shocked to the very essence of her innermost self by this most unwarranted attack on her very person, Ms. Li-Wong literally withdrew from Andrei's verbal assault into the chair behind her. Not that she was actually afraid of the inexplicably angry father now raging away at her. Dumbfounded would be a better description of her feelings. Having dealt in the past with irate parents of both sexes she knew perfectly well how to handle such eventualities:

NO…

What really gave her pause was the radical departure from his normal behavior this vehement outburst really signified, having been called before to Mai's office concerning minor infractions of the rules.

Usually involving the twins, however, it was nonetheless nothing serious: Just the usual childish acting up…

And on each of those given occasions the always polite young man now standing before her behaved himself in a respectful manner befitting a proper laddie, conducting himself as a proper laddie was both expected to and should.

Never once had she known him to be anything other than courteous when in her company, mild-mannered to a fault. Nor was she was able to imagine anything happening able to provoke the normally soft-spoken, amiable young father now looming over her to fly so off the handle.

Mai Li-Wong wasn't the only person there dumbstruck by Andrei's unprecedented hostility, poor J.J. at a complete loss seeing her father in such a crazed, manic state. Shrinking away from him into her own seat as well, drawing her legs up beneath her, the terrified seven-year-old began to flee from the world around her like a turtle retreating from a danger into its shell. Like her principal she never witnessed either such bizarre conduct on her father's part:

Oh, sure, there were times Andrei might get angry whenever the children were unruly, or disobedient. However, by that very same token, he never *ever* gave them reason to truly, honestly fear him. Even when naturally upset with them Andrei always managed to remain calm, cool, and rational.

Never seeing him lose control of himself with such wild abandon before it was like some fearful stranger was now in complete, absolute possession of that one man her innocent young heart loved above all others. Staring at him in wide-eyed dismay, feeling lost and alone like never before in her short, sweet life it was all she could do to hold back the tears now demanding bitter release.

One thing was for certain as far as Ms. Li-Wong was concerned: Whatever happened previously to the distraught young man now scowling down at her, eyes ablaze with righteous indignation, it *must* have been much more serious than just some mere automobile accident. Clearly something quite disturbing recently occurred just prior to his arrival.

And while J.J.'s thoughts were less coherent than her principal's, less well organized, she experienced even so one of those frequent insights children often have when dealing with their parents: Something really, **REALLY**, awful must have happened to her father since she last saw him.

"I can assure you, Mr. Saphira, that the young girl caught abusing her brother is in much more serious trouble than your daughter", Ms. Li-Wong guaranteed him, quite sincere:

"In fact I promise you she'll be seriously dealt with", she managed to maintain an even, patient voice once having recovered from her initial bewilderment. Gradually penetrating the angry haze holding Andrei so firmly in its grip, cutting through the blind rage which up to now gripped him firmly in its grasp, Mai's words were beginning to make inroads upon his awareness.

Nevertheless it was the plaintive voice of his little girl reaching out to him which, like a rousing slap in the face, brought him back at long last to bitter reality:

"Please Daddy", she begged him, frightened out of her wits: "*Pleeeaaase* don't be mad".

Hearing J.J.'s imploring voice, the absolute desperation contained therein, was like being awakened from a terrible nightmare. Immediately aware of what just transpired, struck at once by the bad show he just put on—the sorry spectacle he just now made of himself—it was then all the energy was siphoned straightaway out of him. Visibly shaking, ashen with shock, Andrei staggered backwards, sinking once more into his chair like a marionette, its strings just cut.

It wasn't until after moments of stunned silence filling the room all around him Andrei raised his head, buried in trembling hands until that very moment:

"I deeply apologize for that shameful display, that horrid performance, and humbly beg your forgiveness", he humbled himself in utter remorse before both his daughter and her School Administrator:

"I have no excuse for such poor conduct", he added, taking several deep, hitching breaths in hopes of better centering himself.

"That's perfectly all right, Sir", Ms. Li-Wong smiled, mercifully: "All is forgiven. I've dealt with irate parents before and have seen my fair share".

However, even as she said this, Mai couldn't help but wonder what in Heaven's sweet name could have brought about such a dramatic outburst from an otherwise normally gentle, quiet, peaceful soul. With that in mind she thought right about then it might be best for all concerned if she were to just bring this meeting to a rapid close.

Doing so as soon as humanly possible, she was still somewhat shaken after what just took place. If nothing else, it would do at least *her* worlds of good to personally put this whole sorry, miserable incident behind her.

"And I want to say sorry to you, too, sweetie", Andrei continued in a soft, penitent voice turning now his full attention to J.J.:

"It was really wrong of Daddy to behave like that and I should've never exposed you to such a wretched tirade", he added; feeling inside both utterly vanquished, withered up, and deflated:

"I hope you, too, will forgive me".

"Yeah, sure", J.J. whispered in a small, shaky voice. In many ways this bitter self-recrimination, defeat, and abject misery on both Andrei's face and in his voice disturbed her even moreso than his frightful conduct of before.

Then again there was at least one small comfort to be found here. Understanding her father was yet again at her side, that fearsome doppelganger in full possession of him was banished once more to whatever dark recesses it came from.

"Please continue Ms. Li-Wong", Andrei sighed following yet another slight pause. Turning his weary gaze back towards J.J.'s principal he sounded now completely lifeless: "You were saying…?"

"Would you perhaps care for some sort of refreshment instead?", Mai changed the subject, her concern evident for all to see: "Some coffee perhaps, or tea?"

"No, Ma'am. Thank you for asking, though, but I'm fine as is", Andrei assured her, the colour returning once more to his cheeks: "Please continue with what you were saying".

"Well …", she began over again; "what I was basically trying to tell you before was that the other girl involved will be disciplined while you can likewise rest assured young J.J. here isn't in any real trouble. It's just that, as I said before, we do require that the child in question… meaning here young

Jenniboni, of course... be sent home for the rest of the day. Once again I promise you this isn't some form of punishment, but merely a cooling-off period.

"Actually, to be quite honest, I both sympathize with your daughter's reaction and even find it commendable in its own sort of way. Indeed, it is to the credit of both your wife and yourself she has such a strong sense of right and wrong, such a strong desire for justice. Therefore it's not her motives I'm calling into question here, but her methods.

"Instead of just walking up to the other girl, just hitting her straight away, I feel young J.J. here should have first sought out the assistance of either a teacher, or another adult in resolving the matter, reporting what was happening at that particular moment.

"At the very least she should have told the other girl to back off first and leave her brother alone, giving the other party involved the opportunity to retreat on her own behalf instead of just striking her forthwith: A sort of declaration of war before actual combat as it were", Ms. Li-Wong further elaborated with a certain trace of wry humor.

Upon hearing this it suddenly occurred to Andrei that Frances herself also took a similar 'time-out' to warn his abuser off before just lashing out:

"Yes, once again I see your point", he conceded yet again, still penitent, clearing his throat while doing so: "You're quite right, Ma'am. So what do you suggest we do now?"

"Simply put we would like you to take J.J. home now for the rest of the day and, as far as any possible punishment is concerned, I leave that to both you and your wife to decide".

"Thank you. And I appreciate once more all the many kindnesses and understanding you've shown the both of us concerning *everything* that transpired today".

"You're quite welcome, I assure you", Ms. Li-Wong smiled in complete sympathy. Certain what Andrei was getting at subtly stressing the word *'everything'*, she wanted all the same to bring this particular parent/principal conference to a speedier conclusion. As the contrite young father seated across the way from her began to get up, apologizing for having taken up so much of her valuable time, Mai promised him none of what transpired there that day would ever leave the confines of her office, escorting him thereafter to her door.

Thanking her for this little kindness as well, sighing with relief upon hearing so, Andrei took as well J.J.'s small hand in his. Yet turning to leave, reaching just then her office door, he heard Mai speak up behind him yet one more time:

"By the way, Mr. Saphira, I just want to assure you that the 'Code of Feminine Chivalry' is both rigorously taught, and strictly enforced in this institution", she confided in hopes of putting Andrei's mind further to rest. With yet another pang of remorse over past words and conduct, promptly leaving right thereafter, Andrei expressed aloud his sincerest regret for even suggesting Mai was remiss in the protection of all her students.

****

Forsaking the increasingly restrictive confines of the school's interior now behind him, J.J.'s small hand still in his, Andrei paused for a moment just outside the large double doors to the buildings main entrance. Closing his eyes while standing atop of the steps leading to the broad path ahead he took a deep, cleansing breath… slowly exhaling… willing the lingering tension still within to vacate his very body.

"All you all right Father?"

Even able to hear the evident worry in his little girl's voice Andrei still found himself smiling at her use of the word "Father" instead of "Daddy". Proof positive she recovered sufficiently from her own sense of inner turmoil, reassuming once more her cherished affectation of mature adulthood. All in all a good sign she, too, was starting to feel somewhat better.

"Yes, dear: I am".

Realizing he was truly starting to feel better; Andrei opened his eyes once acclimated to the light outside, giving J.J. a comforting smile before deciding at last to move along.

*　*　*　*

Proceeding together down the wide pathway to the widish boulevard beyond, both sides of the street lined with tall artificial pine trees arranged in perfect single-file, he actively sought out with diligent eyes any sign of either his or Naomi's car.

It wasn't until both father and daughter were well beyond the complex jungle gym situated to their immediate left Andrei had a clear, unobstructed view of the street ahead. Pleased to discover his faithful little blue car waiting patiently for him where Frances originally parked he was somewhat disappointed nevertheless his two benefactors were nowhere to be seen, having hoped for the chance to introduce both to J.J.

Then again, on second thought, maybe it was simply better to let sleeping dogs lay. Even while hoping to meet his wife's sheroic security chief just one more time Andrei had also to admit it might prove difficult explaining to his young daughter how exactly they happened to meet.

One particular can of worms he dreaded the very thought of opening, another problem deserving serious consideration was the possible moment J.J. might let slip to her mother how she actually met Frances Straker for herself. It wasn't until reaching the sidewalk running alongside the road Andrei was able to see a small piece of folded white paper tucked away beneath his passenger side windshield wiper.

At first glance he had the sinking impression it was some form of traffic citation but, upon drawing even closer, he could clearly see it was something else entirely. Letting go of J.J.'s hand at long last it was then Andrei carefully removed it from its resting place with just a trace of deliberate caution. Unsure at first what it might contain he held it firmly in his increasing grip, reading the

130

message it bore:

"What is it?" J.J. asked, Andrei feeling his eyes grow misty.

"Nothing, dear", he smiled at her with trembling lips, moved deeply by his benefactor's thoughtful message: "Just a short note from a very dear Gentlewoman who lent your silly old father a much appreciated helping hand when he needed it most".

Gently folding up again the piece of paper containing said message he slipped it carefully into the inside breast pocket of his black leather jacket. Unable to even imagine throwing it away he planned to tuck it away directly upon getting home in a very special, very private hiding place so long as he should live.

"I don't think you're silly", J.J. objected strenuously.

"Well; maybe 'poor' then", Andrei conceded with a light chuckle.

"Are we poor?" she jumped in with both feet:

"I thought we were rich!", she added, wearing a puzzled frown.

"That's not the kind of poor I was referring to", her father explained, gently laughing as he did:

"However, to put your mind to rest, we are indeed quite well off to say the very least", he assured her.

"And in many more ways than just a monetary one!", he added, thoughtful. A joyful warmth welling up in his heart it occurred to him right then and there just how rich they really were.

"What's 'well-off' mean?"

"Well, for one thing it means we can afford to go to the Crystal Gardens for a little afternoon treat before it's time for your brother and sister to get out of school", Andrei offered, grinning at the expression of sheer delight appearing with a sudden flash on his daughter's face.

"All right!", J.J. practically squealed with eager anticipation, her infectious good spirits likewise spreading to him.

"Splendid", he laughed with merry zest, feeling both renewed and invigorated at the very same time: "In that case why don't we just hop on in and be on our way".

Needing no further encouragement than this, J.J. leapt into the front passenger seat of their waiting car like a shot from cannon, any pretense at maturity thrown to the four winds in her unbridled enthusiasm to be on the move. Pleased with her reaction, most happy when seeing in his eldest an honest-to-goodness child enjoying her all-to-brief youth, Andrei ventured out into the quiet street, circling their parked vehicle to the driver's side with a joyful bounce to his step.

Chapter 21

"CMDR STASHA NIKAROV"

Informing her of the meeting Jenniboni called for later that evening, Stasha soon severed all communications with the last department chief on her list. Nor was it long after doing so Maccs interrupted her private meditations, doing so by way of the internal comm. unit built into the crescent-shaped desk at which she now sat:

"Cmdr. Nikarov?"

"Yes, Maccs?"

"You asked me to inform you when Commodore Saphira arrived onboard. Her shuttle has just completed final docking procedures".

"Thank you, Maccs".

"You're welcome, Ma'am. Will that be all?"

"Yes", StarChild's X.O. assured him.

"Very good, Ma'am: Over and out".

Lapsing yet again into utter silence that synthetic intelligence referred to by his fellow shipmates as 'Master Young Maccs StarChild' left Stasha once more to her private thoughts. Waiting with an anticipatory smile those revelations she knew were soon forthcoming, being kept in the dark was something she didn't care for in the very least!

Yet, even so, she nevertheless trusted Jenniboni's good judgment in the matter, having come to know her like a sister after all these many years. If her oldest, dearest friend in the entire System refused to relinquish any pertinent data even over the most secure of all available comm. channels, then her reasons for not doing so must be valid.

Right from the very start the very first day they initially met some twelve years ago Stasha learned to trust without fail in both Jenniboni's natural intuitiveness and inborn wisdom. Even though Stasha was, at that time, the other woman's senior in both rank and position she could likewise see in her junior partner someone whose opinion she could trust.

Remembering it all as if only yesterday the year back then was 2903, Stasha having served in the Protectorate ever since moving to Earth some four years earlier, leaving her hometown of New Moskva on Mars. Stationed in St. Tammy City shortly after graduating from the Academy she was later assigned a junior partner straight-out of training herself, a rookie officer answering to the obvious name of Jenniboni Saphira.

An eager go-getter first assigned to Stasha for a little on-the-job training it was apparent right from the very start she not only possessed both the immense drive and ambition to go far, but the innate good judgment to do so as well.

Truth be told it was both Jenniboni Saphira and a chance mishap with some nocturnal 'ne'er-do-well' leading to where she was that very day. Called in on a routine burglary attempt in progress it was back then Stasha lost her right eye during an angry exchange of weapons fire with said prowler, swiftly followed by Jenniboni taking the perp down with lightning reflexes.

However, it wasn't until after her final release from intensive care she soon found herself faced with what she considered a fate worse than death, permanent desk duty thanks to her so-called 'physical impairment'. Bitter over this unfair turn of events Stasha originally opted for sub-quark cybernetic surgery, allowing her to remain on active patrol. With an optical implant truly indistinguishable in both appearance and function Stasha would have been allowed to continue doing that which she loved so well.

It wasn't her fault she was one of those infinitesimal few whose natural immune system rejected such sub-micro-bionics, or nano-quark biomechanics.

Despondent, unable to even imagine being relegated to a desk-job for the rest of her life, Stasha turned to that one practical source of sage advice she could always rely on in the past. Glad to have done so Jenniboni's council, true to form, left her not wanting.

Intimately acquainted with her former partner's sincere interest in the topic of xenology, an amateur expert passionate about the subject since early childhood, Jenniboni's advice came as Heaven-sent just when Stasha needed it most. Too close to the problem to see it for herself, Stasha never really thought of turning what was always a favored intellectual pastime into an actual career all on its own.

Not knowing today why it never originally occurred to her she'd never forget the happy times she and Jenniboni shared with one-another their opinions and insights on the subject during lulls in their regular patrol duties. And thanks to both Jenniboni and a disability clause in Protectorate regulations Stasha was able to follow her dearest friend's wise council.

Resigning from the C.C.P.F., she went instead back to school, pursuing a degree in what was nothing at first but a cherished hobby. Yet no matter how busy Stasha was over the next few years with her scholastic endeavors she made as well a sincere effort to stay in close touch with the Saphira's, always finding time on a regular basis to remain an active part of all their lives.

It wasn't always easy, but she managed nevertheless to do so. Taking time out of her burdensome schedule to serve as Godmother for the couple's three children, she even stood up for them in the very same cathedral where she stood as 'Best Woman' alongside Jenniboni at her wedding. As it was both J.J. and the twins likewise looked forward to whenever "Aunt Stasha" came to visit, doting on them in the process to the point of spoiling them rotten.

And in return Jenniboni continued likewise to take an active interest in her life, playing as well a major role in Stasha's future. Just how major Stasha learned soon enough upon graduating with high honours from the likewise prestigious University of Ahnteekah.

Having stayed in the C.C.P.F. while her former partner studied long and hard for her doctorate, Jenniboni had joined the Protectorate's 'Strategic Air-Space Defense' division not long after their previous working relationship came to an end. Staying there for nearly four more years before joining the newly developed 'Star Exploration Administration' she was even allowed to keep her Captain's rank earned during her time as a Protector, promoted soon after that to the rank of Commodore.

Given command of StarChild, always keeping as well Stasha in her thoughts, she wasted no time using her newly conferred powers as ship's C.O. to secure for her dearest friend a meaningful position as both StarChild's Chief Science Officer and second-in-command. Truth be told Jenniboni went to Admiral Sellers so quickly with her recommendations on Stasha's behalf she even forgot to inform the beneficiary of her impulsive generosity what she had in mind, unable for once to contain her enthusiasm long enough to do so.

Needless to say Stasha was quite startled to find herself on the receiving end of such a magnificent offer, no advance warning whatsoever, in recognition of both her excellent scholastic achievements and exceptional career as a former Protector.

Personally contacted by no less than S.E.A. High Command itself!

No sense of surprise existed on Jenniboni's part however, aware from the very start of Melissa's desire to fill both positions with a highly trained xenologist who knew her stuff. Luckily the Star Exploration Administration had no restrictions like the Protectorate concerning members with such 'limitations' as Stasha's missing eye. And the fact Stasha was likewise a highly decorated former Protector was another factor she knew would be a major selling point in her favor.

Which is probably why Stasha sometimes resented it when others sometimes doubted her, expressing disbelief when told who she was, divulging both her function and high-ranking position aboard Womankind's very first starship.

Having nothing to do though with Stasha's physical 'handicap' however, the real reason for their initial disbelief was due actually to both Stasha's youthful good looks and powerful build. Twin factors contributing to her appearing even younger than her 35 years a passion for weights left Stasha endowed with a mighty physique worthy of any professional athlete while a cheerful, youthful expression and definite glow of inner health left her looking likewise several years younger.

All in all she even competed on behalf of her former alma-mater at several inter-university meets, managing as well to place first in her division on more than one occasion—a situation that, despite certain obvious advantages, proved as well cause for the occasional misunderstanding on the part of both others as well as Stasha herself.

While earning her both the respect and appreciation of those she competed against it would nevertheless appear that, sadly enough, there remained even in these enlightened times those few unfortunate individuals who saw both brains and brawn as mutually exclusive—unable to grasp the simple premise that one could be strong in both body and mind!

Then again, what with her winsome feminine muscles and sweet countenance, Stasha encountered very little trouble in attracting the laddies. Not when one also took into account other such womanly features as her superior intelligence, strong personality, and self-assured manner. Even her eye-patch was a source of certain appeal according to those few men she actually found the time to date, granting her what they often described as an adventurous, exciting, and even exotic air of both mystery and romance.

Sometimes disappointed that her busy schedule left so little time for such off-duty dalliance's, Stasha nevertheless found it little cause for regret. The crimp it put in her social life was a small price she was more than willing to pay if it meant being involved in something as monumental in Human herstory as Project StarChild.

Happy in her new life she guessed it was even worth sitting on a few pins and needles awaiting Jenniboni's arrival—glad all-the-same when Jenniboni finally appeared outside her door, arriving with all those answers to that myriad flow of questions flooding now every fiber of her being.

****

Upon entering her X.O.'s office Jenniboni motioned the other woman to remain seated. Insisting there was no need to stand on formality with just the two of them present she took a seat in one of three chairs close to Stasha's desk.

No sooner had she done so Jenniboni found herself bombarded with a whole slew of probing inquiries demanding further explanation:

"So now that we're all alone I hope you feel free at last to tell me what's going on?", Stasha insisted with a certain amount of trepidation. Although curious she likewise had to admit feeling a wee bit nervous, having never seen her commanding officer behave before in such a pensive manner:

"So what's the big mystery? Must be serious".

"Oh, yes, it's serious all right", Jenniboni agreed with both a slight nod and dour expression. Proceeding to just dive in she revealed all she learned in Melissa's office.

The stunned look Stasha wore as her C.O. told her all there was to tell revealed a shock similar to that Jenniboni also experienced when Melissa shared with her the same revelations. Taking several moments to recover from what she just heard, Stasha voiced then her own concerns once having done so:

136

"Well, as far as StarChild is concerned, the ship himself is all ready to leave on Friday. No problem there", she confided, expressing a certain amount of confusion while speaking further:

"Even so I don't see the reason for all this rushing about. What real difference can moving up our departure date a couple of weeks make to those colonists after sending that message nearly five years ago? After all this time I seriously doubt there's anything we can do for them at this late stage of the game".

"True", Jenniboni confided with a certain amount of hesitant concern:

"Although I've a nagging suspicion we're going to learn soon enough that isn't why we're being asked to leave so early. No doubt we'll find out quite differently once aboard the Prime Arch Matri's private cruiser, but I think this imperative has more to do with our own welfare that of the colonists. And by 'our' I mean the entire Matriarchate".

"I see", Stasha frowned, the true meaning of Jenniboni's words inescapable: "So you and the Admiral think this lost colony's misfortune might be the direct result of some hostile alien power attempting to expand their territory in our direction, using Alpha Centauri as a springboard for possible invasion?"

"I think that a likely hypothesis", StarChild's C.O. readily agreed, crossing her legs, balancing on her knee the ei-pad Darren gave her earlier: "It would make perfect sense given how our unwomaned survey probes never scanned *any* viable indication of *any* current civilization just some eight odd years ago.

"And now we learn of not only a formerly unknown colony... and Human at that!... being destroyed out there, but that they were also destroyed by some sort of hostile unknowns just two years later. Unfortunately parts of the message they sent were faded, so we don't quite know for certain what really happened out there".

"Well, at least we know why none of our unwomaned drone probes ever revealed any sign of this colony during their initial survey", Stasha mused aloud: "Those ancient pioneers couldn't have arrived there until at least a year after our probes completed their mission. By then they'd already begun their return trip home at near-light speed".

"Agreed", Jenniboni nodded with a weary sigh: "And given both our distance from Alpha Centauri, and the time it would have taken their transmission to reach us just this year, that means they had to have sent their emergency message just a little less than five years ago.

"That would make their arrival date sometime in the year 2908, a fact the colonists themselves confirm when claiming they reached their new world just two years before. By that time our survey probes were already a year into their return journey back to the Commonwealth".

"Must have passed one another by like ships in the night", Stasha chuckled, her crooked grin registering a subtle trace of sour amusement: "Pity our probes never detected their sleeper vessel at their closest trajectory to one-another. Not that we could've actually rendered them any assistance had we known they even existed even way back then. Even at our closest approach to their ship they were no doubt beyond our range of detection. Pity".

"Pity, indeed", Jenniboni's clear, decisive voice cut through the ensuing silence following immediately thereafter: "Not that such concerns matter right now. No point in berating ourselves wondering what might, or might not have occurred under such circumstances. All that matters now is the obvious worst-case scenario both the Supreme Mother and the other, various government branches seem to fear.

"If they weren't so clearly worried about what we might be facing out there I'm sure they'd have already informed us of the colony's message sooner than this. No doubt convening emergency sessions of both the Parliament, Senate, and even the Supreme Council of Matriarchs. Wouldn't surprise me if they actually consulted the Supreme Archbishop herself while at it".

"Who knows? Maybe they did", Stasha offered with a half-hearted laugh, displaying a similar sense of moral outrage: "Either way, as I indicated before, the ship is all ready to leave by the new departure date while, according to both Engineering and Security, all our weapons systems are likewise up-and-running at peak efficiency. The same goes as well for both Maccs and Sickbay".

"Excellent! So did you manage to likewise contact all the Department Chiefs concerning the emergency get-together I requested for tonight?"

"Yes, Ma'am! Some, like Dr. Wei-Chang and myself, were already onboard while others were either on the base, or in Chiron City. I managed to reach Lt.'s Netra and Matthias straight away, but had a little bit of trouble getting in touch with both Lt. Cmdr.'s Marlowe and Straker...

"At least at first.

"Don't worry, though. I managed to get through to them in the end. The important thing is they'll all be here in time for the meeting".

"Excellent!"

"And, with your approval I think we should likewise contact the dry-dock commander, inform her as well of our new departure date. No doubt Captain Stevens and her people will also need to work double shifts alongside ours just to get all their final maintenance checks and diagnostic surveys taken care of by this Friday.

"Dear Lord", Stasha groaned aloud, feeling all-of-a-sudden quite overwhelmed by everything now transpiring all around her: "That's only three days away!"

"Indeed", Jenniboni granted, also feeling more than just a little put-upon:

"As-a-matter-of-fact I was thinking just that very same thing during my final approach here".

"So I guess that takes care of everything except the teleporters".

"I know. So when were the final parts scheduled to arrive from Earth?"

"This coming Monday the 18th. Needless to say our dear Ms. Marlowe isn't going to be all too happy. She was really looking forward to getting those units up-and-running. As excited as a little girl on Christmas day I dare say", Stasha laughed more readily this time around.

"I can just imagine", Jenniboni found herself equally amused, knowing what her Chief Engineer could be like when all wasn't in perfect order concerning either her department, or StarChild himself.

"Can't really blame her, though", she concluded.

At first Jenniboni resented the S.E.A. High Command's rather arbitrary decision, using both her ship and crew as guinea pigs for what still remained little more than an experimental procedure to begin with. Only later, having had greater opportunity to consider the matter further, could she see the overall practical applications behind such a possible method of near instantaneous transportation. Even more so now, given what a perilous mission this was shaping up to be.

Lapsing at this point into a moment of silent reflection, each woman taking a brief time-out to conduct a mental survey of anything else they might need to consider during the little time remaining, Jenniboni was the first to speak her mind. Instructing Stasha to stock up further on extra supplies from the dry dock above when discussing with them StarChild's new departure date, the requisitions she recommended ran the gambit from both technical to medical in nature.

As was to be expected much of the technical hardware ran along such predictable lines as extra weaponry and spare parts for both defensive and offensive systems—including more smart-metal armored suits.

Yet, when Stasha confided a similar desire to put in a requisition form for extra transport shuttles in lieu of teleporters, Jenniboni reminded her with regret they, too, required a six-day delivery period.

So—proposing instead they strengthen weapons, increase engine output, and refortify shields already in their possession—Jenniboni made an even further counter-proposal they order as well extra drone probes, arming them for mass deployment as remote-controlled fighter-craft.

But even as StarChild's two senior-most command personnel went about brainstorming for the immediate future, taking into consideration every possible contingency, they couldn't help but exchange a pair of sour, 'just-who's-kidding-who' glances between them.

No matter how many brilliant plans they came up with, no matter what ingenious precautions each might suggest, there was no getting around the simple fact there were no legitimate measures with which to prepare themselves for effective combat. At least not against those overwhelming forces their superiors seemed to fear.

Although StarChild was equipped well enough to handle any skirmish involving perhaps as many as three times his number—High Command having at least enough foresight to consider such a possibility—there was still no legitimate way they could've ever predicted one, single starship might be expected to take on an entire alien invasion fleet all on its very own!

"Just between the two of us I'm finding all this quite hard to deal with right now", Stasha finally confessed, slowly, shaking her head.

"Join the club", Jenniboni sighed before adding in a more sympathetic manner: "Look, I realize this is a lot to dump on you at such short notice, but please remember I learned about all this no more than a couple of hours ago myself".

Able to understand her first Officer's obvious consternation on both a professional and personal level, there was still no way either of them could've ever imagined their mission… originally intended to be one of both peaceful exploration and scientific research… turning into an actual interstellar re-enactment of the ancient, herstorical "Charge of the Light Brigade".

Or, put another way, it was both the scale and magnitude of what they might actually be going up against, not the actual concept of danger itself, that left StarChild's honourable X.O. so concerned. With this in mind Jenniboni continued with all due consideration, giving her old friend an understanding smile full of obvious compassion:

"I guess that, in the end, all we can really do is hope for the best and prepare for the worst", she humbly offered for all it was worth.

Not much when thinking about it.

"Funny, but I never thought of you as a fatalist before", Stasha responded with a bemused grin.

"I prefer the term 'realist' myself", Jenniboni likewise smiled.

"Have it your way".

"Well, no matter which way we look at it, the simple fact still remains I don't want the rest of the crew to know what we might be facing until *after* our departure. For now I think it best to keep this between just the two of us and those various Department Heads attending tonight's briefing.

"Otherwise, we do our best to downplay any probable significance the rest of the crew will naturally try and attribute to our new launch schedule. The last thing we need on our hands right now is an anxious crew".

"Agreed".

"Excellent. And having taken care of that may I further suggest you get in touch right away with Captain Stevens, see to those requisitions we discussed, while I take care of this", Jenniboni concluded, indicating the E.I. Pad she'd been balancing on her knee until that very moment. No time to dilly-dally was her primary thought, leaving Stasha's office immediately thereafter.

Turning left down the corridor beyond towards her own, neighbouring office Jenniboni took a seat behind her own desk once behind closed doors, pausing from the work ahead just long enough to give the nearby photo of Andrei and their three children both a cursory glance and fleeting smile.

Chapter 22

"A FATHER/DAUGHTER HEART-TO-HEART"

Ever since a routine shopping expedition no more than a year ago the Crystal Gardens were definitely the 'absolute bestest' were you to ask the Saphira children their humble opinion, each having led their father on a merry chase the first time he ever brought them there on the pretext of new clothes.

Nevertheless Andrei grew to love as well this mammoth shopping complex almost as much as they, maintaining nevertheless a tighter rein since then on his rambunctious offspring least they try again running him ragged. However, loving it for different reasons, their pleasure sprang from such childish rationale as all the gaming centers, restaurants, cinema's, toy and candy stores, and other 'fun stuff' while their father's justification for liking this ponderous retail Mecca lay elsewhere.

One reason for his enthusiasm was how even J.J. would temporarily abandon her premature, self-imposed adulthood in this particular environment, giving free rein to that small child within Andrei always wanted to see more of.

Another reason for so heartily endorsing this place regardless of the considerable work it involved, despite the tiresome effort just keeping his little brood gathered all about in some reasonable semblance of order, had nothing to do however with loving fatherhood.

Often visiting the Crystal Gardens even without his children in tow the basic truth was that Andrei's main enjoyment of this almost carnival-like atmosphere stemmed from both pure nostalgia and a certain amount of natural homesickness, a desire to relive younger days back on Earth.

For him this bustling temple built for the almost religious pursuit of commerce was a joyous reminder of similar establishments he relished whiling away the hours in back on the Prime Mother world, a pleasant escape from those occasional trials and tribulations of present-day life.

Taking him back to simpler times it was a fact that, while he harbored no ill-feelings, or regret over Jenniboni's decision to move them all to the outer-System, there were still those sometimes difficult patches during which Andrei missed those cherished people and places of yesteryear.

141

Designed to provide for the shopping and entertainment needs of the entire family the Crystal Gardens consisted of a diverse compilation of various stores, eateries, and theatres—a whole plethora of assorted mercantile and amusements brought together under a high-vaulted, creamy white crystalline arcade not unlike a multi-tiered cathedral in design.

The ground level of this glittery menagerie consisting of a wide pavilion well over two kilometers in length it was lined upwards on either side as well by even more levels yet.

Each set back slightly from the one directly below, complete with a similar promenade all its own running the arcade's entire length, each upper pavilion was connected also to the one directly across from it by an intricate series of long, wide bridges comprised of sparkling blue glass contained and framed in a latticework of glistening silver chrome.

And bordering the outer edge of each upper promenade set above the main floor were row-upon-row of both colourful, multi-hued flowers and other assorted plants imported from such life-bearing inner-System worlds as Earth, Mars, and even Venus.

Creating a decorative partition between inner walkways and outer railings on each and every level these veritable hanging gardens of Babylon were, in all honesty, the only practical concentration of living flora gathered together in all of Chiron City.

Their sweet fragrance filling the entire arcade with a quite heavenly scent it was yet another little touch of Earth Andrei appreciated… thank you oh so very much… along with the tranquil artificial breeze keeping those leafy fronds and delicate blooms swaying gently back and forth.

No doubt it was such continuous little reminders of the inner-System explaining why the Crystal Gardens were so popular across the whole length and breadth of Demeter, if not the entire tri-planetary alliance itself.

Nor would it surprise Andrei in the least were he to discover the most frequent visitors here were likewise former inhabitants of either Earth, Mars, and/or Venus—the last two Mother worlds, each terraformed for centuries now, possessing both their own breathable atmosphere along with indigenous flora and fauna originally transported there from the first.

Nevertheless the greatest concentration of variant-hued greenery was still situated all throughout the ground-level pavilion running along the arcade's very center. It was there dozens of large, verdant gardens flourished quite literally with both a wide assortment of rainbow-hued flowers and other such specimens of varied plant life, all ranging from one-another in both size, shape, and height ringed with glazed brown brick barriers no higher than waist level.

Reaching from almost one side of the grand pavilion to the opposite other, each rich gathering of blooming flora reached within just ten or so meters of those many sundry business concerns arrayed alongside either side of that grand arcade—a majestic, crystal-clear water fountain rising from the very center of each round garden giving drink to the plant-life below in the form of a gentle, powder-fine mist.

****

Seated next to one of these exquisite miniature rainforests at what might be described as an indoor sidewalk café Andrei and his eldest enjoyed a light familial repast, their table arranged so close to the nearest garden they could reach out, touching the vivid floral display so near at hand.

Placed before both father and daughter the food their diligent waiter brought them only moments ago consisted of a steaming cup of cafe mocha for Andrei complete with just a dollop of whipped cream floating on top along with a small plate upon which sat a light, flaky, croissant stuffed with a sweet layer of almond icing while a large bowl of frosty ice cream sat before J.J..

Going practically ignored however there were several layers of the delectable concoction liberally topped with both sliced bananas, chocolate chips, and a healthy serving of whipped cream topped with a few strategically placed maraschino cherries.

As Andrei took a delicate bite from one slender end of that airy pastry set before him, he glanced up from his mid-afternoon treat only to notice the despondent little girl across the way frowning down upon her otherwise all-time favorite—her father watching with mounting concern as J.J. stirred listlessly the melting ice cream around-and-about with the tip of her long-handled desert spoon.

Watching as well one of her lonesome cherries slide gradually down an avalanche of sweet, smooth whipped cream to the very edge of the heavily laden bowl set before her, it tumbled almost to the table's waiting surface directly below.

"Sooo… are you going to just sit there moping about, or are you finally going to tell your dear old dad what's troubling you so?" Andrei asked with an inquisitive little smile: "I know something's wrong when you just sit there while your all-time favorite dish goes practically untouched for so long".

"Nothin' really", she muttered in reply.

"Come, now. You know you can trust me", Andrei vowed, reaching out, taking her free hand in his:

"Please tell me", he pleaded.

Able to detect the obvious concern in her father's worried voice J.J. answered at long last in a still, small voice, eyes still downcast:

"It's what happened in Ms. Li-Wong's office today".

"Ohhh, Darling", Andrei groaned in utter dismay, giving her hand a comforting squeeze: "Daddy's so very, very sorry about being so cross today with your principal. I had a really bad, bad day today, but that's no excuse. I'm really, really sorry I scared you so. It was very wrong of me, I know. Please forgive me".

"That's not what I'm talkin' about", she spoke up this time around in a somewhat clearer voice: "I mean I was scared but I'm not anymore. That's not what I mean".

"Then what, Sweetie?" he asked once more, this time truly perplexed.

143

"It's what Ms. Li-Wong said about letting you and Mother punish me", J.J. sighed.

"Ahhh, I see. So you're worried about what we're going to do to you!"

"Yes, Sir".

"So you want to know what we're going to do to you?" Andrei asked, leaning back in his chair, giving the matter a little further thought. Squeezing his eyes tightly shut he began tapping each forefinger against his temples in an exaggerated parody of deep concentration:

"Geeee… let's see. What to do? What to do?? …

"I've got it!!" his eyes popped open soon thereafter in an equally humorous affectation of sudden thought, snapping his fingers in feigned triumph as they did so:

"First we'll take you back to the apartment and dig out that secret torture rack your Mother and I've been saving at the back of our closet for just this very occasion. Then we'll handcuff you to it and dig out that big old bullwhip and, after we beat you all night with it, we'll put those trusty old thumbscrews to you and…"

Not needing to finish his fantastic litany of imaginary horrors before it had its desired effect, J.J. burst out giggling straightaway:

"Oh, Father, really! Don't be so silly!"

"Now that's what I like to see" Andrei beamed from ear-to-ear: "I always love seeing that beautiful smile of yours".

"Thanks, Daddy", she happily blushed, continuing in a more serious voice soon after: "So what're you *really* gonna do to me?"

"Absolutely nothing!" he assured her this time in deadly earnest, leaning forward yet once more, looking her straight in the eye.

"What do you mean?" J.J. shook her head, full of innocent disbelief: "Is this another joke?"

"No joke! Promise!" Andrei assured her with such obvious sincerity she knew from the very moment he opened his mouth he was telling her nothing, but the truth: "No punishment! The way I see it we've both had a really bad day today and, the sooner we put it behind us, the better".

"Great", she let loose with such a raucous cheer it drew startled looks from other cafe patrons, her face clouding up all-the-same soon thereafter: "But what about Mother? What'll *she* do?"

"She won't do anything either", he promised her for a second time in a row: "Especially since neither of us is going to tell her anything about what happened today!"

"You mean just say nothing", J.J.'s jaw dropped a country mile, incredulous beyond belief: "How can we just not tell her?"

"I think right about now would be a good time for the two of us to have a serious little father, daughter chat", Andrei suggested, still looking her straight in the eye, giving her hand yet another tender squeeze.

"Okay…" she allowed, sounding somewhat wary, all-of-a-sudden feeling unsure.

"Well… it has to do with a man's role in society", he began in a slow, hesitant, fashion.

"Oh, you mean like doin' the laundry, cookin', and all that kind of stuff?"

"Yes, well, that's part of what I'm trying to get at", Andrei agreed in part, proceeding carefully as he tried to explain further: "As you already know it's your mother's role in society as the woman of the house to manage our little family, provide for our every need, and go out into the System each and every day to do 'battle' for us".

"Oh, you mean like when she used to go out all the time and catch crimm's when she used to be a Protector?"

"Sort of, but not exactly", Andrei smiled ever so gently, struggling hard to convey to her what he wanted so desperately to get across: "Actually I'm referring to how she goes to work every day to put food on the table, clothes on our backs, and a roof over our heads.

"And then there's also the way she's in charge, how she makes the big decisions that have such a major effect on our lives, making everything better. In other words she's the 'rule maker'".

"Yeah, sure; I know what you mean".

"Good. And, as a man, it's likewise my role in life to take good care of both our home and family to the very best of my ability. As both a husband and father it's my responsibility to handle all those various duties you mentioned before, clean house and see to it that the rest of my family is both healthy and well cared for, seeing to it that everyone is happy, that all is kept in perfect running order.

"It's not always easy, but I still take both great pride and satisfaction in a job well done.

"And then there's the same way that, like your mother, it's also my job to teach you right from wrong, seeing to it you stay out of trouble, stay out of harm's way, and grow up to be responsible, contributing, members of society.

"And, since I'm the one who spends most of my time day with you, this responsibility often ends up falling on my shoulders more than it does her, making sure that her rules are being obeyed and that order is maintained at all times when she's away".

Taking a brief time-out to catch his breath, taking as well another sip of cafe mocha, Andrei could tell from her attentive expression she basically understood... so far... what he was driving at, aware at the very same time he was getting as well just a little off-track.

"Basically my point is this; that it's my role in life as a man to see to it that all your mother's wants, needs, and desires are fulfilled to the best of my ability, serving her as best I can whether, or not she's at home. And a big part of doing so means providing her with a happy home so she doesn't have to fret over us whenever she's not there. Do you understand?"

Although the look she gave him indicated comprehension, Andrei was happy nonetheless to hear her say so:

"And this is why I'd like to keep our hardships of this particular day just our little secret between just the two of us. What with everything else your mother has to deal with right now I'd really like to spare her the further burden of having to worry about us as well. Especially when she'll be away from home for such a long time, unable to be with us for so long. No need to remind you of everything going on in her life right now, or what she'll be doing soon? Right, hon?"

"No", J.J. reassured him, quite aware of both her mother's fame and importance as C.O. of the Matriarchate's very first starship preparing for its bachelor voyage in just two weeks' time.

"Good, because this likewise means your mother has even more to worry about with her career than most women. Therefore, I don't want her worrying about how we're going to get along without her as well while she's away, whether or not we can take care of ourselves during her absence.

"Try looking at it this way", Andrei demonstrated even further, using an illustration sure without fail to make his point for him:

"Let's pretend that our home is a starship, and our family is the crew making your mother, as the woman of the house, our commanding officer, while I—as both your father and her husband—am the First Officer.

"And as I'm sure you're fully aware, it's the First Officer's duty to make sure discipline is maintained at all times, that all runs smoothly onboard ship, and that the crew stays out of trouble.

"However, if the C.O. is worried her X.O. isn't up to the job, isn't performing to the best of her abilities, she'll be too busy worrying about her ship and crew whenever away to perform to the best of her own abilities.

"And, if that's the case, then the entire ship suffers. Do you see what I'm trying to say?"

"Yes, Father", J.J. giggled. Although quite able to grasp his meaning the very idea of a man actually being allowed to serve aboard any vessel in any administrative capacity, much less as First Officer aboard an actual starship, nevertheless amused her:

"So what does that make my rank?"

"Hmmm… I'd say Lieutenant".

"So when do I get to be a Lt. Cmdr.?"

"That depends on your mother", Andrei grinned in reply, giving his daughter a wry little wink: "After all, she is our Commanding Officer".

"Aye, aye, Ma'a… I mean 'Sir'", J.J. laughed, giving her father a jaunty little salute.

"Sooo… does this mean you're feeling any better now?" he asked, giving her hand yet another affectionate squeeze. Assuring him in all honesty she felt much better there was no denying her father's special knack for always being able to cheer her up no matter the situation.

Then again, at the very same time, she couldn't help but feel there was nevertheless some tiny flaw in both his analogy and reasoning, some childhood instinct telling her it lay not in what her father said, but instead in what he didn't.

Something he, himself, had overlooked.

However, seeing as well she just couldn't quite put her finger on what it was to begin with, J.J. decided in the end to just let the entire matter drop.

"Good. So does that mean we both agree not to discuss what happened with your mother?"

"Yeah, sure", J.J. agreed without further delay, neither father nor daughter saying much of anything for the moment. At least not until Andrei heard her enquire as to whether, or not this meant he actually approved now of what she did.

Sitting further back in his chair before rendering his final verdict, folding both arms across his chest, Andrei gave the young girl in question a critical look, giving her renewed pause for concern:

"Let's just say, for the moment, it would be more accurate to say I understand what you did, and why, rather than saying I actually condone your recent behavior", he confided rather cautiously, giving the entire matter some further thought. Noting the look of utter confusion appearing now on the bewildered child's face, Andrei explained in greater detail:

"Let's just say I understand why you got into that fight, why you got mad, and I'm proud of you for coming to that little boy's rescue.

"All-the-same, though, I likewise feel your principal had a valid point when she said you should've at least tried to tell that other girl to back-off before just hitting her, given her a chance to back off on her own accord before resorting to actual fisticuffs.

"Then again the actual, ideal situation would've been for you to go find a playground supervisor, or some other adult, reporting the situation to them instead of taking the law as it were into your own hands. Does that answer your question?"

"Sure, I guess so".

"Good", Andrei wasted no time smiling; "then maybe you can answer a question for me".

"Okay".

"Well...", he enquired with a wry little grin, watching J.J.'s ice cream melt away into a messy, rainbow coloured goo: "Are you going to actually consume your repast, or has it been all for naught?"

"What?" she exclaimed, completely baffled.

"Sorry", Andrei chuckled, shaking his head more at himself than her: "Just something your grandparents would ask when I was your age".

"That's strange", J.J. responded, slowly, a puzzled frown appearing, clearly trying to remember something: "I don't ever remember Grandpa Raoul saying that".

"Not your Grandpa Saphira", Andrei smiled once more: "That's your mother's father. I'm referring to my parents, Joannah-Ruth and Colm Harold Sollos".

"Yeah, that's right. Grandma Sollos! She's the real rich one who always sends us the real cool Christmas and birthday presents all the time".

"Exactly: The one back on Earth in St. Tammy City".

"Yeah", J.J. sallied forth, full of naked awe: "Your mother's a lot richer than Grandma Saphira ever was".

"Now wait just a minute there, young Gentlewoman", Andrei wasted no time correcting her: "You make it sound as if your mother's side of the family were all a bunch of worthless tramps without a single krodit to their name".

"That's not what I meant!" J.J. hastily assured him, considerable dismay in her voice.

"I should hope not, my dear young Ms...." her father teased, chastisement turning to humor, a subtle smile beginning to form at each corner of his mouth:

"Because if so I'll have you know that the Saphira family has always been well thought of in Protectorate circles, along with being financially well off as well. My mother might be even more so, seeing as she is both President and C.E.O. of several major conglomerates, but your Grandmother Saphira was likewise a highly respected senior-ranking official in the C.C.P.F....

"Not only that but I'll have you know even further that both my parents were quite impressed with your Grandma Elissa, honoured to have her eldest daughter marry their only begotten son, namely me!"

Realizing her father wasn't really upset with her after all, J.J. likewise smiled in reply:

"Yeah, I see your point".

"Good girl", Andrei patted the back of her hand:

"Now, are you going to eat that sloppy, gooey mess or shall I", he teased even further, making an insincere, comical grab for that sticky bowl between them.

"No! I'll eat it", she shot back, laughing merrily, wrapping her arms around the dish before her in a purely instinctive gesture.

"All right, all right", he laughed, holding his hands up in feigned surrender as J.J. began shoveling the sweet, syrupy slop into her waiting mouth as if there were no tomorrow:

"So can I at least have one of your cherries?"

"But they're mine", J.J. declared with childish possessiveness around a mouthful of semi-frozen desert.

"Gee, that's no fair", Andrei protested with a playful little pout: "You're just being mean".

"Oh, all right", she rolled her eyes, sighing over what she often considered her father's somewhat silly sense of humor:

"Here".

Lifting one of the shiny red fruits up from within a thick layer of whipped cream, she held it out to him between both thumb and forefinger by its slender, delicate, stem.

"Thank you, oh kind and generous Gentlewoman", Andrei accepted with a jocular little bow from the waist up, consuming it with an expression of great relish on his face:

"Mmmm! Nice and sweet—just like you!" he continued smiling in her direction.

"Oh, cut it out", she giggled, both amused and embarrassed at the very same time, her father reaching as well for another sip of cafe mocha, partaking of the melted cream on top while enjoying another savory bite of his partially eaten croissant.

"Hey, you got whipped cream all over your moustache", J.J. snickered, pointing an accusing finger in his direction.

"Don't point", Andrei corrected her, tenderly, wiping it away with a nearby napkin: "It's not polite".

"Okay: So what are we going to do after we pick the twins up from school?", she asked after a few shared minutes of mutual silence—each enjoying both the pleasure of each other's company, the unique ambiance of their present surroundings, and what remained as well of their afternoon treats:

"Can we come back here and play some A.R. games?" she pressed on in hopeful anticipation.

"'Fraid not", her father apologized, caught in the act of leaning sideways to smell a fragrant violet alongside the nearby garden's edge: "I still have to do the laundry since I never got a chance to do it earlier. Then I've got to get dinner ready.

"Besides, I'm afraid I'll also be needing your help with the laundry, watching the twins, since I don't have anyone to watch you guys in the apartment while I'm doing wash down in the basement".

"Oh", J.J. began sulking almost at once: "I was hoping to watch some 3-DV when we got home: 'Ernie' comes on at 16:00 hours".

"Sorry, but I'm sure that 'Ernie; the amazing, tap-dancing, telepathic bat' will understand", Andrei sighed. Wearing even so an understanding smile he employed as well her favourite fictional 3-DV character's full name, a popular childhood favourite based on the 'Sarah Small books' by that very same name:

"After all he is telepathic, isn't he?"

"But I thought you said I wasn't going to be punished"; she persisted with childish disappointment, her voice starting to acquire a definite whine.

Her attitude quickly working its way under his skin, soon grating on his nerves, Andrei managed nevertheless to shrug it off with otherwise relative ease, keeping in mind that no matter how mature she acted most of the time, she was still but a seven-year-old child.

Therefore, making allowances for her somewhat petulant behavior, he answered her not with anger but tolerant amusement instead:

"Hey, Sweetie: Don't think of it as a punishment but a rare, once in a lifetime opportunity to see how the other half lives".

"I guess so", she finally replied, less despondent after mulling it over.

Occurring to her that the main reason her father hadn't already seen to his daily chores was because he had to bail her out at school, it dawned further on J.J. with a more reasonable, adult flash of recognition that she definitely 'owed him one'.

More than just one taking into account the fact he was just as ready to keep what happened at school a deep, dark secret from her mother.

So, mindful of this, she gave him a bright smile.

Choosing right then to ask him something that just came to mind, it was a question inspired by both his reference to 'the other half' alongside their earlier conversation concerning his role as a man in 'proper society':

"Father?"

"Yes, dear?"

"What's it like being a man?", she asked with such innocent, wide-eyed, naivety she might as well have been asking some strange alien entity from far beyond Womankind's home System what it was like being from another star.

Briefly stunned by such an unanticipated question coming so clearly out of nowhere, Andrei found himself at a momentary loss, unsure at first how to respond.

It wasn't until taking a deep breath, hoping to regain some former sense of composure, he finally countered by asking for further clarification:

"Are you asking what it's like physically, being naturally shorter and weaker than women are, or are you referring to something else?"

After both World War III and the resulting Yesinia R-Beta plague over 800 years ago… not to mention the method chosen back then to save humanity from final extinction… it was only understandable in hindsight a mostly unexpected reverse dichotomy would have occurred between the sexes, women now naturally taller and stronger.

Then again it could be his little girl was asking after those 'other' physical differences between the genders remaining exactly the same both visually and internally ever since the Good Lord first created Womankind oh-so long ago.

Confident however this wasn't the actual case here, Andrei at least hoped not. Or at least not yet!

"I mean what's it like doing men's stuff? Living as a man?", J.J. bombarded him with question after question. Staring at her father with such frank, raw, naked curiosity it left him feeling a moment's discomfort like some schoolgirl specimen under some high- powered magnifying glass.

Gazing back at her with similar wonder, Andrei was not at first certain where to begin. All he knew for sure was he didn't want to fail her with an inadequate response. Not when looking into her expectant face so full of both rapt attention and great expectation.

Therefore it was with both meticulous care, and absolute precision, he chose every word that followed, speaking straight from the heart with every ounce of purest love dwelling therein.

Chapter 23

"TENSIONS"

Going yet again over everything contained on the ei-pad Darren gave her just earlier that day, Jenniboni read and re-read the information stream passing now in front of weary eyes, hoping in vain to keep her wandering mind on track.

However, finally admitting defeat, she let go of the wafer thin data storage device in hand. Letting it clatter noisily to the surface of her desk, she rubbed instead her hot, tired eyes. No getting around it: She just couldn't just sit around like some useless bump on a log twiddling her thumbs, the tension within mounting to almost tortuous levels.

Having always found rigorous physical activity the best way to deal with such pent-up frustration Jenniboni decided to forsake the secluded privacy of her office, take instead an extended tour of her entire ship going now through its final preparations for their new departure date.

A direct, hands-on approach to command she concluded with a wry little smile, planning to spend what remained of her day inspecting each and every department onboard. Asking in a purely casual tone of voice about the relative progress of their individual tasks she found time as well to converse with several crewwomen going about their various duty assignments.

Given the circumstances at hand Jenniboni made a noble effort to keep her inquiries sounding as innocuous as humanly possible. Yet even while naturally flattered by their commanding officer's undivided attention, those women she spoke to found themselves growing rather uneasy not long after Jenniboni began conversing with them.

Knowing her to be both a consummate perfectionist and devoted leader with a professional bearing in all she did, there was nevertheless something all-the-same leading behind otherwise casual inquiries—each crewwoman able to detect at the center of her probing questions something extending far beyond their Commanding Officer's usual devotion to duty, her constant desire to ensure maximum efficiency.

Able to sense as well from her every mannerism something suspicious in the air, some sort of difficulty they were as yet unaware of, its very mystery made each woman increasingly nervous. Nor did it take Jenniboni long in likewise picking up on *their* discomfort, understanding as well her singularity of purpose was making the rest of her ship's compliment wary, her sense of impending disaster beginning to rub off.

And seeing how an edgy crew was the very last thing she wanted, Jenniboni decided instead to check on Stasha's current progress, her first officer still hard at work ordering the supplies each of them decided upon earlier.

****

Hunched over the ship-to-ship comm. unit built directly into her desk, deep in conversation with the requisitions officer on the dry dock above, Stasha entered simultaneously each requested item into the P.C. located to her left, ascertaining even further if each was indeed available.

And by the time Jenniboni arrived unannounced in her Executive Officer's private shipboard office, Stasha was wrapping up already the final details of their mutual business with that large space station directly overhead. Doing so she gestured with an upraised palm for Jenniboni to remain silent, typing up in her private data-base the very last entry:

"There: All done", she announced soon thereafter, looking up at long last from the P.C.'s display screen.

"From the satisfied gleam in your eye may I assume you were able to get all we wanted", Jenniboni asked, a noticeable trace of hope in her otherwise jocular tone.

"Yes, indeed", Stasha nodded, leaning back in her chair with a triumphant grin all her own. Hands folded behind her head, Stasha affected about her an air of almost relaxed indolence: "What's more it's all being rushed over here—A.S.A.P.!—right as we speak".

"Excellent", Jenniboni congratulated her, clearly pleased, suggesting the two of them oversee their newly arrived cargo all the way from its initial delivery to final storage. Once again a matter of 'who's-kidding-who-here', both senior personnel knew from whence this suggestion came.

Fully aware StarChild's crew were sufficient enough in both numbers and capability to handle such an operation without any further guidance, each woman understood as well Jenniboni's suggestion stemmed from a personal desire to feel needed, not an actual problem with those under her command.

Understanding after all these years Jenniboni's almost compulsive need for perpetual motion when under emotional duress Stasha agreed all-the-same to accompany her C.O., no mention of the fact their joint-supervision was otherwise pointless

****

152

Arriving in StarChild's hangar bay not long after the first transport vehicles from Captain Stevens began to arrive, both C.O. and X.O. followed each group of precious supplies to their varied destinations. Not wanting an unfortunate repeat of what happened just earlier Jenniboni went out of her way to manifest instead a casual air of confident ease.

This time however Jenniboni's efforts failed through no fault of her own. Undisturbed by their commanding officer's actual deportment their mounting concern was inspired this time by the plainly marked packing crates each group of cargo specialists were ultimately responsible for.

Troubled by the clearly defensive applications of each piece of technical hardware they were shuffling about from one area of the ship to the other, the obvious implications were inescapable—the similar increase of medical supplies being shuttled back and forth to Dr. Wei-Chang in sickbay serving only to amplify further their increasing anxiety.

Wishing above all else she could have avoided this from the very beginning, Jenniboni realized nonetheless this reaction on their part was both as unavoidable as it was unfortunate. Trusting though in their silence, she was nevertheless sure her crew would rise to the occasion, maintaining their professional bearing.

No matter their obvious misgivings Jenniboni still had complete and utter confidence in their ability to behave responsibly, sure they would carry on in the performance of their assigned duties with efficient calm despite their initial trepidation. It wasn't that which troubled their C.O. as much as how all this mandatory secretiveness would compromise her own ability to ensure their continued peace-of-mind—her obligation to both maintain and sustain morale amongst those women serving beneath her.

****

By 18:00 hours Jenniboni's aching feet were literally throbbing in her boots from all the time she spent on them, feeling positively swollen to bursting, while suffering a similar group of painful rumblings deep in the pit of her stomach.

An otherwise fitting companion for the creeping discomfort already crawling up her legs only then did she decide on a quick bite, heading straightaway for StarChild's bow with Stasha in tow. Realizing as she did so she hadn't eaten since breakfast Jenniboni planned to remedy this as quickly as possible before the meeting she herself scheduled within an hour.

Dubbed the 'Star Stage' by the crew's greater majority, they arrived in the officer's mess on deck B-6 only to discover the ship's cook was one of those currently planet-side, forcing them to resort to those food duplicators found in the mess's 'food prep' area.

Approaching one of the small counter-top appliances without any real enthusiasm whatsoever, placing her order by verbal command, Jenniboni watched with languid disinterest her meal appear before her out of thin air.

Reconstituted at the sub-atomic level to assume whatever edible form she might so desire, carrying their fresh food and drink into the dining section, both women sat down soon after at one of five triangular tables nearest the broad forward viewing-port from whence the 'Star Stage' acquired its specific moniker.

Jenniboni assuming a position allowing her a clear, unobstructed view of the planet Demeter's pale grey-white orb... its starry backdrop close behind... she washed down a bland forkful of beef Wellington with a sip of some equally insipid coffee.

Noting the time, glancing up at that nearby world, it occurred to her right about then both Andrei and the children were no doubt sitting down back home to a sumptuous home-cooked meal.

"Just tolerable", she muttered more to herself than her dinner companion.

Stasha, confident as to what Jenniboni was referring to, passed likewise similar judgment on her less than satisfying 'feast'.

"And I'm not at all pleased with what I saw today, either", Jenniboni spoke up yet again, scowling across the table at the starscape lying directly beyond StarChild's narrow prow.

"I don't understand", Stasha's voice rose in confused protest: "We were able to requisition everything we need, and in record time! Captain Stevens really came through for us".

"That's not what I'm referring to", Jenniboni confided, lowering her voice to an almost conspiratorial whisper. While having the entire officer's mess to just themselves that could change at any given moment:

"It's the mounting tension aboard this ship that has me concerned right now. I'm sure you noticed from the very look in their eyes what was running through everyone's mind unloading those supplies. They know something's up and I'm afraid I've only helped exasperate matters even further with my earlier prowling about. The very last thing we need right now is a jumpy crew".

"No argument here. So what do you have in mind?"

"Well... for starters we can't just let this anxiety spread from those already onboard to the rest of the crew when they begin reporting back tomorrow for duty. As far as I'm concerned it's unfair to the point of being cruel keeping them in the dark like this, letting their imaginations run amok".

"Yes... so?"

"So once we've dropped our little bombshell on the Department Chiefs in less than an hour's time, we'll instruct them right after that to inform first those members of their departments already onboard what's going on.

"Then, as the rest of the crew reports back in the morning from shore-leave, we'll have them likewise report to their immediate supervisors for similar briefings: Do so before they're infected with the same tensions without at least the benefit of knowing what little we know".

"Sounds like a plan to me", Stasha approved.

"At least as far as it goes", Jenniboni sighed, agreeing only in part. The events of the day catching up at long last with her, she felt weighed down even further than before:

"At least they'll know for the moment just as much as we do. I'm afraid that's about as much as we can do for now until the meeting tomorrow night aboard the Supreme Mother's private cruiser. Hopefully we'll learn more there".

"Maybe so", Stasha agreed, something else giving her reason for concern, listening to her C.O. and what she had in mind. Taking note of the worried look now appearing in her eyes Jenniboni realized something was wrong. Nor did she have long to wait before finding out what had her ship's X.O. so preoccupied:

"And on that note may I further suggest confining the entire crew aboard ship until our departure, forbidding them any unauthorized contact with the outside".

While not really caring much for such draconian measures Jenniboni could nevertheless see the practicality behind such a recommendation. Giving her reluctant approval she even authorized the further monitoring of all outgoing communiqués, permitting even the censorship of any private transmissions dealing with anything of a sensitive nature.

Hearing this it was then Stasha's turn to suggest Maccs be instructed to monitor *all* outgoing messages, filtering out any references whatsoever to any classified material:

"Good idea. You'd better get on that straight away. And since you already know what's on the agenda for tonight's briefing, it might be another good idea for you to program Maccs while I handle the meeting".

Stasha just nodded her willing acquiescence, both senior personnel finishing soon thereafter their somewhat adequate but unremarkable meals.

While duplicators might be an impressive technological advancement both women had to agree nonetheless it was a pity the nourishment they provided couldn't taste just a tad more flavorful.

Chapter 24

"A MAN'S-EYE-VIEW"

"Well", Andrei began slowly, keeping a watchful eye on J.J.'s expectant face: "If you're asking me if I'm happy with my lot in life as a man, performing my masculine duties, then I'd have to say that the answer to your question is a definite '*yes*'…

"Oh sure: I admit there are times I find life a bit difficult, times I find it hard to keep on going, although I'm sure the same likewise applies to women. Like women men, too, can feel bad inside when they feel they're not appreciated. Sometimes we, too, can feel like giving up, that life just isn't worth the hassle, and it's at times like these that I often feel angry or frustrated whenever things go wrong, don't work out exactly the way I want.

"But, in the end, those feelings always go away. Or at least they do for me, the important thing being that the good feelings mostly outweigh the bad.

"So, having said all that, I likewise look upon my role in society as a man… my role as a husband, father, and homemaker… to be both a very important and fulfilling one. It gives me both great pleasure, happiness, and an overwhelming sense of satisfaction to both serve, and take care of my family.

"I love you, your mother, and the twins very, very much and take great pride in a job well done. Therefore it pleases me to take care of you all, giving me great joy in life to serve your mother and provide her with a warm, tranquil loving home life where she can find sanctuary from all the many difficulties she might encounter elsewhere in life.

"Don't forget that Saint Tammy herself wrote in **The New Matriarchate** that a man's role in society is a very important, vital, and even sacred one blessed by God Almighty Himself, worthy of both great respect and consideration".

Pointing this out to the little girl gazing at him across the table, hanging onto his every word with rapt attention, Andrei was reminded at once how their parish priest back on Earth once pointed out in one of her sermons that even the

156

Lord Jesus had come Himself not to dominate Humanity, but to serve Womankind.

Using the blessed Savior as a positive role model for all men, the Church Mothers would often stress His role as a nurturer, healing the sick, feeding the hungry, and comforting both the downtrodden and poor in spirit, basically living amongst Womankind as a servant.

In fact Jesus' own words backed this assertion upon claiming "the Son of Man did not come to be served, but to serve":[§§]

"So despite the few necessary restrictions men might face in our society today, I nevertheless feel we've actually gained so much more in life than we ever lost, something that applies likewise to the rest of Womankind. Of course this is probably due to the simple fact that women are, by their very nature, superior to men in their ability to lead, better fit for administrative positions."

Andrei testified to this simple truth with neither reservation, nor any intention to depreciate his own gender. For him it was merely a statement of fact. In his opinion admitting to female superiority in the realm of the 'leadership principal' wasn't to either diminish, or denigrate the male of the species.

Having too much respect for both himself and the rest of his sex to see recognizing the superior abilities of one as casting doubt on either the importance, or intrinsic value of the other Andrei was just too secure, too confident, in his own manhood to feel so threatened by the oh-so-obvious truth:

"Of course I know you've already learned all the herstorical proofs of female superiority in school; how there's been no war, famine, poverty, or civil unrest since the formation of both the Tammyite Matriarchate and the Commonwealth over 800 years ago. So I won't bother going into all that.

"Nor will I bore you with all the medical, biological, and psychological evidence that women are naturally superior. Actually, as a man, the greatest proof of female superiority to me is how women treat us with kindness, courtesy, and the deepest respect.

"Of course I'll admit that there might be a couple of exceptions to the rule but, in my opinion, these sad and pathetic few are so rare in number as to be considered freaks of nature! The real women, the ones who really count, are those like you and your mother—caring, loving, supportive and chivalrous in their treatment of men.

"Which is why I'm just as confident you'll grow up someday to be a truly remarkable young gentlewoman, someone I'll always be able to look up to with both great pride, admiration, and even respect just as no husband could ask for a better wife than your mother!

"And so, in conclusion, may I say just once more that my answer to your question is an unconditional 'yes!': I am indeed happy to be a man, enjoying my life as such very much…

"So Sweetie, have I answered your question to your satisfaction?" Andrei ended with a hopeful little smile.

[§§] Matthew 20:28 (*NKJV*: "New King James Version"). Read Matthew 20:20-28 for a fuller understanding of this quote.

"Yes, Daddy", J.J. whispered in absolute awe, a mingling of both frank admiration and raw fascination appearing on her young face: "I never knew you felt that way".

Although she always loved her father with all her untried heart she still never knew him before so intimately as another Human being. And able to see all this in her expression, Andrei decided right then and there to strike while the iron was hot:

"In that case I was wondering if you could do Daddy a real big favor and try to remember everything he just said."

"Of course I will!!", J.J. promised, no hesitation whatsoever, wondering how she could ever forget in the very first place.

Unaware of the profound effect both that day and the next would have on each their lives, J.J. realized all the same that both just took a giant step forward not only as parent and child, but in their relationship also as fellow Human beings.

And so it was then, feeling for the immediate moment nothing more needed saying, they just sat there together in loving silence, finishing what remained of the tasty treats still before each. Having a lot less to polish off than his daughter Andrei had to likewise confess feeling much closer to his eldest child, always having felt closer to her than the twins.

Sometimes feeling a certain sense of inescapable guilt over this simple predilection on his part, there were times he wondered if it had anything to do with the just-as-simple fact J.J. possessed a more well-developed personality he'd known for longer than the others—a greater sense of 'self ' as an individual— someone with which he could relate to on a more personal basis.

Wiping sticky residue from her face with a paper napkin upon consuming the last spoonful of her ice-cream extravaganza, J.J. looked up from the empty bowl before her just in time to catch Andrei in the middle of running fingers through thick, black luxurious hair—pausing just long enough to give his daughter an embarrassed little smile, realizing he'd been caught in the act of checking himself out:

"And speaking of what it's like to be a man, I think it's high time your old man here got himself a haircut before it gets too far beyond socially acceptable lengths", he offered by way of explanation. Women encouraged to wear their hair long as a symbol of both their power and authority, a crown of glory, men were likewise expected to keep theirs short as an equal reminder of submissiveness.

"And while we're also at it we might as well stop by that little fabric store next to the barbershop, pick up a couple of invisible patches. Even at this angle I can make out some obvious tears in your dress. No doubt acquired during your previous altercation of today. Better repair them as soon as possible before your mother notices.

"So, when we get home, I want you to slip into something else while I repair your present attire. Then, once it's gone through the wash all nice and clean, you can put it back on so she won't notice anything out of the ordinary".

"Hey Father! I never knew you were so sneaky before", J.J. giggled her sly approval.

"Hey, Honey! When you're raising three children you definitely learn a few tricks of the trade", Andrei informed her with a similar chuckle: "So let that serve as a warning for all three of you; you have to get up pretty early in the morning to put one over on your dear old Dad".

"Yeah", she laughed with a wicked little grin all her own: "And you should see the other girl"

"J.J.! I don't like hearing you talk like that. As I said before I understand why you got into that fight, and I admire your singular desire for justice, but that doesn't mean you should actually take pleasure in what you did.

"Physical combat should be employed only when every other avenue of choice proves otherwise fruitless. It's one thing to stand up for both yourself as well as others, but it's another thing entirely to actually enjoy hurting people.

"No matter how vindicated you might feel in what you did, no matter how justified it might have been, that still doesn't give you the right to derive actual pleasure from it! Have I made myself perfectly clear, young woman?"

"Yes, Sir!"

"Very good, then", Andrei smiled once more, no longer upset now his point was made: "In that case are we both agreed we'll put everything that happened today behind us, make no more mention of it?"

"Agreed".

Chapter 25

"FRANK'S PLACE'

Having spent a mutually enjoyable time together in the park, it wasn't long after the concert reached its inevitable climax Gloria suggested they grab somewhere nearby a bite to eat. And not wanting to pose a financial burden on his young date, it was then Frank's turn to recommend a tasteful, yet inexpensive little restaurant he knew about likewise nearby.

Spending first a little while waiting for the other concert-goers to thin out before likewise leaving, Chiron's dome orb was beginning already to wane, approaching its less luminous night cycle by the time they reached Frank's modestly priced little eatery.

Able to secure a private table just to themselves pleasant meals were accompanied by equally warm, satisfying dinner conversation, the young couple discovering many shared interests including several musical performances during the park recital they both enjoyed.

So preoccupied with the simple pleasure of each other's company they never even noticed night had fallen all the way until leaving the restaurant's cozy confines, the dome-orb above having reached at last its lowest luminosity, the stars beyond finally visible.

Reluctant to part ways quite so soon however with the rather intriguing young gentlewoman by his side, Frank suggested right about then it might be a nice idea to take instead a leisurely drive about town.

Aware of how much Gloria enjoyed driving his car, the feeling of power she experienced at the Lembarchini's controls, he likewise found the stars above to be quite romantic, wanting the pleasure of sharing them with her while cruising about as well beneath their crystal-clear sparkle.

And except for the gentle music flowing forth from the car's quadraphonic speaker units, they drove about for the most part in a state of utter quiet.

However, far from being an awkward silence, it was in reality that special sort of warm, satisfying quiet when a couple realizes no verbal exchange is necessary, the very presence of one-another stimulation enough.

In the end, though, it was Gloria's voice that finally pierced the tranquil calm proposing over the still, soft music all about them that they head back to Frank's place. The slight note of hesitation, as if worried how her suggestion might be interpreted, reminded Frank they were swiftly approaching that crucial point in their all too brief relationship.

Being the more experienced when it came to matters of the heart, somewhat uneasy himself over how to handle the entire situation, he agreed to her proposal with a similar trace of hesitant concern, aware he'd have to handle the rest of their time together with kid gloves so neither party came away hurt from this particular experience…

Especially Gloria!

Nor was the subtle irony of this situation lost on him, Frank's lot from this point onward being to play that role in their relationship usually reserved for the woman—the role of initiator—placing upon his shoulders an extra burden of responsibility he'd never known before.

Not that it really bothered him, though. In Frank's eyes the young gentlewoman sitting next to him was well worth the effort.

****

Pausing for a moment outside the door to his 7th floor apartment complex, fumbling about for his keys, Frank experienced a sudden rush of panic searching the various pockets of his white 3-piece suit.

Growing more and more distraught, each pocket proving itself 'key-less', Frank was too busy fighting his ever-increasing sense of alarm to notice that amused grin playing at each corner of Gloria's lips:

"You wouldn't by any chance be searching so diligently for these, would you?", he heard her finally ask, playfully. Looking up at long last in her direction, taking note as well of the nearby jingle of metal against metal, Frank was immediately brought up short.

Upon sight of his missing keys dangling back and forth from her outstretched hand, dangling mid-air just inches from his nose, a sheepish expression appeared at once.

Forgetting he surrendered them earlier into her safekeeping at the beginning of their date, he accepted them slowly from between thumb and forefinger with an embarrassed "thank you", amusing his young date all the more.

Feeling an absolute idiot Frank then opened the way into his humble abode, reaching into the darkness beyond to activate the light switch just inside his front door.

Inviting Gloria to go on in ahead of him, the resulting glow from within revealed a long, narrow hallway replete with both light brown carpeting and cream white walls—a series of large watercolours paced evenly along both sides of the passageway ahead, each framed in a simple yet timely gold-plated frame.

Noting a little further down the narrow hall ahead a partially open door leading into what appeared a bedroom, a casual peek inside revealed the same cream white walls, light tan carpet, and similar artwork encased likewise in the same golden framework—noticing as well a large bed with dark green covers, a highly polished dresser bureau made of genuine maple wood, and another door leading yet still into a small bathroom.

Locking the front door to the small apartment behind them Frank offered Gloria an opportunity to look around while he changed into "something more comfortable", startling her right about then out of her silent reverie.

Realizing almost at once such an expression could be taken more than one way Frank backtracked at once, making it understood all he wanted was to slip out of his present waiter's outfit, replacing it with something both more casual as well as practical.

"Sure: No problem", Gloria granted: "I'll be quite fine on my own".

"If you like, please feel free to help yourself to some refreshment. I have a wide assortment of nibbles and drinks in the refrigeration unit in the kitchen", he added in the same hospitable vein:

"So please make yourself to home".

Giving her further instructions on how to find her way about, not so very hard by the sounds of it, he retired right about then to his private bedchamber, closing the door behind him.

Not really interested in anything to eat, or drink Gloria nevertheless availed herself of Frank's generous invitation to take a good look around, starting with the various paintings proudly displayed all around her.

Observing their soft lighting, bright colours, and gentle brush strokes what struck her most was the subject matter of each any every object-de-art within sight, every piece sharing the same basic theme of love and romance. No matter which picture Gloria examined each involved the central figures of a woman and man sharing special moments both intimate and chaste.

In one they were wrapped in each other's arms in a loving embrace while, in others, they were involved in such private moments as walking hand-in-hand along a secluded beach or sitting in a love seat… the woman's arm around the man's shoulder… sharing a tender kiss both sensual and innocent.

Yet, despite her otherwise shy nature, Gloria felt neither any discomfort, nor embarrassment whatsoever gazing upon them. On the contrary she actually found every artistic piece gathered about to be both brilliantly rendered and emotionally pleasing to both the outer eye and inner self.

In fact she'd go even one further, claiming on her own life the feelings they evoked were more spiritual than physical, appealing more to the higher senses rather than simple, base, prurient desires. Then again one reason for this might have been the exchange of facial expressions between the two subjects in each painting:

That of the purest love, adoration, and respect imaginable.

Just seeing them gave her an even warmer, more positive feeling about Frank than she already had. In her own humble opinion the very fact her date would display so boldly… so readily… such works in his most private place of residence spoke highly of the "new laddie" in her life.

Be that as it may Gloria was in for an even bigger surprise when, curious as to whom the artist of these magnificent works might be, she found the individual's signature right there in the lower right-hand corner of each piece—the name "Mas. Frank Weller" written there with a proud, masculine flair under the title of each.

Swiftly recalling Frank and Naomi's discussion concerning the young laddie's most recent artistic endeavors, Gloria never imagined anything like this. Although true she saw him as a very nice, sweet and sensitive young man right from the very start, Gloria never realized he had such as this dwelling also within him.

And so, with this in mind, she set out with all due haste in order to see what else she might discover about this exceptional soul it was her sheer good fortune to be out with.

Making her way down the narrow hallway to where it opened up on her right, Gloria found herself at once in a small, but cozy living room area—a large 3-DV cube with a series of glistening glass shelves up against the closer of two walls, the wall on the room's other side occupied instead by a long picture window spanning the room's entire length.

Able to look out it's crystal-clear transparency at half the entire city Gloria took note as well of a wide, plush black leather couch directly beneath.

Complete with coffee table it reached towards the room's far end, a small island counter just beyond separating the main living area from a little kitchenette.

Complete with an intimate little breakfast nook for two, a small stove-top cooker, and a compact refrigeration unit Gloria saw likewise several sculptures arranged with loving care along the flat countertop separating both 'rooms'.

Waiting for Frank to make his grand reappearance, she proceeded without delay over to the little island to have a quick look-see at those assorted pieces displayed there with such exacting devotion.

Noting how some were decorated in soft, soothing pastel colours while others were a plain white, Gloria noted as well they all shared the same common theme, the same overall motif as that of the paintings she'd been admiring as well just moments ago.

And from the signature carved within the base of each plaster mold it was just as clear they were also creations by the same artist, Gloria delighted to find herself faced further with even more three-dimensional images crafted by the same hand.

Nor did it end there, inspecting further to her right the chrome and glass shelves situated between the kitchenette entrance and the well-proportioned 3-DV unit.

Finding even more arranged there with loving exactitude, each beautiful in own special, singular way—perfect in both form and substance—the one having the most profound effect on her very soul, her very inner being, was a simple piece mostly white with just a hint of gold overlay.

Consisting of a perfectly detailed representation of a man's hand laying palm-down, a woman's hand resting gently on top in loving repose, both wore simple gold wedding bands on each their ring fingers, the only feature of the entire piece other than white.

Drawn to it like a very magnet Gloria found it well-nigh impossible to take her eyes off it, entranced by both its simple eloquence and purity of heart. Of all the many diverse samples of Frank's artistic genius arranged throughout every nook and cranny of his private abode, this was the one that spoke to her the loudest.

Then again, at the very same time, it seemed to hint likewise at a certain loneliness dwelling within the innermost core of that very person responsible for its creation.

Something Gloria could relate to, it occurred to her right about then like lightning from a clear blue sky that—for all his gorgeous, good looks, winning personality, and the doubtless throng of feminine admirers surely lined up six-deep just to court him—Frank was also, down deep, a somewhat lonely person.

A revelation that both surprised, and even saddened her there remained even more discoveries likewise in store concerning the young laddie in question, able at last to divert her attention from those white plaster hands having such a powerful hold on her.

Taking note of those other nearby items next to them she discovered as well articles of a more sacred nature, telling her even more about this special new man in her life. The closest of these a black leather-bound tome with Hebrew lettering engraved upon it in solid gold leaf, other such articles of a similar religious theme were likewise gathered there in the immediate vicinity.

These included such items as a navy-blue yarmulke with silver trim, a glistening bronze menorah possessing nine branches... decorated with a blue Star of David on its trunk... and a close-by tri-dee photo in which she could make out two women, a man, and a little boy no more than 12 or 13 years old.

Standing all together with the front of a synagogue serving as backdrop to the familial gathering, all five individuals dressed in what was clearly formal attire—both man and boy wore yarmulkes just like that on the shelf before her, the two women wearing likewise blue and white prayer shawls upon their heads.

And even though the small boy in the picture was at least ten years younger than her present escort, there was no mistaking him for anyone else but Frank Weller himself.

Not only that but Gloria was just as certain the man standing in back of young Frank, hands upon the handsome laddie's shoulders, was no doubt his father, one of the women positioned on either side of father and son just as likely the little boy's mother.

****

Completing her little tour of Frank's apartment with a brief inspection of his kitchenette, Gloria soon heard the door to his private chambers open... then close... making it back into the living room area just as he rounded the hallway corner, appearing at the opposite end of the room from the passageway beyond.

Giving his current attire an appreciative once-over, Frank wore now both a pair of dark blue pants and matching pullover turtleneck sweater accessorized with a pair of black shoes and belt—Gloria finding his outfit to be just like his place of residence; simple, tasteful, and most assuredly masculine:

"You look really nice", Gloria blurted out all at once, saying the very first thing that came to mind. Pleased with his overall appearance it wasn't until later her usual inhibitions emerged once more to the immediate surface.

"Why thank you, Dear Gentlewoman. Very kind of you to say", Frank accepted with a gracious smile and little bow all his own:

"And I hope you didn't mind the extended wait, but it always takes a while to change out of that work suit of mine", he then offered by way of simple explanation:

"Biggest hassle is actually storing it away each night so it doesn't end up with any creases, or wrinkles in it", he rambled on: "My new boss is a real stickler when it comes to how her waiters look working the floor".

Not really caring all that much for either the clientele, or his new boss at 'The Dark Room', Frank had already come to the definite conclusion he was better off at his former place of employ.

And to heck with the resulting decrease in both pay and benefits!!!

"Hey, no problem! As it is I was really enjoying looking around", Gloria assured him, her eyes wandering back yet again to the many examples of Frank's creative genius arrayed all about them.

Following her attentive gaze there was no mistaking the emotional impact his work had upon the impressionable young gentlewoman practically devouring each piece with her very eyes:

"So I see you've been admiring my little collection", Frank smiled once more, releasing from within his date a veritable torrent of unconditional praise.

Insisting he could make a fortune just selling his work, Gloria's gushing soliloquy on how brilliant he was ending only after some time to come, it was praise Frank found both gratifying and even humbling at the very same time:

"Well, to be perfectly honest, several friends and I do rent a converted studio down in the storage sector of the city where we produce a few modest pieces we actually sell from time to time at various art fairs", Frank confided once able to get a word in edgewise:

"Yet even so we all have other jobs, usually raising only enough money from our artwork to pay for the loft and other sundry expenses. After all you must keep in mind we create because we love to. It's not something we do for money.

"And when it comes to these pieces gathered here, I could never sell them: Give them maybe to someone I really care for, someone I really love, but not just sell them for money. I know it sounds a bit trite, a bit cliché, but it would be too much like selling my own children".

Having no problem understanding what he was trying to say, Gloria realized it was pretty much the same with her and her love of engineering, creating and designing new technologies, while likewise working with her hands in their practical application.

Even if she never secured her position with *'Project StarChild'* Gloria would still have accepted any job—anywhere—allowing her to pursue her consummate love of the mechanical sciences.

The pay didn't really matter!

It was just her good fortune that the same profession she loved so dearly ensured her as well a bright future in the area of financial security.

"I know what you mean", she assured him in a positive tone of voice: "It's the same with me and what I do. Even though my work isn't really all that pleasing to the eye when compared to what you do, it still gives me all-the-same a similar sense of inner satisfaction".

"I thought you might understand", Frank smiled, no delay, none at all:

"And I wouldn't be so sure about your kind of work not being so pleasing to the eye, or even moving to the soul. Technology can also possess a certain artistic beauty all of its own, especially when it's the product of someone like yourself who clearly loves what she's doing.

"After all, look at your reaction to my car", he added with a sly little wink.

"You have such a wonderful way of looking at things", Gloria marveled, her admiration sincere: "Of course I could already tell that from just looking at your work. Especially this piece".

Saying that she then reached out an appreciative hand, gently brushing the carving of the two hands, wedding bands included, with her fingertips.

"Ah, yes", he smiled, warmly: "I could tell from the way you were looking at it just moments ago you were quite taken with it. A perfect example of what I was talking about when I said it would be too much like selling my children… how I could only give it to someone I truly loved, really cared for… someone I know for sure would love it as much as I".

"Yeah, love", Gloria spoke up this time in a more hesitant voice, her face beginning to cloud up, her eyes taking on more of a distant look:

"I just want to let you know that I've really enjoyed our time together in so many ways I never thought possible before. I never realized that just being out with a man, just talking to a man, could be both so stimulating and even satisfying at the very same time.

"This date has turned into a real eye-opener, and I just don't want it to ever end…

"But unfortunately, I know it has to…

"But how?

"What I mean is… well… the point is I think you're really attractive, really sweet, and really, really intelligent, but all the same I just don't think I can… you know …" her voice trailed off before finding the courage to add further:

"I know this was supposed to be an all-night affair… key word, 'affair'", she giggled nervously; "and deep, deep down I really want to, but …"

"Wait a minute", Frank interrupted her with raised hand, realizing they reached at long last that dreaded moment in their short time together demanding all the tact and sensitivity he could possibly muster:

"I think it best if we sit down when having this particular discussion", he suggested, indicating the plush couch in front of the just-as-large picture window—that transparency looking out on both bright city lights as well as the stars far beyond Chiron's now transparent dome.

Turning her gaze in the direction Frank indicated Gloria peered out at the city during its present night cycle, Demeter's frozen surface visible beyond that.

"I think I'll have a drink after all", Frank announced: "How about you?"

"Sure", she muttered absent-mindedly, rounding the coffee table between her and the couch, taking a seat.

"What would you like?" he asked, making his way instead to the nearby kitchenette.

"I don't care", Gloria sighed with a wan little smile: "It doesn't matter. Whatever you want is fine by me".

Chapter 26

"THE BRIEFING"

Catching the ag-pod from deck's B-6 to B-5 Jenniboni made a special point of arriving in the senior officer's conference chamber next to her office at least fifteen minutes before the actual meeting itself.

Taking a seat in her rightful place at the head of the rectangular conference table Jenniboni was, true to form, the first to arrive—the second putting in her timely appearance being StarChild's elderly Chief Medical Officer, Dr. Eartha Wei-Chang:

And following her at six minutes to the hour the next Dept. Chiefs to make their grand entrance were Lt. Cmdr.'s Straker and Marlowe, the rest bringing up the rear soon thereafter—all of them, to a single woman, wearing similar expressions of mild confusion.

Calling the meeting to order once everyone summoned there took a seat, Jenniboni wasted no time recounting all those revelations made known to her earlier that very same day in Admiral Sellers' office.

Beginning with the message from Alpha-Centauri this quickly led to the Prime Arch Matri's impending arrival tomorrow night, how they were all expected aboard her private cruiser where, hopefully, more light would be shed on the matter. Only then did Jenniboni inform everyone present of their new departure date, how they were expected to leave on the 15th instead of Friday, March the first.

Including how they might be facing an actual combat situation with hostile alien forces, using that as a springboard to discuss further the extra provisions requisitioned just hours before, explaining why Stasha wasn't there for this very important briefing. Hearing all this Naomi was about to pose some questions of her own, beaten to the punch by StarChild's rather curmudgeonly chief surgeon:

"That at least explains all those extra medical supplies piled to the very rafters in my sick bay as we speak", the elderly Asian gentlewoman grumbled cantankerously in her usual fashion: "Heaven only knows how long it'll take to sort it all out".

Even while Jenniboni viewed the other woman as an excellent doctor with a skilled bedside manner, unable to think of anyone else she'd rather have see to all her medical needs, her occasional disrespect for proper authority rankled nevertheless at Jenniboni's inborn sense of proper protocol:

"Correct, Doctor", Jenniboni's almost tart reply came at once, clearly irritated: "As Chief Medical Officer I'm sure you'd agree it's better to play it safe when dealing with any potentially dangerous unknown such as what we're facing here. Correct?"

"Yes Ma'am. Point taken", Eartha humbly acknowledged, feeling quite put in her place.

"Please, Commodore, if I may?", Naomi spoke up, choosing that very same moment to strike while the iron was hot.

"Yes, Ms. Marlowe?"

"Forgive me for asking, but does this mean we won't be able to get the teleportation units up-and-running before our new time of departure?"

Expecting her dedicated Chief Engineer to bring up this particular subject right from the very get-go... and at her earliest convenience, too... Jenniboni's lips curled upwards ever so slightly, a subtle smile, even while delivering the bad news:

"Yes, Ms. Marlowe; I'm afraid so".

"Excuse me for saying so, Ma'am, but if the danger we face is as severe as you suggest, I don't see why the High Command can't wait until all our shipboard systems are completely operational before sending us on our way", Naomi nonetheless persisted in the face of obvious defeat:

"The way I see it teleporters would be extremely beneficial given the new parameters involved now in our current mission".

"I'm sorry Ms. Marlowe but, once again, I'm afraid you'll just have to wait for further details until our meeting tomorrow aboard 'Stellar-One' with the Supreme Mother", Jenniboni practically apologized, sympathizing with the other woman's apparent frustration:

"Otherwise I have nothing more to offer by way of explanation".

"I beg pardon, but, if I may", Frances availed herself of this chance to address her commanding officer. Regretting the fact she didn't know better her chief security officer on a more personal level the tall, thin woman now speaking her mind impressed Jenniboni as being both an excellent officer and tactician.

So much so that, next to Stasha, she trusted in Frances Straker's professional expertise and superior abilities most amongst her senior personnel. Based on her personal record Jenniboni chose Frances right from the very start to serve as both StarChild's second officer and 'third-in-command', following just Stasha and Jenniboni in both rank and position.

And on a totally unrelated matter, Jenniboni was likewise intrigued to see the erstwhile Ms. Straker wearing her long, raven-black hair flowing freely down about her shoulders instead of up in that severe bun she usually wore it in.

A definite improvement in Jenniboni's opinion, granting her a more approachable, less intimidating appearance. Mustn't have had enough time to put it back up in its customary do upon returning from shore leave.

"Yes, Ms. Straker. You may".

"Thank you, Ma'am. With all due respect to Lt. Cmdr. Marlowe, I don't really see the teleporters as making all that much of a difference. Not if the danger we face is as serious as our superiors seem to believe. To be perfectly honest I can see no practical means by which we can defend ourselves against the obvious alien numbers they seem to expect.

"Therefore I was wondering if it's safe to assume our mission will be one of pure reconnaissance, resorting to actual combat only on the remote chance our being there might actually be discovered", Frances pressed on… no trace of either worry, or consternation in either voice, or manner… only a sincere display of true professionalism.

"I'm afraid I can't answer that question to your satisfaction, either", StarChild's C.O. confessed, wondering that very same thing herself:

"As in the case of Ms. Marlowe all I can officially recommend is that you wait until aboard the Supreme Mother's private vessel tomorrow for further clarification concerning such matters.

"Unofficially, however, I would assume our mission to be one of a more convert nature while, at the very same time, preparing for every possible eventuality. If that's of any help to you, Lt. Cmdr."

"Yes, Ma'am", Frances nodded in perfect understanding.

"Good, then. Any more questions, Gentlewomen?"

"Just one, Commodore".

"Yes, Lt. N'dhambi?"

"I was curious as to where in Lt. Cmdr. Marlowe's jurisdiction you wish 'Services' to deposit the extra drone probes requisitioned so Engineering can fit them with the added weapons likewise requested?"

"I suggest you consult with both Lt. Cmdr.'s Marlowe and Straker on the allocation of such supplies after this meeting, seeing as it will be their particular departments handling all such refits.

"Likewise StarChild is hereby placed on permanent communications blackout until further notice; no communiqués unauthorized by either myself, Cmdr. Nikarov, or Lt. Cmdr. Straker allowed to leave the ship".

While this last order applied to everyone present, Jenniboni directed her steely gaze towards one Lt. Phyllis Matthias in particular when making this specific announcement. As StarChild's Chief of Communications it would be her unique responsibility above all others to ensure total compliance with this singular command decision.

"What about any incoming messages from Base Central?", came the young officer's immediate reply.

"All incoming messages will also need to be cleared by myself, Cmdr. Nikarov, and/or Lt. Cmdr. Straker", Jenniboni instructed, changing the subject soon thereafter, focusing now her undivided attention upon yet another of her senior personnel.

"Admitting Lt. Cmdr. Straker has a valid point regarding our inability to combat such superior forces that might await us upon reaching Alpha-Centauri, that still doesn't mean we shouldn't at least do our best to ready ourselves for any possible contingency", Jenniboni insisted, leaving no room for further debate:

"Therefore, while both Engineering and Security go about preparing our ship-to-ship defenses, Security and Planetary Exploration will likewise join forces in an extended effort to effectively co-ordinate internal defenses should the need arise.

"And while I'm all-the-same aware Exploration personnel already possess basic combat training, I want them to report to either Lt. Cmdr. Straker or her deputy, Lt. Baynes, for more extensive refresher courses".

"Does this mean 'Planetary Exploration' will be allocated to Security as a mere extension of their defenses", Lt. Cmdr. Toni Oftesfs, Chief of that department, asked in an uncertain voice suggesting just a hint of annoyance.

Anticipating all along that Ms. Oftesfs would make such an enquiry without any considerable delay, Jenniboni was just as ready with an otherwise reassuring answer. Besides being a consummate nature enthusiast bordering on the fanatic, the muscular young black woman at the table's opposite end could prove equally territorial where the myriad concerns of her specific department were involved.

One of the many qualities contributing to her being such an excellent officer, this was something with which Jenniboni could easily relate:

"No. Each department will remain independent of the other. All-the-same, though, I still recommend both you and Lt. Cmdr. Straker get together; arrange a suitable schedule by which you can best co-ordinate your efforts", Jenniboni advised still further.

"Yes, Ma'am", the other woman expressed her understanding, Exploration serving as backup to Security should the need arise.

"Excellent", Jenniboni continued in further hopes of clearing the air least any future misunderstandings likewise cropped up: "In that case are there any other problems, or concerns anyone here wishes to discuss before I officially declare this meeting at an end? Anyone here have anything further she wishes to get off her chest?"

It wasn't long after asking Jenniboni found herself greeted with an otherwise positive round of either "No, Ma'am"; or "No, Commodore"; allowing Jenniboni a renewed sense of hope for the first time since her earlier conference with Admiral Sellers just that very same morning.

"Excellent, Gentlewomen! In that case you all have your duty assignments and may leave all your various progress reports with Cmdr. Nikarov.

"That's all! Dismissed!"

Chapter 27

"GLORIA"

Returning to the living room area with a tall, cool glass of something orange in each hand—beads of condensation forming already on the outer surface of each crystal-clear container—Frank handed Gloria hers before taking a seat on the couch off to her immediate right:

"What is it?" she asked with just the slightest hint of concern.

"Just a wee bit of vodka with a whole lot of orange juice", he was quick to assure her, noting Gloria's apprehension in the subtle way she sniffed at her drink in hand:

"Don't worry. I only put in a little. What with all my experience in bars I've learned how to mix a drink so it will help brace you while not getting you drunk…

"I thought you might be able to use it".

Taking a tiny exploratory sip from the glass she held onto so tightly without even realizing it, Gloria finally relaxed her guard. Smiling after what seemed like an eternity, she continued on from where she left off only moments ago:

"As I was trying to say before I really like you a whole lot, and our time together has meant more to me than you can ever imagine, but I just can't sleep with you. It's not that I don't think you're really, really attractive", she was quick to add, fortifying herself with yet another small hit of liquid courage:

"It's just that I'm not ready yet for that kind of serious commitment in my life. I really hope you're not disappointed in me".

Relieved to learn she felt this way, Frank realized also an urgent need to word his reply very carefully from then on out. Fearful she might misconstrue such apparent relief as a sign he found her unattractive nothing could be farther from the truth, finding her instead *very* desirable!

All-the-same though, Frank was just as confident such physical intimacy at this early stage of any relationship was a grave error in judgment. Leading in most cases to nothing but eventual pain and ultimate heartache, neither of them was suited to such casual liaisons:

"Not at all. I could never be disappointed in someone as noble and unselfish as yourself", Frank was quick to reassure her: "I respect your feelings in the matter and agree it would be way too soon for either of us".

"Exactly!" Gloria let loose with an almost explosive burst of sheer delight:

"I've always felt the same way myself, but didn't know if you'd think any the less of me for doing so".

"Never!" he vowed: "Truth be told I think even more of you for feeling the way you do".

"Great", Gloria sighed, a burdensome weight lifted magically from upon her shoulders: "You don't know how happy I am to hear you say that".

"I think I have a pretty good idea how you feel", Frank smiled in complete understanding. Nodding, his pleasant expression soon disappeared however hearing her very next words:

"It's just that I've always admired Naomi for her ability to pick up men so naturally", she explained with another wee sigh, envy registering both loud and clear in both face and voice: "I've always wanted to be just like her, to get on so famously with the opposite sex".

"Oh, honey; don't ever wish you were more like her!", Frank groaned outright, concern mingled with an overwhelming sense of immense pity: "I can understand how you might admire her for her technical expertise, but *please* never tell me you want to be more like her when it comes to how she treats men!"

"You don't really care much for her, do you?" Gloria asked in a shy, hesitant, voice: "I could tell something was up back in the bar but was afraid to ask what it was all about".

"As far as I'm concerned the '*great*' Naomi Marlowe is nothing but a selfish, conniving, manipulative, insensitive 'KALBA'!", Frank spat in bitter reply, hurt resentment rearing momentarily its ugly head. Often were the times he wondered why StarChild's chief engineer didn't just buy herself a 'mandroid' and be done with it.

Sure they didn't have the same intellectual or emotional capabilities as the real thing, but it was with another bright flair of acidic scorn Frank couldn't imagine Naomi caring as much about what existed either above a man's shoulders ... or in his heart... as much as what clearly existed between his legs.

And as un-conversant as she was in the Hebrew tongue, Gloria still needed no translator to realize her immediate superior had nonetheless been insulted.

Startled by such vehemence from someone otherwise so gentle in his sensibilities, her first natural inclination to likewise shrink away from the angry young laddie beside her. Retreating into the well-padded armrest behind her, the contents of her drink almost sloshed over the rim of her glass onto the black leather couch upon which they sat.

And seeing this reaction on her part Frank lamented his sudden, regrettable lack of control:

"As far as I'm concerned you're ten times the Gentlewoman she could ever hope to be", Frank hurried forth in a more tender, soothing voice realizing right thereafter he owed her further explanation for his sad loss of temper:

"I guess it's no secret Naomi and I share a somewhat sad and sordid past, having probably guessed that much already. Therefore I guess I might as well come clean with you even further.

"That's if Naomi herself hasn't already bragged about the whole affair.

"Yes! It's true that she and I slept together but, no matter what she might have told you to the contrary, it was a brief affair only. After I learned what she was all about I refused to have anything more to do with her:

"So I guess it's now my turn to hope you don't think any-the-less of *me*", he added, confessing after this to everything he swore earlier to never speak aloud.

Yet even while disclosing all that transpired, detailing how he found himself a victim of Naomi's persuasive charms, Frank felt it only fair in his user's case to freely admit his own blame in the matter—the weak smile as he proceeded further a poor disguise at best for both the obvious remorse in his voice and regret in his eyes.

However, while accepting the blame that was just as rightfully his, wrapping up all the loose ends concerning his past and present relationship with the erstwhile Ms. Marlowe, there was nevertheless one thing Frank refused to divulge: Never *ever* would he tell the young woman listening to him with such apparent sympathy how Naomi blackmailed him into their current little get-together, certain as he was learning this would cut poor Gloria to the quick.

Needless to say Frank didn't want her walking away with the erroneous belief that the *only* reason he went out with her was coercion. Heaven only knew what such an assumption would do to her already fragile ego, believing that the only way she'd ever get a man to be with her would be against his will.

And feeling for her part the pain in Frank's eyes as surely as if it were her own, Gloria reached out an understanding hand. Resting it gently upon his chest, she struggled to hold back sympathetic tears. Brimming with compassion for the hurt visible in his eyes she tried to comfort him as best she could:

"Ohhh, no. I could never think badly of you. Not ever! And I swear Naomi never said a thing. *I promise*!! I'm so, very, very sorry!"

"That's all right", he managed a more positive front this time around, taking her tender, caring hand in his: "I didn't tell you all this just to gain your sympathy, appreciated though it is. The only reason I really told you all this is to discourage you from further wanting to be more like *her*, especially when it comes to how she treats men!"

"Yeah, I guess so", Gloria smiled in return: "Although I still can't help but wish I was at least as beautiful as she".

"See; there you go again", Frank shook his head, grinning ruefully: "Can't you see that you're already just as attractive as she, if not even more so!"

"You really think so??"

"Yes! I really think so!" he insisted, resolute and determined.

"How do you mean?", she practically begged him in hopeful, eager anticipation.

'Fishing for compliments, huh?' Frank couldn't help but smile within:

'Well, why not!', he decided not unkindly, concluding it was high time she heard the absolute truth from someone:

"Well… to begin with you have bright, beautiful, sparkling eyes, full lips, and a very sweet, open, honest face", he confided out loud, listing one-by-one with obvious enthusiasm each of her positive attributes:

"Not only that, but you also have a cute little button nose, well-defined cheekbones, and an adorable smile so full of purity, innocence, and life it's absolutely radiant with a special life all its own.

"And to top it all off you have really fantastic hair so full-bodied and luxurious with a rich, lustrous, colour and healthy glow all its own".

Unable to resist the urge to do so after having said all this Frank then reached out an exploratory hand. Running gently his fingers through silky brown strands he set as he did so Gloria's heart all aflutter. Blushing with embarrassed delight, leaning into his tender touch, she encouraged him in her silence to continue what he was both doing and saying:

"In fact I even find the way your glasses give you a look of wide-eyed innocence quite appealing. Highlighting your already exquisite facial features, they lend you as well a most fitting intellectual air while the few freckles you have scattered across both your nose and rosy cheeks give you a fresh, youthful, girl-next-door quality", he grinned.

Diverting his attention from Gloria's dark brown hair complete with sable sheen, he brushed instead each individual freckle with playful fingertips. As he did so Gloria experienced yet another rush of sheer pleasure run throughout every excited fiber of her being. Her already rosy cheeks turned a bright, cherry red full of absolute delight as Frank continued listing all that she had going for her:

"And if all that's still not enough for you, you also have a very attractive figure—subtle, svelte, and very feminine that could never be mistaken for manly. You are definitely all woman, and a darned attractive one at that!" he concluded on a most emphatic note:

"So there's no need for you to go about wishing you looked more like Naomi Marlowe. Nor should you go about wishing you were more like her when it comes to her way of handling men.

"The way I see it you're already quite special just the way you are right now, possessing both a lovely blend of intelligence, innocence, and humour complete with a special knack all your own when it comes to handling men— relating to them on an individual, emotional basis Naomi could never hope to in a million Martian years—even though this is your first time actually out on a date with one".

The positive sensations welling up within began to both wither and die soon enough though, overcome by feelings Gloria neither desired nor found herself able to curb. An emotional knee-jerk reaction to what followed they were feelings such as self-pity, righteous indignation, and a certain amount of acidic scorn all her own hearing Frank's very next words:

"In fact I really hope you don't mind me offering you just a wee bit of personal advise seeing as we've known each other for such a short time, but I honestly think you should forget trying to be like others and just try being yourself", Frank ventured forth with uncharacteristic timidity, fearful how such advise might be taken.

Not all that well as things turned out!

"All you really need is a little more self-confidence, a more positive outlook, while learning also to be more assertive. Once you…"

"Don't you think I know all that??" Gloria cut him off, hurt and defiant, a slight whine of self-pity creeping as well into her voice…

Filled with an overwhelming sense of utter self-loathing, a bilious contempt for everything about her own self at that particular moment, this was an unfortunate side of her personality she neither cared for, nor found herself able to control.

"Don't you think I know what I need?!" she continued in that same bitter, acrimonious vein, taking out on the hapless young laddie next to her all those latent feelings of both rage and self-recrimination pent up now for so very long:

"But it hasn't been easy, let me tell you! So if I just so happen to be lacking self-confidence and assertiveness, you can blame it all on the miserable life I had growing up back on Mars and not on me!

"First off there were those miserable…"

However, instead of making any feeble attempt to mollify her, divert her from such impassioned protests on her own behalf, Frank just let her rail on, allowing her to use him as a target for all those repressed emotions already bottled up for way too long.

Understanding her need to vent at long last, Frank just let her unburden herself before continuing as before:

"I know, hon. Naomi told me all about your past and, after listening to what she had to say, I can really appreciate how you must feel after all those years of negative reinforcement, all the self-doubt you were no doubt forced to endure", he carried on in that same understanding vein, his gentle eyes taking on an even sadder cast:

"All I'm trying to say in my own clumsy way I suppose is that your past is now all behind you.

"Now it's time to start looking within yourself, forget what was, and begin exploring all the inner strength you clearly possess, all the wonders you have dwelling already within you, while exploring likewise what lies beyond the known worlds.

"After all, I honestly doubt you would have come as far as you so clearly have at such a tender age if you were really such an obvious loser. It must have taken a lot of inner strength, true grit, and boundless confidence—not to mention superior intelligence and skill—to be made Deputy Chief Engineer of Womankind's first ever starship.

"I honestly doubt your superiors would have granted such a position of obvious power and authority to such an equally obvious non-entity".

"I know you're right", Gloria confessed at long last, following that up with a despondent little sigh: "But knowing it in your head versus knowing it in your heart are two different things".

"Try looking at it this way then", Frank offered, cupping with affection her chin in his hand: "If you were really such a major loser I would have never agreed to go out with you in the very first place, much less allowed this little date of ours to go this far.

"As-a-matter of fact, to be quite honest, I truly believe the only reason you've never been out on an actual date before this is because you simply lacked the confidence to get out there and circulate. Don't forget that although, if interested, we laddies might drop hints in a gentlewoman's direction, it's still up to the woman in question to pick up on all our signals, do the asking".

Upon hearing this Frank's last words came as a cruel breeze sweeping away mental cobwebs. Masking until now previous recollections, Gloria remembered with growing regret more than just a couple of boys back in school who did drop in fact such hints in her direction.

And not so subtle ones at that!

Every missed opportunity suddenly apparent, seen in a whole new light, Gloria couldn't help but feel a sudden stab of remorse over lost fortunes that could have been hers for the asking, bitter pangs of shame.

It was a hurt impossible to hide, a remorse so profound, Frank had no trouble seeing it in her eyes as Gloria looked deep into his:

"What's the matter?"

"How could I have been so stupid; so blind?", she answered him with a question of her own, asked in a voice full of simple self-contempt, self-recrimination, explaining what had her so upset.

"I hope you'll forgive me for saying so, but it sounds like you brought at least part of it on yourself by buying into all their lies and abuse", he finally answered her... softly... sadly:

"Not surprising after the way your uncle had you cowed for so long. The other kids must have figured you for an easy target".

Glassy-eyed, Gloria just sat there—motionless—staring ahead of her into pure nothingness. Lost in her own private world for several moments the vacant expression on her face started to worry Frank, feelings of concern growing soon into a definite sense of alarm.

Almost ready to take her hand in his, hoping to awaken her from this veritable trance-like state, it was only then Gloria began at last showing some sign of conscious awareness. From trembling lips he heard her mutter something about wasted opportunities, berating herself for all those years she spent living as such a coward, letting others convince her she was so utterly worthless:

"It's all true! Everything! God, I was such a lousy, stupid..." she gasped in jagged, hitching breaths sobbing openly at long last, bitter tears inching their way down flushed cheeks. Gently relieving the weeping woman of both her drink and eyewear Frank lay each on the nearby coffee table, reaching out to her, enfolding her in a tender embrace.

Drawing her to his side, Gloria's head resting upon his chest, warm tears penetrated the soft fabric of Frank's pull-over, nuzzling up as she did to him with her right cheek.

Stroking tenderly stray hairs from her face it was then Frank felt Gloria slip her arms around his waist in a timid, needful embrace all her own, clinging to him like a small child seeking comfort:

"It's all right, Sweetie", he cradled her in gentle, nurturing arms: "Take all the time in the worlds you need: Just let it all out".

Holding on to him in lonely desperation, letting Frank's comforting presence support her both physically and spiritually, Gloria could feel his one hand begin to gently rub her back, the other stroking her head. Admitting to herself it actually felt good just to be so near him, even those tears she shed helped her feel better inside, flushing out almost all the pain and hurt of past events better forgotten.

Feeling a subtle hint of embarrassment having him see her in such an awkward state, feeling more than a trifle naked, it was nevertheless a comfort realizing there was someone else with whom she could be so vulnerable... someone who'd never judge her for doing so... making her feel less like a woman.

Truth be told it was the first time in her entire life Gloria could actually remember anyone with whom she could actually let her guard down so completely, her entire life spent in secret longing for that special someone who'd hold her in their arms just like this. And now that her dream had finally come true Gloria was just as reluctant to relinquish that comforting warmth of his body now close to hers, someone with whom she could share all her pain and suffering.

Even after her tears subsided, ceasing for the moment their cleansing flow, it still felt so beautiful just being in a man's arms like this, sharing such intimacy on a level both physical and even spiritual at the very same time. As if awakening from some horrid nightmare after all these years it was only then she realized something she always hoped was true to begin with—that Uncle Les was the freak of nature, *not her*!!

Resting her cheek upon his chest, weeping replaced for the very first time with a brilliant inner glow of utter peace... true contentment... Gloria heard Frank address her yet again in that same reassuring tone as before:

"And for what it's worth, I also want to let you know I think you're totally off the mark about being such an unfeminine coward".

"Huh??"

Tilting her head upwards at long last she looked yet again into those smiling, affectionate eyes of his:

"I'm serious", he assured her in answer to her probing gaze, wiping away from searching eyes those last remaining tears, guiding her back once more into a more seated position:

"You have much more strength of spirit, a lot more courage, than you give yourself credit for: Please! Let me finish", he insisted when it seemed she was about to contradict him: "The way I see it is that it took a lot of courage, strength, and self determination to not only survive the kind of abusive past you endured, but to actually persevere as well in the face of such adversity, to succeed in life as you so obviously have.

"And if all that doesn't help consider this as well: All those other girls who tormented you over the years are probably working now at boring, menial jobs while you're sitting here wearing that grand uniform leading the exciting life you always dreamt of... a new life full of fame and glory... about to embark upon the greatest adventure in Womankind's herstory doing something you really love".

"And let's not forget how I'm also out on the town with a really handsome, wonderful and exciting laddie", Gloria added on a more positive note, grinning from ear-to-ear, taking with giddy delight Frank's every word to heart.

"Well... modesty prevented me from saying so", the laddie in question smiled an impish grin: "But I'm glad at least *you* made mention of the obvious".

"And this uniform really does look good on me", Gloria asserted even further, gazing down with renewed confidence at her green and gold attire.

"Simply exquisite", he agreed, giving her an approving wink: "As they say, 'living well is the best revenge', and there's no denying that you're living very well indeed!"

"And you should see my formal dress uniform", Gloria continued in the same proud vein: "It has a full crimson cape, high peaked cap, and ankle-length dress".

"You know what. I'd really love to see that", Frank assured her, quite intrigued, sincere awe apparent in both voice and face:

"Maybe you could model it for me sometime", he suggested, hoping she'd pick up on such a not-so-subtle hint.

"I bet you cookies to krodits that Trevor Hanson would definitely take notice of me if I were to return to Mars wearing it", she speculated under her breath, a calculating gleam in her eyes, just loud enough to be heard by her date.

"Trevor?" Frank asked in truly innocent curiosity: "Was he someone you knew back in school?"

'Great going, Bonehead!' he silently scolded himself, seeing Gloria's face cloud up immediately thereafter:

'You really put your foot in it this time', Frank chewed himself out even further, apologizing at once for dredging up what seemed a clearly painful memory.

"No, that's all right", Gloria was just as quick to reassure him, wearing all the same a bittersweet smile: "Besides, it was a long time ago. I'm feeling a lot better now. Especially after meeting you!"

"Why, thank you", Frank beamed, both touched and relieved at the very same time.

"You're entirely welcome", Gloria smiled sweetly: "The way I see it we've only one problem left now".

"And that would be..." Frank enquired with just a trace of puzzled concern.

"What're we going to do about Naomi? She's expecting this to be an all-night thing and I just know she's going to..."

"No need to continue", Frank stopped her, mid-sentence:

"We both know what Naomi's like and what she's expecting to happen here", he finished for her, disgust evident in both voice and face.

As far as Frank was concerned, Gloria should tell her immediate superior to take a flying leap into deep space, sans space suit, out of one of StarChild's no doubt many airlocks.

No point though in suggesting that to the timid young gentlewoman sitting beside him. The way things stood for the present, he realized she still lacked the confidence to go up toe-to-toe against the likes of Lt. Cmdr. Naomi Marlowe.

With this in mind Frank realized it was up to the two of them to put their heads together, see if they could come up with a practical solution to Gloria's dilemma—an obvious way to get Naomi off both their backs once-and-for-all.

And no sooner had Frank reached such a conclusion the answer likewise came to him swift as lightening, appearing out of thin air with such crystal clarity he could have kicked himself for not having thought of it even earlier.

"Don't worry, hon", he comforted her with a triumphant grin: "All we have to do is sleep together in my bed—fully clothed, of course!—and tomorrow you can honestly tell her we slept together".

The short-lived sense of overwhelming relief Gloria felt hearing this proposal soon vanished though, along with the brief smile she wore, another important consideration coming as well to mind.

His magnanimous offer might save her good name but what about his?

"No", she sighed, all the same reluctant to refuse: "That's very kind of you, but I couldn't! What about *your* reputation??"

"Don't worry about all that", Frank smiled wistfully in her direction, moved by her natural gallantry while unable to deny the truth:

"I appreciate your thoughtfulness, but it doesn't really matter. Don't forget that, as far as Naomi is concerned, my honour has already been compromised", he reminded her with a certain hint of remaining bitterness:

"Besides, it would be well worth it to teach her a thing, or two", he added, reaching out to gently caress Gloria's cheek in loving recognition of her chivalrous attitude.

"Only if you're absolutely certain", she accepted with a troubled frown, herself still uncertain.

"*I am*!" Frank insisted, quite emphatic, before Gloria thought of yet another little problem still:

"Great", she giggled with all due modesty: "But I think it only fair to warn you that I've never been able to sleep fully clothed".

"Simple enough", Frank offered in good humored reply:

"We'll just sleep in our underwear. I do assume you're at least wearing a bra and panties?" he enquired even further in playful repose.

"Of course", she blushed, all the while grinning.

"All right, then", Frank declared in a most decisive manner: "All settled. I'll just wear my briefs then and, in the morning, we'll just…"

Before finishing that particular thought Frank's voice trailed off quickly enough into oblivion, a wicked smile appearing instead, accompanied by an equally cunning twinkle in his dark brown eyes. Almost able to see actual wheels turning around and about in his head, Gloria pleaded straight away to be let in on whatever clever scheme it was Frank had in mind.

"Oh, yes! That sounds perfect!" Gloria gave his plan her unreserved approval, laughing gleefully while doing so: "I can't wait to see her reaction. I just hope we can actually pull it off".

"Don't worry: Revenge is a great motivator", Frank chuckled at the very thought of Naomi's face in the morning.

Basking for the moment in the simple pleasure of each other's company they finished their drinks, sharing yet another brief moment of perfect silence. It was Frank who first rekindled conversation, asking out of complete left field if Gloria knew how to dance.

"Sure. At least I know how", she informed him in greater detail: "I've taken lessons and know all the moves. I've just never had anyone with which to share them before".

This last true confession on Gloria's part gave rise to a disappointed little sigh... pouting... clearly regretting that missed opportunity, too.

"Great!" Frank leapt in at once with both feet, ready to remedy this particular oversight on her part: "Because I think a little dancing would be a perfect way to round out an already wonderful evening".

"Are you asking me to dance?" she asked, both eager yet bashful at the very same time.

"No", Frank assured her with a mischievous little grin: "**You** are going to ask **me!** After all, it's your duty as the woman to ask the man. Just look upon this as an excellent opportunity for a little 'on site' practice: That and I'm curious what you might be like on the dance floor".

"Sure", Gloria agreed quite readily, quickly warming to the idea of being in charge: "To be perfectly honest I've always wanted to put those lessons to some practical use. I guess they're the one and only thing Uncle Les was right about when he insisted I learn."

"Well, then, I guess that just leaves the proper atmosphere. What do you say to a little dancing in moonlight?", Frank smiled, reaching for a small console sitting on the coffee table alongside a neatly stacked pile of ei-pad periodicals.

Putting her glasses back on as he did, Gloria was at a momentary loss when the regular lights above went off, replaced instead by a luminous silver glow, pale shafts of silvery moonlight coming from across the room. Seeking out its place of origin she was even further startled by the unexpected sight of a bright lunar orb suspended just a scant meter or so above the floor, right across the room from where she sat.

Recognizing it from residing on Earth during her academy days, it's only natural satellite, the fact it was only a perfectly rendered hologram appearing in Frank's 3-DV set made it no less romantic. It was as if the young laddie at her side managed to whisk it somehow from across the entire System for the sole purpose of their own private amusement.

Bathing them in shimmering moonlight sweet, slow dance music coming from the set served as well to further enhance the intimate mood already provided by its gossamer glow.

"Fantastic!" Gloria whispered, truly awestruck; enraptured.

"I hope you don't mind, but I used to love slow-dancing by the light of a full moon back on Earth", Frank offered by way of further explanation.

"Not at all!" Gloria barely managed with breathless wonder: "It's lovely!"

The sphere before her filling the entire cube, it looked even larger than the original had from Earth's own nighttime surface.

"Great: I'm glad it meets with your approval. So now that the mood's set I guess that leaves just one more matter to be taken care of ", Frank declared with both a sly grin and slight raise of his left eyebrow.

"Absolutely", Gloria agreed, his meaning well taken. Rising from his side, assuming a proud, regal stance she stood before him with head held high, reaching out to him with extended hand, palm up:

"Would you do me the very great honour, Dear Laddie, of permitting me this dance?", she then asked in a most gracious manner, smiling down upon the source of her renewed confidence with an increasing sense of her own womanhood.

Now his turn to be enraptured Frank was totally swept away by the sudden transformation in the dashing young starship lieutenant standing before him, deeply impressed with both her noble bearing and growing sense of assertiveness.

Appearing more confident in herself, more in charge of not only herself but those around her, she even seemed taller. Captivated by her chivalrous posture Frank looked up now at her full of admiration, placing his hand in hers:

"I'd be most delighted to accept your gracious invitation, my dear Gentlewoman!" he likewise allowed with sincere reverence.

Leading him out into the middle of the living room floor Gloria wasted no time in placing her right arm gently but firmly around his waist, her other hand against the small of his back. Guiding him along in a quite effortless fashion, she skillfully maneuvered him in whatever direction she so desired.

'Those lessons were definitely worth whatever they cost', Frank mused within, completely taken by her eloquent style, the natural ease she so clearly demonstrated when it came to her ability to lead.

Swept off his feet in more discernible ways than just one, gazing into each other's eyes, the admiration she likewise witnessed in his filled Gloria to overflowing with a joyous new belief in herself she never knew before—the growing passion in her eyes leaving Frank equally dumbstruck by what a radiant beauty she truly was.

Even the way each individual moonbeam was reflected back at him in her glasses lent Gloria's eyes a sprightly sparkle... a burning intensity he found absolutely breathtaking... what came next a surprise both as welcome as it was unexpected.

Gently tilting her head to the side while guiding him as well through a likewise graceful turn it was then Gloria pressed warm, soft lips to his, granting her unsuspecting dance partner a sweet kiss both passionate and innocent in its pure intensity of genuine feeling.

"I hope you don't mind, but it just felt so right", she almost begged his understanding. Withdrawing her mouth from his she tried to gage Frank's reaction, looking deep into his eyes. With the honey-sweet taste of her lips still upon his Frank was at a momentary loss for words, having never experienced such a kiss despite the numerous attempts of others to penetrate in similar fashion his outer defenses.

Burrowing deep into the very depths of his innermost self it left him stirred to the very core of his being. Unable to imagine ever being moved quite that way ever again, he was left feeling both shaken and giddy at the very same time.

It wasn't until finding the precise words with which to convey what he felt so deep within Frank reassured the young woman he didn't mind in the least— not at all—confessing aloud it was probably the most beautiful kiss he'd ever known during all his otherwise young life.

Unable to miss the veracity of what he said in either Frank's expression, or the way in which he addressed her with such humble awe, Gloria sighed with contented delight, resting her cheek upon his shoulder, his resting gently against the back of her head.

Enjoying the soft silkiness of her hair against his skin Frank breathed deeply of its fresh, subtle spring scent; Gloria reveling likewise in the close proximity of the handsome young laddie in her arms... his trim, elegant form pressed up against hers... the heady aroma of his mild cologne leaving her quite intoxicated... each consumed by their growing affection for one-another.

And so it was they held onto each other in a close, tender embrace gliding slowly about the room through silvery moonbeams—neither aware they both wore the same expression of loving bliss as the subjects depicted in all of Frank's work.

Chapter 28

"HOME AT LAST"

Pre-programming the automatic coffee maker for Jenniboni's breakfast the next morning, Andrei likewise set about preparing her a light meal in anticipation of her return from StarChild. What with the children already in bed for a while now, he decided to spend his remaining free time preparing for her imminent arrival.

Yes, he'd seen the message she left him on their answering machine earlier but, after the hard day she no doubt had, Andrei wanted Jenniboni to have something nice waiting for her when she finally got home.

Having heard countless times before his wife's caustic remarks on the quality of duplicated food, Andrei just couldn't bear the idea of the poor woman having nothing on her stomach after a trying day but what she, herself referred to as 'mediocre slop'.

Wrapping up the final touches on her late supper it was only then he noticed by the kitchen clock it was already 22:30 hours, hearing at that very moment the apartment door open at last.

Making his way out of the kitchen with all due haste he asked at once how her day went, seeing the answer in her eyes the very moment he reached up, kissing her on the cheek.

"It was more hectic than expected. Some new situation aboard ship that kept us all pretty preoccupied", Jenniboni explained with a weary little sigh, clearly bushed, instructing him in a somewhat firmer voice she didn't want him pursuing the matter any further.

Having no need of further warning Andrei, as per his wife's request, likewise dropped at once the entire subject.

"Would you like something to eat or drink?", he asked instead, changing the subject.

"Maybe some herbal tea", she accepted, too exhausted to deal with much else: "Nothing more".

Dragging her limp body past both husband and the nearby dining room table, Jenniboni continued on a shaky course for the darkened corner of the room furthest from the kitchen, plopping herself down in one of the plush easy chairs near the 3-DV set, opposite the couch next to J.J.'s closed bedroom door.

"Oh well", Andrei smiled, nonchalant, greeted on his return to the kitchen by the ready sight of the dinner he prepared in honour of Jenniboni's return.

Deciding instead to save it for a mid-day snack the next day, he slipped it into the refrigeration unit before preparing Jenniboni's tea. Serving it to her where she sat in gloomy silence, he then took a seat on the aforementioned couch.

Sipping daintily from the edge of her proffered cup, resting her feet on the coffee table between them, the pain she was clearly in was obvious in the very way Jenniboni scrunched up her face, the very act of raising her legs a burdensome task. Even in the semidarkness all about them her obvious discomfort didn't fail to capture Andrei's keen notice. Attentive as he was to her every need, it elicited from him a worried query as to what the problem might be.

"Nothing much ... really!", she assured him with a dismissive little wave of her hand, able to detect the immediate concern in his attentive voice: "Just sore feet. That's all".

"Would you like me to rub them for you?"

"I'd appreciate it very much if you did", Jenniboni confided: "But only if it's no trouble".

"No trouble at all!", he promised with a pert little grin: "If the smell proves too much to handle I'll just hold my breath until passing out from the effort".

"Why you cheeky little scamp!" Jenniboni laughed, wide-eyed with startled amusement. Feeling more relaxed doing so she could feel already the stress and strain of the day-gone-by begin to seep away, her spirit beginning to feel free at last.

Clearing ample space between them with which to continue Andrei shoved to his right the low table upon which Jenniboni's tired legs rested just a moment before, almost bumping it into the nearby 3-DV unit before kneeling at her feet.

Setting the stage for what came next he eased with tender, loving care her boots from each foot, placing them off to the side. Free at last from the restrictive confines of her just cumbersome footwear Jenniboni reveled in her newfound liberty.

Wiggling her toes around and about in a quite lazy fashion, the cool air against her lower extremities struck her as being a complete Godsend.

"Mmmm, that feels downright fantastic", she purred.

"And I haven't even started yet", Andrei chuckled, placing her left foot upon his lap. Applying tender therapeutic pressure against the arch of her sole with the ball of each thumb, he massaged as well the top of her foot with a gentle back and forth motion of his fingers.

Moaning aloud in sheer delight Jenniboni's pleasure was quite audible. Closing her eyes she leaned back into the ample cushioning of the easy chair behind her.

"That feels soooo good I wish you could go on doing that forever", she giggled: "I bet I could turn a tidy little profit renting you out as a professional masseur".

"You? Jenniboni Kaye Saphira?? Proud defender of tradition and staunch champion of absolute propriety!!", Andrei exclaimed, feigning complete moral outrage:

"You're the very last person in this whole wide System I would ever imagine willing to endure either the shame, or the utter social stigma of having a husband work outside the home for actual pay".

Laughing uproariously at the very idea of his always proper wife even considering such an arrangement, Andrei decided right then and there to have a little fun of his own, having her on for a change:

"All right: You've got yourself a deal", he played along, pretending to eagerly accept her impetuous proposal: "I'll ask your father to baby-sit the children after school while I start looking for work first thing tomorrow.

"Unfortunately though, that still leaves us with the teeny, weensy, little problem of who we're going to get to do everything I do around here on a permanent basis. After all I don't think it's fair to expect your father to shoulder such a continual burden, and there's no one else I can think of we could ask.

"No. The way I see it we'll definitely have to hire someone to come in here and do all the housework. So, my dear, I'm afraid that takes care of your 'tidy little profit' right then and there. Sorry".

"Hmmm? Maybe it wasn't such a good idea after all. Pity", Jenniboni pouted, affecting a disappointed little frown: "After all, there's nobody alive in all the worlds who could ever do all the wonderful things you do around here each and every day. I'm afraid this family just couldn't hope to survive on its own without you".

Despite the otherwise jocular manner in which she said this there was no denying the likewise equal amount of abiding love, and sincerest respect, in every word she seemed to otherwise speak in jest. And hearing all this in what his wife just said Andrei experienced a warm glow of consummate satisfaction; immense, immediate gratification. Feelings dissipating soon enough however hearing what came next, that one question he hoped above all else to avoid:

"And how was your day, today, Sweet-pea?"

All things considered Andrei hid well his uneasiness, answering her with the expert aplomb of a seasoned politician caught in the middle of a bare-faced lie. Assuring her all went well without missing a beat in the foot massage he was still conducting, he avoided likewise any mention of all the "unpleasantries" both he and J.J. encountered just that day.

Rationalizing away the increasing sense of simple guilt he felt over this particular lie of omission, Andrei actually tricked himself into believing it was for her own good—convincing himself it wouldn't be fair to burden her any further given the rough day she already had, her current state of utter exhaustion.

Lying even more so to himself than her however, Andrei's stubborn refusal to face the simple truth continued unabated. Denying the obvious fact there was no way he could ever see himself revealing to anyone the torment inflicted on him in that horrid place, there existed in his own mind's eye the equal belief that the mere mention of those events would prove as traumatic as the actual experience itself.

Once more Andrei chose to handle it 'like a man', make believe nothing really happened, suppressing all that transpired so even he need not deal with it!

TOTAL self-denial!!

Glad to think at least one of them had a good day Jenniboni found it a comfort knowing all was well at least on the home front, attentive to both her husband's oral report and physical ministrations. Removing her left foot from his lap once Andrei finished with his little narrative, she replaced it with her other, wiggling her toes at him indicating her desire.

Readily understanding, repeating the same procedure as before, it wasn't that subtle hint that left him puzzled so much as Jenniboni's next request. Opening her eyes she then instructed him with a cozy little smile to select from his extensive wardrobe something really nice to for tomorrow night:

Peering up at her from what he was doing Andrei recognized quite well that tone from past times when she had a special surprise in store for him sure to please. It was that playful, mysterious, fun-loving, 'I-know-something-you-don't' voice reserved for very special occasions. And following her lead yet again Andrei also realized from past experience Jenniboni couldn't be rushed when in this particular, playful mood revealing all in her own good time.

"And why is that, dear?", he asked, full of innocent curiosity.

"Because I'm taking you somewhere very special tomorrow", she strung him along in that same playful fashion: "Somewhere I'm sure you'll want to look your best".

"Is it a formal occasion?" he allowed, excitement mounting.

"Oooo, I'd definitely call it formal".

"Soooo, I take it there'll be a lot of other important people there besides your own 'dear self '?", he teased as well.

"Very important!" she planted the hook even deeper, increasing the suspense.

"Who", he practically begged: "Please tell me".

"All right, Sweetie", she smiled with tender mercy upon the confounded young man kneeling before her: "In addition to both Admiral Sellers, my senior officers, and ourselves there'll also be none other than 'Ms. Anita Carlin' herself! How's that for important?"

Believing for a moment he didn't really hear her right he just gazed upwards into her lively eyes so full of mischievous good humor, confusion written all over his face. Swiftly replaced with startled delight Andrei soon enough found his tongue yet again:

"You mean the *Prime Arch Matri*? *The Supreme Mother* herself ??", he gasped in utter disbelief, staring at her with eyes as round as saucers.

"Yes, indeed", Jenniboni giggled, pleased beyond measure with his reaction: "And you, my dearest, will be attending her aboard 'Stellar-One' himself. If that's of any interest".

"Of course it is", Andrei exclaimed, joyful to the max: "I can't believe I'm actually going to meet the Supreme Mother herself aboard her very own private cruiser. Why is she even coming here in the first place?"

"Well... she apparently wants to discuss a few last-minute details with command personnel concerning our up-and-coming mission".

Too excited to notice now Jenniboni's own evasive manner, letting her deliberate avoidance of any particulars slip him by, Andrei likewise forgot all about rubbing her foot. Instead he chattered on at a rapid pace about picking out his absolute best outfit, asking Raoul if he could mind the children tomorrow evening, whether or not the P.A.M.'s husband would also be there, and what the other men might be wearing.

"I thought you might enjoy that little tidbit", Jenniboni grinned sweetly:

"After all I know how much you've always admired her".

"Wait a minute there", Andrei came back at once with a similar chortle: "If memory serves right you also lent a hand down at her campaign headquarters".

"Touché", she readily accepted, both wife and husband avid supporters of Humanity's present leader right from the very get-go. Starting some eight years ago with the last Commonwealth elections the young couple were married for a little over two years when the last Prime Arch Matri passed away, her Vice-Prime holding office until a general election could be held.

And of all the assorted candidates presented for consideration by the masses the one whose political credentials impressed the starry-eyed Saphira's most was one 'Ms. Anita Carlin'. Gaining rapid popularity during previous years as 'Planetary Matri' for her own home world... Venus... she gained likewise a sterling reputation during later years, serving as well on the 'Supreme Council of Matriarchs'.

So much so that Andrei wasted no time asking Jenniboni's permission to serve as a volunteer down at her cross-town campaign headquarters—all this in addition to an already hectic schedule as both a full-time househusband and volunteer tour guide for the 'Susan Canfield Central Art Museum' back in St. Tammy City.

Being at a time before J.J. was born Jenniboni saw no harm in allowing him to do so, likewise joining him at campaign headquarters whenever her own busy schedule as a Lieutenant Protector allowed.

While true men themselves were forbidden to hold political office, they were nevertheless allowed to support their candidate of choice, therefore granting them an active part in the voting process. Guaranteeing men a fair voice in how women run Human affairs, the vote was their primary means of having a say in Womankind's immediate future, expressing likewise their own particular concerns.

Already a civic-minded young man to begin with, quite a little activist when push came to shove, this only added fuel to Andrei's fire given Anita Carlin's efforts on behalf of the male populace. Right from the very beginning of her political career the future Prime Arch Matri proved herself already sensitive to both their particular problems and issues as men.

Nor had his enthusiasm dimmed any since then, still an avid supporter.

Smiling down upon his eager countenance, quite gladsome over his exuberant reaction, Jenniboni was filled to the brim with boundless love for the young man now at her feet. Happy to see him so excited he always made coming home something to look forward to at the end of each and every day, realizing at that very moment just how much she'd miss him this coming Friday when time to say good-bye.

Almost spilling the beans right then and there concerning the advancement in StarChild's departure date, Jenniboni nevertheless held her tongue. No need to break his heart at such a joyous time. He'd find out soon enough when finally allowed to tell him after the gathering aboard the Prime Arch Matri's official cruiser tomorrow.

"Oh, yes: I almost forgot", she announced further, suddenly, something else likewise occurring to her: "The party starts at 20:00 hours, which means we'll have to leave here no later than 19:00 hours. Do you think you can be ready by then?"

"Sure thing! No problem!"

"I had a feeling you'd say so", Jenniboni grinned, wriggling her foot in silent request he continue as before. Surrendering to wild impulse it was then that Andrei lifted it to his face. Kissing her right above the arch the loving devotion behind this otherwise jocular move was obvious.

And seeing this in the equally rakish grin he bestowed upon her Jenniboni leaned forward to affectionately tousle his hair, experiencing however a sharp, sudden pain between her temples while doing so. Unable to hide it from Andrei's immediate notice she visibly winced, shutting her eyes in a tight squeeze, retreating back into the cushioned chair in back of her.

"What's wrong?" Andrei looked up, full of alarm.

"No need to fret so", she grimaced through tears of pain already forming:

"Nothing serious: Just a pesky little headache I've been trying to shake for the last few hours".

"Well, no need to suffer any further", he offered, sympathetic; "because I have the perfect solution. "So why don't the two of us just retire to the mistress bedroom and, after you take a pain pill, we'll both get undressed and climb into bed while I …"

"Oh honey", Jenniboni interrupted him with an apologetic smile and groan all her own: "You know how much I love making love with you. Any other night for sure, but not tonight. I'm just too beat".

"Needless to say I appreciate both the compliment, not to mention the rain-check, but that's *not* what I have in mind", he informed her, grinning, with a little shake of his head.

"Really?", she couldn't help but ask. Eyebrows arched she was curious to say the very least: "So what do you really have in mind?"

"That's for me to know and for you to find out", he teased her this time in his own mysterious way: "However, for the moment, why don't you just retire for the night, take a pain killer, and slip into your most comfortable nightie".

"I must admit you have me intrigued", she confessed once Andrei helped her up.

"Good. In that case just scoot", he advised; "and I'll be joining you in a few minutes after tidying up out here".

****

Closing the bedroom door behind him Andrei turned down as well the lights to their lowest setting, depositing Jenniboni's abandoned footwear from before in the nearby walk-in closet. By the time she emerged from their bathroom in the night attire he suggested Andrei was now stripped down in the dimly lit room beyond, turning down their bed by the time Jenniboni joined him.

Watching him fold back the covers to his usual exacting standards, arranging the pillows with equal care against the headboard in a makeshift backrest, Jenniboni noticed her hairbrush sitting also on his nightstand alongside where he now stood. Having at last her first inkling what he was really up to she smiled a dreamy smile, sure she'd no doubt enjoy what he had in mind:

"So what am I going to use for a pillow seeing as you've taken them all for yourself ?", she giggled once Andrei climbed into bed, reclining against those very cushions in question.

"That's easy, Love: Me!" he informed her, a sly wink, instructing her likewise to have a seat.

Doing so he spread wide his legs, patting the bed itself between them, positioning her between firm, supple thighs. Submitting without reservation to whatever he asked, Jenniboni followed his instructions to the letter, resting her weight on shapely buttocks while sitting there, her back to him.

Hands resting on the bed at either side of her, Jenniboni's lips formed a pleasured smile as he removed her brush from its resting place, proceeding to brush out her long, silky, honey blonde hair with slow, soothing strokes.

Giving voice to an unabashed sigh of utter content, former aches melting away at long last, Jenniboni felt a growing sense of utter comfort transform previous suffering into an equal sense of sweet relief—Andrei gaining almost as much pleasure from brushing out his wife's full, wavy, hair as she.

Always looking forward to those special occasions on which she'd allow him to do so he always viewed her hair as looking like spun gold, the simple joy he derived from performing this particular act truly sensual on his part. Burying many times his face in the golden strands, he would breathe deeply of her fresh, sweet, honeysuckle scent.

However, tonight, his only desire was to bring a swift and immediate conclusion to her discomfort, banishing at once her pain.

"That feels sooo wonderful!", she confided with a throaty moan; Andrei continuing with one hand to brush her hair, stroking gently her scalp with the other, before announcing it was time to move on.

Setting the brush to one side of them, reclining once more into the pillows behind him, it was not long after this Andrei drew her even closer, Jenniboni resting her back against him, head against his manly chest:

"Now just close your eyes and let yourself go completely limp", he guided her with a loving touch through what followed, supporting her body with his.

Able to discern her muscles relax even further, Jenniboni's head resting still against him, Andrei could tell quite rightly she was ready to proceed even further.

Massaging her temples with gentle fingertips it was then he began to serenade her in that deep, mellow, soothing voice of his, grazing both her forehead and the bridge of her petite, graceful nose with a feathery light technique.

Responding well to such tender, therapeutic caresses Jenniboni's divine countenance relaxed even more so, a tranquil expression spreading quickly across her sweet face. Lulled into an even deeper state of absolute peace yet another happy sigh escaped full, parted lips.

Humming now a soft, sweet melody Andrei went back again to rubbing her temples in lazy, circular patterns. The almost hypnotic techniques he employed having their desired effect, he coaxed his wife into a quite profound, restful sleep. And as Jenniboni slept against her husband's bare chest he reached out to the right, drawing the bedcovers he folded back just a short while ago over the superb swell of her luscious breasts.

Taking great care in doing so least he disturb her slumber, Andrei froze in mid-reach upon noticing her stir ever so slightly, proceeding as before when finally sure she was still quite asleep.

Granting then his wife a devoted kiss upon her peaceful brow once sure she was all nestled in for the night ahead, it was only then Andrei allowed himself the similar luxury of leaning back in sweet repose. Doing so he followed her into sweet, gentle, tender oblivion.

Chapter 29

"THE MORNING AFTER"

Ascending towards wakefulness at a slow, leisurely rate Frank gradually discovered himself lying on his back; a warm, reassuring presence cuddled up alongside him in the near dark.

It was during that fleeting moment between utter rest and total awareness, that special domain where confusion reigns supreme, Frank found immediate cause for alarm, unable at first to recall the young gentlewoman snuggled up next to him under the sheets.

However, before panic could take immediate hold over his startled brain, the day before came flooding back like an incoming tide. Finally able to remember all the memory of good times spent in the attractive, young lieutenant's company filled him with a joyous sensation.

Frank's left arm resting against her back, his hand resting on the tender swell of her left hip just above the waistband of her white cotton panties, Gloria's head lay lightly as well on his shoulder, arm draped across his chest in a most casual manner.

Wandering about in that pleasant dreamland she still occupied the soft exhale of her warm, sweet breath against his chest felt like the gentle flutter of a butterfly's wings against bare skin: An experience both innocent and sensual at the very same time.

Tilting his head sideways to better glimpse her sleeping person, studying the young woman's face in tranquil repose, Frank felt his previous affection for her blossom as well into something even deeper, richer, and more meaningful than even he could've ever imagined.

Even in this state of total relaxation he could nevertheless see in her delicate, girlish features that oh-so unique combination of innocence, chivalry, intelligence, and even strength-of-character he noticed there just the day before.

Appealing to all his higher senses beyond measure Gloria Greensley was, in more ways than just one, unlike any other woman Frank ever knew possessing a rare blend of both purity, integrity, vulnerability, and courage he found quite compelling.

Sharing his bed with a woman for the very first time without sex being involved it occurred to him just being here with her was a more satisfying experience, more stimulating, than the mere physical relationships he shared with the previous two.

Realizing like an immediate revelation from on high he'd actually fallen head-over-heels in love with her why her more than all the others—a woman who, until just yesterday, meant nothing more to him than a mere mercy date?!

Not that it really mattered.

No turning his back now on how he felt, unable to deny his true feelings once known, the 'damage' was done! And realizing this Frank wished with all his heart this precious moment could last forever.

Unfortunately that just wasn't meant to be, crushed to learn what time it really was. Glancing soon to his immediate left it was already 07:00 hours according to the nearby timepiece atop of his small nightstand, its luminous face visible in the almost semi-dark:

Time soon for Naomi's pending arrival.

No sooner did StarChild's Chief Engineer come to mind Frank wanted to be sure all was in perfect readiness for later. Looking forward with vengeful glee to the hopeful success of his wicked little scheme, he felt it only proper to make her squirm more than just a little after what she tried to do.

Able to forgive Naomi for virtually blackmailing him into this little date in light of how it actually turned out, it wasn't that which left Frank feeling so nonetheless peeved, so increasingly resentful.

NO!

It was what Naomi attempted in the unfortunate case of the young officer next to him that left Frank feeling as he did. Such as she should never be hounded into giving up something oh-so dear to them such as their innocence, pressured into something they were just not ready for.

In Frank's humble opinion it was high time Naomi learned—once-and-for-all—both purity and innocence weren't qualities one either trifled with, or so rudely scorned.

"Ahtsmot zakhl!" Frank cursed the mistress-mind responsible for all this. Deciding right then to wake Gloria up from her present slumber he did so as gently as possible. Removing at the very same time his hand from her hip, he ran instead his fingers ever so lightly through her sleep-tossed hair:

"Come, Glory: Sorry, but it's time to get up", he whispered. GLORY?? Where in Heaven's sweet name did that come from?

No matter!

It still felt right regardless where it came from, knowing her as such from then-on-out in his deepest, purest, heart-of-hearts.

A dreamy smile appearing as well on Gloria's lips at the very sound of Frank's soft voice gentle fingertips stroked now his bare chest in lazy circles. Moaning with pleasure while caressing his naked flesh Gloria's expression of unbridled pleasure turned soon enough into one of startled concern, sleepy eyes wide open at last. Suddenly aware of her situation, propping herself up on her right side, Gloria noticed at once their state of near undress:

"Oh no! We didn't... I mean did I... well... you know... take advantage of..." her voice trailed off in a timorous stutter, sudden remorse over assumed transgressions.

"No need to fear", Frank helped sooth her anxious spirit, understanding what troubled her so: "You were a decent gentlewoman all night, not trying anything improper".

Hearing this, an immediate sigh of blessed relief practically burst forth from grateful lips as Frank spoke even further:

"Well... now I've helped put your worried mind to rest may I also suggest we get ready to put 'Operation Rattle Naomi's Cage' into full effect", he offered with a devilish little grin.

"For sure!", she agreed with utmost enthusiasm: "Sooner the better! So when do we start?"

"Whoa, there", he chuckled with similar delight: "All in good time...

"First though, I think it might be a good idea for you to shower while I prepare a little something for you to eat", he added in the same merry vein, pointing towards the bathroom door off likewise to the near left of where they lay in bed:

"And while you're doing that I'll likewise slip your clothes in the sonic wash. All should be in complete readiness by the time you've taken care of 'other matters'".

"I can't let you do all that", Gloria insisted with a renewed sense of guilt, afraid to impose on Frank's generous nature any more than certain she already had.

"Don't concern yourself any more than necessary", he insisted, understanding once more her problem: "My pleasure, believe me".

"I don't know", Gloria hesitated yet again, albeit this time less reluctant:

"As is I already owe you so much".

"Nonsense", he assured her, full of firm resolve: "Truth be told, it's I who really owe *you* for such a wonderful time yesterday. I really enjoyed myself. Honest!"

No denying his sincerity in either voice or face Gloria couldn't help but blush in silent reply. And captivated by this reaction on her part Frank was likewise moved, having rarely met anyone who blushed quite so easily. Made her look almost like a pixie, like something fresh out of some ancient fairy tale:

"So, if that's all settled, I suggest we get started. Just slip into the bathroom and toss out your bra and panties for me to wash".

"But won't I need them for when Naomi arrives?"

"No", he patiently reminded her: "The whole idea is to make her think we went 'all-the-way' last night. Of course she'll be expecting me to be wearing something when I answer the door, knowing quite well she'll never see *me* naked again.

"At least not as long as I have any say in the matter! Even these briefs will be less than she's expecting.

"However, by that very same token, you'll have to look completely relaxed and 'all-natural' for our little plan to work. So, with that in mind, I think it's just about high time we get on with the day ahead. Agreed?"

"Sure thing", Gloria gave his suggestion her glad approval.

Accepting his advice with willing exuberance Gloria made her merry way into the other room, Frank gathering up her uniform at the very same time from the far opposite corner of his bedchamber.

Removing it from over the back of a wooden chair replete with dark green upholstery, he substituted it for just his own attire neatly draped there.

Waiting outside the bathroom door for what remained of her laundry Frank averted his eyes least he by chance compromise her privacy. Soon hearing the shower beyond the young gentlewoman's underwear followed not long thereafter, flung across the bathroom threshold to the waiting laddie standing nearby.

Collecting them up from where they landed on the floor in a tiny heap Frank added them to the rest of her former attire, departing straightaway to make her breakfast first. A diabolical grin appearing Frank looked forward with eager anticipation to the new day about to unfold—the wee, little performance he and Gloria were about to stage for Naomi's 'benefit'.

****

Retrieving Gloria's just-laundered outfit from the wash Frank went about arranging as well the last touches to her breakfast tray, folding her freshly laundered attire in a tidy stack while the beneficiary of this special treatment went about drying herself off.

Having completed her shower only moments before, climbing back into Frank's bed soon thereafter, it wasn't long after doing so Gloria could hear Frank's steady approach down the hall, having just rearranged the covers over herself.

Almost right outside the partly open bedroom door Frank made sure to give Gloria fair warning he was about to make his grand entrance, delaying a good minute or so before pushing his way into the room beyond. Hands already occupied, he used instead his left shoulder.

Doing so it was only when crossing the threshold Frank was able to spot Gloria sitting upright in the very center of his bed, bedcovers held securely in place under her arms drawn up over perky, rounded breasts. Observing how Gloria's hair was clearly mussed up from a hasty toweling off Frank couldn't help but feel it a nice little added touch, window dressing for the festivities rapidly approaching.

"That smells Divine", Gloria beamed at her host soon upon arrival, tray in hand, her crisply laundered uniform draped beneath a pristine cloth napkin slung over his right arm. Standing off to one side Frank tilted the metal blue server he carried ever so slightly in Gloria's direction, allowing her to further inspect its assorted contents.

Licking her lips in ravenous anticipation she devoured with eager eyes the

195

food arrayed before her with such loving care, unaware until just that very moment how hungry she really was.

Making a complete and thorough survey of each item arranged before her with such exactitude the first to capture Gloria's immediate notice was a plate of scrambled eggs alongside a medium-rare breakfast steak, dollar pancakes, and a small stack of lightly buttered toast:

A variety of other equally appetizing items likewise gathered about, these included a transparent bowl heaped to the rim with freshly cut strawberries, heavily laden with liberal amounts of velvety whipped-cream handmade just moments ago:

"My, but that looks tasty", she readily accepted: "I never even realized how hungry I was until just now".

"Good, then. In that case why don't you just drop those sheets so I can place it before you"?

"Are you sure?", she asked in a shy little voice.

"Yes… of course", he smiled, understanding: "You needn't worry for sake of embarrassing me. Don't forget that I've been down that particular road before. Besides, I don't want any of this getting all over my clean sheets. That and it will help if Naomi sees you topless".

"Point taken", Gloria giggled. Lowering the sheets right thereafter, she gathered them around her waist instead:

"With all this wonderful food here she completely slipped my mind".

"Reasonable response", Frank conceded, placing the tray in hand directly before her, its legs suspending it mere inches above her thighs:

"And I hope you enjoy eating it as much as you apparently do just sniffing at it, dear Gentlewoman"; he added with an equally jocular grin. Arranging the silk napkin draped over his right forearm on the bed beside her, he explained further what other breakfast delights awaited her pleasure:

"I didn't know if you prefer coffee, tea, or orange juice in the morning, so I brought you all three. Likewise I didn't know what kind of syrup, or spread you might like on your toast and pancakes so I brought a little of whatever I had.

"And just in case you don't like your coffee or tea black, there's also some cream and sugar here and here", he explained, pointing out two small silver containers resting next to the cups of hot brew sitting atop China saucers.

"This is all so, so…", Gloria didn't know quite where to begin, lifting a fork-full of scrambled eggs to eager lips:

"I don't know how to ever thank you", she added upon further reflection, having just devoured her first mouthful.

"No need", Frank allowed, granting her a dismissive shrug:

"I enjoy watching people enjoy their food. Maybe that's why I became a waiter", he added, giving it some further thought as she studied with appreciation the meal before her. And spotting right away the aforementioned berries and cream, Gloria reached for them with similar gusto.

Thwarted in her efforts however, the nearby laddie removed them from her immediate grasp:

"Sorry, hon; but they're for later when 'you-know-who' arrives. I guess I should put them out of temptation's way", he grinned with wry amusement, setting them atop of the dresser bureau next to the bathroom door.

"Oh, yeah, I forgot", she humbly confessed with an awkward grin all her own: "They just looked so good I didn't know what I was thinking".

"No problem", he assured her, laying out the clothes he still held over the corner chair.

"It's just that you're such a fantastic cook. NO! Make that an honest-to-Gosh chef!", she insisted soon thereafter with waxing effervescence, expounding on this basic theme in greater detail—Frank returning once more to the nearby dresser, searching for something in particular within its various sliding compartments:

"Maybe that's what you should consider doing instead of being a waiter. Prepare food instead of just serving it!"

"To be perfectly honest I've given it serious thought on more than just one occasion", Frank confided after a silent moment's deliberation: "The only downside being that I honestly doubt I could withstand the heat of a professional kitchen for over eight hours straight.

"Then again there's also the added consideration I like being out on the floor too much, dealing on a one-to-one basis with the actual customers. Hard to do that while cooped up all day in some hot, hectic, overcrowded kitchen all day.

"No, I'm afraid I enjoy cooking too much to actually think of making a career out of it".

Truly perplexed, Gloria made it quite clear she didn't understand at all Frank's last remark.

"Well, it's like this", he explained in greater detail, still rummaging about his dresser drawers with increasing fervor:

"Some people do what they love as a career, making their career something they actually love. Then you have others who try to turn what's fun into a full-time occupation only to end up hating what they originally loved, no longer finding any joy in it. Fortunately for you you're one of the former, whereas I'm afraid I'm one of the latter".

Able at last to truly appreciate what he was trying to say Gloria couldn't help, but wonder if that was the real reason Frank didn't try making a similar full-time career out of his artwork. Assuring him in all sincerity she understood what he really meant she also found it sad.

"Besides, I prefer cooking in much more intimate surroundings for those I truly care for. More pleasurable that way, actually able to watch them enjoy what I've prepared with my own two hands. Sooo... if you'd really like to see what I'm really capable of in the kitchen, you should come over for dinner sometime soon".

Hoping at that moment Frank's offer was an honest-to-gosh invitation Gloria was nonetheless afraid to ask. Fearful of further rejection she asked instead another question just coming to mind:

"Aren't you going to have anything to eat yourself ? I feel rather guilty enjoying all this wonderful food by myself while you go without".

"No need to fret so on my account. I'm perfectly all right", he assured her, encouraging her to continue as before:

"Ah, found it!", he announced right thereafter, a triumphant gleam in his eye. Talking more to himself than her, he retrieved from his dresser bureau what seemed to be a small clipboard complete with pen and paper.

Returning soon after that to the previous subject at hand, he sat down once more in the same chair as before. Doing so he explained in a somewhat absent-minded fashion how he really didn't care much eating before noon.

Noting his thoughtful expression, penning something unknown on the smallish pad he now held, Gloria couldn't help but ask what it was that had him so occupied, highly intent on whatever he was writing to the exclusion of all else.

"Oh; this?" Frank looked up: "Well, I hope you don't think me too forward or unladdie-like for this, but I just wanted to give you my V-Phone number and address. I realize how presumptuous this might seem, but I'd really like to see you again…

"I hope you don't mind", he added, his turn now to fear rejection.

'Don't mind?? ME???', she rejoiced at the very thought in silent reflection.

More than she dared hope from the very beginning, it was all Gloria could do to manage an even voice when responding.

"Sure: Sounds fine by me. No problem", she assured him. Struggling to maintain an air of pure calm she suppressed a powerful urge to cheer him on.

"Don't worry", Frank sped on in great haste, still worried in light of such blatant impropriety:

"There's no pressure to call. No undue expectations. I'm still enough of a laddie to wait for you to make the first move. I just wanted you to have this just in case".

"Sure", she reiterated as before with the same forced calm, her heart racing all the while with sheer joy.

"Good, then. In that case I'll just slip this in the breast pocket of your uniform behind me. With your permission of course!"

"Fine by me", Gloria radiated joyful acceptance, hearing him sigh with similar relief receiving her reply. Watching him get to his feet Gloria held her breath in wistful anticipation, Frank folding the piece of paper in question.

Turning about he slipped it gently in the right breast pocket of her official green and gold attire. With great care he made sure it was securely shut, clasp well-fastened, least its precious contents might somehow fall out.

Returning then the green jumpsuit portion of her casual dress S.E.A. uniform to its former resting place over the back of his chair, Frank glanced after that in Gloria's direction, observing her finish the last of her meal.

Removing the empty tray from just above her lap it wasn't long after placing it atop of the nearby dresser, right alongside the strawberries from before, they both heard the apartment door-chime ring out from down the outer hall.

"That must be Naomi", he muttered, his voice dripping with righteous disdain.

"I'm not sure I can go through with this", Gloria blurted out, suffering an immediate case of the jitters.

"Fear not, hon", Frank reassured her, sounding quite certain: "If you get stuck just follow my lead. And if it helps any just keep in mind how sweet revenge can be. Not to mention how fun it'll be to mess with her mind".

"Yessss", Gloria smiled now with savage glee, confidence restored: "Bring her on. I'm ready!!"

Chapter 30

"REPRIMANDS AND REVELATIONS"

Waking up with a wee crick in the small of his back Andrei was nonetheless grateful to see a clearly refreshed, energetic Jenniboni going cheerfully about her usual preparations for the day ahead: 'Feeling like a whole new woman' she declared. Helping him up from their bed she bestowed on him a loving kiss full of sincere appreciation.

Watching her from behind make her way into the bathroom it wasn't long after Andrei likewise went about his daily routine, serving the children breakfast before calling his father-in-law.

Agreeing at once to baby-sit his three grandchildren for the night, Raoul wasted no time as well congratulating the younger Saphira man on his audience with the Supreme Mother later that evening. Including his daughter as well when discussing the young couple's good fortune it was then Jenniboni appeared from down the hall.

Resplendent in her casual dress uniform, catching the tail end of their conversation, she paused on her way to the breakfast table just long enough to say hello. Enquiring after her father's well-being she then handed the VP back to her somewhat stiff-and-sore husband.

Continuing steadfast on her way to the table beyond after a brief but pleasant conversation, taking her rightful place at the table's head, Jenniboni was pleased as well to find both her customary coffee and fresh donuts already waiting. In the meanwhile Andrei concluded at last his 'chin wag' with Raoul, joining the rest of his family at the other end of the large dining table.

Consuming his favorite chocolate fudge energy drink at a leisurely pace, taking his own sweet time about it, Andrei would likewise pause while doing so just long enough to keep up his end of the various dialogues taking place around the family table.

Ranging in content from such domestic matters as Jenniboni asking him to clean her uniform from the previous day to how Grandpa Raoul would be sitting up with the children that night, this inevitably lead to the revelation their parents would be visiting the Supreme Mother that very same night aboard her private cruiser.

Naturally awestruck learning this both J.J. and the twins couldn't stop chattering back and forth about how they'd impress for sure all their friends at school with the same, exceptional news flash.

So relaxed, so comfortable, and so content with all that happening around him, Andrei was too busy just basking in the pleasant glow of that familial scene to notice angry storm clouds beginning only now to gather on distant horizons…

First appearing when Tammy asked J.J. if she planned to do any bragging where 'that other girl' was concerned, it wasn't until hearing Jenniboni Sr. ask in all innocence 'what girl' that Andrei first realized trouble was on the way.

Swallowing the last of his morning meal with an elevated sense of approaching disaster, watching his wife polish off the first half of her second donut with a sip of coffee, the sinking sensation in the pit of his stomach steadily increased.

With a clear sense of mounting trepidation Andrei cast a furtive glance in J.J.'s direction. Hoping to gage how she was likewise holding up J.J.'s troubled expression proved she could see as well the approaching brouhaha in her mother's otherwise casual question. The look of matching desperation she gave her father was proof enough she knew as well the 'jig was up'.

"So to what other girl are we referring?", wife, mother, and family matriarch persisted even further in the same unsuspecting vein. Unfortunately it was young Tammy Saphira who spoke up once more in her sister's place, the approaching squall arriving at last:

"Wow, you should have seen it Mommy. I heard J.J. totally beat her up!"

Andrei's heart, already pounding away in fearful anticipation, leapt like a panicked bird thrashing against the bars of its cage when Tommy made matters even worse, adding his own two centi's worth to the general conversation:

"Yeah, I heard she broke the other girl's nose and jaw", he included, quite eager to share all he 'learned' the previous day via the official playground rumor mill: "Blood all over the place! She even got kicked out of school for good!"

"Hush up, the both of you!", Andrei hissed, having already endured more than enough.

Dumbstruck in the presence of such uncharacteristic vehemence on his part they just stared at him with wide-eyed dismay. Unlike yesterday morning both twins paid immediate heed to their father's impassioned orders.

"So young Gentlewoman what do you have to say for yourself in light of such damaging testimony", Jenniboni asked, diverting her attention from the twins' side of the table to where J.J. sat now in nervous anticipation of the very worst:

"You know very well how both your father and I feel about you indulging in such physical altercations".

"But I just had to hit her", J.J. burst forth at long last in her own self-defense: "She was beating up her little brother. Besides, I never broke nothing!

Just gave her a black eye is all!"

His heart going out at once to the little girl to his left Andrei also knew he couldn't just sit there, letting her take the inevitable fall for simply following his own misguided advise right from the very start.

"It was nothing, really", he was quick to speak up, trying to pacify his wife's increasing ire: "Even her principal said J.J. wouldn't be punished for her part in what happened. She just suggested she go home yesterday for the remainder of the day. She was *not* thrown out of school and Ms. Li-Wong was very understanding about the whole affair.

"And, after we both left her office yesterday J.J. and I had a long talk in which she promised to handle herself better in the future".

"Soooo… you knew all about this to begin with?!", Jenniboni proceeded now to interrogate her husband. Glaring at him through narrowed eyes she gave him a frosty stare from the table's other end: "And when, pray tell, were you going to be so kind as to inform me of what took place".

"Well… seeing as the whole matter was finally resolved to everyone's satisfaction, I saw no need to trouble you further with any details concerning what happened", Andrei spoke up with a little smile bordering on the tremulous.

"Sooo… that's what you took it upon yourself to assume, is it?", she continued to glower at him, arms folded across her chest, leaning back in her chair.

"Well, yes", Andrei confided, his resolve now somewhat firmer, projecting as well an additional calm he likewise didn't feel:

"I figured that, since all this was already put to rest, there would-be no additional need to bother you with any further particulars. In the end I decided it might be best to simply let the whole matter drop".

"I see", Jenniboni pressed on, her tone increasingly sardonic: "And may I be so bold as to enquire what penalty our little pugilist is currently facing?"

"Oh, Father said I wouldn't be punished", J.J. leapt in with both feet, giving Andrei an adoring look, before realizing her innocent blunder. Too late by the time she did, the damage already done, she gave her father a look of sincere apology.

"I see", her mother smiled, her previous expression replaced by a look of deceptive, serene acceptance:

"Wellll… since your father has managed to handle this whole sordid affair to everyone's apparent satisfaction, and with such obvious wisdom I might add, I guess there's nothing left for me to say in the matter.

"Therefore, with that in mind, I think it best you children just continue eating while we all forget this entire incident ever took place", Jenniboni added for the assumed benefit of all three offspring: "And when you're all finished with that you can watch some 3-DV until it's time for your father to take you to school. How does that sound?"

"Great!", the twins cheered out loud, giving her suggestion their hearty approval.

"Sounds fine, Mother", J.J. muttered, truly despondent.

Eyes downcast she just stared at the almost empty breakfast dish before her. Feeling more than just a little poorly on her father's behalf, she somehow knew quite well this wasn't the end of it. Not as far as he was concerned.

"Excellent, then", Jenniboni carried on in that same pseudo festive fashion, turning her rigid gaze back towards her husband. Confident he knew what was coming Andrei was almost expecting her very next words:

"Oh, by the way dear, there's a spot on my other uniform back in our room which I'd like to show you. Thought I'd better point it out to you right now so you won't miss it in the wash today".

Getting up from the table without any further ado Jenniboni hadn't long to wait before Andrei, reading her signals loud and clear, followed her obvious example.

Commenting he was sure he could get "that pesky old stain out in a jiff ", both husband and wife made their way back to the mistress bedroom down the nearby hall—Jenniboni leading the way with a tenacious stride while Andrei followed close behind, affecting both a jaunty gait and carefree attitude poorly masking his inner worry.

And as for the beneficiaries of this little show, all three children waited fretfully for the sure sound of their parents' door being shut, daring only then to speak:

"I think Daddy's in trouble", Tommy observed with hushed consternation, their mother's subterfuge having fooled no one at all.

"Of course he is!", J.J. snarled across the way at both her younger siblings:

"And it's all your fault, you two blabbermouths! Why couldn't you two just keep your big yaps shut?!" she practically wept, feeling her own keen sense of guilt concerning their father's present situation.

Seeing how they both withdrew from her anger into the chairs in back of them, both likewise on the verge of tears in response to such utter ferocity, J.J. merely snorted at each with utter contempt:

"Just sit there and don't move", she grumbled further in their general direction, showing them both the same contempt as before.

Too stunned to even imagine crossing the irate young girl on the other side of the table both younger Saphira's remained exactly as they were, their older sister taking right then her immediate leave of each.

*　*　*　*

Ushering her husband across the threshold before her Jenniboni made quite sure the bedroom door was securely locked behind them. Aware that children will always be children, neither father or mother cared at all to quarrel in front of their three offspring.

Given each parent's current state of mind it was understandable they'd feel this way now more than usual, Andrei more fearful of recounting yesterday's events in *'THE DARK ROOM'* than he was of his wife's current anger. And for her part Jenniboni, already worried enough about her new mission parameters, felt her world grow now only more chaotic with this new development at home.

"Before we really get into it I want to first start out by assuring you I've no plans to reverse at all your decision concerning either J.J.'s punishment, or lack thereof ", Jenniboni assured him, remaining quite reasonable in both tone and manner.

"Needless to say we both know what the result would be if I did", she added, turning around, facing him at last.

Thanking her for saying so Andrei understood as well what Jenniboni meant by 'the result'; the possible weakening of his position with the children, fostering within them the perpetual attitude of "Mommy will let me", or "I don't have to listen to you".

Likewise there was also the added burden Jenniboni would encounter were she saddled with being their sole disciplinarian. Worse yet for his wife the children would end up living in nervous dread of her return home as opposed to discipline being handled in timely fashion by their father.

Not fair to either them, or Jenniboni to turn her into an object of fearful expectation in their eyes.

"All the same though I still think we need to have a little talk about including me in such family decisions, problems that might arise—what is, and isn't acceptable conduct!"

"I understand fully", he insisted, "and I explained to J.J. how she mishandled the situation and she assured me it wouldn't happen again".

"I'm **not** referring right now to our daughter, but **you**!", Jenniboni stated most emphatically: "I'm not at all happy with how you handled this entire matter".

"Understood", Andrei felt it better to agree than not. Worried she might dig into the matter even further if he didn't, he worried more for himself than her having to relive out loud **all** that really happened the day before:

"And I'm sorry".

"Excellent", she favored him this time with a sparse little smile.

Suffering already a certain amount of angst, worried over what turned just yesterday into a probable suicide mission from which she might never return, it seemed now to Jenniboni's beleaguered senses all her troubles outside the home were plotting to sully as well this last source of inner refuge she counted on for final sanctuary—her family!

Starting to feel the walls closing in on her this seemed like nothing less than a further betrayal by dumb luck. A betrayal she couldn't help, but take as a personal insult:

"This isn't like hiding a burned pot-roast from me or needing to get the 3-DV unit fixed. This is our daughter we're talking about, not some ruined meal or household appliance.

"But what hurts most is how you've given the children the mistaken idea it's perfectly acceptable to hide important matters from my attention, going behind my back to you.

"Now they'll think it perfectly acceptable to perform with your blessing a complete end-run on me. Can you imagine how this makes me feel, or what sort of position this puts me in? How this undermines my authority with them, not to mention their trust in me?

"I've always respected your right as their father to know when something's wrong. *Never* have I hidden any problems from you, no matter how trivial. Nor have I ever contradicted your rightful authority over them as their father. And I *darn* well expect you to show me the same respect as both their mother and *family matriarch!* ...

"In the end that's what it all comes down to—*respect*!"

Unable to deny the hurt outrage now appearing in her voice alongside the obvious, righteous anger Andrei lowered his gaze in shamefaced avoidance of her eyes, the emotional injury he heard there unmistakable.

Focusing instead on the patch of blue shag carpeting between his feet Andrei could always hold his own in the face of her sometimes fiery temper. It was more the idea of ever hurting, or disappointing her which caused him grief, preferring some angry exchange than feeling the way he did at that very same moment...

No fear now.

Just genuine remorse.

However, mistaking shame for defiance, Jenniboni's mood merely worsened thinking he was trying to ignore her, staring so intently at the floor during her impassioned discourse.

"Look at me when I'm addressing you!!", she demanded sharply, grasping Andrei's chin between thumb and forefinger with a gentle yet firm touch.

Angling his face upwards in her direction it was only then Jenniboni noticed his pained expression. Anger dissolving into mere confusion it was then she asked him at long last to explain:

"First and foremost I need you to believe me when I pledge with all my heart and soul that I *do* indeed respect you very much", Andrei began in a fashion both concise and contrite. Even the idea Jenniboni could ever doubt his manifest respect for her wounded him deeply.

No different than questioning his unabated love for her, seeing as one can't exist without the other, such thoughts inspired an even greater sense of genuine remorse, wounding her so carelessly as well as compromising her lawful authority as rightful head of their little household.

The obvious contrition registering loud and clear on Jenniboni's receptive ears just listening to him inspired a tender smile of clear forgiveness, leaving nothing in its wake but simple bewilderment:

"So why didn't you tell me about J.J. last night when the opportunity first presented itself? Why all this secrecy??"

"I just couldn't tell you. Not then! Not after the way you came home so clearly beat into the ground. Any fool or blind dog could tell you had a really bad day yesterday. That's why I didn't want to add any further worries to those you already had".

Explaining how he wanted to prove himself, showing his wife how he could handle any eventuality that might arise during her prolonged absence, Andrei nevertheless denied her the whole truth. Telling Jenniboni how he didn't want her to lose faith in his abilities he nevertheless refused her any mention of his key reason for deceiving her, the one ugly truth he hoped to keep forever hidden from all—including himself!!

"Oh, Sweet-pea! Don't you know I could never lose faith in you", she promised the angst-ridden young man sitting now on the edge of their bed:

"Especially over something as trivial as some childhood tiff at school. Children get into fights from time-to-time, and I understand how it goes.

"Don't you realize by now just how much I truly admire, and respect the wonderful job you continue to do around here on a daily basis. I've always admired you your intelligence, devotion, and all the loving care you put into every single thing you do for this family.

"Which is why it hurts so much when you don't trust me to have similar faith in you, to believe in you as much as I so clearly do.

"I realize I was tired last night, but… all the same… I'm never too tired to listen to you, to make time for you, whenever you need an understanding ear. All you had to do was tell me what happened, how you solved the problem, and I would have happily left it at that.

"So *please* have more faith in me in the future, and feel free to come to me whenever you *do* have a problem".

Almost crying aloud for her to stop, a sharpened dagger burrowing deep in his heart, Andrei begged her within to leave this one remaining issue to himself, let him bury it so deep out of sight where it could fester and rot in eternal darkness. The very idea of ever sharing that nightmare with his wife filled him with ceaseless revulsion:

"You're absolutely right", Andrei forced himself to look her straight in the eye, just managing with all his might to remain calm despite an overwhelming urge to scream: "And I'm sorry I didn't trust in you from the very beginning, didn't have faith in you. I give you my solemn word it will never happen again".

Momentarily thrown for a loop by something she saw flash by in her husband's clear blue eyes, something faintly familiar, Jenniboni regained quickly enough her composure. Despite whatever it was, it was already gone by the time she noticed it:

"All rightie, then", she reassured him in a soothing tone of voice not unlike a velvet caress: "Let's just chalk this whole incident up to an unfortunate misunderstanding".

"Sure thing", he exhaled… deeply… unaware until that very moment he'd been holding his breath. The sense of certain reprieve Andrei was beginning to experience soon soured though, hearing Jenniboni's next words:

"Even so, there's still just one little thing bothering me I was wondering if you could explain".

"Yes?"

"It concerns the matter off J.J.'s lack of punishment", she insisted, a mite suspicious: "Don't fret. I meant what I said about not reversing your decision. It's just that I'm a bit confused why you didn't even bother handing out a token penalty.

"While I understand how you must have naturally empathized with that little boy she was defending, I just can't help but wonder if there's more to this story than meets the eye. Am I right?"

"Yes, love".

Once again it was there, that mysterious flash in his eyes while answering her. Disappearing once more before she could make a positive identification, it nevertheless struck her as familiar. And its very familiarity was, in itself, a cause for worry.

Convinced he was still keeping secrets from her Jenniboni was by this time no longer angry, only scared. Those keen instincts developed during long years in the Protectorate told her in no uncertain terms something was wrong: Wrong with the one man she so dearly loved above and beyond all others:

Something seriously wrong!

No longer a matter of mere curiosity it was now of prime importance she solve this mystery as quickly as possible—more for his sake she somehow realized than hers:

"I thought so", she persisted in that calm, tranquil, reassuring voice first cultivated as a former Protector for special use with frightened witnesses: "In fact would I be correct in assuming we've reached the crux of the whole matter concerning your secretive behavior".

"Yes, love", he confirmed her initial suspicions all along, his voice growing rather subdued… almost inaudible… while doing so.

"Good", she smiled: "Now, Sweet-pea: I want you to keep in mind your solemn oath and tell me the real reason you've been so secretive".

"Well, I didn't feel it proper to reveal J.J.'s trouble… or punish her… after what happened to me: The little scrape I got into yesterday".

"That's all right, dear. Please continue", she gently nudged him along, aware how clearly difficult this was for him.

Slowly recounting all which befell him just that day before, Andrei began at the very beginning…

Starting with his visit at Raoul's, how he called home to retrieve the messages on their answering machine, he proceeded from there even further, telling her as well about the detour, how his car broke down, and his ensuing search for a public V-Phone.

Noting however his immediate reluctance to relive out-loud what happened next inside the bar itself, Jenniboni felt herself compelled to once more urge him on. Fearful he might stop right then and there in his already halting narrative she pushed him this time a tad more firm:

"So you went into this 'Dark Room' to look for a VP?"

"I had to! I had no choice!", Andrei insisted. Most emphatic at this point, his nervous agitation increased exponentially:

"I couldn't just sit around that laundromat for two hours waiting for theirs to be repaired while J.J. just sat around there all alone in her principal's office all scared and in trouble. I just couldn't!", he almost wept.

Rushing forward to pacify him yet again Jenniboni realized at once what it was that just set him off so:

Or so she thought.

"Shhh, it's all right darling. I'm not mad at you for going into that bar unescorted if that's what has you so worried. I understand completely. So just relax and continue please with what you were saying".

"Wellll… that's when I went in there to use their VP and got into trouble".

"What kind of trouble?" she persisted with dogged patience, so very close!

"Please, dear, couldn't we just leave it at that", he begged her in one, last, final desperate attempt to avoid reliving that ultimate degradation of his very soul:

"It was all my fault anyway so can't we just *please* drop it", he groaned in abject misery…

"*PLEEAAASE*!!"

This had her stymied. All his fault?

Could that have been gilt she'd seen in his eyes all along? No, she didn't think so.

Still, though… what else could have been all his fault?

There was only one thing she could ever imagine happening in some strange bar he could have reason to feel guilty about, only one thing he knew beyond a shadow of a doubt would earn him her complete disapproval. And although completely, totally out of character for the devoted young family man sitting in front of her so was all this furtive, cagy behavior:

"Did they actually serve you alcohol there without any female escort, or supervision? Did you get drunk and do something improper while there? Is that what you're so afraid to confess to?"

The very idea of him 'indulging' was as inconceivable as it was unconscionable. Especially with his little girl in such apparent trouble, waiting for him all that time.

Then again she just didn't know what else to think. Not after his almost frantic, heartfelt confession all this assumed chaos was somehow his fault to begin with. Under any other circumstance her next question would have been fired point blank at him in fiery reproach:

Not so now!

Quite concerned with his obvious emotional duress Jenniboni's inquiry was put forth with nothing more than confused sympathy, perplexed. Too distraught however to hear anything but her actual words the feeling behind them didn't register at all upon Andrei's troubled mind.

Hearing instead nothing but a base accusation his temper soared beyond all limits like a skyrocket launched into the wild blue yonder. Deeply insulted Jenniboni could even suspect him of any indecency, whatsoever, her very use of the word "improper" in regards to his actions of yesterday likewise rankled beyond belief.

No! Not him!!

It wasn't *HIS* conduct which was so terribly out of all moral bounds in that horrid place the day before. The very suggestion such were the case served only to dredge up even further all those feelings of helpless anger, degradation, and utter defilement he suffered from like some festering pustule—some open sore.

"*NO!*" he blew up at long last, red-faced, livid with an all-encompassing rage holding him fast in its relentless grip:

"I WASN"T DRINKING! I WAS TOO BUSY BEING DETAINED AGAINST MY WILL, MOLLESTED, AND ALMOST KILLED BY SOME STINKING, FILTHY BAR HAG TO EVEN THINK ABOUT GETTING DRUNK!!"

Glaring at her, wild eyes full of angry outrage, chest heaving with all the violent passions churning around and about inside him—breathing labored—it were as though Andrei dared his hapless wife to cross him any further in the matter.

Numb with absolute horror, heart lodged firmly in her throat, Jenniboni stared into his tortured eyes and saw yet again that same look for a third time now...

This time, however, it remained.

Finally able to recognize it for what it really was she remembered it as that haunted, hunted, tortured resentment unique to those special victims of violent crime and abuse—the brutally violated so rare in society for so many centuries now.

So rare she encountered only a mere handful during her otherwise extensive career in law enforcement. Engraved upon her very soul, unable to ever forget it, Jenniboni never dreamt though she'd actually see it again in the innocent eyes of one she so dearly loved:

"What did you say?", she barely managed, a strangled gasp, dropping to her very knees before him.

"*You heard me*", he answered in a hard, cold voice sending a panicked thrill throughout every fiber and sinew of her being, setting Jenniboni to shudder.

"Please Andrei", it was now her turn to plead with him, taking his hands ever so gently in hers: "Please tell me what happened. I can see clearly how it's tearing you apart inside and, if you continue refusing to just let it all out, it's only going to get all that much worse, tearing you apart from the very inside out.

"Ohhh, Sweetie, I'm begging you to let me help!"

Able at last to hear the loving concern in her voice through the murky fog of his own emotional turmoil, noting her pain at seeing him suffer so, it finally burst forth from trembling lips like water from a ruptured dam.

Begging her forgiveness for losing all control just moments ago he openly wept upon doing so, telling Jenniboni all which took place at his abuser's hands. Revealing how she approached him Andrei then told her how he was physically restrained, how she tried to grab him, and how his tormentor then proceeded to verbally sodomize him.

While revealing no particulars concerning what was actually said Andrei was all the same successful in conveying to her the frightful obscenity of all his abuser's utterances, how they made him feel.

"Oh, Sweet-pea", Jenniboni likewise wept, gathering him up in loving arms: "Please forgive me for being so short with you before. No wonder you wanted to keep this secret.

"But how can you say any of that was your fault?"

"Because if I hadn't been foolish enough to go in there in the first place nothing would have happened. I brought it all on myself", Andrei censured himself most bitterly.

Grabbing him tightly by the shoulders in a rather sudden move Jenniboni held him at arm's length hearing him say this:

"Now you listen to me, Dear", Jenniboni commanded in a stern yet compassionate voice: "Just because you were in a wrong place at the wrong time didn't give that vile creature the right to do what she did. The only reason you were there at all was because you love your daughter, making you guilty of nothing more than being a good father.

"However, no matter what your reasons for being there, whether or not you should have been there in the first place, that doesn't give anyone the right to do to you what she did. No one has the right to violate, or desecrate the sanctity of your body, your personal space, in such a beastly fashion.

"What she did was nothing less than criminal, beyond all common decency, making you completely innocent of any wrong doing, whatsoever!!"

INNOCENT!!

It was only then it dawned at last to Andrei what really hurt the most, that inescapable feeling some priceless measure of sweet innocence was brutally stolen from him, never to be regained:

"I know", he moaned in abject misery; "but she made me feel so absolutely dirty, so obscene inside when she spoke to me. I felt like such complete and utter garbage like I was filth, like I had no right to live, or even breathe.

"She made me feel so... SOOOO... guilty", Andrei sobbed; "like I did something wrong by just listening to her!"

Lost in an endless ocean of absolute pity at the very sight of her husband's forlorn expression, Jenniboni was likewise overcome by an equal undertow of crimson hate for the monster responsible for violating that one, great love of her life.

Painfully aware how Andrei actively avoided telling her what that horrid creature actually said she was grateful to him for doing so. It must have been hard enough for someone as decent as him to hear such degrading obscenities without having to actually repeat them aloud.

Fearing what she might do hearing for herself the totality of what took place Jenniboni was tempted already to employ the considerable resources at her command to ferret out her beloved's despoiler. And little did she realize Andrei feared that very same thing. That's why he withheld his assailant's vile, bestial utterances from her, afraid his wife might be driven by absolute rage to exact bloody revenge.

"Look at me, Sweet-pea, because I have something to tell you I want you to know", she instructed with firm and abiding love. Cupping gently his chin in the palm of her hand her heart was full of nothing but tender compassion. Once sure of his undivided attention it was only then Jenniboni proceeded further, picking up where she just left off:

"You are without doubt the most caring, loving, and sensitive Human being I've ever had the honour of knowing throughout my entire life. If there's anyone in this whole, wide System who should **not** feel less about themselves it's you. The happiest days in my life were those upon which I both met you and said 'I do' before all our family and friends.

"You were so young, pure, and innocent then", she insisted in a voice beginning to crack with deep feeling, fresh tears beginning to flow; "and I'll have you know something else. You have just as much purity and innocence now as you did then. If you didn't you wouldn't have been so traumatized by what that vicious sot said.

"That's something I've always admired about you, always loved.

"That, and your incredible strength of character. The fact that you were able to keep all that bottled up inside you for so long shows a lot of courage I both admire and respect".

Andrei just had to smile hearing this, honoured someone like Jenniboni, in whom he always admired those very same qualities, would feel the exact same way about him.

"So I want you to stop feeling you have something to feel bad about, something of which to be ashamed. Of all Womankind there's no one else I can think of who deserves to feel better about themselves than you do. You are without doubt the most wonderful, beautiful, and noble man I've ever met and I never want you to forget just how miraculous you really are. That's an order, my man", she gently cajoled him towards better spirits.

And from the grateful smile he graced her with it seemed to be working:

"And I think your something pretty wonderful, too, my dear gentlewoman", Andrei was quick to rejoin: "Not to mention the fact that I love you, too".

"Now there's the smile I look forward to every day I come home", Jenniboni was swift to comment, brushing his lips with loving fingertips: "I'm just so very grateful you were able to make good your eventual escape from that loathsome brute".

Andrei's reply to her heartfelt declaration of final relief came as a complete surprise however, coming as it did out of complete left field:

"To be perfectly honest I almost didn't get away", he confided now that all else was just as out in the open; "and I honestly think I might have really been killed if both Frances Straker and Naomi Marlowe hadn't come to my immediate rescue".

"Are you referring to Lt. Cmdr.'s Straker and Marlowe? My officers?" Jenniboni asked in a startled voice.

"Yes", Andrei nodded: "They were just about to take leave of that vile place… I suppose… when they saw what was happening to me".

Recounting all that occurred straight away after Frances' initial appearance… as if from out of nowhere 'like a knight in shining armor'… he took his wife right up to the point where he found his champion's note waiting for him, tucked away securely under the left windshield wiper of his car.

Giving her a blow-by-blow description of how Frances dealt so brilliantly with his attacker, this act of utter sheroism quickly followed by an equally positive recounting of how she so gently calmed him down.

Giving his wife a glowing testimonial as to both Frances' innate sensitivity and basic, overall compassion he described in great detail the tender way in which she brought him out of that state of emotional withdrawal Andrei found himself almost slipping into.

Nor did he leave out of his narrative how Naomi so generously repaired his car while the noble Ms. Straker escorted him to her vehicle, looking after him all the way to his final destination. Recognizing as well a certain note of sincere shero worship coming to life in her husband's voice Jenniboni found it both compelling, understandable, and even endearing in its childlike innocence.

Listening to him she was shown a side to both her senior personnel she found both quite revealing as well as unexpected, realizing just how much she owed each for the many kindness' they'd shown her beloved.

Nor was it long after this Andrei finished his narrative, asking her as well if he could, perchance, see his rescuers yet one more time—in Jenniboni's company, of course—stressing how both he and Frances each agreed they should seek her approval first.

"Always the proper, respectable, young laddie. That's what you are", she teased with both gentle goodness and loving humor.

"And they were quite the proper gentlewomen, the both of them, I can assure you", he sighed with starry-eyed admiration.

"Now wait just a mite-pickin' minute here", Jenniboni laughed, teasing yet again: "Do I actually sense some competition here I should know about?"

"Please, Love", Andrei rolled his eyes, sighing out loud in bogus exasperation:

"You should know by now that you're the only woman for me. Still, though, I have to admit finding them quite appealing", he toyed with her in kind: "Especially Frances!"

Jenniboni's eyebrows rose in startled amusement upon hearing this, her husband having clearly seen something in her two officers she just as plainly missed.

Maybe it had something to do with his being a man.

Then again it likewise explained all those rumors she'd heard aboard ship attesting to her Chief of Security's assumed popularity with the opposite sex despite what Jenniboni considered less-than-stellar good looks. And after listening to Andrei's glowing account of her more-than-noble nature it seemed now perfectly reasonable men would be drawn so to such an obvious 'paragon of female virtue'.

Yet even so Jenniboni was even more interested to learn about Naomi's considerable propriety, her gentlewomanly behavior in relationship to her husband. Could it be because he was a married man, or might it be Jenniboni was guilty all this time of misjudging the other woman in question. Up until now Naomi Marlowe struck her at times of being something of a lecherous, disrespectful playgirl in her attitude towards the weaker sex.

Be that as it may though, she always trusted Andrei's honest appraisal of character, his own fundamental innocence granting him the power to see the good in others she might often miss. With this in mind maybe Jenniboni owed her Chief engineer another look-see, agreeing at once to Andrei's petition both gentlewomen be invited into the Saphira home sometime in the near future:

'Especially Frances'.

Only one issue still remained however, gnawing away as it did at the very edge of her heightened awareness:

"I wonder why neither one of them told me anything whatsoever about all this commotion last night", Jenniboni wondered aloud, a wee bit miffed. Understanding Andrei's reluctance in discussing the previous day didn't excuse such neglect on the part of those serving under her command.

"Please don't be upset with them", Andrei was quick to speak up on behalf of each gallant officer now 'under fire': "The only reason they didn't tell you about what happened yesterday was because I begged them not to. I didn't want you to worry about me, so I asked Frances to keep silent.

"So none of this is their fault, only mine. I could tell right from the very start she was reluctant to hold back such information from you, doing so only out of pity for me.

"So please don't scold them any. They only kept quiet for me".

Scold?! Strange word to use in reference to grown women. Nevertheless it was his use of this word in connection to both Frances and Naomi which struck a chord, filling in the last missing piece of the puzzle still in back of Jenniboni's mind:

"That's it!", she exclaimed, sweetly tickled: "*That's* why you didn't really punish J.J.. You saw her in the role of Frances Straker, didn't you?"

"Yes", Andrei confessed once more, revealing what fevered thoughts occurred to him learning why their daughter was summoned before her principal. It was with no undue chagrin Andrei likewise revealed his absolute loss of self-control, adding with equal rapidity how forgiving Ms. Li- Wong was in the whole matter.

"Sounds like both you and our elder daughter had a most eventful day yesterday", Jenniboni smiled most tenderly, quite sympathetic: "And if you don't feel up to tonight's audience with the Supreme Mother, I'll understand if you'd rather make time for yourself, go ahead and take some time out to just rest, recuperate from yesterday's ordeal.

"That's more than all right with me. I'll just give her your apologies".

Quite moved by such a magnanimous offer on her part Andrei was likewise aware how it would reflect badly on his poor wife, appearing before the Prime Arch Matri 'sans husband'. There was no way she could possibly tell the Supreme Mother the real reason for his absence—such excuses as an illness or headache sounding likewise as contrived as they would, in all actuality, be.

Therefore, although quite touched by her natural largess, Andrei just couldn't allow her to make such a sacrifice on his behalf.

Then again he was just as honest with himself to admit his reasons for turning her down weren't so purely altruistic after all, slightly tempted though he was. It wasn't every day one had handed to them as nicely as this the great good fortune to meet in person the actual, elected leader of all Womankind.

Handed to him on a veritable silver platter as it were, the main highlight to an otherwise dismal time of it, this very special occasion was one Andrei was looking quite forward to.

"Thanks, but no. I appreciate your generous offer, but still wish to be there at your side", Andrei confided most heartily, flagging spirits already improving at the mere thought: "Besides, after all I've recently endured, I'm really looking forward to this little pick-me-up as it were".

"Only if you're absolutely sure".

While her offer was an honest one Jenniboni was grateful nonetheless to hear this, a hopeful sign he was on his way now to a speedy recovery.

"No doubt about it", he whispered gentle assurance, reaching out, running loving fingers through her golden hair, caressing her cheek.

"All rightie, then", she smiled back, getting once more to her feet before looking back down at him:

"In that case I want you to at least take the rest of the day off. Spend it completely on yourself. No housework! I want you to just relax and take it easy. Do whatever comes to mind; play your guitar, listen to your music, or watch some 3-DV if you have a mind to.

"Even if you just want to take a nap all day, do so!

"The point is I want you to take a complete and utter physical, mental, and emotional holiday today! That's an order".

"Yes, Love", he agreed without need for further encouragement, giving her a wry wink: "Message received".

"And so you can start your own day to yourself off right away, I'll take the children to school myself and have Darren bring them home. I'm sure he won't mind a little break of his own.

"I'll even ask him if he'll be so kind to take them to that place the four of you love so much... the 'Crystal Gardens' isn't it?... for the rest of the day. Maybe even get them dinner there so you won't have to cook", Jenniboni suggested even further, taking charge in her usual confident manner:

"Then, by the time they return, it'll be time for them all to retire... almost time for my father to arrive... so all you'll need to do is choose which outfit you want to wear to the party tonight.

"So how does all that sound?"

"Wonderful!", Andrei confided, always impressed with his wife's superior command abilities, her ability to remain forever in control no matter what the situation. Among the many things he admired his wife for, her impeccable talent for improvisation during any given crisis was surely one of these.

Nevertheless Andrei could also tell there was still more on Jenniboni's active mind. The grim stare she fixed him with was proof positive, a similar frown also appearing. Knowing that look from previous experience it was painfully obvious she had still more to say, also aware it wouldn't be to his liking. The only times in which she wore such a dour expression were those on which she planned to discuss something to which she knew he'd object.

With arms once more folded across her chest, her smile gone now for sure, Andrei learned soon enough Jenniboni's reason for the pensive stare she focused upon him.

"To be perfectly honest I'd rest a lot easier if I knew you had some means of self-defense, something with which to protect yourself ", she sallied forth, reluctant, knowing quite well his feelings in such matters:

"While confident what happened yesterday won't be repeated, I'd still rest more easy knowing you had at least some sort of extra protection. Something you could rely on during any other, similar hypothetical situation.

"Therefore, if for no more reason than my own peace of mind, I plan to get you a private stunner programmed to operate according to none other than your own, personal electro-neuron impulses—this allowing no one else but you to use it—something I want you to keep close to you at all times whenever leaving the base

"Will you *please* allow me at least this much?"

"Yes, Love", he gave her petition his grudging consent, calling forth a cheery smile with which to reassure her.

Caring quite little for the very idea of going about armed it left Andrei feeling less certain of himself, less like a real man able to handle any of life's little problems without the need of such obvious crutches.

Still... macho hang-ups aside... his other reason for not wanting such an emotional albatross around his neck was how it would serve as, by its very presence alone, a constant reminder of the day before. Yet even so he was still willing to make such small sacrifices if doing so meant easing his wife's troubled state of mind, the look of desperate entreaty she gave him swaying at last his decision:

"Thank you, dear", she sighed with sweet, evident relief: "Let's go and tell the children I'll be the one taking them to school today. We can even tell them about..."

Disturbed in mid-sentence Jenniboni's head snapped about in swift alarm, staring bug-eyed at the bedroom door, hearing on the other side the obvious sound of small feet running away. And from the distinct volume of their impact in the hallway beyond there was no doubt who it was eavesdropping just now on their oh-so very private conversation:

"Oh Dear Lord in Heaven, NO!!", Andrei moaned, plunged once more into the lowest depths of absolute misery. Face buried in hands he felt both despoiled, decimated and downright defeated to the very core of his inner being. Swept away on an endless tsunami of bilious unreality it left him feeling quite ill to the depths of his eternal soul.

"I'd better go to her", Jenniboni declared, resolute, turning at once towards the bedroom door. Stopped before she could take but a single step however Andrei grabbed her instead by the hand, a powerful grip taking her by complete surprise:

"No: I better take care of this myself ", she heard him sigh, heavy-hearted.

"Are you really sure that's really such a good idea?" she asked. Being J.J.'s mother Jenniboni naturally felt it her place to handle this particular problem, worried as much for his sake as their young daughter's.

It was only her husband's next words which convinced her otherwise, delivered this time around in a more steady voice:

"Yes, I'm sure. Given how she must be feeling right about now she'll need someone who understands what she's going through. And since I'm the one who actually suffered everything she just heard us talking about it's only right I be the one to go to her.

"After all", he ended on a more positive note, "who better than the victim to render solace?"

Nodding in gentle agreement she was unsure what to say in the face of such selfless love, such mettlesome determination. Smiling down with tender eyes at the remarkable young man seated before her Jenniboni took his hands in hers, full of sincere admiration.

Helping him up from the edge of their bed it was then Andrei gazed up as well into her loving countenance with an equal sense of eternal respect, asking Jenniboni to wish him luck when once more steady on his own two feet.

Slipping loving arms around him immediately thereafter, tilting her face down towards his, she did so with a tender kiss ripe with ceaseless adoration.

Chapter 31

"STRAWBERRY VENGEANCE"

Waiting anxiously outside the door to Frank's apartment Naomi's sense of nervous trepidation trebled by leaps and bounds, enduring all this for several minutes before hearing someone approach from the other side.

Moments that seemed like an eternity.

Yet even after suffering what seemed like a life-sentence just standing there, her initial sense of relief hearing the door-lock deactivated from the other side proved short-lived, further confounded by the sight of Frank Weller standing before her in such a scandalous state of near undress.

"How terribly nice to see you again, my dear Gentlewoman", the young laddie in question greeted her with both a frosty stare and a clearly manifest air of mocking disdain: "I assume you're here to collect Gloria. Very considerate of you, I must say".

Ever since *all* those tragic events occurring in the *"Dark Room"* just yesterday Naomi had rehearsed a lengthy apology for having so shamefully maneuvered the young man standing before her into his present situation—not to mention her similar transgression trying to force both he and Gloria into that very special sort of intimacy neither was yet ready for.

Unfortunately this otherwise fine plan was quickly dashed however by a sudden mental paralysis leaving the hapless woman too tongue-tied to speak. Between Frank's scantily clad body and cool, ice-prince treatment Naomi found herself just too rattled to deliver that carefully worded speech she already labored over so mightily:

"Uh, yeah, sure… just like I promised", was all she could manage, uttered after a brief moment in a still, small, humbled voice practically non-existent.

"Ah, lovely. Guess you might as well come in then", her host granted in that same frosty tone Naomi feared would be all she'd ever hear from him ever again: "Please follow me once securing the door behind you. Gloria's in the bedroom.

"I'm sure *you* remember where the bedroom is", Frank delivered as one final parting shot, Naomi almost wincing in reply. With a sauntering gait meant to be provocative from the very start he led her down the hall gradually increasing the pressure.

Having it's desired effect, barely hidden from sight by a pair of exquisitely brief briefs, viewing Frank's perfectly sculptured torso from her current position gave rise to clear feelings of blatant desire. Feelings helping to only increase Naomi's already heightened sense of guilt trailing close behind him.

All lustful thoughts on her part were soon doused quite well however following the object of her unwanted passions into his private bedchamber, met as she was by the unanticipated sight of Gloria Greensley sitting smack-dab in the middle of Frank's bed, naked from the waist up.

Almost staring at her junior assistant like some dimwitted fool in open-mouthed shock, it occurred to her right about then she was most likely naked as well under the sheets—Naomi's sense of self-reproach soaring now to dizzying heights, convinced beyond doubt she pushed the two of them into that which no one should be.

"Uh, well, yes, well… I came to pick you up like I promised I would", she announced, wearing but a feeble smile doing nothing to hide her penitent unease. Feeling both quite disoriented as well as discomforted she couldn't think of anything else to say, floundering about in vain hopes of reorganizing her scattered thoughts.

"That can wait for now", Frank declared, contemptuously, in response to Naomi's obvious distress: "As you can see Lt. Greensley isn't quite ready to leave yet.

"And she won't be until she finishes breakfast. Right honey-bunny?", he gave Gloria an adoring glance that, unbeknownst to any of them, wasn't purely show.

"As right as rain, Sweetie-pie", Gloria shot back just as quickly, sounding quite chipper indeed, as Frank finally removed the long-suffering bowl of strawberries from atop of his dresser bureau, taking a seat next to her on the bed.

Observing all this in embarrassed silence as he plucked a sliced berry from its container, swirling it slowly about in whipped cream, Naomi watched even further as he likewise popped it in Gloria's waiting mouth. Accepting it from almost servile fingers as if it were her due, she closed her eyes upon receiving it, an expression of avid delight mingled on her face with that of lusty relish.

This continued for a good while in hushed silence, each giving the other lingering glances full of static sexual tension as he twirled about in creamy white froth each luscious piece of juicy red fruit. Swirling each around-and-around in a highly suggestive manner lazy, graceful movements bordered well on the erotic.

And then there was the shameless way in which Gloria would likewise pause after consuming each dainty morsel, taking Frank's serving hand in hers. Adding to the sensual intimacy of the little tableau played out before her, Naomi watched on in both helpless disbelief and a certain amount of sick fascination as Gloria, replete with amorous jubilation, held his hand firmly in place.

Licking and sucking from his fingers sticky sweet cream, offering as well the object of her clearly carnal desire such amorous looks, Naomi came away feeling like some arrant voyeur just being there:

Just as bad as how Frank gazed upon the woman he so lovingly tended with such slavish devotion, almost making wild, passionate love to her right then and there with his very eyes, Naomi was consumed by the burning sensation she was some sort of degenerate Peeping Jane just breathing the very same air.

Already passionate as it was this amorous performance only reached new heights of rapture when, once Gloria devoured the very last berry, Frank scraped up with his middle finger the last few telltale traces of whipped cream from the empty container.

Positioning it before her lips it was then that she leaned forward, accepting his cream-covered finger in her greedy mouth. Wrapping her lips securely around its base Gloria closed her eyes, wearing an expression of sheer ecstasy while Frank withdrew it with slow, seductive, deliberate ease—the encore to this little scene arriving when he likewise leaned into her, gracing Gloria with a lingering kiss full of smoldering passion.

Having already reached a state of shame-faced humiliation she'd never known before; Naomi was even further shamefaced to discover herself actually blushing in her obvious disgrace. Only then did Frank draw back at last from the unwavering focus of his amorous attentions, addressing Gloria after what seemed like an endless eternity of unabashed foreplay:

"Very nice, my love, but not as sweet as the natural essence of your savory lips all on their own", he declared in a deep, throaty voice replete with lusty appreciation:

"Just one more little matter that needs tending", he soon added in Gloria's waiting ear, getting up from the edge of his bed. Headed for the nearby bathroom, leaving his two gentlewomen guests alone for a brief spell, it wasn't until 'sans laddie' Gloria addressed her superior at last.

"Now *that* was *verrrry* enjoyable", Gloria purred, giving her dept. Chief a brazen leer. Stretching her arms out to either side in lazy satisfaction she drilled holes with her very eyes through Naomi very being

Left feeling as though her very soul was just gutted like some recently hooked sea bass, crushed under the awesome weight of her own helpless disbelief, Naomi watched in mute silence as Gloria arched her back. Hands clasped behind her head, perky breasts thrust forward in the other woman's direction, she gave Naomi both a lascivious grin and derisive little laugh.

Almost welcoming Frank's return with a nervous giggle Naomi's relief was yet again ill-fated, the young laddie asking his bed partner from the night before to scoot forward.

Climbing back into bed alongside her, a hairbrush in hand, Frank began to straighten up her disheveled hair, dashing Naomi's fond hope this endless display of bawdy affection was nearing its end. Assuring her she had such full, lovely hair Frank continued brushing it out with careful, delicate strokes, Gloria keeping the bed sheets wrapped securely around her middle:

"I just can't let you leave without making sure you look your absolute best. After all it's all my fault it got so mussed up in the first place", he offered by way of humble apology: "I'm really, really sorry but it looked so thick and luxuriant last night I just couldn't help running my fingers all through it".

"No need to fret so on my account, lover-boy", Gloria giggled: "Perfectly understandable. After all, things did get pretty wild last night".

Finding it difficult to even breath, feeling more and more claustrophobic with each passing second, Naomi felt she might actually swoon if she didn't vacate the immediate vicinity as soon as humanly possible, overwhelmed by such powerful emotions she might actually pass out.

Having reached at long last her final breaking point Naomi quickly excused herself, announcing she'd wait elsewhere for the young Lieutenant, immensely joyful just to be free of that suffocating environment.

****

Once closing the front door to Frank's apartment behind her, leaning instead against the doorjamb in the public hallway just beyond, Naomi took several deep, hitching breaths.

Struggling against the many emotions welling up within she struggled in desperate hope of regaining... somehow... a sense of composure she felt sure she'd never feel again.

Wondering in silent reflection if this was indeed how she made each of them feel with her continual teasing, pushing, and—in Frank's case—her 'playful', but unwelcome advances, Naomi didn't need to ponder long before seeing for herself the ugly truth ...

"YES!!!"

Realizing as well it didn't matter if she really meant any actual harm, or malicious intent Naomi was swamped by such feelings of both utter shame and absolute remorse the likes of which she never felt before.

'Sooo... now that you got what you originally wanted, how does it feel???' she grilled herself with an all-powerful sense of self-loathing. Feeling like some sort of paid assassin having just murdered something precious, no taking it back—the damage already done—tears began to trickle down flushed cheeks.

****

Sitting together in stunned silence soon after Naomi's rather hasty departure it was Gloria who first spoke up:

"Did you see the look on her face?", she asked in hushed awe: "I never thought it would actually work. I mean, after how she made me feel like that before, I hoped it would. But, now ..."

"Uh, huh", Frank nodded: "I know what you mean".

220

No less subdued than she he now wondered if they truly did the right thing, aware as well Gloria was asking herself that very same question.

"At least I don't think we need ever worry again about Naomi trying anything with either of us", he tried to comfort the both of them, remaining at the same time a bit uncertain.

"Yeah, right", Gloria replied, sounding a bit subdued: "I really think she's learned her lesson this time. To be perfectly honest I wasn't sure for a moment there I could even go through with it":

"I understand", Frank smiled, managing a bright facade for both their sakes: "Although you carried it off quite well: Very realistic".

"Thanks", Glorias confessed: "To be perfectly honest some of it was a little embarrassing, but there were also parts of it I also really liked, too. For instance, I really liked the way you brushed my hair. And the strawberries tasted real good, too".

"Well, truth be told, I also have to admit I really enjoyed serving them to you", Frank likewise confessed to just some of the guilty little pleasures they both just shared only moments ago, not all their performance as faked as either might have the other believe:

"And I meant what I said about liking your hair. It's quite lovely".

"Why, thank you my dear laddie", Gloria laughed rather merrily, already feeling in better spirits: "And yours is quite nice as well. Sort of reminds me of the golden wheat fields back on Mars that seemed to just go on forever, one of the few pleasant memories of Telis-Ville I actually have".

Blushing as she did so it was only then she confided in him a hidden desire to run *her* fingers through *his* hair, a secret longing she had since first meeting him:

"In that case I think you should. Go ahead", Frank granted with an understanding smile. Making it easier to do so he lay on his side next to her, well within arm's length, propped up on his right elbow. Looking deep into the shy young gentlewoman's eyes he wasted no time encouraging her to feel free, indulge herself, and give way at last to temptation's sweet call:

"I just don't know", Gloria dallied about... bashful... unsure.

"I would think after that little scene with the strawberries this would be child's play", he teased with gentle good humor.

"But that was just play-acting", Gloria objected.

While the both of them knew that wasn't exactly true Frank nevertheless kept quiet, refusing to contradict her. Instead he just waited in loving patience for Gloria to make her next move.

All-in-all it came quite soon enough when, slowly reaching out to him with hesitant fingers, she slipped them deep into Frank's thick, curly, golden-blonde strands. And as she ran her fingers through it Frank gave her an inviting smile confined not just to his lips, spreading as well to his lively, soulful eyes.

Gazing into those beautiful dark brown windows to his very soul Gloria felt an overwhelming sense of joyful privilege just being there with him. Her explorations of his tawny crown growing bolder, more enthusiastic, she savored the feel of soft, silky hair between slender fingers. Growing even more daring yet Gloria soon let her hand likewise slip down to his cheek, feeling his beard.

Caressing gently his jaw line with open palm, she stroked with the ball of her thumb Frank's moustache:

"I've always wondered what a man's beard felt like", she informed him, a little smile dancing at each corner of her mouth.

"Is it what you expected?" Frank asked in amused curiosity.

"Not exactly. Actually, it feels a lot nicer than I thought it would, softer. Then again I thought it might when we first met".

No sooner had she said so however her hand came to an abrupt rest upon his face, her smile faltering, turning instead into a disappointed frown.

"What's wrong?", Frank rushed to ask the very moment her hand grew still.

"I don't want to go", she felt almost like crying, fighting back tears now seeking release: "I've loved our time together so much I just don't want it to ever end. One day just isn't enough!"

"Oh, Sweetheart", he soothed Gloria's pain with tender words of comfort, caressing gently her cheek: "Don't you see that it doesn't have to end.

"That's why I gave you my number. Just because our time together now is over doesn't mean we can't be together again", he pleaded for her complete understanding:

"Yes", she smiled weakly, still clearly upset: "I guess you're right".

Rising slowly from the bed they shared, Frank looked down at her with an affectionate gaze full of gentle compassion, seeing she needed some time alone to gather herself together:

"I'll just wait for you outside while you get dressed", he informed her in a soft, tender voice: "Take your time and, when you're finally ready, I'll show you out".

Turning away from her side, reluctant all the same to do so, Frank nevertheless left, closing the door between them.

****

Opening together the front door of his apartment, Frank and Gloria found Naomi waiting for them on the other side wearing all the while a tremulous little smile. It was a contrite expression neither would've dreamt possible for the clearly distraught woman just standing there.

Seeing the obvious remorse in her bright emerald eyes, all the brighter from crying, Frank's ice-prince facade melted straight away.

Realizing what the two of them just put her through, sure by just looking at Naomi's forlorn expression she was indeed sorry for all past misdeeds, he felt more kindly disposed towards the mournful gentlewoman waiting on his doorstep:

"It's good to see you again, Naomi", he assured her, affecting his warmest smile possible: "I just want to let you know I wish you all the best, wanting to thank you from the bottom of my heart for introducing me to Gloria".

"Thank you. I really appreciate your saying that", Naomi smiled in a timorous, shaky, fashion totally new to her very essence—grateful yet repentant all at the very same time.

Shifting his gaze back to Gloria's soon thereafter, standing now next to her immediate superior in their matching green and gold S.E.A. uniforms, Frank felt an immediate, powerful tug at his heart witnessing the glum expression in her downcast eyes.

"Please don't look so sad, hon. As I said before you can see me again any time you want. You know how to find me, so this isn't really 'good-bye', just 'so-long-for-now'. However, before you go, I just want thank you for a truly wonderful time which I will always treasure".

Hoping to drive home in no uncertain terms the sincerity of every word he spoke Frank stepped forward, pressing his lips to hers in a very special kiss conveying more than any verbal proclamation of love ever could. Nor did he ever take his eyes of her when, after stepping back once more inside his apartment, Frank began closing the front door between them:

"***Please*** remember that ***you're always welcome here***", he almost begged in a voice full of honest entreaty just as the door finally came to a close between them, separating the young couple with a tiny little click.

No kiss was necessary to convince Naomi however of either the sincere display of emotion in Frank's voice, or eyes as he said to his date 'so-long-for-now'. Having planned before yesterday morning to press Gloria for "all the juicy details" involving her time in the young laddie's company all that had changed, such plans now abandoned.

Not wishing to intrude any further on such a special moment she merely followed in total silence the younger gentlewoman in question, head bowed in quiet reverence for all that just occurred.

****

Alone once more Frank took a shower, got dressed at long last, and carried out to the nearby living room Gloria's breakfast tray of empty dishes.

Setting it down on the island between both there and the adjoining kitchenette, he caught sight as well of the crystal shelves to his immediate right, the various articles of faith displayed there.

Inspired to petition the Almighty he closed his eyes, praying in earnest for the young Lieutenant he just spent such a moving time with. Asking for both her continued safety and ultimate happiness, Frank likewise prayed she would most surely come back to him. An invocation full of fondest hope, love, and even desire not just for the near future but for the rest of his life he concluded his devotions only when sure he'd explored with the Almighty everything in his heart.

Only then did he once more open his eyes, spotting straightaway yet another object on that nearby shelf. It was then, as if receiving a definite reply to all his heartfelt prayers, Frank knew right then and there what to do.

Chapter 32

"THE FALLOUT"

Seeing their older sister appear from down the hallway leading to both their parent's bedroom… her horror-stricken face drenched in harsh, stinging tears as she sped on by… an identical pair of smug, self-satisfied grins appeared on the faces of both twins.

Assuming she was likewise in trouble they felt more than just a little bit vindicated by her grief given the way she spoke so sharply to them earlier on. Too immature to know any better their smiles remained firmly in place, J.J. slamming the door to her room right next to the couch on which they both sat watching 3-DV.

Their satisfied expressions of childish spite soon faltered however, turning into those of uneasy apprehension, catching soon after that the dramatic sight of their father's quick approach. Never in their young, innocent lives had they ever seen such absolute misery, such utter dismay, engraved upon his every feature.

All they knew for sure was that something real bad was up…

Something they didn't understand.

And like all small children faced with such unpleasantries in life beyond their youthful comprehension they grew quite anxious indeed. Watching him with cautious eyes full of nervous trepidation neither missed the clearly plaintive voice Andrei employed, knocking on J.J.'s door:

"Please, Sweetie, please let me in", he implored her in a most heartrending fashion. And when no immediate reply was forthcoming, Andrei knocked yet again: "Please, Honey, I really need to talk to you. Please say I can come in. I promise you you're not in trouble: None at all!"

It wasn't until after yet another lengthy pause he heard at long last a muffled voice weep in reply:

"Okay, come in".

****

Easing open the door to J.J.'s room with his own similar sense of anxious worry, Andrei was greeted soon enough by the sad sight of his daughter lying face-down on her bed. Her entire body all atremble, wracked by violent sobs, she wept hot, scalding tears into her favourite pillow.

Closing the door behind him, securing it well least two certain 'little cube-watchers' decided to intrude, he walked straightaway to her bedside, sitting next to her prostrate form. Turning sideways he reached out and, gently rubbing her back in a paternal effort to offer at least some small comfort, he carried on in a voice full of profound regret:

"I take it you heard everything".

Without speaking a single word J.J. made her answer known, nodding her head, remaining face-down in her tear-soaked pillow.

"Both your mother and I are very, very sorry you had to overhear what we said. I know what you heard really scared and upset you, but I promise you you'll feel a lot better if we just talk it out together. Believe me. I know from experience".

No words were spoken for several minutes after that: Just the painful sound of the little girl's desperate weeping as her father waited in patient silence, gently stroking her long, flaxen hair. It wasn't until after what seemed a painful eternity on Andrei's part J.J. finally rolled over on her side, lifting her reddened face to him:

"How can anyone do that?" she cried, puffy eyes looking straight at him in confounded fear: "How can anyone be so mean and nasty. Especially to you?!"

"I honestly don't know, hon", he confessed, smiling a weak smile, realizing to whom she was referring:

"Maybe it was because she was just too drunk to know any better. Or maybe it was because…"

Almost ready to suggest his assailant was more likely than not mentally ill Andrei stopped himself right then-and-there, fearing this would only serve to frighten her all the more:

"I honestly don't know dear. I guess that some people are just naturally mean. Like that girl at school yesterday… 'Evelyn' was it?"

"Yeah", J.J. responded, her tears beginning to subside: "But she's just a kid. That woman who hurt you was a grown-up. Aren't grown-ups supposed to know better?" she asked with large eyes full of innocent wonder.

"Yes, Hon; they're supposed to", her father agreed: "And most of them do. Still though there are those very few…", his sad voice trailed away.

"Yeah, I know what you mean", she added this time in a firm, angry voice cynical beyond her years: "It's just that I can't stand the idea of anyone hurting you".

"I know", he thanked her softly, brushing away stray hairs from in front of her face: "Unfortunately, though, there isn't much we can do about it".

"Yes there is!", she snarled in a hard, cold, voice. A look of boundless animosity creeping into her eyes, Andrei's heart froze with honest dread just seeing it: "I can hunt her down and kill her. Rip her head off. I hate her and want to kill her. Hurt her like she hurt you!!"

"Oh, no, J.J.", Andrei groaned: "Please don't say such things. I can understand your anger. I felt it, too. But please don't say such things".

"But why??", she gasped, truly bewildered, a tone of voice demanding immediate explanation.

"Because it would kill *me* to imagine you so consumed with hate you'd actually take a life, especially in *my* name! It would kill me inside to see you take the law into your own hands, committing such violence because of me…

"If I couldn't stand the idea of Frances Straker hurting anyone on my behalf then how could I ever bear the idea of my own wonderful, beautiful daughter doing so? I've always loved, admired, and even respected the noteworthy woman you're already growing up to be and just couldn't live with the thought of my precious little girl sinking to such deplorable depths.

"It would truly tear my poor heart in two thinking of you as some sort of bloodthirsty savage staining your soul with the blood of another just to avenge some wrong they did me", Andrei wept anew, catching J.J.'s attention like never before:

"I'd feel so low, so very unhappy; I don't know if I could go on living. It would just hurt too much…

"So much so in fact that I just want you to know that, if you ever hurt anyone for hurting me, soiling your very inner-self in such a monstrous way, you'd be hurting me more than them. I'd be a victim of your violence more than they…

"So please don't ever hurt me like that".

"Oh, Daddy, I'd never do anything to hurt you", J.J. cried out, horrified at the very thought. Jumping up, she flung her arms around Andrei's neck and shoulders, proving the honesty of her heartfelt declaration with a mighty hug possessing all the power love granted her childish limbs.

Clinging unto him she likewise wept: "I love you, Daddy! Really I do!!"

"I know you do; Sweetie", he spoke softly, wrapping his arms around her, returning her ardent embrace with a similar one of his very own. Feeling her face pressed up against his shoulder, warm tears freely flowing, he gently stroked the back of his daughter's head, addressing her in a healing voice replete with boundless affection:

"I know you love me, dear. Just as I love you. Which is why I want you to give me your solemn word you'll never take the law into your own hands. Promise me you'll never go out in a rage and hurt someone, especially for me, because that's the day I'll surely die inside.

"It's one thing to seek justice through legal means, but it's another thing entirely to become a lone vigilante outside the purview of official law enforcement".

"I promise, Daddy", she vowed, "I'll do what you say. I promise! I never want to see you die".

While able to see she didn't fully understand his reasoning, Andrei likewise knew she really meant it when giving him her solemn oath. With an audible sigh of sincere relief he gave her a gentle, tender kiss on the cheek, thanking her right thereafter.

It wasn't until she finally removed herself from the tender security of her father's arms, kneeling on her bed in front of him, he soon saw in her puzzled expression there was even more on J.J.'s curious young mind:

"Yes, dear?" he asked: "I can tell there's still something bothering you".

Giving her father a hard, speculative look she got straight to the problem with all the simple confidence of pure youth, challenging him outright in a dubious tone of voice:

"How can you say you enjoy being a man like you did when things like that happen?"

"I think you're forgetting something else very important I said during that very same conversation", Andrei pressed on with patient understanding.

"Like?"

"Like how I said I respect and admire the way women both run things and treat men. Remember when I told you that, while there might be a few women out there who actually mistreat men, I consider them to be such a minority as to be freaks of nature?"

"Yes?!"

"Well, I was actually referring to that particular woman when I mentioned such 'freaks of nature'. I still remain convinced that the vast majority of women are just like you, your mother, and Frances Straker—chivalrous and upstanding in their treatment of the weaker sex.

"So dear, does that answer your question?"

Like a sudden light revealing even the darkest recesses of her young mind it then dawned on J.J. where her real destiny lay. No longer would she seek command of her own starship wearing the green and gold, the S.E.A. holding now no more interest for her. From this day onward her young feet were now set on another path leading straight to the crimson and gold of the Protectorate, defending those such as her father in need:

"Yeah, it does!", she marveled aloud, gifted at such a tender age with the distinct foreknowledge of where life's sure road would ultimately lead her:

"And I'd really like to meet Frances Straker, too".

"You know what, dear", Andrei smiled: "I, too, would really like you to meet her. And you might just get your wish when your mother returns from Alpha Centauri.

"So, are you feeling any better now?"

"Yeah, I guess so", she assured him, feeling quite better indeed.

"I'm really glad to hear you say that", he nearly laughed, almost giddy with relief. Getting up from the edge of her bed with a revitalized bounce in his step Andrei swung about, lifting her high into the air:

"Central Control, we have launch", he grinned quite merrily, sending J.J. into a similar fit of giggles while placing her back down on the floor.

Smiling down upon his daughter now standing before him, spirits renewed, it was only then she hit him with an unexpected question chilling his blood like an evil arctic blast, his heart skipping more than just one beat:

"By the way, what did that woman really say to you?" J.J. asked in all pure innocence, staring up at him with nothing but harmless inquiry.

Suddenly unsteady Andrei closed his eyes, feeling as though, in one fell-swoop, someone just pulled the rug out from under his entire universe. It was all he could do to remain standing, a wave of sudden nausea crashing down on him with relentless force, feeling quite dizzy.

It wasn't so much the memory of what was said that left Andrei quite so upset as it was the very idea of the sweet young girl standing before him being defiled by hearing such dreadful filth, such vile obscenities. In all reality he'd much rather die, struck dead at that very same moment, than reveal what inconceivable filth was forced upon him to the innocent child now waiting.

"No, Sweetheart, I'm not going to tell you that", Andrei swallowed, sounding quite sick indeed, eyes still closed: "What she said will forever remain between just her, me, and the Good Lord Above. That's all. I won't even tell your mother, much less you.

"Let's just say that it was really, really bad and if it shook me up so much I don't even want to think what it might do to you".

There was no mistaking either the revulsion in his voice, or the horror written all over her father's face, turning quite pale in his extreme consternation. Nor did J.J. miss the way Andrei's body trembled ever so slightly upon hearing what she asked, suddenly worried more for his sake than anything else:

"Forget it, Father. I don't really want to know", she was quick to reassure him, giving him a comforting hug. With her arms still around his waist, trying to sound as casual as possible, she gently rested her head against his stomach.

"Thank you, hon", Andrei expressed his sincere gratitude, holding her close, choosing right then and there to change the subject:

"And as I'm sure you already know your mother will be driving you to school today instead of me. Won't that be fun?", he asked, his voice sounding up beat: "You've been wanting more time with her and this will give you the perfect opportunity".

"Yeah, that sound's great", she smiled. Stepping back, gazing up at him, she added further with a wry little grin: "By the way, Mother really chewed you out. But I'm glad she wasn't still mad at you in the end. I'm sorry you got in trouble 'cause of me".

"Firstly, I did *not* get in trouble because of you", Andrei contradicted her in a firm, no-nonsense, voice. So forget all about feeling guilty. It was my entire fault for trying to keep secrets from her when I should have known better. She was right about that.

"And I owe you an apology, too, for asking you to likewise hide such things from her. As both your father *and* an adult I should have known better. From now on we both need to be more honest with her, having more faith in her, without underestimating her. After all she proved herself most understanding when dealing with me only moments ago".

Certainly both fair and just enough to make time for him whenever having opinions, or grievances of his own he wished to air. Always taking Andrei's feelings into account, Jenniboni would often admit seeing his point of view.

"Yeah, I see what you mean", J.J. readily accepted, "although I still feel guilty about what happened to you yesterday".

"I'm afraid I'm not following you", Andrei told her quite frankly, a worried frown dawning.

"Well, what I mean is if it wasn't for me that woman yesterday wouldn't have hurt you. The only reason you were there was to call Ms. Li-Wong because of me. So, if I hadn't..."

"*No*, J.J.", he cut her off more than just a little bit sharply, objecting most strenuously: "Don't ever say that. Don't even *think* it! The only person to blame for what happened in that horrid place was that woman.

"Not me and certainly *not you.*

"Don't forget that, until your mother pointed out otherwise, I made the same mistake by blaming myself. However, in the end, each of us is responsible for our own choices in life. And that includes how we treat others.

"So when it comes to what happened yesterday it's only that woman in the bar who's to blame for what she did to me, neither me or you. Have I made myself perfectly clear?"

Assuring her father that his message was indeed received both loud and clear, this was likewise manifest in the simple way J.J.'s body relaxed upon hearing such positive words. Her feelings of guilt quickly dispelled; they were replaced straightaway by an equally persuasive rush of sudden relief.

"Good", Andrei smiled once more, breathing more freely: "In that case I suggest we go see how your mother's doing. I've no doubt she's worried right about now about the both of us".

"Sure thing", J.J. agreed, asking if it were likewise true her mother was really getting him a stunner.

"Yes", he sighed; still somewhat dismayed in regards to that particular subject: "So it would seem".

"Great", she cheered: "That means you can stun all the kids in school I don't like!"

"Jenniboni Elissa Saphira!" Andrei exclaimed, both shocked and amused at the very same time.

"Sorry, Father", J.J. giggled: "Just a thought".

"Well, young gentlewoman", Andrei likewise chuckled: "You can get that ever-lovin' thought right outta your ever-lovin' mind!"

Chapter 33

"REPURIFICATION"

Leaving her room together, J.J.'s small hand in his, both father and daughter discovered Jenniboni waiting for them on the couch to their immediate right. Sitting between the twins, arms draped around each, all three were found watching some animated 3-DV kid's show involving the Protectorate.

Hardly paying any attention to the show however both children listened instead to their mother with rapt attention, Jenniboni spinning them select true-life stories about her own former existence as a real-life Protector.

Caring rather little for the cartoonish show they were presently watching, too sensationalist and unrealistic for Jenniboni's taste, she was nevertheless unable to see anything really objectionable in its content. However, while not so entertained by the actual program itself, she found herself nonetheless enjoying this very special time with both twins while likewise waiting for both her husband and elder daughter.

Their innocent questions concerning her past in law enforcement, quite profound in their childlike simplicity, proved as well quite thought provoking, Jenniboni deriving as much pleasure from their conversation as they. Both talking and laughing with one-another it was then she found herself wanting to spend more time with each, planning to do just that very thing upon her *hopeful* return from Alpha-Centauri.

Coming to this decision it was right about then she heard J.J.'s door open directly to her left, both father and daughter appearing at the very same time.

Taking her leave of both the couch and the twins, getting up instead, Jenniboni wasted no time asking both new arrivals how each was doing:

"Oh, we're okay", J.J. informed her as if without a single, solitary care throughout the whole entire System.

"Yes", Andrei reassured his anxious wife, noting the way she turned to him for even further confirmation. "It was a little dicey there for a little while but, all in all, we had a quite productive little talk during which we got everything settled".

"Thank you, Sweet-pea", Jenniboni smiled with an appreciative little sigh, loving gratitude apparent in the very way she now looked at him. Elated, overcome with jubilant relief, she clapped her hands together with a loud report.

Focusing now her attention on all three children gathered before her she announced with obvious enthusiasm it was time for them… one-and-all… to be on their way:

"And since I was really enjoying my little talk here with both Tommy and Tammy so much, I've hereby decided to drive all of you to school today so we can continue having such a good time together".

Perking up straight away over this wee bit of news, both twins demonstrated their clear delight with a raucous cheer brimming with childish effervescence. Moved by this reaction on their part Jenniboni's resolve to spend more time with her family was cemented further, quite touched by this honest outpouring of heartfelt joy.

"And since your Daddy has a little tummy ache, he'll be staying home for the rest of the day. So, after school, your Uncle Darren from Mommy's office will be taking all three of you to the Crystal Gardens to play some games and have dinner before he brings you home.

"All rightie, then", she continued in the same light vein, her second announcement receiving the same boisterous endorsement as her first: "In that case we'd better be on our way. But not before each of you give your father both a big hug, and kiss good-bye".

The twins were actually first to bid him farewell, rushing into Andrei's outstretched arms upon his crouching down to welcome them.

Exchanging firm, affectionate kisses it was only then that they withdrew from their father's gentle embrace, J.J.'s turn now to give him another powerful hug of her own, kissing him also on the cheek.

Moving out of the way soon enough, the children made way for their mother—Jenniboni stepping forward now as her husband stood up, raising himself up to full height.

Finalizing the family's farewell ritual she slipped strong yet gentle arms around Andrei's waist. Holding him close, pressing her mouth to his, she gave her willing spouse a lingering kiss, his arms likewise encircled her.

Finally withdrawing her soft, tender lips from his she then leaned forward, whispering something in his right ear:

"Now remember what I said about taking it easy today: This is *your* day. Promise?"

"I promise", he likewise whispered in reply.

"Good, then", she smiled, gazing deep into clear blue eyes:

"I love you", she added in a sweet voice not unlike a warm summer's breeze.

"And I love you, too", he assured her as well with all his heart.

*****

Left all to himself with only his innermost thoughts to keep him company, Andrei was at a momentary loss when it came to choosing what to do next. The apartment seemed so very empty… so quiet… and with nothing to do now, no housework, he felt a little bit disoriented.

Staring absent-mindedly though at the large 3-DV unit up against the nearby wall, he was at least certain of what he didn't want to do. Picking up the remote from the coffee table next to him, he switched the cube off without giving it any further thought.

Like his wife, Andrei cared little for children's programming.

Except, maybe, for *'Ernie; the Amazing, Tap Dancing, Telepathic Bat'* he smiled to himself.

Turning around now with no further objective in mind when, unsure what to do next, his attention was drawn now to the dark wood dining room table at the room's far end. Staring at that morning's dirty dishes sitting atop of its polished oak surface he wouldn't *really* be disobeying Jenniboni's orders if he just put them in the kitchen sink to soak.

Would he??

Although they owned a sonic dishwasher, not unlike a sonic washing machine in principal, Andrei still preferred the personal satisfaction of doing a job well done on each and every one of them.

Besides… for some inexplicable reason he couldn't quite put his finger on… he actually began to encounter feelings of absolute repugnance just at the mere sight of all that messy kitchenware. Never before had he suffered such an extreme, abnormal aversion to such untidiness as at that very moment.

****

Originally planning to leave them just soaking once having loaded them in the kitchen sink he still couldn't stand seeing them there afterwards, knowing they remained so dirty under all that soapy water. Realizing he was being irrational didn't help any as he began scrubbing away, tackling each and every blessed one with a manic zeal bordering on the desperate.

Using the rough side of the sponge reserved for this very same chore Andrei proceeded from there. Stacking each clean eating utensil in the waiting dish rack to his immediate left he planned at first to simply let them drip-dry all on their lonesome.

No such luck, though.

Again unable to just leave them out in plain sight, scrambling about for a nearby dish cloth while leaving the kitchen tap likewise running, he dried each item with meticulous care before stacking it away in its customary place. Only after every single article in question was fully out of sight was Andrei content, returning then to the sink itself.

Reaching out to turn it off his hand froze in mid-air before able to do so, practically mesmerized by the mere sight of that sparkling stream of luke-warm water splashing into the glistening silver chrome basin below. He didn't even think any more about what he was doing, operating by this time on automatic pilot only. Reclaiming the sponge from its nearby tray, he plunged once more his hands into the running tap water.

Applying liberal doses of dish soap to his skin Andrei began scouring himself all the way up each arm in a demented frenzy, scrubbing away quite furiously at both limbs. Effectively rubbing himself quite raw it was then Andrei burst out laughing, his arms now a dark, angry red from the rough side of the same dish sponge as mentioned before.

A brittle, jagged, hysterical laugh it was triggered by a schoolboy memory leaping to mind with a sudden jolt, a famous line from an ancient stage play called "Macbeth":

"OUT DAMMED SPOT!!"

Devoting the greater majority of his efforts to the palm of his right hand, Andrei was as yet unaware of the actual significance behind this simple obsession...

At least not consciously...

Not yet.

****

Still functioning on a purely instinctive level all he knew at the moment was that he felt incredibly dirty, suddenly overcome with a supreme, powerful urge to scour his entire body. Giving it no further thought once turning off the running sink, he hastened straightaway for the bathroom adjacent to the mistress bedroom both he and Jenniboni shared.

With both sponge and dish soap in tow, stripping himself bare with an urgent need, a desperate desire almost lunatic in its intensity, Andrei climbed without delay into the nearby bathtub. Almost tripping himself up over its edge, he slammed shut the frosted Plexiglas partition behind him.

Sealed off now from the rest of the adjoining washroom by the speckled transparency now firmly in place, Andrei was quite alone now in his vulnerability.

Setting the showerhead directly above him to emit a continual spray of cleansing water at the hottest degree he could possibly endure, it stung him head to toe, the concentrated stream of fine moisture stinging his naked flesh with merciless force.

The water droplets from on high scourging him like burning hail Andrei likewise doused himself with copious amounts of liquid detergent, letting the now empty soap bottle clatter noisily to the bottom of the tub below. Only then did he really get down to it, practically attacking the rest of his defenseless body with the same coarse surface as before.

Just as he didn't notice his previous obsession with the palm of his right hand Andrei was no more aware now how he focused his frantic, desperate efforts on the left side of his face—that very side where his abuser breathed upon him, uttering her foul verbiage in his helpless ear.

Nor did it occur to him why he was so intent on purifying himself between even his legs, devoting extra time to that part of his anatomy she tried to grab before slapping her hand away from his sex:

No!

Truth be told it wasn't until almost yielding to the crazy urge to actually crack his skull wide open, hoping to simply scrub away all memory of what happened with actual soap and water, it finally hit him like a sucker-punch straight to the gut.

Realizing at long last from whence this frenzied compulsion came, Andrei slumped against the nearby wall opposite the sliding glass barrier. Sliding now to the bottom of the tub below, the immediate result was as if all his muscles just turned to mere jelly.

Mingling now with the hot, cruel water droplets from above assailing his sorely tried skin, scalding tears likewise ran down his face. Beginning to quake all over, face buried in his hands, he was wracked all over with bitter sobs not unlike J.J.'s only an hour ago.

****

Just sitting there as the shower began to gradually cool, feeling separated from the rest of Womankind in spirit as well as body, it was with a similar sense of urgency Andrei went about racking his beleaguered mind, looking for a new way by which to re-purify himself—purge his soul.

Understanding as well no physical means would suffice it didn't really take all that long to come to him in all its simple eloquence. In a dramatic burst of sudden inspiration the answer appeared soon enough in all its shining glory. Even if unable to literally remove the top of his head in order to scrub away all the poison left there, there nevertheless remained to him another course of action.

A private little ritual having always helped him deal with previous trials and tribulations he made it once more to his feet, getting up in a rapid haste. With a definite sense of oncoming deliverance he left behind him the still-running shower, making a mad dash instead for the neighbouring bedroom.

Too anxious for final closure Andrei didn't even bother drying himself off in the frantic scramble for the room beyond, forgoing as well the silken bathrobe he normally donned after having bathed.

Hurrying instead to that corner of the mistress bedroom where he got dressed each and every morning he flung instead his dripping wet body into the nearby chair. Almost knocking it over with the sheer force of his sudden arrival no sooner was he settled in place Andrei snatched up the guitar he always kept close by.

Propped up within arm's reach against the wall closest to him, a treasured possession given him by his maternal grandfather long ago, it rested there like a faithful puppy standing at attention, awaiting its owner's nimble fingers to summon forth the music dwelling deep within each of them.

However, as Andrei called this time upon his singular musical genius, he

234

forewent the soft, gentle melodies the likes of which he lulled to sleep both his wife and children just that very night before. For this particular process of self-reclamation to actually work he didn't play the sweet love songs or light, festive numbers he was famous for among his select group of both family and friends.

On the contrary his fingers struck chords with rapid, hard, even violent precision bringing to life a musical archetype both beautiful and terrifying in its loud, abrasive complexity and the exceptional dexterity needed with which to summon it forth.

A gentle, peaceful, quietly joyful person in nature replete with his own positive take on life, it was a form of music Andrei rarely played, rarely needing to, the vast majority of his days replete with happy contentment. Yet even so there still remained those few times in which he found himself in need of such emotional, if not spiritual healing.

And so it was that, as this gifted virtuoso called upon the needed chords, they awoke in him emotions both dark and passionate—emotions able to both exalt, and even destroy in their fearful intensity—feelings needed with which to finally drive out from within those unclean sensations still squirming about:

Passions with which to purify his sullied psyche of those infectious images planted there only yesterday.

Throwing himself quite literally into this all-consuming process he sang as well lyrics reflecting these dread emotions, emotions he brought to the surface only to flush them from his system, his gifted singing voice manifesting each in the hash, strident, angry quality it now possessed.

Soon though the act of crying robbed him likewise of his ability to vocalize, Andrei's throat paralyzed with the violent power of those feelings being regurgitated like so much bile. Not that this hindered any his guitar playing, tears flowing once more in heated rivulets.

Certain now his plan was working he could feel all that emotional baggage being washed away by those very same, special tears. Surely they were healing tears, empowering him as much as the music he played. Proof positive of their beneficial qualities the increasing sense of release he felt told him salvation was now in plain sight.

No longer playing in pain alone, hope also present, Andrei pushed himself all-the-same even further. Not ready yet to quit he was aware from previous experience what was required for ultimate deliverance, he pressed ever onward. Hoping to achieve a state of both utter physical and emotional exhaustion he knew it was then, and only then he'd achieve that final freedom which he so desperately sought.

****

Ultimate emancipation from his inner torment was only won at last when the tears would no longer come. His body feeling as though encased in lead, his spirit felt nonetheless both liberated and reborn even with his physical being left feeling both tired and numb. Only then did he cease playing, returning his loyal companion to its customary resting place, dragging himself instead to the foot of the nearby bed.

Once there Andrei let himself collapse smack-dab right in the middle, not even bothering to gather back the sheets. Having made the bed earlier that morning he didn't even trouble himself with so much as a pillow. Curled up instead in a naked ball of weary flesh, his head resting against his arm, sleep followed immediately thereafter without any further ado.

****

Brought back to the waking world by the soft yet persistent door-chime from down the hall Andrei looked over at the nearby nightstand, the timepiece there informing him he'd been asleep for nearly five hours. Rested and refreshed he quickly grabbed his bathrobe from the nearby walk-in closet, wrapping it around his naked form.

Heading down the hallway beyond, tying a silken chord belt around his middle, Andrei called out to his unknown visitor someone was in fact on their way, reaching the front door only a moment later.

Hearing a woman's muffled voice respond from the other side, unable to make out her precise words, he activated the small security screen embedded in the lefthand doorjamb. Met by the clear image of a young gentlewoman barely out of her teens she held a large bouquet of red roses accompanied by a wide, flat, square parcel wrapped in silver paper:

"Yes?" Andrei addressed her via the intercom located beneath the small screen: "How may I help you?"

"I have a delivery here from a 'Commodore Jenniboni Saphira' for a 'Mister Andrei Saphira'", she announced in a pleasant voice, holding up further a Base Pass picture I.D. for his inspection:

"Yes, of course", he responded rather clumsily, loath to talk with others through that darned thing. Oh well: Better safe than sorry! After earlier that very same day he was sure Jenniboni would want him to likewise observe such little precautions:

"I'm sorry about that", Andrei apologized all-the-same to the young woman upon opening the door.

"That's all right, Sir", she assured him, blushing, quickly averting her gaze from his immediate direction: "Perfectly understandable. And I'm sorry as well if I've caught you at an awkward moment".

Glancing down at his own person, understanding now the reason for her newfound discomfort, Andrei informed the bashful delivery woman he was about to get ready for a party later that night. Not wishing to sound like some sort of pretentious name-dropper he chose on purpose not to mention neither where, nor with who.

"Yes, Sir, of course. Hope you have a good time", she proceeded. Still rather timid in her newfound embarrassment she announced further he'd have to sign for the delivery at hand.

Having no further wish to embarrass either of them, concerned the front of his long, blue silk robe might slip open were he to even try and relieve her of her 'burden', he asked the shy young gentlewoman to just set the new arrivals on the nearby dining-room table behind him.

Placing carefully both flowers and parcel where requested, she retrieved afterwards a small stylus and ei-pad from the back pocket of her workwoman's coveralls. Taking each from her hand Andrei signed his name where instructed, asking her to wait yet another moment after giving them back.

Stepping over to the coat rack next to the front door, his black leather jacket hanging from one of the lower pegs, he collected from inside his wallet a ten-krodit note.

"Here: For your trouble", he looked up at her, smiling kindly.

Handing her the rainbow-hued money its holographic 3-D images sparkled in the artificial lighting from above, engraved with laser precision on its flexible plasti-metal fibers.

"Why thank you, Sir".

Pleasantly surprised receiving such a generous gratuity the young delivery woman appeared to make an otherwise rapid recovery regarding her previous discomfort. All in all the reaction Andrei was hoping for, presenting it to her just before she left.

****

Left again to his own devices, enwrapped once more in the familiar warmth of his immediate surroundings, Andrei wasted no time inspecting now the new arrivals sent courtesy of a thoughtful wife.

Arrayed before him on the large family table, providing a colourful contrast to its dark wood surface, he was quick to discover two dozen long stemmed roses and a mysterious package clad in silver wrapping paper, blue ribbon with bow on top tied around its middle.

Eager to discover what delights were resting beneath its glistening cover, Andrei was presented with a goodly-sized box of his favorite candy, maraschino cherries complete with crushed almonds encased in liberal amounts of dark chocolate.

Longing to try at least one as soon as possible he resisted all the same temptation's sweet call, choosing first to put the flowers in water. Not wanting them to wilt any he collected from the kitchen a tall, elegantly detailed crystal vase from over the family refrigeration unit.

Filling the lead glass container halfway with cool water he then stirred into it a packet of powder sold under the otherwise trite brand name; "*Flower Power*". While the product name struck him as sounding rather insipid Andrei had to admit it still lived up to its claim, prolonging the endurance of cut flowers, keeping them both fresh and blooming longer.

Peeling away green tissue paper from around their stems, arranging them neatly in their new home, it was then something fell to the table's surface infront of him. Landing right-side-up it was a richly textured, cream-coloured vellum envelope addressed simply "To Andrei" in Jenniboni's clear, bold, feminine handwriting.

Turning it over to open it from the other side he couldn't help but take note of a full, seductive lip print smack-dab right over the back flap—a pair of full, ripe, feminine lips wearing the same distinctive shade of pink as his wife's very own preferred brand of lipstick.

Literally sealed with a kiss, Andrei found it a singularly beautiful gesture of affection giving birth to warm feelings of joyful appreciation born of the simple knowledge he was truly loved, truly cared for, like no other:

Loved by someone also like no other!

Not wanting to damage this simple yet expressive sign of her eternal devotion he opened it instead from the top, gently tearing it open with the tip of his thumb under the edge of the envelope's back flap.

Folded neatly within Andrei found a note written on the same kind of thick paper as envelope it came in. And reading each sweet line of the short message contained therein he grew quite misty-eyed doing so. Brief in content the sentiment expressed there couldn't have been more potent were it the longest love sonnet ever written and… reading it several times over… he savored each tender word as one might relish a fine Bordeaux.

Better in fact than even that it warmed him deeper, and satisfied longer, than anything else ever could:

"My Beloved Andrei.

These modest gifts I send your way are but poor tokens of my never-ending love for you. While I dearly hope they bring you great pleasure I fear it will never rival the endless joy you've given me all these years by simply being the same wonderful, loving, and continually giving man I've come to care for more than life itself.

You make coming home the high point of my day and leaving each morning the most difficult thing I do.

So I send you these symbols of my everlasting devotion as a reminder that you are a truly beautiful and remarkable person whom I shall always cherish.

—With Undying Love, Jenniboni"

It was with a certain amount of deep reluctance Andrei placed the note back in its vellum casing. Bending over with eyes closed to breathe deeply of the flowers before him, their intoxicating perfume filling the senses, all his thoughts were centered now on the exquisite woman who sent them.

Her generosity matched only by her modesty he knew how dear her gifts truly were, long stemmed roses worth a queen's ransom alone so far removed from the inner planets. Especially here on one of the outermost worlds of the outer system.

Yet, while treasuring both flowers and candy, the small note still in hand was worth even moreso in his eyes—planning to tuck it away in a very special hiding place where he kept similar keepsakes likewise meaning the worlds to him. Holding forever a very dear place in his heart it should come as no surprise the majority of these valued mementos were all from Jenniboni herself, honoured reminders she loved him with the same depth of passion with which he loved her.

Right from the day they first met she became the very center of his existence Unwilling to even imagine the thought of living without her he refused to even try, such a life in his opinion worthless. So many magnificent attributes about her to love Andrei couldn't even list them all, treasuring nevertheless each and every one of them.

Opening the box of chocolates soon thereafter he plucked one from its individual cellophane wrapper, taking a bite from its thick, chocolate-almond shell. Sucking out the sticky sweet cherry within while likewise getting all of the syrup that came along with it, Andrei was put in mind of a Bible quote reminding him so well of Jenniboni:

"Out of the Strong came forth sweetness".

That and the Biblical reference to a good wife being worth more than all the gold and precious jewels in the world suited her to a 'T'.

Eating the rest of the tiny confectionery between thumb and forefinger an idea for something else quite delicious soon came to mind. Something he knew from past experience sure to give his wife both great pleasure and enjoyment of her own. And tomorrow would be the perfect night to spring it on her: Thursday, February the 14th…

Valentine's day!

Knowing already she was planning a very special celebration for their 10th Valentines together, what he had in mind would help make for a perfect climax to their romantic interlude

Resisting the urge to partake of yet another sweet morsel in the flat container before him Andrei slipped instead the box of chocolates into the kitchen refrigeration unit—doing so right next to a tapered bottle of sparkling cider destined also for tomorrow's festivities.

Closing the cooler's door immediately thereafter he wore a mischievous little smile picturing the expression on Jenniboni's face when learning what he had in mind.

Chapter 34

"PREPARATIONS"

When the children finally came home early that evening from their afternoon adventure at the Crystal Gardens Andrei, having missed them more than anticipated, was happy to have them back. Listening with undivided attention to their exuberant chatter he took as much fatherly pleasure in hearing about their day as they took childish delight in the telling.

Even J.J. forewent her usual display of mature reserve when recounting all the fun they had on their outing with "Uncle Darrin".

'Note to self ', Andrei silently mused: 'Tell Jenniboni to give her secretary a raise!'…

Wanting his entire family with him before the day's end, he let all three children stay up long enough to wish their mother *good-night* upon her arrival home. Giving them a reasonable amount of time with her before putting them to bed, Jenniboni prepared right thereafter for their own eagerly anticipated visit aboard the Prime Arch Matri's private cruiser.

Hanging up her casual-dress uniform back in the closet before discarding bra and panties in a nearby laundry hamper, Jenniboni listened as well as Andrei sang the children to sleep down the hall. Able to hear him begin this particular tradition with a perky, spirited little tune this was followed soon by a tender ballad replete with loving sentiment accompanied on Spanish guitar.

Just standing there in the middle of the mistress bedroom she listened, enraptured, rooted to the spot. Captivated by the very sound of her husband's deep, beautiful, singing voice and the soothing way in which he played Jenniboni regretted the necessity of donning instead her shower cap, climbing into the shower before hearing him complete this nightly family musical ritual.

Only with the children lulled to sleep, Raoul yet to arrive, did Andrei take a similar shower once Jenniboni proved done with hers.

Taking one only because it was his usual custom that time of day however, he didn't want Jenniboni growing suspicious should he vary his routine on this of all nights. Realizing with rueful humour one wasn't necessary after the dramatic events of that very same morning what took place earlier was a private, personal affair resolved once and for all. No need to worry her further whether, or not he was coping.

****

Stepping directly out of the shower into the nearby dryer booth, Andrei waited until both hair and skin were moisture-free before slipping on as well his bathrobe.

Tying it loosely about his trim, flat mid-section he made his way into the adjoining bedroom, sitting at the vanity table both he and Jenniboni shared—brushing his hair while she employed the full-length mirror to his immediate left, applying the final touches to her grand, full-dress S.E.A. uniform.

Reserved for official functions and ceremonial occasions it was comprised of the same green/gold colour scheme as her other. However, unlike that one, this consisted of green tie, gold shirt, and an ankle-length dress of the same deep-forest green—a close-set row of gold buttons running down its center while a pair of elegant tan, brown knee-high boots remained visible just beneath its hem.

Tailored from the waist-up in the distinct style of a military jacket replete with widened lapels and gold braid about the cuffs this, like her other, came complete also with the impressive golden-yellow fempacem armbands and multi-hued ribbons over her left breast denoting both rank and position.

Even Jenniboni's three sparkling medals were back in their customary place, positioned right below her other aforementioned laurels, while a crimson sash secured firmly about her waist helped accentuate her curvaceous hour-glass figure.

Two other final touches helping to likewise round out her striking ensemble one was a majestic, floor-length crimson cape with gold trim draped over her shoulders alongside a high-peaked green and gold cap of an imposing design commanding absolute respect.

Having yet to don these last two items, however, Jenniboni thought it best to wait until dealing first with both her hair and make-up—Andrei fussing still over both his hair and goatee, anxious for every single strand to be just so for his introduction to the Supreme Mother.

Applying a quick sprits of men's hair spray only when sure all else was taken care of to his complete satisfaction, restoring at last all his toiletries to their previous station, he then asked Jenniboni if she wished to take his place:

"Yes, Sweet-thing. Thank you", she answered him, taking her turn at the table. Sliding open the various drawers, she removed from within both her make-up case, brushes, and comb:

"Once you get dressed, and I finish up here, we'll be ready to leave", she continued, spreading out her cosmetics before her in a tidy arrangement as Andrei sat himself down on the corner of their bed.

Even though beyond her direct range of vision Jenniboni knew with a pert little grin he was watching, always intrigued by the application of her make-up.

241

Anticipating this from the very beginning she even factored into her original calculations the delay involved when deciding the best time to leave. Although aware she could put an end to all this by just telling him to stop dawdling and get dressed she still didn't have the heart to pull 'gender rank' on him. After recent events she just couldn't bring herself to deny him such a simple, little personal pleasure.

Then again, as long as her preparations had his undivided attention, he wouldn't be fretting so over his own up-and-coming audience with the Supreme Mother. Although he hid it well, Jenniboni could nonetheless detect quite well those telltale signs of anxiety.

Then again, nerves aside, she had yet another good reason for wanting to keep him happy as long as possible. Convinced he'd have a wonderful time once actually meeting the P.A.M., Jenniboni knew as well he wouldn't be in such high spirits after telling him she was leaving early once back home.

A painful task she dreaded already; it was one she'd have to deal with soon enough. And an awesome personal burden to begin with, it was only further complicated by the certain fact she couldn't reveal why.

While knowing she'd be given permission to tell him of her new departure time Jenniboni was just as certain she'd be forbidden as well to explain why she must leave so much sooner—a grim reality made only worse by the additional fact her husband, no dummy by any stretch of the imagination, would readily see through any otherwise clever cover-story concocted for public consumption.

Extra emotional turmoil she'd be heaping on top of the certain disappointment he'd already be feeling, she endured a certain amount of emotional turmoil herself over both the twin aspects of their new mission parameters as well as breaking the bad news to her unsuspecting husband. An uneasiness she nevertheless hid well Jenniboni finished applying her cosmetics, facing at last the young man watching her with such loving devotion:

"So, precious, how do I look?", she asked, getting up from her seat.

"Absolutely fantastic", Andrei assured her in a voice full of honest appreciation: "Achingly beautiful as always!"

"You always know the right thing to say, Sweet-pea", she smiled a broad smile replete with an immediate sigh of relief. Stepping towards him Jenniboni graced her husband with an affectionate pat on the cheek, her touch always filling him with such utter jubilation he just wanted it to last forever.

Just wanting to hold that exquisitely manicured hand to his face for the remainder of the evening, Andrei resisted all-the-same the compelling urge to do so as she removed it from against his flesh.

"Come now, Mr. Saphira! Time for you to get dressed", she teased, holding both hands out to him. Assuming a stern countenance for purely comical affect her otherwise grim demeanor was belied only by the lively, good-humored sparkle dancing about in rich, dark, mahogany eyes: "Now that you've had your fun watching me *power-up* my father will be arriving shortly".

Starting to blush, feeling now rather self-conscious being so obvious in his simple adoration, this endearing reaction on his part inspired his wife to smile even more so, taking his hands in hers. Letting her help him off the bed,

Jenniboni pulling him up quite easily to his feet, not once did he take his eyes off her sweet, loving expression.

Wanting so much to just reach up and kiss her once firmly on his feet her lips looked so soft, moist, and utterly inviting it inspired such feelings of intense longing it set his entire body all aflame, looking equally so dashing in her regal vestments:

So especially sheroic.

Realizing however she wouldn't appreciate him smudging up the otherwise excellent job she achieved in her cosmetics, empowering herself for such an important gala event as tonight, he fought instead that irresistible urge to kiss her. Calling upon all his considerable willpower doing so he gave Jenniboni instead a snappy, comical salute:

"Yes, Ma'am!", Andrei responded to her last declaration in the same jocular vein she used earlier with him.

Glancing down at the knotted silken cord tied around his waist, undoing it at once, he removed his shimmering dressing gown from about his shoulders, tossing it in a casual manner on the bed. Wearing not a stitch he passed by her on his way to the closet only to have Jenniboni give him a playful little smack with the back of her hand on his firm, bare derriere:

"Hey, you break it, you bought it", he laughed over his shoulder in her direction.

"I'll have you know that I already 'bought it' the day I put that ring on your finger and said, 'I do'", Jenniboni giggled in merry rely.

"Yeah, right: You think you're all that".

"Hey, I already *know* I'm all that—*and more*!", she shot back with similar amusement as Andrei drew apart the slatted sliding doors to the sizable walk-in closet beyond. Selecting a pair of briefs from the dresser inside he could hear her enquire as he slipped them on as to what he planned to wear for the evening ahead:

"It was hard to choose but, if you have no objections, I think I've come up with just the very thing", he offered, stepping even farther into the large storage space until soon out of sight. For a while all she could hear was the clear, audible, rustling sound of clothes being sorted through while still hanging on the rack, her husband reappearing shortly after—outfit in hand.

Slung over one shoulder Andrei carried his main attire on a sturdy padded hanger, a pair of black patent leather shoes and rolled up dress socks cradled in his other arm. Plopping the later items down on the bed he then removed the others from their hanger, laying them out with great care for her inspection.

The first article of men's finery placed on display was a crushed velvet Edwardian jacket, dark blue, alongside a light violet shirt. Replete with ruffles this was followed by a pair of crisply tailored trousers the same colour and material as the jacket—a navy blue ascot and black leather belt complete with gold buckle adding an extra touch of class to an already splendid array.

All-in-all his chosen attire for their appearance before the Supreme Mother had about it an air of masculine grace, culture, civility, and dignified elegance, such antiquities in men's styles being all the current rage.

"So what do you think?" he asked in hopeful anticipation.

"Perfect!" Jenniboni purred her approval: "You'll be the most handsome, best dressed laddie there".

"Thanks love", he breathed a grateful sigh, relief evident in the very way his entire face now relaxed.

Gathering up each item from its current resting place Andrei set about getting dressed, standing before the same mirror Jenniboni used putting on her uniform. Watching as he adjusted his clothes, turning every which way to check himself out at every angle possible, she could easily spot the tense apprehension gnawing away at him in the stiff, hesitant way he moved about.

Having always taken pride in his appearance, meticulous without being in any way narcissistic, she still couldn't remember any other occasion seeing him fuss just quite so.

Usually so sure of himself, Jenniboni sympathized with his temporary lack of confidence. Not only was he to meet the duly elected leader of all Womankind in less than a couple of hours he also faced the extra pressure of knowing how he looked... along with how he behaved... would naturally reflect either one way or the other on his wife.

Sensitive to such an understandable case of nerves Jenniboni favored him with both a supportive little smile, and the ancient "thumbs-up" sign when looking to her for positive reinforcement. Appearing content at last he arranged his navy ascot just so, slipping it about his neck, before turning back in her direction.

Approaching her however, Jenniboni stopped him dead in his tracks, gently laying her hand upon his chest.

"What's wrong", he looked up at her, both confused and worried at the very same time.

"No. On second thought that ascot just doesn't quite fit. Not with that outfit", she informed him with an introspective little pout:

"Wait right there: Don't move", she instructed him, giving Andrei a playful little tap on the tip of his nose. Heading straight away for his side of the closet she soon returned with a white satin scarf, same general design as the one Andrei now wore, removing the first from about his neck.

Holding it with extended arm over their bed, letting the little piece of blue finery go, it floated leisurely on the air towards its eventual resting place. Replacing it with that new one of her own choosing Jenniboni arranged it in place ever so smartly, tucking both ends under the top of his ruffled shirt.

"There. Perfect. White goes with just about everything", she cooed most playfully:

"Besides, the cool of white will offset that natural glow you seem to have just acquired. You do know, don't you, that you're absolutely adorable when you blush", Jenniboni added with a tender smile, Andrei blushing then even moreso.

Having taken care of that Jenniboni then returned once more to their full-length looking glass, taking care of the final touches to her own attire. Positioning her cap just so she gathered up as well her crimson cape from atop of the nearby bed, arranging it about her shoulders with a flourish of motion, it was then she heard the door chime from down the hall.

"And that, my dear Sir, is our cue to leave", Jenniboni declared.

Opening the bedroom door, bowing as well ever so slightly, she ushered across the threshold her comely young escort for the evening, doing so with both a cheery smile and courtly little wave of her hand.

****

Making their way down the hallway past the closed doors to each twin's bedroom both wife and husband were careful to keep silent, making their way to the front door.

"Hope I'm not late", Raoul greeted each as Jenniboni let him in: "I had some difficulty with traffic outside the shelter".

"Not at all", his daughter was quick to assure him: "Right on time as usual".

"Glad to hear it. Hate to think I held up either of you for your audience with the Supreme Mother", Raoul breathed more easily, smiling at last:

"Oh well, now that I'm here, I'll be sure to take good care of my grandchildren", he added, clapping his hands together in jovial good humour.

"I'm sure you will", Jenniboni smiled as well, giving his upper arm an affectionate little squeeze: "And we really appreciate your staying with them on such short notice".

"Think nothing of it. My pleasure: You two kids just go now and have a good time", her father encouraged the young couple before him in that deep, rich, cultivated voice of his—adding that they both looked "quite splendid indeed" for their evening out with Humanity's supreme leader.

Thanking him for the heartfelt complement, making her way across the small vestibule between their front door and the elevator unit beyond, Jenniboni pushed the lift button while looking at her wristwatch:

"It looks like we'll make the shuttle on time but we still need to hurry", she announced, waiting for her husband's response. Looking to her side when no reply was forthcoming, expecting Andrei to be beside her, she was somewhat concerned to learn differently.

Turning about quickly, her red cape swishing majestically about her legs, she found him quickly enough in deep conversation with her father, standing just outside their apartment door.

"Oh, for pity's sake, Andrei: Stop dawdling and come along **right now**!", she summoned him with an irritated sigh; "or else we'll be late".

The last thing she needed was to be found tardy for one of the most important meetings of her life because of a chatty husband.

"In a moment, Dear", he promised her over his shoulder, turning then his full attention back to Raoul:

"Just a few last minute details I need to further discuss with your father".

"NO!", she exclaimed: "It's time to go. I'm sure my father knows on his own what to do".

Appearing for a brief moment Andrei wasn't going to budge, loath to obey, she marched with a determined stride straight towards him. While understanding his hesitant behavior might be a subconscious case of the jitters meeting the Prime Arch Matri, Jenniboni had nonetheless no time to spare coaxing him along with reassuring words of comfort.

Being sure to be as temperate in her touch as much as possible Jenniboni placed her hand against the small of his back, applying persuasive force.

Turning him about with unwavering determination, letting up not once on the gentle pressure guiding him now towards the open lift, she left Andrei barely enough time to call out "good-bye" as the lift doors slid likewise shut behind them.

Alone to himself, closing the front door, Raoul was amused to notice how much Jenniboni reminded him of her late mother:

"Just like her", he chortled, shaking his head.

Chapter 35

"THE PRIME ARCH MATRI"

Along with StarChild's senior command staff aboard the private shuttle destined for Stellar-One were Admiral Sellers and her husband, Charlie, who was as usual coolly polite to Andrei—nothing more.

No skin off his nose however if Charlie Sellers had no time for him, the feeling quite mutual. In Andrei's eyes the 'great' Mr. Sellers was nothing but an obsequious little toady seeking prestige on the hem of his wife's dress, trying also to ingratiate himself to those possessing both power and influence of their own.

Probably why, despite his own personal trepidations, Andrei found himself actually smiling at the very thought of Charlie Sellers meeting the Supreme Mother.

'This'll surely be a sight to behold', he laughed to himself, only one other man in addition to both Andrei and Charlie present—only one of Jenniboni's senior officers able to secure a date on such short notice.

Nor did it come as any surprise to Andrei's way of thinking that Frances proved herself that one, very special someone able to find an escort on such short notice—her companion for the evening one '*Master Shotoku Imoko*'.

A handsome young Asian laddie from 'Asuka-Nara City' he was from one of those original Japanese colonies established in Ahnteekah just before its current tropical climes, back in those ancient days when still known as '*Antarctica*'.

Sitting next to his wife in one of the shuttle's front row passenger seats Andrei could feel her hand slip around his, giving it a comforting squeeze. Turning to look at her however, Andrei's gaze was captured instead by a large spacecraft looming into sight. Coming into view through the passenger window next to Jenniboni's seat it was a long, sleek, magnificent ship putting him in mind of a giant dragonfly.

Interested how women seemed to design space-faring vessels to resemble actual winged creatures he was enraptured by the very sight of it, its resemblance to a dragonfly only further enhanced by the expansive solar sails to either side. Looking so much like graceful, gossamer wings they employed solar winds to propel the cosmic cruiser once standard engines achieved desired velocity.

Conserving in this way other, more easily exhaustible power sources, able to shift position in order to steer the vessel in any given direction, Andrei watched them tilt upwards now in frank amazement, revealing as they did so a well-lit hangar-bay entrance:

"Fantastic!", he whispered aloud: "Is that it?"

"Indeed he is", Jenniboni nodded: "'Stellar-One'".

Upon closer scrutiny Andrei was able to make out now the name **'STELLAR-ONE'** printed along the ship's impressive prow in large, proud, block letters situated just above the official state emblem for the entire Commonwealth of all Womankind—a fempacem with the faces of a man and woman on either side, facing away from one another in profile, the initials **'C.T.C.I.M.W.'** ('Colonial Terran Commonwealth of Interplanetary Matriarchate Worlds') emblazoned directly beneath.

Implementing right about then an immediate course change, the small shuttle angled itself on a trajectory for the larger craft's open docking port. And sensing her husband's apprehension increase as Stellar-One now blocked out the stars with its massive bulk, Jenniboni gave him a reassuring little pat on the back of the hand:

"Don't worry, Sweet-pea: You'll be just fine. I'm sure you'll do both of us proud. I'm sure the Supreme Mother will love you as much as I", she beamed him a great smile full of boundless confidence: "Which is why I'm not worried in the least".

Returning her smile with one of his own, Jenniboni's kind words helped ease for the most part Andrei's troubled mind.

At least for the moment.

However, even so, he couldn't help but wonder if she was being completely honest with him regarding her own current state of mind. While true he couldn't detect any trace of either anxiety, or concern whatsoever in her strong, confident features, he wondered nonetheless how she couldn't be at least a little bit nervous.

After all this was the Prime Arch Matri they were talking about!

****

Once their shuttle came to its eventual resting place smack-dab in the very center of that stark landing bay's glistening white interior, its engines now quiet, the passengers onboard proceeded without delay to disembark.

Doing so according to rank, the first to emerge was Melissa Sellers followed soon after by Jenniboni, Stasha, and Frances—those gentlewomen with escorts pausing upon stepping out into the hanger bay's grand expanse, assisting their men in stepping down from the smaller craft's entryway.

Nor had they long to wait mulling about their nearby vehicle, greeted soon after by a distinguished-looking middle-aged laddie with hazel eyes and wavy brown hair liberally streaked with grey.

Clad in a well-tailored, form-fitting silver and black servant's uniform he wasted no time introducing himself as 'Eric', the P.A.M.'s chief manservant aboard Stellar-One.

Requesting with courteous efficiency they accompany him to the nearby Hall of Audiences he informed them likewise they'd be greeted there by the Rime Arch Matri and her family. According to Eric these included her husband, the Prime Laddie, alongside her daughter and son-in-law.

With the P.A.M.'s head manservant leading the way, the new arrivals followed close behind. Departing the cavernous landing bay for an equally spacious corridor Jenniboni offered Andrei her arm, leading him along behind their guide. Side-by-side with the Sellers', Charlie likewise on his wife's arm, the two couples lead the way ahead of the other delegates from StarChild.

Envying Jenniboni her proud regal stance, striding along as if without any care in the System, Andrei wasn't even aware his hold on her upper arm was beginning to slowly tighten. Impressed with how magnificent she looked in her forceful attire; so dignified, empowered, and serene... head held high... Andrei had no idea he was causing her any discomfort.

At least not until she leaned towards him, voice low:

"Darling, I know you're nervous", she whispered discreetly in his ear; "but would you please be so kind as to loosen up that vice-like grip of yours?"

Doing as she asked, making a concerted effort to maintain as gentle a grasp as possible, Jenniboni returned her gaze forwards as he likewise tried taking his mind off those annoying hummingbirds in the pit of his stomach.

Studying instead his immediate surroundings, a continuous triangular passageway wider than it was high, the walls on either side of them angled inwards to meet directly above. And embedded into each slanting wall a row of bright, rounded lighting panels lit their way; the floor upon which they trod carpeted in a heavy duty short weaved fabric a regal red in colour.

After a while though the grand hallway soon came to an end, a triangular door made of some sort of highly polished wood barring their way.

Divided down the middle into two equal halves, each half of the broad entry possessed a round, frosted plate-glass window. And unable to see through the surface of either cloudy portal, Andrei knew all-the-same his moment of truth had finally come.

Nor was it long in coming when Eric stepped forward. Activating a pale green access panel just right of the impressive entranceway the solid, tan wood doors slid apart to reveal on the other side a welcoming committee of four.

****

No mistaking the one on the far right for anyone other than Ms. Anita Carlin herself, Andrei's starry-eyed gaze was drawn to the highly respected leader of all Humanity like a veritable magnet. Standing there in all her awesome glory no more than a few meters away was none other than the Supreme Mother herself.

"Well, here goes nothing", Andrei braced himself: "So don't go screwing up".

First to enter the Hall of Audiences was Eric. Positioning himself out of the way he began to announce straight after that each new arrival in a clear, formal, punctilious voice:

"Admiral and Mr. Melissa Sellers".

In observance of proper protocol the senior couple present stepped up to the Supreme Mother to be formally introduced, moving down the line to greet the other members of her entourage:

"Commodore and Mr. Jenniboni Saphira".

Immersed in private thought, paying no heed at all to Eric's introduction, Andrei was at a momentary loss when Jenniboni stepped forward. Startled by the sudden tug at his hand he didn't realize what was happening until only a couple of meters away from the Supreme Mother herself:

Disengaging him from her arm, approaching the other woman first, Jenniboni gave her a solemn bow—Andrei making the most of this unique opportunity to observe up close the stately leader of all Womankind, the entire Matriarchate.

Standing at a little over six feet in height the proud black woman in her dignified purple robes of office was about average height for someone of her gender, the only average feature of this rather imposing Matriarch already in deep conversation with his wife.

Although she might have been an inch, or two shorter than Jenniboni, she still managed to eclipse StarChild's commanding officer with her monumental girth. Yet it wasn't her considerable size that fired Andrei's imagination so much as it was the overwhelming absence of any discernible weakness whatsoever in either face or form...

Everything about Anita Carlin's physical presence screamed both power, strength, authority, and control. Her face, although quite round, was in no way jowly, but firm possessing both smooth dark skin, broad dignified features, and a confident expression born of a steadfast belief in both oneself and one's own talents.

In many ways she reminded him of a series of highly skilled, intricately detailed woodcarvings he'd seen during his stint as a volunteer tour guide in that museum back on Earth—renderings from ancient Africa of proud African Queens and Matriarchs.

Believing back then they were exaggerated in design Andrei had found it hard to believe that anyone could look so perfect, so splendidly regal. At least not until that very moment. Even her grey hair was reminiscent of a majestic, silver crown. Nor was that all, comforted to see as well in her eyes both kindness and sensitivity alongside her obvious intelligence, clear strength of will, and her intimidating grandeur.

So very taken in fact with the very being of this woman standing before him, Andrei almost missed Jenniboni's presentation:

"... and it gives me great pleasure, Supreme Mother, to introduce to you my husband: Mr. Andrei Saphira".

Almost blowing his cue he nevertheless affected a swift recovery, humbly approaching her with all the calm he could possibly muster under such circumstances. Bowing like his wife before him, he told her as well upon rising what an honour and privilege it was to be making her acquaintance:

One contributing factor to Anita Carlin's excellent leadership skills was her superior ability to read the feelings of others, able to detect their emotional state with unerring accuracy, mindful of how those coming into her orbit might feel uneasy in her company.

Aware that her very physical presence commanded both a natural respect and deferring awe, she picked up quite easily on the anxiety permeating the young man standing before her. Then again she had to confess with an inward smile he hid it well, better than many others regardless their gender, this indication of inner-strength earning Andrei her immediate esteem.

Something else which made Anita both a wise and thoughtful leader was her similar talent for putting people at ease while with her. Helping them to feel more comfortable, more relaxed, with themselves while in her company, she utilized that special skill now.

Taking Andrei's hand in hers, looking him straight in the eye, she bestowed as well upon the nervous young laddie a convivial smile full of sincere warmth. Speaking to him in a familial voice, expressing as well her pleasure in making his acquaintance, she even complimented him on his 'magnificent attire' while confiding in him her sincere admiration for Jenniboni.

With that the tension flowed quite literally from out of his entire body, replaced with a sure sense of giddy delight, moved by how the Supreme Mother was talking to him now as though they were indeed equals.

Reigning in all-the-same his exuberance least he come across as either a blathering idiot, or fawning sycophant he told her nonetheless how both he and Jenniboni were appreciative admirers. Revealing how each of them served on her election campaign, Andrei also confided in her his fond appreciation for her positive stand on various men's issues, citing those nearest and dearest to his heart.

Concluding what he wanted to say, keeping his conversation brief least he hold up the rest of the procession, he ended with his sincerest thanks for having been invited to this evening's special gathering. Moving along down the line to greet the other three members of the Supreme Mother's entourage the next to welcome him aboard Stellar-One was the Supreme Mother's husband, Daniel Carlin, the Prime Laddie himself.

About the same height as Andrei the other Carlin was a solidly-built man whose close-cropped hair, like his wife's, was starting to turn grey—that which stood out the most about him being however his kindly manner, refinement, and witty intelligence—the P.A.M.'s son-in-law following soon thereafter:

Introducing himself as Timothy Carlin he was a wavy-haired, redheaded laddie no more than just a couple of years older than Andrei. Possessing a gentle, good-natured, twinkle in his pale blue eyes he had as well about him a quite Viking-like appearance—a modern-day Leif Erickson in an expensive, three-piece, evening suit standing next to the Prime Arch Matri's daughter, Ms. Candace Carlin.

Resplendent in the same crimson and gold formal-dress Protectorate uniform Jenniboni wore at their wedding replete with gold-trimmed green cape—red and gold cap likewise present—the many ribbons on her chest denoted also a rank comparable to Jenniboni's.

Easily the tallest of the four she was an achingly beautiful woman somewhere around her early-to-mid 30's. If her mother reminded Andrei of a proud African queen then she was a regal African princess with a strong, graceful figure and winsome face:

Smiling down upon him he was awestruck by her finely sculptured cheekbones, expressive wide eyes, full lips, and radiant countenance—her long, glistening jet-black hair cascading down about her shoulders, breasts, and back in finely braided dreadlocks—her beautiful ebony skin complimented by the crimson and gold she so proudly wore.

Embarrassed to admit it even to himself Andrei discovered himself quite reluctant to move along when it came time for the next person in line to meet the dashing, red-clad woman standing there before him.

****

Once the initial formalities of welcome were thoroughly seen to the party-goers mingled then among one-another in the Hall of Audiences—waiters in smart silver and black attire circulating about the brightly decorated room with its tasteful décor carrying golden trays from which they offered guests hor d'oeuvres and fine champagne in fluted crystal glasses.

Making the most of this unique opportunity to meet the other officers comprising his wife's senior command staff Andrei managed brief, but pleasant talks with each. While finding each to be both quite affable and intriguing in her own special right he still enjoyed his talks with Naomi, Stasha, and Frances most.

Although Naomi's conversation centered for the most part on matters of a more technical level at least she managed to keep her subjects both entertaining and easy to understand. And as for Stasha she was an old and dear friend, allowing them a past to share when conversing.

Nevertheless it was Frances with whom he looked forward to speaking with the most, finding her after a short while… arm around her young date… gazing out the large, picturesque viewing port arrayed along one entire side of the vast chamber.

Approaching them further however it was only then it occurred to him he might be intruding upon a very private moment, turning around at once in order to leave. No such luck though. Having clearly heard his approach Frances and her young laddie for the evening turning about to see who was there.

"I'm very sorry to have intruded on either of you", Andrei apologized, feeling rather awkward: "I didn't mean to disturb you".

"You needn't apologize", she held her hand up in gentle protest, introducing him to her escort.

Complimenting the other man on the smashing gold and black kimono he'd chosen for that evening's celebration, fashioned in a style worn by ancient Japanese royalty. Commenting on how its neo-tencel fabric had about it an almost iridescent shimmer, the two men had taken to talking just as Jenniboni joined the trio, making them a quartet.

Once again Frances introduced Shotoku, this time to her commanding officer. Slipping her arm about Andrei's waist Jenniboni told the other laddie it was a pleasure to meet him, expressing her honest hope he was enjoying himself as much as they. Clearly as star-struck at meeting her as Andrei was when introduced to the Prime Arch Matri, he was used to this reaction on the part of other men when first making her acquaintance.

Finding it all a trifle amusing, it was right then Andrei wondered if the Prime Laddie found his own awe upon meeting the Supreme Mother an equal source of subtle humor.

Soon shifting her attention from Shotoku however, Jenniboni then extended her sincerest thanks to Frances for all she'd done for her husband, the other woman declaring it an honour to have rendered any assistance she could.

Once having done so however neither gentlewoman spoke any further on the matter least they cause Andrei any additional discomfort in the reminding. Each now aware the other knew also about the event in question a silent agreement was reached to drop the subject.

Changing the topic of conversation for his sake it was then Jenniboni invited her over to their place instead, informing her both she and Andrei would consider it a great honour should she partake of their hospitality—Frances, accepting with evident pleasure, assuring them it would be an honour on her part to accept their gracious offer.

With that Jenniboni excused herself, wishing both Frances and Shotoku an enjoyable evening. Having no further desire to intrude upon their time together she steering Andrei away from their general vicinity, her arm still around his middle. Only then, once sure they were all alone, did she whisper something in her husband's ear:

"I just thought you might like to know that you handled yourself most brilliantly with the P.A.M."

"Lord, I hope so. I just hope she didn't think me some sort of empty-headed chatterbox".

"On the contrary my dear Sir I'll have you know that she told me, and I quote, she thought you were '… a most charming, intelligent, handsome, and well-spoken young laddie with both style and grace'".

"Really?" Andrei all but gawked at her, her words sounding just too good to be true.

"Really! She even informed me that I was, to be sure, a very lucky woman just to have you", Jenniboni confided, sweetly smiling. Gazing up into those sparking eyes so full of honest praise he was quite overjoyed to see by her gentle expression she was being completely honest with him:

"Well, now. Haven't I been telling you just that very thing for several years now?", he teased her with a soft laugh, feeling as though on cloud nine.

"Quite", Jenniboni giggled: "Then again, I wasn't worried in the least. I knew all that aristocratic blue-blood of yours would see you through".

"Well… if we're going to discuss family backgrounds I wouldn't rightly call the Saphira's gutter trash, either", Andrei quipped, wearing a most convivial grin. Overcome with a strong need to celebrate his good fortune he didn't even think twice about plucking a glass of champagne from a passing waiter's tray. Hesitating only when raising it to his lips, he looked up instead at his wife:

"Go ahead", she indulged: "You've earned it".

Taking a small sip Andrei closed his eyes, relishing the warm glow soon flowing throughout his entire being. Welling up from the pit of his stomach, bubbles tickling his nose, he heard Jenniboni whisper all-the-same tender council in his ear:

"Just don't forget the rules. You may have one glass now, and one later, but that's all. So you might want to make it last awhile. Alrightie, then?"

Understanding her concern, aware of his own penchant towards silliness when in his cups, he agreed readily not to forget. The very last thing he wanted to do was embarrass either one of them here of all places!

"That's my boy", she smiled with loving affection just as Andrei noticed Naomi out of the corner of his eye, deep in conversation with Dr. Wei-Chang.

Pointing her out to Jenniboni just as the other two women parted company he suggested right then and there they take this opportunity to invite Naomi as well to visit their home. Nor was it long after Jenniboni thanked her for the role she also played in his rescue the day before Eric appeared; announcing in that crisp, punctilious voice of his dinner was now being served in Stellar-One's formal banquet hall.

Chapter 36

"DINNER AND DISCUSSIONS"

Arriving on Jenniboni's arm in the formal dining area Andrei was struck right away by the sharp contrast between this room and the last. Whereas the former had a light, colourful contemporary spirit about it, this one possessed a dark, somber elegance harking back to a bygone era long past:

Dark wood paneling on the walls, crystal chandeliers, and equally dark oak furniture lending it a truly Victorian air, the floor was carpeted as well in the same burgundy hue as the red velvet padding on the solid chairs arranged about the grand dining-room table.

Looking about in simple admiration at both the lavish place settings and sumptuous array before them it also occurred to Andrei when taking a seat that, while the Hall of Audiences had a more feminine touch to it, this display of frank opulence possessed a somewhat masculine feel. And glancing down the long table to where the Prime Laddie now sat in similar period attire, Andrei was pretty sure who the interior decorator here had to be.

Once again waiters went about serving alcoholic beverages to the dinner guests, Andrei politely refusing this time around just as the Supreme Mother rose from her station at the table's head. Announcing her desire to propose a toast a hushed silence fell at once upon the entire room as she continued in a clear, precise, stateswoman-like voice:

"It is at this time I wish to once more welcome everyone here aboard Stellar-One for this very special celebration in honour of Womankind's first voyage beyond its home System.

"And as we push back the current boundaries of our civilization to all points previously unknown, I feel it only fitting we acknowledge both the courage, fortitude, and dedication of those daring officers and gentlewomen gathered here on this very special occasion.

"Having volunteered one-and-all for this landmark mission, they are nothing less than the torchbearers of our entire society braving new trails well beyond our home worlds in Humanity's name. Whatever may come their memory shall be honoured, their accomplishments never forgotten, in the long annals of Human herstory.

"And, on a similar note I likewise wish to salute both the bravery, devotion, and dedication of the men they leave behind to keep the home fires burning. I dedicate this toast as much to the laddies remaining here as I do to the intrepid gentlewomen going forth in the name of Commonwealth".

Raising her glass in tribute the Supreme Mother then took a sip, everyone there following suit as she sat down.

While setting his drink back down on the table before him Andrei couldn't help but feel rather uncertain about her little speech. Giving him cause for a vague sense of uneasy ambivalence, he found her words both inspiring and rather ominous at the very same time.

The part about 'the laddies left behind' reminding him of his impending separation from Jenniboni, Andrei was painfully aware he was the only laddie present whose wife was soon embarking on said 'landmark mission'.

However it was her reference to 'whatever may come' that really troubled him. Phrases such as 'their memory shall be honoured', and 'their accomplishments never forgotten' sounded more like some sort of premature eulogy for some sort of suicide mission, not a salute to one dedicated to mere exploration and scientific discovery.

Of course it was possible she was referring just to the inherent perils of the unknown in general, and the fate of Womankind as a whole, but... down deep in his very own heart of hearts... he didn't think so.

Could there be some other hidden meaning behind her carefully chosen words of which Andrei was as yet unaware?

Mulling it over a little further just as the first course was set before him, a most delightful Caesar salad freshly prepared only moments ago, it wasn't long after this he finally reached a simple conclusion:

Certain he would discover soon enough what was actually afoot he decided right then and there to put any further speculation on the back burner. Wishing for now to postpone any unpleasantries beyond his control, Andrei came to the firm resolve to just make the most of the evening ahead.

Realizing there wasn't much he could really do if something unpleasant was in the actual making Andrei decided to have a good time while possible, enjoying both the excellent food and splendid dinner company fate saw fit to grace him with.

As things turned out he'd proven fortunate enough in their pre-arranged seating plan, positioned between both Jenniboni and Dr. Wei-Chang. Although hoping to find himself stationed next to Frances he was pleased nevertheless to discover in StarChild's Chief Medical Officer a most entertaining conversationalist.

Even so however Andrei wasn't too thrilled about being seated directly across the table from no less than Charlie Sellers himself. Luckily for him the other man in question appeared just as happy to ignore Andrei's very existence, casting envious glances now-and-again in the Supreme Mother's direction. Not at all difficult to figure out at whose side Charlie really wanted to be at. How galling it must have been for the Admiral's husband not to have the grand matriarch's full and undivided attention.

As far as Andrei was concerned the other man should have been just as satisfied with the simple knowledge at least his wife sat at the majestic ruler's right hand. The person he really pitied here was Candace Carlin, not Charlie. Having had the grave misfortune of being situated alongside the annoying Mr. Sellers, it was apparent the latter consoled himself having at least the Supreme Mother's daughter as a captive audience.

From the polite yet bored expression on the beautiful Protector's face, it was clearly all she could do to suffer the man's constant, self-serving prattle in the name of simple courtesy. Recognizing that look in those lovely eyes of being so utterly trapped Andrei's heart went out to her, flashing her an encouraging smile when she cast a despairing look in his direction.

A smile she returned with one of her own, understanding there was at least someone there who sympathized with her 'plight'.

And so it was that, while dinner was indeed superb, Andrei enjoyed even moreso the equally splendid conversation all about him. Paying less attention to his food, both the trifle and after-dinner coffee served at the banquet's close went practically unnoticed as the Prime Arch Matri once more rose to her feet.

Reinforcing his earlier suspicions the real motive behind this gathering was other than social right from the very beginning, her next words brought their meal to an effective end before Andrei even knew what was happening:

"Gentlewomen; I believe the time has come to take leave of our charming male dinner companions so that we may discuss a few particulars concerning StarChild's bachelor voyage.

"So, with my apologies to the dear laddies, we shall adjourn now to my private conference chamber while I place both the dining room and Hall of Audiences at their disposal for the remainder of their stay".

Her attentions, now focused on all the men present at her table, included as well a most gracious smile:

"However, before we leave I wish to let each and every one of you know I've enjoyed the pleasure of your company and promise not to keep your escorts any longer than necessary. The staff is at your complete disposal as we gentlewomen dispense with a few routine matters.

"So feel free to request whatever you may desire while still aboard Stellar-One".

No sooner had she finished than the other women also present likewise rose to their feet, their men remaining where they were:

"Don't worry, dear. Nothing you need fret over. Just a few last minute details", Jenniboni whispered in Andrei's ear just before leaving with the rest.

If only he could believe her!!

*****

Possessing neither the cheery hospitality of the Hall of Audiences, nor the dining room's somber elegance, the conference chamber was stark in its functional utilitarianism.

Brightly lit its plain white walls and oval conference table made it clear this was a space reserved for serious matters-of-state *only*. And with the P.A.M. seated at one end of the table, Jenniboni and Admiral Sellers at either side of her, the other officers in attendance arranged themselves about the table in no particular order.

No time spared in calling their meeting together the Supreme Mother proceeded straight away to the very heart of the matter:

"As you are no doubt aware by now the departure date for your mission has been advanced from Friday, March 1st, to the day after tomorrow, this Friday the 15th.

"And in addition to the reasons already given there are a couple of others I felt it prudent to keep confidential until this very moment: The first being that, no matter what security precautions we might take, we face the very real possibility of the media getting wind of all this beforehand, exposing the serious threat our entire Commonwealth might be facing.

"Therefore, the government wants StarChild to be on its new fact-finding assignment—and back—as soon as humanly possible before the press gets hold of anything that might compromise our current position. Spin control will be a lot easier if we are in full possession of *all* the facts before anything of any real consequence is leaked to the public. There'll be a lot less panic in the streets if we can offer the general populace concrete facts and figures instead of mere speculation".

Everyone present nodded their silent agreement upon hearing this, the Prime Arch Matri continuing:

"Our second reason for moving up your departure time is because your mission reports will also be vital in determining whether or not we'll need to convert our entire economy to an immediate war-time status beginning with both troop deployment, arms production, and fortification of civilian defenses.

"And the sooner we know the better. Preliminary preparations have already been set in motion for the conversion of existing forces into a united military organization replete with full-scale battle capabilities just in case our worst-case scenario turns out to be fact".

"If I may, Ma'am, what preparations have been made up to this point?", Jenniboni queried, certain obstacles coming to mind:

Chief amongst these being if a civilization geared towards a peace-time, social democratic, free enterprise economy for nearly seven centuries could accomplish such an abrupt transformation virtually overnight: Other problems she likewise foresaw on the immediate horizon were forced conscription in a democratic society, the immediate establishment of extensive war-time production facilities, and civilian defense all in that short window of opportunity currently available.

Expressing these concerns though she soon found them being addressed not by the Prime Arch Matri, but her daughter. Seated next to Melissa Sellers, it was only then Jenniboni realized the purpose for Protector-Colonel Candace Carlin being in attendance at this particular meeting:

"I can assure you, Commodore Saphira, that all your concerns have already been taken into account", the junior Ms. Carlin informed her: "Even ancient patriarchal societies facing similar situations were able to cope on equally short notice".

'Oh lovely', Naomi mused to herself with silent scorn: 'Now we're taking lessons from the 'Ancient Patriarchates'.

'And look what happened to them!

'The Losers!!'

Their ultimate self-annihilation at the end of World War Three, not to mention the devastating effect it had on the entire Earth's surface, was all the proof needed since then that men lacked the essential temperament required for either total leadership or any other position of high authority.

'Or, put another way, they just didn't have the estrogen needed for the job', Naomi reflected in silence, sardonic:

'Nor the ovaries.

'Never did… never would… never will'.

"Of course we'll need to ensure both the cooperation and support of the general population in the eventuality of total war. However, once they realize that the very existence of the entire Commonwealth is at stake, I'm sure we'll have no problem in enlisting their full support", Candace assumed with a subtle trace of smug arrogance grating on Jenniboni's nerves.

No more so than it annoyed Dr. Wei-Chang, the first sarcastic thought leaping to the brusque old woman's mind being 'why not revive some catchy old war slogans from ancient herstory while we're at it'. Slogans such as 'Guns before butter', 'Slip of a lip…', and 'Tittle-tattle will lose the battle' came to mind.

Holding though her acidic tongue for once in her life, she just listened as the beautiful Protector Colonel went on listing further preparations for war:

"Plans are now being drawn up for an amalgamation of both the Star Exploration Administration and the air-space division of the C.C.P.F. into a united military combat force—Protectorate ground forces remaining in control of civil order unless the landing of invasion forces should occur on any of our worlds. If the enemy *should manage* to reach any of their surfaces then civilian defense forces will also be involved in military combat.

"However, we are still hopeful we'll be able to keep the fighting off-world, already stepping up production of faster-than-light propulsion systems to be installed in C.C.P.F. fatherships. Individual fighter craft will have to wait until near-light engines small enough to install are finally designed, but such designs are nevertheless near completion.

"Likewise, construction of other starships like StarChild have already begun, the only difference with these brotherships being that they will be more heavily armed. And as the newly appointed liaison between both the C.C.P.F.

and S.E.A., I will be working very closely from here on out with Admiral Sellers in order to co-ordinate efforts between our two organizations.

"Meanwhile if you'll take now a look at the monitors before each of you you'll see now what preparations are either currently underway, or shall soon be implemented:

"The red points of light are both S.E.A. and C.C.P.F. production facilities already in existence; the only modifications required being an expansion of both weapons manufacture and engine production, extra family living-units for those men summoned to work there, and day-care facilities for their children, while the greater majority of our female populace is involved in the actual fighting.

"In the meantime the green points are additional war production plants already in the planning stage, the blue military strike-force bases—both orbital and planet-side—also in the planning stage, while the gold are both S.E.A. and C.C.P.F. bases already in existence".

No sooner had she said all this the small viewing screens situated before each woman came to life with images of each Commonwealth world, a series of spots appearing on their surfaces as though some bizarre pox, an interplanetary malignancy infecting actual planets.

As each celestial body made its dramatic appearance, along with whatever subsequent natural satellites it might possess, something struck Jenniboni as especially odd—a peculiarity that didn't escape as well the notice of either Stasha Nikarov, or Frances Straker.

Unlike the other worlds making up Womankind's system, there were neither any green or blue pinpricks seen anywhere on neither Earth, Mars, nor Venus themselves—only a smattering of red and gold—unable to likewise detect any green orbiting either of those three worlds, only a few blue.

Questioning the other woman across the table concerning this obvious discrepancy, Jenniboni hadn't long to wait for an immediate answer:

"Because it was decided upon further consideration not to give the enemy any further incentive to bombard the surfaces of these particular worlds. On the remote chance they might succeed in eliminating our orbital defenses we are confident relief forces from other sources will arrive in time to render assistance.

"In the meantime however ground forces already established should be sufficient enough to repel any hostile occupation forces that might land before additional relief forces arrive".

"I'm afraid I don't understand", Jenniboni confessed, rather puzzled: "Why not simply increase both our military forces and war production facilities on both Earth, Mars, and Venus as you plan to throughout the rest of the System?"

"Because, as I said before, we don't want to risk any further devastation of their surfaces than necessary. Less motivation for any possible alien force to inflict further damage to valuable land. As the only three terraformed worlds in the entire Commonwealth, the only planets able to support life by natural means, they are also our main sources of food.

"So, while current ground forces are more than capable of handling hostile occupation forces until help arrives, further installations would only risk provoking increased destruction of critical food supplies".

Aha! So that was it! Sounding like a practical course of action the surface Jenniboni could nevertheless see the one glaring fault in an otherwise sound line of reasoning. A tactical error she was swift to point out much to Candace Carlin's utter chagrin:

"But what if the enemy decides not to launch any occupation force first once having neutralized our orbital defenses? What if they choose instead to initiate a 'scorched earth' policy before our own relief efforts arrive in time to launch any sort of effective orbital counter-strike?"

"Excuse me, Commodore?" There was no missing the other senior-ranking officer's confusion in either voice or face.

"In other words, what if the enemy chooses to eliminate our only food sources rather than claim them on their own behalf ?", Jenniboni illustrated in greater detail: "What if they come to the eventual conclusion we can't be defeated by regular military means, choosing instead to starve us into capitulation? As you say both Earth, Mars, and Venus are Womankind's very 'breadbaskets' as it were.

"So, instead of going to all the bother of trying to occupy those worlds after taking out their orbital defenses, might they not decide on a more expedient course of action such as just eliminating all life on each? Several swift and easy methods come to mind they could employ from the relative safety of any orbital position before Commonwealth forces might have any chance to intervene".

Thrown for a momentary loop no one spoke. Not until the Supreme Mother's clear, decisive voice cut through the silent pall all about them:

"Commodore Saphira raises a very important tactical concern which I plan to bring to the attention of the Strategic High Command. Thank you, Commodore", she acknowledged with an appreciative nod:

"However, I also wish to stress at this particular juncture we hope to avoid such a worst case scenario wherever possible. Unfortunately though only time will tell: Which is why we need StarChild's mission reports—A.S.A.P.! Only then will we know for sure, one way or another, what we're up against.

"Therefore, with all this in mind, we also want you to initiate peaceful contact wherever possible with the duly appointed representatives of whatever civilization you might encounter. While your primary mission remains one of a covert nature we nevertheless realize you run the risk of being discovered—a possible eventuality we want you to use as an opportunity to enter into a meaningful dialogue with whoever, or whatever might actually be out there.

"That's without risking, if at all possible, the lives of either you, your ship, or your crew. Don't forget that your primary concern, your first duty, is to return to the Commonwealth as soon as humanly possible with your report.

"And so, in conclusion, I have the distinct honour of informing you, Commodore Saphira, that—by authorization of both the Parliament, Senate, and the Supreme Council of Matriarchs—you are hereby appointed our official representative for *The Colonial Terran Commonwealth of Interplanetary Matriarchate Worlds*', its government, and its people.

"You are hereby empowered to speak on behalf of all Womankind during any negotiations that may arise *without* compromising either our moral standards, or integrity as a society! Is that understood?"

"Yes, Ma'am!", came Jenniboni's definite response, delivered without any hesitation whatsoever.

"Good, Commodore", the Prime Arch Matri smiled: "I was sure you'd understand, and have complete faith in both you and your crew".

"Thank you, Ma'am. And I can assure you we are almost ready to leave, and will be when the time comes".

"Good, then: In that case let us discuss both your ship's current status and the preparations already underway for your new mission parameters".

Reviewing the various procedures already under way in anticipation of any given contingency, Jenniboni soon allowed each of her senior officers the floor, all informing the P.A.M. as to the continued progress of each their individual departments.

****

"Well, seeing as my wife has effectively left me in charge, may I suggest we repair to the Hall of Audiences", Daniel Carlin addressed the other laddies scattered about the large dining room table: "Allow the servants a chance to clean up unobstructed".

Lost in thought Andrei paid little attention to the Prime Laddie's recommendation, momentarily confused to see the others get up from their chairs. Rapidly rejoining the world around him he rushed the last of his after-dinner coffee in a couple of hurried gulps, taking his almost empty champagne glass with him:

With only a few drops remaining Andrei set out in quick pursuit of the other members of his party. Last to reach the 'Hall of Audiences' he noticed how the other men had already broken up into two groups of two—Charlie in all his *obsequious glory* chatting up the Prime Laddie near the large viewing port occupying the broad far side of the impressive chamber beyond.

A wide transparency through which Andrei could see as well Demeter's northern hemisphere he was able to make out both Chiron City and the Project StarChild Base from this distance, their dome orbs still visible at their lowest luminosity.

In the meantime however both Shotoku and Timothy Carlin were assembled near the counter bar on the other side of the room, deep in conversation, a nearby bartender in silver and black serving each laddie a drink.

Unable to face the dismal prospect of either Charlie Sellers, or his insipid chatter the choice of which couple to join was an easy one. Hoping to be included in their discussion Andrei headed straightaway over to the two younger men, invited without reservation by each to join them.

Remembering Jenniboni's directive of before he agreed to just one more glass of bubbly when asked by the attending barkeep behind the counter between them, calling it quits immediately after that.

As it was Andrei's drink went practically untouched, both he and Shotoku more interested in hearing further from Timothy about current events back on Earth—his being from Soupol City serving only to make the gossip all that more juicy:

Situated smack-dab in central Ahnteekah, Soupol was the Matriarchate's capital, the hub of Humanity's very political existence and, although politics was no longer the sordid affair it was during the 'Ancient Patriarchates', there were still enough amusing anecdotes to keep all three men amused.

Not only that but the fact that Timothy's wife was a Protector gave Andrei even more in common with the other man, allowing them further ground on which to hold a meaningful conversation.

Just too bad he didn't know the exact details concerning her involvement with the Star Exploration Administration, sure it would go a long way towards explaining what their womenfolk were up to right now in that conference chamber of theirs.

Then again, on a totally unrelated subject, Andrei was just as surprised to discover Daniel Carlin wasn't originally from Venus. Mistakenly assuming that the Prime Laddie was from the same world as his wife he was interested to learn instead the senior Mr. Carlin was actually from Earth. And more than that he was from Andrei's very on hometown... St. Tammy City'... a beautiful jewel resting on the golden-white sands of Ahnteekah's eastern shore.

Soon remembering though the third member of their group Andrei felt rather poorly how the other man had been relegated for the most part to the role of mere listener. Forasmuch as Shotoku didn't seem to mind this unfortunate discrepancy Andrei still made a more concerted effort to include him in their conversation.

Delighted to learn of similar interests they both shared it just so happened Shotoku was an assistant photographer in a professional portrait studio, Andrei likewise something of an amateur shutterbug ever since Jenniboni gave him an expensive set of camera equipment several Christmas's ago.

Quite proficient in the art his work even appeared on stellar-wide 3-DV, the occasion being Andrei's recent interview on the popular early morning men's talk show; "Good Morning Laddies!"

Admittedly a fluff piece from the very beginning most all the questions ran along such obvious lines like "... how is your family finally adjusting to life on Demeter?...", and "... what's it like being married to the Commodore?..."

Expecting nothing else right from the very beginning at least the show's producers used several still-life's he took on previous occasions as an eventual back-drop to his actual interview. They even gave Andrei a photographer's credit at the program's end—Andrei selecting beforehand only those pics other family members wouldn't mind on public display, screening every choice with his wife and children first.

Not that he'd ever take any picture anyone in their right mind might deem inappropriate. It's just that he understood there might be those few pics certain family members might find personally embarrassing. Especially when displayed on a chat show broadcast to every single, inhabited planet, moon, and even asteroid in the entire blessed System.

One good example being a still-life he once took of Jenniboni's sleeping form, just her head sticking out in peaceful repose from under the covers, it was surely one of his absolute favorites. Reminding him so much of a veritable angel at rest Andrei was confident all-the-same it would have earned him his wife's enduring wrath were it to actually appear within every cube across the entire Commonwealth!

And so it was both he and Shotoku spent a most pleasant moment, or two conversing about wide angles versus narrow, the best type of film depending on exposure, and the merits of the more antiquated 2-Dee style when compared to 3-Dee.

Nor was that all, the other laddie revealing as well how he first met Frances Straker at his place of employ a couple of years ago—what began as a routine shoot for a simple picture I.D. developing into a fast and firm friendship with the dashing, gallant S.E.A. officer in question.

Mildly curious as to just how deeply involved the handsome young Master Imoko really was with StarChild's Chief of Security, Andrei never-the-less curbed his tongue. Aware that such an inquiry would be quite amiss he chose instead to simply convey to Frances' escort his mutual admiration for Shotoku's gentlewoman-caller for the evening.

Doing so Andrei fell into the unwitting trap of revealing however the unfortunate circumstances behind their initial encounter in the first place. While not going into any painful details concerning what actually transpired, he none-the-less found it easier to talk about it with others of his gender. Both men quite sympathetic, promised to keep Andrei' misfortune of yesterday a secret. And as far as Shotoku was concerned, Frances' gallant rescue came as no surprise.

What confused Andrei though was the other laddie's less-than-accepting attitude in connection with his second 'savior', Shotoku seeming rather skeptical… and amusedly so… hearing Andrei's just as glowing report dealing with both Naomi's upstanding behaviour and virtuous deeds.

About to question the other man even further on the matter he stopped however, noticing out of the corner of his eye Charlie Sellers still pestering the Prime Laddie. Can't that man *ever* tell when his attentions aren't welcome, Andrei seethed. Like at dinner before his immediate response was a profound sense of pity for Charlie's captive audience, accompanied by an equal measure of bitter contempt for Mr. Sellers himself.

"I think it well about high time we rescue your father-in-law from a fate worse than death", Andrei told Timothy, nodding in the direction of the other two men in question. While Andrei's hands were bound by proper etiquette during dinner, unable to assist the unlucky junior Ms. Carlin regarding Charlie's unwanted prattling on, such limitations were no longer binding where her father was concerned.

"Now here's what I have in mind".

****

Staging their own little cavalry charge with Timothy in the lead, Shotoku and Andrei trailing close behind, they set out across the room between them in swift deliverance of the senior Mr. Carlin.

Witnessing the diametrically opposed expressions appearing on the faces of each older laddie in response to their approach, a derisive little smirk came at once to Andrei's lips. There was no mistaking Charlie's obvious annoyance while the Prime Laddie's eyes registered an equally clear sense of outright relief, if not downright gratitude.

"Yes, son, what is it I can do for you?" Daniel was quick to ask, giving Timothy a broad smile once they reached his position.

"Please pardon the intrusion, Sir, but I was telling Mr. Saphira how you're from St. Tammy City and, as fate would have it, he's also from the Holy City. Which is why, if it's no imposition, he was wondering if you'd care to discuss your life there and perhaps compare notes".

"Why, of course", the Prime Laddie beamed in Andrei's direction: "I can always find time to reminisce with a fellow 'Saint Tammyite' about home".

"But, Sir", Charlie protested: "I thought we were…"

"Ah, yes", Daniel replied. Seemingly startled by the other man's voice he recovered his former composure quickly enough:

"I humbly apologize for this unfortunate interruption, Mr. Sellers, as I have truly enjoyed our fascinating talk. However, as resident host in my wife's absence, I'm obligated to spend some time as well with our other guests.

"Besides, I feel rather guilty over how I've so unjustly monopolized as is your precious time".

Beautifully handled, Andrei couldn't help an appreciative smile over such a mistressful display of consummate diplomacy.

One for the herstory books!

When it appeared for a brief moment the despondent Mr. Sellers was about to object even further, all Andrei could think to himself was '… for Heaven's sake, Charlie, can't you ever just shut up and accept defeat gracefully?'

Luckily it would seem the Admiral's husband chose to remain silent after all, deciding in the end it might be in *his* best interests to pursue such a policy. Meanwhile Andrei and the Prime Laddie took a little stroll down memory lane, sharing recollections of their mutual birthplace, Christendom's most sacred site since the late 21st century.

Known in ancient times as 'New Manchester' it was there St. Tammy herself founded the "Holy Church of Christ" during her later years, serving as both first Supreme Arch Bishop as well as Womankind's first Prime Arch Matri. The Matriarchate's first and last 'Priest/Queen' in the sacred order of Melchizedek, it was only after the 'Great Saint's' death the offices of Supreme Mother and Holy Mother were then separated.

And so it was both Daniel and Andrei shared memories of both a religious and secular nature, recounting both the clergywomen in their bright, priestly, vestments as well as bonfire parties by the ocean.

Each remembering their first beach party, the first girl they kissed while lying on a blanket by the surf, and how the moonlight glistened on each wave gently crashing on the shore, both men recalled as well the Supreme Arch Bishop's Easter and Christmas benedictions delivered by the Holy Mother to the multitudes from her balcony at the Sacred Palace. All-in-all a rich tapestry of life in a city where both the spiritual and mundane were celebrated with an equal sense of joyful reverence—a unique state of existence unparalleled elsewhere throughout the entire System.

Mostly Andrei just let Daniel do all the talking, saying just enough himself to keep up his end of the general conversation—Charlie standing all-the-while nearby, fuming in utter silence, grinding his teeth in impotent rage. Realizing all-the-same there might be one, or two repercussions down the road for this night's little act of subterfuge Andrei cared little nonetheless.

Nor did it occur to him that, although antagonizing the husband of his wife's immediate superior, he'd all the same gained the obvious favor of the Supreme Mother's. Fascinated with the Prime Laddie's verbal memoirs, his interest captured by what the older man had to say, Andrei paid little attention to anything else.

Oblivious in fact to his all his other surroundings, unaware their womenfolk just returned from their private 'war council', he nearly jumped out of his skin, Jenniboni laying her hand softly on his shoulder:

"Sorry, Dear", she apologized, observing the start she just gave him, "but I'm afraid it's time to leave".

Chapter 37

"ANDREI'S TURN"

Returning her full-dress uniform to its usual, honoured position in their bedroom walk-in closet, Jenniboni listened to her husband's adventures at tonight's soiree as he likewise turned down their bed. With her back to him she could hear Andrei fluffing up their pillows, all the while delighted he had such a wonderful time.

Pleased to hear he made a new friend in Master Shotoku Imoko, how they exchanged V.P. numbers in hopes of getting together again, Jenniboni laughed outright when hearing how her brilliant husband trounced so cleverly Charlie Sellers at his own game.

Feeling like he did concerning Melissa's obsequious spouse she could just picture the other man's face, frustrated in his status-seeking efforts. Trading places with Andrei, she sat on the edge of their bed once undressed while he went about putting away his suit.

Listening even further to his merry chatter though, Jenniboni soon found his buoyant effervescence starting to weigh heavy on her heart. No longer any way to avoid telling him, she nevertheless hated herself for doing so when he was in so happy a mood:

"Would you please come sit by me a spell, dear?", she asked, patting the area of their bed right next to her side: "I have something I really need to tell you".

Having just taken his clothes off Andrei was just turning about when hearing her request, the pained look on her face setting off an internal warning bell as he complied. Sitting at her side Andrei could feel Jenniboni's hand begin stroking his back in a soothing manner, something she did only when trying to break to him some sort of ugly news.

Quite unable to look at him she just stared instead at the floor, telling him of her need to leave the day after tomorrow, confessing as well she knew all about this since just this Tuesday. When asked why she had to leave so terribly soon it was then Jenniboni lied, feeling dirty all the while doing so. Nor did it ease her acute feelings of guilt doing so under direct orders from the P.A.M. herself:

"Astronomers have recently uncovered a rare spatial anomaly near Alpha Centauri's two yellow suns. According to them it releases an unusual energy burst once very millennium, due to do so in less than two weeks' time.

"So they want StarChild to monitor this phenomenon at close range.

"They believe it might be of major scientific import and, since the Supreme Mother agrees, they've moved up our departure time in order to examine it while in progress.

"Don't worry, though. I've been assured this will pose no threat at all… whatsoever… to either us or the ship".

Able at once to feel the muscles in his back bunch up in tense anger, aware how much he loathed being touched when so upset, Jenniboni snatched her hand away from Andrei's now rigid body. Casting a furtive glance in his direction she saw his jaw clench, eyes focused on nothing in particular, staring instead into cold, blank space.

Wearing a hard, cold expression he didn't speak for what seemed an eternity, Jenniboni actually praying he'd yell at her—rant, rave, scream, and get it out of his system. Sure he knew she was lying anything would be better than this harsh, frigid, silent treatment.

Little did she realize how very close he actually came to letting her 'have it', ready to blast her for even more than she imagined. Part of his resentment stemmed of course from her unfair choice of time to drop this particular little bombshell in his lap. After feeling so up, so very happy, only moments ago her news hit him all that much harder.

All the same though what angered him most was how she scolded him just earlier that very same day, his turn now to be upset with her! *How dare she* chew him out for keeping secrets when hiding at the very same time one like this. And the knowledge she was *still* hiding something from him added only further insult to injury! Even while revealing one ugly truth, she continued lying with her very next words.

Not believing for a split second her hen-and-heifer story Andrei had no doubt the secret she continued hiding could end up impacting their entire family much more than anything he kept from her. At least—when push came to shove—he told her everything. He didn't reveal one dirty little secret just to keep hiding another.

Okay: So there was no such thing as a perfect fifty/fifty marriage arrangement. All right! So such a concept was a Utopian fantasy no matter what herstorical time period one lived in.

Fine!!

But that still didn't change the fact there was supposed to be a certain give-and-take, a certain understanding upon which a lasting trust could be based. A trust Jenniboni just violated as far as he was concerned.

After all, respect was a two-way street!!!

His anger didn't last long however, dissipating soon after it flared up, realizing there was still one little difference between them: Whereas his secrecy was voluntary, Jenniboni's was forced upon her by those under which she served.

No different than when she was a Protector.

Almost having forgotten the sleepless nights spent worrying about her, her former career likewise required she keep secrets from him. As Raoul once put it; "all part of being a 'husband of the Protectorate'".

And so it seemed now the same held true being "married" to the S.E.A..

Given the nature of her occupation it was unrealistic, if not downright unreasonable of him to expect her to share those confidential matters with him that would inevitably crop up in her career.

Witnessing the bitter expression on Andrei's face begin to soften, the muscles in his body beginning to likewise relax, Jenniboni felt an immense flood of absolute relief. Thankful she wasn't being 'sent to Coventry' after all, she was doubly gladsome when he finally spoke:

"I have to admit that this 'spatial anomaly' of yours sounds quite fascinating. I hope you'll bring back some pictures if it for both the children and me", he asked, putting on his brightest face more for her sake than his:

"If you're not too busy, that is. I'm sure we'd all find it most interesting".

"I'll do my very best to remember", she promised, her tone of voice a grateful one. Fully aware he knew her cover story was a lie, she loved him all the more for pretending:

"And at least we still have our special Valentine's celebration to look forward to tomorrow. So I guess we should just make the very most of the time we've got left before you have to leave", he smiled up into her eyes, giving her silky thigh an affectionate caress.

"And, since you're leaving early, I guess that means you'll just be back all that sooner: Right?"

"Right, Sweet-pea", she tenderly vowed.

Lifting his hand from her naked thigh she pressed it firmly to her lips, Andrei able to detect her sincere appreciation for his clear willingness to accept the inevitable with such good grace.

"And we'll make every minute we're together count for the best".

Enwrapped in perfect silence neither could help, but wonder what in fact the future held in store. Afraid to express their concerns with one-another, they each knew it would serve no useful purpose—the only result being to worry the love next to them over something neither could control.

No turning back, their fates were both set now on a certain course!

"Well, if that's all, I guess we better get some sleep", Jenniboni was the first to speak, the hushed quiet growing at last too much for her: "I have a pretty good idea we'll both be very busy tomorrow before our little night out on the town together".

Giving his knee a gentle pat soon thereafter she then got up, walking about to her side of their bed.

****

Lying on his side Andrei was no closer to sleep than since turning out the lights almost an hour ago, his wife clearly enduring the same difficulty.

"Are you asleep yet, Sweet-pea?" she asked from next to him.

"No", he sighed, doubtful he'd get any sleep *at all* that night.

"In that case would you like to snuggle up close for the rest of the night?"

Sounding more like a hesitant plea than an actual offer Andrei could hear the obvious need in her soft, almost halting voice. Answering her with action instead of words Andrei sought her out in the dark. Finding her easily enough Jenniboni had already stretched her arm out, ready to welcome him to her side in hopeful anticipation.

Cuddling up next to her he lay his head against her shoulder, resting just above the tender swell of her left breast. Putting his arm around her waist Andrei felt her hold him close as well in a loving embrace, his body relaxing against hers.

At first sure he'd be awake all night, Andrei nevertheless found himself drifting away next to the soothing warmth of her soft skin, her strong arms encircling him with all her love—the light sound of her relaxed heartbeat, her gentle breathing, and the rhythmic rise and fall of her tender breast against his cheek all helping to finally lull him to sleep.

Chapter 38

"VALENTINES DAY"
(THURSDAY, FEBRUARY 14TH, 2915 AD)

Spending the greater part of her morning in her shipboard office aboard StarChild, Jenniboni went over a large stack of interdepartmental status reports, breaking for a brief lunch only.

Then it was on to other such pressing matters—concerns like meeting with each departmental head in person, dealing with possible last minute details not included in their reports, and making double sure all the extra supplies requisitioned were delivered as promised.

Yet, hectic as her day was, Jenniboni still experienced a certain peace of mind when it finally came time to return home, confident both her ship and crew were ready indeed for their early departure, their arduous voyage ahead.

Meanwhile, back on Demeter, Andrei busied himself with matters of home and hearth, taking care of his usual daily routine… going over such last minute details for the evening ahead like picking the children up at school and dropping them off at the Men's Shelter for their little sleep over at Grandpa Raoul's… all before heading straight home.

With their overnight visitor's passes tucked safely away in the inside pocket of his leather jacket, Andrei finished loading their supplies in the trunk of his little blue car when it came time at last to collect them.

At first Andrei had second thoughts about imposing any further on his father-in-law's generous nature two nights in a row but—worrying in the end for nothing—it seemed the older Saphira was actually looking forward as much as they to having his grandchildren stay the night.

Offering to bring them back in the morning so Andrei wouldn't have to make an extra trip into the city, he even arranged for the night ahead an "old-fashioned camp-out" in his living room replete with holo-fire and ghost stories.

So making one last check, sure that all the children's 'camping gear' was present and accounted for, Andrei was soon on his way before returning immediately thereafter, getting everything in perfect readiness for Jenniboni's return home.

****

Anticipating a wonderful night right from the very start Jenniboni nevertheless had no idea how special it would really be until Andrei first welcomed her home. Exquisitely arrayed in his finest apparel, he greeted her arrival at the front door with both an ardent kiss and firm embrace.

"My-oh-my, but you look absolutely gorgeous", she purred, holding him at arm's length, giving Andrei an appreciative once-over: "Simply Divine".

"Why, thank you Dear Gentlewoman", he acknowledged her sincere praise with a generous smile of his own: "How very gallant of you to notice".

How could she NOT notice?

No matter how many times Jenniboni saw him decked out in his present attire there was just no getting over how truly fabulous he looked, the custom-tailored suit designed specifically for his well-sculptured body by the prestigious 'House of Olmontei'.

A sheer work of art with its stylish cut and elegant butter-soft material shimmering in the light he was—along with his red silk shirt, white vest, and black tie—a walking fantasy come true! And as she looked him both up and down with adoring eyes Andrei took her hand in his, leading Jenniboni down the hall to their bedroom.

Announcing quite simply he'd drawn her a bath what she found upon her arrival there left her truly speechless. Having quite clearly gone to great lengths setting up the sensual scene before her his satisfied expression when seeing her honest delight was, in Jenniboni's humble opinion, more than quite justified.

Crossing the threshold into the bathroom beyond the only source of light gathered all about came from countless pink and white scented candles thrilling the senses with both their seductive glow and enticing aroma. And approaching the tub itself Jenniboni was quick to notice dozens of tiny, delicate, feathery, red objects floating about in slow, lazy, patterns on the water's languid surface—noting on closer examination they were actually scores of fresh rose petals.

Wondering at first if he actually used those very flowers she sent him just yesterday Jenniboni realized soon enough that couldn't be the case, having just seen them moments ago. Still in their vase on the dining room table upon returning home she had no doubt Andrei used his own money for all of this, further confident it must have set him back a pretty centi indeed.

Gently lighting her fingers upon the water's still surface it wasn't only the prefect temperature, but likewise perfumed with all her very favorite bath oils, a heavenly treat quite unexpected.

"Oh, Sweet-pea", she whispered, her voice tremulous with profound feeling: "This is all so very wonderful. Thank you".

"Thought you might enjoy it", Andrei granted her yet another bright smile, glad his efforts were met with such obvious enthusiasm: "After the hard day

272

you no doubt had, I was sure you'd appreciate this little opportunity to relax before proceeding further with the beautiful evening you've already planned for both of us".

"Yes, of course!", she exclaimed with boundless pleasure.

"Well then; don't you think it a good idea to climb on in while the water's still just right", he grinned, clearly pleased by her reaction: "Just leave your uniform on the bed. I'll see to it later".

Leaving before she could thank him yet again Andrei was already on the move for parts unknown, Jenniboni alone now to partake of this wonderful treat so lovingly prepared. Easing the many little aches and pains throughout her entire body, every tired muscle of her entire being soothed by their many therapeutic properties, Jenniboni let the warm, fragrant waters wash all over her.

Leaning back into them she closed her eyes. Wearing a dreamy smile full of blissful contentment, slowly wriggling her fingers and toes, she breathed in deeply the sensual aromas courtesy of the many scented candled displayed all about. Luxuriating in the almost decadent environment her husband had so carefully orchestrated for her own private delight, she found their flickering glow upon closed eyelids a source of even further relaxation.

So it was with tender thoughts focused on just how very, very lucky she was to have someone like Andrei in her life Jenniboni heard right about then his soft approach. Opening her eyes once more to see him standing at her side, he held out to her further offerings in either hand as if some angel from on high.

Holding in one hand a small silver platter, a long-stemmed champagne glass full of sparkling cider in the other, he went about handing her the glass in complete silence. Placing within reach beside the tub a small stand tucked beneath his arm he placed further the small silver platter on top. And on top of that Jenniboni noticed five of the dark chocolates she sent him the day before, all waiting there for her alone on its highly polished surface:

"Oh, Sweet-pea", she said with an appreciative little shake of her head:

"All this special treatment is most wonderful, but I know how much you love them".

"Please take them", he encouraged her with a tender smile full of sweet entreaty: "I know how much you also like them, and love you even more. Besides it was a big box you sent. So enjoy, and feel free to take your time".

Once again Andrei left before giving her a chance to thank him, convinced she'd rather luxuriate in the solitude of her own private thoughts.

Alone again, wrapped in perfect quiet, Jenniboni plucked up one of the dainty little confectioneries between thumb and forefinger, nibbling slowly at it. Taking a delicate sip as well from the drink in her other hand she took her own leisurely time about it. Polishing off each exquisite tidbit she relished both their sweetness on her tongue alongside the erotic tingle spreading throughout her entire body.

Feeling both totally refreshed and relaxed Jenniboni couldn't shake however a guilty twinge beginning to take form, thinking of her poor husband waiting out there all alone. While believing him sincere in his desire she take her time, Jenniboni still didn't feel quite right just letting him wait around elsewhere all by himself. She meant this evening to be just as much about him as her.

Removing herself from the tub, drying off, she made her way into the mistress bedroom to select her wardrobe for the evening ahead. Something she knew for sure Andrei would enjoy seeing her in. And doing so it was then Andrei appeared from down the hall.

"I'd better put out the candles in there and clean up", he told her on his way to the bathroom.

"No need", she informed him, gently resting her hand upon his chest, stopping him in mid-stride: "I've already taken care of the candles, and the rest can wait 'till later. So why don't you just sit yourself down on the edge of the bed while I give you a little sneak preview of what I plan to wear tonight.

"Perhaps you could even render your opinion".

Watching her walk over to their closet wearing nothing but what the Good Lord gave her at birth, a jocular little grin sprang at once to Andrei's lips:

"Personally, I love it. Very stimulating! However, don't you think you might want to put on something else over it. No doubt the restaurant you're taking us to has some sort of minimum dress code", Andrei commented with a raised eyebrow at sight of her splendid state of absolute undress.

"Don't be such a cheeky little monkey", Jenniboni giggled, opening the closet door.

Choosing a pair of black, open-toed dress shoes she followed these with a strapless, floor-length red sequin evening gown, an alluring side-vent on the left side reaching up to mid-thigh.

Complimenting her ample breasts and hour-glass figure quite nicely, accentuating her every sensuous curve to its fullest, she picked after that her final accessories—a black velvet choker and a pair of chic, black, silk evening gloves ending midway up her upper arms.

Complete with a pink silk rose she decided on the choker simply because it went so well with her dress. However, when it came to the gloves, they were chosen with just Andrei in mind. Remembering how he enjoyed their feel whenever she touched him Jenniboni came to the ultimate conclusion it was high time to trot them out yet again for yet another repeat performance.

Saving however these last items until after seeing to both her hair and make-up she set them instead to one side on the vanity table before her, taking special note of Andrei's reflection in the mirror while donning a pair of black, silk stockings.

As with the night before he watched her in the application of her cosmetics, riveted by the sight, when Jenniboni decided right then and there to wear her hair swept up, revealing her graceful neck in that particular style he found so captivating.

Smiling to herself it occurred to Jenniboni just about then that this was surely a special treat for him— two nights in a row! Usually reserved for only special occasions she didn't use make-up so very much, giving Andrei little opportunity to watch her power-up in this manner.

Nevertheless Jenniboni noticed a new expression on his face alongside that loving reverence usually present during such times. Glancing at her husband's reflection in the mirror's highly reflective surface, Jenniboni was able to observe as well the same secretive smile he wore when leading her earlier into the bathroom.

Given his proven ability to anticipate both her likes and desires so very well, recognizing that look for what it really meant, an expectant glow of warm excitement came over her. Nor did she need to wait long for his next surprise, coming soon enough after she fastened the velvet choker about her graceful neck.

Applying a light sprits of rose-scented toilet water to the silken flower arrayed there Jenniboni then removed the small diamond ear studs she usually wore, choosing instead a set of emerald earrings from her jewelry case.

About to put them on, however, Andrei stopped her:

"Nooo, I don't think so".

"Excuse me?!"

"What I mean is don't put on your earrings. At least not until I first give you your Valentine's day present".

Slowly rising from where he sat on the bed's edge Andrei sauntered over to her current position, a most winsome smile radiating forth from his handsome countenance.

"Soooo, what did you get me, Sweet-pea?", she asked in a playful little voice all her own as he now stood behind her.

"How about I give you a little hint first?"

Resting his hands upon satiny soft shoulders Andrei then leaned over, gracing her right ear lobe with a most tender kiss, repeating this gesture with the same seductive ease as before, pressing likewise his gentle lips to her left.

"I thought you might like to give these a little bachelor voyage of their own at dinner tonight", he offered, pulling a flat, rectangular jewelry case with a black velvet covering from his suit's inside breast pocket.

Once more pulling himself up to full height before giving it to her, no sooner had he done so Jenniboni's attention was drawn immediately to the stylized writing upon its lid—the name "GULTASHAI" printed in gold italics right there in its lower right-hand corner. One of the most renowned jewelry firms in the entire System she knew her husband wasn't the type to offer her such a container from such a prestigious establishment unless its contents were likewise from that very same place.

"Oh my", she gasped, her voice reduced to nothing but an astonished whisper. Gazing at what lay within her bewildered eyes sprung open so wide she feared they might literally pop right out of her very head.

"They're incredible! Absolutely marvelous! But you shou…", she almost blurted in her amazement, stopping herself at the very last moment least she sound either ungrateful, or unappreciative. Nestled against the container's padded bottom lay two heart-shaped earrings of purest gold, two brilliant sapphires mounted side-by-side upon each. One the purest of blue's, the other a rarest of passionate pink's, each precious gem was encircled by a ring of tiny diamonds arranged together to create an infinity symbol exquisitely formed with perfect precision. Tears coming to light in the corners of each eye the blatant symbolism behind this particular design wasn't lost in the least on her.

"They are so, so, beautiful darling. I love them. Of course I'll wear them", she assured him, a definite quiver to her voice putting them on.

Admiring their unique design in the mirror before her she couldn't help but wonder how, by mere chance, he managed to discover in any jewelry store—much less one so exclusive as Gultashai's—such a specific design so descriptive of the special relationship they both shared as woman and husband.

Only then, with a burst if sudden insight born of years as a professional investigator, did it finally dawn on her astonished mind:

'Good Heavens', she thought to herself:

'Custom-made by Gultashai's!'

Jenniboni could only imagine how much they cost!

Although more generous than many wives he must have been saving even so his marital allowance for an eternity to even afford such an extravagant gift.

Moved beyond words she slipped her gloves on almost absent-mindedly, paying no heed to what she was doing as he leaned over, kissing her on the nape of her lovely neck:

"You don't know how very happy it makes me to see you enjoy them so", Andrei whispered, gently: "I really wanted to give you something certain to show you how much I both love and appreciate you".

"Don't worry, Precious. I already know how much you love me by everything you do around here every day", she vowed, struggling to keep her voice from cracking, stroking his cheek with a gloved hand. "Nevertheless, I swear to always treasure these exquisite tokens of your affection".

Gratified by her response he smiled, his heart full, just as she announced it was time they left for the city.

While each knew there was no way anyone would give away any reservation made by *the* Commodore Jenniboni Kaye Saphira—no matter how late they might be! —she considered it even so only proper good manners to show up on time.

* * * *

Arriving at the same posh dinner/dance club to which she took him to on his last birthday, Andrei entered proudly that very same establishment on Jenniboni's arm.

Aware of the many stares focused in their direction he was confident their gaze was inspired by the sight of StarChild's already famous commanding officer appearing in their midst—liking all-the-same to imagine they envied him also, being out on the town in the company of the most beautiful, exquisite woman to ever grace their presence.

Escorted to their table by a clearly awestruck waiter continually asking if there be anything he could possibly bring them, Jenniboni held out Andrei's chair for him, seating herself directly across the way.

Dismissing all-the-while the young, starry-eyed servant she insisted instead they be given first a chance to read their menu's. Given her popularity Andrei had to admit the other customers behaved themselves quite well, respecting their privacy, going about their own business.

Still though there were nevertheless a couple of individuals to approach their table, asking for her autograph in shy, hesitant voices. Not put out by this however, he accepted it with good-natured resignation. Actually quite proud of his wife, watching Jenniboni receive the adoration he felt she so richly deserved, he remained all the same glad the autograph hounds were few, aware how her newly acquired celebrity status made Jenniboni at times uncomfortable.

One that truly floored him though, amusing him to no end, was an elderly laddie who, upon securing Jenniboni's signature, proceeded also to ask him for his. Claiming he'd loved Andrei's interview on *'Good Morning Laddies!'*, he enquired even further if Andrei planned to do any more talk shows.

The whole incident didn't last long though and, once the older man departed, Jenniboni leaned forward, giving him a sly little wink:

"So now you know how it feels. How do *you* like it?", she teased.

Her smile only broadened upon his shy admission it actually felt kind of nice, having enjoyed the whole experience. And so it was their evening grew all the more sweeter, having a truly wonderful time together, Andrei unable to help but reiterate how truly beautiful she was.

Not able to take his eyes off of her he felt quite honoured by all the trouble Jenniboni went to with both her sumptuous attire and hair. While their meal was truly divine, tastefully presented upon gold-rimmed fine-bone china, it was his wife's attentions that kept Andrei both enthralled—even enraptured.

Allowing him to order all his very favorite dishes for himself she even relaxed her rules on imbibing, allowing him to order any alcoholic beverage he might so desire. Appreciating none-the-less her generous offer he still chose not to indulge, wishing to be under the influence of nothing save her own natural sensuality.

This was one night above all others Andrei wanted to remain clear-headed, intoxicated as he was by her very presence alone.

Not only that but he also appreciated how Jenniboni avoided any mention of StarChild, her early departure, or any other reminder of her work that might mar this special time together. And touched by her tender sensitivity in the matter he avoided likewise such topics as housework, the children, and all those other domestic concerns comprising as well his every day.

Instead of discussing such routine, daily matters they simply shared a conversation much more intimate in nature—declarations of their innermost feelings accompanied by reminiscences of a loving past shared in each other's company.

When their meal reached its eventual conclusion, left with nothing save their after-dinner coffee, they merely held hands in loving adoration. Taking simple pleasure in the silent still of their gracious surroundings, enjoying one-another's company, they never even noticed their waiter's light approach, oblivious as they were to all else.

"Will there be anything further, Ma'am? Sir?" he asked, visibly abashed to have found himself intruding on such a private moment.

"Dear?", Jenniboni gave Andrei a curious smile, gazing at him across the tapered candles flickering between them. Upon returning her look with a little shake of his head she soon settled the bill, including with the amount due a generous gratuity for the young man who served them so well.

Quickly departing upon having thanked her, leaving the courting couple once more to their private discourse, Jenniboni sat back in her chair. Peering out from their present vantage point across the elegant dinner/dance theater she noticed almost at once a broad hardwood dance floor virtually uncrowded in the relative distance.

A more accomplished dancer than she, well versed in all forms of the art, she suggested to Andrei they avail themselves of this opportunity—Jenniboni all the same quite skilled, too—their talents combining in a most delightful way.

Knowing how much he loved to dance she regretted how her hectic schedule as of late left her so little time for such simple pleasures. Vowing at once to remedy that situation right then and there, rising at once from the table at which they sat, she took her husband's hand in hers.

Escorting him across the impressive sized dining area down towards the highly polished sunken dance floor beyond, the few other couples likewise present made upon their arrival immediate way for both.

Slipping her arm around Andrei's trim form, drawing him close in a tender embrace, Jenniboni held his one hand close to her chest, beginning to move in step with the light music from above—able to feel as well his firm yet supple body surrender willingly… with delight… to her lead.

Guiding him along, her other hand steering him softly by the small of his back, they cherished what they saw looking into each other's eyes, neither paying any heed to the admiring crowd gathered all about watching with frank admiration their graceful, flowing moves.

Wishing this evening could last forever Andrei could see the same desire reflected in Jenniboni's expression as she beheld his.

Yearning for nothing more than to spend all eternity in her loving arms he rejoiced silently at the warmth of her body against his, the love literally radiating from her filling his very soul to overflowing—Jenniboni able to read as well her husband's feelings in those oh-so expressive blue eyes so full of gentle devotion, wanting likewise nothing more than to hold him close in her strong yet tender embrace.

Finally overcome with the mounting affection he felt for his wife at that very moment Andrei pressed his lips to her cheek in a light kiss, pausing just long enough to breath heavily of the sweetly scented silken rose about her graceful neck.

Closing his eyes, resting his head with a soft sigh of sweet, joyful bliss gently against her shoulder, husband and wife danced on into the night ahead.

****

Parting temporarily, going their separate ways returning home later that evening, Jenniboni sashayed her way down the hall toward the mistress bedroom. With both a jaunty little saunter and anticipatory smile she closed the bedroom door behind her, Andrei likewise making his way with a purposeful stride to J.J.'s room.

Once there he proceeded to remove all his clothes, laying them atop his absent daughter's bed before donning a full-length, black velour bathrobe covering from top to bottom his naked form.

Tying the belt just tight enough to hide what lay below, making sure it wasn't so secure as to defy the efforts of roaming fingers, he slid then the robe's hood partially over his head just far enough to add a little air of mystery while, at the very same time, not obscuring his face.

Leaving his daughter's room once sure everything was in place, he then went about seeing to all the other preparations ahead in anticipation of Jenniboni's imminent return. Removing from the refrigeration unit both the bottle of sparkling cider and box of chocolate cherries from before, he also collected two champagne glasses left there to chill likewise just yesterday.

Carrying them into the living room area Andrei arranged each item in precise order on the waiting coffee table's transparent surface. Opening the box of candy in promise of his wife's eventual return there remained only one other order of business:

Activating the 3-DV unit he inserted a holo-wafer from the storage compartment below into the unit's play slot, the family entertainment device miraculously transformed into a perfect replica of a quite cheery fireplace roaring to life.

Complete with both dancing flames, and the crisp sound of crackling wood, it added that final intimate touch to an already romantic interlude within each other's company.

The only source of light now present it would add quite nicely to the special ambiance he had in mind for this, the final stage of their private celebration. Running through a swift mental checklist, making sure all was in place, he soon heard the mistress bedroom door finally open.

Turning about just in time to see Jenniboni appear at the hallway's far end she left open as well the darkened bedroom door in back of her. Drawing nearer with hands hidden behind her Jenniboni had an almost shy, even demure, quality about her.

Nothing shy or reserved though about the saucy smile or lively twinkle in her eyes. Nor was there anything modest about the sheer, lacy white silk peignoir she scarcely wore. Leaving little to the imagination, it revealed more of her voluptuous figure than it hid.

"Absolutely exquisite", Andrei sighed, overcome with feelings of intense longing, breathless with desire for the scantily clad angel before him.

"I see you wore it", Jenniboni remarked upon reaching his position, caressing in a highly suggestive manner the soft fabric over his chest.

"Your wish is my command", he chuckled with a jovial little bow in her direction.

"And don't you forget it, my man", she giggled merrily, crossing her long, shapely legs upon taking a seat at the couch's far end.

"Oh, I won't", Andrei grinned, pouring them both a drink.

Doing so he failed to notice her stuff something behind her back down between two seat cushions in a quick, furtive motion all done by the time he handed Jenniboni her glass. Positioning within reach the box of chocolates before sitting at her side she lifted her glass to his, tapping them gently together in a silent toast.

"So what are we drinking to?" he asked, curious, when she didn't say a single word.

"Oh, darling, don't be such an old silly", she giggled yet again, giving him a wanton smile: "You know very well what".

"Very well. And on that note I have a little something here to help get us in the mood", he announced, plucking a wee candy from the nearby table.

"Hey, Babe, I'm game for whatever it is you have in mind. All-the-same though, I'll have you know that I'm already in the mood".

"Well then…" he offered her the sweet little confectionery, holding it up to her in silent supplication between both thumb and forefinger.

"What is it tonight with you and all the chocolates, anyway?" she arched her eyebrows in quizzical good humour: "You wouldn't be trying to get me fat now, would you?"

"You? Fat? Never!" Andrei gasped, feigning absolute horror: "You could never be anything but perfect. For one thing you're just too active to ever get fat".

"And I promise to show you later on just how active I can really be", she winked at him in coy promise of future delights soon on the way.

"So you've got nothing to worry about then", he teased with a pert little grin:

"There's no conspiracy involved. I just thought it might be fun to share a couple", he explained, illustrating in greater detail what he had in mind.

"Well, then…", she consented, Andrei still holding up to her his little offering.

Parting slowly full, red lips, wrapping them around the tasty little treat right up to his fingers, she bit it clean in half—Andrei popping soon after the rest of the rich, dark chocolate into her waiting mouth, tilting what remained in such a way as to prevent both cherry and syrup from falling out.

However, stretching his hand out for yet another, Jenniboni beat him to the punch. Snatching one up from the nearby box before he even knew what was happening it was her turn now to hold one up to him:

"Go ahead, Sweet-pea", Jenniboni instructed him in playful fashion:

"Turnabout is fair play. Besides, I bought these for you and have yet to see you eat a single, blessed one".

"Point taken", he agreed, smiling as he accepted it from her outstretched hand. Biting down Andrei could feel some of the thick, gooey liquid inside trickle down his chin.

"That's a good boy", she cooed, collecting up with the tip of her finger the sticky syrup now running down his chin:

"Come, now. I want you to finish it all", she encouraged him even further, holding her finger up to his face within less than an inch.

Licking up the sticky sweet substance as told he then suggested something rather different, arranging a third chocolate between his lips before leaning into her, eyes shut. Guessing straight away what playful mischief he had in mind Jenniboni accepted quite readily, pressing around the small edible her lips to his.

Biting down on it in unison things didn't go quite as planned however, the small red fruit within escaping from between their candied kiss. Slipping away from between pressed lips it landed instead with swift accuracy upon Jenniboni's chest, right above her ample cleavage:

"Andrei!" she exclaimed, breaking contact, her eyes flying open in utter surprise. Following her startled gaze ever downward he spied without delay the tiny little cherry sliding already even further down her person.

"No need to worry, Love. I know exactly what to do", he assured her with a sly little laugh, burying his face between her full, ripe breasts right where the plunging neckline of her gossamer peignoir soon began.

Scooping up the candied fruit with his tongue, Andrei took as well his own sweet time while down there—taking great care to clean up each and every miniscule fleck of syrupy chocolate having accompanied the tiny cherry on its speedy decent.

Nor did he pull away from her warm, supple flesh until sure he'd gathered up with his tongue every single trace of the tasty mess from her warm, full, ripe bosom.

"There you go, Love: All taken care of ", he guaranteed with a pert little grin.

"Excellent work, my dear Sir. Such devotion to duty calls for a little reward", Jenniboni giggled, instructing him to close his eyes:

"No peeking!"

Taking his champagne glass from him, setting it down beside hers on the nearby coffee table, Jenniboni then set about retrieving the mysterious item she'd hidden from between the couch cushions in back of her:

"I think you'll want both hands free for this", she explained, telling him he could open his eyes upon placing in his upraised palms a flat, rectangular jewelry box.

Recognizing it from the same fine establishment where he purchased her earrings Andrei opened the elegant container most carefully indeed. Seeing what waited for him inside, the holo-fire's flickering light reflecting off its highly polished metallic surface, his eyes bugged out in complete disbelief.

Shutting the case with a sudden, sharp snap he just gazed at his wife in wide-eyed wonder, too stunned to reply.

"So how do you like it?", she smiled at his reaction.

"I don't like it. I *love* it!", he burst forth at last, leaping into her arms, giving her a joyous kiss.

"Sooo… I take it from your enthusiastic response you don't want me to take it back for a refund", she teased.

"Not on your life!" he laughed, giddy with delight, opening the black velvet box to look again at her generous gift:

"It's so beautiful", Andrei marveled: "But how did you know?"

"How could I not know?" she rolled her eyes, amused: "Especially after all the times you stopped to stare at it whenever we strolled by their display window".

Unable to take his eyes off of it, Andrei just couldn't believe it was really his now. Spotting it one day when window shopping down town he'd fallen in love with the sleek, stream-lined compu-watch the very moment he first laid eyes on it. The very moment he first saw it it's simple, stylish design and wafer-thin body captured his imagination.

Comprised mainly of a tiny square computer system a little under two inches wide, it's otherwise blank platinum surface possessed at its center a voice-activated sensor in the form of a green emerald—the wrist-band, likewise platinum, composed of an equally broad flexible mesh so refined, so delicate, its threaded texture was as silk.

Surrendering to impulse one day Andrei had even gone into the store, asking the sales clerk for further information, learning it was capable of much more than just verbally telling the time in every time-zone on every world in the Commonwealth.

Learning in fact it could arrange also daily schedules, keep addresses and V-phone numbers, he was told it even contained as well a general memo-storage wafer for personal messages of a more private, confidential, nature.

Coming complete with its own private access code the ingenious little device was also practically indestructible, bonded molecularly on the sub-atomic level, powered by the electro-magnetic impulses of the wearer's body.

Able to be worn at all times, in all situations, it was perfectly self-contained, no power source that needed changing.

Lifting the feather-light time piece from its container for an even closer look-see Andrei listened to Jenniboni list its many functions, its many abilities, with great relish. Taking as much pleasure in the giving as did he in the receiving Andrei hadn't the heart to spoil her fun, keeping silent instead.

Yet even so there was still one feature, a personally added touch, which took him quite unawares.

Following Jenniboni's instructions to look at the back of his newly acquired treasure, he held it up to the flickering light of the pseudo-fire from behind. Only then was he able to read on its underside her own special addition engraved in bold, fiery, script:

"To My Beloved Andrei:

"You brought both great joy and meaning into my life: My undying love and devotion shall be yours— forever and always!

Claiming it was a shame to hide such a beautiful message he actually raised his voice in mild protest when she requested the honour of placing it around her beloved's wrist:

"No need to worry", she smiled in full understanding: "I also had it verbally engraved so you can listen to it any time you want".

Taking it from him, Jenniboni slipped it over his right wrist. Too loose at first it soon fit however with snug comfort, putting her lips within a couple of inches of the small voice-operated device:

"Secure wristband", she commanded.

"What do you mean by 'verbally engraved'?", he asked, feeling the fine mesh band contract to just the right fit.

"Why don't you see for yourself ", she smiled sweetly: "Just say into it 'play verbal engraving'".

Doing so he heard his wife's sweet, tender voice repeat the same heartfelt proclamation of love he read just moments ago—the obvious sincerity he could hear having upon him an effect both deep and profound.

Wanting desperately to tell her how very much he adored her, Andrei feared in honest his heart might burst from all the feelings welling up inside if not able to express them all aloud—each and every one!

More than anything else he wanted to tell her of all the gratitude he possessed not only for her generous gift, but for just having someone like her in his very life. Try as hard as he might though, he just couldn't get the words out. Stirred too deeply by her own words now next to his flesh for all eternity tears began to form, struggling hard to speak.

No verbal declarations of love necessary as far as Jenniboni was concerned Andrei's eyes spoke volumes all on their own, conveying beyond a shadow of doubt what truly dwelt within his deepest soul. Aware of what he was trying so hard to say silently moving his lips she reached out with loving fingers, pressing them lightly to his mouth:

"No need, Sweet-pea", she comforted him in a soft whisper, wiping away gently the tears now forming in the corners of his eyes: "No need. I know how you feel... I know".

Letting then her fingertips travel across his face in a tender caress, Jenniboni couldn't resist the urge to explore all his manly features in greater detail, adoring both his chiseled good looks and the smooth softness of his skin.

Studying every exquisite detail with admiring eyes Jenniboni gave each a delicate brush, his swarthy olive-complected skin inherited from his Latin foremothers such a pleasure to touch, an exotic contrast to the sparkling blue eyes passed on down from his father's Gaelic ancestors.

Along with a well-defined square jaw and manly Roman nose, these likewise helped reflect both his natural strength of character along with the sensitive, caring side he possessed in such abundance.

Running her fingers over his lips she also enjoyed stroking both his neatly kept moustache and goatee, each lending him a rather intriguing 'bad boy' quality belied only by the guileless innocence of his natural expression.

Continuing her intimate explorations Jenniboni soon surrendered to an equally powerful temptation to light gently upon his eyelashes with only the slightest of touches. So long, thick, and yet masculine at the very same time she found them quite irresistible. Especially when he'd flutter them in such a flirtatious manner whenever brushed. Quite endearing given the fact this was pure reflex on his part, no conscious effort involved.

Closing his eyes in silent reply Jenniboni leaned forward, kissing his eyelids ever so lightly. Doing so Andrei felt his passion likewise flair, a fire burning in the pit of his stomach quickly spreading throughout his entire body.

Drawing her full, ripe lips away from his face Jenniboni continued by running her fingers through his thick, luxurious raven's black hair as he began nibbling on one of her broad, feminine shoulders. Soon working his way up her neck, showering her with eager, ardent kisses it wasn't long after that Andrei felt his wife's roaming fingers likewise leave his head, slipping under his robe, playing slowly now with his chest.

Running them with lazy precision through the hair likewise there as he caressed her soft, smooth, bare shoulders it was from there his right hand soon slipped ever downward across one of her perfectly rounded breasts, her right nipple hardening.

A low, throaty moan escaping moist, parted lips an almost electric jolt of absolute pleasure rocked her entire being to the very core. Erotic chills coursing throughout every fiber and sinew of her body Andrei continued his leisurely journey along her trim, firm stomach and the luscious swell of her left hip.

Exploring hungrily every perfect inch of her womanly body with both mouth and hands, Jenniboni found herself reflecting upon what a blessing it was to have a man who not only knew all his wants and desires, but could anticipate hers without likewise having to be told what to do.

Not so surprising given that he'd always proven himself an enthusiastic partner when it came to the sensual side of their marriage as well as the more spiritual. Never would she forget their first coupling on their wedding night as both woman and husband—each having come to the marriage bed chaste, neither really knowing what to expect but eager anyway to give themselves to one-another.

Even at the tender age of just seventeen Andrei still possessed a passionate nature that would only ripen with age, whatever they imagined paling in comparison to what actually took place that very first night. Jenniboni would always remember with absolute fondness looking down into her new husband's sweet, innocent face, his head resting on pillows in back of him.

Reaching up to her in sexual supplication it was then she noticed the mixture of emotions in the young man's eyes—an expression of reverent awe, a look of dawning awareness, alongside the understandable desire also there— the consummation of their union proving itself as spiritually gratifying for the both of them as it was physically satisfying.

Reaching together at the very same time that ultimate plateau of sheer ecstasy, Jenniboni would forever cherish the vivid memory of how tears of joy made their way down Andrei's young cheeks, stirred to the very depths of his soul.

Bestowing just then upon her such a look of pure love and utter devotion she, too, began to weep… part of her when realizing how deeply she'd moved him inside… another part weeping because she, too, was just as moved as he by what they both just shared.

Afraid to let go following all this they just held onto one another quite tightly, confessing their undying love for each other with both tender words and kisses. And now, ten years later, Jenniboni was just as grateful to realize their love for one another hadn't diminished in the least, having instead blossomed into something broader, more profound than either could have ever hoped.

Andrei's hand now reaching her silken thigh he could likewise feel his wife's loving fingers continue their light decent from his chest, down across his trim mid-section, grazing his leg ever so gently.

Coming at last to a complete rest upon his inner thigh she gave it a tender squeeze; a thrill of total, absolute arousal passing through him as he leaned into her. Pressing his mouth firmly to hers, parting his lips, he brushed the tip of his tongue against hers, sensing as well a similar quiver of consummate delight spread likewise throughout Jenniboni's entire body.

Overwhelmed by the immediate intimacy of the moment Andrei was therefore at a complete loss, unable to comprehend what was happening, when she began to pull away. Looking up at her with plaintive eyes full of silent entreaty, Jenniboni now standing over him, Andrei almost cried up at her; "What's wrong? Where are you going?"

His confusion didn't last long however when she leaned over, reaching down for him. Confident what was to come he surrendered himself to her with joyful anticipation, Jenniboni slipping one arm under his knees, the other around his back, lifting him with easy grace from where he looked up at her.

Quickly grabbing three chocolates before draping his arm about her neck Andrei's swift seizure of all three bon-bon's escaped not her notice:

"They're for later", he told her by way of explanation, noting her look of immediate confusion gathering him up in her arms. Lifting him quite effortlessly from the couch her puzzled expression remained until he added, wearing a truly impish grin:

"Of course they'll have to soften up a bit first before we can use them. Just like last time". Hearing this, a broad smile of recognition sprang at once to Jenniboni's lips, inspired by an exquisite memory of sensual delights most scintillating in its crystalline clarity.

Carrying him off to the mistress bedroom with simple ease it occurred once more to her how very lucky she was to have such a creative, innovative husband.

And as it did she made her way down the hall with a most jaunty, carefree, little bounce to her step.

Chapter 39

"DEPARTURE"
(Friday, February 15th, 2915 AD)

The time on StarChild's oval bridge was '14:40 hours'—a fact confirmed by both the digital chronometer located directly above the ship's main forward viewer alongside the disembodied voice from the '*Project StarChild Command Base*' back on Demeter's frozen surface:

"Base Command to StarChild: We now stand at 'T'-minus twenty minutes and counting. All systems are presently green and go: Over".

"Base Command, this is StarChild: Transmission received", Jenniboni acknowledged. "All shipboard systems likewise green and go. Ready to proceed with secondary disembarkation procedures: Over."

"Authorization to proceed is given, Commodore: Godspeed to both you and your crew: Over and out".

Severing her link with Base Command it was Jenniboni's fondest hope to minimize any possible risk of being overheard by *any* non-authorized civilian communications systems... none whatsoever... wherever able to do so.

So far proving lucky the media had yet to discover StarChild was already leaving at this earlier time. Nor were they about to due to any slip-ups on her part, accidentally picking up on any off-ship communiqués:

Not if she had any say in the matter!

Over the last couple of days, ever since learning of their early departure, Jenniboni overheard some of her crew express in hushed whispers their profound disappointment regarding how they wouldn't be receiving the grand press coverage initially scheduled for StarChild's spectacular exit from both System and Commonwealth.

Not sharing their sentiments in the least Jenniboni had absolutely no interest in the media circus originally scheduled in great detail for the commencement of StarChild's bachelor voyage. Having no emotional need for such grandiose hoopla Jenniboni Saphira wasn't the type who needed such public attention given her every move to bolster any her ego.

Viewing her recently acquired celebrity status a tiresome compromise in otherwise achieving her main goals of both exploration and command, StarChild's supreme commander didn't require public adoration to remind her of the significant role she was now playing in the herstorical events currently unfolding.

"All right, Lieutenant Matthias: Contact the '*Project Dry Dock*' and have them release magnetic mooring clamps".

"Aye, aye; Ma'am", Phyllis obeyed, seated at her station just right of the main viewer ahead. A slight shudder running through StarChild's titanium-alloy skin, it was free in just a few minutes of all restraints.

The leggy magnetic claps from above curling up out of the way, retreating back from StarChild's outer hull, the spider-like space station directly above looked now like some dead insect lying on its back.

"Lt. Commander Marlowe; activate position stabilizers and power-up sub-light engines", Jenniboni continued, directing her attention off to the far right of StarChild's wide bridge—Naomi's current position at her engineering console.

Receiving from her the same reply as from Lt. Matthias Jenniboni soon leaned back in her grand command chair, crossing her legs in a both confident and even relaxed posture. Able to sense the low vibration of StarChild's engines now humming to life, it felt as though the same energy pulsating now throughout every metallic fiber of her ship was coursing as well now throughout her body, too.

Empowering Jenniboni likewise with its awesome energy other sensations were soon to follow... sensations such as mounting excitement, great expectation, and a clearly understandable sense of personal satisfaction... Jenniboni sitting like a ruler of state center-stage of StarChild's busy command center.

For the last three years of her life nearly all her considerable time and energies were spent in preparation of this particular event, this particular moment. Honing all her remarkable command skills and leadership abilities to a razor-sharp edge of absolute precision this was what all the physical, technical, and even psychological training had been in final preparation of.

Yet even so Jenniboni proved honest enough with her innermost self to acknowledge as well other feelings beginning to surface—feelings of both great power and exaltation—a growing sense of great personal honour, and even privilege, to be at the immediate forefront of this next major step in Womankind's development.

Keenly aware of the grand role she was playing in the future expansion of Human civilization she felt a strong, almost giddy, sense of her own personal power even as StarChild began to likewise realize his own considerable potential.

However, while allowing herself to enjoy these truly heady emotions, Jenniboni was nevertheless more than able to maintain firm discipline over each, reigning all of them in least they overwhelm her in their intensity.

Personal control quite evident now in the calm, cool exterior she conveyed Jenniboni's obvious self-possession was evident in both face and form—seated as she was in her elevated command post positioned smack-dab in the middle of StarChild's highly charged command center.

Nor was it long after released from dry dock Naomi announced soon enough sub-light drive ready for activation.

With a pleased smile Jenniboni wasted no time ordering an 'all-ahead at quarter-light speed' until certain they were beyond all present hazard-zones.

Recently proving the existence of UltraSpace, Womankind soon developed technology allowing access to this particular state of 'hyper-reality'. And gaining entrance to that other state of being through the creation of 'hyper-portals', they designed as well ships able to travel many times the speed of light once there.

Yet no sooner had such an artificial passageway been achieved, certain deadly side-effects came to immediate notice—dangers necessitating the declaration of certain obvious 'hazard-zones' to protect both nearby celestial bodies and stellar craft not in possession of Ultra-drive capabilities.

Were StarChild to activate such a passageway too near either one of these, the resulting disruption to the space-time continuum generated by the natural energy fields surrounding hyper-portals would rip the unprotected object to utter shreds.

Womankind's first Starship remaining safe-and-sound from those destructive side effects, others however would be decimated—their tattered, helpless remains sucked directly into the gaping maw of that alternate reality just beyond.

Upon receiving further, final confirmation it was now safe to engage Ultra-drive, Jenniboni noticed there were still five minutes remaining until their scheduled early departure at 15:00 hours. Cutting it rather close she nevertheless ordered a 'steady-ahead' at both their present course and speed until achieving even more distance between both her ship and what lay now in back of them.

Any possible mishap, especially at this most early juncture, struck Jenniboni as a most tragic way of starting out a mission.

Especially one already fraught with as much peril as this.

However, when the chronometer ahead of her current position finally read '14:58 hours', Jenniboni decided the time had come at last to begin their uncertain voyage in earnest.

Pivoting her chair to one side Jenniboni ordered straightaway Lt. Miranda Netra, the ship's senior navigations officer, to plot their next course change into Maccs' programmed trajectory—Ms. Netra's duty station situated towards the rear of StarChild's bridge, in back of Jenniboni's stately command chair, off to her right.

"Course laid in, Ma'am. Maccs confirms all systems operating at peak efficiency", Lt. Netra announced following status reports from both Stasha and Frances, each seated at their respective stations for both Science and Security.

"Excellent!" Jenniboni nodded her approval: "Lt. Cmdr. Marlowe, power-up Ultra-drive: Ensign Fielding, once the portal is open lay in our course, taking us into the passageway".

Directing her last command towards the young helmswoman on duty in back of her, stationed to the left of Lt. Netra, it wasn't long before Jenniboni could feel yet another mighty energy pulse surge throughout every metal fiber of her ship.

Coursing likewise throughout her body as well, Jenniboni turned then her attention back towards the main viewer. Doing so as Ensign Fielding announced right then and there the hyper-rift was beginning to form, she experienced once more that same heady sense of absolute power.

"Thank you, Ms. Fielding".

Gazing at the field of stars before her, Jenniboni was soon able to spot a ripple effect taking place directly off StarChild's bow some hundred kilometers away.

Growing even more pronounced as the stars closest to the phenomena seemed to begin dancing, swaying to and fro, a diagonal rip... or tear... in the very fabric of space appeared soon thereafter, taking on both form and substance directly in the path of StarChild's plotted course.

Starting out as nothing more than a jagged blue-white line positioned smack-dab in the middle of the main viewing screen directly ahead, StarChild's entire bridge crew watched it quickly expand into a brilliant triangular display of every colour imaginable, an incredible menagerie of pure light setting the most beautiful rainbow to utter shame.

Cascading now through the main viewer's wide expanse with a certain fluid quality the entire ship's bridge was soon saturated with its infinite splendor. Every colour in the visible spectrum penetrating the oval chamber's otherwise stark, white walls and light blue deck the otherwise functional white consoles at which each bridge officer sat glowed now with its fiery brilliance.

A sight guaranteed to move even the coldest, hardest heart to tears Jenniboni all the same maintained her composure, ordering instead Ensign Fielding to engage ultra-light engines.

Rushing headlong into the multi-hued portal ahead like a sleek, graceful race horse bolting eagerly from its starting gate StarChild then vanished into that alternate state of existence known only as 'UltraSpace'.

****

Andrei stood in back of the large theatre of operations comprising the Project StarChild Base's 'Central Command Chamber', Admiral Sellers standing alongside both him and the Saphira children.

Consisting of row-upon-row of computer consoles, each row on a progressively lower level approaching the far wall opposite of where Andrei stood, the "C.C.C." was crowded with nearly a hundred women in S.E.A. uniform. Each stationed at every console present all were responsible for the many different operational procedures involved in StarChild's early launch.

However, ignoring each and every one of them, it was the Command Chamber's far wall that garnished instead the majority of Andrei's attention.

Blanketed with a series of display screens ranging in size, each

289

broadcasting a different image from varied locations, the opposite wall's upper half was dominated by two giant rectangular viewers equal in width.

On the right was a clear shot of Jenniboni seated in profile in her majestic command chair, replete with regal satisfaction while, on the left, Andrei caught sight of StarChild's glistening exterior.

Enraptured more so by what he saw on the right, watching his wife in preparation of all for their early departure, Andrei was glad now he'd chosen to be there, having almost deciding otherwise.

Nor was it long ago, right about the same time Jenniboni first approached him about the very real possibility of watching StarChild's disembarkation procedures for himself. In fact it was right after gaining permission from the Admiral for both he and the children to be there... in person... for this very special event.

Almost refusing her generosity he feared at first the pain it might cause him seeing her leave like this. So much so it resulted in Andrei almost denying both himself and the children this very special opportunity.

Realizing though that to do so would be an act of pure selfishness on his part, he decided upon further consideration there was no way he could possibly rob them all of this special gift courtesy of Jenniboni's own procuring.

Not after all the trouble she so clearly went to securing permission from both Admiral Sellers, and even S.E.A. High Command for her family to be there. Jenniboni deserved for her loved ones to be present for such a momentous herstorical event in her life—Andrei likewise wanting one, last glimpse of the most important person in their lives before she took as well her leave of them.

Actually glad now to have accepted this unique opportunity courtesy of a loving wife, it likewise gave him this singular opportunity to witness Jenniboni in her natural element aboard StarChild regardless how painful it remained just watching her leave.

A revelation both revealing, and even comforting at the very same time he paid little heed when some nearby entity soon announced "'T' minus twenty minutes", quite riveted instead by the very sight of Jenniboni's face.

Having never seen her aboard StarChild before, until now only able to imagine what she was like when in command of her ship, he now realized from where most of his fears really stemmed. Especially those concerning her safety traversing the great unknown.

Nor was it the orders she gave, or anything she actually did which explained Andrei's newfound peace of mind as much as it was the very aura now radiating from within her, blazing forth with those positive feminine virtues he always admired in her at an intensity he never saw before.

Such womanly qualities as her great courage, strength, determination, superior intelligence, and natural belief in her own remarkable command abilities. Nurtured within her right from childhood on by attentive, caring parents there was no doubting Jenniboni's superior leadership skills when so painfully obvious just gazing at her on that large monitor before him.

Now there was a woman ready to tackle any problem fate might send her way, sure to come away victorious.

Enraptured by the very sight of her, able to see magnified now in his amazing wife both the devoted explorer and battle-savvy warrior he always admired in her before, Andrei couldn't help but feel his already mounting love for the incredible woman on the large screen before him grow to such an overwhelming extent it made his poor heart ache for her all that much more.

Yet, even though truly happy for the intrepid starship commander now taking her leave of one and all, Andrei still had to confess there were times he was really jealous of Jenniboni's command, honestly seeing StarChild as a rival for his wife's affections—the "other man" in her life!

Heck: they even referred to the darn thing by such proper masculine pronouns as "he" and/or "him". So what if it was only tradition to describe such vessels—whether sea going, or even space faring—in such manly terms. It still didn't help ease any Andrei's occasional bitterness knowing this.

Be that as it may however, all that had just changed. No longer resentful in the least he actually felt a sense of quiet joy welling up inside him, able now to see a similar sense of inner fulfillment on Jenniboni's face. Happy to know now she had such as this in her life helping her feel more complete, Andrei could see now in her expression that which no one else ever could, the incredible sense of personal power... even excitement... Jenniboni was now celebrating within.

After all the years spent loving her, closer to his wife than anyone else, he could see about her that which no one else ever could, the sheer happiness he saw at that very moment within her eyes pleasing him to no end.

Unfortunately this didn't help with the immediate stab of sudden fear, the anxious worry Andrei now experienced noting a sudden burst of multi-hued light now flowing all around her—a fluid technicolour rainbow swirling around and about his wife in both liquid eddies and languid currents as if in slow motion.

A beautiful display of every colour imaginable, he might have actually seen it that way were it not for how it startled him, appearing as if out of nowhere. Nor did it help ease his anxiety any when the picture up on that large screen before one and all began to grow quite distorted, fading out before his very eyes, taking Jenniboni's lovely image with it.

"What's happening?" Andrei called out, clearly alarmed.

"Don't worry. It's just the energy flow from the hyper-rift now in progress", Melissa assured him, standing at his side: "It's starting to surround StarChild from UltraSpace, preparing to draw him in, interfering with the onboard signal he's now transmitting".

No sooner had the Admiral finished saying this than she started out on a rather lengthy, detailed, description of that other reality. Quite unnecessary seeing as Jenniboni had already taken time explaining its many unique properties to him.

Also referring to it as "Hyper-reality" the particulars he found most relevant was that it was another state of alternate existence beyond the already proven space-time continuum comprising the "normal" universe Womankind now existed in. To him this was more important than anything else since, according to Jenniboni, it also meant 'ship-time' would pass for her at the same orderly rate as for him on Demeter.

Nullifying Einstein's theory of relativity the fact she'd be traveling at velocities far beyond the speed of light seemed to matter very little, allowing her more than anything else to return home and find as well her entire family just as much older—no more and no less.

Impressing his adventurous wife most was how this clearly opened up all the cosmos for further personal, hands-on exploration while likewise preserving the temporal continuity of Human civilization for said explorers upon their return home, returning to the exact-same herstorical timeline they left behind.

However, as far as Andrei was concerned, the most significant thing about this was how it meant Jenniboni... personally... would be returning home to him sooner than later. Unfortunately taking comfort in this hadn't gone far preparing him for the unsettling effect of seeing her face grow so distorted, fading away before his very eyes.

Nor did it help any when Admiral Sellers pointed at the large screen to the immediate left of this disturbing image, what he saw there proving in some ways even more distressing to look at.

Whatever the broadcast's point of origin was it must have been slightly above the sleek, avian vessel as well as to its rear. Beginning as a routine, rear-view shot during StarChild's approach of the hyper-portal ahead Andrei could clearly see both the ship's upper decks, narrowed beak-like prow, and massive stern grow even longer yet.

His consternation only increased as the ship seemed to literally 'stretch' forwards as though StarChild were no more than so much warm taffy in some possessive child's tug-of-war, growing even longer at its slender yet sturdy neck. Once more Andrei just listened, Melissa explaining how this was merely an optical illusion created by distortions in the space-time continuum now surrounding StarChild on his final approach to UltraSpace.

Listening to her compare it to the similar effect witnessed in objects likewise approaching the event-horizon of 'your typical Black Hole', Andrei realized already on a purely intellectual level he had nothing to worry about when witnessing this strange apparition.

All the same though that didn't help any when given the emotional effect such a disquieting scene had upon the higher senses. Especially when the triangular gateway StarChild was now approaching likewise grabbed the nearing vessel with wild, frenzied rainbow tentacles growing out of its ragged, torn edges—pulling the hapless ship into its gaping maw—quickly devouring StarChild before Andrei's very eyes.

Having little time however to let his eyes dwell upon this peculiar sight it was then his wife's starship vanished into UltraSpace, drawn into that other state of existence like some tiny fish swallowed up by a giant, multi-coloured squid. And at that the hyper-portal likewise collapsed in on itself with a brilliant flash, nothing visible now but the normal starscape of regular space.

As it did a loud cheer went up from all those present, rejoicing over the successful launch of Humanity's first starship upon its bachelor voyage, Andrei understanding their high spirits... their jubilation... over the triumph this represented not only for them, but for all Womankind.

The culmination of all the hard work they put into Project StarChild over the last several years, all the countless womanhours devoted to this one specific endeavor, even J.J. and the twins let forth with a joyful chorus—adding their voices to the overall din all around at the magnificent sight of their very own mother's grand departure from the Tammyite Matriarchate's home system.

While understanding it was indeed a great success story for all Womankind, all Andrei could manage for the moment was a little, bittersweet smile, overcome all at once by dark premonitions of danger ahead. Although happy Jenniboni could play such an important role in Human herstory, truly proud of his brave and noble wife, he was all the same overcome with feelings of impending trouble on her immediate horizon.

Understanding what a great honour—even privilege—it was to just be there at that very auspicious moment in Human herstory Andrei nevertheless gave Melissa his sincerest apologies, asked if he'd care to join in on the Command Center's post-departure celebration.

Doing so quite gracefully he was nevertheless concerned over the likely damper he might put on their otherwise fine time together, ending up a virtual wet blanket were he to attend their happy gathering.

From the sympathetic smile on her usually dour, jowly face it was obvious as well the good Admiral understood.

"That's all right, Andrei", she assured him, recognizing his present need for utter solitude: "I'm just glad you could share this most special time with us".

Expressing likewise his sincere gratitude for this splendid opportunity she'd given as well his entire family, Andrei gathered up all three children.

Taking the younger two each by the hand, J.J. followed close-by at their side.

Turning however towards the impressive Command Chamber's rear exit the young father of three was taken somewhat aback, the two security guards posted on either side of those double doors snapping all-of-a-sudden to immediate attention—both officers granting him a smart salute, holding open each wide door before him.

Stirred deeply by their silent tribute Andrei acknowledged this noble act of silent recognition with the warmest of smiles, nodding in the direction of each gallant woman before heading home down the long corridor beyond, children in tow.

Part 2

"THE EMEROG"

Friday, February 15th, 2915 AD
To
Saturday, February 23rd, 2915 AD

"To expand without fear Womankind's
civilization, knowledge, and personal experience—
to grow beyond both the known and even unknown"

—Official S.E.A Motto

****

"The Devil comes in many disguises,
So beware the beast within".

—Anonymous

****

"Never say 'die' until ten minutes *after* you're dead".

—Lt. Cmdr. Frances Miriam Straker

A Quote from **_The New Matriarchate:_**

"Many assert that all the world's past ills can be traced to such natural Human traits as aggressiveness and an inborn need to compete with others. Nowhere is this more evident than when discussing the now defunct patriarchates and their bygone masculine leaders throughout Human herstory.

"However, while such claims **do** possess a certain kernel of truth, it must also be kept in mind that these very same basic traits are likewise responsible for many of Womankind's greatest achievements crucial for our continued growth, progress, and even advancement not only as a civilization, but as a very species itself.

"The only reason these natural Human traits **did** wreak such havoc in past times is because it was usually just men who were given free rein to them, to put them to their practical application—the only problem with this being that men were never meant to either rule, or hold such eventual positions of ultimate power.

"Admittedly there were still those female exceptions to the above rule who, likewise holding power back then, proved themselves just as corrupt, just as irresponsible in the performance of their duties as any man.

"Often motivated by both feelings of anger, resentment, and a deep-seated desire for revenge when competing with their masculine contemporaries, their biggest mistake was in denying their femininity—not only ignoring but even neglecting those womanly qualities that, by their very virtue of being feminine, would have made them superior leaders.

"Yet, even while having said all this, there nevertheless existed even then those female leaders who proved themselves superior to their masculine counterparts during those bygone days of male domination: Women who remembered their feminine side, tempering their aggressive, competitive natures with both tenderness and compassion.

"So now that women have been restored to their rightful place as both Humanity's ultimate leaders, and rulers they must never forget to balance their aggression with compassion, control with love, competitiveness with sensitivity, and leadership with both mercy and justice for **ALL**!"

—**The** Rt. Reverend Tammy E. Garfield.
THE NEW MATRIARCHATE
—*2056 AD*—

****

A Quote from ***The New Matriarchate:***

"No one can really be certain how both male domination and the patriarchal system really got their start so very long ago. All we know for sure is that both seem to have originated some 6,000 years past in connection with the rather sudden development of Earth's first city-states.

"Why such a mass concentration of Human populations under a more municipal authority should result in such a dramatic, unnatural shift of power between the sexes remains a perpetual mystery right to this very day.

"Nevertheless we can still remain confident that the first Human societies known to exist were essentially matriarchal in nature, having been so since the first appearance of Womankind over 40,000 years ago."

—***The*** Rt. Reverend Tammy E. Garfield.
THE NEW MATRIARCHATE
—2056 AD—

Chapter 40

"GETTING TO KNOW YOU"
(Friday, February 15th, 2915 AD to Sunday, February 17th, 2915AD)

Once safely in UltraSpace Jenniboni ordered yet another routine diagnostic of all ship's key systems, making sure all was operating at peak efficiency in absolute keeping with her own exacting standards.

Upon receiving final confirmation all was running in perfect accord with her own high expectations, this left her with yet another essential duty before continuing any further the rest of their already perilous voyage ahead.

Activating the internal comm. system securely embedded in the left armrest of her command chair, Jenniboni then set about addressing her entire crew. Everyone aboard, officer and N.C.O. alike, were able to hear their ship C.O.'s crisp, clear voice ring forth throughout every quarter of StarChild's vast interior.

Presenting them only now with every new aspect of their mission ahead as revealed to her aboard Stellar-One, she likewise emphasized in no uncertain terms the major importance of their new task ahead. Emphasizing how she expected each and every crewwoman aboard ship to perform according to the very best of her ability, it was only then she ended on a more positive note both strong and reassuring at the very same time:

"And so, in conclusion, I likewise wish to confide in all those listening my complete confidence in each and every one of you to reach new heights of excellence in the performance of your assigned duties.

"While the current mission ahead isn't quite the one we originally hoped, I remain all-the-same confident in the sure ability of each and every one of you to adapt, to meet these new challenges now facing us all, with flying colours— everyone aboard StarChild chosen to serve aboard him because she is the very best Womankind has to offer.

"Therefore, although this might be our first deep space assignment as both commander and crew, I nevertheless remain confident we shall prove ourselves triumphant over whatever hardships we may encounter. Both honoured and even proud as I am to be your commanding officer I trust firmly in our ability to rely on one-another seeing us all safely home again, returning to the affectionate bosom of loved-ones trusting in our certain return.

"Commodore Saphira over and out".

Switching off once more the active comm. link between her and the rest of StarChild's crew, Jenniboni merely stared out before her at the kaleidoscope of brilliant colours now occupying all this alternate reality known as UltraSpace.

Hoping her entire ship's compliment was just as aware of the sincere feeling behind her parting words ending her ship-wide address, Jenniboni hoped as well the final conclusion to her little speech offered them at least some small measure of comfort given the otherwise disturbing news she just gave them.

Nevertheless she was also more than realistic enough to realize it would take more than just a few meager reassurances to ready both ship and crew for whatever lay ahead. Involving as well both a lot of hard work and dedication on her part, it was likewise work she couldn't accomplish by merely staying put, sitting there like some worthless potentate on her... um... 'bridge'!

Therefore, informing Stasha she now had temporary command, Jenniboni decided it was already more than high time she set a positive example for all those aboard ship, rolling up her sleeves along with everyone else in preparation of what that might await them in Womankind's closest neighbouring System.

Leaving her current position by way of the ag-pod in back of StarChild's bridge, asking Maccs for a brief run down on his immediate operational status, she traversed both the length and breadth of her entire ship listening to the resonant timbre of StarChild's deep, masculine voice before inspecting all departmental preparations now underway—doing so in cautious anticipation of whatever danger lurked on their distant horizon.

****

Sunday services commenced at precisely 10:00 hours in the ship's chapel located on deck S-11 and Jenniboni was there as might be expected, seated up front in the very first row of participants in that crowded sanctuary. Surrounded by others of her crew, participating along with them in the shipboard service, she nevertheless felt inside a trifle disoriented.

Nor was it the actual service or her chaplain's words which left StarChild's C.O. so wanting, thanking in-fact Mother Shauna afterwards for her inspirational service. Given the emotional uncertainty of their present condition Rev. McSteele's service was actually quite uplifting, Jenniboni having to confess considerable respect for the way the older woman went about the superior dispensation of her clerical responsibilities.

Although not well acquainted on a more personal basis with her shipboard priest, she all-the-same heard nothing but good from the rest of her crew in regards to StarChild's spiritual guide, taking some welcome comfort from the present proceedings.

Nooo… what actually left Jenniboni feeling rather disconnected, removed from all those around her, was expecting to see the rest of her loved-ones at her side only to find them missing—this the first time since their wedding day she could remember ever attending church without Andrei there at her side.

And so it was with him in mind she left the ship's chapel in search of both Frances and Naomi, deciding it was more than high time to better acquaint herself with these two exceptional women. Feeling she owed it as much to herself as them given all their tender mercies, the generosity each showed her family, Andrei's positive endorsement of each was only part of her reason for doing so.

Having granted much of her crew this one day off Jenniboni had even so a pretty good idea from what she already knew about each where both Lt. Cmdr.'s Marlowe and Straker would most likely be.

Granting Naomi a brief respite from her duties in Engineering, encouraging her dedicated Chief Engineer to take a much earned break, Jenniboni was pleasantly surprised to discover in the other woman a quite intelligent, outgoing conversationalist with both a quick and ready wit.

Finding in her someone to go to whenever needing a quick pick-me-up, Naomi struck her likewise as a well-mannered individual both polite and respectful. Maybe the rumors of her rather sordid, unseemly off-duty behavior were unjustified after all.

Then again, by their very nature, such rumors usually were.

Regardless one way or the other Jenniboni was, at least for the time being, willing to give the congenial Ms. Marlowe the current benefit of the doubt.

Yet, even while impressed with her intrepid and industrious head of Engineering, it was Jenniboni's Chief of Security who ultimately captured her undivided attention. Doing so from the very onset it didn't take very long either to discover in that tall, gaunt, and even severe-looking woman someone with whom she could develop a firm and abiding friendship sure to endure any test of time.

Sharing many traits in common there resided in each the same passion for both order and justice, holding in high esteem the many traditions, principals, and mores upon which both the Tammyite Matriarchate and its Commonwealth were likewise established.

Happy as well to discover how each shared both the same basic pleasures and pastimes, both Frances and Jenniboni were delighted as well to learn of their shared passion for both high adventure, exploration, and even the discovery of that which dwelt within their own inner-selves alongside whatever existed beyond their own personal experience.

Whether it be their similar love of athletic competition, games of both great skill and great intelligence, or even their common interest in the same variety of music, art, and literature each was equally pleased to find in her companion both the same general sensibilities and high standards of personal excellence.

Nor was that all, discovering within one-another just as many variations adding that extra sense of discovery to their initial meeting essential to any newly-acquired friendship—that tantalizing sense of uncharted horizons in each that any really significant, meaningful, relationship needs in order to both survive and even grow.

For example, while it was true they both shared a similar interest in classical pre-tech literature, Jenniboni possessed a greater interest in the collective works of both Shakespeare, Bacon, and Chaucer alongside the philosophical musings of such as Sartre, Camus, and Voltaire while Frances' on the other hand seemed to favor both the unique social commentary, literary genius, and even deep spiritual insight of such latter-day authors as Koontz, King, Whitman, Wilde, Dickens, and even St. Thomas Aquinas.

And from their initial get-together following her previous get-together with Naomi,w it didn't take long on Jenniboni's part to find Frances hard at work in StarChild's 'Security Training Facility'.

****

Right across from Jenniboni's initial starting point in StarChild's chapel the "S.T.F." was a walled-off section of the crew gymnasium in which the object of her search was more than quite busy indeed, training a goodly-sized segment of StarChild's engineering department in the proper use of their newly acquired 'Smart-Armor'.

On her arrival Jenniboni found over a dozen crewwomen already gathered about in neat order for a thorough demonstration, Frances making her way over to a row of 'smart-suits' arranged on a series of magnetic security hooks hanging on the far wall.

Staying out of her subordinate's way near the room's only entrance Jenniboni watched instead in utter silence. Herself quite proficient in the use of such protective apparel she was interested in seeing how her people would likewise cope.

Aware that her arrival caught Frances' immediate notice right from the very start, Jenniboni approved as well how her senior officer ignored her unexpected presence, proceeding with the lesson at hand with such professional detachment.

'Smart armor', composed entirely of a highly polished white titanium alloy, was called such not only for both its superior design and advanced combat capabilities, but also for how it operated on the telepathic commands of its wearer.

Consisting of sturdy anti-grav boots, helmet, and defensive gauntlets reaching from wrist to elbow, all these various components were likewise joined to one-another by a large suit of protective armor composed of overlapping disks reminiscent of scales, some no wider than an inch—the gleaming armor possessing as well a brilliant gold fempacem upon the chest.

Replete with the moniker "*S.E.A.S.S. STARCHILD*" written in proud style both above and below, 'Smart Armor' provided its wearer as well with defensive capabilities consisting of a long, sleek, spike-shaped laser running along the back of each forearm—each ending in a tapered, slender blue crystalline tip protruding several inches beyond each wrist.

So when Frances called upon all those present for a volunteer with which to demonstrate the intricate armor's many abilities, Jenniboni was more than a wee bit doubtful watching Lt. Gloria Greensley step forward. Having certain reservations when it came to the matter of her youngest officer it wasn't Gloria's skill, or intelligence which gave Jenniboni such pause for concern.

Nor was it her age.

What really troubled her was the other woman's apparent lack of authority, her inability to assert herself, required for both the important rank and position she currently held. Going over status reports on the young gentlewoman's work performance, Jenniboni couldn't fault Lt. Greensley on either her technical expertise, or the otherwise outstanding performance of her material duties.

Having no problem with the young tech officer's many other skills, her ability as a top-notch engineer quite apparent, Jenniboni's only concern involved Gloria's seeming refusal to take effective charge of those serving under her—an issue worthy of major concern should there be any likely situation demanding such obvious skills.

Which is why, although it pained her to do so, Jenniboni came recently to the sad conclusion it might be best to offer Lt. Greensley the unfortunate choice of either a demotion to some position of both lower rank and authority, a discreet transfer to the Project StarChild Base back on Demeter, or even a complete honourable discharge from the entire Star Exploration Administration.

Wishing to be fair though Jenniboni was nonetheless willing to wait until their eventual return to the actual Commonwealth itself before making her final decision, giving the young woman more than an even chance to prove herself.

However, if matters turned out otherwise, then that was that! Charity was one thing, but the bottom line would always remain the ultimate well-being, the continued safety, of her entire ship and crew as a complete and undivided body. And if any member of her ship's compliment wasn't up to the peak performance of their assigned responsibilities aboard him, Jenniboni wouldn't have her serving at all aboard StarChild.

Therefore it was with studious interest she watched Gloria slip on her protective battle gear, curious to see how she'd weather this particular test, her sample armor's initial fit bringing even so an amused smile to Jenniboni's lips. Many sizes too large for her when first donning the glistening suit, seeing how it hung in fact from the young woman's body, put Jenniboni in mind of a recent incident involving her young son back home.

Catching by chance little Tommy going through Andrei's half of their bedroom closet, playing dress-up as little boys sometimes do, he was all decked out in one of his father's finest outfits. Looking so adorable staring up at his mother, wide-eyed with utter surprise at being caught so in the act, he looked so precious, so completely adorable, lost in Andrei's best.

Not so cute however as to stop her from snatching a pair of large scissors from out of his possession, the mischievous little scamp about ready to cut down-to-size his father's prize apparel—Gloria looking just as lost in that bright metal armor she now wore. All one could see of the small Martian woman were her eyes peering through the sophisticated helmet's transparent viewing strip.

Comprised of a hardy titanium alloy reaching clear from temple-to-temple, the sturdy helmet's dense visor ended just inches from a set of round, gold mesh grids transmitting sound to the wearer within—three other sparkling metal grids made of the same metal, triangular in appearance, positioned directly beneath the protective viewing screen.

Arranged in an even larger triangular pattern, located directly over the wearer's nose and mouth, the upper grid served the person within as both an air filter and adjuster. Purifying the outside atmosphere of harmful toxins it regulated as well oxygen-rare environments to the wearer's comfort while the lower two units, positioned side-by-side, served the user as combination speaker/transmitters. And to "top it all off" the smart-armor helmet possessed likewise one more added feature, a domed light fixture like those found on a miner's headgear located right above the helmet's broad, narrow visor.

"Are you ready now to continue, Lieutenant?", Frances asked her young volunteer.

Replying in the affirmative Gloria's voice took on an almost distinctive mechanical quality, the young ship's engineer told immediately thereafter to 'think' the smart-suit down to a less awkward size.

Closing her eyes before doing anything else, Gloria ordered the telepathic quark-bots embedded in the armored-plating to do her mental bidding. Doing so with no delay they picked up on her silent orders, the outfit once so bulky shrinking in now around her body, providing Gloria with a snug yet comfortable fit.

Receiving still further instruction to move about, get used to her new attire, she did as she was intructedqq—Frances lecturing now the rest of her class on the gifted outfit's many other brilliant abilities.

Ending with the anti-grav padding on the soles of each booted foot, StarChild's senior security officer explained in great detail how such added features helped counteract the suit's otherwise cumbersome weight, permitting the user to likewise repel foreign objects when kicking outward.

Calling on Gloria to demonstrate this last of its many capabilities, Frances lead her over to a dark-grey practice dummy standing dead center of the surrounding chamber both tall, still and upright—Lt. Greensley approaching the stark, silent, nondescript humanoid form in a rather timid fashion.

Already Jenniboni could foresee the final outcome even as the other woman leapt only then into action. Jumping upwards, thrusting both feet out before her in an otherwise accurate martial arts maneuver, her mistaken attempt to connect with the bland figure's solar plexus ended rather poorly.

Without any support beneath her Gloria's upper body tilted immediately in back of her under the smart suit's unexpected weight, bringing the hapless young woman down with a most awkward clunk. Landing rather ignominiously on her pert, little derriere several other crewwomen present began giggling, Frances' deputy bursting forth with fits of uproarious laughter at the smaller woman's expense.

Scowling deeply over this most discourteous display, Jenniboni never cared much right from the very beginning for Lt. Cecilia Baynes. Her 'Assistant Chief of Security' striking her as having a definite mean streak, Jenniboni's only problem was that the woman now laughing uproariously never did anything out in the open.

At least nothing Jenniboni could actually use against her.

Despite all the periodic scuttlebutt circulating about ship in regards to her junior officer's alleged cruelty Jenniboni's hands were unfortunately tied, prevented by S.E.A. rules and regulations from taking any official action, whatsoever. And having heard all these rumors, StarChild's C.O. heard stories also to the effect poor Lt. Greensley was the preferred target of that other woman's disagreeable behavior.

Sadly though it came as no surprise, the object of Lt. Baynes' whispered cruelty quite unwilling—or so it seemed—to take any official stand on her own behalf, filing official charges with her superiors. Something Jenniboni regretted most sincerely, unable to take any legal sanctions against Gloria's tormentor despite her burning desire to do so.

"*THAT WILL BE ENOUGH*!!!" Frances roared, fixing all those laughing with a furious gaze—her countenance, already severe, assuming now an almost vampire-like cast. Even Jenniboni was quite jolted, startled out of her silent ruminations by that fearsome look on the angry teacher's face, the previous tittering dying away just as quickly as it began.

Yet, as forbidding as Frances suddenly appeared, so did her expression soften now to one of gentle sympathy, assisting Gloria back to her feet:

"Your mistake, Lieutenant, was in trying to kick with both feet", Frances informed her fallen pupil before addressing the rest of her class in sterner tones:

"So let that be a lesson to *all* of you! What just happened here is a common error many beginners often make. Always be sure to keep at least one foot planted firmly on the ground or else your A.G. padding won't help counterbalance the otherwise cumbersome weight of your armor".

Demonstrating the proper way to kick once finished, Frances kept her left foot firmly planted beneath her. Thrusting her other long, slender leg out in a blinding swift, flawlessly executed sideways kick it was then she told Gloria to try yet again—the smaller woman's fear of further humiliation crystal clear in the hesitant way she approached once more the bland, grey practice dummy.

This time young Gloria acquitted herself of said task however with flying colours, repeating Frances' exact move with lightning precision. Her right foot making direct contact with the waiting target's firm, flat midsection the dark lifeless test dummy careened swiftly across the training center's light blue deck.

Crashing into the far white bulkhead to Jenniboni's immediate right, it tumbled down to the blue-grey floor with a dull thud, Gloria now wearing a quite satisfied grin under her protective head-gear.

Complimenting Lt. Greensley on her outstanding performance, Frances then ordered the other trainees gathered about to likewise don a smart suit of their own—each armor-plated item still hanging from its very own security hook on the far wall opposite Jenniboni's current position.

Only after instructing Lt. Baynes to take over for the remainder of this particular session did Frances make her way over to Jenniboni. As she did so the other crewwomen gathered about between them parted like the Red Sea at her rapid approach, granting Frances swift passage wherever she so desired:

"Good day, Commodore", she greeted the other woman now standing right before her: "How may I be of service?"

"Actually, to be perfectly honest, I just thought I'd stop by and ask if you have perchance an upcoming break period in your otherwise busy schedule. After all the great kindness you've shown my family I just wanted to make use of this opportunity in order to better make your acquaintance".

"I'd be most honoured, Ma'am", Frances assured her superior, a quite sincere smile delivered alongside her appreciative reply: "As-a-matter-of-fact it just so happens I have such a break coming up in just a few minutes and, if you'd care to likewise join me, I was planning to get in a little fencing practice".

Preferring competition with another to practicing on her own Frances was glad for Jenniboni's company. Sparing her a solitary workout she also appreciated her commanding officer's participation, learning Commodore Saphira was likewise class fencing champion during her days in the Protectorate.

Pleased to learn of their similar passion for the sport Frances often despaired of ever finding a worthy sparring partner equal in the womanly art to her own superior talent.

****

Situated on deck B-7 smack-dab in the ship's forward section, the officer's gymnasium was currently unoccupied, allowing StarChild's two senior officers' complete, unobstructed, access to all the facilities.

Just five levels below the mighty starship's bridge it was there they exchanged their routine uniforms for the padded fencing suits stored in the adjacent storage depot right next to the empty gym's likewise vacant locker room.

Repairing then to the actual gym itself after having suited up, both women having already collected their foils, each proved just as interested as the other in seeing what her companion had going for her in a fair and honest competition.

Giving the contest at hand their absolute best it was the very first time, *ever*, either champion of past times couldn't honestly recall an opponent comparing so well in skill to her own similar prowess with the blade.

Likewise each officer took as well this opportunity to compare personal herstories, never dropping her guard while learning as well all about those many attributes they held in common regardless their different backgrounds. Foils made swift contact while voices compared notes in rhythmic harmony, blending most easily with the sharp, crisp clatter of sword-against sword:

As if already dear old friends from the very start they shared with each other their personal philosophies, comparing with one-another their similar hopes for the future... their personal goals in life... alongside more mundane subject matter as in the case of general hobbies, interests, and personal pasts.

Both impressed with what each heard about the other, a sisterly bond developed with remarkable ease between both women, each talking and competing at the very same time—their match drawing to a close when each agreed to declare whoever scored next the winner, each having scored two hits off her opponent.

Regardless how much they were enjoying each other's company other shipboard duties likewise called. And just when it seemed each would have to concede an unfortunate stalemate, neither able to get the upper hand, it was then Frances made a most unanticipated move on her opponent's part.

Feigning a sudden dart to the right, diverting Jenniboni's attention from her true intent for less than a mere second, it still proved all the time Frances needed to both win, place, and show.

Shifting her entire body leftwards with the same agile dexterity as always, dropping to one knee with a quickly dispatched underhand thrust, she attacked from just under the other woman's guard. Making immediate contact with the dense padding of Jenniboni's suit, her foil curved upward in a distinct arch, the tip of her blade scored a direct hit right above the vanquished woman's heart!

"The Cortez Maneuver!", Jenniboni exclaimed, looking down at where her opponent's weapon made swift contact.

Having had the distinct pleasure of attending the 'Stellar Fencing Finals' on Earth just a little over five years ago, it was then she had the unique good fortune to see the exact same move used. Done so against the then-reigning Stellar champion, Ms. Angela Doreen Crosby, her rival at the time was a newcomer by the name of Margarite Juanita Cortez.

Making good use of that very same gambit to become the present 'Commonwealth Fencing Queen' it threw the attending crowd into a complete uproar. Lasting several minutes before the ruckus died down it was just long enough to hear the judges' final ruling; Ms. Cortez declared the obvious winner.

Nevertheless it still took Jenniboni by complete surprise, having never seen that exact same move used again until just that very moment:

"Impressive", she conceded most graciously, marked respect evident in both face and voice as Frances once more made it to her feet: "Until now I've never had the distinct pleasure of actually crossing swords with another living soul to make use of the 'Cortez Maneuver' during competition".

"Yes, indeed", Frances confessed with all due humility, likewise complimenting Jenniboni on her own considerable skill: "Ms. Cortez has always been a personal favorite of mine. As-a-matter of fact, if you care to view them, I have all her heats on 3-D.V. storage wafer. I even study them from time-to-time in hopes of further enhancing my performance".

Noting the obvious sincerity in Frances' voice, assuring her that she appreciated such an offer, Jenniboni could never stand at all those who lost to her by either design or—worse yet—paid her insincere tribute after winning an honest competition as if actually apologizing for being victorious!

Which is why it was with great pleasure Jenniboni saw in both her Second Officer and venerable Chief of Security an individual of singular integrity who not only played within the rules, but likewise felt no need to either denigrate her own honourable success' or—in the process—depreciate her opponents'. And by that very same token Frances appreciated as well Jenniboni's honest thanks for a most stimulating match, even inviting her former 'opponent' to dinner in the aforementioned "Star Stage" on deck B-6.

Gracious in defeat as well as magnanimous in victory, their mutual respect for one-another only deepened, cementing their newfound friendship just that much more.

And as good luck would have it they were further delighted to find an actual chef on duty in the Star Stage's nearby kitchen, serving each a freshly prepared, quite excellent meal—this good fortune sparing both women the unappetizing mishap of dining together over bland, duplicator-generated food.

Chapter 41

"JEEPERS WEPT"

Gloria arrived in the large chamber at precisely 19:45 hours, ready to assist Lt. Cmdr. Marlowe in arming the unwomaned survey probes discussed earlier by both Jenniboni and Stasha. With no further space in 'Drone Storage' Commodore Saphira's next logical choice was to store the additional probes requisitioned from before just six levels below that on deck S-12, the same location as StarChild's assembly teleporters.

Seeing as said teleportation units were currently inoperable, Jenniboni came to the logical conclusion this would prove a practical location in which to work on them. The entire area quite deserted on Gloria's arrival it was likewise silent as the grave with the single exception of just two, lone voices.

Spending the entire morning overseeing routine operations in Main Engineering, the afternoon spent training in the use of smart armor, Gloria broke for only the briefest evening meal she could manage.

Just finished with her quickly eaten 'repast' it was then she was informed by Maccs Naomi wished to, quote: "make use of your technical expertise at your earliest convenience".

Knowing fully well what that meant, stepping off the ag-pod at a rapid pace, it was directly upon doing so she found her immediate superior knee-deep in the middle of a vast display of drones.

All in various stages of final conversion, working all alone in the grand expanse all about her, Naomi had open before her one of those flat, oblong, egg shaped devices replete with well rounded edges.

Oblivious to Gloria's sudden appearance directly in back of her, unaware anyone else was indeed present, she laboured over the remodifications in progress while likewise carrying on with Maccs a rather personal conversation:

"And whose my most favorite laddie in the entire universe?", Gloria heard Naomi ask in a highly flirtatious, fun-loving tone of voice.

"I am!", came Maccs StarChild's chipper reply, descending from on high.

"And who loves you the very most?"

"You do, Ma'am".

"That's right! And who…"

"You're the only person I know who can actually carry on a romantic tête-à-tête with some machine", Gloria couldn't help, but finally interrupt with a little good-natured laugh.

Shaking her head she approached further Naomi's position.

"Oh… hi, 'Glow-worm'", the other woman working there smiled quite amiably, slightly startled at being caught so in the act by her newly arrived work-mate.

Her back still turned to her approaching subordinate, Naomi referred to Gloria by the affectionate moniker she bestowed upon her young Deputy Chief not long after their initial meeting. Given in recognition of both her superior intelligence and obvious technical skills, Naomi was impressed right from the very get-go by her amazing deputy's quite evident skill.

"What do you expect? After all, I am Chief Engineer", Naomi continued with another giggle, glancing up at last from her present endeavors—assuring her assistant even further her relationship with StarChild's synthetic awareness was 'purely maternal' in nature.

"And *I'll* have you know, Lt. Greensley, that I'm not just *any* machine!!", that third entity all around them spoke up quickly in his own haughty defense, feeling more than just a wee bit slighted by the very idea:

"I am a first generation 'M.A.C.C.S.-XI A.I. Syntha-Sentient' capable of…"

"Oh, hush up, Maccs", Gloria cut him off mid-stride with a tiny, amused grin and giggle all her own: "We all know very well what you are!"

"Yes, Ma'am", the masculine voice complied from above, sounding both hurt and despondent at the very same time, lapsing once more into complete and utter silence.

"So where would you like me to begin?", Gloria asked then her superior, positioning herself on the drone's other side, having just dealt with that sometimes pesky being oft referred to as 'Master Young Maccs StarChild'.

"First you can hand me a strip of muscle wire", Naomi answered her, looking back down at the work still before them: "Then you can install the M.E.M.S. remote control unit now next to it in the forward cavity".

Finding the first atop of the toolbox alongside the probes nose cone, Gloria lowered herself further to the ground. Crouching down right across that very same drone from Naomi she handed her the nickel-titanium shape-memory chord she just requested.

After a short time of working together on the intricate mechanism between them, it wasn't long after this Gloria heard Naomi ask in a voice brimming with grim humor:

"So Glow-Worm, what do you think of this 'wee little collection' of ours, huh? Got more fireworks here than an actual Commonwealth Day celebration: And it isn't even the 5th of August yet!"

"Not much", the other woman frowned, a deep scowl now marring her otherwise wide-eyed, innocent features—an expression of disapproval lending her a much older, more cynical cast than fitting one of such tender, fragile years.

No. Not at all!

That's how much Gloria appreciated the impressive arsenal now on display all around them…

Not at all!!

Nothing but a constant reminder how a mission dedicated at first to both scientific research and peaceful discovery had turned now into nothing but a possible risk of ambush, a prelude to war's inevitable end. After over eight centuries of unparalleled peace Womankind faced once more the grim possibility of armed conflict, this time on an unprecedented scale heretofore unimagined!!

"Yeah, I know what you mean", Naomi sighed in gloomy accord:

"Besides, my favorite parts of Commonwealth Day are the lawn parties and outdoor barbecues anyway".

Having little more to say on the matter except to ask for either some needed tool, or piece of technical hardware each senior officer soon lapsed into a state of total silence. The only sound to be heard was the subtle noise of their work at hand.

Nevertheless Gloria still noticed a look of reluctant curiosity in her companion's expression, realizing soon enough Naomi had something troublesome on her mind whenever requesting some needed tool, or piece of hardware.

And understanding even further it had nothing to do with their present physical endeavors, she likewise knew it had to be something of a more personal nature. Something even quite sensitive, clearly painful given the other woman's facial expression to even think about discussing it aloud.

Yet, while naturally curious as to what this hidden matter might be, Gloria still chose to wait until Naomi found at last the courage to speak. Not sure she really wanted to hear what the problem might be anyway; Gloria chose to let sleeping dogs lie as long as humanly possible. And as sure as sure can be Naomi was indeed first to speak her mind, beginning in a matter both hesitant and contrite at the very same time:

"I'm not going to ask you what happened on your date with Frank. I have no wish to pry", her superior assured her in a most humble fashion Gloria didn't think possible for Naomi to manage unless hearing it for herself—able from the very start to see what a struggle it was for her to even talk:

"All I really want to say is that I'm so very, very sorry for having pushed the two of you into such an awkward situation the way I did. I just hope the both of you can someday find it in both your heart's to forgive me".

Understanding how difficult such an obvious act of contrition must have been for someone like her, what incredible strength of character it must have taken, Gloria gave the apologetic woman before her a most forgiving smile.

Overcome with a new sense of overwhelming sympathy, noting the look of sincere repentance Naomi now gave her, she proved grateful for this clear sign of not only remorse but even respect, feeling now a whole new spirit of generosity well up within her.

"Don't worry, Ma'am. We both had a real good time and have forgiven you", Gloria was quick to comfort her, saying little more on the matter than that. While seeing no harm in confessing all went well in general she still thought it a betrayal of Frank's trust to divulge any specifics, not sure which particulars might upset him were they discussed aloud.

"You don't know how happy it makes me to hear that", Naomi practically gushed, letting out with a joyous sigh of utter relief. Feeling as though a mighty weight were just lifted from her troubled soul she asked soon after in a timid, but hopeful voice if Gloria planned to further court her young date of last week:

"Not that I'm asking for any details", she was quick to add: "I'm just curious if you plan to ask him out on a second date. That's all! I swear!!"

"I don't know", Gloria confided after a somewhat reluctant pause of her own, almost unable to continue:

"I mean... well... he's really nice, really sweet. Maybe that's the problem", she added, hesitant.

"I'm afraid I'm not getting this", Naomi shook her head in complete bewilderment, quite confounded to say the very least.

"Well, it's like this, Ma'am", Gloria explained, clearly depressed. Struggling to choose every word most carefully a note of self-pity began creeping its way into her slow, but steady voice:

"What I mean to say is, well, how do I really know he really wants to see me again, or if he's saying so only out of pity. Seeing how naturally nice he is how do I know he wasn't just trying to be nice like when he slipped that piece of paper in my pocket with his address and V.P. number on it, asking me to see him anytime.

"What I mean is... well... how do I know he really..."

Lowering her eyes in gloomy dismay, staring now at the drone probe upon which they just stopped working, Gloria didn't see the look of utter contempt now quite evident in Naomi's expression.

However, hearing it loud-and-clear in her voice, Naomi did nothing to hide her otherwise obvious disgust, indignant as heck:

"JEEPERS WEPT!!"

"What's wrong?", Gloria's head snapped up, both stunned and confused at the very same time.

"Honestly, Greensley, I don't know what to make of you", Naomi hissed most vehemently across the scout probe still between them: "Are you purposely blind, or just plain stupid?"

"I don't understand!", Gloria protested in baffled dismay.

"Of course not", her accuser sneered, proceeding with mounting rage.

How dare this pathetic creature opposite her throw away such a golden opportunity at possible love when so clearly hers for the taking—a shot at true happiness Naomi realized only now she was foolish enough to cast adrift. And not only any chance at that, but a chance Naomi herself was instrumental in arranging for this worthless ingrate now casting doubt on the oh-so obvious.

Not knowing which hurt more Naomi sailed on, full steam ahead, further berating the clear target of her increasing ire:

"How could such an ignorant, self-evasive, pitiful little nothing like you understand anything. Well then, since you are such a simpering fool, let me explain even further...

"First of all no man like Frank Weller would ever commit such an obvious breach of social etiquette, giving a young gentlewoman he just met his personal V-phone number, unless he was absolutely, positively serious about her. Take it from me: I know the laddies well enough to know that a proper one like Frank Weller would never take another such risk if he didn't honestly mean it.

"Jeepers Crispy!! I don't even need to hear about that darn piece of paper to know he's quite taken with you. Although, after hearing all this, I can't for the life of me see why.

"Heck, the way he looked at you with such obvious adoration, kissing you good-bye should've been more than enough proof for anyone with eyes to see and ears to hear! That was no game of 'let's pretend', no display of mere play-acting on his part. He really meant it!!

"Honestly, Lt.", Naomi insisted with continued force: "It's about high time you start asserting yourself as both a woman and S.E.A. officer, start having more confidence in yourself because, if you don't, I doubt you'll continue longer being Deputy Chief of Engineering aboard either this, or any other ship.

"Heck, forget that! If you don't start asserting yourself, taking charge more when it comes to obvious command situations, I'm afraid you won't be wearing for much longer that precious uniform you seem to love so much, either!

"All right! Fine!! So you had a miserable childhood growing upon Mars. The other kids were all a bunch of vicious little swine, and your Uncle was nothing but a cold, cruel, ice-king—the original Martian icicle!

"Fine!!

"But for crying out loud, that was over three years ago. So stop wallowing in all that self-pity of yours and start pulling yourself together. You're an S.E.A. officer holding a position of both power and prestige aboard Womankind's very first starship and it's darn-well time you started acting like it! Or can you even hear what I'm saying, so full of self-pity as you are??"

Noting it at once when Gloria hung low her head in apparent shame, staring at the small patch of floor directly before her, Naomi's first thought at that very moment was... 'So help me, if she starts crying, I'll reach over there and strangle her with my own two hands'.

Even with dark brown strands getting in the way of her face, Gloria's hair hiding her face from full view, Naomi could still see quite well from the other woman's rapid breathing, the way her chest both rose and fell, that she was clearly upset.

However, be that as it may, there was no sign at all of any self-pity in Gloria's steely gaze, looking up at long last into Naomi's waiting eyes:

No tears at all!

Only a fiery expression of burning hate smoldering within, a look almost able to kill in its severity:

"Oh, yes, I can hear you! Loud and clear", the young woman snarled through clenched teeth: "And, with that in mind, I'll prove to both you and everyone else aboard this lousy ship I more than deserve to wear this uniform, to be here in the very first place. From now on you'll see in me all the confidence, all the self-assertion, you could ever want...

"And more!

"And, having said all that, may I speak freely?"

"Of course, Lieutenant", Naomi granted, a definite smile beginning to form at each corner of her mouth. With dawning admiration for this sudden transformation she was fully aware that, were she to even try and refuse her young deputy such permission, she would have failed quite miserably doing so.

"Thank you, Ma'am", Gloria smiled in turn. Her expression replete with both a hash, icy-cool stare and escalating contempt, she proceeded even further in a sarcastic tone both frosty and even at the very same time:

"And, on that note, let me likewise assure you that I've always admired you, even respected you, as both a mentor and, dare I say it, colleague. I've always respected you for both your great intellect and technical expertise. I'm even grateful to you for all you've taught me during our time together.

"So help me, I even admired you your outgoing, upbeat personality and various people skills...

"Yet be that as it may, may I also say you're something of a miserable swine, too, Ma'am! And considering what I've recently learned about your considerable track record with the Laddies, may I likewise suggest you keep your miserable, lousy advice on men to yourself!!

"Frank told me *all* about you—every dirty little detail—so, if you're really right about him being so crazy in love with me, then all I can say is I plan to treat him like a proper laddie should be. I'd never hurt him, treating him like garbage the same shameful way you did...

"And so, in conclusion, may I also say that, while we did indeed have a very good time together, I also assure you that if you ever—*ever*—ambush me with another blind date like that *ever again* you'll most surely rue the day you were ever born, Ma'am!!! ...

"Have I made *myself* perfectly clear??!!"

"Is that all, Lt.?" Naomi asked, grinning from ear-to-ear with wide-eyed satisfaction. While true that remark about how she treated Frank hurt deeply, unable to deny its validity making it all the more painful, Naomi couldn't help but feel as well a sense of increasing satisfaction. Maybe there was some hope for her otherwise timorous young deputy after all, taking note of this first, clear-cut indication of actual backbone.

"Yes: Ma'am!", Gloria quickly rejoined, grinning as well with pert satisfaction: "At least for now, Ma'am".

"Very good, Lieutenant", Naomi pressed on in hopes of getting back to other, more official matters:

"In that case may I continue by suggesting we get back to the previous job at hand", she added, giving the waiting scout probe between them a meaningful glance.

"Quite right: Ma'am. So what do you think we should do next?"

"Well, if you've already managed to install the..."

Chapter 42

"GLORIA STRIKES BACK"
(Monday, February 18th, 2915 AD)

With over half the probes now ready for possible combat Gloria labored now all on her own, the rest of her work detail not yet scheduled to appear.

Preferring such solitude when dealing with such 'hands on' responsibilities, enjoying utter privacy, this was one of her few chances to do so—working in the wee morning hours where she and Naomi toiled together only several hours before.

Inserting yet another micro-memory system in yet another nose cone of yet another drone probe, repeating herself over and over again, Gloria found herself growing quite tired of this particular procedure... losing herself in private thoughts... when momentarily startled by Maccs making a special, general announcement for the benefit of 'all-hands-aboard'.

Addressing the entire ship's compliment in mellow tones it was then, at precisely 03:00 hours, he informed everyone concerned that maximum Ultra-drive velocity had been achieved—deceleration to commence in just a few minutes—a few minutes during which the major part of their interstellar voyage will have taken place.

Doing so it never ceased to amaze the young tech officer, currently up to her armpits in some blasted scout probe, how the greater part of their journey to the stars could be traversed within such a minimal period of time—a trip to the red giant, Betelgeuse, taking only a few hours longer than their present jaunt to nearby Alpha Centauri.

The greater portion of their travel time devoted to either acceleration, or deceleration it didn't even matter the former was some sixty times more distant from the Matriarchate than the latter—this opening up the entire galaxy to both Womankind's exploration and colonization all within the same short period of travel.

Nor was it long after Maccs StarChild's last communiqué he made yet

314

another ship-wide announcement. Telling everyone this time around ship deceleration had now begun, he interrupted yet again Gloria's silent musings on the different laws of quantum mechanics, their direct application to UltraSpace.

Even so however that officious little A.I. bio-computer all about them was hardly as annoying as the next distraction appearing right then on Gloria's immediate horizon, Lt. Cecilia Baynes stepping off a distant ag-pod lift far across the room.

Catching sight of her sudden arrival, looking up at the familiar sound of pod-lift doors swooshing open, Gloria's familiar sense of cold dread whenever in Cecilia's company was accompanied as well by an immediate rush of intense anger. Resenting bitterly Cecilia's very existence this should come as no surprise given how the other woman literally went out of her way at every single opportunity to make Gloria's life a sheer misery.

Starting quite soon after their initial encounter at the S.E.A. Officers Training Academy it was then the dark-haired Jovian beauty from Europa singled out the shy, withdrawn, yet brilliant young Martian tech officer as her favorite target for what seemed an aggressive mean streak a billion miles wide.

Then again, being true to herself, the smoldering young engineer still working hard had to admit she, too, was at least partly responsible for that hateful crewwoman's continued torment. Having not stood up for herself well before this Gloria realized soon enough she was just as guilty in the matter as her protagonist.

Providing Cecilia in the past with an easy target for her most venomous, spiteful hate it was right then and there Gloria decided it was more than high time to draw the proverbial line—standing up for herself at long, long last—telling the detestable object of her long-standing ire:

'THIS FAR AND NO FARTHER!!!'

Then again there still remained a small but persistent part of her wishing to avoid even so any possible confrontation, an unfortunate part of her hoping appeasement might still do the trick.

Wishing to discourage her antagonist from any further unpleasantries by just ignoring her, pretending Cecilia didn't even exist, it was then Gloria kept her eyes focused solely on the work before her—listening with a sense of nervous trepidation to the hollow echo of Cecilia's crisp, clear approach cease from directly across the drone probe now between them.

"Here!" Cecilia offered, tapping her foot... impatient... holding out for Gloria's inspection a slender, wafer thin 6" by 9" ei-pad: "I have an update request from security concerning the expected time of completion for all these here scouts".

"Fine: Just put it down right over there", the young tech-officer answered her unwanted company... deadpan... pointing towards the rear compartment of that very same probe she likewise labored over.

Refusing the other woman any further recognition whatsoever of her very existence, struggling instead to remain perfectly calm, Gloria kept her main attention focused on nothing but the complex technology before her. Skilled hands carried on even further with the many modifications in progress, doing so as though possessing a separate mind all their very own.

Soldering one example of intricate circuitry to yet another, employing a compact laser torch, it was right then Cecilia chose to let go of that same ei-pad she arrived with just moments ago. Holding it no more than a mere couple of feet above the probe between them it clattered rather noisily against the pale white probe's well-rounded tail section, sliding in no time flat onto Gloria's side to the floor.

While slightly rattled by this rather unexpected display of childish behavior, she all the same ignored with relative success this rather feeble attempt to get under her skin, proceeding as if nothing happened at all.

Starting to climb with a volatile quality all its own, her preferred victim of choice refusing to take the bait, it was Cecelia instead who ended up vexed, her naturally volatile temper climbing at a steady rate the more and more she thought of it. The more Gloria tried to ignore her very existence, the more she pretended Cecelia wasn't even there, the more irate her tormentor grew, quite outraged by such 'inconsiderate' treatment, such 'inappropriate' behavior!

'How dare she??' she seethed, her growing hate both bubbling and even churning around and about in the very pit of her stomach.

How so very intolerable!!

How dare this unworthy worm treat **her** in such a disgraceful manner, treating her as if she, **Cecilia Baynes**, were in fact the one beneath contempt?

She just had to… **HAD TO!**… get Gloria to take immediate notice.

Needing to no end a truly emotional response from that favored target of her ignorant prejudice, her inability to accept anyone which existed outside her narrow-minded concept of the accepted norm, pushed her even further towards the extreme. Hating to no end anyone she couldn't cram inside her tiny, box-like concept of true Womanhood she racked her twisted brain for some sure-fire method by which to penetrate Gloria's affected indifference.

At first it occurred to her to taunt her prey with how she slipped up so bad during the smart-armor session just yesterday, falling so shamefully on her very keister not only in front of her very own department, but even Commodore Saphira herself!

However, forgetting with swift abandon this idea when something even better came to mind, it wasn't long ago she recalled overhearing just yesterday a juicy little morsel in the Officer's Mess. Knowing right then and there she'd found the perfect tool with which to defeat Gloria's assumed calm, to attack her via her soft underbelly, she readied herself with the most spiteful glee to rip young Gloria limb-from-limb:

"By the way, Greensley, I heard some interesting little trivia from one of the crew just the other day. According to her it seems you were recently seen in the company of '… a very handsome young laddie …' just last week at a concert in Chiron City.

"So how about it, Greensley? Was he a **professional whore**, or just so desperate for sex he was willing to slum with **even you**??"

With a most cruel little smirk Cecilia knew at once her nasty little insinuation struck pay dirt in a very big way, indeed!

With warm satisfaction at long last she watched Gloria's hands cease in the performance of their assigned duties, beginning to snicker as the other woman lay her tools down with most careful precision on top of the scout probe still between them.

Getting to her feet in a slow approach—head hung low, fists clenched tight—Gloria made then her way around the intricate device left now on its own, standing now toe-to-toe with Frank's foul accuser. Turning to meet her head-on Lt. Cecilia Baynes giggled only that much louder, waiting with impatient lust to see better Gloria's face, hoping to glimpse better the mortified expression she was certain beyond doubt would be there.

So darn sure Gloria would be acting soon quite hysterical indeed, weeping in absolute shame, quite humiliated beyond all reason, she relished that singular moment with the sure-fire delight of some emotional predator feasting on the wounded hearts of others.

Certain her victim would soon raise '*its*' head in hopeless protest, crying in vain hope of lodging complaint, pleading her absolute innocence like so many times before, ***NEVER IN HER LIFE*** had the great Cecilia Baynes ever... ***EVER***... screwed up quite so badly!!

Insulting her was one thing, maligning Frank Weller was another!! Had her vile accuser remained content to cast doubt on just her own darn virtue, Gloria would have been willing to settle for a mere verbal confrontation only—a dressing-down limited to nothing more than some stream of heated words delivered not in shame, but with righteous indignation.

Not any more though, more drastic action now called for, an angry volley of heated comebacks would no longer suffice.

The situation at hand having taken a rather dramatic turn for the worse there was no way, ***WHATSOEVER***, she'd ever allow anyone at all, much less this pathetic monster, to cast ***ANY*** disparaging word against either Frank Weller's good name, reputation, or character—casting doubt on the very dear virtue of someone who, at that very moment, meant more to Gloria than even life itself!

Drawing herself up to full height, looking at long last into Cecilia's expectant face, whacking her ***hard*** upside the head, the back of Gloria's clenched fist wiped clean the cruel grin from Cecilia's waiting lips in no uncertain terms, impacting with considerable force right below the other woman's waiting eye.

Leaving in its wake a mighty welt soon followed by an equally impressive black/blue bruise, Gloria didn't stop there:

"Don't you ever, ***EVER***, say anything about the young laddie in question ever again or, so help me... ***so help me... I will KILL you***!!!!! Do you hear me?", Gloria spat up at Cecilia in venomous reply, jabbing her antagonist over and over again with a sharp, manicured forefinger.

Paralyzed with absolute shock, Lt. Baynes couldn't have been more stymied, confounded, or even horrified had a scampering mouse turned itself somehow into a rampaging, Bengal tiger right before her very eyes. Looking down at Gloria's flushed cheeks, the murderous glare in those stormy eyes, she could see there no sign at all of either degradation, or humiliation… only a livid, purple rage… intense hatred burning out of all control.

Unable for the blessed life of her to figure out where she'd so obviously gone wrong, at a total loss to understand what was now unfolding before her very eyes, all she could do was swiftly nod her head in both mute understanding and absolute fear. No sooner had Lt. Baynes done so Gloria continued her verbal assault; her menacing tone joined now by a most livid, lop-sided grin spreading mightily across her angry features

"Good! Because I've always hated you, loathed you, and despised you ever since the very first day we ever met. Therefore, since your continued presence is no longer desired, or even required, get the *'sanguinary freakin' heck'* outta here!!!"

Confused and even disoriented by this most sudden, unexpected reversal of fortune Cecilia could think of nothing else to do, but obey the former object of her base ridicule. Fleeing in the face of Gloria's obvious triumph, wanting nothing more right then than to be as far away as possible from the immediate vicinity, she didn't even wait for the same ag-pod upon which she arrived, scrambling instead for a nearby stairwell.

Watching Cecilia beat a hasty retreat with equal disbelief, witnessing for herself the unexpected sight of her former tormentor flee the scene of her ultimate downfall, Gloria marveled as well. Naturally elated, Cecelia's reign of terror overcome at last, Gloria felt most liberated indeed!!

Feeling now quite larger than life she returned to work immediately thereafter, convinced now she could carry on for weeks on end without a single, solitary break.

Chapter 43

"ALPHA CENTAURI"
(Thursday, February 21st, 2915 AD)

Asleep in her quarters on deck S-4 Jenniboni's rest was far from peaceful, haunted at the very same time by images both mysterious and disturbing.

Woken from her slumber with no small sense of sweet relief Stasha's punctual voice put an end to her troubled sleep, coming across her private intercom from StarChild's distant bridge:

"Yes, Cmdr. Nikarov?"

"Yes, Ma'am: As per your instructions I'm waking you an hour beforehand, informing you we'll be leaving UltraSpace at 03:00 hours, arriving on the outer rim of the Centauri system".

"Excellent, Cmdr.", Jenniboni smiled in the surrounding darkness, severing soon the comm. link with StarChild's distant bow: "I'll be there shortly".

Sitting by now on the edge of her bed Jenniboni ordered Maccs to activate all lights in her private quarters, likewise shielding her eyes just before doing so. Lowering her hand only when having acclimated to the new found luminosity all around her, Jenniboni glanced up soon after that at the door to her private washroom next to a nearby closet.

"Just enough time for a shower", she muttered, selecting from the close-by cabinet a fresh uniform, laying it flat on her bed for when done.

****

A continuous spray of warm water running down bare skin, a numerous series of progressive rivulets, it drove from Jenniboni's waking mind every last vestige of lingering sleep. Unable to remember the exact details, what it was about her recent dream that left her feeling so troubled, all she could remember for certain were sickly pale green stars moving about in a dark, alien sky.

That alongside the cold dread they seemed to inspire.

319

Rarely enduring such unpleasant dreams, much less actual nightmares inspiring such feelings of sweet relief to just wake up, she couldn't help but feel this nocturnal vision significant.

But why? Why should the likes of such as green stars fill her with such obvious trepidation?

FOOLISH!!

Although an astronomical impossibility they were still no cause for such an overwhelming sense of utter anxiety, such cold flights of unreasonable panic.

Banishing at once such nonsensical worries from her every thought Jenniboni turned off the running water still raining down upon her naked body, doing so with a most decisive twist of her wrist.

Having more pressing matters to deal with than such meaningless messages from her apparent subconscious, she brought the invigorating mist from close on high to an immediate end, drying off in a nearby hot-air booth.

****

Stepping off the ag-pod lift reaching the other end of her ship Jenniboni was greeted at once by the anticipated sight of all her senior bridge officers in complete attendance, each having taken a seat at her usual station. Technically the graveyard shift, a time for most command personnel to stand down, it didn't surprise Jenniboni one iota each officer made a personal point of being present for Womankind's first arrival in another star system.

Well… maybe not the first:

Not if you counted as well those lost colonists who likewise sent that distress call back to their distant world of origin nearly five years ago.

This time however, Jenniboni remained adamant her ship and crew wouldn't meet with that same unknown fate they did.

Planning to return home upon immediate completion of their present assignment Jenniboni remained determined her team of well-chosen explorers prove victorious, triumphant over whatever dark force no doubt claimed those other, less fortunate lives.

Looking about her at all those other good women currently present and accounted for Jenniboni readily saw Lt. Miranda Netra, hair pulled back from her face in a make-shift pony tail, examining with intense precision the complex data-stream appearing now on her well-lit console at Navigations.

Standing just to the right of Jenniboni's current location next to the lift entrance in back of StarChild's bridge, three meters or so in front of her, Lt. Netra stood in front of her seat right next to Lt. Carla Shaddock—Carla also quite busy, hunched forward in her seat at Helm control off to Jenniboni's forward left.

Reading out loud a quite detailed list of co-ordinates for the benefit of some hidden entity beyond Jenniboni's momentary range of vision her display of professional detachment slipped just slightly when announcing the fact they were now traveling at '*Roemer-3*', an observation likewise confirmed by Lt. Cmdr. Naomi Marlowe.

320

Reaching Jenniboni ears from next to the starboard bulkhead of StarChild's expectant bridge Naomi's crisp, clear voice traveled well, adding likewise for the benefit of everyone present the fact they'd soon be traveling at speeds of just '*Roemer-1*'. Employing as well the same established term for light speed it was a term derived in honour of the laddie scientist who discovered its velocity way back during ancient patriarchate times, 'Olaf Roemer'.

In the meantime however, Frances Straker sat as well at her Security station, face marked with grim determination, ready for whatever danger might await them upon re-entering normal space. Poised both still and quiet over the intricate features of that very console it was her honour to operate, the severe cast of her narrowed eyes provided Jenniboni an actual source of reassurance.

Seated directly opposite Naomi's position next to the impressive command chamber's port-side bulkhead, there was no mistaking Lt. Cmdr. Straker's determined, steely expression for anything else than what it actually was—an obvious indication of the dedicated, battle-ready warrior dwelling within.

No less ready than she for any possible contingency just seeing such a hardened look of pure determination inspired in Jenniboni an even greater confidence in the ultimate success of their recently modified mission assignment.

Leaving only two more of Jenniboni's command crew unaccounted for, Lt. Phyllis Matthias was nevertheless present, quite visible at her communications console stationed across the way from Jenniboni's present location, opposite StarChild's bridge from the ag-pod in front of which she still stood.

Surveying all those gathered about Jenniboni had no difficulty spotting at all her gifted Chief Communications Officer, leaving only Cmdr. Stasha Nikarov conspicuously absent.

Not situated at her Science station just left of that dominant main viewer monopolizing most of that grand command center's forward bulkhead, the opposite side of the impressive viewing screen from Lt. Matthias' comm. station, Stasha's posting was the only one currently unwomaned:

A discrepancy both understood, and even expected however, Jenniboni remained certain where her missing X.O. could be found. Nor was she mistaken when, circling the interconnected Helm and Navigation stations directly before her, she caught immediate sight of Stasha Nikarov's powerful form sitting cross-legged in Jenniboni's very own elevated command chair.

Her command post visible dead center of the ship's fair-sized bridge Jenniboni drew ever closer from its left hand side.

"I hand command over to you, Commodore", Stasha relinquished temporary control over their immediate surroundings, Jenniboni now reaching her position.

Having already acknowledged both Carla and Naomi's previous reports she now left it in Jenniboni's purview to continue further:

"Accepted, Commander", came her superior's likewise official reply:

"You may reassume now your regular post", Jenniboni added, requesting as well a further update from Lt. Shaddock upon assuming her rightful place.

"Commodore, we're now at Roemer-1, leaving UltraSpace in only ten minutes", came Carla's dutiful reply.

"Excellent, Lieutenant: Continue as is".

Staring at the rainbow ribbons of light still streaming through StarChild's main viewer, flowing about her bridge in fluid, liquid motions like some multi-hued whirlpool replete with both tides and eddies, Jenniboni then instructed Frances to order general quarters, addressing thereafter her entire ship:

"Bridge to all personnel: This is Commodore Saphira. We are now at 'Code Yellow', about to re-enter normal space/time on the outer perimeter of the Alpha-Centauri system in less than ten minutes. We are still unsure as to what we might encounter upon immediate arrival so stay alert at all times: Saphira, out".

It wasn't more than a few minutes after that the chronometer prominent above StarChild's main viewer read "03:00 hours", a fact quickly followed by a most brilliant flash of white light requiring a wee bit of time to recover from.

Both ship and crew finding themselves yet again in normal space, having now reached their scheduled destination, the first thing everyone noticed was the distinct lack of colour filling only seconds ago the entire bridge.

The swirling mass of fluid pyrotechnics having just vanished, the liquid-like light filling the bridge from UltraSpace gone now, the walls were yet again a plain, sterile white—the frosted light fixture comprising the entire ceiling once again the only visible light source, providing the entire bridge a gentle yet pervasive glow.

Disoriented by this abrupt change in their immediate surroundings Jenniboni found it nevertheless amusing how one found it so easy to acclimate oneself to new situations often to the point of felling a wee bit disoriented when returning to otherwise old, familiar 'stomping grounds'.

Only the inky black of regular space visible now on the main viewing screen ahead, the usual smattering of distant stars scattered throughout, it was for all intents and purposes a rather innocuous sight to behold.

Nothing visible to raise immediate suspicion this still didn't stop Jenniboni from ordering a most thorough scan of the entire vicinity, waiting no longer than it took for everyone else to acclimate themselves to the change. After so many years of dealing day-by-day with such situations on a professional basis, she learned the hard way that what went unseen proved more-often-than-not the greater threat.

Then again that still didn't quell the simple awe she likewise felt just being where she was, gazing at this totally new System so far removed from Womankind's own. And observing every other bridge officer likewise present Jenniboni couldn't help but notice the same expression of reverent awe and subtle apprehension alongside their ever-vigilant stance.

Quite ready for any possible fate destiny might throw their way, Jenniboni found herself feeling a most definite sense of pride concerning the way her people were now comporting themselves in the face of such probable danger:

In the far center of this particular system its two yellow suns, "Centauri-A" and "Centauri-B", appeared no larger than any other star in the great heavens beyond; the red dwarf simply known now as "Centauri-C" possessing greater form, greater substance than the first two. Well rounded, closer than its compatriots, it glowed a dull, ruby red located in the main viewer's upper left-hand corner.

Once known as "Proxima Centauri" it rested at 20 times closer to the other two suns than the Oort cloud and Kuiper belt surrounding Womankind's own solar-system was to Earth's sun. And it was around "Centauri-C" Jenniboni remembered their first unwomaned scouts discovered a single, dying 'M'-class world just eight years ago.

Dubbed simply "C-1" it was there they discovered as well an interconnected network of alien ruins scattered across its barren surface, mega-cities all deserted now for millennia.

So why did Lt. Matthias choose that very same moment to inform one-and-all she was receiving a repeat audio-comm signal aimed at them from that long-dead world. None of Womankind's initial probes ever picked up any such broadcast:

"May I suggest, Commodore, that this might in all probability be an automatic auto-repeat 'message' programmed for activation only when an object as large as StarChild comes within such close proximity", Phyllis further offered by way of a logical hypothesis. .

Preferring for the moment to work with such a theory, Jenniboni ordered her to copy all further transmissions, sending duplicates over to Stasha's location at Sciences. Hopefully her and Lt. Matthias' departments together might prove able to translate it with a greater chance of success.

"Well Gentlewomen, time to get on with the job at hand", Jenniboni then announced to everyone present in a decisive, crystal clear tone of voice: "Time to see what's actually out there".

Instructing helm to bring StarChild to a full stop, stabilizers activated, Jenniboni ordered as well the launching of four scout probes, her ship anchored at its present location as each individual drone left on its merry way.

Trailing in back of them white tails of bright energy discharged at enormous speeds, they resembled nothing less than shooting stars set on a detailed course for the waiting system ahead. Only then did Jenniboni prep herself for what she considered the most tense, nerve-wracking element of any assignment well-done—waiting patiently for the results.

Settling back into her chair as they grew yet fainter and fainter the further they traveled each scout was, by her command, pre-programmed to orbit every available planet, gather all data possible, and return at once to StarChild immediately thereafter.

Implementing an evasive path all throughout their perilous journey this last directive was given in hopes of reducing the risk of any alien hostiles nearby using their return trajectory to track StarChild's current location. While confessing there were still no sure guarantees Jenniboni wanted even so to make it as darn difficult as possible for anyone else out there to find them.

Meaning however they'd not return until late afternoon this would leave StarChild at general quarters for hours on end, leaving her crew likewise on tenterhooks during all that time.

Deciding right then and there to likewise remain longer at her current post than previously intended this also was an added burden to keep in mind, realizing that neither she nor anyone else would get any meaningful, honest rest until their hopeful return.

Still though…

"Cmdr. Nikarov? Have you managed yet to download on wafer those signals from 'C-1'?"

"Yes, Commodore".

"Excellent: In that case would you please be so kind as to bring it here?"

Reaching her side, wafer in hand, Jenniboni instructed her however to lean in closer with a subtle 'come-over-here' wiggle of her left index finger. Only then did Stasha realize her C.O. had even more on her mind:

"How long have you been pulling bridge duty since the beginning of your regular shift?", Jenniboni whispered discretely in her ear.

"Since about 18:00 Hours yesterday", Stasha confessed in a likewise hushed voice.

"Just as I thought: In that case I want you to go straight to your quarters, right now, and get some sleep. I'll stay here until 12:00 Hours, at which point you can once more relieve me".

"But what about the wafer?"

"Give it to one of your linguistics experts to decipher. As of right now I want you to go take a break. Get some sleep. I want at least one of us rested, mentally alert, and operating at peak efficiency at all times".

When it seemed for a brief moment her second-in-command might protest the matter further, Jenniboni brought her to a grinding halt. Fully aware of Stasha's habit of sometimes pushing herself to the very limit, she brought any further debate to an immediate conclusion, employing both an upraised palm and stern glance:

"That's an order, Commander!!"

"Yes, Ma'am", Stasha obeyed without further discussion.

Within seconds after that Jenniboni could hear the pod-lift doors in back of her swoosh open… then shut… the other woman quietly accepting her defeat with grace.

Chapter 44

"INITIAL FINDINGS"

It was 10:00 hours; all still quiet as StarChild continued holding its initial position just beyond Centauri-C. No sign of any hostile forces in the immediate area, Jenniboni could nevertheless detect the strain their prolonged wait was having on the rest of her crew.

Although hiding it well she could spy even so those subtle hints of stress such awkward situations give rise to, taking on both form and substance in all those around her.

Realizing that both their morale, and even performance might be compromised if nothing was done to ease the pressure already building, Jenniboni ordered at once an immediate cessation of 'general quarters'. Yet while hoping to offer those beneath her a brief respite from mounting tensions—tensions almost palatable in the very air all around them—she still felt it prudent to place both ship and crew on 'stand by' alert.

Although logical to assume any possible enemy in the immediate vicinity would have launched by now at least some sort of exploratory attack Jenniboni remained even so uncertain, not wishing her people caught off guard. Thanks to the immediate downgrade in alert status she could sense a definite improvement in their overall situation by the time Stasha made her grand entrance, appearing just in the nick of time to relieve her.

Their concern still obvious, at least they weren't going about their various routines as though walking on eggshells.

****

Having left the bridge Jenniboni now found herself too keyed up to get any meaningful rest despite her own reduction in their alert status, deciding to remedy this clear dilemma the best way she knew. Always proven to do the trick, a tried and true solution, she chose to pursue straight away a rigorous workout in the Officers Gym before heading back to her quarters.

Finding release from her own personal anxieties through strenuous physical activity, a private session of high-impact aerobics followed by equal time indulging in weights left her with a pleasant type of weariness some fifty-odd minutes later.

Returning only then to her quarters, following a warm shower immediately thereafter, she lay down for a quick nap. Drifting off the very moment her head made contact with the pillow below, Jenniboni discovered herself even further blessed, no unpleasant dreams like before disturbing this time her sleep.

****

"Commodore?"

"Yes, Cmdr. Nikarov?"

"Its 18:00 Hours and our scout probes have just returned. Their memory banks are already being downloaded into Maccs for complete analysis as we speak".

"Excellent. How long before he's managed to correlate all the pertinent data for further study?"

"All should be ready for your inspection within the hour, Ma'am".

"Excellent! In that case have all Dept. Chiefs gather for a briefing in the Senior Officer's Conference Room at 19:00 Hours. I'll have a quick bite to eat and meet you there".

"Very good, Ma'am".

****

Jenniboni wasn't the only one to put in an early appearance, the rest of her senior staff just as eager to learn the truth about what waited for them beyond their current position—each curious what that mysterious collection of worlds held in store.

Quite mindful of this herself, no different than those women serving beneath her, Jenniboni called the meeting to prompt order, taking her rightful place at the senior officers briefing table around which they now gathered:

"Cmdr. Nikarov has already made a preliminary examination of all the information gathered by our survey probes and, seeing as this is the case, I'll hand now these proceedings over to her".

"Thank you, Commodore: And on that note, I likewise wish to begin these proceedings by informing everyone here our earlier worries of hostile invasion forces in this system have seemingly proven false. From the data recovered this system would appear completely uninhabited except for one, single occupant I'll discuss in a moment.

"In short Gentlewomen all would seem just as our original unwomaned scouts reported on their return home just eight years ago. Only two planets display any indication of former habitation, these being 'C-1' and 'AB-1.5'—the fifth moon orbiting the gas giant, 'AB-1', orbiting in turn both Centauri 'A'

326

and 'B'.

"Now, if you'll all please direct your immediate attention to the data screens before each of you, we can commence further with a more detailed analysis of the visual information just gathered.

"Beginning with 'C-1' we can see here a world in the continuing grip of an endless ice age, a dying planet showing no sign of any recent, sentient habitation whatsoever.

"All we can detect there are traces of lower life-forms all in the process of becoming extinct—the atmosphere, although still breathable, likewise in the further process of growing more rarefied. In short a once quite Earth-like world on its gradual way to becoming more like pre-terraformed Mars during the previous millennium.

"Here we can see that 'C-1' is covered with the remains of several large cities which clearly suffered major devastation some seven thousand years ago. Probably the result of some catastrophic war bringing about the immediate demise of those who once lived here alongside the prolonged death throws the rest of that world is suffering.

"Except for the automatic signal we first received upon our immediate arrival here there is no other evidence of active artificial energy being generated anywhere else on the planet's surface. Which is why we're assuming for now the message sent us was nothing more than a simple warning to 'Stay Away' set on continual repeat.

"Unfortunately though we still remain in the dark as to whether or not this was a deliberate act of xenophobia on their part. Or could it have been actual worry on the behalf of others, leaving us with the puzzle of what worried them if they were so concerned for the safety of others.

"If so, whatever it was must surely be long-lived for them to set up such a warning system meant to still warn away others after all this time. Fortunately we can find no evidence of harmful microscopic organisms on the planet's surface, able to assume it safe to eliminate the possibility of some lingering disease—either natural or woman-made—still living on the planet's surface".

Hearing this there was an audible sigh of relief from around the entire conference table as Stasha continued her presentation, no one having any wish to encounter some virulent alien version of something like the 'Yesinia-R Beta' plague.

"And here we have the alien signal's place of origin", she announced even further; an aerial shot of some large, conical structure appearing on each data screen present. A magnified close-up taken from above the monstrous edifice shown seemed to almost break through each transparent viewing screen in vain hopes of making actual, physical contact.

Resting dead center of a shadowy mass of buildings arranged in circular configurations, a metropolis of truly ponderous proportions, Stasha continued, announcing it was located in 'C-1's northern hemisphere:

"Scans of this structure likewise show a massive concentration of artificially generated energy no doubt maintaining a steady power flow to some complex mechanism still in existence within its walls. Something its creators wanted to remain operational for an indefinite period of time, our best guess for the moment is that it's some complex system of stored information, a library of sorts maintained for future posterity.

"Therefore it seems only logical to assume that all the answers to all our questions concerning what happened here should be contained within its walls".

No sooner had Stasha finished her report concerning 'C-1' than the scene on each woman's screen changed most abruptly to 'AB-1.5', the crumbling remains of three communities now visible. Although the two larger settlements were clearly miniatures of the same alien design as the cities on C-1 the smaller one, while likewise circular in configuration, possessed at least a more familiar feel to it:

"You are now observing the only visible evidence sentient life ever existed on this 'moon-world' known for the moment as only 'AB-1.5'.

"And from both their design, not to mention their present state of eventual decay, it's even further apparent the two larger settlements were built by the former denizens of 'C-1' not long before the ultimate demise of their entire civilization…

"They, too, have suffered the same general damage at the very same time as their counterparts back on 'C-1' itself.

"Yet while both worlds no doubt perished during the same conflict we still don't know whether this conflict was the result of some sort of internal struggle among the actual inhabitants of 'C-1', or a greater battle with another alien race from still elsewhere.

"Therefore we've decided to stick with the former hypothesis until clear proof to the contrary makes itself available.

"And as you've no doubt guessed by now this is what we believe to be the Terran colony referred to in its broadcast as nothing but 'Paradise'", Stasha offered further—no pause—the image on everyone's screen zooming in now on a fuzzy close-up of the smallest settlement there.

Easily the lesser of all three at least this small community seemed in better repair than its alien counterparts. Then again it was hard to tell for certain given such poor, sad picture quality:

"Due to electro-magnetic interference in the planet's upper ionosphere a more precise image is, much to our regret, impossible. Still though, you should have all been able to take note earlier on that 'Paradise' is situated just south of the larger alien metropolis, likewise farther east of the other.

"And having said all that life-scans likewise reveal just one, lone Human inhabitant on 'AB-1.5's' surface. Both age, sex, and even general physical condition of said inhabitant remain impossible to determine, the electro-magnetic disruption in the moon's upper atmosphere making a more detailed analysis impossible.

"All we can ascertain for certain is that said individual is, without doubt, Human—no doubt a single, lone survivor of whatever calamity befell the rest of her compatriots".

Then, smiling rather wryly in Naomi's direction, Stasha added: "So, since the ionosphere there is so highly charged with electro-magnetic particles, I'm afraid your teleportation units would prove useless in reaching this particular moon-world's surface".

All those present likewise smiled hearing this. Everyone there could remember their Chief Engineer's profound disappointment learning StarChild's newest mode of transport would still be... much to her sincere regret... inoperable by the time of their earlier departure time.

Even Naomi, herself able to see the poetic irony, smiled ever so slightly in reply:

"And on a similar note 'AB-1.5' has some additional peculiarities likewise requiring further discussion", Stasha added, the green moon's disk now filling each woman's screen—its giant parent world, 'AB-1', visible also in the background.

Replete with splendid golden rings circling its massive circumference the much larger planet hovered there in the immediate distance like some bloated crimson sentinel—a beautiful, but somehow ominous sight:

"And all these abnormal traits in 'AB-1.5's' very makeup can be traced quite readily to the large Jovian world it now orbits.

"For example, the electro-magnetic disturbances bedeviling its fifth moon are all the direct result of mass electrical discharges extending from 'AB-1' itself. Interestingly enough this has likewise resulted in an unusually dense ozone layer surrounding the entire moon's surface, a layer even denser than that of Earth's since the late 21st century.

"Likewise we think this might explain finding as well what appear to be billions of miniscule energy forms in the lower atmosphere possessing many qualities similar to 'St. Elmo's fire'. For the moment we theorize these might be additional particles of electro-magnetic energy heavier still than those forming the denser energy field further above. Our current hypotheses is that these aforementioned particles broke free from said energy field, trapped now as we said in this unique moon's lower atmosphere.

"Yet even so 'AB-1.5' remains a truly remarkable world no matter what obvious problems it poses for further exploration, possessing as it does lush vegetation, abundant animal life, and an oxygen-rich atmosphere in many ways not unlike Ahnteekah back on Earth—only more so.

"And with 'AB-1.5's' unusually dense ozone layer filtering out all harmful solar rays from both this system's twin yellow-white suns—'Centauri-A' and 'B'—it's no wonder the colonists from Earth called their new home 'Paradise'", Stasha confessed in conclusion, her voice expressing a certain hint of sure appreciation.

No more appreciative however than Lt. Cmdr. Oftesfs, the muscular black Chief of StarChild's Scout and Exploration Department. Announcing straightaway she wouldn't mind in the least settling there herself, she referred even further to this new world as 'Prime real-estate'.

"Before you start surveying land for your future 'dream home' may I remind you three colonies both alien and Human have all met violent ends down there at the hands of forces as yet unknown", Frances wasted no time in cautioning her, her solemn voice possessing just a trace of grim humor.

"Indeed; Lt. Cmdr.", Jenniboni readily agreed, doing so in a voice leaving no room for contradiction: "So before we all start planning summer homes in this newest 'Garden of Eden' let us not forget that this garden would seem to possess in its wake at least one deadly serpent.

"While it would seem fortunate we no longer face some hostile alien invasion force from somewhere else whatever really occurred here might prove just as formidable a threat. I find it rather peculiar that both the former inhabitants of 'C-1' as well as the colonists from Earth sent us the same basic message seven thousand years apart warning us to stay away.

"And while I freely admit that the deaths of the first might have nothing to do with the latter we still can't rule out such a likely possibility. Even if we no longer face the same kind of enemy we first anticipated, we still have to solve the very real mystery what really happened here.

"If whatever brought about the destruction of 'C-1's' people is responsible as well for the almost total annihilation of 'Paradise' just five years ago, that means we are facing both the double threat of something not only quite dangerous, but quite long-lived.

"Therefore, all said and done, I'm afraid an even further examination of both 'C-1' and 'AB-1.5' is in order. If the cause of 'C-1's demise is the same as for 'Paradise' who knows what danger it poses not just for us and our people but for anyone else who might also pass this way. The only way to further determine what really happened here is a more thorough, hands-on examination of both dead worlds.

"Any suggestions, Gentlewomen?"

"Yes, Ma'am; if I may", Frances was first to offer:

"Firstly, I'd like to recommend all members of each landing party wear full-dress, combat ready Smart Armor suits every step of the way from the moment they leave StarChild to the exact moment they return—no one leaving the safe confines of either shuttle we use unless doing so in teams of either two, or more personnel".

Hearing this Naomi was next to speak up:

"And on that note, Ma'am, my department has already performed complete upgrades so far on at least three shuttles including both weapons, shields, and propulsion. Therefore, I suggest we use two of these for the away mission in question, keeping the third in reserve, ready for immediate launch if needed in case of emergency".

It wasn't until both Naomi and Frances received final approval for their recommendations, ironing out a few extra details with most of those other senior officers present, Lt. Phyllis Matthias brought to the forum a particular concern of her own.

Taking into consideration what Stasha told them concerning the magnetic disturbances in 'AB-1.5's' upper atmosphere, StarChild's Chief of Communications realized such interference would raise as well another problem as yet unresolved. And having once brought the problem to everyone's immediate attention, Phyllis was just as ready to offer a solution both unique and viable:

"Yes, Commodore. The way I see it is that I should be a member of the away team destined for 'AB-1.5', my sister remaining onboard, taking my place on the bridge. Then, whenever the landing party there needs to send messages back and forth to StarChild, Maytina and I can use our special ability to relay messages from one point to another, the interference in 'AB-1.5's' atmosphere unlikely to cause any problem.

"Then, if we need send any further communiqués to 'C-1', Maytina can send them off to the landing party there… and visa-versa… via conventional means".

"Very Good, Lt.", Jenniboni was quick to grant. Nodding her full approval, an appreciative smile also came to light:

"Quite ingenious", she added, everyone there quite aware of that 'special ability' to which Phyllis referred. Aware from the very start both she and her sister were identical twins in every conceivable way, this included as well their ability to send and receive telepathic messages between them no matter how great the distance—both she and Maytina full-fledged telepaths as well as senior communications officers aboard Womankind's very first starship.

"Yes, and on that note I have yet another recommendation", Naomi spoke up yet again: "Since the computer network on 'C-1' appears still operational I therefore suggest we rig up a long-range transmitter to transfer all available information directly to Maccs' central memory storage banks.

"Since neither our portable scanners nor onboard shuttle systems possess the adequate memory space to contain such vast amounts of general information, I see this as our only safe assurance we gather all the information we need from 'C-1'.

"Which is why I therefore suggest something portable, providing a direct link between both Maccs and the central memory system still operational planet-side.

"And if their system contains too much information for Maccs to download given his present ability, he can simply use his better judgment scanning all incoming data, discarding all that which proves irrelevant given our present situation. In fact, given Lt. Greensley's expert assistance, I'm sure we could have such a portable memory retrieval system ready for deployment in just a few hours".

Once having given Naomi's plan her immediate approval Jenniboni soon focused her direct attention on yet one last important matter requiring all due consideration—the pressing decision as to who *exactly* would take part in each away team.

By her very tone of voice it was clear to all those present Jenniboni wasn't in search of any further recommendations, having already reached beforehand her final decision:

"Therefore, concerning the away team to 'C-1', it will consist of both Lt. Commander's Marlowe and Straker accompanied by three security personnel of Lt. Cmdr. Straker's choosing—Lt. Cmdr. Straker in charge.

"And as for the landing party to 'AB-1.5' it will likewise consist of both myself, Lieutenants Baynes and Greensley, Dr. Wei-Chang, and Lt. Cmdr.

Oftesfs accompanied by two scouts of her choosing. I will be in command of this particular team while Dr. Wei-Chang brings along a full medical field-kit just in case that Human survivor there needs immediate medical attention. So if that's all …"

"Excuse me Commodore but don't you think it more fitting that I, instead, lead the away team to 'AB-1.5'", Stasha interrupted straightaway, her concern obvious.

"No, Commander", Jenniboni insisted, giving Stasha's protest no further consideration. Already certain her ship's X.O. would object to Jenniboni's decision to begin with she was just as ready for such an obvious eventuality, insisting Stasha remain in temporary command aboard StarChild during her absence.

Aware Stasha was quite right to object Jenniboni's natural spirit of adventure alongside her natural, inborn curiosity nevertheless prevented her the option of just staying behind. No way would she deny herself this unique opportunity to see, close up and in person, what really happened here.

Then again, curiosity aside, Jenniboni had even so a much more sound reason for insisting she herself lead this critical mission to 'AB-1.5'.

As the duly chosen Spokeswoman for the entire Commonwealth she considered it her solemn duty to be there should they encounter any alien task force that might have somehow avoided their initial probes. It was she, not Stasha, who was appointed by the Supreme Mother official representative of all Womankind, imbued with the authority to act on her own initiative, empowered by the Matriarchate itself to speak on its behalf:

"So unless there's anything else anyone here wishes to add before bringing this meeting to an end, I hereby declare this meeting concluded", Jenniboni added, no one else there raising their voice in further protest:

"Excellent. In that case we leave tomorrow morning at 09:00 hours. And since I'm sure tomorrow will prove itself a quite busy day for all concerned, I hereby insist everyone present get beforehand some meaningful rest. That's all.

"Dismissed!"

Chapter 45

"PARADISE REVISTED"
(Friday, February 22nd, 2915 AD)

By 19:00 hours StarChild's hangar deck was quite busy indeed with orchestrated activity, each of the two landing parties immersed completely in their preparations for immediate departure.

Both Naomi and Gloria, making sure all was in perfect readiness, put each shuttle to be used through a most brisk, thorough examination of all its onboard systems—both primary, secondary, and even tertiary—giving likewise the supplies for each away team equal scrutiny.

Everything most thoroughly tested before loaded aboard each ship-to-surface transport, this left just the smart armor suits to be taken care of. Each member of both expeditions donned her protective gear after it received as well a most thorough examination—pondering all the while what lay in wait for them beyond StarChild's "safe confines".

And so it was the sleek little shuttle destined for 'AB-1.5' was first to take leave of its young fathership, traveling the starship's entire length before picking up speed just beyond its narrowed prow. Meanwhile the vessel carrying both Frances and Naomi to 'C-1' followed likewise the same trajectory from both stern to bow, swinging full about immediately thereafter on an opposite course towards its own final objective.

Having given specific orders earlier that day for StarChild to take up a stationary position between both 'C-1' and 'AB-1.5', Jenniboni wanted to cut down wherever possible on the distance each away team would need to travel, allowing for speedier returns should rapid retreats prove necessary.

As cosmic fortune would have it the two worlds each shuttle now headed for were positioned closest to one another in their individual orbits, Naomi wistfully smiling with maternal affection out one of her shuttle's portside viewing ports. Admiring quite readily StarChild's graceful avian features—his bold, elegant lines—it was then she silently promised him she'd surely return no matter what may come:

'Don't worry old boy, Mama plans to be back in a jiff!'

Doing so without the vaguest hint of any reservation Naomi found herself unable to even entertain the thought of anything keeping her away on a more permanent basis—Commodore Jenniboni Saphira also refusing aboard her own shuttle to entertain the thought of anything keeping her from returning.

Leaving now her ship on a possible collision course with the still unknown such wild flights of fancy were, in her opinion, counterproductive—any such fantasies over what might go wrong banished once-and-for-all the very moment they likewise came to mind.

Choosing rather to rationally meditate on what might lay ahead Jenniboni summoned to mind instead every reasonable, possible hypothesis; her nimble mental reflexes deducing viable solutions to each likely scenario.

Leaping from one possible danger to the other with brilliant strategic insight no matter what came to mind she was nevertheless interrupted after a while by the crisp, clear sound of Lt. Greensley's voice filtered through the hearing units in her helmet:

"Commodore, we are now entering stationary orbit over 'AB-1.5'. However, due to electro-magnetic interference in the moon's upper atmosphere, I'm afraid I can't promise a smooth entry".

"That's quite all right, Lt.", Jenniboni assured her young pilot for the duration of this mission, glancing at the young woman seated to her immediate right: "I have every confidence in your ability".

"Thank you, Ma'am".

Angling the small craft on a gentle trajectory so the crescent horizon of the lush green moon below rested in the lower portion of their transport's forward viewer, Gloria eased their shuttle gently downward, its nose tilted at a gradual incline towards the moon-world's surface now below.

Growing steadily closer the solid black of deep space turned at a rapid rate bluish-green. The sky growing brighter all around them given their continual rate of decent, this was soon followed by the likewise increasing turbulence of which Gloria just warned her commanding officer.

Although it did indeed shake things up a bit Jenniboni was all that more impressed with the expert manner with which young Lt. Greensley handled their shuttle's controls this very first time out with her. Glancing at the energy readings appearing on the sensor screen before her they could've been thrown about a heck of a lot worse according to available data.

Thinking about it even further Jenniboni experienced a certain, definite admiration as well for what it must have taken those unknown pilots seven years earlier to manage such rough skies, arriving at long last at the future sight of their own little 'Paradise'. Given the primitive, archaic technology of pre-Matriarchate Earth, all that was sadly available leaving the Prime Mother World way back in the early 21st century, such an accomplishment struck her as no less the incredible feat it truly was.

Equally noteworthy was both the courage and fortitude (or was it desperation??) leading those colonists to travel nearly 900 years in cryogenic slumber. To say the very least it couldn't have been easy given such dire limitations. So much more to pity that, after such an inspirational struggle for life itself, such noble efforts earned them nothing more than obvious heartbreak.

* * * *

Entering the lower atmosphere over the smallish moon's equator Jenniboni instructed Gloria to make soon after that a standard fly-by survey of the two larger alien communities before continuing further on to Paradise. Even in their clearly dilapidated condition she could readily see in those alien habitations a marked vestige of their former majesty.

Turning ever southward towards the Terran colony they planned to visit last Jenniboni's shuttle passed as well over a large spaceport just outside the northern 'C-1' city… three derelict space-craft sitting in its center.

Little else anywhere near them in that broad, flat, paved expanse they were ugly, squat, bulky-looking vehicles appearing almost new despite the obvious millennia they no doubt spent just crouching there. Each about a quarter of StarChild's own considerable size Jenniboni couldn't help but wonder as to their exact function, what ancient purpose they no doubt served.

Long discarded and no doubt inoperable was it for combat, or something else more benign. Exposed to the natural elements so beneficial to life but equally detrimental to the continued welfare of machinery, their dead hulks possessed an eerie semblance to archaic land tanks employed by the many ancient patriarchates during herstorical battles long ago.

No matter which Jenniboni didn't have long to ponder however those remnants of a long gone past, Gloria announcing immediately thereafter their final destination—the speaker unit in her smart armor helmet lending the other woman's voice a quite synthetic resonance:

"Dead ahead… Paradise!"

"Excellent, Lieutenant: Bring us to within a hundred meters of the colony, landing us on the most level site available".

"Yes, Ma'am".

****

Hovering right above their eventual resting place Jenniboni found the immediate scene quite tranquil—even bucolic—in its rather 'down-home' country appearance, approaching even so the Terran colony at a lower-than-standard altitude.

Trying to avoid detection by those possible hostiles from elsewhere still undiscovered, not quite able to make out what lay at the colony's very heart, 'Paradise' was surrounded by a series of small, metal living units turning now a dingy, faded white.

Set up side-by-broad-side in two concentric rings, one arrayed well within the other, the blunt end of each pointed inwards towards the colony's center.

335

Single-leveled rectangular affairs they surrounded whatever lay at the lifeless heart of this recently defunct community.

Effectively blocking off all view of what lay just beyond, the only thing visible at all of the inner settlement were just the tops of a few scant larger, taller buildings. Each constructed of the same grayish-blue metal they were covered now with cracked and peeling paint the same faded white as the aging living units closer-by:

"Not much to look at", Jenniboni mused to herself.

Rather ungenerous in thought she chastised herself swiftly thereafter for such 'un-kindliness' in spirit.

Let's be fair now! All things being equal it appeared these people did a quite remarkable job setting up a viable, working community given the meager resources they were no doubt limited to. Especially doing so in just two years' time.

And in that very same vein there was even further evidence of that ancient, traditional 'Pioneer Work Ethic' clearly motivating these people to even greater feats of labor—large, well-organized fields of varied crops growing along the far shores of a broad river flowing at a most leisurely pace in the near distance.

Clearly well cultivated not so very long ago they'd grown now quite wild after nearly five years of continual neglect. Growing quite freely they spilled over into nearby pasture lands where a few remaining livestock meandered even now rather lazily about.

Left to their own devices they also seemed to be faring well, rooting about in golden shafts of wheat as if without a single care in their whole, entire world. Startled briefly by her shuttle's dramatic arrival within their own little 'paradise' they returned soon enough to their previous behavior patterns, grazing around and about not long thereafter.

As for other buildings across the river all Jenniboni could make out on its other side were a few scattered barns complete with grain silo's. From what she could tell they appeared to be constructed as well of at least both wood and metal. Painted a bright, festive red that seemed to better weather the elements than the white used in the settlement proper three wide bridges spanned as well the broad, languid, crystal blue waters separating farmlands from the colony proper.

All said and done the entire area manifested a clear illusion of being nothing more than a cozy, little, self-contained world all of its very own nestled as it was between two low-lying mountain ranges to both the north and south.

All-in-all a secluded little Eden where all seemed quite perfect indeed.

Not fooled for a second though Jenniboni could tell already there was something quite off-kilter here, more than just a wee bit wrong, the lack of any Human habitation proof enough something was amiss. Nor was this any less than she expected as Lt. Greensley set their shuttle down at last in the middle of an otherwise flat patch of grass, a level playing field already long-gone to seed.

****

Ordering at once her intrepid little band of explorers to remain alert at all times, taking nothing at all for granted, Jenniboni wasted no time whatsoever organizing them all together just outside their shuttle.

Posting one of Lt. Oftesfs' two scouts on continual guard duty right next to their vehicle, she requested as well Dr. Wei-Chang run a complete and thorough examination of their immediate vicinity.

Utilizing the medical scanner the elderly chief medic still wore slung over her shoulder since leaving StarChild, Eartha managed to work with relative ease its more-or-less complex controls despite the somewhat cumbersome gloves likewise a part of her smart armor suit:

"According to these readings there are absolutely no harmful micro-organisms, or air-borne contagions detectable posing any threat", Eartha announced, relaying soon enough the information now appearing on her scanner's glare-insulated display screen:

"From what I can already determine here 'AB-1.5' would seem quite hospitable to Human life. I can't even locate any traces of harmful solar radiation None at all".

"It would appear Cmdr. Nikarov was quite accurate in her assessment of the density of the ozone layer above", Jenniboni added; "its superior properties of insulation".

"Indeed", Eartha agreed: "I'm even able to detect oxygen levels 10% richer than back on Earth".

"Unless you have anything further to report Doctor I'd say we've learned all we're going to just standing here. With that in mind I suggest you collect the portable medical unit you likewise brought along from inside the shuttle:

"Time to move out".

Setting out no sooner than Eartha returned, P.M.U. in hand, Jenniboni left behind one of Toni's scouts to stand guard over their only means of escape, the rest of the landing party following close behind.

Flanking their ship's C.O. on either side, their armed gauntlets poised at the ready, both Lt. Baynes and Lt. Cmdr. Oftesfs were dedicated without fail to the continued protection of both Jenniboni and the rest—Gloria, Phyllis, Eartha, and the other remaining scout following close behind in constant guard of their rear flanks.

Gazing out with longing eyes at the rich, lusty scenery all about her Toni Oftesfs actually felt a wee bit cheated by the durable, smart-armor uniform encasing her entire body, understanding the wisdom in wearing it doing little to ease her resentment.

Rather disappointed how it cut her off from the immediate climate all around her, restricting her ability to enjoy the many natural pleasures this unique little world must surely have to offer, the main irony being that Toni first joined the S.E.A. for the very sole purpose of experiencing to its fullest what such an alien world might have to offer.

It was to experience the feel of an alien breeze against her very skin, the warmth of another System's sun against her flesh, she signed up for duty aboard StarChild—her face tilted upwards, eyes closed, relishing the scent of a whole new world's very air filling her senses to their absolute fullest, meeting it all head on.

And now that she was finally standing on that brave new world in question, wanting nothing more at that very moment than to indulge every tactile sensation possible with whatever this newest environment had to offer, Toni was now denied her one and only chance to do so by some lousy suit of armor standing in her every way.

No solar warmth able to penetrate its highly polished surface, no summer's breeze able to work its gentle way through, even every morsel of air she breathed was filtered through the quite efficient breathing apparatus also a part of her extensive gear.

Then again StarChild's *'Chief Planetary Scout and Exploration Officer'* found herself able to find at least some little comfort in the wondrous sights everywhere to be seen, enchanted by both the incredible landscape all about her alongside the equally gorgeous skies above—sparkling turquoise horizons dominated by the grand sight of 'AB-1.5's' parent-world rising in the far distance over all the rest of this bountiful new land.

Providing a most scintillating contract to all the lush greenery all around them the Jovian globe's reddish orb, complete with swirling clouds a vibrant yellow/orange, occupied nearly a quarter of this new moon-world's late afternoon sky—its incredible amber/gold rings appearing to reach out in vain hope of making direct contact with the very land upon which Toni now trod.

Already making her way through the inner ring of living units… cracked, dirty windows keeping everyone there from seeing what might lurk inside… Toni nonetheless paid no attention, her mind so tightly wrapped around such warm daydreams…

Oh, how that splendid world must look in this smaller ones' nightly sky. The starry sky beyond providing a quite ample backdrop to an already romantic scene that ringed world above would cast no doubt a most exotic, rose-tinged light over the entire land.

Able to imagine such an exquisite setting quite easily Toni found it no more difficult to likewise see herself walking along some secluded avenue bathed in its crimson glow; a handsome, attentive laddie on her arm. A couple she knew back home would do quite nicely indeed.

The landing party passing through a narrow passage formed by the broadside of two outer dwellings not even shabby surroundings like these disturbed the pleasant thoughts occupying her entire awareness, white weather-beaten paint peeling back from rusty metal exteriors.

Perhaps a midnight stroll along the shores of that river just beyond Paradise, gentle waters lapping against the shoreline, the scent of nocturnal blooms adding an extra sensual spice to a light night breeze against mostly bare skin…

Paradise beyond question just the very thought of it nearly took her breath away!

Emerging though from the narrow passage between derelict living units, seeing at last what lay strewn all about the community green belt beyond, all scintillating daydreams of lusty romance vanished at long last. A sight as far from romantic as it was horrific it was *this instead* that took Toni's very breath away!

Chapter 46

"WHITE KNIGHTS"

As in the case of Toni before her Naomi cared neither for the rather 'snug', if not downright claustrophobic confines of the smart armor gear encasing now her lush, rubenesque form—her feelings performing soon enough a most dramatic 'about-face'.

Catching at last her first up-close, personal glimpse of what awaited them on 'C-1's quite desolate surface, piloting the compact shuttle carrying the second away team from StarChild ever closer, a shiver ran all throughout her entire body.

Approaching even closer their final destination on one, final orbital approach of the planet below, its entire surface was nothing but a frozen wasteland. A dying world blanketed in perpetual darkness both quite cold and inhospitable at the very same time, it was a 'ghost-world' in every sense of the term—the cities likewise awaiting their arrival nothing but vast necropolis':

Dwellings of the utter dead.

Occupying their shuttle's cramped cockpit it soon occurred to Naomi upon further reflection their armor evoked the noble image of white knights going into battle; a fanciful, modern-day version of St. Tammy's very own 'Sisterhood'.

Scanning the bleak landscape all around them, Frances seated at her left managing their small craft's navigational controls, all they lacked were a few dragons to slay, seeking that conical alien edifice possessing the answers to questions both complex as they were vexatious.

As a little girl there were many a time she and her classmates on Ceres pretended they were members of the chivalrous '*Sisterhood of the Knights of Garfield*', personally knowing Rev. Garfield herself long before both her subsequent death and posthumous canonization by the very church she helped reorganize.

However, revealing such lofty day-dreams to the other woman beside her, they elicited nothing at all from Frances but a quite sour reply, StarChild's

Chief of Security making it clear in no uncertain terms she wanted to avoid any and all possible mishaps during their current assignment—*any whatsoever*—a sentiment with which Naomi most heartily agreed:

"There it is! That's where we're headed", Frances announced soon thereafter, pointing a gloved index finger to the right directly ahead of them.

Following the direction in which she did so, peering out the forward viewer in the very direction her 'sister-knight' indicated, Naomi noticed quite readily a tall, cone-shaped tower rising far above all those others gathered about in its weighty shadow.

Resting smack-dab in the very center of that grand group of other ruins spread out all about it, the monstrous skyscraper seemed to have survived whatever destruction befell the others, appearing less scathed in appearance.

No minor accomplishment noting the pockmarked evidence of general warfare scattered throughout the rest of the ancient city below them. Only when growing closer still did it become evident that, quite to the contrary, the alien behemoth now dead ahead didn't really escape so free from harm after all.

Circling the grand complex on a somewhat closer trajectory both senior officers sitting side-by-side noted quite readily now a series of ancient blast marks—ancient impact marks resulting in long, narrow fissures spread upwards from the tower's broad base like a collection of varicose veins halfway to its very peak:

"I just hope that building's still structurally sound", Naomi sighed rather pessimistically.

"Don't worry. I'm sure we'll find out one way or another soon enough", Frances assured her with a most definite hint of gallows humor in her otherwise serious tone of voice: "However, in the meantime, I suggest we look about for somewhere nearby to affect an otherwise safe landing".

"Your wish is my command", Naomi grinned. Steering their small craft away this time from the tower in an ever-increasing arc, she came across what seemed to be a medium-sized town square after several minutes of circling the entire vicinity.

Bordered on every side by broad avenues leading away both east and west, as well as north and south, the greater majority of this temporary, make-shift space-port seemed still mostly paved as well as reasonably clear of surrounding debris:

"How about there?", Naomi asked, her choice for touch down possessing the added benefit of being only a few cities blocks from their prime objective.

Gaining her immediate superior's approval, Frances agreeing to land where Naomi indicated, both senior officers made their way back into to the passenger area of their tiny craft once safely on the ground.

Waiting there for further instruction from both senior personnel the only way Naomi could tell the other three members of their landing party apart were the magnetic nameplates affixed to each woman's armor-plated chest, situated just upper right of the golden fempacem adorning each battle-ready outfit:

"Ensign's Wilson and Umbota will accompany both Lt. Cmdr.'s Marlowe and myself to the tower; Ensign Fazara remaining here on guard", Frances instructed each of her three security personnel all present and accounted for.

Doing so in a most succinct manner, asking anyone else if they had anything further to ask—any points needing further clarification—it was then she gave everyone gathered about their immediate marching orders, no one voicing any further concerns.

****

The only sound to be heard all around them was the shrill whistle of a brutal arctic wind more often than not blowing up thick clouds of perpetual dust in the streets, Naomi dwelling for the umpteenth time on just how bitterly cold that piercing wind must be.

Further reason for now blessing the protective armor protecting every inch of her otherwise vulnerable person, the only cause for further complaint she could find was its otherwise complex breathing apparatus.

Even with the air-processing units built into all their protective headgear working at peak efficiency, regulating and even enhancing both the mean temperature and oxygen levels beyond, Naomi was able to determine all the same a certain lack of both density and warmth in the very air they breathed.

In the meantime Ensigns Wilson and Umbota monitored the immediate remains of the dead city all about them. Security scanners in hand both remained on the continual, immediate lookout for any suspicious movements, or energy traces of either a natural or artificial nature.

With no moon in that inky black night sky above them to cast any additional light on those ruins to either side the cold, cruel light of those distant stars did nothing at all to dispel the eternal darkness. Their built-in motion detectors were all they had to warn them of any possible attack from within that solid, inky blackness beyond smashed windows and door-less entrances lining the street down which they walked.

Keeping to the exact middle of that wide boulevard leading all the way to their prime objective, all four visitors to this gloomy world made a most prudent point of remaining close to each other while making their way towards that ponderous tower directly ahead.

Not even those otherwise efficient light fixtures built into the forehead of each of their sturdy helmets proved able to reveal those mysteries hidden just beyond vacant portals. Focusing her immediate attention on the tower's ominous bulk ahead, a shadowy dagger thrust upwards towards the cold indigo skies right above, Naomi felt a rather distinct chill run both up and down her very spine.

Her already overactive imagination getting quite the better of her it were as though the myriad incorporeal eyes of countless phantasmal entities lay in eternal wait all about them, watching their each and every move with hateful, malignant intent.

Almost able to actually feel all those numerous specters staring at her with evil desire from just beyond each and every empty doorway, every glassless window frame, it were as though they envied the four lone women from on high

342

their very flesh and blood bodies.

No doubt about it!

This was a graveyard—a home for all those ghosts, goblins, and other cohabitants of eternal nightmare hiding beneath blankets of endless night, stalking their hapless prey hidden well under the cover of countless shadows—the very wind howling past all four women nothing less than the irate voice of some Banshee queen crying out in loud protest against all four interlopers intruding now upon her most private domain.

Nor was Naomi the only one there to experience such a certain sense of unrest, a powerful discontent simply being where they were, each and every one of her compatriots disillusioned as well with their present location. Even Frances, although she didn't show it in the least, found this city of the dead as disturbing as did her three companions.

Always an on-duty professional remaining in control of whatever fear she might on occasion experience nobody could tell from both her purposeful stride, cool eyes, and calm exterior she was also uneasy with her current situation.

However, be that as it may, her disquiet didn't originate with such fanciful thoughts as occupied the deepest recesses of StarChild's brilliant Chief Engineer, things that go 'bump in the night' holding no dread at all for the honourable Lt. Cmdr. Straker.

For Frances this city was home for something a lot worse than any fantastic thought of the supernatural ever could be, this very metroplex all about her the home of both utter chaos and absolute disorder. For her it was a place where justice, discipline and sweet reason were forever abandoned in favor of endless anarchy—a monstrous monument to both sanity and peace being defeated forever at the brutal hand of lunatic violence.

The only peace to be found here was in the eternal still of an endless graveyard, a dismal setting where the only opposite of rampant chaos was to be found in the perfect still of absolute death, the final peace of absolute lifelessness.

To her that was more troublesome than any ponderance of mere spooks could ever be, more horrific than any fanciful haunt. Whatever happened here must never be allowed to likewise take place back home, the defense of Womankind's home System an absolute imperative against whatever evil force held sway here.

If still an active threat after all these countless years whatever was guilty of what happened here must never be allowed to spread, reaching out by whatever pernicious means at its ready command to the very heart and soul of Womankind's very Commonwealth—the Tammyite Matriarchate!

Reaching at last the dull-white tower to which they journeyed, its pock-marked surface worn mightily after so many millennia of air-borne particles whipping by, all four away team members found their only means of entrance blocked by a colossal metallic seal truly mammoth in design.

Reaching both far above them as well as to either side the armor-plated barrier, a smoky grey in hue, blocked most surely their only certain passage into that mountainous high-rise before them.

****

Having determined to the best of her abilities there were no hidden security measures, no booby-traps awaiting their arrival on the barrier's other side, it was only then Frances gave StarChild's resident genius in all matters technical her full blessing to continue as she saw fit.

Wasting no time in removing the well-stocked tool kit slung over her left shoulder Naomi placed it with great care on the ground, kneeling soon after that at the portal's edge, tools of her trade all at the ready. Opening the kit to the immediate right of where the slate grey door met with the faded building's neglected exterior, Naomi had very little trouble locating the enormous barrier's rather small locking mechanism.

Realizing she found it when noting a square protrusion subtle in design less than a meter above the ground, it was buried almost alive in the entryway's otherwise nondescript doorjamb.

Pressed up to the very edge of the armor-plated egress barring their way it was sheltered rather well from the quite harsh elements everywhere around them. And even though dealing with alien technology well beyond previous experience, Naomi was nevertheless confident she could decipher its unforeseen components once exposed to the shining light of pure reason.

Nor was this unshakable conviction born out of any undue sense of ego, originating instead with the simple realization there were certain practical, mathematical absolutes constant throughout all reality governing the many laws of her profession—certain engineering principals applying to all mechanical enterprises no matter how simple, or complex:

Laws, rules, and principals easy to both recognize and even interpret by someone given both Naomi's superior genius and natural ability. Being one of those gifted individuals ready to instinctively understand the complex workings of any contraption by just looking at it Naomi was in fact a virtual Mozart of all things mechanical, an engineering virtuoso beyond compare.

Removing with professional dispatch a laser cutter from among her assorted tools, following a brief scan of what lay just beyond the locking mechanism's protective cover, she was sure beyond any shadow of doubt now how to proceed. Running the cutter's thin, blue beam with great care around the covering's outermost edge—all four sides—Naomi did so least she damage the unseen mechanism buried snug within.

Nor did it really take so very long before the metal barrier barring her way fell to the ground below, emitting as it did so a dull clang, revealing against a well-lit backdrop the complicated circuitry it had sheltered now for over seven millennia.

Knowing at a mere glance what to do next Naomi snipped at once three thin wires, reconnecting them instead to a couple of wee, tiny microchips situated just left of a rather complex circuit board almost right behind it. Telling everyone else to step well back she pressed the very tip of her right index finger against a small, creamy-yellow crystalline diode in the direct forefront,

344

snapping the sparkly, spangly little device with an intense flash of pent-up energy.

With both a low rumble and gritty groan the massive metal egress once barring their way into the tower itself slid slowly upwards into the broad lintel far above, revealing just beyond it a bright, powerfully-lit corridor of equally grandiose proportions stretching out before them into the far distance.

Built it seemed to impress others with mere size itself the hallway ahead possessed smooth, glistening walls and high vaulted ceiling all blank and featureless except for a series of plain grey doors. Exact miniatures of the portal Naomi just opened they were arranged in uniform rows on either side of the grand hall—a wide, solid cylindrical strip of luminous properties lighting their way embedded in the ceiling above.

Composed of some glassy, milky substance not unlike the crystalline component she snapped clean in half just minutes before, it also seemed able to conduct energy in the form of a bright light without benefit of any internal mechanism.

****

Hearing Frances instruct everyone to stay alert in their search for hidden security measures, commanding them even further to 'move out' in pursuit of their primary target, each member of their little team found herself preferring even so this well-lit setting to that in back of them—that cold, dark, vacant corpse of a once proud metropolis.

Listening to the rather solitary sound of their lone footsteps echoing all about them in such desolate territory, sheltered from the harsh environment from which they just came, at least their new surroundings—no matter their intimidating grandeur—were bright as bright could be. And from the overall data retrieved just yesterday from StarChild's scout probes they were able to determine with reasonable accuracy their primary goal lay somewhere ahead at the very core of this most impressive structure.

Reaching however the very end of this first corridor all four women from above were met by the blank, featureless surface of yet another glistening, pearly white wall—a curved passage branching off to either side of their present situation. Using their scanners to determine which way to turn they soon reached yet another straight hall like the first leading even further into the alien skyscraper.

Nor did it end there, another blank wall leading to yet another curved corridor, leading to yet another straight one leading them even closer... ad-infinitum... to the very center of this quite monotonous mega-structure.

Forming an impressive array of concentric rings growing ever smaller the closer each grew to the central nucleus of this quite ponderous place it was an endless collective of straight passageways connecting each to the other. And whether straight or circular each and every one possessed the same sterile, monolithic, somehow inhuman feel as the last—bright Spartan décor and larger-than-life architecture added.

No surprise then that, although a definite step up from the menacing climes of their previous environment, this newest of surroundings was likewise not very conducive to either feelings of warmth, or an overall sense of general intimacy—Frances alluding to this simple fact in response to some casual comment on Naomi's part:

"A little *too* impressive if you ask me", she made her feelings known, subtle disdain evident: "Personally I've never really cared much for such grandiose architecture. Smacks of egotism bordering on the megalomaniac if you ask me".

"Maybe so, Maybe so", Naomi rolled her eyes in comic frustration, granting that in a somewhat weary fashion: "But this building clearly served some major purpose in the daily lives of these people and, if I were to go about designing such to convey such, then *this* is how I'd do it".

"I guess you have a point", Frances relented but just a little; "but that doesn't mean I have to like it!"

At this Naomi never even bothered trying to hide her obvious amusement, likewise confessing with a generous chuckle she as well didn't quite care much either for it.

"Getting cold feet, Lt. Cmdr. Marlowe?"

"More like a cold body, Lt. Cmdr. Straker".

Trading back and forth such friendly banter they realized soon enough their lengthy search was finally over when, turning yet another sharp corner in this seemingly endless warren of many corridors, they were met by a similar grey portal like before—albeit a tad smaller—at the far end of yet another straight passageway.

Nor did it take Naomi very long to secure quick entry, clearing their way as surely as before. Struck at once, overcome with incredulous wonder, she could but just stare at the awesome image now greeting her:

"Bingo", Frances grinned, her broad smile almost audible over the very speaker units built into her complicated headgear: "I think we're finally where we want to be".

"I don't care what you say", Naomi whistled, finding her voice at long last: "Now *that's* impressive!"

Chapter 47

"GENDERCIDE"

Calling at once an abrupt halt to their immediate advance Jenniboni could only gaze in numb, utter horror at the decayed and decaying killing field now occupying infront of them the entire colony's immediate interior. While true they all anticipated on an intellectual level something along these very same lines, doing so right from the very start, the emotional response when actually faced with such atrocity was another thing entirely.

No way around it, one quite different from the other, there was no honest way in either Heaven above or the worlds below to emotionally steel oneself for such a sight.

No way at all!!

This was one of those occasions when able to come to emotional grips with what you previously expected only after witnessing it in real time.

Strewn about like so much garbage the very last remains of all those deceased colonists lay all about in tortured repose, scattered about as though some vast graveyard vomited up all its many contents. Left to decompose right where they first fell there was no doubt as to how they all died, a sight not seen in Womankind's herstory for nearly a full millennium.

By Jenniboni's keen estimation there must have been well over several hundred examples of butchered humanity flung about them throughout the entire colony, the weapons likewise scattered around them answering the question of how they died.

Nor was there any doubt in the minds of all seven women now standing there the former denizens of this so-called 'Paradise' each suffered a most violent demise, the obvious means of their self-inflicted mass destruction bearing witness to that.

Even after nearly five years of just lying there the very positions in which they lay, rotting under the alien sky above, proved each and every one of them died in both great fear and certain pain. All that remained now of these people were their twisted bones, most still intact, all picked clean by whatever wee scavengers might be native to this brave new world.

Even the time of the day added to the horror before them, the lengthening shadows cast by the setting suns lending this already fearsome sight an even more sinister touch—their only death shrouds being the tattered, torn remains of whatever clothing each wore at the time they died.

Only just mid-morning aboard StarChild it was nevertheless late afternoon here and now in 'Paradise'.

Looking all round her at the tortured remains of past carnage it couldn't help but occur to Jenniboni's beleaguered reason that, whenever people gave their new homes such hubristic monikers as 'Utopia', 'Heaven', 'Perfection', or—as in this particular case—'Paradise', it always seemed to end rather poorly for such boastful individuals.

More like "Paradise Lost" it then occurred to her, reflecting upon this in a most scornful fashion. Keeping such feelings to herself, it were as though fate itself struck down such boastful individuals.

Even while completely in the dark concerning the full story what really happened here both she and the rest of her team wanted nothing more now than to be done with their current mission in record time, Jenniboni giving the immediate command to move out.

****

Cutting across what appeared to be a large community greenbelt gone to seed everyone there was keenly aware of her immediate surroundings, making their way for this Hellish colony's very heart. Alert to every single sight, every blessed sound all around her, Toni was no longer resentful in the very least concerning her smart armor uniform.

Quite the contrary she felt both quite secure, even comforted, by its clinging confines.

Holding her clenched fists thrust out before her in a most aggressive stance she had no wish to be caught off-guard by anything either imaginable, or unimaginable. With appreciative eyes she studied with intense satisfaction the spiked weapons fixed to the back of each gauntlet-bearing arm—their blue crystal tips reaching well beyond the extended limits of protected hands encased as well in glistening, highly reflective, flexible titanium-alloy gloves.

Never before was Toni so very grateful to be so heavily armed. Glancing about at all the others—each and every one of her other six sisters-in-arms—she noted as well they were likewise at the ready, laser gauntlets poised likewise for combat.

****

Halfway between both the inner-ring of dilapidated living units and this latter-day ghost town's actual nucleus Jenniboni heard from behind a hesitant voice requesting a pause, breaking for a brief moment from their continued progress:

348

"Yes, Lt. Greensley? What is it?", Jenniboni was quick to ask. Turning around she fixed the younger woman with a rather curious gaze.

"Yes, Ma'am: I was wondering if it might be a good idea to take one of these alien weapons back to StarChild with us for further examination", her young tech officer began at first in a somewhat hesitant manner, pointing at one of those strange weapons littering here and there the entire compound:

Weapons of clearly non-Human design.

And as she grew more confident of the wisdom behind such a recommendation Gloria's voice grew more steady. Unable to help but notice the obvious battlefield droppings lying about everyone knew already what Gloria was referring to, the many unfamiliar weapons resting alongside a number of the skeletal corpses.

Although many of these people availed themselves of firearms clearly of 20th/21st century patriarchate design, the rest seemed to have acquired at the same time weapons of clearly non-Terran manufacture. Heavy, bulky rifle-like weapons they looked quite lethal no matter what they were actually capable of.

Gathering up one of those alienesque contraptions from the long grass all around them, Gloria gave it a most thorough examination once given Jenniboni's permission to do so:

"Interesting", she said aloud, employing a voice loud enough for everyone to hear: "Not only too advanced for pre-matriarchate Earth, but easily comparable to present-day technology.

"Yet the design parameters are not quite like ours in output".

"May I have a look, Lt. Greensley?", Cecilia asked, her tone respectful almost to the point of subservient. Meekly waiting for the other woman to first offer it up she then took it from Gloria with all due caution, accepting the bulky device with the greatest of natural care.

Giving it a most complete, thorough examination of her own Cecilia was about to likewise hand it back, Gloria stopping her before she had a chance:

"As senior security offer present I think it might be best for you to take charge of it until we're once more back on StarChild—with the Commodore's permission, of course!", Gloria was most hasty to add, forgetting herself just briefly when making this particular proposal.

"Permission granted", Jenniboni allowed, a grin lurking at the corners of her mouth, hidden only by her helmet.

"Thank you", Cecilia accepted with uncharacteristic deference escaping no one's notice: "I'll be most sure to return it to you when we get back. I'm sure you'll want your people to run a complete diagnostic on it as soon as we get back".

Smiling inside without reservation at this verbal exchange, Lt. Baynes' recent conduct in the matter of Lt. Greensley earned her Jenniboni's immediate attention. Even before their recent departure from StarChild the way her Asst. Chief of Security went about treating the former object of her absolute scorn captured Jenniboni's immediate notice—Lt. Baynes treating the smaller woman with a nervous respect teetering on the very brink of utter obsequiousness.

Nor was the obvious explanation for this abrupt turn-about hard to see, as painfully obvious as both the violent bruise and mighty welt visible to everyone present. Suspecting from the very start her disagreeable security officer finally pushed someone else aboard ship a "tad too far", Jenniboni didn't believe for a single second Cecilia's official excuse for the distinctive mark on her person:

Her claim of a clumsy mishap during a private workout fooled no one.

Yet, until now, StarChild's reigning C.O. never assumed Lt. Greensley was the one who delivered that fearsome blow, leaving its indelible mark on Lt. Baynes' very person. Whatever she either said or did must have been truly horrid to have elicited such an extreme, uncharacteristic outburst on the part of her usually timid Asst. Chief Engineer.

Either that or Lt. Greensley simply reached her final breaking point, unwilling at all to tolerate any more foul abuse. An encouraging sign in anyone's opinion, Jenniboni's included. Under any other circumstances she would never condone such outrageous conduct on the part of anyone under her command, willing just this once to make a minor exception.

Besides, if Lt. Baynes chose not to file an official complaint, there was nothing Jenniboni could do on her behalf. Again she smiled. This time 'out in the open' her expression of quiet mirth was masked only by the defensive smart armor helmet she wore, its faceplate hiding all but her eyes.

No wonder the other woman conjured up such a flimsy explanation for how she came about her apparent injury. Jenniboni could only imagine the incredible mockery Cecilia would no doubt suffer if the rest of her crew learned it was—of all people—Lt. Greensley who finally took her to task.

****

Continuing with this not-so-pleasant away mission each member of Jenniboni's team now indulged herself in practical speculation, all out-loud, as to what must have happened here no more than just five years ago:

No turning back now!

Drawing ever closer to the dead heart of this increasingly wretched settlement, searching still for answers to those questions bringing them here in the very first place, it was quite obvious to everyone a large number of colonists discovered an equally generous cache of weapons left on this sad moon by 'C-1's former inhabitants.

Turning them against the rest of their fellow Human beings for reasons as yet unknown it was equally obvious the rest, having only weapons brought with them from Earth, were forced out of the very blue to defend themselves the best they could, the hapless victims of some inexplicable ambush conducted without mercy by their murderous brethren:

End result? Total annihilation!!

No longer was there any doubt in the minds of all those present that, whatever the reason, what happened here was the end result of some internal struggle from which no one but one single, solitary settler was exempt:

A bloody battle involving just human against human.

Or at least it seemed for the moment.

No visible evidence of direct alien influence involved in what happened here just five years ago the only mystery remaining was that of a viable motive, Dr. Wei-Chang adding her own suggestion to those of the rest. Rendering her shocking verdict with such calm, cool professional detachment it was hard to tell which was worse, what she suggested or the tone with which she did so:

"We might never know what exactly it was that triggered this fatal conflict, but we at least know one thing for certain".

"Yes, Doctor", Jenniboni was first to enquire: "And what might that be?"

"That this massacre was based on gender; a 'sexual civil war' if you may".

"If that's some kind of sick joke Doctor I'm not amused", Jenniboni snapped in vehement reply—outraged—refusing to even entertain such a possibility.

"I assure you Ma'am I'm not in possession of such a diseased sense of humor as to consider such a possibility even remotely amusing", Eartha lodged in bitter complaint, no less vexed by the very idea: "Especially given our present situation!".

No sooner had Eartha finished speaking the entire landing party came to a sudden, rapid halt. Spinning about 180 degrees, confronting her devoted C.M.O. head on, Jenniboni performed an immediate 'about face':

"In that case, Doctor, maybe you'd care to offer even more evidence in defense of such an odious assertion".

"If you wish, Ma'am: Fine", Eartha spoke up even further, defiant, feeling as though her very reputation was now on trial.

Finding such a motive for mass-murder equally disturbing as her Commanding officer Eartha Wei-Chang nonetheless felt it her solemn duty to press onward even so:

"To start at the very beginning I can tell you quite readily, given the size of each skeleton, factoring also into consideration the pelvic structure of each and every one, which were female versus which were male. Taking into account the reverse dichotomy existing between each gender in the late 20th, early 21st centuries it's not too difficult to deduce which set of remains belongs to which sex.

"Even the few scant remains of clothing they wore help determine somewhat their gender.

"Moreover, given the ratio of each individual represented here, their distribution pattern, and the weapons they used, it's most evident to me that the colony's women were gathered about the community's exact center, having nothing at their disposal but those weapons they brought here from Earth.

"And arranged all the while in a defensive position as the men approached from outside the colony, this would indicate just as clearly the men here were attacking the women with all those alien weapons scattered about in such apparent numbers...

"No doubt some sneak attack that clearly 'failed' it's also quite clear the only reason the women of Paradise proved able to neutralize the men at all...

despite their inferior weapons… was due to both their superior numbers and the simple fact they were gathered together in such a compact, defensive formation".

Not knowing how to reply in the face of such undaunting, relentless logic—such rational, sound reasoning—Jenniboni turned instead to Cecilia Baynes, putting her now on the spot:

"You're Assistant Chief of Security!! So what's your opinion? Is what our good Doctor here claims really possible? Could it be as she insists??"

"Well, I wouldn't presume to question Dr. Wei-Chang in either her medical expertise, or her ability to determine from the given evidence what happened", Cecilia proceeded with all due caution, able to note straightaway the almost desperate tone in Jenniboni's voice:

"Therefore, in light of all this, I have to confess her given hypothesis as to what actually happened here is, in all probability, a valid one".

"I read about the so-called 'battle-of-the-sexes' back in the old pre-Tammyite days in Herstory class", Gloria spoke up right after, doing so with a just a hint of frightened protest: "But never anything like this!"

Jenniboni understand quite readily her youngest officer's unwillingness to accept such a radical concept. Shaken herself to the very core sexual conflict was reduced dramatically ever since the final restoration of the natural order over eight hundred years ago. As with sexual violence its ugly existence was curtailed greatly after the rise of the Tammyite Matriarchate from the end of the 21st century onward.

Oh… sure… there might be private, personal disputes between individual members of each gender but, even so, there was no longer any major discontent… any social unrest, or public agitation between the sexes… all such organized gender-bashing now a mere memory in Womankind's distant past.

Even when there had been a so-called "battle of-the-sexes" there were no reports way back then of anything so utterly brutal, so all-encompassing as this.

"Let's get a move-on", Jenniboni commanded the rest of her small party, her forceful voice replete with both a certain loathing and angry dismay: "We still have too much to do here to just stand around like this, engaged in idle speculation".

****

Reaching at very last the true heart of Paradise, Jenniboni heard the not-too-distant sound of battered cloth fluttering about in the moderate breeze of late afternoon, coming from the opposite side of what was once the hefty forward portion of some ancient ship clearly Terran in design.

Stepping back but a few more paces from the former command module situated dead center of 'Paradise Lost', the other buildings making up the colony's interior gathered around it a few dozen meters or so away, Jenniboni could see quite readily a tall, sturdy flagpole—flapping around atop of it a torn flag both red, white, and blue.

From such obvious colours it wasn't long after that she likewise

352

recognized it as the former emblem of a once-famous patriarchate nation now relegated to the mere pages of ancient herstory, the once proud "United States of America":

"Sooo", Jenniboni mused just under her very breath; "this colony was American".

One of the most advanced, most powerful, of all the old patriarchates it stood to reason they would have made it this far more likely than many other bygone nations. And gazing at that faded symbol of such a noble, adventurous, fiercely independent people Jenniboni felt quite soon a strong tug at her very heart... moved quite deeply at sight of its tattered, torn, weather-beaten remains.

In great distress the aging cloth, abandoned to the cruelty of the natural elements, was ripped asunder almost to where its faded field of fifty stars soon began. Suffering nearly five years of continual neglect the red and white stripes before that were shredded to the point of ribbons, whipping about in the alien wind.

To Jenniboni this forgotten relic of a land long past was just too painful, too tragic a sight for anyone to bear, flying still in faded glory over the twisted bones of its last patriots. Averting her eyes instead from that sad image so close by she focused instead her immediate attention on those gathered about, waiting patiently further instruction.

Dividing them all into three separate groups she likewise gave them their next set of 'marching orders'... Toni, her remaining scout, and Eartha sent out in one party to investigate those buildings off to their left... Cecilia and Phyllis given orders to explore those on their right... leaving Jenniboni and Gloria to investigate the ancient forward command module, all that was left of the sleeper ship which brought the late citizens of Paradise to this, their ultimate fate.

****

Traversing dark, narrow passages turning both one way and another their only source of reliable light guiding their every step were the bright, round, luminous head lamps built into that part of their headgear just above their clear, transparent metal visors—Jenniboni leading their way in search of what was once this ancient derelict's very nerve center, the main bridge once servicing this entire, now defunct vessel.

Nor was there any doubt they found it when locating a large concavity greater in size than StarChild's own bridge, both women finding themselves standing in back of an ample chamber looking down a steep incline, the entire area reminiscent of some ancient amphitheater.

Pitch black save where the bright rays of their own strong 'headlights' might fall, both Jenniboni and Gloria set about inspecting that rather bulky network of dilapidated control panels arrayed to the rear of their current location. A gathering of archaic computer consoles lining the wall space all about in a rather exact horseshoe pattern, it was Gloria who discovered first the precise object of their determined search.

353

Announcing she did so just minutes after their initial arrival, sure she found no other than this ancient relic's data storage units, Jenniboni instructed her at once to download all the relevant information they might contain, tucked away in cold, dusty memory banks.

"I'm afraid I can't, Ma'am", Gloria apologized not long after a mere moment's examination.

"What seems the problem, Lieutenant?"

"Two problems actually, Ma'am, the first being the power source for the entire memory retrieval system. Due to both advanced age and continual use the batteries powering this particular system are completely drained, this archaic technology not allowing for 'cold scans' of recorded information.

"Not only that but, even if it did, the interfering energy discharge from the magnetic field surrounding 'AB-1.5' is already beginning to play havoc with my scanner, this making accurate readings problematic at best. Trying to retrieve detailed information stored in such an antiquated system would prove highly unlikely even if possible".

"Understood: In that case do you think it possible to remove the actual, physical data chips from the rest of the system: Take them back to StarChild with us and retrieve the information there aboard ship?"

"Yes, Commodore: However, in order to gain access to all their contents, it would likewise require their physical integration into our own memory systems, creating a direct link between them and Maccs. Once again this technology doesn't allow remote data transfer from actual storage chips without an added 'Information Relay Terminal'—or 'IRT'—set-up.

"Unfortunately the one here seems to have suffered some sort of energy feedback overload. Probably when this system passed through that same magnetic energy barrier we encountered entering the upper atmosphere".

"Understood, Lieutenant. That's all right. Do the best you can to remove whatever you need. Then, when we get back, you can download the information there. In the meantime I'll inspect the rest of this vessel's interior compartments while you take care of that".

****

Placing the last ancient data chip required in the compact tool kit she brought along, doing so with the utmost delicacy, Gloria heard Jenniboni's commanding tone call out from elsewhere in the dilapidated sleeper ship's forward command module.

Snapping quickly shut the carrying case in question she arranged its strap once more over her left shoulder. Nor did she pay much attention when it likewise bumped up quite harmlessly against the engineering scanner she still carried as well, setting out instead with all due haste.

Having little trouble at all finding her ship's C.O. Gloria found her as well standing smack dap in the center of a smallish chamber, examining with narrowed eyes a row of badly vandalized panel boards. Communications equipment damaged on purpose beyond all chances of repair.

Peppered in key locations with numerous holes, countless indentations, the damage at hand seemed inflicted by an old-style rapid-fire projectile weapon. No doubt one of those currently strewn about the compound outside, littering the colony proper alongside the bones of former owners:

"Well, Lt. Greensley, I'd hazard to guess we just discovered the origin point of the message these people sent us. I assume you agree?"

"Yes, Ma'am: And, by the looks of things, I'd likewise suggest whoever sent it did this in order to prevent any further transmissions being sent".

"Agreed. Guess that also explains why the message was cut-off in such an abrupt manner during mid-repeat. No doubt the sender meant to continue sending her warning on automatic repeat. However, when the colony's men began their sneak attack, she destroyed this chamber to prevent them from sending us any messages of their own".

"Yes, Commodore", Gloria nodded, sighing, depressed beyond all measure even entertaining such a thought.

Ugly as it was there were no longer any way they could deny any further the simple truth staring each and every one of them straight in the eye. While such a conflict between the genders was as inconceivable as it was likewise repugnant to all the higher senses, there was still no denying any of the overwhelming evidence proving now Eartha's Wei-Chang's earlier claim.

From here on out her earlier hypothesis the carnage outside was gender inspired passed now from the realm of mere conjecture into that of irrefutable fact. However, even so, this did nothing but leave them with an even greater mystery. Posing even more questions than it answered, Gloria was first to voice aloud what troubled them both:

"Granted there was some sort of 'sexual civil war' here as Dr. Wei-Chang put it, the women here sending us their message before dying. That still doesn't explain the motive behind what happened here, or what it has to do with what happened to the people of 'C-1' nearly seven thousand years ago. What, if there's any connection, destroyed them too??".

"Oh, I'm sure there is, indeed, a connection. I'm sure of it!" Jenniboni declared, resolute: "However, whatever it might be, I doubt the answer's here. Maybe, hopefully, we'll find something more on those storage chips. Did you manage to recover all of them?"

"Yes, Ma'am!"

"Excellent, then. In that case I think we've achieved here all we're going to. Let's go see now how the others have also fared in our absence, what their investigations have likewise uncovered".

****

Leaving the command module's stale, dark interior both Commodore and Lieutenant found themselves greeted at once by the sight of the other members in their party. Gathered about the ancient relic's only way in they were clearly waiting on the reappearance of their ship's C.O..

While each officer present waited in quiet anticipation of giving Jenniboni her own, particular report there wasn't really that much to tell, both Phyllis and Cecilia first to offer up their initial findings.

Having discovered nothing more than some community warehouse stocked with all those items one would expect to find there anyway, they reported likewise a fair-sized garage alongside it, a wide variety of all-terrain vehicles gathering a thick layer of fine dust inside its murky confines. And being the consummate engineer she always was, is, and forever would be Gloria wished at once she could sneak if possible a quick peak at such vintage relics—a desire enhanced when learning as well they were all in equally mint condition.

Unfortunately she'd have to settle for some four-wheel land rover some forty meters away left these last few years to the outside environment. Badly rusted from the inside-out it included the skeletal remains of what Dr. Wei-Chang assured them were four men resting either inside, or lying about on the close-by ground.

Disappointing as that might have been Gloria... along with everyone else... was nevertheless interested in learning how neither Phyllis, nor Cecilia's thorough investigation of either building turned up any further sign of such meaningless carnage.

Nor did their interest wane upon learning the same held true for those other buildings toured by both Dr. Wei-Chang, Toni, and Ens. Olivia Patterson—one of Toni's other scouts. Giving their report with professional dispatch all three women revealed an equal lack of any dead in all those rustic structures they likewise searched from top to bottom.

Touring both a quaint little town hall, community hospital, church, and combination commissary/grange the only time Eartha's calm exterior faltered even a little bit was during a quite elaborate summary of all she'd seen touring the colony's rather well-stocked medical-aid facilities.

Only then did Jenniboni find it rather incumbent on her part to interrupt the good doctor's report least the other woman continued forever, describing with mounting enthusiasm each obsolete tool of her profession contained therein. All Jenniboni wanted now, having heard now all she needed to, was to find that last surviving member of this Gosh-forsaken colony and get off that lousy moon-world as soon as possible.

Unless those silicon chips now in Lt. Greensley's tool kit held in store some similar treasure trove of information revealing what happened here, Jenniboni remained now confident the last settler left standing here could tell them far more. Or at least far more than they could ever learn just hanging about at their present location, easy targets for whatever dark forces might still linger thereabouts, lying out there in possible wait for their very lives.

Beginning at once on Jenniboni's sharp command a most thorough scan of the entire area, seeking any sign whatsoever of Human life, it was only a few moments later Eartha announced the object of their search just some six-hundred meters away. From the direction she likewise indicated this placed the elusive individual in question somewhere across the nearby river, lying low it would seem in the tangled farmland growing wild on the opposite bank:

"Excellent", Jenniboni responded, full of grim resolve: "Very good. In that case let's just vacate this miserable mortuary, try to rescue some life from out of all this death!"

Regardless however their common desire to leave the entire vicinity behind them Jenniboni still found herself unable to do so, stopping one last time to remedy just one last, personal concern. Circling about that remaining bit of derelict spacecraft still between her and the final goal of their joint mission, hoping at first to simply take leave of such miserable surroundings, it was also then she found herself quite unable to.

Cutting a wide path around the aforementioned command module, having quite forgotten about what she saw fluttering in the wind earlier that very same hour, Jenniboni was all the same brought up short by a long, spindly shadow falling right across her immediate path.

Taking time to rediscover what it might be she was likewise met with a tall flagpole, the familiar sound of tattered cloth fluttering in the breeze high above her head. Gazing up at that battered flag from before, moved yet again by its wretched condition, Jenniboni found herself quite unable to just leave it behind, leaving it once more to such a sad, ignoble fate.

Feeling it would be both a disgrace and even a travesty to just leave it up there like so much forgotten trash, it was with similar resolve she decided to take it with them. Maybe there was nothing StarChild could do for the pitiable dead lying all about her, but maybe there was something she could do at least for that battle-weary symbol of all they held dear—that constant reminder of cherished friends, family, and former homes back on Earth.

Knowing how she'd likewise feel if that were the Tammyite 'Rose Banner' of all Womankind flying up there—its green, pink, and even gold surface in such a mournful state (a proud, gold fempacem overlapping a double-pink Rose set against a field of deep forest green) there was no doubt in the name of all that was holy what she had to do.

Speaking out in a strong voice full of profound emotion, almost too choked-up to speak at all, Jenniboni spoke out in memory of both these people and their lost homeland resting now beneath miles of deepest ocean:

"Before we do anything else, Gentlewomen, I want that flag taken down from there at once ... *right now*! ... show it at long last some decent respect. We'll take it back home with us to where it will be treated once more with full honours!!"

Ordering Toni to lower it from where it kept silent vigil for so very long it was right about then, soon after her last proclamation, Jenniboni decided it most fitting to present this object of former veneration to *'The Institute for Stellar Exploration'* back on Earth—its faded red, white, and blue almost the only thing of these vanquished people that would survive this ruinous world.

There it would be well-kept, lovingly preserved, and shown great deference by all those who came to see it. In this special way the noble memory of these forgotten people would also be kept. Jenniboni's resonant voice rang out once more, full of ultimate authority, deciding to treat this occasion with all the proper decorum it so richly deserved:

"Attention!" she commanded, quite brisk, giving the command to salute.

Everyone there doing so, eyes focused straight ahead, each officer present understood just as well the deep, rich significance of this precious moment as those long neglected stars-and-stripes of days gone by completed their final journey down that tall pole.

Reaching bottom, having performed these many years so far above the very call of duty, Toni removed it ever so gently from its former post, doing the best she could considering its delicate, fragile condition. Taking equal care least it touch the ground she then proceeded to fold the ancient cloth the best she could according to strict protocol, handing it soon thereafter to Jenniboni.

StarChild's C.O., accepting it likewise with heartfelt deference, summoned as well to her side Dr. Wei-Chang, requesting her ship's C.M.O. bring over the compact, streamlined, portable medical unit she brought along 'just in case'.

Assuming correctly what her commanding officer had in mind, Eartha opened wide the flat P.M.U. complete with gold caduceus on its highly polished surface as Jenniboni slipped the fragile cloth inside that snug, protective flap built right into the medical briefcase's glistening, black lid.

Sealing secure once more that solid transport now serving as official flag-bearer Jenniboni set out yet again in search of that one last colonist still alive. Seeking out that one last resident of 'Paradise Lost' the rest of her party followed close-by in tight formation.

Chapter 48

"DRAGONS"

"I don't care what you say", Naomi confided, whistling quite loud in absolute awe: "Now THAT'S impressive!!"

Beyond the grand entranceway at which they all stood, staring with beleaguered senses at what lay before them on 'C-1', each member of the away team was taken aback at the sight of a vast circular chamber of incredible proportions curved along its outer rim as far as the eye could see.

A cavernous expanse appearing to stretch forever into the farthest distance, every square inch of available wall space was lined with row-upon-row of glistening computer consoles replete with multi-purpose access terminals.

And at the center of all this they were each greeted as well by the sight of a massive pit no more than some twenty-five meters away.

Perfectly rounded at its very edge it occupied as well the vast majority of this immense complex, an infernal opening at whose very center a wide cylinder possessing the same grotesque grandeur as everything else reached high above them—a monstrous 'tube' containing within its transparent casing a churning mass of energy plasma swirling about in quite luminous blue/green patterns.

Drawing ever closer to the guardrail encompassing that hellish pit all four women peered over its very edge.

Appearing quite bottomless in its obscene dimensions that awful tube at that colossal crater's very center seemed to likewise vanish quite readily into this dead world's very bowels—reaching likewise upward in the same exaggerated fashion until seeming as well to disappear at the very pinnacle of the grand tower in which they all now stood:

"Hope nobody here has vertigo", Naomi quipped, her voice somewhat shaky from absolute awe:

"Amazing", she whispered, already scanning that dazzling cylinder now the primary focus of her considerable attention: "According to my readings here the energy level inside that colossal contraption haven't dropped more than

0.0000000001 percent since this power matrix was first activated seven millennia ago".

"Excuse me, Ma'am, but what exactly does that mean?", Naomi heard Ensign Umbota speak for the very first time since landing on this dark, frigid planet.

"It means Ensign that this thing's power source has a greater life expectancy than either 'Centauri-A', 'B', and/or 'C' combined!"

"It also means that whoever built this giant gizmo meant it to last forever", Frances added. Although hidden from sight under her smart armor the scowl she wore was nevertheless reflected in her very tone:

"So if the main reason for this tower was some sort of warning buoy this would prove as well its builders had equally good reason to believe in the indestructible nature of whatever it was that destroyed them here. Clearly they were confident it would pose an equal threat to anyone else foolish enough to come here no matter how far in the future".

"Maybe not", Naomi offered hopefully: "Not if this entire edifice was built any time before what happened here".

"Maybe so, maybe not", Frances allowed, rather surly: "But be that as it may I don't plan for any of us to stick around here long enough to find out. So I suggest most strenuously we do what we came here for in the first place, leaving here just as quickly".

Taking up defensive positions, wasting no time deciding how they should proceed further, both Frances and her two security personnel began at once to guard Naomi on every side—Naomi herself seeking the exact relay granting free access to all the alien data stored up on their every side, sending it back as well to Maccs once having found it.

Finding the exact object of her search soon enough she took out right thereafter the data transfer modem from her portable tool kit both she and Gloria worked on the night before, hooking it up with equal speed to that alien array of complex technology all around them.

Doing so Naomi found herself likewise wondering how her young deputy was likewise fairing alongside the rest of that other away team now exploring 'AB-1.5'. However, upon completion of her work, thoughts switched instead to StarChild's bridge, contacting them through use of that long-range comm. unit in her helmet.

Informing Stasha all was now ready for final transfer confirmation wasn't long in coming, Stasha giving Naomi her complete 'go-ahead' to begin.

Watching with intense interest the various lights embedded in those alien display panels come to brilliant life, flashing and flickering on and off now in multi-uniform patterns, it was with a sense of silent reverence Naomi now found herself immersed in deep speculation.

Wondering as to the hidden content of all that alien knowledge now in the process of being downloaded aboard StarChild himself, she remained confident she'd know more upon gaining access to the deepest recesses of Maccs' biosynthetic memory.

Listening to the soft hum of complex technology seemingly everywhere, transfixed by the intricate glory of it all, Naomi wasn't aware of the danger barreling down that very moment on one-and-all. At least not until Frances' rather calm voice intruded on her silent reverie:

"Well, 'White Knight', I think your 'dragons' have just arrived".

****

Such a bizarre comment, both cryptic and provocative at the very same time, couldn't help but capture Naomi's complete attention. Turning about in the direction of yet another sound now roaring down upon them like some runaway locomotive, her eyes were at first unable to comprehend what exactly it was they were looking at:

Or at least not for the briefest of seconds.

However, the moment it finally sank in what those blasted things really were, the first caustic remark leaping to mind was…

"Yeah, and they're even uglier than anything out of any story book!"

All four women watched now two massive forms both red and black enter that colossal chamber from distant gateways.

Situated on either side of that vast pit in front of them, separated by that ponderous distance between, each bizarre monstrosity approached StarChild's away team with lightening rapidity from opposite sides of the nearby pit. Nor was there any denying both their deadly intent, their hostile purpose, alongside their awesome girth.

"Frances was right!" Naomi muttered, full of bitter irony: "Didn't these people ever think small?"

"Sentry robots!" it was now Frances' turn to insist, doing so in a brisk, analytical voice almost devoid of all panic. Remaining calm in the face of such apparent danger she simply calculated her next logical move with the cool, level headedness of a professional strategist planning her next counter-strike.

"So how did they manage to avoid your expert security scans", Naomi wasted no time asking, almost accusatory.

"Must have some sort of hidden sensor camouflage built into their deepest hardware".

"Oh, lovely", Naomi muttered yet again, quite facetious in the face of advancing peril, the two alien monsters closing in even more on their tightly knit position. Barreling down on them on three gigantic wheels they were as bizarre in their appearance as they were ugly.

Their bodies hunched forward like that of a cyclist making a mad dash for the finish line eight snake-like tentacles ran likewise down each side of their elongated torsos, all whipping back and forth in a most highly agitated manner.

Yet even with all that 'going for them', the most disturbing aspect concerning their beastly features had to be their bulbous heads. Shaped like bloated tear-drops, two gaping 'nostrils' at the end of each their pointed snouts, a saurian crest rose up likewise from the back of each their heads.

Fanning out to form a single, cyclopean eye right on top of each mechanized horror they were both bulbous and milky white in both form and substance, bringing to mind nothing less than a monstrous cataract.

Standing nearly ten meters in height, glossy black bodies replete with tiger-like red stripes, it was all too apparent these terrible titans were designed on purpose to strike fear into the hearts of all those daring to intrude upon their specific territory.

Quite successfully, too, Naomi had to confess.

Everyone present inching their way back to the open egress through which they first entered this forbidding chamber, the stripped behemoth approaching from the left was easily the closest.

Packing away her precious tools as quickly as possible it was this hostile sentry that posed the greatest threat to Naomi's already precarious situation, Ensign Umbota raising her armed gauntlets in defense of StarChild's Chief Engineer.

Standing right between Naomi and the charging monster both Frances and Ensign Wilson joined in, opening simultaneous fire on the intruding titan. The approaching creature's massive head snapping to min their direction, it likewise returned on all four women trespassing on its home turf.

Twin beams of burning light soaring at them with a high-pitched whine from its very nostrils they struck Ensign Umbota right in the stomach, throwing her back with considerable force right into that computer panel at which Naomi still stood.

Turning about, swinging into action the moment this happened, Naomi still experienced a certain amount of happy relief noticing her protector was all the same undamaged. Despite such brutal force employed against her very person Lt. Umbota's armour nevertheless provided her ample protection against the otherwise deadly weapons fire.

Left no more than a wee bit stunned Naomi helped the battered woman remain all-the-same steady on her own two feet. Grabbing her tool kit in one hand, clutching the case by its padded shoulder strap, Naomi likewise put her other arm around Ensign Umbota's waist, the other woman draping her right arm around Naomi's shoulder.

Only then did Naomi realize she forgot the data transfer unit still sending information back to StarChild:

"Freak it!" Naomi hissed in reply to such otherwise trivial concerns, still helping along the young Afro-Ahnteekahn security guard at her side. Might as well let it continue broadcasting as long as possible.

Glancing up instead in the very direction they were now headed Naomi took immediate note of the second sentry now within firing range, targeting with her right arm—her laser gauntlet—the oncoming monster quite intent now on blocking off their only escape route.

Ensign Umbota taking similar aim with her left, both women hurled at that beastly mechanoid a mighty barrage of blue-white laser pulses—Frances and Ensign Wilson opening equal fire behind them on that first enemy Cyclops threatening their already precarious position from the opposite direction.

Striking their target smack-dab in the very center of its slick, black chest Naomi experienced a brief moment's jubilation at sight of the deep cuts their rapid discharge left in its considerable wake. It was a moments exultation that turned sour soon enough though, realizing they failed to penetrate the thick armor-plating protecting that rampaging obscenity's very interior.

Knocking the nasty apparition back nothing more than a little bit in its determined stride, feeling at the very same time quite cheated indeed, all she and Ensign Umbota achieved in the end was nothing more than a momentary head start already diminishing. Reaching first their escape route, the exit to that now deadly chamber behind them, Naomi looked over her shoulder.

Calling out to Frances to get a move-on the other two security personnel were still defending their position, following close behind just a couple of scant meters away. It wasn't until all four away team members crossed that broad threshold back into the corridor beyond, Naomi saw that first nightmare from before attack the little data relay unit she was forced to abandon.

Lashing out at the defenseless little mechanism with one of its frantic tentacles, the tiny little link-up burst into flames at first contact. Giving voice as well to a loud, crackling whine its many parts went flying about like some sad little balsa-wood toy crushed instead under the awful wheels of some rampaging truck.

"Oh, well", Naomi grinned, rather philosophical in light of all which just happened, propping up as well the still dazed Ensign Umbota against the nearest available wall:

"So much for several hours hard work".

Once sure her young sister-in-arms was quite all right all on her own Naomi went about sealing up as well the way they just came. Giving that now her full attention her fondest hope was to at least delay for a while those death machines almost right on top of them. This time she didn't bother with her tool kit, using instead one of those armed gauntlets almost a very part of her.

Bringing down yet again that immense blockade barring their way earlier into the very same chamber they now fled, Naomi pressed the crystal-blue tip of her narrow weapon against one of those exposed circuits she re-wired earlier on, releasing a carefully channeled burst of energy into that very same mechanism.

Sparks flying all about, the heavy grey seal rumbling this time down from above, it blocked their enemy's way with nary a moment to spare. Nor did she stop there. Standing back a little further she fired off yet another round of bright blue fire. Welding together every working part of the alien door lock least anyone, or anything else ever try opening it again she hoped to prevent forever its ability to be re-opened:

"Cutting it a little close, wouldn't you say"; Frances asked with just a trace of wry humor.

"Well you know how I like to add a pinch of spice to every occasion no matter how mundane", Naomi answered in like, her broad grin most audible in both tone and timbre.

"And how are you doing, Ensign? How do you feel?", Frances turned now more serious, her attention focused now on Ens. Umbota.

"I'm all right, Ma'am: Just a little dizzy, a little sore. I'm just lucky Lt.

Cmdr. Marlowe was there to save me".

"Think nothing of it, girlfriend", Naomi smiled, feeling rather awkward on the receiving end of such praise: "My pleasure".

"Will you be able to make it on your own now, or do you still need further assistance?", Frances continued in a quite understanding fashion, motioning Ensign Wilson to her side.

"No, thank you, Ma'am", Ens. Umbota assured her: "I can make it".

Standing up straight now, forsaking the ample support of the wall she was now just leaning up against, Ms. Umbota wasted no time at all waving away the other junior security officer just before Ens. Wilson reached her.

"I hate to interrupt", Naomi cut in nonetheless, "but shouldn't we contact the ship and let both them and Commodore Saphira know of our situation?"

"Yes. Of course", Frances agreed, straightaway. Having not long to wait for a reply Frances passed on soon enough Jenniboni's explicit orders to abandon at once their current position, returning just as quickly to StarChild.

"*Look, Cmdr. Straker!*" Ensign Wilson called out no sooner had Frances finished, her voice carrying with it a clear hint of alarm.

Looking at once in the direction she indicated everyone else took equal notice of what caught Ms. Wilson's undivided attention, a pair of sizzling white pin-pricks appearing now on either side of that grey partition separating women from sentry-bots.

Two points of light appearing first at the portal's base, metal sparks shooting forth in rapid stream, each pinprick was soon joined by an equally loud hissing. Bright streaks of molten-hot light soon forming, they moved ever upward in steady progression.

"Little creeps sure don't give up, do they?!" Naomi sneered just as Frances gave sharp instructions to move out: "And at that rate they'll be right on top of us in no time!!"

Chapter 49

"RODNEY AND THE ANDROIDS"

None of the away team to 'AB-1.5' could deny her intense feelings of utter relief leaving behind them the colony proper, leaving also behind them its constant reminder of tortured lives ending in tragic death.

Although each woman present was just as unable to observe the different expression each of her sisters likewise wore beneath her protective armor, every one of them remained just as certain the others were no less glad than she to reach the river's other side.

'Paradise' now divided from their present position by that flowing river separating it from the farmland ahead they stopped at the edge of a dense cornfield. Having just traversed one of the three bridges they spied earlier during their shuttle's first approach Dr. Wei-Chang found herself close enough to the corn ahead to hear each dusty, yellow/brown stalk swaying about.

She could even hear it growing in the late afternoon/early evening breeze, a subtle yet audible crackling sound quite distinct. Not having long to ponder it further though, Jenniboni ordered Eartha right about then to put down the P.M.U. she still carried, telling her to search instead the broad patch of tall corn for any signs of human life.

Telling her to do so with her medical scanner like before Eartha searched that thicket of dense vegetation for any signs whatsoever of Human life hiding among all those grayish stalks. Everyone else remaining quiet in mounting anticipation of the final result, each tried as well to catch her own distinct hint of whatever might be lurking out there.

Having intimate acquaintance with such agrarian surroundings the first among them all to note anything out of place was, of course, one Lt. Gloria J. Greensley. Unable to see with her eyes anything out of place she was able nonetheless to hear the light, subtle sound of someone close-by, hidden as they were in all that dense vegetation.

Hard to hear much over all that rustling, crackling corn growing in those early twilight hours Gloria proved herself able even so to hear someone close-by, someone trying their darndest to remain as-quiet-as-quiet-can-be while unable at the very same time to resist the natural strain of tired, aching muscles.

Forcing from that individual some movement no matter how small the more that mysterious individual tried to remain still, frozen in one position, the more their weary body required of them some manner of physical activity no matter how slight.

Confident her ears weren't deceiving her, needing little time to convince herself, Gloria told the Commodore all she 'knew' just seconds before Eartha announced as well the results of the search she was likewise conducting:

"Are you sure, Lieutenant?", Jenniboni asked. A wee bit dubious she found it hard to believe anyone at all could hear something so unobtrusive over the sound of all those crops stirring about in the pre-twilight breeze.

"Yes, Ma'am: Where I grew up on Mars we had both corn and wheat fields outside the town I lived in and, when we were children, we'd play hide-n-go-seek in them. After a while you just ended up able to tell where..."

"She's right!", Eartha cut in right about then with her own professional findings. Even though Dr. Wei-Chang just backed her up with the results of her own expert investigation, Gloria felt nonetheless a slight stab of petty resentment being cut-off so right in mid-sentence, feeling as though the older woman just stole her thunder.

Even so her brief disappointment didn't last all too long, mollified as it was when Commodore Saphira complimented Gloria on her both her excellent powers of hearing as well as her superior talent for deductive reasoning.

"There's someone less than a dozen meters ahead of us just to the right of our current position", Eartha announced, continuing where she just left off.

"Can you determine anything more than the mere fact they're Human?"

"No. Sorry, Commodore. The magnetic interference from above is still proving itself a most effective deterrent in achieving more accurate information".

Assuring the conscientious woman next to her she understood completely, Jenniboni turned then the focus of her immediate attention toward that mystery person in hiding. Calling out to the hidden colonist, doing so in a loud voice, she commanded them to come forth.

Wondering if that reluctant entity out there might in fact pose some risk she added quickly in a most calm, even voice that, although they meant no harm, each one of them was, if need be, capable of self-defense. About to include the fact they were also from the Tammyite Matriarchate Jenniboni changed her mind, announcing instead they were from Earth. Doing so, she realized no one from ancient 21st century America would know the current name for Womankind's entire civilization.

Feeling as though hanging from tenterhooks after their C.O. finished talking everyone there likewise held her breath before anything else really happened, waiting for a good while in utter suspense until hearing at last the timid, hesitant approach of someone pushing their way through brittle vegetation.

First to appear were a pair of grubby, dirty, dust-streaked hands spreading aside the last remaining crops between both them and Jenniboni's party… these slowly followed by the bronzed form of a young, prepubescent boy staring at them with wary eyes.

Leaping back yet again into hiding at the very sight of those seven armor-clad women standing now right before him, a look of sheer fright spread quickly across his entire face:

"Honey, Sweetie, wait!!" Jenniboni cried out, full of compassion, seeing the poor man-child's vivid terror: "We're here to help you, take you back to Earth with us!"

Aware right away what must have frightened the poor young laddie, seeing only one real way in which to gain his trust, Jenniboni nevertheless warned her officers not to follow suit.

At least he didn't retreat any further upon last hearing her voice. That in itself was encouragement enough to proceed even further, remaining all-the-same cautious every step of the way.

Feeling as though treading barefoot on broken glass Jenniboni crouched down on her shapely haunches in a low, squatting position removing her helmet with similar caution.

Breathing in the unfiltered air of this new moon-world all around her she noticed first the fragrant scent of blooming flora, the familiar perfume of lush plant-life she found herself often missing on Demeter—a warm summer's breeze reminiscent also of life before StarChild brushing her cheek in light caress:

"See, hon", Jenniboni spoke again in gentle voice to the scared child back once more in timid seclusion, her voice possessing no longer that strange mechanical quality courtesy of those speaker units an intricate part of her armor-plated headgear:

"You have nothing to fear from any of us", she promised. Biding her time, waiting quite patiently for him to take the initiative… make that crucial first move… Jenniboni's patience was rewarded at last when the young boy in hiding finally stepped out in the open.

Doing so in a most timid, fearful way like some gun-shy fawn revealing himself to her, the young man-child had golden-brown skin and bleached-blonde hair thanks to constant exposure to the twin yellow suns beginning now to set on the distant horizon.

His only real clothing a pair of faded, dirty blue-jeans two sizes too small for him—nearly in rags—his body was streaked as well with both dust and grime while, beneath a full head of long, stringy hair his pale, ice-blue eyes possessed an almost wild, feral quality mingled with his remaining doubt.

Dirt and long hair aside he looked nonetheless quite healthy on the surface, not to mention rather comely under all that mess. A diamond in the rough with an already handsome, angular face and trim, graceful physique Jenniboni could already to see in the young pre-teen no more than just eleven… or maybe twelve… the handsome young laddie he was sure to grow into.

Nor did it escape her keen powers of observation that, subtracting from this estimate the time it likewise took his people's warning to reach the Commonwealth, this would have made him the tender age of just six, or seven when the rest of his people met their mournful end.

No older than J.J. was now at the time they all died it tore at Jenniboni's heart to think of someone so very young, so very innocent, having to witness such brutal carnage, his parents no doubt among the other dead back there in Paradise.

Oh, how he must have suffered so terribly living all these years since then in such utter isolation, no Human company whatsoever to draw comfort from.

Quite overcome with deep pity Jenniboni realized nonetheless she had to proceed with all due caution. Waiting for him to act first on his own initiative she was careful not to make any sudden move he might interpret as a threat, that might "spook" him.

Therefore it should come as no surprise that, when he finally chose to do so, opening his mouth at long last, his first words after so very long threw her for an absolute loop:

"Are you all girls?", he verily stuttered, as unused as he was to conversing with others after nearly five years. Peculiar first question to ask after all these years isolated from the rest of Womankind…

Especially when posed by such a young child.

Then again maybe it wasn't so very odd after all. Not with all his people massacred in what her ship's C.M.O. dubbed a 'sexual civil war'.

"Well, we're all 'women' if that's what you mean", Jenniboni smiled, sweetly, rather tickled by the boy's childish choice of words. It wasn't until hearing his following reply however Jenniboni started to wonder, quite perplexed.

If gendercide is indeed what occurred here then that would surely place him as it were in the "enemy camp". So why was his reaction one of obvious relief, a clearly audible gasp of sheer delight bursting forth from his very lips?

"Yeah! Sure! That's fine!! That'll be okay!", he gushed with great excitement in a rather strange, thick, twangy accent that, from what they already knew, had to be ancient American.

"Why is that okay?", Jenniboni felt herself compelled to ask, a note of puzzled worry creeping its way into her voice. Such a blatant display of unbridled joy in response to her somewhat simple answer seemed quite unwarranted.

However, wanting to question him further on the matter, she decided all-the-same not to when seeing the sudden return of abject fear in his eyes:

"Oh nothing", he mumbled now in a most evasive fashion: "Don't matter".

Unwilling then to scare him off by pursuing this particular line of questioning any further , Jenniboni concluded instead this was as good a time as any to ask him his name.

For a moment there it seemed the young laddie couldn't even remember, unsure of the answer to a question most take for granted. It was without-a-doubt heart-wrenching watching him struggle so hard for something so simple as the mere memory of just his own identity, the expression of absolute triumph when it finally came to mind almost as pathetic:

"My name is… 'Rodney'… 'Rodney Roderick'!"

"I'm very pleased to meet you, Rodney. My name is 'Commodore Jenniboni Saphira' and these are some members of my crew aboard 'StarChild', the ship we came here on", it was now Jenniboni's turn to introduce her staff, doing so with both a gentle smile and tender voice.

And when he soon asked her all about StarChild, Rodney listened to all she had to say with rapt, wide-eyed fascination. Telling him all she could think of which he might understand, Jenniboni began with the simple facts that StarChild was a research/exploration vessel able to travel faster than the speed of light.

And telling him it took only a few days to get here from Earth, she also mentioned its size and the fact that there were a little under 250 people—both officer and enlisted—serving aboard him.

Hearing this Rodney asked yet again in a voice full of hesitant curiosity, "And everyone there are gir… 'women' too?"

"Yes, Dear; they are", she soothed in the same gentle manner, all the while warning bells beginning to chime. This obsessive, almost paranoid preoccupation with the very gender of her crew began to make her more than just a wee bit apprehensive.

"Yeah! That'll be okay, too", he declared with yet another joyful exhale.

Enough was enough!!! With that Jenniboni made up her mind, beyond all doubt, to ask why, exactly, '… that'll be okay, too'.

Not getting the chance however she failed to do so when, noticing something from the corner of his eye, Rodney turned quite pale, numb with utter terror.

Staring over her left shoulder in the direction of 'Paradise', trembling all over like some little cold, wet puppy, he was overcome with such a stark expression of frantic horror mixed with sheer despair it froze Jenniboni's very soul with icy dread.

Saying not a word he just spun about right thereafter, fleeing back into that cornfield from whence he came, running for his very life as fast as his young legs could carry him.

"No, Rodney, don't go!" she called out in a plaintive voice, calling after him before even knowing what it was that spooked him so.

No use, however.

Listening to his rapid retreat through those dusty, dense cornstalks it was quite apparent he planned not to return.

Ordering both Toni and her remaining scout to find at once that retreating child growing further and further away Jenniboni also got swiftly to her own feet, turning about to see what so quickly scared him off.

The cause of his alarm quite obvious once spotted, Jenniboni wasted no time at all putting back on her sturdy helmet, fastening it most surely to the rest of her armor at the very sight of them.

Assuming with haste a defensive posture, aiming the slender lasers affixed to the back of each arm back across the river towards 'Paradise', the other four officers under her command followed likewise Jenniboni's lead.

Watching intently those dark apparitions appearing now across the river between them, all five women present were more than ready to do battle.

****

Ten in all, humanoid in form, they moved with slow progress towards that very bridge Jenniboni's landing party crossed just earlier. None of them in any apparent hurry they just plodded along, one and all, in close-knit formation.

"Stop right there!", Jenniboni raised her voice more so than originally intended, full of stern authority: "Our meaning here is peaceful but we are nonetheless quite capable of defending ourselves".

Taking heed right then-and-there of her warning those shadowy beings paused now in on the river's other side, keeping now quite still:

"We are also peaceful and wish only to meet with you in conversation", one of those spectral entities called out from the river's other side.

Having no real reason yet to doubt them in either word, or deed other than Rodney's frightened reaction to their sudden appearance, Jenniboni nonetheless took no pleasure in how they stood now between both her people and their initial escape route.

And taking note of this put her likewise in mind of their shuttle, mentally activating the telepathic comm. unit inside her helmet. Asking the remaining scout still standing guard there for an impromptu status report, it was with a certain sense of relief Jenniboni discovered all was at least well there, no trouble to report.

Not that this changed the fact Jenniboni didn't like those intimidating creatures in their current position, instructing her junior officer to likewise remain on constant alert. Better to have them on this side of the river between them, allowing her own people the fair option of hasty retreat across one of those other bridges remaining to their rear.

If these new arrivals did, in spite of their reassuring words, prove themselves hostile, she wanted at least a decent head start to the river's other side.

"Agreed, then. You may cross over this way and meet us here. Yet keep in mind we are both armed and, if need be, ready to defend ourselves".

With a lumbering gait rather ungainly at first the new arrivals did as Jenniboni ordered, crossing the bridge ahead in the same tight formation as before.

Caring little at all for their superior numbers Jenniboni instructed young Gloria to begin a most thorough, continuous scan of each of those unexpected visitors while the rest were instructed to keep their weapons likewise at the ready.

With both Toni and her well-versed scout unavoidably elsewhere this gave the advancing behemoths a tactical advantage of two-to-one. Even though Jenniboni had complete faith in both the expert skill and complete ability of all her crew, she still didn't appreciate having to operate on such an uneven keel.

370

It was only when each and every one of them reached the same riverbank as the team from StarChild Jenniboni could hear the distinctive hum of technology. The whirring sound of complex machinery in play, it grew ever louder with their continued approach.

Just as her original instinct told her the very first time she heard their flat, lifeless tone of voice: mechanoid's! These unwanted interlopers some sort of service 'droid. Ones that, by both the very sight and sound of them, seemed in need of further maintenance—something evident in both their awkward gait and loud, wheezing components in continual play.

Nor was their artificial status lost on Lt. Greensley, Gloria's initial scans confirming likewise Jenniboni's suspicions. Despite the endless magnetic interference experienced by all their scanning apparatus' this much was quite apparent right from the very get-go.

However, only partially comforted... her initial assumptions confirmed... Jenniboni maintained all-the-same her defensive posture.

Although such artificial life-forms were in the long run more predicable in action than their flesh-and-blood counterparts she had little way of knowing what their intended function was to begin with.

All she knew for certain was that they must have been built by the former inhabitants of 'C-1' millennia ago, such synthetic entities likewise beyond the primitive know-how of pre-Matriarchate Earth.

Then again, regardless, they still must have had some sort of previous contact with the colonists, the colonists from Earth no doubt the ones responsible for getting these mechanical beings up-and-running yet again. Jenniboni couldn't imagine an alien race from some seven millennia ago programming such creatures with a Terran dialect existing for little more than just one millennia ago.

Finding it amazing such ancient hardware was still operational in the very first place there still remained the nagging question whether, or not their original planners programmed these impressive examples of their handiwork with their own version of Asimov's 'Three Laws of Robotics'.

If not, depending on what function these long-lived creatures were first created for, they might all end up in really big trouble. Nor did their awesome physical proportions do much to quell Jenniboni's almost instinctual misgivings at the very sight of them drawing closer.

Standing nearly eight feet in height, broad in width with heavy armor-plating all their own they were solid, sturdy entities in their basic design. Their powerful legs, like burdensome tree-trunks growing ever wider upon their decent, ended likewise in flat, rounded feet while long, powerful arms resembling Human limbs likewise ended in mighty hands just as large.

Lacking neither in the torso, their hips narrowed upward at the wait only to widen out yet again, forming both massive chests and the broadest of shoulders.

Possessing from there on up short, thick necks topped off with large, domed heads, appendages not unlike the brim of some sports cap jutted out from just above their faces. Sheltering them from the light these extensions reached from temple-to-temple, lending their strange faces below a shadowy quality.

Granting them to be sure a most malevolent air as it was, needing no further assistance in their innate power to intimidate, such was… to Jenniboni's way of thinking… overkill. Almost insectoid in appearance their large, multi-faceted eyes glowed with a rather pale green light also shining forth from various air holes all arranged in circular patterns, openings where both a mouth and nose would normally go.

'Oozed forth' would be more precise a description of the way that sickly green luminosity flowed out of their every mechanical orifice, every exposed opening an integral part of their original design parameters.

Completely devoid of all Humanity, all recognizable expression, they were more than anything else like the walking dead. No wonder such artificial monstrosities never caught on in the Commonwealth, never gained popular acceptance. No technophobe by any stretch of the imagination Jenniboni nevertheless caught herself feeling these creatures were more than just unnatural, but unwholesome as well.

That sickly green luminescence spilling forth from behind metal faceplates bothered her the most, their mechanical features granting them no pleasant appearance to begin with. To her that ghostly green light had about it a quite distinct, putrescent quality bordering as well on the pernicious.

More than anything else maybe this would explain Jenniboni's somewhat snappish behavior, one of them reaching closer to her current position than she really cared for. Nine members of the advancing horde coming to an immediate halt some twelve yards away the tenth monster, now clearly in the lead, plodded even closer yet to both she and her crew.

"Stop right there!" Jenniboni called out, sharply. The nearing monster reaching within just five meters of where she stood, StarChild's commanding officer found herself more than ready to do battle:

"That's close enough for all of us to hear well what you have to say!"

"We understand your concern", the mechanoid in question tried reassuring her in a flat, dead voice truly devoid of all emotion: "However, at the same time, I assure you we are all quite harmless".

"Be that as it may I still want you to remain right where you are", it was now Jenniboni's turn to address the other.

"No problem", the entity now clearly 'Spokes' droid' for the rest of its group wasted no time giving her its guarantee: "We are simply here to serve. That is our only purpose in life".

"You have my full attention", Jenniboni granted. No less wary of these mechanicals she was willing all-the-same to give them the temporary benefit of the doubt:

Very temporary!!

"If at all possible I'd like to hear even more yet about both yourselves and what happened to all the people here".

Needing no further invitation to speak out on both accounts, the metal titan launched without delay into a short explanation of who exactly they were.

Nothing but a motley group of service 'droids built by the original settlers from 'C-1', mechanoids dwelling now in the northern Zelmorlite city, it likewise revealed during its flat, unfeeling monologue that those inhabitants of 'C-1' called their dead world 'Zelmorl', referring also to themselves as 'Zelmorlites'.

And in similar fashion Jenniboni soon learned 'AB-1.5' was known back then as 'Bandros', having now at her command actual names for these wretched new worlds.

Following this she was soon told Zelmorl was divided during its last days into two major spheres of influence—each highly antagonistic towards the other—a static, cold-war animosity resulting even later in open warfare for both possession and final control of Bandros.

Nor did Jenniboni need further clarification to guess the final outcome, the final result of this alien lust for power still quite obvious after no less than seven millennia.

Then, jumping ahead in the same dead monotone as always, the mechanical narrator of this tragic tale told her about the colonists from Earth, its account of their last days beginning with their discovery of the androids now before her.

Found at first inactive in the smaller, less intact alien city to the east of their position, all in a state of utter disrepair after several long millennia of sad neglect, they were likewise brought back to artificial 'life' by the will of those Terran explorers needing similar help building their own special, little 'Paradise'.

Paradise soon found itself "Paradise Lost" though when all those from Earth discovered themselves suffering a degenerative brain disorder following their lengthy journey from home, a malady brought about by their prolonged stay in cryogenic suspension.

Realizing there was nothing at all they could do to remedy this unfortunate circumstance, each and every one of them tried instead under such adverse conditions to simply carry on the best they could—insanity gaining control of their very lives by the time the male colonists stumbled over a subterranean cache of lethal arms left behind by Zelmorlite forces, repairing said instruments of mass destruction just as they had the androids.

According to the oppressive-seeming individual relating all this to Jenniboni the final showdown between the genders occurred here when, after a heated discussion between the community's men versus women, the female populace took exception to the male idea of adding these new weapons to their already existing armory brought all this way from Earth.

Claiming they were already in possession of enough arms to suit their present needs, the women likewise cared little for the most formidable power of these rather unpleasant alien additions. Taking quickly their leave of Paradise in quite an obvious huff the men all-the-same returned, attacking the women with their newly restored 'treasures'.

Inspired by a state of paranoid schizophrenia resulting from the aforementioned degenerative tissue damage to their cerebral cortex's, sure beyond all doubt each and every woman there was plotting against them, what followed for the female populace turned out nothing less than some doomed struggle for their very survival.

Taken by utter surprise by such ambush tactics, the women barely had time to distribute among themselves the contents of their own armory from Earth. Taking control of all Terran arms at the colony's disposal, the story that service droid told them from then on bore a strong resemblance to that earlier chain of events Dr. Wei-Chang likewise described.

Once more the physical evidence, without question, spoke for itself.

No less disturbing though was how the metal creature relating all this information fell silent yet again without any further preamble, having told Jenniboni all it seemed willing to say.

Instead it waited, mute and motionless, as though expecting now some sort of simple reply. Ignoring straightaway that lifeless hunk of mere metal Jenniboni addressed instead her erstwhile C.M.O., asking Eartha in a somewhat pensive voice for her own medical opinion concerning all they just heard:

"Personally, Commodore, I've never heard of anything like this occurring as a direct result of cryogenic suspension. Saying that however, I must also confess such methods of artificial life suspension were never attempted before for such long periods of time. At least not that I've heard of until now", Eartha felt compelled to add; hesitant, confused:

"Therefore, without the opportunity to run at this moment a more detailed time-lapse simulation of what really happened, I'm truly unable to say more concerning the definite results of over 800 years spent in such cryogenic hibernation", she continued.

Both disappointed... even disgusted... with herself for not being able to provide her direct superior more certain information, her feelings were quite evident in her very voice:

"Therefore, it could be just as our new 'friend' here says".

Picking up at once on Dr. Wei-Chang's emotional duress Jenniboni tried rendering her at least some small comfort, assuring the other woman she understood quite well her obvious dilemma.

Yet even so such news still left Jenniboni herself feeling both empty and depressed. What she just heard explained all, including even the colony's message to Earth replete with warnings of alien mischief afoot. No doubt it likewise shed light on Rodney's bizarre questions, his bizarre behavior, filling Jenniboni's heart with immense sorrow at the very thought of that poor boy being likewise afflicted.

Startled however by that lead 'droid once more addressing her, immersed as she was in her own sad musings, Jenniboni was surprised to hear it ask in similar fashion if her crew likewise traveled to Bandros in cryogenic slumber.

While still uncomfortable with these rather ominous beings of dark metal she could likewise see no real harm in telling them the truth, holding back nonetheless additional information on the subject of how exactly they got there.

Why she took such an immediate dislike to these creatures was, even to Jenniboni, as inexplicable as it was intense. Maybe it was the almost instinctual, even primordial nature of her feelings which defied all self-analysis: logic dictating that, as mere automatons, they were without question incapable of either lies, or any other act of outright duplicity.

Walking tools incapable of actual, intentional deceit on their part they were above all suspicion of any treachery, whatsoever. The most they could ever be accused of would be an honest error in their many electronic calculations, relaying faulty information by no fault of their own—this resting more in the purview of a mere malfunction of unreliable software than any malicious intent.

So why again was it Jenniboni found herself beyond any ability to trust any of these artificial life-forms still in her company; both revolted, and even repulsed, to the innermost core of her very being by their continued presence.

Nor did Jenniboni know at that very moment Gloria likewise felt uneasy in their company, also sure something here was amiss. Or, as the young people back home might put it, something 'Mega-Max Un-Right'!! As in the case of her ship's C.O. the young lieutenant still monitoring those metal titans couldn't give herself an exact reason for the way she felt.

All she knew for certain was that it had something to do with the rather anomalous readings her scanner provided in relationship to their complex internal structure, their many intricate components.

As it was she found it hard enough to simply manage any clear readings at all given all that electro-magnetic interference from above. All she knew for certain was that her mistrust stemmed strangely enough from their very speech patterns, the very words they spoke, unable even so to put her finger on what it was that bothered her most. All she knew for certain was that it had more to do with what they said, not the way they said it.

Her anxiety only doubled hearing that dread mechanoid's toneless reply to Jenniboni's previous remarks, her guarantee that her crew didn't come to Bandros in suspended animation. It was then Gloria's new-found sense of 'Mega-Max Un-Rightness' skyrocketed to the very heavens, hearing that automated monstrosity in the lead declare in its usual, normal, dispassionate manner:

"We are pleased to hear this, sure in our opinion Bandros still remains a perfect choice for colonization by your people. And if your people find themselves in need of any further help at all making this world theirs, they may consider us at their complete and utter disposal".

Gloria's sense of something wrong was joined in essence by Jenniboni's own case of the creepy-crawlies. Hearing that same dark creature offer up such a strange proposal, her already suspicious mind screamed a clear warning of immediate danger.

Nor was it a lie in any way to say that, for at least one insane moment right then and there, Jenniboni felt her immortal soul in absolute jeopardy just listening to such an otherwise innocuous offer—employing every ounce of will-power at her own considerable command to otherwise hide from them her undue sense of alarm.

Not wanting any of those leviathans before her to guess at her true feelings Jenniboni exercised complete control in the exact modulation of her voice—its very tone and timbre—when giving them her answer in as relaxed, as pleasant a manner as humanly possible:

"I can see no reason why those who sent us here would object to your most generous offer", Jenniboni gave assurance in more than agreeable terms:

"However, I'm not empowered at this time to speak on the matter so unilaterally without their unanimous consent. First I need to return to my ship, contacting our home worlds for further instruction in the matter".

"Understood", the obvious spokes 'droid for the rest of its party agreed, no hesitation at all: "Until then you know where to find us. We await your final decision".

Saying no more after this all ten mechanoids standing in front of the away team just took their immediate leave of one-and-all. Turning about on those same giant legs as before, they just wandered off in that very same direction they recently came.

Quite bewildered over all that just occurred Jenniboni likewise let them go with nary a word. Glad to just see them leave it wasn't until after that she thought it odd none of those automated entities asked at all why they were there, why she and her crew were trespassing on their home turf in the very first place. Instead they all just plodded off, mute, in the direction they came from right from the very beginning.

Considering from the start all those other questions they raised why didn't they ask more? About to solicit further opinion from those beneath her, gage as well each of their reactions to all they just heard, Jenniboni was brought up short instead by Lt. Matthias's look of utter shock—her eyes bulging wide on the other side of the narrow viewing strip part of her armored headgear.

"Commodore Saphira!", she blurted out in all due haste, her very tone an urgent one: "I've just received an important communiqué from Lt. Cmdr. Straker!!"

Chapter 50

"FALLEN KNIGHT"

Corridor followed corridor in swift progression when a raucous clamor thundered all about them. Reverberating from behind throughout the entire tower, followed soon thereafter by a quite jarring vibration passing through the very soles of their insulated titanium footwear, the sound of dense metal-against-metal followed swiftly thereafter.

Those two sentry-bots from before!

Free now to continue the hunt, drawing ever closer in swift pursuit, they made very good time indeed.

'Too good', Frances was painfully aware, the entire landing party turning yet another sharp corner into yet another curved passage.

Likewise aware there was no real hope of outrunning those lethal nightmares still hot on their trail it was then she chose with equal resolve to just turn and fight, stand their ground regardless.

"But our weapons can't penetrate their outer defenses", Naomi soon warned her, hearing what Frances had in mind.

"I know we can't do any serious damage to their armor plating, but would I be correct in assuming those milky white orbs on top of their heads are some sort of motion detector?"

"Yes!" Naomi shot back, a gleam of triumphant hope, realizing what it was Frances had in mind.

"Very good, then", it was now Frances's turn, explaining further.

Speeding along down that very same hall from which they just came the rumbling approach of their mechanized enemy was joined as well now by a pair of lengthy shadows headed their way.

Turning about in the direction of those charging watchdogs giving chase to all four women, each of the away team members took careful aim just as the first sentry rounded the sharp corner between them. Taking aim together at the first metal titan before it had a fair chance to complete its turn around that exact same corner, all four fired their weapons in a coordinated effort.

Doing so while both its massive head and pointed snout remained in full profile four fine, brilliant blue beams struck with utter perfection that particular titan's one and only eye, that cyclopean appendage bursting with a mighty pop like some water-filled balloon.

Both sparks and partial fragments of what remained flying now in every which direction, the injured device crashed instead into the pearly white wall directly in its way, both blind and unable to slow down its forward momentum.

Careening out of control with a mighty, ear-splitting crash worthy of some ten-car pile-up it lost all at once its precarious balance, going down **hard**. A fallen goliath it lashed out at anything in its reach like some demented psycho-child pitching some insane fit, tentacles whipping around in a frenzy at the very air around it.

Whipping and rolling about, throwing a quite hysterical tantrum, it occupied the entire corridor's grand width, blocking the other guard 'bot's very path, the second 'bot appearing just seconds after.

Attempting to repeat their earlier success with this sentry as well the away team soon discovered it was the 'smarter' of the two. Swiveling its head to both the left and right it prevented them from taking proper aim at its only legitimate Achilles Heel. Firing about in wild determination it hindered only further all their noble efforts.

Bright laser-fire plowing deep grooves into both walls and ceiling it filled the entire passage with burning discharge from its devilish nostrils. Although hardly co-coordinated in its choice of aim that didn't stop it from getting in at least one good shot, stray laser-fire catching Ensign Wilson off-guard.

One nasty round of burning discharge slamming straightaway into her protective headgear, it impacted with the transparent visor through which she viewed the world around her. Made out of clear titanium alloy formed to withstand such intense heat the young Ensign proved lucky enough, managing to withstand that energy pulse lifting her otherwise off the ground.

Spinning her about as she went sprawling backwards she landed with a loud thud fully intact.

Yet, while luckily uninjured, the extreme heat of that alien discharge managed to blacken that once crystal clear metal. Leaving in its wake a brutal scorch mark the poor woman staggered yet again to her feet, Ens. Wilson's back turned now to that remaining leviathan. Utterly blind she had no way of knowing her attacker had yet another foul trick up its proverbial sleeve.

Even with it's somewhat limited awareness that simple automaton wreaking so much havoc realized soon enough it couldn't eradicate its prey with any greater efficiency.

At least not at its present rate, continuing in the protection of its own imperiled vision. This all-consuming thought occupying its very one-track mind it chose at that exact same moment to switch tactics—releasing a dense series of slender, highly lethal darts from hidden storage units deep within its many tentacles.

Resembling more than anything else crystalline quills from some giant porcupine they rained down in steady procession on the white-clad bipeds thwarting its further progress. Rebounding quite harmless off their compact, skin-tight armor none of those brave individuals fighting now for their very lives could even feel *in the least* all those otherwise deadly projectiles bouncing off them.

Better however for the hapless young ensign had she proven able to feel at least something, some small hint of what was going on all about her—some sort of warning, no matter how slight, of the very great danger she was in.

Unaware of anything *at all* but her inability to see all she wanted at that very moment was to simply remove that current obstruction to her vision. An automatic reflex born more out of temporary panic than higher reason what she did next was an act of pure instinct.

And in her both confused, and even disoriented state of mind it would likewise prove her very last… ***most fatal***… error in judgment.

"NO, ENSIGN", Frances cried out in dire warning, seeing for herself what her foolish underling had in mind:

"DON'T TAKE OFF THAT HELMET!!!!"

Too late though, Ens. Wilson having already activated the release mechanism in back of her head. Frances could only watch in numb disbelief, a growing sense of absolute horror, as her young subordinate begin removing her protective headpiece from the rest of her armored attire.

By the time her commanding officer's urgent order registered on her beleaguered mind her life was already forfeit. Giving her no further chance to obey a razor-sharp dart burrowed its way deep into her flesh. Slamming at once into the very base of her skull the crystalline projectile severed as well her spinal cord.

Plunging its way deep into her brain, hands shooting upwards in absolute surprise at a straight angle before her, Ms. Wilson's now useless helmet went soaring into the air. Landing with a dull thud midway between both her and those stunned shipmates she now left behind, the others could only stare in sick horror.

Watching her eyes pop open wide as she fell now to her knees, the young woman's startled lips forming a rounded "O" of utter surprise, her abandoned helmet went briefly rolling across the floor to where Frances still stood, stopping at her feet.

Each of the survivors she left behind could easily recognize that very spark of life once there in her eyes now die, their fallen comrade already dead as she fell forward. And knowing all the same she could do nothing now to save the other woman's life, Frances rushed nonetheless over to that motionless body lying there in bitter repose.

"What are you doing? There's nothing you can do. We need to get out of here", Naomi called after her.

While not insensitive to how her dearest friend now felt, the practical pragmatist dwelling at the root of Naomi's very person considered it more prudent to make good their escape while possible. She and Ens. Umbota still maintaining a rapid barrage of steady laser-fire aimed at the remaining death machine, its progress was held up at least for the moment by the prone body of its fallen twin.

"We'll go soon enough", Frances shot back, both angry and defiant: "but we're taking her with us. There's no way, come Heck or high water, I'm going to leave her to the tender mercy of those … those … **things**!!"

Saying no more than that, feeling nothing more was needed, she crouched down at Ens. Wilson's side. Averting her eyes from the tortured sight of that lethal dart anchored deep in her fallen officer's skull Frances lifted instead her lifeless subordinate up from the floor. Ignoring the nasty protrusion she rested instead the fallen ensign over her shoulder in a powerful firewoman's carry.

"**Now** we may leave", Frances granted at long last. Leading the way with her painful burden both Naomi and Ens. Umbota brought up the rear, delaying their relentless foe with yet another heavy barrage of continuous laser-fire.

Still firing round after round at their mindless adversary, last one to turn the next sharp corner into yet another Spartan corridor, Naomi remained likewise in defensive mode when witnessing something that made her gorge rise, wanting as she did at that very moment to heave.

Dawning on the beastly contraption at long last why it was getting nowhere it liquidated its fallen comrade with swift barbarism. Slamming all its many tentacles down upon its blind twin it made short work of that other juggernaut's pointless thrashing about.

Not content with just bashing its companion's head in though, its crushed collection of ruined bits flying about every which way, the second red/black monster kept whipping away still yet at what remained. It didn't matter that the first of those two behemoths lay now perfectly still, it's useless struggle already brought to an immediate end.

No matter to the one still standing its dead ally ceased already its frenzied, frantic flailing away at every single thing within its immediate reach, it's now limp tentacles lying useless at both sides.

No pity at all in fact as the second monster kept on hammering away at the first, squashing flat the metal cadaver in hopes of creating an easy path.

Taking her leave soon enough, wanting no more of that violent tableau, she caught up at once with her waiting shipmates. After all she just saw Naomi was certain she'd soon feel quite ill.

No matter the fact they were just machines, aware as well anthropomorphism was a personal failing of hers—a hazard of her profession—Naomi found even so such cold-hearted, ruthless savagery committed against one's own kind quite troubling a concept to fathom.

****

Reaching that vile tower's weather-beaten, wind-worn exterior it was then Naomi paused yet again just long enough to once more seal that outer entrance—a delay tactic she hoped might buy them at least some little time in which to escape this tragic world, a gloomy wasteland already the site of so much death.

Left now all on its own it stood to reason that horrid Hellhound still nipping at their heals would require at least twice the time needed before cutting its way through that thick, grey barrier—its dead companion no longer able to offer assistance.

Or at least Naomi hoped so, blasting also to bits the portal's locking mechanism once that colossal egress was sealed tight between them, its grand barricade firmly shut again in its rightful, proper place. Still retreating the away team made their way down those same dark, sinister streets of that same cold, dead city as before fleeing that dark, frigid, horrible world.

Too busy this time just trying to survive they found no time to indulge like before in paranoid musings of nearby haunts. Wild flights of fancy concerning ghosts, goblins and other improbable specters proved themselves now rather superfluous in light of their present situation.

That very real threat still in jealous pursuit of their very lives was more than enough to suffice, each focusing her every effort—both physical and mental—on just escaping instead that nefarious landscape.

Even Ensign Fazara, still back aboard the small shuttle which brought them all there, readied herself likewise for their speedy departure.

Going over the final launch procedures in the small shuttle's just-as-tiny cockpit, receiving implicit orders just seconds ago from Lt. Cmdr. Straker, it wasn't long at all before spotting the rest of her party in their mad dash for safety.

Seeing all this through the small viewing portal to her immediate left, getting up in all due haste from the console at which she sat, it wasn't until then however Ens. Fazara noticed an added nightmare likewise headed her way.

Not sure what that monstrous apparition might be, opening instead the rear hatchway to the compact shuttle now ready for take-off, its greater bulk remained hidden in surrounding shadows:

"Oh sanguinary heck; what the freak is that??!!", Ens. Fazara just stared with a audible gasp at its distant approach.

Relieving Frances of that lifeless burden she still bore, asking all-the-while what was chasing them, it was Naomi instead who answered in breathless reply, the others all climbing aboard:

"No time for all that, Ensign! Just get us off this Gosh-forsaken rock. And step on it!!", Naomi hissed most vehemently, that very nightmare in question rolling towards them at a most furious rate, closing in even quicker on their current position.

Obeying at once, no further delay, Ensign Fazara leapt straightaway back into their shuttle's cramped cockpit. Activating at last the pre-programmed departure code their vessel soon lurched upwards, away from the ground below.

Climbing toward the heavens, hearing at once Frances Straker's crisp, clear voice order her to raise shields, Ensign Fazara caught at last one, clear glimpse of what threatened so their very lives.

Doing so when that phantom figure outside raised its misshapen head, hurling at them bright bolts of lethal energy from its narrow snout, the very discharge from that fearsome barrage backwashed their antagonist in a sudden flash of light.

Shrouded in perpetual dark until that one brief moment, unveiling at last that hideous leviathan in all its Hellish glory, it was a glimpse of its true nature that, as brief as it was, would last the poor woman seeing it the rest of her life.

"What happened?", she heard Naomi Marlowe snap right about then in angry alarm, enemy fire from below rocking to-and-fro their fragile craft just seconds before Ensign Fazara was able to raise shields.

Still gaining altitude, she was nevertheless joined up front by the other woman just growling at her seconds ago. Taking up more permanent residence at the navigation console to Ens. Fazara's immediate right Naomi didn't wait however for any reply, running instead an emergency self-diagnostic on all their various on-board systems.

Taking not long at all to determine what damage was done she warned Frances straightaway all outer starboard propulsion units were now leaking power:

"Will we make it back all the way to StarChild?", Frances wasted no time, appearing at the tiny cockpit's only way in.

"'Fraid not", Naomi told her at once with a weary, frustrated sigh: "As it is we'll use up most our energy reserves just breaking free from this stinkin' planet's gravity. After that we're left with just barely enough to get us halfway back to the ship".

"In that case contact Commander Nikarov and request she immediately send another shuttle to tow us in the rest of the way. After that you might as well have them notify Commodore Saphira of our current situation".

Climbing ever higher into that night sky blanketing 'C-1' in perpetual dark Frances noticed, despite their present situation, a mounting sense of relief dawning among all those gathered about—a feeling of hope now they were StarChild bound.

While sharing as well a certain sense of similar relief over their return shipside Frances felt nonetheless an equal sense of both remorse and even guilt, her mind dwelling now in continual thought on Ensign Wilson—all that remained now of that unfortunate woman laid out behind her in silent repose.

And letting her mind wallow in such morbid imagery Frances likewise came to the firm conclusion, the definite conviction, that—all things considered—she just proved herself a pathetic, dismal failure during this, her first command.

Chapter 51

"APPREHENDED"

Not once did Rodney halt his frantic run, running without pause even when feeling his lungs were on fire, heart pounding away in his fragile chest as if ready to explode. The brittle leaves of corn slapping at his entire body, stinging him all over, he could still hear those armor-clad women chasing him, calling after him to come back.

Assuring him neither meant him any harm, promising they were in fact there to help, it wasn't because he doubted their honesty young Rodney kept going so frantically in the opposite direction.

Confident in fact those women in back of him were quite sincere in their heartfelt guarantees it wasn't that which kept him on the retreat, having no time to explain it wasn't them he wanted so desperately to escape…

Not they, but the *'Others'*!!

Concerning those very same women he now fled it was no lie that, when little Rodney first saw that beautiful blonde woman in charge of them all *sans helmet*, he believed for a brief moment his long nightmare had finally reached some unexpected conclusion, an end as unanticipated as it was Heaven-sent.

Just listening to her sweet, almost musical sing-song voice talk to him in that strange yet precious foreign-sounding accent so full of tender affection, he experienced for the first time somewhere deep inside him a certain sense of ultimate hope so alien to all he knew—a feeling of approaching salvation the likes of which he never before imagined.

Of course it was right then and there, the moment those cursed 'Others' arrived, he remembered how there was in fact no such thing as salvation, no such mythical being as hope, no deliverance ever from those many tortures doled out by 'the Others'.

Truth be told it was his original assumption those seven women in white were nothing in fact but some new version of android he somehow missed until that very moment, planning at first sight to flee them even then. It was only their voices that changed his mind. Possessing unlike the 'Others' both feeling and emotion when they spoke, they captured his undivided attention with their very Humanity no matter how well hidden under all that armor-plating.

Giving him valid pause, wondering about their actual nature, he was likewise taken back to dim memories of when he knew both the actual love and fellowship of other Human beings: A love that, in its entirety, Rodney almost forgot the very nature of—its very existence.

Yet even so some lingering doubt still remained during that initial period, seeing in them the final realization of his every dream come true only when the one calling herself *'Commodore'* revealed to him her true identity.

In doing so it was those dreams in which his mother came for him Rodney remembered most, those in which Raechal Roderick reveals right then and there she never really died, returning to take him somewhere far removed from his current situation—somewhere they could both live happily ever after.

Yeah, right! Sure!

That in itself should have served as enough warning something was amiss, that something was surely wrong:

Dreams *never* come true …

ONLY NIGHTMARES!

There were no 'happily-ever-after's…

Only misery and heartache!

The 'Others' proved this ample time-after-time, abusing both Rodney's very body and soul for nothing more than their own cruel delight, the gratification of their own sadistic pleasure!

And so he now ran. Not because he entertained any vain hope of ever escaping the Others but simply unable, even unwilling, to put more stock in such reassuring words as those drifting now after him on the twilight breeze.

Knowing full well he'd never find sweet pardon from the abusive control of those twisted others, their crazy manipulations, it wasn't against this which he rebelled, but the very idea of watching yet another precious dream—no matter how vainglorious—murdered at the very hands of those who dominated him now for oh, so very long.

For all he knew those two women still after him were the only survivors left now of their entire group:

As of right now there was no doubt in poor Rodney's mind both the beautiful blonde woman from before, alongside those other armored ladies in her party, lay about dead: Slain at that ruthless whim Rodney's fiendish masters loved so much to indulge, a fate no different than that suffered by both his parents joined long ago in eternal damnation by the rest of his people.

Oh why, oh why had his mother not let him return with her all those five long years ago to Paradise, preferring as he anticipated even then the thought of such death versus the life he now led. Sometimes ashamed of how he hated her even given such 'abandonment' when Rodney needed her most, it was also true he loathed at times Raechal Roderick with a purple passion almost as tortured as that of his hellish masters.

Clearing at last that thick stretch of corn, chest heaving as he struggled hard to catch his breath, he wasted very little time before continuing his mad dash across a field of stubby grass now resting between both him and the edge of a large thicket—the outermost territory of a dense, coniferous forest climbing a jagged mountain range nearly a quarter mile from his current position.

Regardless physical fatigue distance was no problem at all, courtesy of the panic-generated adrenaline rush driving him onward.

Paying little head whatsoever all to that short, spiky, dirty grass native to Bandros now cutting his feet he pressed on, forward bound. That stubby grayish grassland ending soon enough anyway, Rodney reached the forest's edge in which he now sought refuge.

Losing himself once there in a thick clump of tall, furry 'pine' trees their close-knit branches blocked out all light from the setting suns. Swerving once there to both the left and right a thick blanket of dead pine leaves once blue-green, but now quite brown softened his path.

Beginning a long up-hill climb, running an obstacle course around broad, dark, furry tree trunks it was right about then young Rodney's poor leg muscles began to spasm:

Beginning to seize up, they forced him at long last to slow down. Yet even that wasn't what brought his frantic run to a most tragic, ignoble conclusion. Running with his eyes cast downward, watching the ground, his chin almost touching his chest, Rodney found it just as hard to breathe as he was finding it hard to run.

Raising his head at long last just to give tired lungs a little easier time of it, it was only then he saw as well what lay just ahead. Noting quite readily what "stood" in his way no more than a few yards away it was then that, tripping over his feet in a blind, futile attempt to alter course he fell backwards.

Landing instead with a painful thud on his lean behind, looking up at that horrid being now approaching him, there was no mistaking that awful entity for anything else than one of those 'Others' that made life such an endless morass of utter despair.

All he could manage at that fearful moment was a feeling of quiet remorse, a sense of growing disappointment. No more struggling, no more futile attempts to fight the inevitable, Rodney understood yet again what he should have known better right from the very start.

Escape?

There was no escaping their torment!

Deliverance?

There was no deliverance from their almighty will!

Hopes and dreams were all a Chimera!... a fairy-tale!... the only reality both hopelessness and despair!!

All the above now unavoidable truths, Rodney could see as well no other choice but to surrender himself once more over to his vile users, reconciling himself yet again to whatever similar fate this 'Other' likewise had in mind:

Nothing would, or even could, stop the 'Others'!!

They were as invincible as they were sadistic!!!

Increasing during their pursuit the anti-grav support in their mechanized footwear, this helped some both Toni and her just-as-determined scout trying to keep up with their elusive catch.

Not going all that far in relieving those stress-related aches and pains both women suffered now in their relentless pursuit of duty, they still ignored such 'inconveniences' in light of how they were closing the gap at last between both they and their 'quarry'.

Every little bit helping when the object of their pursuit had such a clear home-court advantage, it hurt the boy's cause even less he had no cumbersome armor weighing him down, this realization forcing from Toni a sardonic grin regardless her many aches.

Following him mostly by the very same path he cut through both corn and grass they followed that obvious trail of bent, broken foliage to the very edge of a broad, low-lying mountain range—a thick forest meeting them upon their arrival.

Almost as dark inside its crowded undergrowth as the darkest of moonless nights each woman activated the 'headlights' embedded in their armored helmets before proceeding any further.

Following a minute trail of blood smears leading them further on into that grand assortment of forbidding trees they each continued their determined hunt, those ochre stains telling both 'huntresses' where their elusive 'prey' went alongside the simple fact he was hurting:

"Can't be too far now", Toni mused just under her breath, not really expecting any sort of reply.

Sure enough, calling it with expert precision, both she and her erstwhile scout found the young laddie in question just a scant thirty yards further. Still as the grave he sat in a small clearing lit only by that very same luminous headgear both women wore.

Making nary a move regardless the sound of their approach... his young, bronzed, naked back turned towards them... he seemed quite docile indeed, only the back of his head visible at their present angle:

'Too exhausted now to struggle anymore', was Toni's own considered opinion, especially in the face of such obvious defeat:

'No fight left to him'.

However, still exercising all due caution, both she and her junior officer approached him even further, taking nothing at all for granted.

Too much the consummate professionals to do otherwise both women likewise displayed such professional tactics when given their present situation, unwilling to take any undue chances given this nasty moon-world's rather ugly past:

"Well, well, my dear young laddie", Toni managed a pleasant chuckle, keeping her voice both light and care-free: "You certainly led us on one very merry little chase".

"I'm sorry", young Master Roderick apologized, doing so in a rather flat, uneasy tone of voice: "but I wasn't quite sure if I could trust you".

"Can we therefore assume you've decided to co-operate", Toni asked even further, both she and her young subordinate standing now in front of their weary 'prize': "That you won't be giving us any more trouble".

"No, I won't", the object of their chase now gave them his solemn promise, looking Toni straight in the eye: "I'm ready to go with you now, peaceably, returning with you to your ship".

Sounding quite reasonable, quite calm now that he had no other apparent choice, Toni still chose to play it cool while exercising extreme caution, deciding to do so when finding it quite hard to read his emotions.

Having always possessed a keen eye for those hidden feelings others might try to conceal, children his age often the easiest to interpret, Toni now found it rather disconcerting that... after studying close and hard that young laddie's face... she found him all-the-same quite inscrutable.

No longer that frightened, timid, fawn-like youth he came across as before running away, there was now some ominous difference about him extending far beyond such simple considerations as his both redness of face, his rapid breathing and weary, watery, glassy eyes.

Sheer exhaustion both physical and emotional quite easy to decipher, this went far beyond any obvious signs of mere fatigue.

Indecipherable, having radically changed since last they saw him, it appeared almost to her probing gaze like a cold heartless void, a poverty-stricken emptiness of spirit, now hiding in the deepest recesses of those little-boy eyes:

"Are you up to any further walking, or should we help?", Toni altered her chain of thought, getting back with a kind, gentle voice to her original purpose for being there...

The boy himself.

"I don't think I can walk anymore", his reply came at once, that dead voice beginning as well to spook her: "My legs and feet feel too sore".

"That's okay, hon", Toni offered without a moment's hesitation, uneasy however at the very idea of even touching that waiting child: "We can take turns carrying you back to our shuttle".

"That will suffice", Rodney stated, that irksome monotone abating not once as his 'ride' likewise lifted him up from the leafy ground.

Forgetting her natural disquiet soon enough though, Toni cradling him now in her arms, her attention was suddenly diverted elsewhere—the crisp, clear sound of Jenniboni's voice addressing her now via those comm. speakers within her helmet:

"Have you found the boy yet?"

"Yes, Ma'am: In fact we've just secured his person, returning now to your position: Seems he's quite willing now to co-operate".

"Excellent work, Ms. Oftesfs! Report back at once to the shuttle. We'll rendezvous with you there while I, personally, up-date you on current events".

Detecting without hesitation an undercurrent of obvious worry in her C.O.'s otherwise brisk, professional tone Toni soon learned soon enough the reason for such disquiet, hearing further what happened since parting company with the rest. Understanding at once the subtle strain she perceived in Jenniboni's voice, her own concern also mounted hearing about the androids, what they said earlier concerning what took place both there and on 'C-1'.

Nor did it ease Toni's mind any further learning about the similar loss of life among Lt. Cmdr. Straker's away team far away on that other dead world, mention of the alleged brain damage suffered by the colonists from Earth giving her equal pause for thought.

Maybe it was this, and nothing more, explaining Rodney's recent immunity to her own personal powers of astute observation.

Or was it?

Chapter 52

"THE GUEST"

The returning shuttle from Zelmorl, already in the process of being towed back to its Fathership, was now completing its final approach to StarChild's waiting hangar bay. And with her returning shuttle from Bandros likewise waiting its turn at disembarkation, parked in a stationary position high above StarChild's narrow prow, Jenniboni watched with intense interest the entire procedure.

Surrounded on her part by solemn quiet she monitored all that transpired from her starship's opposite end, the third shuttle towing the first severing now its energy-link to that injured craft. Moving instead now off to StarChild's starboard side, another invisible tow-line originating from within StarChild himself brought now the small vessel back from Zelmorl all the way home.

Watching now that wounded shuttle come to its final resting place, Jenniboni watched as well the passengers aboard that smaller ship disembark before its final decent. Landing atop of the 'small-craft elevator' pad to the port-side of StarChild's waiting hangar bay, the small transport vessel began soon its ride down one level below only after every passenger aboard was safely elsewhere.

Unable to observe much at first other than four small shadows step down from inside that first shuttle, Jenniboni leaned forward even further yet. Squinting hard for a better look-see she rested her full weight against the navigations control panel in front of where she stood.

Not much detail involved other than those small, indistinct shapes seen from a higher angle, Jenniboni could see them even so carrying between them a fifth individual.

Horizontal, inactive, and surely quite dead it was then they were joined as well by several other individuals from parts unknown, two of those carrying between them a medical stretcher.

Focusing now all her attention upon that lifeless form being taken away, that injured vessel having already made its final decent to her ship's

'Storage/Repair' deck one level below, Jenniboni was taken completely unaware by another—a third individual joining now both her and Lt. Greensley in their own shuttle's smallish cockpit:

"It's interesting how the universe works", Dr. Wei-Chang's sudden arrival caught Jenniboni briefly by surprise, giving StarChild's C.O. a momentary start:

"It's simple, yet eloquent checks and balances.

"For example we find one life on 'AB-1.5'... or, should I say now 'Bandros'... while another is taken on 'C-1', or 'Zelmorl': a fact that, while it is regrettable, we must try to accept as all part of life's greater, unavoidable cycle".

"How may I help you, Doctor?" Jenniboni asked now in snappish reply, both quite curt and to the point. Eartha's philosophical observation, offered as it was in an awkward attempt to render comfort, fell even so on deaf ears.

The fact that Eartha's observation struck her as both cold, cruel, and even cynical served to fuel only further Jenniboni's mounting ire. Quite irked anyway by this sudden intrusion on private thoughts, the other woman's obvious effort to console her mattered not.

"I apologize for the intrusion", Eartha added. Rather hesitant she was able to pick up at once on Jenniboni's cloudy mood; "but I recommend we clean the boy up at once when back aboard StarChild before running any complete physical on the young laddie in the Officer's sick-bay. After all that interference our scanners endured on Bandros, I don't trust at all the P.M.U. diagnostic I already ran while there".

"Agreed, Doctor", Jenniboni allowed. Eyes still focused on that distant landing bay her voice sounded just as far-off: "Anything else?"

"Yes: As-a-matter-of-fact there is".

"Proceed".

"I'd also like Ensign Wilson's body brought at once to the medical pathology lab on Deck B-4 so I can examine the cause of death there in greater detail".

"Yes... yes... of course", Jenniboni spoke yet again rather sharply, leaving no doubt in Eartha's mind what bothered her.

Having squared away anyway all she had to say Dr. Wei-Chang saw it as likewise prudent to just leave. Leaving her superior once more to her own private angst, her own inner contemplations, it was then their shuttle received at last from StarChild official disembarkation notice—authorization to likewise dock onboard.

Looking over her shoulder Jenniboni ordered Gloria to begin at last their final approach, noticing by then just one, lone, solitary person waiting their arrival in that very same hangar bay.

Watching that single, solitary figure just standing there grow a wee bit closer Jenniboni found herself all-of-a-sudden grinning, recognizing even from where she was Cmdr. Stasha Nikarov waiting patiently to welcome their shuttle home.

It was with flawless precision Gloria landed their returning shuttle on the small-craft elevator already back from its voyage one deck below, Jenniboni making her way back to their shuttle's already open hatch. Greeted at once by her waiting X.O. waiting right outside the smaller vessel she removed her helmet, handing it off to Lt. Baynes as Cecilia passed her by on her way elsewhere.

"Welcome home, Commodore", Stasha acknowledged her commanding officer with both a cheerful nod and smile.

"Thank you, Cmdr. Nikarov. Good indeed to be back!", she returned, at least sounding just as up-beat.

Amazing how they got used so quickly to thinking of StarChild as 'home' Jenniboni smiled, stepping down at once from the small ship they just returned on. Moving away a short distance in StarChild's bright landing bay Stasha remained at Jenniboni's side, giving her weary C.O. a brief, but concise report on all their goings on aboard ship since she left.

Not much to tell, Stasha moved on soon enough to the subject of the previous shuttle just back from 'C-1'. Informing her how that other landing party seemed so solemn, subdued, and even grim as both Frances and Ens. Fazara carried Ens. Wilson's final remains off that tiny vessel, Stasha was concerned how little the entire landing party had to say as a pair of stretcher-bearing orderlies took possession of their fallen sister.

Saying very little at all in fact Naomi volunteered instead to sift now through all that alien data transmitted from 'C-1' to Maccs while Frances proved likewise reticent, expressing only her wish to begin at once an official, in-depth report on the 'whole entire mess'. It was then Stasha related even further to Jenniboni what she saw in Frances Straker's gaunt face—those large, dark eyes most of all—Frances clearly upset despite her affected stoicism and cool, even voice.

"I better see to her at once right after we get our new arrival to sick-bay", Jenniboni voiced her own concern, frowning in sympathetic reply.

"Ah, yes", Stasha smiled, most quizzical: "So where is our newest addition?"

No sooner did she ask than Dr. Wei-Chang chose that very moment to appear at the returning shuttle's open hatch, Rodney's young hand in hers, Stasha looking over Jenniboni's left shoulder in their very direction.

Assisting the small figure down from the shuttle to the stark grey/white landing bay in which it now sat Eartha lead him over as well to the other two women discussing now his very whereabouts:

"Here Doctor; let me take that for you", Stasha offered straightaway, Eartha removing right about then her cumbersome smart armor headgear.

"And how might you be young laddie?", she addressed the little boy now staring up at her, looking down likewise at the disheveled youth standing in their midst.

Pleased at first to see in his expression no expression of alarm concerning her facial disfigurements, both her eye-patch and the scar running down the right side of Stasha's face from forehead to lower cheek, this warm feeling of unexpected acceptance on his part soon soured.

What she thought to be at first the mere absence of childish alarm appeared now to be an even more troubling hint of something cold, hostile and not so very human.

Bedeviling Stasha's senses there seemed now something else in the boy's expression, something almost malignant in its rather unbalanced, calculating gaze. A certain maturity unnatural for such a child of such tender years it was a cunning wisdom she now saw there striking her as even unwholesome in its very nature.

Yet, speaking of nature, it was likewise Stasha's very nature to deal in the practical, the logical, giving little heed to such personal 'flights of fancy' even in herself. So in keeping with her own unique foibles, not then recognizing them as such, Stasha dismissed instead all such 'emotional considerations', deciding she was reading too much into Rodney's strange expression.

Nor did it take all that long to justify the young laddie's peculiar gaze, passing it off now to her rational mind as nothing more than the final result of his unfortunate past. Or at least that coupled also with the possible cerebral damage, his likely mental impairment, Jenniboni communicated to her just earlier during her return from Bandros.

'Poor, poor, child', she reflected, overcome with pity now that she saw him in such a new light, this reminding her also of something else important: "By the way I'm also curious about those androids you mentioned on your way back home, the serious doubt you expressed concerning their intent".

Riding the 'target drone elevator' right across the landing bay, across the way from that other lift to the level immediately below them, Jenniboni didn't really know where to begin.

At least not without sounding quite paranoid indeed!

Gazing out the hangar bay doors, watching instead that tow-shuttle from before make its final approach—its registered designation, "*Gene III*", printed along its portside in fair sized letters—it wasn't until after reaching that other deck below that Jenniboni began.

Describing at long last that pernicious green glow emanating from right behind each sinister mechanoid's dark faceplate Jenniboni's confession of utter doubt didn't end there. Continuing her narrative as they stepped forth into a nearby ag-pod, she made it quite obvious just how much she didn't trust them.

"Well… I'll admit they sound strange", Stasha took her time in reflection, traversing the greater of length of StarChild towards his narrow bow.

Astonished by such an emotional response on Jenniboni's part to what sounded like nothing more than a motley group of service 'droids Stasha found herself at a momentary loss, having yet to see her dearest friend behave in such a skittish manner. Remaining nonetheless her usual, practical self she soon found herself arguing in gentle fashion these otherwise articulate examples of alien design were, in the long run, mere machines—simple automatons incapable of deliberate misrepresentation.

Undaunted even while listening to echoes of her own rationale just hours before, Jenniboni remained even so resolute in her feelings as to the contrary:

"You weren't there, Commander. You didn't feel what it was like in their very company, their *very* close proximity", she persisted, steadfast in her convictions even in the face of her own earlier pragmatism reflected now back at her in Stasha's oh-so practical manner—her reasonable words and soothing voice.

"And I'll tell you something else, Stasha. As far as I'm concerned there's something definitely off-kilter about that entire moon. Beautiful, but ominous.

"Frankly I don't plan to have anything further to do with any of those wretched things. Nor do I plan to let anyone else go back there until we've at least examined all the pertinent data gathered from both Bandros *and* Zelmorl", Jenniboni vowed. Quite adamant all three officers present payed little heed to that childish pair of ears now hanging on their every word.

"Speaking of information," it was now Stasha's turn to offer, starting now to feel uneasy; "maybe I should likewise assist Lt. Cmdr. Marlowe in her examination of all such intelligence gathered from 'C-1'".

"Zelmorl", Jenniboni corrected her with gentle good humor.

"Yes, of course", Stasha nodded, lips pursed, lost in thought: "And while I'm at it, I'll have Stellar Cartography change the official designation for both 'C-1' and 'AB-1.5' to both 'Zelmorl' and 'Bandros'".

Knowing at once where to find Naomi Marlowe, Stasha had Maccs stop the ag-pod stop on deck S-9, right next to the Special Studies laboratory at the base of StarChild's slender yet sturdy neck. Continuing after that its way through StarChild's neck, Jenniboni and Eartha alone now with their young guest, the lift approached now his smaller forward section—his 'head'.

"And as far as you're concerned young Master Roderick our first order of business is to get you all cleaned up nice and spiffy", Jenniboni gave the young boy standing between both her and StarChild's elderly C.M.O. a most sweet, affectionate smile:

"First we'll start with a good scrub-down, followed by both a haircut and duplicated clothes more fitting a modest young laddie your age. And once all that's seen to Dr. Wei-Chang here will likewise give you a most complete, thorough examination. Make sure you're as fit as a fiddle for your trip soon back to Earth".

Mistaking for worry that strange look he gave her it was then, at first glance, Jenniboni promised him a painless exam, assuring the young boy there was nothing to fear.

It wasn't until yet another passing moment she saw not anxiety in those cool blue eyes but a look that gave her goosebumps, a heartless expression of cold calculation:

"Fine", came his simple reply, delivered in a flat monotone devoid in every way of all true feeling. Pondering those empty eyes still staring up at her it was then her troubled mind wandered back to their first encounter; both his wary, cautious curiosity and wild, almost feral expression. At least that was reasonable, making perfect sense given his obvious past, his current behavior striking her conversely as different Even perverse, it was a dramatic change from that original personality she first met.

Trying on the other hand to convince herself she was being irrational, suffering nothing more than a delayed reaction to all those recent horrors previously witnessed, Jenniboni racked her uneasy brain for a simple, logical reason why Rodney might seem now so very different.

Rather easy to find giving the matter just a little more thought maybe he was simply tired, all tuckered-out after his long sprint to the forest. Maybe he was suffering nothing more than a delayed stress syndrome all his own, overwhelmed as he must be by their sudden appearance in his life.

After all it was only a few hours ago they yanked him away from the only home he knew, no matter how lacking, and brought him here. More than reasonable cause for strange behavior Jenniboni decided right then-and-there to have Janelle Higgins, the ship's Psychologist, spend a little time with him.

Of course there remained yet another possible explanation for any strange behavior the boy might exhibit, Jenniboni still loath to even consider however such a grim eventuality—the sad possibility those decrepit, horrid androids back on Bandros were, all said and done, telling the truth!

What if Rodney was just showing those same telltale symptoms of that same wretched malady they say drove all the rest of the boy's people to actual murder itself!

While such a mournful prospect disheartened her Jenniboni still found a small part of her almost hoping it was true, that being the only valid cause she could accept for that gross example of "gendercide" committed there.

Then again, if that were indeed true, that meant Rodney likewise faced the same sad fate, doomed to a degenerative disorder of the Human brain as lethal as it was tragic. For his sake, and his sake alone, Jenniboni found herself either hoping those dreadful 'droids were in honest error, or that her brilliant Chief Medical Officer might prove herself up to saving Rodney's very life.

****

Stepping off the ag-pod onto deck B-4, the Officer's Sickbay, they crossed the pale green corridor immediately there into the medical receptionist's office.

Looking up at the sound of new arrivals the young on-duty receptionist behind that far desk did a brief double take at sight of both her Dept. Chief and Commodore Saphira, each wearing smart-armor protection, escorting between them a scruffy-looking young boy barely in his teens.

Regaining her composure soon enough though, Lt. Cornett gave their new arrival a warm smile. Bidding him welcome Dr. Wei-Chang instructed her at the very same time to assist both she and Jenniboni in cleaning up the young, grimy-faced laddie in question—Ms. Cornett following her superiors into the I.C.U. chamber adjacent to the sick-bay reception area just left of her desk.

Giving him a thorough scrubbing in the fully equipped washroom opposite the I.C.U. from where they entered... a complete physical to follow... all three officers saw to both his grooming and attire before proceeding further with

Rodney's medical. Their young 'patient', co-operative throughout the entire process almost to the point of zombie-like compliance, said nothing at all throughout the entire procedure.

Doing what was asked of him with the almost plodding body language of some habitual sleep-walker, Rodney's uncharacteristic, un-childish acquiescence to such an 'odious' ritual as 'bath-time' struck Jenniboni as rather unnatural—a mother of three who knew from helping their father just how trying children could be during such a tedious chore.

However, even despite those distant warning bells ringing almost by instinct in the very back of her mind, Jenniboni meanwhile managed to dismiss such odd behavior. Chalking it up yet again to mere physical/emotional exhaustion on the part of their new little visitor, she convinced herself yet again it was the simple shock to Rodney's natural system brought on by their sudden arrival in his otherwise lonely life.

Dispensing after a short while with his grooming, Eartha chose right then and there to conduct Rodney's complete physical in the neighbouring surroundings of her well-equipped I.C.U.. Aware he didn't require intensive care it remained nevertheless the most logical choice given the fact it possessed the most extensive range of diagnostic equipment.

Wanting to conduct an exacting medical examination leaving no stone unturned Eartha kept Jenniboni updated as well every step of the way, Lt. Cornett serving as both nurse and assistant treating Rodney's few cuts and scrapes.

Watching on with keen interest from the foot of his bed, listening with mixed emotions to every step-by-step up-date Eartha provided, Jenniboni waited with bated breath for the final, overall results—Rodney sitting on the bed's edge, still compliant, silent as the grave, as her ship's C.M.O. ran a whole slew of exhaustive examinations detailing every possible aspect of his entire being.

As each result of each test was read-out-loud the young, flaxen-haired boy's overall prognoses improved by both leaps and bounds, every test 'negative' across the board! Although truly happy for Rodney's sake Jenniboni was still left frowning, left now with an even more disquieting mystery.

More than one to be exact!

Noting at once her worried look, the way those large, expressive mahogany eyes narrowed in such a troubled fashion, Eartha jumped right in with a plausible explanation for what she knew bothered her immediate superior most:

"All things taken into consideration it may be that, due to Master Roderick's young age at the time of his cryogenic suspension, he was spared the unfortunate side-effects suffered by the rest of his people. From what I could also tell from all the available evidence Rodney was no doubt the only child in their entire community.

"It could be possible those superior recuperative abilities small children often possess allowed him a greater chance of recovery from that cellular trauma those 'droids below described while the rest of his people..."

"Perhaps, Doctor: Maybe so", Jenniboni permitted. Cutting her off, her sour expression persisted even in the face of what she just heard: "Nevertheless, that still leaves us with several other unpleasant questions as yet unanswered. Don't get me wrong. I couldn't be happier for the young laddie…"

At this she gave the young subject of her talk a most encouraging smile:

"… but relief over the boy's good fortune doesn't change the fact that those 'droids appear now even less trustworthy than before, casting even greater doubt on their so-called 'good word'.

"And if those… those… things!… are the intentional liars I fear them to be, then what *exactly* is it they're trying to hide? Not knowing could very well prove our eventual downfall!"

"Well, all I can tell you from my own thorough examination is that young Rodney here is in perfect health. Other than that I have no more to offer on the subject", Eartha offered in her own somewhat gruff' n' grumbly manner. Frustrated she couldn't address Jenniboni's concerns in that more helpful fashion her commanding officer so clearly desired, she wasn't certain where to even begin:

"All he needs now is plenty of rest".

Talking amongst themselves, totally preoccupied, nobody there took notice of that smug, devious grin full of evil plotting flashing at once across young Rodney's face—a look of cunning calculation gone by the time Jenniboni turned her attention back once more to him.

An expression having no place in the innocent heart of a child isolated for so long, lacking all communion with others, it was gone as quickly as it first appeared.

"Well, my dear Sir", Jenniboni beamed the boy a maternal smile full of motherly affection: "Now that we've seen to both your personal hygiene, grooming, and clean bill of health I think it also high time you get some rest. I'm sure Dr. Wei-Change has a comfy bed nearby, so why don't you just hop down from…"

"I want to see your ship", Rodney chose that very moment to interrupt, talking out-loud at long last. Still doing so in that strange, bland, almost comatose voice it was the same voice he employed on those very few occasions he chose to speak at all since brought back from the edge of that hilly forest back on Bandros.

"Maybe later", Jenniboni smiled yet again: "However, for the time being, I believe Dr. Wei-Chang's right. You need your sleep".

"I mean right now", Rodney spoke again, a spark of dark emotion now appearing.

"No, Hon", Jenniboni lowered her voice, assuming at once a more firm hand: "I'm sure it's well beyond whatever bedtime you're accustomed to back 'home', having had I'm sure a most eventful day. So, with that in mind, I think it best…"

"I don't care what you think", the small child blew up, acting out in hot reply: "I want to see this ship of yours at once, right this very moment".

Making allowances for the type of barren existence he no doubt led these last, few formative years in his sad, pathetic life—lacking any adult supervision whatsoever—Jenniboni nonetheless refused to permit such improper conduct in her presence. Realizing it might prove a hard adjustment it was no doubt one he'd have to make anyway if rejoining the rest of Womankind as a functional, proper member of decent society learning once-and-for-all what was, and wasn't acceptable behavior.

Needing to learn as soon as possible such proper deportment, how to behave himself in a more fitting manner, Jenniboni decided straightaway there was no time like the present to teach him such basic etiquette, setting at last those much needed boundaries:

"You better start caring what I say, young man", she declared in firm reply, "seeing as I'm the final authority aboard this very ship you want to see, giving the orders here".

Managing to keep her cool while nonetheless stern, what came next strained all-the-same her weary patience almost to breaking:

"I *demand* to see your ship, *right now*!!!", Rodney almost screamed at the top of his lungs, livid, the sound of his extreme response causing Lt. Cornett a startled reaction. Even the venerable Dr. Wei-Chang, normally as cool a customer as you could ever imagine, just stared—gasping in sheer disbelief at this almost psychotic display of manic rage.

"Now *you* listen to *ME*, young Laddie", Jenniboni glared down at him, eyes burning. Hands on hips she leaned forward, standing over him:

"*You* don't give orders aboard this ship—*I DO*!! All you may do here is make requests which I... at my discretion... might, or might not allow! Understood?!"

"FREAK YOU, WITCH!! GO TO SANGUINARY HECK!!", Rodney chose that very moment to snarl back at her, doing so with such bestial hate it rocked the object of his anger to the very core, Jenniboni's mind starting to swim.

Even so the hurt injustice she felt over such brutal abuse soon found itself pushed aside, replaced in one almighty surge by an equal flash of righteous indignation, a burning sense of utter rage over such foul injustice. The entire situation getting way too out of hand such hateful animosity was as unwarranted in her opinion as it was intolerable, as unfair as it was inappropriate.

Wondering now if young 'Master Roderick' might be as 'touched in the head' as they feared at first, Jenniboni nevertheless decided more drastic measures were all-the-same needed if hoping to regain at all some decent measure of sweet control. What was needed this very moment was to take swift charge of such a bizarre turn for the worse, restoring at once both law and order!!

"That's it!", Jenniboni growled at once through clenched teeth. Leaning in even closer, her face was now nose-to-nose with his: "I've just had more than enough out of you, young Master!"

Hands still on hips Jenniboni followed this right away with even further assertions of impending doom, laying down in deadly voice the absolute law aboard StarChild:

"Nor will I tolerate any such disrespect and/or insubordination aboard my ship, not from any of those under my command much less a snot-nosed little brat such as yourself. You are merely a guest aboard this ship and don't you forget it.

"So unless you start minding your P's and Q's, doing just as I say, I'll send at once for a ready detachment from security, have them drag you at once by a lock of your hair down to *my ship's* brig. Once there you'll be held in complete isolation, locked away in some tiny cell until handing you over to the proper authorities back on Earth! Do I make myself perfectly clear?!"

Whether or not it was the stormy anger in her eyes, or the honest fury apparent in her commanding tone, it was quite obvious by the sudden worry appearing in otherwise scheming eyes Rodney knew she wasn't bluffing. Backing down at once, he was now as quickly docile as he was at first aggressive:

"Okay, okay. I'm sorry. I'll do whatever you say. Just don't lock me up!"

"All right, then", Jenniboni stood up straight again, now smiling: "That's better".

Observing right then from the corner of her eye Dr. Wei-Chang approach them both, returning now from the I.C.U. chamber's far side, it wasn't until then Jenniboni even noticed her absence in the very first place. Distracted as she was by the boy's foul temper it was only then she paid any attention to Eartha's return. Bringing in one hand two small pills at the bottom of a clear, shallow container she carried in the other a glass of water:

"All right, Rodney", Eartha instructed him once reaching their side: "I want you to take these".

"What are they?" her young patient eyed suspiciously both pills and water.

"Well, if you must know, the green one is a general antibiotic while the brown one is a multi-supplemental".

Consuming each with a slow, hesitant sip of water from the glass she still held he accepted them only reluctantly from Eartha's care. No sooner had he swallowed both Eartha instructed him to open his mouth, giving her commanding officer a solemn nod once sure he swallowed both.

"All rightie, then", it was now Jenniboni's turn to address him, smiling down now at their young 'houseguest': "In that case it's time for all good little boys aboard ship to be getting their rest".

Helping him down right after that from the examination table upon which he still sat, resting then her hands upon sinewy, lean shoulders Jenniboni steered young Rodney across that pale green corridor mentioned earlier into a smallish recovery ward situated just opposite the I.C.U.

Once there, surveying all the available beds in that empty facility, having even so the entire room to themselves, Jenniboni likewise pointed her young charge in the very direction of one of two sleeping units situated up against the back wall—the boy's every step growing now quite uncertain, wobbly indeed, under her gentle direction.

Sensing this at once, realizing right then what wily "double-cross" Eartha no doubt just pulled, Jenniboni lifted him at once off his unsteady feet. Bearing now the sleeping child in her arms, the other woman turned down the sheets to their newest arrival's temporary 'home'. Temporary that was until they could find him quarters aboard ship more fitting a young laddie of Rodney's delicate circumstance, Jenniboni leaving him to rest on the soft mattress now supporting his slender build.

Gazing also at his peaceful expression, taking immediate note of what a lovely child he really was, she went about removing her armed gauntlets once his gentle form lay at rest. Proving unable to deny that maternal urge welling within she brushed away as well pale blonde hair from that winsome child's sun-bronzed face.

Brushing it back in a most loving fashion from his graceful features it struck Jenniboni right then and there that, more than just handsome, the young boy before her was truly beatific—radiant—as though an absolute angel resting there in gentle repose:

"Those weren't just some 'General Antibiotic', or 'Multi-Supplemental' you just slipped him. Were they?", she finally glanced up from young Rodney's direction, rather amused:

"Be honest, Doctor", she grinned across the bed at Eartha's own aged, craggy face.

"'General Antibiotic'? 'Multi-Supplemental'? Sedatives!!!", Eartha confessed, a sly little twinkle in the corners of each eye: "Why quibble over semantics?"

"Under normal circumstances I'd consider such conduct a violation of the doctor/patient ethic. However, in this particular instance, I'm willing to turn a blind eye. Thank you, Doctor".

"You're welcome, Commodore. I had a feeling you might approve".

"How could this now be the same child so violent just moments ago?", Jenniboni once more changed the subject at hand, wondering aloud more to herself than her faithful C.M.O..

Studying in reverent silence Rodney's tranquil expression, moved at once by that almost divine innocence she perceived there yet again, Jenniboni contemplated with equal affection the way lush, delicate eyelashes rested against rosy, tanned cheeks, the slight parting of the lips, and the look of serene passivity he now wore.

"I wouldn't worry myself too much over such matters", Eartha claimed without further delay, offering in absolute confidence her professional diagnosis:

"Nothing more no doubt than extreme fatigue coupled with both the obvious upheaval we represent in his life; our sudden arrival, removing him now from the only home he's ever known, and the wild existence he's lead now over the past several years.

"Such bizarre behavior is to be expected after all the emotional upsets he's no doubt endured right up to this very moment".

"Perhaps, Doctor", Jenniboni gave her grudging consent, clearly uncertain, remembering that brief look of lunatic hate she saw only moments ago in this very child now so seraphic in sweet expression:

'No!', she thought further on the matter. There had to be more going on here than just some cranky, overwrought youth acting out under the influence of some quite understandable trauma. Something more so than even a possible state of mental duress… instability even!… brought on by physical damage to those key areas of Rodney's brain dealing with one's powers of higher reason.

No, no and once again 'no' it came then to Jenniboni a nagging sensation that, far from dealing with the reasonable alternatives given above, she was dealing in the boy's behavior with some other probability.

"Perhaps, Doctor: Perhaps", she reiterated, more firm this time: "But I still want both doors to this room sealed, two security personnel posted at each, until further notice!"

"Yes, Commodore", it was Eartha's turn to sound unsure, even hesitant. Admitting the boy's conduct left her feeling as well a wee bit spooked she still couldn't help but feel her ship's C.O. was a trifle over-reacting, erring more than just a little on the side of over-cautious.

Then again, as a good ship's commander, Eartha understood it was likewise Jenniboni Saphira's conscientious duty to see first to the safety of her crew, taking into consideration anything odd—no matter how trivial—which might pose some future threat.

"How long in your opinion should he remain out?", Jenniboni asked soon thereafter, stroking tenderly with the back of her hand the sleeping boy's cheek.

"Several hours at least. The sedatives I gave him weren't all that strong but, taking into consideration his obvious state of utter fatigue, he should sleep for some time yet".

"Excellent! In that case notify me at once the very moment he wakes up".

"Yes, Ma'am".

"In the meantime, however, I think it time I change out of all this armor", Jenniboni observed, looking up again from Rodney's silent form:

"And while we're at it doctor may I suggest you do the same", she added in wry conclusion: "I'm sure your many patients might feel less ill-at-ease if their attending physician looked less like she was charging into battle!"

Chapter 53

"TO CONSOLE AND CONFRONT"

Returning her smart armor to its assigned storage unit in Security it occurred to her not long after she hadn't eaten since early morning, Jenniboni choosing to remedy that situation with a quick hop, skip, and jump to the previously mentioned "Star-Stage".

And arriving at approximately 17:00 Hours… ship-time… it was her initial belief she had at first the entire place to herself. At least that was until, turning the corner to her immediate right, she saw at once Frances Straker sitting by herself, all alone, at a far table:

Positioned near the darkened entry to their chief cook's now vacant galley there was no mistaking in Jenniboni's opinion her stark, severe Spartan-featured Security Chief for anyone else aboard ship. Even with her back now to her there was no mistaking that darkest of raven black hair pulled up in that strict, almost too painful to even look at bun Frances so liked to sport.

From the angle at which she now sat it was clear Jenniboni's reclusive officer wanted likewise no company at all, wishing nothing to do either with that wide observation port gazing out at the stars to her immediate left, a broad expanse occupying that entire bulkhead.

Passing by her on way to that empty galley just beyond, lights there turned down low, it was Jenniboni's first inclination to respect that lone woman's right to utter privacy, leaving Frances to indulge sullen reflections of her own choosing.

However, catching sight at last of her despairing expression, Jenniboni decided right then-and-there it might be better in the long run were she to intrude on Ms. Straker during this rather unfortunate situation.

Returning herself from the aforementioned galley with her own less-than-stellar late-day meal, that look of glum defeat Frances wore transformed her usual, somber visage into that where she looked more like some grave old crone aged well beyond her 31 years.

"Mind if I join you, Lt. Cmdr.?" Jenniboni requested in gentle fashion, her second officer just staring at the plate before her. Going mostly untouched, it looked no more appetizing than the similar fare arranged about on Jenniboni's tray.

"Not at all, Ma'am: Please; have a seat", Frances allowed, hollow-voiced, picking rather listlessly at her food if even touching it at all.

"I don't blame you in the least, showing so little interest in this mediocre slop", the new arrival offered as way of an icebreaker, having just taken a seat at the same three-sided table:

"We should surely lodge complaint with whatever mistressmind designed those horrid duplicators", Jenniboni quipped, sitting now next to her lost companion.

"I've had worse".

"Now there's a depressing thought".

"Do you think we'll ever really get used to it?", Frances looked up at her commanding officer after just a wee bit of mutual silence, asking in almost too casual a voice.

"Dear Lord, I hope not!" Jenniboni rejoined. Most emphatic she understood quite well what Frances was referring to. Young Ensign Wilson was even more so under her command than Ms. Straker's and it was now Jenniboni's sad duty as StarChild's C.O. to inform the dead woman's family of their tragic loss, a responsibility she anticipated with a clear sense of sick dread.

With a solemn nod Frances approved her commanding officer's heartfelt sentiment, likewise aware what Jenniboni meant. As former members of the Protectorate back home both women at that table saw it happen on previous occasions—other Protectors who became so desensitized to the pain they encountered during the performance of their duties their humanity likewise diminished over the course of years until only shadows of their former selves!

It didn't matter in such cases that the crime rate during Commonwealth herstory was only a fraction of its former self during the old Patriarchates...

It didn't matter that, when compared to the level of violent crime back in those dark millennia, such criminal violence was much less in the Tammyite Matriarchate.

So what if, when compared to the dark days of male-dominated societies, the crime level during the last 800 years was minimal in comparison.

Despite all that there were still those women, those Protectors who, during exposure to all that subtle injustice, that deviant cruel streak still a persistent aspect of Human nature, found themselves just as unable to cope, letting their hearts turn to stone.

So much so there was even an old Protectorate motto that, in its simple eloquence, summed up quite nicely such sad cases: A philosophy to which both Jenniboni and Frances subscribed:

***A Hard Heart is a Useless Heart*!!"**

"Somehow I can't help but feel I somehow honestly failed her, that I'm indirectly responsible for her death", Frances confided, subdued.

"How so?" Jenniboni leaned forward, curious.

"Well, for one thing, I've always tried to factor in every possible contingency involving equipment impairment during combat procedures when training my staff in the use of all battle gear. Yet, at the very same time, I never took into consideration such an unlikely scenario as being hit in the visor by stray weapon's fire.

"Especially when each and every armored suit was put already through an intensive, exhaustive test in order to determine beforehand the chances of that very same thing happening. According to the results of all such tests those visors were supposed to be damage proof.

"Therefore all I can only assume sitting here thinking about it, running it all over and over again in my beleaguered mind, is that the base energy level of all that alien weapon's fire back on 'C-1' was much more intense than anything we've so far encountered. It just has to be!"

"But you did instruct them on how to handle their panic?", Jenniboni asked, rhetorically, confident already of the answer.

"Of course", Frances insisted, somewhat indignant, as if her very reputation was in question: "I *always* told them that, no matter what, they weren't to remove any segment of their armor during combat procedures. I always told them to request assistance from a sister-officer if somehow incapacitated, to wait for help, and keep their heads down.

"How could she be so stupid, so gosh-darn foolish", Frances all-of-a-sudden hissed through clenched teeth, sensing now with her last enquiry what Jenniboni was hinting at: "If she only waited, kept her wits about her, I was just about to send Ens. Umbota after her, back to help her. Why didn't she request assistance? She must have known ..."

"Maybe she did panic", Jenniboni offered, her point now taken: "Or maybe it was a purely instinctive reaction on her part, a simple attempt to remove the obstruction to her vision before thinking better of it.

"Truth-be-told we'll never know for absolute sure. I could just as easily blame myself for sending an away team to Zelmorl in the first place: No different than you blaming yourself for somehow letting your juniors down, not anticipating some one-in-a-million chance shot to their visor units: An event that shouldn't have affected her vision to begin with.

"Let's face facts: Everyone aboard this ship knew serving aboard him would entail some sort of risk the very moment we all joined the S.E.A..

"So while it's only right... only Human... to regret our losses, we can't at the same time let them eat away at our insides to the point where our fear of loss incapacitates us. Not only won't that bring back our dead, it would also go a long way to failing our duty to the living".

"What can I say? When your right, your right", Frances confessed with just a slight smile: "However, at the same time, it still bothers me. Sorry".

"No need to apologize. If it didn't bother you, you wouldn't be Human. Just as long as you don't let it tear you apart".

"Once again; when you're right, you're right".

"Sooo, are you feeling any better now?"

"Well... let's just say I'm feeling a lot better than before", Frances conceded with just a little grin, something else Jenniboni said registering only now: "Wait a minute. Did you just refer to 'C-1' as 'Zelmorl'?"

"That's a long story", Jenniboni sighed: "In fact I'm planning to convene a meeting of all Dept. heads once all the pertinent information attained on each world has been correlated in proper sequence. However, seeing as you are both my Chief of Security as well as right here right now, I might as well let you in... in advance... on what we've discovered on 'Bandros', the name we now have for 'AB-1.5'".

"Great", Frances quipped in sour response: "Now we have actual names for these eternal horrors".

Recapping after that all which transpired on Bandros Jenniboni's account lacked for nothing, both the colony's massacre and Dr. Wei-Chang's certain theory of 'Gendercide' eliciting from Frances both a look of utter horror mingled with obvious disgust.

And on a similar note Jenniboni's recounting of their first encounter with Rodney, his strange questions, the sudden appearance of all ten androids, and their continued experience with those metal titans coaxed as well from Frances a similar expression of grave mistrust.

Voiced aloud for Jenniboni's benefit there was likewise no attempt on Frances' part to convince her C.O. they were only machines encountered while planet-side, sharing with Jenniboni an equal distrust concerning those strange automatons.

Unlike Stasha, Jenniboni's 'third-in-command' shared the same instinctual distrust, the same deep-seated misgivings, just hearing about those very same synthetic beings.

Sight unseen she experienced the same creepy sensation just listening to her dinner companion describe them that Jenniboni experienced as well during her actual encounter, unable even so to likewise justify her own dark feelings of grave misfortune.

And when it came time for Frances to recount her dark happenings on Zelmorl she rendered an equally detailed report, both women returning soon to their meals in absolute quiet.

Wondering in all reality what they'd gotten themselves into, the two of them dwelling all alone in that silent lounge on one unpleasant hypothesis after another, it was Frances who chose at last to break free of that pointless trap each now found herself falling into, injecting into their current mood a lighter air.

"I'd sure hate to live on this... this... duplicator generated garbage for the rest of my life", she threw out there, hoping to lighten their mood.

"Hey, don't come whining to me about this pathetic slop", Jenniboni rejoined in a similar, lighter vein: "Maybe you should see if our resident wizard of all things mechanical, the gifted Ms. Marlowe, can re-program the gosh-darn things".

****

It wasn't long after Jenniboni joined Frances at her table Gloria finished as

404

well a no more appetizing meal in the Officer's Mess on deck B-5 just one deck below. Paying little to any heed to the food passing her lips her attention was focused instead on going over all that information retrieved from the defunct colony ship back on Bandros—picking over the data gathered from its memory banks proving itself a more scintillating proposition right about then than the food she ate.

Wasting no more time once done eating Gloria made way at once for deck S-2. Located at StarChild's opposite end, the ag-pod she rode dropped her off once there in a small, plainly decorated lobby just outside the ship's 'General Research Room'.

Taking a sharp turn left directly opposite 'Internal Security' Gloria crossed the small foyer there with an eager stride full of purpose. The door behind her sliding shut once there she was pleased to note just three other crewwomen likewise using the compact research facility.

Reserved for on-duty personnel to pursue non-specified assignments, taking her place at a computer access terminal nearest that chamber's only entrance, the 'General Research Room' allowed personnel direct access to Maccs' very own memory core—an area off-limits to anyone without her own proper, authorized access code.

Under normal circumstances Gloria would have preferred using for the task ahead the private terminal granted her in her own personal quarters, an option not available at the present time.

Although downloading the data from her scanner into Maccs proved itself a snap the memory chips removed from the derelict sleeper-ship in Paradise proved however a more difficult nut to crack. So difficult in fact Gloria was compelled to dismantle the compact P.C. in her private quarters in order to physically integrate those very same memory chips from Bandros into its own, particular input/output user-control system.

Anticipating beforehand the problems of working with primitive patriarchate technology, especially when it came to the speed of data retrieval, she had to let the information they possessed quite literally seep its way into Maccs slowly, but surely. A time-consuming procedure it was also one that rendered her poor P.C. quite useless for the direct retrieval of all that data contained.

At least not until she had time to repair it.

Time she loathed wasting, however. Sure that Commodore Saphira wanted soon the results of her thorough investigation—*A.S.A.P.*—it was then she decided to access here all that hard-earned information instead. The only reason she even took a break to eat was the time she knew it would take downloading as well everything on those archaic silicon chips into StarChild's omnitronic Q.P.Q.[**] matrix:

"It's time, Maccs", she whispered aloud, more to herself than her ship's synthetic soul: "Let's see what we got".

Calling up on her display screen *all* the information gathered from Paradise

---

[**] Q.P.Q.: "Quantum Protean Quark"

the first item of business appearing from the colony's official record was a complete crew/passenger roster listing each of the colony's former inhabitants, each name accompanied by a brief dossier alongside a corresponding photo I.D..

Scrolling down through that lengthy collection of ancient biographies she wasn't really all that interested in what she saw, pausing even so when reaching Rodney's name—delaying just long enough to read the fact sheet appearing directly below...

Not much there:

"AGE: 5 years; BORN: March 19th, 2030..." followed by a no-less-pithy, right-to-the-point, physical description including both medical records and official photograph.

"Cute little tyke", Gloria muttered, studying that little-boy face full of innocent hope smiling right back at her.

Rodney's parents, Raechal and Braddock Roderick, also present and accounted for there was no denying the strong family resemblance, the young laddie surely possessing both his father's clear blue eyes alongside his mother's angular features and light blonde hair...

Noting as well with a lopsided grin that, while Raechal bore a certain resemblance to Commodore Saphira, she was also during life not that much taller than Gloria herself. The singular irony of this fact wasn't lost on the young woman now reading their life's story.

Transferring all that personal information onto a couple of ei-pads she brought along for that very same reason, Gloria found herself now transfixed by those now-dead faces flickering by in steady procession.

Her interest now peaked, she wondered idly which face went with which set of rotting bones she saw scattered before all around her in Paradise. Not realizing until then she possessed within her such a fearsome morbid streak, Gloria doubted all-the-same she'd ever forget what she bore witness to back in that pitiable community.

Try as hard as she might it was burned nevertheless forever into her deepest memory.

Reaching at last the end of that crew roster, she'd grown rather intrigued with that roll-call of lost souls. And following right after that was a considerable collection of personal communiqués sent to those very same colonists by long-gone friends and family back on Earth:

"Messages in a bottle", was the first image that leapt quite naturally to Gloria's questing mind.

Sent no doubt while those meant to see them journeyed forth in cryogenic slumber, letters from bygone loved-ones followed one-another in quick procession on her active screen. Feeling after a while like some sort of voyeuristic intruder violating their very privacy she nevertheless read on, trying to pardon herself on the simple grounds it was only duty compelling her.

"Yeah right. Who's kidding who?", she snickered in good-natured self-reproach. Giving her reflection on the screen before her a sarcastic glance she was at least honest enough with herself to admit to more personal reasons.

After all... and let's be fair here!... it wasn't everyday one was granted such a rare, private glimpse into the very far past by those very individuals living way back then. Events that never made their way into the herstory books were now made known to her, and her alone, by authentic contemporaries living during that most horrific period in Womankind's tumultuous past...

****

**"... and I shall drown them all in their own blood
and vomit, lay barren all the land, and lay claim
to the very throne of God Almighty Himself over
and upon their rotting flesh and bones".**

—Colonel Philippe Silas Scarlett

World War Three, born out of a minor conflagration in the middle east, coming to light during the early summer of 2029, was an unprecedented time in Human herstory during which the old patriarchate nations brought about true hell on Earth. Concentration camps on the outskirts of nearly every major city across the globe, the rotting bodies of plague victims littered the entire world in their billions, humanity choking on the foul stench of such almighty pestilence, such unprecedented death.

It were as though all the world now reveled in some twisted worship of death almighty, complete lawlessness, the ashes of its many victims cremated in charnel pits... world-wide... turning the entire planet a murky twilight grey. The sky so saturated by such airborne debris the entire Earth was plunged into perpetual night for well then over three years, lasting some time even after the 'Great Patriarchate War'.[***]

Referred to from then on out as 'Death-Camp Winter' this short-lived but horrific phenomena resembled quite well in many aspects 'Nuclear Winter', the normal temperature across the entire world plunging from its mean average in the low 70's Fahrenheit to somewhere in the mid-20's—bands of nomad tribes displaced now by the misfortunes of war turning cannibal.

Living on the fallen wherever they might be just to survive, some of these starving groups feasted as well upon the living, at least one such 'cannibal nation' boasting over a million members.

And as if all this insanity wasn't already enough, the entire world one mass graveyard, one global "Auschwitz", there was also the new-age occult tyrant, Colonel Philippe 'Sanguinary' Scarlett, to deal with:

Born in Bristol, England this leader of the greatest, most powerful, of these long-past male-oriented societies—the *United European Empire*—this 'Man Of Sin', Scarlett, was a world leader obsessed beyond all reason with personal victory at *ANY* cost.

[***] By war's end in late 2038 the global crematoria had disposed of over 3 million dead every day for well over an entire year.

So much so that this unparalleled madman, having no equal throughout the entire span of Human herstory, raised quite literally demonic legions from the lowest depths of eternal Hell-fire to fight on his side.

Doing so under the guise of raising the dead, a truly Satanic hoax unsurpassed since the original fall of all Womankind, this twisted necromancer… this darkest of all warlocks… was just as fooled as anyone else, believing that *THAT* was *ALL* he'd really done, unleashing as he did all of Hell's very worst on an unsuspecting world.

Already a war unique in having no real side, no neutral parties, each of the old patriarchate nations were at one-another's throats… willy-nilly… a pack of rabid wolves infected by an absolute blood lust reaching epidemic proportions hitherto unknown in the long annals of recorded warfare.

And as frenzied a situation as it already was Colonel Scarlett's successful dabbling in the dark arts served only to drive those other leaders-of-state way back then even further over the edge.

Watching what appeared to be Scarlett's many dead troops come back to unholy life, doing so in their various degrees of decomposition, only then did they deploy at long last that very last doomsday weapon at their immediate disposal.

Occurring right then to one-and-all no more practical tools of conventional warfare could now deliver them from this actual, supernatural, diabolic catastrophe courtesy of that prophesied 'Man of Lawlessness'[†††]—none other than Scarlett himself—it was then they all signed at last their ultimate death warrant.

What with their predominantly masculine armies already decimated by the twin forces of both combat and plague, lying all about them in tattered ruins, the last male leaders of all Womankind reacted now to one act of stupid folly with yet another. Escalating the conflict even further, they called forth the 'Lions'.

Although the official designation for these newest angels of death was 'Orbital Sonic Cannon', they were more oft referred to as 'Lions' by the general public—this moniker given in honour of that fearsome, ear-splitting roar they were reported to emit, raining down total annihilation upon their hapless victims.

Promoted in the end as a cleaner, safer alternative to nuclear arms this unique method of mass destruction involved the highly focused deployment of amplified sound waves directed down upon the Earth's surface from positions high above. Shattering enemy cities in one explosive blow, they did so in one fell-swoop as though nothing but fragile glass.

However, as dumb luck would have it, they were never tested before in such fatal numbers until that one crucial, pivotal moment in all of Human herstory. It was then both World War Three and male domination came to a rather ignoble, if not apocalyptic climax during the late fall of 2038, deployed as they were by those last 'Sons of Perdition', those last men allowed by Divine Will rule of the Human race.

[†††]   2nd Thessalonians—Chapter 2: Verses 1 to 12

              ****

...And as dumb luck would likewise have it the letters Gloria skimmed with such frank interest came as well to their own unfortunate end, the disappointed lieutenant regretting now her inability to read each and every one in greater detail.

Left now with nothing, but some boring old cargo manifest she kept on recording even so that data stream pouring into each ei-pad, remembering well the Commodore's explicit command to deliver to her *every* single scrap of information retrieved from the dilapidated command module back on Bandros.

Even so Gloria had her own, personal doubts as to whether or not she'd uncover anything of any great significance in the following information.

Boredom aside what actually caused Gloria to momentarily divert her attention from said monitor was a dull ache forming just behind her eyes, the oncoming sensation of a full-blown headache thanks to the light reflecting off her screen hitting as well her glasses.

Removing the offending eyewear from where they exerted pressure on the bridge of her nose Gloria looked briefly away, massaging closed lids with both thumb and forefinger, resting her eyes. Wishing she wasn't allergic to corrective vision drops... then she wouldn't have to wear the gosh-darn things... she cursed in silence her misfortune, paying no immediate attention to her work.

"Oh, well", she sighed, resigning herself to sad circumstance, placing her glasses back on just in time to catch sight of something odd flash by on her system's monitor. Gone in the wink of an eye, passing by with lightning speed, it appeared nonetheless to be some strange energy "blip" emitting a distinct form of peculiar energy all its own.

Not so quick however as to avoid Gloria's own rapid reflexes, forgetting as she did everything else. Activating at once her terminal's 'private modem diagnostic program', she managed by the very skin of her teeth to capture for future posterity that mysterious intruder's independent energy patterns.

Prevented from examining what she just proved lucky enough to catch on wafer while downloading as well all the colony data though, Gloria found herself at a momentary loss concerning how to proceed—the answer to her dilemma appearing soon enough however in the unwitting form of a junior petty officer, 2nd Class, straight out of her very own department.

Having left her own terminal only a fleeting moment ago the other woman in question was already making swift progress for the room's only exit, Gloria bringing her at once to a grinding halt, calling out to her from where she sat.

"Yes, Ma'am?", the lesser crewwoman paused, approaching her superior.

"Yes, Ms. Naylor: I need your assistance", Gloria explained, holding the results of her hasty recording by its slender edge.

Describing each specific test she desired at that very moment... a detailed analysis even she confessed might involve some significant time... she instructed the older woman to run as well a precise comparison check for anything like her 'mystery blip' recorded by chance in Maccs' memory.

Nor was that all, expressing even further her personal concern there might be some hostile, unidentified systems virus aboard StarChild.

"Probably just some random energy pulse from another system also in use", her subordinate offered straight away in a somewhat blasé manner bordering right on the edge of condescending.

"I don't think so, Ms. Naylor", came her superior's quick response, patient, controlling her temper. Irritated at once by this crewwoman's inappropriate attitude Gloria nevertheless managed her ire, suppressing her natural inclination towards anger as she proceeded even further:

"I think this might, in fact, prove important. Therefore I want you to run the complete spectrum analysis I've requested".

"As you just said, Ma'am, this might take a while. So maybe we should get instead Lt. Cmdr. Marlowe's permission first", Petty Officer Naylor then had the nerve to suggest, moving away now towards the research chamber's only exit without even the benefit of Gloria's dismissal.

Leaping up at once from her chair, Gloria's blood beginning to boil, she wasted no time darting out in front of her insolent N.C.O..

Although the greater majority of those crewmembers under her direction seemed to respect Gloria's rank there were nevertheless a couple of those under her direct command who felt it acceptable to sometimes disregard her rightful directives. Probably resenting her superior position of power at such a young age, not believing in her many abilities, they'd often go right over her head.

Bypassing her authority in favor of Naomi, Gloria's girlish appearance and diminutive stature helped her case even less, giving her an even younger air than her actual twenty years.

Letting it slide in the past however, wishing to avoid any unpleasantries all together, it was back then her original intention to win her detractors over with a simple display of her superior technical expertise, hoping they'd learn to respect her authority once seeing how well she handled her other duties:

BIG MISTAKE!!!

Understanding right then like never before Command was also one of her primary responsibilities, a duty she was guilty of neglecting now for so very long, it occurred to her high time at last she remedy that situation. Blocking at once the other woman's exit, moving with swift alacrity, Gloria looked up with fiery determination into the older non-comm.'s eyes.

"This has nothing to do with Lt. Cmdr. Marlowe seeing as I'm also your superior in charge of engineering. And just as I answer to her, Ms. Naylor, you answer to me", Gloria told her at the very same time in a firm, even voice ill concealing her burning rage.

"No longer will I permit, or even tolerate anyone in *my* department trying to perform any sort of run-around, circumventing either the proper chain of command or *my rightful authority*! Do I make myself perfectly clear?", Gloria read her haughty underling the full riot act in no uncertain terms. Managing all the while to control herself she vented nevertheless her justified anger:

"Now, Ms. Naylor, I have given you a direct order and, by all that's holy, I expect you to carry it out right now! Otherwise, if not, if you persist in this insubordinate behavior, questioning my rightful authority, it will be I, not you, lodging a complaint with Lt. Cmdr. Marlowe.

"And if that doesn't help remedy your attitude, put an end to such disrespect from those under my rightful command, then I guess I'll be left with no other alternative than to file on you an official disciplinary report with Commodore Saphira herself. Do you hear me Ms. Naylor?"

"Yes, Ma'am!!"

Satisfied her point was made, seeing the look of nervous apprehension in Ms. Naylor's eyes at the very mention of Jenniboni Saphira, Gloria was now confident she'd have no more trouble with her unruly subordinate. Holding up in Ms. Naylor's face the wafer she still held between them Gloria continued, now full of calm authority:

"Very good then: In that case I want you to take this, analyze the energy reading contained, run a comparison check on it with anything else on file, and locate both its point of origin as well as its final destination.

"And I want all this done—*A.S.A.P.*—with the results brought to me immediately upon completion! Meanwhile, I'll likewise finish up my work here. Understood?"

"Yes, Ma'am!", Ms. Naylor snapped yet again to immediate attention, anxious anticipation still quite obvious in her now obedient manner.

"Very good", Gloria continued, smiling: "In that case you have permission to begin: That will be all, Ms. Naylor!"

"Yes, Ma'am! Thank you, Ma'am!"

Watching her subordinate return now—quickly—to her own recent terminal Gloria wasn't embarrassed in the least, noticing those other occupants likewise using the research room staring at her.

Embarrassed? Not at all!!

Glad in fact they observed everything that just occurred she had no doubt at all how fast this little incident would get around ship. Now, perhaps, people would get the clear idea Lt. Gloria Greensley was no longer to be trifled with.

Seeming to have rectified at least that little problem Gloria returned once more to what she was doing before. Downloading the memory banks from the colony ship, reviewing as well all the information gathered on scanner during their brief time on Bandros, she included that also for Jenniboni on ei-pad.

Chapter 54

"THE EMEROG"

Situated on deck S-9, positioned before a terminal of her own in the 'Special Studies Lab', Naomi scrutinized in deep concentration the lengthy stream of complex data transferred to Maccs from Zelmorl. And standing right behind her Stasha peered as well over her shoulder, the only other person with her in that narrow room, sharing the bright display screen before them.

Breathing almost down her very neck it more often than not irked Naomi when other people stood behind her while trying to work. Not this time though, more understanding this time around, Naomi couldn't blame her given the situation at hand.

Captivated as she was by moving images left them by a bona-fide alien civilization flashing before her very eyes, captured on audio-image playback for future posterity, she could forgive this time quite easily Cmdr. Nikarov's intrusive proximity.

A record of daily life courtesy of that first non-Terran species discovered beyond Womankind's own home System Naomi was confident her companion was as spellbound as she by this detailed chronicle involving every aspect of their past existence. Just a shame neither of them could understand that alien voice explaining now in such obvious detail each and every scene they were now privy to. Both Maccs and Stasha's experts in linguistics were still trying to translate the Zelmorlite tongue, but were still having no luck.

'Oh well', Naomi pondered that ancient expression: 'A single picture is worth a thousand words'.

And taking into consideration all those visual findings now available, appearing before their very eyes, this meant they were privy now to over a billion words worth of valuable information, countless trillobytes of precious detail.

Taking more than just a little comfort from what they actually had, one feature that came to immediate light was the obvious fact that these

"Zelmorlites" were, in their day, quite Human in their general appearance. The only notable differences were their higher foreheads, narrower noses more angular in shape, and slightly larger eyes more round in circumference.

Nor was that all, another valuable fact soon revealing itself. This society was also a Matriarchate civilization. And observing this Stasha expounded upon a xeno-anthropological debate she participated in back during her university days.

Doing so for Naomi's benefit Stasha told her companion how the forum discussed whether, or not alien societies would be patriarchal, or matriarchal in nature. Given the obvious fact Human herstory proved the Matriarchate system more in keeping with the natural order of things Stasha had argued for the matriarchal viewpoint.

"But what if we someday encounter an alien race composed entirely of hermaphrodites?" Naomi countered, wearing all the while a jocular grin.

"I'm sure there are exceptions to every rule", Stasha gave way with a similar smile all her own: "However, as far as my humble opinion is concerned, such a society composed of such beings would no doubt prove a most boring place to live".

Giggling her amusement, agreeing with this assessment of such a theoretical civilization, another question likewise came to Naomi's probing intellect:

"So how do you, personally, think the old Patriarchates ever got their start on Earth in the very first place?"

"There are many viable theories on the matter", Stasha frowned, appearing perturbed by the very thought: "But, personally, I'm not certain to which I subscribe".

And when StarChild's learned X.O. said no more on the matter, Naomi decided it best to just let that particular subject drop, turning her attention back to that visual display from ancient Zelmorl.

"And at this rate we'll be here forever", Stasha complained, frustrated even more so by their apparent lack of progress: "As fascinating as all this is we have yet to determine what was responsible for their final demise!"

Intrigued as she was by the images passing by in great detail, especially those dealing with her own profession, Naomi was enjoying the 'show' very much. Reluctant to see it end she had to agree nonetheless this was getting them nowhere.

"No problem. All we need to do is check the final entry made into their system. I'm sure that'll contain what we're looking for".

"Can you actually do that?" Stasha asked, skeptical: "Were you able to send the data stream back in its proper chronological order?"

"No", Naomi confided: "The information in question was drawn from several different memory banks, each possessing its own individual matrix: A built-in redundancy should any storage unit suffer permanent deactivation, the information contained shunted on automatic into another fail-safe. The very minute we reached the very last entry in one, our transfer system picked up again with the first of another".

"Just as I thought", Stasha sighed, resting her good eye, shaking her head.

"However, I have found what appears to be an entry code buried in their original transmit signal", Naomi confessed, sounding optimistic: "It shows up on my diagnostic display board as a subliminal counter buried deep, just beyond the visible spectrum. Correlating in essence to a similar system employed by Maccs as a private means of entry verification time it would seem to be some sort of calendar. Here: Let me demonstrate".

Even as she spoke Naomi was already in the process of doing so, instructing Maccs to bring up the hidden signal so both women could view it for themselves. Appearing in the upper left-hand corner of that display screen they both shared each could make it out quite clearly now, Stasha leaning even further over Naomi's shoulder in hopes of a better look-see:

Yes!

There they were!

A tiny set of alien symbols!!

"For a while I couldn't figure them out", Naomi was careful to explain in greater detail: "At least not until it occurred to me to be some progressive number chart.

"Then, realizing that, I also noticed they seemed to employ a 'base 12' system listing the month before day then followed by the year: A system reminiscent of a similar progression employed by Rodney's very own people living back in ancient America.

"However, what really had me running around in circles is how their numbers are in reverse, arranged it seems from right to left not unlike certain Semitic writings.

"So, taking all this into consideration, all we have to do is feed now into Maccs the proper sequence code, its Commonwealth equivalent, and have Maccs search for the most recent entry".

Fingers dancing across her keyboard in eager anticipation, taking her less than a minute to do what she promised, it wasn't long before Naomi cried out in triumph:

"Voila. And there it is: Their final entry!"

Following that a split second of utter silence accompanied a blank screen, new images replacing now the previous display. And as each woman watched now what appeared before them, stunned into absolute quiet by all they saw, both Stasha and Naomi realized with mounting horror they found the ultimate object of their diligent search.

Nor did it prove necessary for either to understand what it was their alien narrator said, understanding at once why she sounded so close to tears.

****

Sedated, beyond fatigue, Rodney's subconscious mind managed nonetheless to inform him he was, within himself, once more alone. That malignant individual just recently in control of his every word, his every deed, had briefly left him, confident now Rodney posed no significant threat to *'Its'* nefarious machinations.

Even in such a quasi-quiescent state young Rodney was painfully aware there remained precious little time before, yet again, he found himself a mere vessel for some alien intelligence as insane as it was almost ageless.

Realizing this was most likely the last chance he'd ever have to save at least those who'd proven so kind, showing him at least some sweet modicum of fleeting hope, Rodney fought like never before.

Utilizing all those meager resources at his command to regain once more full wakefulness, still unable to believe in his own salvation, maybe he could save nonetheless those who brought him to this amazing place.

Who knows? Maybe it was God Almighty Himself who intervened right then on the poor boy's sad behalf, smiling upon his noble efforts.

Then again the answer might have lain in the simple purview of medical science, a sizeable adrenaline rush resulting from his highly agitated subconscious condition.

However, no matter which you choose to believe in—Divine intervention, simple biology, or a more likely combination of both—the final outcome remained nonetheless the same.

Struggling with all he had to regain absolute control of both body and soul there occurred inside his frail form a sudden rush of natural endorphins propelling him ever upward toward the bright light of complete wakefulness.

Like a deep-sea diver rising now from the briny depths, emerging from the ocean's surface on a clear day, Rodney likewise clawed himself all the way back to a full state of conscious awareness—the first individuals alerted to his premature awakening being those two security personnel Jenniboni posted just earlier outside each door to the Recovery Ward...

The same lonely chamber in which Rodney now came around.

Nor did that bloodcurdling scream ripping loose from the very pit of his stomach, passing through a tortured larynx strained to the max, leave in their minds any doubt now the young laddie they stood guard over was most certainly awake, shrieking as he did at the very top of his lungs:

"LOOK OUT FOR THE EMEROOOOOOOG!!!"

****

Prying the sharp, wicked crystal dart from the back of Ensign Wilson's punctured skull in the pathology lab next to her office Eartha was dictating step-by-step her every finding into an overhead audio-comp.

Nor did she need anyone telling her Rodney was already awake well ahead of schedule, forgetting at once the autopsy in progress. Interrupted by that frightful ruckus just a short way down the outside corridor, it was then one of the security detail posted outside his room found StarChild's C.M.O. in her nearby operating room.

"Yes; yes, Ms. Tully: I'm fully aware of the situation", Eartha grumbled over the continuous din, filling a clear injector: "Maccs!"

"Yes, Doctor?", his voice drifted down from above.

"Inform Commodore Saphira that our young guest has managed to wake up early sounding quite perturbed".

"Yes Doctor!"

****

Seconds later, as good as his word, Maccs passed on Eartha's urgent communiqué to Jenniboni herself, Frances still in her company. Still alone in the Star Stage they were discussing possible security precautions should they need return to either Zelmorl, or Bandros:

"You're with me, Lt. Cmdr.!", Jenniboni commanded, on her feet in no time flat. Making her way to the Recovery Ward two decks below she didn't even wait for the ag-pod. Using instead a nearby stairwell she turned to her right once reaching deck B-4.

Spotting at once both Eartha and Ms. Tully waiting for them outside the closer of the two recovery doors, Jenniboni caught sight as well of the medical injector in her C.M.O.'s right hand alongside the stunners each guard now held at the ready:

"Are both doors still secured?", Jenniboni demanded immediately upon arrival.

"Yes, Ma'am!", Ms. Tully assured her right off the bat, the other sentry guarding the other door further away giving her a similar guarantee.

First receiving Dr. Wei-Chang's message from sickbay Jenniboni was sure she'd find young Rodney in the middle of throwing an extreme temper-tantrum concerning his confinement to the small room beyond. After his previous ill conduct she thought it only fair to anticipate such a response.

Yet now she was here Jenniboni could readily hear in the poor child's terrified voice not anger, but unmitigated fear; the young laddie calling out quite plaintively for someone, *anyone*, to listen to whatever it was he had to say:

"All right, Gentlewomen; we're going in!"

Giving the command to proceed with all due caution Jenniboni lead the way, Eartha at her side, while Frances and Ms. Tully followed close behind, that other guard left behind instructed to just remain at her post.

Weapons lowered but at the ready the alarm in Rodney's expression increased at the mere sight of them, eyes wide as silver dollars watching Ms. Tully position herself just inside the door, Frances and Eartha drawing closer still at Jenniboni's side.

Not recognizing the design of each woman's sidearm Rodney had all the same a pretty good idea what they were for, the door all four women came charging through swooshing by now shut behind them.

"Hey, don't shoot me!!! I didn't mean to act so mean before. I couldn't help it", he cried, turning to Jenniboni, all three senior officers present reaching his bed: "I swear! Honest!!"

Seeing sincere regret over past troubles in the imploring look he gave her, Jenniboni mistook immediately Rodney's declaration of absolute innocence as an apology for previous misbehavior:

"That's all right, hon", she rendered gentle comfort in a soft, soothing voice not unlike crushed velvet:

"Don't worry. They won't hurt you", Jenniboni addressed young Rodney's fear, standing now closest to him: "They're only stunners. Do you understand?"

"Yeah, sure. Okay", he answered, calmer but still wary, cautiously afraid.

"Good", StarChild's commanding officer gave him a reassuring smile: "Now what is it you wish to tell us?"

"It's about the Emerog", he rushed on, his hurried voice growing only more and more flustered from one desperate word to the next:

"You gotta watch out for them. They're everywhere on Bandros and they want to take over Earth again just like they tried to last time! They killed all the people on Zelmorl and tried to take over Earth, too. They're really, really crazy… really, really nuts… and really, really mean too. And they also want to…"

"Wait a minute, hon", Jenniboni raised her hands in beleaguered protest:

"You're going way too fast. Slow down. Take a few deep breaths. Okay, Sweetie? Now start at the beginning: Who are the Emerog?"

"Okay! Sure. Yeah!", he willed himself to calm down, to remain calm.

Jenniboni was able to tell what a real effort it was for the scared little boy before her to relax, remain coherent, relating to her what he wanted to say:

"Wellll… it was a real, real long time ago when the people on Zelmorl came to Bandros to make it their own, to live on it like we tried to. The women came there first to build their cities and the Emerog didn't bother them when they came so they thought they were nothing, but a bunch of dumb green blobs of dumb energy floating around in the air…"

Suddenly aware like some noxious epiphany from on high he was referring to all those telltale fragments of nomad energy their probes detected just yesterday in the lower atmosphere—*billions of them!*—Jenniboni found herself ready to question him even further on the matter.

Changing her mind at the very last moment though, reigning in her natural curiosity least she interrupt his already fragile train of thought, Jenniboni decided better, seeing for herself the hard time the young laddie was having just trying to express himself in as coherent a manner as possible:

"Nothing bad really happened to the women until after they built their cities there and brung their men there. That's when the Emerog started making real trouble, taking over all their men, getting inside all their bodies just like bad ghosts, or demons in a scary movie …"

Rodney 'knew' all about demons. His father, Braddock Roderick, let him watch once a censored version of "The Exorcist" when he was much younger. Of course, censored or not, his mother pitched one 'Heck' of a major fit when finding out soon thereafter, giving her husband one heck of a royal chewing out.

Actually, truth be told, the movie didn't really scare him. Or at least not too much. The only thing that really 'grossed him out' were all the 'puke scenes'.

Yet, be that as it may, Jenniboni's first reaction hearing all this was to pray quite fervently that the poor child was either lying, making all this up or, failing that, quite crazy. Even that would be preferable to the obvious alternative, forced to concede sadly enough after listening further neither was the case.

Both the very tone of his young voice and reluctant expression relating all this frightful information told her in the unfortunate end that, fond hopes to the contrary, he was telling the absolute truth.

Nor did the rest of young Rodney's very demeanor suggest at all any mental impairment—neither ranting, raving nor gibbering about in some uncontrollable manner—remaining instead quite calm, coherent and even steady despite the obvious toll just remembering all this had on him.

There was no way Jenniboni could imagine such a young child, left to his own devises during such a significant time in his early development, coming up on his very own with such a fantastic, highly elaborate, complex tale. *No!!* This was no dark flight of twisted fancy Jenniboni now listened to with mounting horror. This was fact, as pure and simple as the frightened child detailing every sad event:

"So after they took over all the men there, and some of them went back to Zelmorl, the Emerog inside them went back there with them, too, and started to grow more and more there, taking over all the other men there, too.

"They like split themselves up like those tiny, little, animals back on Earth my mother told me about".

"Amoebas?" Jenniboni heard Dr. Wei-Chang ask, still close by.

"Yeah, right; I guess so??", Rodney gave Eartha a curious glance before turning his full attention back to Jenniboni:

"Well… whatever… the women back then never knew about the Emerog until it was too late. By the time they found out it was only 'cause the Emerog in the men got really mean and wanted to take over everything even though the women there were always nice to them, always fair...

"Nice to the men I mean...

"So when the women said 'no' to the men the men all started a war, breaking things and blowing them up, killing the women even though the women didn't want to hurt the men. Not even when they found out about all the Emerog in them.

"But they had to. So both sides started killing each over all over the place until they wiped everybody out just like my folks did!

"But some men with Emerog in 'em did escape from here and went to Earth", Rodney declared, outright, unaware of the shocked expressions of those listening:

"The people on Zelmorl knew about Earth as well as Bandros, but never went there. They even built a ship that could travel fast enough to get there real quick, the only one they had that fast, but no one went there until the men with Emerog in 'em stole it and took it there.

"But when they got there they found out that the women on Earth ran everything on Earth, too, like the women on Zelmorl did. They even treated men there okay, too...

"But when the Emerog got to Earth inside the men from Zelmorl found out the people on Earth were more primitive and thought they were gods. So they pretended they were gods, even telling the people on Earth they could be gods, too, while the Emerog started splitting themselves up again even more and more so they could take over all the men on Earth, too.

"And when they got inside all the Earth men, too, they tried to take things over there, too, and make the women on Earth do what they all said like they tried to on Zelmorl

"But 'cause the Earth people way back then didn't have any of the fancy stuff like they did on Zelmorl, too primitive, the women back then couldn't fight back like they did on Zelmorl.

"So 'cause they didn't have all the smart, fancy guns 'n' stuff like Zelmorl the Emerog *did* take over everything on Earth 'cause the men and women there didn't have the power to wipe everyone out!"

"Please, Sweetie. Please tell us what finally happened to all the Emerog on both Earth and Zelmorl", Jenniboni couldn't help but beseech him, Rodney taking as he did a brief pause in his horrific narrative. A story which sounded quite preposterous from the lips of any adult took on a most chilling quality of absolute realism related by a simple child employing a simple child's vocabulary:

"Well..., they all died off. The Emerog I mean. They don't even know why, but they can only live for real long on Bandros. But because they can talk anywhere to each other with their brains the ones on Bandros were able to talk to the others and find out when the others on Earth and Zelmorl all started to die off...

"Well, when they all died on Earth the men they didn't take over after that thought that men were meant to run everything 'cause that's what they saw happening since they were little kids when the Emerog used to run everything before that, bossing all the women around.

"They didn't know it was the Emerog that made all the men before them do that, so they didn't know they weren't doin' right running things, telling all the women what to do, instead of doing what the women said like they were always suppose to ...

"But In some places the women did remember the way things were supposed to be and took over again, but everywhere else the men stayed the bosses right up to today".

Confused by the amused grin on Jenniboni's lips hearing his last declaration, he asked her what was so funny, unable to see anything humorous in anything he told her. Explaining to him further about the Tammyite Matriarchate, she then let him in on how women once more ran all of Human civilization since over 800 years ago.

Fascinated by this revelation Rodney's eyes grew ever wider, amazed, feeling even then a certain sense of subtle relief:

"Really? Wow! So are the women back there nice to the men?", a trace of nervous apprehension creeping still into his voice.

"Yes Dear. We try to be as nice as nice can be to them", Jenniboni gave him quick assurance: "I'm sure you'll like it there very much".

To put his mind even further at ease, understanding the reason for his obvious concern, Jenniboni beamed him a great big smile quite sweet, giving him a brief but thorough breakdown of life in the Commonwealth.

Describing especially those things a young man-child of Rodney's tender years would likely find the most important, it was proof indeed Human affairs improved most remarkably since his own day.

"Wow. Yeah. Cool", came at once his enthusiastic reply: "That sounds great".

Smiling even more so at this simple expression of youthful exuberance Jenniboni heard yet again Dr. Wei-Chang, intrigued, musing out loud in a soft voice:

"So that's how the ancient patriarchates all got their start", she marveled: "Wait until all the Herstorians back home get wind of this, not to mention both the anthropologists and sociologists!"

Choosing not to comment Jenniboni asked instead Rodney another question:

"Honey, why did the Emerog take over just the men on both Earth and Zelmorl, not the women, and act so mean?"

"It's because they all wanted bodies like they used to have", he answered her slowly, carefully, wanting above all else to make sure he got it all quite right:

"Well..., they came to Bandros over ten thousand years ago in a spaceship from far away from here. And where they came from they all had bodies just like us.

"Didn't look the same, you know. They looked like aliens. But they still had regular bodies that could feel things like ours, and could die. They could feel things, taste things, smell things, and all that just like we can. And they liked doing all that kinda stuff, too!

"But when they came to Bandros they couldn't do none of those things no more 'cause they came thorough some kind a weird, outer-spacey, hole-thing from a whole other universe and got turned into energy..."

'Matter/energy transference', Jenniboni understood in silent reflection.

"...So now they can't feel nothin' no more. They can't even die when they get old like old people do. All they can do now on their own is talk to each other with their brains, figure out what's where with their brains, and move around using their brains.

"So when they found out they could take over all the men everywhere, and use them to do all those things they liked doing when they had their own bodies, they really liked using men to do all that stuff again. But because they didn't feel anything for so long 'cause they had no more bodies of their own, they'd all gone nuts, crazy like in a Looney bin".

An exquisite thrill of unabashed horror ran through all those listening to Rodney's frank narrative concerning Emerog affairs, their more than eccentric mentality, Eartha the most chilled of all:

Having already studied in her younger days the final results of various experiments involving sensory deprivation back home, Eartha was aware even before all this of those many complications both mental and emotional suffered by test subjects forced to endure such conditions for even a few days much less ten millennia!

God only knew, and Eartha could only shudder, trying to imagine the perpetual torment suffered by such individuals robbed of all sensory input, whatsoever, for thousands of years:

Endless torture!—absolute misery!—deprived of such basic necessities without even the hopeful eventuality of utter oblivion, death itself, to count on.

Maybe that was why, for the briefest moment only, Eartha felt an actual sense of overwhelming pity for the Emerog, their miserable condition!

However, not lasting long, it came to a grinding halt considering further all the pain and suffering on at least three worlds these creatures were likewise responsible for—the all-consuming mayhem, mass destruction, they each no doubt wrought since their initial conception.

After this, listening further to Rodney's horrific narrative, Eartha felt no longer any sympathy for the Emerog.

"... So when they took over all the men they were so happy to feel stuff again they hated anyone who tried to stop them, anyone who got in their way. So they killed off everyone who tried to stop them, or control them. None of 'em like being told what to do about anythin'. They only want to tell others what to do all the time, be the bosses all the time.

"They always want to be the bosses. Mean and nasty ones, too. They don't like or love nobody. Only hate. They always feel bad inside".

"Honey, what I don't understand is why the Emerog took over just men. If they want so many bodies so badly why don't they take over women as well?", Jenniboni felt a compulsive need to ask, all the same unsure she really wanted to hear his answer.

Yet even so the honest young laddie's simple reply still came as quite a shock:

"Oh that. That's because they can't take over women's' bodies", he informed her in such a casual, matter-of-fact way it left Jenniboni feeling at a momentary loss.

"Why not?" she frowned, finding once more her tongue.

"'Cause women's' brains and bodies are better made", he added in careful reply... hesitant... expounding the best he could in his childish way on scientific truths he himself barely understood:

"The women on Zelmorl and Earth were the same like that. Their brains were able to do more stuff, made different than men's', and the Emerog couldn't get into them. Just like their bodies. Their bodies are built better than men's' too, able to do more both inside and outside and the Emerog couldn't get into them either.

"I guess it's like trying to break into some regular dumb old house and rob it instead of trying to sneak into some really big, top-secret army base with all its fancy, super-modern security stuff with all its solders with their big guns.

"It's like when I was a little kid and my Dad told me all about the first real computers they had back in real olden days, how they were so slow and stupid when compared to the really modern ones we have now with all they can do and remember".

Jenniboni, amused all the same by the term 'slow and stupid', was nevertheless certain young Rodney never meant to imply his entire gender was either, knowing as well she would never describe men so.

Yet be that as it may, she understood nonetheless what he was getting at, everyone else there—Dr. Wei-Chang especially—likewise 'in the know'.

As far back as the late 20th century medical science had already discovered those varied differences in female/male physiology used nearly a hundred years later, among other obvious considerations, to justify the rebirth of matriarchal rule.

Differences poor Rodney, limited as he was in his simple vocabulary, managed to otherwise convey—his comparison of both to different period computers, their disproportionate ability to access information, proving apt enough.

At least as far as it went.

In this instance Eartha would have included as well the superior capability of later technology to process, store, and even exchange data input.

Not only were women able to learn at more accelerated levels than their masculine counterparts, but the physical corridor connecting both right and left hemispheres of the female brain allowed also a more multi-leveled—multi-lateral—exchange between the two, larger as it was than that connecting both halves of the masculine brain.

Providing as this did a greater flow of synaptic impulses between both hemispheres of the female brain, superior synchronization of the two when compared to men, this meant as well that women were better able to utilize those unique properties of each to an even greater extent than men—a more harmonious balance of that left hemisphere governing the technical, logical, and even mechanical alongside that right side of the brain governing both the artistic, emotional and even creative aspects of human nature.

Nor was this superior co-ordination of the female mind hard to observe, more often than not manifesting itself in a greater variety of both variant skills and interests—a greater blending in women of both the artistic and technical permitting them a more innovative combination of each, men more 'mono-lateral' in both their thinking and creative properties.

A peculiar limitation on the part of the male resulting in that portion of Humanity being labeled either fairly or unfairly as having 'one-track minds', it was likewise an ironic twist granting men a superior talent for greater specialization in nearly every field of Human endeavor.

While true men possessed 'larger' brains in the sense of mere volume, it was nevertheless women who retained a greater count of brain cells. Especially in those areas of the physical mind governing memory, judgment, personality, and planning women even proved themselves able to recall more emotional levels than men, experiencing a wider range of emotions likewise on a more intense level.

However, even so, it must be said in their high honour that no decent woman throughout the entire length, depth, or breadth of the Commonwealth would ever deny men recognition of either their feelings, talent, intelligence, or basic worth as fellow Human beings—Eartha having found for example the Commodore's charming young husband a most witty, knowledgeable, and sensitive dinner companion while aboard the Supreme Mother's private cruiser:

A most delightful young laddie whose company she appreciated very much, likewise taking note of his more than just comely physical features.

Extremely handsome!

Hey, just because StarChild's Chief Medical Officer was a rather cranky old woman with four grandchildren already out of college didn't mean she was dead from the neck down, still able as well to appreciate men for their more physical attributes.

Hard to believe all that was no more than just a mere week, or so ago…

Seemed longer!

And on a similar note Eartha knew as well what her newest patient meant with his comparative references to the female physique. Possessing alongside their superior mental agility both greater physical durability alongside a superior tolerance for pain the female body had as well in its favour a more advanced, complex, hormonal composition resulting in greater stability.

Another obvious plus in the favor of women; a greater built-in control of both the physical, mental, and even emotional.

Truths self-evident for anyone with eyes to see and ears to hear, Eartha would never have guessed though in a million Martian years these same conformations of female superiority proven now by medical science for nearly a thousand years would include as well a natural immunity to alien infestation!

A fat lot of good these natural benefits of womanhood did them, however. Sure didn't protect them from both total annihilation on one world alongside both sexual degradation, complete oppression for over six millennia on another.

And listening even further to the bizarre tale young Rodney still spun it struck Eartha especially ironic that these "Emerog" were, even in their original, physical state an asexual species. Even before their conversion from matter to energy they were never exposed to the 'radical concept' of a two-gender species, assuming during their first encounter with the Zelmorlites that male and female were an indication of two separate races altogether.

Nor did they even consider one sex superior to the other, giving on Earth birth to male domination simply to satisfy their own obsessive lust for absolute power.

All the same though the young laddie's vivid recounting of alien goings-on in the far past reached soon its final conclusion, the weary man-child before her lapsing right thereafter into an anxious, pensive-eyed silence.

Jenniboni, also taking this into account, sat herself then at the end of his bed in front of where he likewise sat, legs crossed. Reaching out to him, placing on Rodney's lean shoulder a placating hand, she proceeded further with great care, posing her next question in as tender a way as possible.

"Rodney, sweetie: I know this is very difficult but could you please tell us what happened to your people five years ago? Anything which might help us fight the Emerog would mean a great deal to us".

Hoping for something in the retelling that might in the end aid them all in combating these alien monstrosities, Jenniboni still hated herself for even asking him this unique favor.

Watching his tragic features cloud up she was no less aware than he this would be harder for him to discuss. Whereas his previous recounting of Emerog atrocities involved herstorical times far removed from his own person, this would be different. This time he'd be forcing himself to re-live the most traumatic experiences in his own recent, personal herstory:

"Well ...", Rodney got off to a slow start, reluctant: "They didn't get really, really super-killin' mean until that very last day...."

Chapter 55

"MEAN AND CRAZY!!!!"

Neither Stasha, nor Naomi could at first fathom the distress in the Zelmorlite voice narrating the visual display they watched with such growing apprehension. The initial scenes on their shared screen appearing quite pleasant, even idyllic, they began as they did with the construction of both Zelmorlite communities on Bandros.

Nevertheless both women taking note of all this from StarChild's 'safe' interior couldn't help, but observe how odd it was that ancient narrator seemed to obsess with almost paranoid frequency on a somewhat strange airborne occurrence—sickly green spheres like a cross between both swamp gas and some peculiar brand of St. Elmo's fire.

Watching those perplexing lights move about in the greenish/blue Bandrosian sky, their every single move growing yet more disquieting than the last, there was no doubt in either Stasha or Naomi's mind those eerie, spectral entities almost dancing about in otherwise tranquil skies would play a most singular role in that Greek tragedy about to unfold:

"I'll bet you cookies to krodits those are the individual energy readings our own shipboard scout probes detected just yesterday", Naomi offered. Scrutinizing their every swift motion it were as though they were almost twirling about in playful frolic:

"No bet here", Stasha turned down her partner's magnanimous offer, examining with studious intent how those jarring creatures of unknown origin seemed to comport themselves with almost sentient purpose. Noting at once the putrid light they gave off she also noted its uncanny resemblance to that rather misty, cloudy glow Jenniboni described during her earlier encounter with those mechanoids spooking her likewise hours ago.

Nor did it escape Stasha's keen powers of observation how those puzzling phenomena exhibited some form of rudimentary intelligence. Their almost hypnotic moves suggesting as well some sort of predatory nature, it was as though they were stalking as it were some intentional prey.

Busy scenes of mass construction were soon followed however by the more tender image of Zelmorlite families. Their day-by-day lives captured for future examination; it was a panoramic display of familial love in all its obvious wonder.

A moving tribute to behold, both peaceful and heartwarming in its very content, this gentle show of alien community struck both Naomi and Stasha quite reminiscent of Womankind's very own back in the Tammyite Matriarchate.

Tender scenes indeed all this gentle living came to a rapid conclusion though, replaced in the blink of an eye by other scenes less bucolic in content: Scenes of both death and destruction wreaking havoc on both Bandros and Zelmorl.

Bearing witness to all that wanton destruction recorded also for future consumption, both StarChild personnel still watching all this stared on in mounting revulsion. Streets bathed now in rivers of alien gore conflict and carnage on a global scale turned every community, both large and small, into a veritable crimson slaughterhouse.

Zelmorl now featured in greater detail, its continual display of social unrest erupted on the lonely screen both Naomi and Stasha shared now in tragic witness. Quite clear that each side doing battle with the other was arranged according to gender it turned into a twisted "Slice 'N' Dice" feature, proving out on an even grander scale Eartha's claim of 'Sexual Civil War' among Rodney's late kin.

Nor was that the end of all the attention-grabbing horror to come, what happened to each and every man that fell in battle clutching both women around the throat like a pair of iron hands.

Glassy eyes staring upward in blank expression at indigo skies, smoky green light snaked its way out from each mortally wounded male's parted lips and nose. Coalescing once more into those same globular entities discovered first on Bandros, each hovered for only a second above those dead bodies they just inhabited, soaring up into dark skies right thereafter.

Only then did the monitor on which both women watched all this go blank. The data stream they were viewing reaching at last its blessed end, each was left now to just themselves.

"What the *'freakin', Gosh-darn, Heck'* is going on here?" Naomi swore, outraged, giving way to an offended shudder.

"I haven't the foggiest", Stasha insisted, herself likewise in deep shock: "But we've got to get all this to Jen… the Commodore… at once!"

"Understood", Naomi agreed, downloading right then all they saw onto ei-pad. Every gruesome detail captured for Jenniboni's future edification, she ordered Maccs as well to file this frightful data under her own, personal, private access code.

And making sure no one would stumble upon it without her personal authorization, Naomi tucked it away even further inside him under the first designation appearing to her creative intelligence:

'Los Diablos!!' …

THE DEVILS!!

****

"Well…", Rodney got off to a slow start, reluctant: "They didn't get really, really super-killin' mean until the very last day when… you know… they killed everyone. Well… they were always mean, even when they started taking all the guys over, but they didn't get… you know… 'killin' mean' until the very last day. They didn't even try to take us over when we first got to Bandros. It was like they were trying to… uh… check us out first if you know what I mean".

Jenniboni just nodded her complete understanding. Letting that suffice for now, Rodney continued on from there:

"So after they checked us out, and liked what they saw, they started to take over all the guys in our group. Couldn't take me over that good way back then, but my mom thought that's because my brain wasn't grown up enough. She figured that out when I finally told her what was going on on the very last day".

"Why did they kill your people on that last day?", Jenniboni felt it her duty to ask at last, proceeding with kid gloves.

"Well, it was because of you guys they did it", he answered her in such a matter-of-fact fashion she felt at first sure she heard him wrong. The very idea they themselves were somehow responsible for all the colony's dead left Jenniboni feeling as heartsick as it did confused.

"It wasn't really you guys here on this ship", Rodney was quick to add, seeing that look of utter bemusement appearing on Jenniboni's face:

"You guys here didn't do nothin' wrong. It was just your T.V. shows".

Bewildered at this point beyond all hope, Jenniboni begged further still for clarification.

"Well, when we first all first got here we all thunk we were the only ones left alive. We thought everyone else was killed in the war, all the people back on Earth. Even after the Emerog started taking over we thought we was the only people left in the whole universe.

"Then, in that bit of our ship we got left in Paradise, we started pickin' up stuff commin' from Earth whenever we got closer to Earth in our orbit, whenever that big red planet with the rings wasn't in the way…

"Well… Mom and Dad were the leaders of the colony, and my Mom was the first to start seein' your shows 'n' stuff from back home. So we knew after that that people still lived there.

"She couldn't hear everything you guys said in your stuff real good, but she watched all the pictures all the time and liked what she saw. She said she could tell from what she saw you guys were real peaceful, nice, and really, really smart; that you knew a lot of new stuff. Things looked a lot better to her there than when we lived there".

Realizing the young laddie was referring to their public, stellar-wide 3-DV broadcasts televised some five years before his people in fact saw them, Jenniboni thought with wry humor how nice it was their shows gave others such a favorable opinion of Womankind's very society—their entire civilization:

"Seeing all your stuff at first she was going to send you a message, but changed her mind. What with all the men starting to act so weird and scary she was afraid the same thing would happen to you guys too if you came here. She didn't know what was really wrong... the Emerog, you know... but she still saw that something' was creepy and she didn't want it to happen to you too if you all came here...

"But my Dad and all the other men with Emerog in them wanted to send you guys a message telling you all this junk about how great it was here, how you guys should all come here, all this made-up stuff so you guys would come here so the Emerog could take over your men, too.

"So all the grown-ups had this town meetin' to vote on what to do and, after my mom and dad each told the people what they wanted to do, almost all the women voted with Mom while the men went along with Dad...

"But because there was a lot more women my mom won. So the men got mad at that and started hangin' out in the alien city in the west 'cause the Emerog always inside them by then made them fix up all this olden stuff there. Stuff like those spacey alien weapons and those androids so they could take them over, too".

At mention of those spectral automatons back on Bandros Jenniboni felt a keen sense of final vindication, all her previous doubts now justified...

" And while they was doin' that my mom was goin' up to the northern city... the big one... 'cause she found this big building shaped like a pointy, up-side-down ice-cream cone with all these computers in a round room in the middle of it in the middle of the city..."

Nor did his mention of that particular design fall either on deaf ears, Frances picking up at once on the young laddie's childish description of that very building his mother used to frequent. Sounding comparable to the tower in which the late, lamented Ms. Wilson lost as well her life, Frances wondered if Rachael Roderick encountered likewise the same metal titan's they did battle with on Zelmorl.

Did she, too, have to fend off such overwhelming odds in her singular explorations and, if so, how? Or were such monsters saved by their makers for just that particular storage bin of alien knowledge Frances led her own small team into?

"... For a long time she couldn't get into all that stuff inside the computers there 'cause she didn't know the right buttons to push. So she just pushed whatever buttons in whatever order she thought might work to see what would happen, keeping notes in a book she had on the ones that didn't work...

"Then after she did that to remember what didn't work, she'd keep trying something else new to see what did to get the right ones in the right order of... whatever. Everybody already knew about the Emerog but the women all thought they were nothin' but a bunch of dumb blobs in the sky until Mom found out the truth on the last day".

Taking a long pause at this point in his narrative, reluctant to continue, it was plain to see Rodney wanted least of all to carry on. Able to see the apparent pain he was in just thinking about it Jenniboni gave him all the time he needed in order to collect himself even further, the boy finding his voice yet again just a few minutes later:

"What happened the last day everyone else was still alive began when Mom and me got up real early in the morning in her room. We locked the bedroom door before going to sleep 'cause my dad and her got into a real big fight about something so he hit her. Real hard, too!

"He never hit her before but the Emerog inside him made him do it. The Emerog made him act real creepy before, but that was the first time I ever saw it make him hit her. So she grabbed me and locked us both in their bedroom ...

"Well, we heard him start yelling a bunch of stuff at us, banging the door, before we heard him leave our living unit so, when we got up in the mornin', my mother grabbed somethin' heavy to hit him with if he tried to hurt us, and searched our whole place for him.

"But he was still gone so she made us breakfast, put a bunch of food in a backpack for later, and took me with her to the big city in the north. The one with all those computers in that funny-looking building...

"But before we left the colony we found out that my dad wasn't the only man gone. None of the men were there anymore and the women didn't know where they all got to. Boy, they all got really weirded out over that one. The women I mean. But none of them knew what to do about it anyway so me and Mom took a land rover to the big city...

"Well, either way, Mom finally got the computer there to tell her what she wanted to know. She couldn't understand the alien talking on it 'cause it only talked alien talk, but she saw what the Emerog did to 'em a long time ago and figured out what was going on with us, too".

Describing in graphic detail all his mother had seen five years ago Rodney had no way of knowing that both Naomi and Stasha Nikarov were, at that very same moment, watching the exact same display of wanton carnage Rachael Roderick witnessed the very same day she, too, died—his audience listening with that self-same mix of both horror and disgust Naomi and Stasha likewise shared in common.

"She also found out the Emerog were sometimes takin' me over, too, exceptin' when they started fixin' up all that alien stuff in that other city..."

Explaining right then and there that such was due to the fact that, while the Emerog could read his mind while in possession of his young body, he could likewise read their every thought while they used his frail flesh for evil intent.

And since they couldn't possess him every single moment at such a tender age, they decided not to risk the possibility of him telling the women their plans when not in absolute control of his every thought, word, and deed.

Relating all this to Jenniboni the poor child revealing all this trembled both suddenly and quite violently, recalling right then how it felt to know their every repulsive, twisted thought and feeling squirming about inside him:

"So that's when she made me tell her all about them. I would' a told her about them sooner but they said they'd kill everyone if I did so I was too scared to", his voice began to also tremble, catching in his throat, overcome as he was with feelings of both absolute guilt and persistent remorse:

"I was only a little kid then and didn't know they'd kill everyone off anyway. Maybe if I told her all about them sooner she could' a stopped them".

Full of self-recrimination, berating himself without mercy, Jenniboni was just as quick responding:

"Oh no sweetie! No! You can't blame yourself for anything that happened down there", she insisted on the very brink of bitter tears herself, feeling his pain as though it were her own: "Nothing they did was your fault!!"

Absorbed however in the recounting of his people's very last hours the young witness she addressed with such fervor heard her not, his own frenzied words pouring out of him in hurried procession... rushed... frantic:

"So Mom ran out to the jeep and used the C.B. in it to call the other women back in Paradise, finding out from them all the men were still gone. So she told them to get all the guns we took with us from Earth and give them to all the women. She wanted to take all the men prisoner if she could when they came back, lock them up in the barns, or somethin' 'till she could figure out what to do with 'em. Mom an' me didn't know about the androids or their spacey, alien super-guns.

"So we got in the jeep and headed back there real fast when Mom says she's goin' to send you guys on Earth a message after all. Not a bunch of made-up junk like the Emerog wanted to send about how nice it was here, but a warnin' to stay away, tell you guys what was really goin' on here.

"But as we're all drivin' along she stops the jeep real fast in the middle of nowhere, only a bunch of dumb grass and trees 'n stuff, and gets out of the jeep not sayin' nothin'. All she did was get the backpack we brung with all the food in it out of the back of the jeep, dumpin' it on the ground:

"So after she did that Mom also grabbed me out of the jeep and dumped me there, too. She said she'd come back for me if everythin' turned out okay, but the Emerog had a spy hiding in the colony—some guy hiding there who heard what the women were going to do and told all the others. I didn't know about all that back then, but I still knew she'd never come back for me".

Discussing out-loud for the very first time in his entire young life what happened five long years ago, all the pain repressed for so long came at last bubbling up to the surface. Weeping for the first time since then, reliving all that hidden hurt with others of his kind, the telling of his pathetic tale became now for Rodney a cathartic function.

Understanding this quite readily herself, having no need of further explanation, Jenniboni let him continue... unabated... cradling him by now in caring arms, stroking his hair as if he were her own:

"So I started screamin', an' kickin', and sayin' 'no', 'cause I didn't want her to leave me all alone, forever and all time, with them. But she said she didn't want me to get hurt if anythin' went wrong back in Paradise. But I wouldn't stop fightin' her, so she shook me to make me stop", Rodney's voice grew now somewhat distant, both urgent yet faraway, reliving now each tortured moment as though it were all taking place yet again:

"Then she started crying, too, holdin' on to me before she let go and got back into the jeep, leaving me behind with just that crummy backpack full of junk. I knew, and so did she, I'd never see her again. I remember thinkin' how I wished she just killed me instead of leaving me all alone with them.

"I always still feel like that".

Fighting back still her own urge to cry, still holding close the little boy telling her all this, the very idea of a child so young hungering after death proved itself too much for Jenniboni's beggared sensibilities. A mother herself the thought of her own children, all back on Demeter with their father, came at once to her active imagination, Rodney no older back then than her elder daughter was right now.

Thinking of that happy little girl back home enduring some tribulation so painful she'd actually choose death over life, it tore at Jenniboni's heart as though a physical ache thinking of both the young boy in her arms as well as his late mother.

Nor was it long after Raechal Roderick came to mind Jenniboni found herself full of admiration for that other mother. What courage it must have taken those many years ago to do what she did, leaving her only child by the wayside in desperate hope of saving his life, knowing all the while in her heart of hearts she'd never see him again.

Jenniboni's own heart went out right then and there to that other woman, no doubt dying all the while she left her own son behind her, aware at the same time she was somehow going to her own death:

"I tried to run after her, to catch her, but it was no use", Rodney carried on through increasing tears: "So I just gave up and waited where she left me for her. I ate the food she left me and walked back to the colony when she didn't come back for me. I knew they were all dead, but didn't find out how they died until later…

"When Mom got back there most of the men came back and killed most of the women. Only Mom, her best friend, Thelma, and three others were left. They were all standing around talkin' about what happened, what to do next, when my Dad drove up in a jeep with three other men and started shootin' at them with those alien guns they got in the alien city.

"Well, they killed one of them, but Mom and the other women left there killed all the men before they could kill them, too.

"Even Dad!!

"He never wanted to kill no one; I swear. It was the Emerog who made him act so mean. He was a real nice guy but couldn't help acting so bad when they took him over", Rodney went to great pains in his late father's defense, stressing to all those listening the point that Brad Roderick was just as much a victim of Emerog maliciousness as his wife.

Needless to say his relief was just as evident, Jenniboni assuring him in no uncertain terms nobody there held his father responsible for anything he did while under alien control. Feeling at least a wee bit better at this, Rodney told them all even further how his mother sent then her message to Earth, setting it on auto-repeat…

"…but she heard a bunch of guns shooting right after that and knew somethin' was wrong, shootin' up the message-sender with a gun Aunt Thelma gave her so nobody could use it anymore. And when she was sure it was totaled she left the inside of what was left of our ship and saw that all the others were dead. Even Aunt Thelma!

"Then she saw the androids with Emerog in them and started to run. They shot her with stuff from their alien guns and hurt her real bad, but she kept on runnin' anyway. She made it to the edge of the colony, but four androids trapped her when she got between two livin' units at either end and blasted her into little pieces anyway with their guns…

"You know how I know all that?", the weeping boy asked without any further preamble, his trembling voice taking on now a more shrill tone teetering on the very border of complete madness itself:

"I know all about what they did to everybody 'cause they like to get inside me and make me watch it over and over again in my head anytime when they want to have some 'mean fun'. Like it's really goin' on in front of my eyes! They like to hurt me over and over again inside when they ain't usin' me for other stuff.

"They make me watch Mom kill Dad first, then make me watch them blow up Mom all the time 'cause they're all mean and crazy… *mean and crazy… **mean and crazy**…*"

Chanting these last three words again and again as though some tortured mantra, his voice rose now to an agonized shriek:

"… mean and crazy… "MEAN AND CRAZY!!!!"

Forced at last to release him from her tender embrace when Rodney began to rock violently back and forth Jenniboni was sure at once he'd hurt himself if not stopped, whipping his head from side to side as though trying in vain to dislodge such memories.

Leaping to her feet as the tortured child, abused now for nearly half his young life, years of living **Hell** coming at long last to the surface, worked himself up now into an absolute frenzy. Jenniboni not the only one sure he might do himself serious injury, Eartha chose that very moment to anticipate her C.O.'s next command.

Rushing at once to his bed she grabbed young Rodney by the upper right arm before the beleaguered youth even knew what was happening. Pressing the hypo still in her hand to the base of his neck the sedative entered swift and sure his entire bloodstream, leaving him no chance at all to protest.

Too late!

Desperate right then to warn them all of the intruder touring now StarChild's every nook and cranny, struggling against those very chemicals now robbing him of every waking thought, he opened his mouth in vain hope of speech.

All to no avail however, slipping back yet again into complete insensibility both mental and physical, Rodney suffered during his last waking moment a clear sense of self-loathing, unable to utter a single word thanks to Eartha's tender ministrations.

Having in his own opinion blown his one and only chance to warn them all of that cruel menace prowling about their ship, his last real opportunity to count for something in this lousy reality, Rodney judged himself a worthless nothing, a pathetic failure!

****

Placing her hand in back of his head, Eartha lay him gently back down on the recovery ward bed. Arranging as before his now-limp body in a more comfortable position all five women left after that the silent room in quiet shock, stunned by all they just heard.

Leaving behind them their young guest to his drug-induced slumber, all three senior officers present crossed the corridor beyond to its far side, the young security guard with them resuming her original post.

"Lord Almighty, what a bugbear like that for a child to live with all these years", Frances was first to break their mutual quiet, talking in just a hushed whisper: "It must have been like being raped each and every day".

"Not 'like' being raped", Eartha growled in savage hate, revolted, her craggy face full of venomous animosity: "It was, and is, rape! Pure and simple! The vilest manner of rape I can imagine, a violation of ones very soul, their innermost self!"

"I actually wish now we did encounter some sort of alien invasion fleet upon our arrival in this contemptible system", Jenniboni spoke up at last, her voice shaky: "A collection of stellar craft like we first anticipated, crewed by flesh and blood creatures like ourselves we could possibly reason with. That at least I could deal with.

"But these… these… *things* aren't just aliens. They're more akin to demons: Denizens of *Hell* itself. No reason, no sanity, no compassion, and no sense of pity whatsoever!!"

Saying all that she was reminded at once of the Bible passage in which the Lord Jesus Christ asked a man possessed by unclean spirits what in fact his name was. The demon's answer…?

"'My name is 'Legion' for we are many!'"[*]

"Legion!", Jenniboni muttered, aloud:

"And there are billions of them down there on Bandros", she added, that new moon-world's very name leaving in her mouth a very bitter taste: "What inner circle of utter damnation have we stumbled across?"

---

[*]   "The Gospel According to Mark"—Chapter 5: Verses 9-10

Unable to think of a fitting answer between them both Eartha and Frances remained instead as silent as the grave, two new arrivals appearing just a few meters away from a nearby ag-pod.

Hurrying over to their current position, Naomi was first to deliver them the recorded news of all they learned but moments ago, the certain truth of what happened to the Zelmorlite people, Stasha following close behind.

"Pray tell", Jenniboni sneered in their very direction, Naomi handing her right then the ei-pad in possession of all their hard-earned research: "A bunch of putrid green blobs that take over the bodies of men, using them to commit sanguinary murder!"

"Yes, Ma'am", Naomi blinked, clearly nonplussed: "But how did you know?"

"The young laddie in there just told us all about them", StarChild's C.O. explained, pointing with her thumb in the Recovery room's nearby direction:

"*ALL* about them", she shivered just thinking about it: "They call themselves the 'Emerog'".

Another name leaving in her mouth a quite bilious taste!

Watching the myriad scenes downloaded onto the Pad now in her possession, its display screen showing her all that Naomi and Stasha saw just earlier, Jenniboni felt quite violated herself realizing that she as well was *also* in their company not so long ago.

No mistaking that unholy glow from android faceplates for anything else than the Emerog themselves she felt right then quite dirty indeed, remembering not long after that how Andrei said he felt during his own ordeal in that horrid bar back on Demeter.

Witnessing for herself the many, many crimes those vile creatures still on Bandros were responsible for, Jenniboni was left feeling quite ill indeed, close to absolute despair:

"Dear Lord, I even talked to those disgusting things".

Feelings of both helpless shock and utter degradation were replaced soon enough however by an even greater sense of pure, unalloyed rage consuming for the moment her entire being. Her heart engulfed in a burning hate smoldering now in her eyes, it was a fiery beacon lighting now the darkest recesses of her innermost psyche:

"Gather ALL department heads for an emergency meeting in the senior officer's briefing room, NOW", Jenniboni ordered, looking up at Stasha from the ei-pad in hand… powerful… in command.

"A strategy session, Ma'am?".

"Yes, Ms. Nikarov. I guess you could call it that", Jenniboni answered her, full of steely resolve: "Then again you could also call it a 'Council of War'".

"War Ma'am?!"

"Yes, Commander: WAR!!", came Jenniboni's immediate reply, full now of cold fury, darkest hate: "Because, as of right now, I'm officially declaring war on the Emerog. And I promise you, Ms. Nikarov, that it'll be a war of total annihilation… *THEIRS!!!*"

Chapter 56

"THE GETAWAY"

"And there you have it, Gentlewomen", Jenniboni continued, keeping all the while a watchful eye on those under her command.

Surveying their varied reactions from the briefing table's immediate head she noted in their expressions everything from an obvious look of righteous indignation to outright revulsion, her senior staff expressing no less an absolute sense of moral outrage over Emerog atrocities than she:

"You've seen both the visual evidence from Zelmorl, heard the testimony given by the young laddie in sick-bay, as well as what we likewise witnessed on Bandros: Dr. Wei-Chang, Lt. Cmdr. Oftesfs, and myself.

"All three of us bore witness to the aftermath of the Emerog-induced 'sexual civil war', as our good C.M.O. has so aptly christened it", Jenniboni testified. She viewed as well Naomi's choice of access code quite appropriate, referring to the grisly file viewed just moments ago:

"Los Diablos"

… Ancient Spanish for "*The Devils*".

"So now we're left with the simple question of what to do next, what course of action with which to proceed against this foul adversary we are now faced with. I doubt anyone here would disagree with the obvious assessment that we cannot allow—*ever*!!—these twisted creatures to leave their current confinement.

"Unfortunately we have at our command no reliable method, or methods however by which we can quarantine the planet in question, preventing without doubt other space-faring races from trying to colonize it in the possible future.

"At least no way that is except risking an interstellar incident ourselves. After all, as Lt. Cmdr. Oftesfs pointed out just yesterday, this otherwise Hellish moon-world seems on the surface 'prime real-estate', a tempting piece of property at first glance for anyone that might pass this way.

"Therefore, I'm afraid we have no other viable option other than to eradicate this new peril we've stumbled upon with all due haste, leaving no trace at all of their very existence.

"And since we know for a fact these devilish creatures are vulnerable to something both Earth and Zelmorl possess in common I suggest this would be our best place to start", Jenniboni offered with cool determination. Void of all feeling, she pressed home with greater passion what followed:

"To be quite blunt Gentlewomen we're not dealing here with a species which can be reasoned with. There is no chance here of a 'meeting of the minds'. No hope of peaceable parley! The herstorical facts of the case, combined with what we've learned of their present state of mind, prove beyond any reasonable doubt these 'Emerog' are quite incapable of either change, or peaceful co-existence:

"In short they are utterly insane with a consummate lust for absolute power beyond any means of dissuasion other than death itself, a mutated species of degraded perverts, sadists, and psychopaths incapable of rational thought. Every one of them!

"Nor does it matter if their present condition is the result of some unfortunate circumstance beyond their control. How they ended up this way, whether or not they are to blame for their present condition, is moot. All that matters right now is the simple fact they are just too dangerous to leave to their own devices, to continue living", Jenniboni added, fierce and relentless, summing up her own position in the matter:

"Any questions, Gentlewomen?"

"To be quite honest, Ma'am, I have no qualms whatsoever liquidating each and every one of these rank abominations", Frances confessed, candid as always: "Not after all I've seen and heard both here and on Zelmorl. In fact the only problem I have here is how to go about doing so".

"Clearly the answer rests in something both Earth and Zelmorl have in common Bandros doesn't", Jenniboni reiterated; "making it our first priority to determine just what, exactly, that might be.

"Therefore, I think our first logical step is to examine every single scrap of relevant information we've gathered so far on this system alongside that we have on file concerning Earth, go over everything possible with a fine-tooth comb. Nothing, no matter how insignificant it might appear on the surface, can be overlooked".

"Agreed", Stasha concurred in reply: "Although I can't in all honesty see anything the other two might possess in common Bandros doesn't have even more of. In short, Bandros has much more going for it in its favor than either Earth, or Zelmorl".

"Fine, then", Jenniboni came back at her; tenacious, resolute: "Maybe the answer lies there. Either way, no matter what, it's imperative we learn as soon as Humanly possible what that answer might be. That's an order!"

"Even so, be that as it may, I still …", Stasha never had a chance to finish; interrupted instead by the unexpected, dramatic arrival of a certain officer intruding on their private council…

No previous announcement whatsoever.

Hurrying over to Jenniboni's side, bounding through the conference-room door wearing a most urgent look, she carried an ei-pad in her outstretched hand, two others under her arm:

"Yes, Lieutenant Greensley??"

****

Still situated at her terminal in the ship's 'General Research facility', still hard at work, Gloria studied further the results of her previous scans on Bandros, planning as well certain comparison checks she hoped would shed further light on questions still bothering her.

Having transferred all the data retrieved from both the colony ship and her scanner onto two ei-pads Gloria chose to examine the latter information first, noting a couple of slight discrepancies right from the very get-go.

"Maccs?" she called out; summoning up with slender, agile fingers one entry in particular.

"Yes, Ma'am?"

"Did you by any chance clean up the magnetic interference from the data-stream I downloaded from my scanner?", she asked, inspecting the varied schematics collected on the androids: "The static distortions due to the electro-magnetic interference surrounding 'AB-1.5'".

"Yes, Ma'am: I did. Was I in error doing so?", Maccs questioned her, both confused and apologetic at the very same time.

"No, no. Not at all!!" Gloria was quick to assure him: "I was just curious if you also saved the original readings".

"Yes, Ma'am: I even arranged it so you could perform side-by-side comparisons on your Pad!", he was just as quick to inform her, sounding quite pleased with himself.

"Why, thank you Maccs. You're a treasure. That was very thoughtful of you", she granted with frank appreciation, smiling.

"I appreciate your saying so, Ma'am", came his chipper reply, Gloria calling up now a comparison of the androids' internal components using both sets of reference material.

"Hmmm", she mused aloud more to herself than anyone else: "Both comparisons have the exact same energy readings".

"Excuse me, Ma'am?"

"Oh, sorry: Just noticed that, even in the data-stream you cleaned up, they still possess that very same electromagnetic energy our unwomaned probes scanned in the lower atmosphere", Gloria explained with furrowed brow, frowning. Like Commodore Saphira she, too, didn't trust those odd mechanoids they met on Bandros.

"So are they anything like me?" Maccs found himself unable to resist.

"No, I'm afraid not", it was now Gloria's turn to apologize, aware at once what StarChild's synthetic bio-mechanical intelligence had on his hopeful mind.

As would any sentient being in his unique situation, Maccs demonstrated on more than one occasion feelings of isolation.

437

The only one of his kind... lonely... he even voiced from time-to-time a certain longing for others like himself, other such constructs with which to converse, to share both a common bond and purpose—other A.I. units with which he had a common background, a similar herstory, allowing them a shared basis for meaningful relationships as equals.

While confident there would be others like him, sure Womankind would build yet more starships like theirs replete with their own A.I.'s, Gloria still thought it sad that—at least for the time being—their "Maccs Unit" had to remain feeling like some pathetic freak so alone in the universe.

A feeling with which Gloria could empathize:

"Sorry, Maccs, but I'm afraid they're nothing but simple service 'droids", she added, sympathetic, examining at the very same time both their simple control systems and those energy readings scanned therein. It was those strange energy readings, quite perplexing, that *really* bothered her, not generated as they were by any discernible power source within the actual mechanoids themselves...

Then again their very bearing likewise, from the very beginning, troubled her.

"Pity, that", Maccs sighed: "I was hoping to talk to them".

"Wouldn't do any good anyway, even if the Commodore *did* allow them aboard ship. Not very likely, however, thank God!", Gloria muttered, pressing on, leaving Maccs no time to ask why she didn't want them aboard StarChild.

"According to their obvious design parameters they were never meant to be anything, but simple laborers. Their 'brains' were never designed for either feeling, or independent thought of any kind. Certainly not up to your high standards, my fine computerized laddie", she teased him, affectionate:

"According to this they can't even initiate conversation, only respond to specific orders. So, unfortunately, I'm afraid that means ...", her voice trailed off into the distance, eyes growing wide in fearful realization.

"What does that mean?"

"Dear Lord, Maccs. That's it! Those machines are simple drones. They shouldn't have been able to initiate with us any sort of dialogue whatsoever, much less offered us any sort of help before the fact.

"Dear Lord, Maccs", Gloria included the Almighty a second time yet: "They were more than just simple service 'droids! They were sentient!!"

Doing so this time in a rather loud voice though, jumping up in a flash from where she still sat, she made a mad dash over to Ms. Naylor, herself hard at work on the assignment Gloria gave her.

Noting as well the confused look Ms. Naylor gave her, having heard as well Gloria's loud exclamation, Gloria asked straightaway if her 'once-insubordinate' subordinate completed already her given task.

"Yes Ma'am! I have it all here, just downloaded onto this Pad, all ready for your inspection Ma'am".

"Thank you, crewwoman", Gloria expressed her appreciation, grabbing it out of Ms. Naylor's proffered hand much to the befuddled N.C.O.'s wide-eyed surprise: "Good work".

Holding up the small E.I. display screen belonging to the unit from Ms. Naylor in one hand to the other E.I. clenched firmly in the other, Gloria studied both with troubled... almost superhuman... intensity.

Just as she feared.

Three identical matches; the energy readings from Bandros's lower atmosphere, the self-same energy signature found in the androids, and the anomalous blip she detected in the ships systems herself.

All present and accounted for!

Even so she couldn't locate however in all of Ms. Naylor's research that exact-same mystery blip's final destination aboard StarChild's entire length and breadth. Try as she might to find '*It*' this was this missing piece of the puzzle Gloria was quick to mention, grilling at once the other woman concerning its apparent absence.

"I'm sorry, Ma'am", her anxious underling was just as quick: "but it just vanished, just disappeared, from all ship's systems. However, I did discover its place of origin. It entered ship's systems on deck B-4, near the Recovery Ward in..."

Gloria's heart began pounding in her chest with painful rapidity, everything coming together at last in one frightful, all-consuming flash.

A sickly green flash at that!

"Maccs!", she cried out, her alarm obvious: "Find Commodore Saphira, Lt. Cmdr. Marlowe, and Lt. Cmdr. Straker—AT ONCE! I must see them right away!!"

"I'm sorry, Ma'am, but they're all on deck B-5—Senior Officer's Briefing Room—not to be disturbed by orders of Commodore Saphira herself ".

"To Heck with that!", Gloria came back at him with considerable force, about to do that which she would have never dreamt of doing just days ago:

"I'm on my way there anyway!!!"

Tucking beneath her arm the first two ei-pads from her own work station, the one given her by Ms. Naylor still in hand, Gloria left 'General Research' with all due haste. Waiting with equal impatience for the ag-pod to StarChild's distant bow, she came close in her mounting impatience to kicking it's closed port-of-entry when the tardy lift didn't appear any sooner.

****

Bringing Its tour of the Human vessel to a speedy conclusion, It returned at record speed to find its helpless host just as It left him before.

Not until back in the little boy's body did It learn what Rodney did, his unfortunate disclosures, revealing as he did the existence of Its entire race, Its plans for Womankind likewise compromised. About to fly into an apoplectic fit over this betrayal on the part of its unwilling vassal, the parasite now securely in place within that Human child forced itself to remain calm instead least It do something It might later regret.

439

Postponing for the moment its vengeance until more convenient, It decided right about then there'd be more than enough time later-on to make its faithless thrall pay for his duplicitous behaviour. Looking forward to doing so with maniacal glee, there were even so other matters to deal with first.

A little change of plan was now in order but, be that as it may, It wasn't worried, manifestly confident as always in Its own natural superiority. Finding the drugs in little Rodney's system too powerful for It to re-awaken him until later It was nonetheless able to use the unknowing child to Its own particular ends, using the various anatomical functions of Rodney's own body as though they were Its own.

Re-animating the boy's heavily sedated form, unknowing eyes sprang open, another entity all-together separate from the young laddie staring out of them at God's own creation. An individual as viscous, malevolent, and ancient as the ages the eyes were the eyes of an absolute zombie. Except for the glint of lunatic sadism buried deep within they possessed the blank expression of one who's been dead in spirit for countless eons.

Gazing upwards from Its supine angle in silent contemplation It saw straight away Its escape route all laid out before It, ready for Its immediate departure. Standing on the hospital bed below It, It laced with a firm grip Rodney's fingers through the latticed grid covering the ventilation duct directly above. Working the grate free of all its moorings It pulled down on it with an inhuman strength born of demonic will.

Quite aware of the two guards left outside the Recovery Ward doors It made no sound, laying the covering at Rodney's feet. Not wanting them to hear what It was up to It lifted Rodney's hijacked body high into the overhead passage, silent as a thief in the night.

****

"Yes, Lieutenant Greensley?", Jenniboni demanded, a trifle more startled than vexed by this unexpected intrusion on what was all-in-all a private 'council of war'. Appearing at first annoyed irritation turned as readily to concern, observing as well Gloria's urgent expression full of worry:

"I apologize, Ma'am, for barging in like this unannounced, but I knew you'd want to see this as soon as possible—A.S.A.P.", Gloria was quick to explain, trying all the same to catch her breath, having just run a fair bit of the way.

Handing now Jenniboni the E.I. device clutched tightly in her hand she still managed to rattle on so in a very excited fashion, telling how she came by all that explosive information placed now in her C.O.'s very own hands.

At least that is until the other woman now inspecting her research ordered Gloria to keep quiet. Jenniboni herself saying nothing but holding up her open hand in Gloria's direction, palm first, proved more than enough to do the trick.

Nor was it long after that, examining with great care all the relevant data, Jenniboni's large brown eyes flew open even wider, a look of incredulous outrage coming there to immediate light:

440

"Are you trying to tell me we have one of those hellish creatures aboard my very ship?" she snarled. Incensed, she leapt up like a coiled spring from where she sat.

"Yes, Ma'am!" Gloria insisted, jumping back, the speed at which the statuesque blonde leapt up from the conference table giving her a momentary start: "And it seems to have entered ship's systems somewhere around the Recovery room on Deck B-4, the Officer's Sick Bay. Therefore, I can only assume ..."

"Maccs! CODE RED!!! All hands to battle stations!", Jenniboni wasted no more time: "This is not a drill ...

"REPEAT! THIS IS NOT A DRILL!!"

No reply expected other than doing as he was told Maccs put the entire ship on emergency alert, a loud klaxon sounding throughout every quarter of StarChild's interior—the status lights arrayed in plain sight above every egress aboard ship blinking away a furious red.

"A Trojan horse!" Jenniboni spat, vehement, every piece of the puzzle now fitting firmly in place—the boy's strange, abusive behavior followed later on by his passionate claim he couldn't help himself .

That was no attempt at saying he was sorry, no apology for previous misconduct! He was referring all along to that vile monster inside him, exploiting him all the way both body and soul.

What really got her goat though was the painful memory how she confided in Stasha her every suspicion concerning the androids, telling her she didn't trust them in the least right in front of the Emerog-infected boy. Now those psychotic parasites knew for certain they couldn't count on Jenniboni's co-operation. No doubt each and every one of them, given what Rodney told her of their telepathic abilities, already knew she had no plans of helping them.

Swept away right then on a rolling tide of sick anger... tired of all their mounting trials and tribulations courtesy of these insidious aberrations of all that was right, natural and even holy... something else also came to mind.

Swinging about, facing now StarChild's Chief Medical Officer, Jenniboni glowered sharply at the hapless woman now on the receiving end of her stern appraisal:

"And why didn't your medical scans of the boy reveal anything of the Emerog inside him", she demanded, furious. Caught off guard Eartha nevertheless understood the intense feeling Jenniboni now vented wasn't really aimed at her in particular, but the situation in which they now found themselves.

However, still at a total loss to explain what might have gone wrong, it took a moment to figure out how that devilish creature might have eluded her professional notice right from the very start:

"It might be the result of the Emerog using a living host instead of some machine, masking perhaps their own energy pattern with the neural energy found in the Human brain while occupying the Human body", Eartha offered, giving the matter some thought: "A sort of natural chameleon effect I suppose".

Jenniboni's harsh expression softened, granting in return her C.M.O. an appreciative nod. Having to confess it made considerable sense given how these horrid things were themselves once flesh and blood, Jenniboni could find no fault at all with Eartha's line of conjecture. Able to come up with no other practical explanation herself her field of expertise was command, not the sciences… medical, or otherwise.

"Pardon me, Ma'am", Frances made herself heard quite well despite the resounding klaxon: "But since the Emerog in question must realize by now it's been discovered it's only logical to assume it'll likewise try to escape, flee the ship. And since it obviously needed the boy to come here, it'll likewise…"

"Understood", Jenniboni cut in, decisive, already on the move:

"You're with me, Ms. Straker!" she demanded, Frances right behind her anyway.

****

Bypassing once more the ag-pod in favor of a nearby stairwell, they reached the Recovery Ward on Deck B-4 in record time:

"We haven't heard a single thing from inside", Ms. Tully was quick to report. Seeing both the head of her own department as well as Commodore Saphira appear out of the corner of her eye their approach was rapid, their shared expression one of alarm:

"He must still be asleep".

"Open that door RIGHT NOW!!", Jenniboni ignored her, forceful, commandeering as well the general-use stunner from Ensign Tully's hip-holster. Doing so with swift alacrity before the other woman even realized what was happening Jenniboni made her way with equal dispatch into the room beyond, both she and Frances greeted at once by both an empty bed alongside the round grating resting atop it.

Looking up they were met as well by the sight of an open-air vent:

"And they run all through the ship", Jenniboni was the first to observe, quite annoyed to say the least:

"By now he could be anywhere! *Find him*!!", she snapped, ordering Maccs to patch her through at once to 'Internal Surveillance'. Put in contact with the current on-duty officer, Lt. Cecilia Baynes, it was Frances however that spoke next:

"Yes, Ma'am?"

"Determine at once the precise location of our young visitor!"

"According to my panel he's on Deck B-4; the Recovery Ward".

"What does your board read?", Frances was quick in demanding, her apparent disbelief audible over the continuing klaxon. Both she and Jenniboni shared a pair of incredulous looks at the sound of Ms. Baynes informing them all was green, nothing out of the ordinary.

Even Cecilia sounded a trifle nonplused, able to tell from the pervasive alarm sounding all around them something aboard ship was indeed amiss.

"What does the ship's internal chronometer read?", Frances was just as prompt, increasingly suspicious.

"Fifteen thirty-six, and fifty-seven seconds", the woman on the other end of their comm. link began: "Fifteen thirty-six, and fifty-eight seconds; fifteen thirty-six, fifty-nine; fifteen thirty six, zero-zero; fifteen thirty-six, zero-one…"

Cecilia's voice trailed off in obvious confusion, announcing after that their internal clock was… for some unknown reason… starting to repeat itself.

"Thank you Lt. Baynes", Frances gave way to a frustrated sigh, disgusted: "Over-and out".

Turning to her ship's C.O. standing next to her Frances knew already what the matter was: "The Emerog must have set our internal monitors on a repeat feed-back loop, replaying recorded results from an earlier period before you declared 'Code Red'".

"Obviously they possess the ability to control our on-board systems just as they do the androids", Jenniboni picked up where her erstwhile companion just left off: "It must have been traveling throughout our all our computer relays at incredible speeds, spying out the lay of the land. And when Lt. Greensley proved lucky enough to catch it on her monitor It realized It was caught in the act when she began her scan of It".

"And, realizing this, It would've likewise beat a hasty retreat after making a little detour into our security matrix, temporarily blinding us to Its whereabouts aboard ship", Frances interjected:

"Then, once done with that It returned full circle here, making good Its escape inside the boy", Frances followed up yet again, passing back and forth a verbal baton between both her and her Jenniboni.

"Heaven only knows what else Its been screwing around with while inside us", she muttered, both women heading now at a rapid pace for the same obvious goal as their enemy.

****

The small craft elevator was already making its steady climb to the hangar bay one deck above by the time both Jenniboni and Frances arrived in 'Shuttle Storage/Maintenance'. Riding now that flat lift to the landing bay directly overhead it was the same shuttle which towed back the second landing party partway from Zelmorl.

In vain hope of preventing its departure both senior personnel hurried for the other lift present, riding in pursuit the 'target drone elevator' opposite the large chamber from the first.

Cursing its slow ascent their only consolation was the equal speed at which the other likewise made its climb. Yet even so Jenniboni felt a definite sinking sensation in the pit of her stomach upon reaching their destination, noting at once the open hangar bay doors.

No chance now of detaining the rogue shuttle, its engines now active, she could only watch its inevitable take-off from the metal deck below it. Piercing the invisible air seal allowing solid matter to pass, already on its way, it plunged forward into the cold vacuum of deep space beyond.

Had the doors been closed, as programmed to be during a ship-wide emergency alert, their cunning adversary might have been detained, preventing its current getaway. Another security precaution their intruder managed to countervail while inside their many onboard systems.

Muttering ugly oaths under her breath Jenniboni watched the green/red running lights in back of the small transport disappear in the distance, mocking their every effort, before contacting the bridge. Ordering Stasha to lay in an immediate intercept course she instructed her first officer as well not to attempt any capture of the renegade vessel until she herself was there.

However, severing her direct com-link to StarChild's main bridge, Jenniboni received only then a rather mysterious communiqué from Naomi requesting her immediate presence in one of many storage bays on deck S-13… the ship's 'Cargo Deck'… some eight decks below their current locale.

Chapter 57

"THEIF AND PURSUIT"

Met at once by Naomi's troubled expression the very moment she stepped off the ag-pod now in back of her, leaving its safe confines on StarChild's well-stocked cargo deck, Jenniboni never saw before her Chief Engineer so clearly upset as she was at that very moment.

The three members of her department standing in back of her seemed nothing more than confused whereas Naomi herself appeared quite angry, both perplexed and hopping mad at the very same time.

"Speak, Lt. Cmdr.", Jenniboni ordered. Her tone as sour as the look on her face, sure she wasn't going to like what she heard, she was right!

"My people just discovered something I knew you'd want to see for yourself", Naomi announced, too irate herself to take note of Jenniboni's similar tone.

Leading the new arrivals down a medium-wide corridor replete with both two right turns, and one left, this lead to yet another passageway… somewhat wider than the first… opening soon into a broad expanse, a well-lit chamber with high ceiling.

Nor was there any doubt where Frances and Jenniboni were concerned what it was Naomi wanted to show them; both women catching immediate sight of several packing crates, all a light grey, strewn about the center of the floor.

Tipped over as well on their sides, their foamy-white packing material tossed about in massive clumps, it was just as clear each ransacked storage bin was looted, its contents pilfered.

"It would seem the young laddie made off with a considerable cache of spare power cells", Naomi made bitter comment, reaching the nearest crate:

"Rather large ones at that!"

"Not the young laddie", her C.O. wasted no time; stern, frustrated, and deeply annoyed: "That vile thing controlling him!"

"Yes, Ma'am", Naomi was quick to apologize, contrite, observing this time

Jenniboni's sour mood.

"Anything else missing?" it was now Frances' turn, confident of the answer even before hearing it.

"Right over here", their hapless tour guide escorted them. No less indignant than before she led them over to yet another large container a dozen or so yards away, **'CRYSTAL REFRACTORS: 100'** stenciled across its side in bold, solid black letters.

"Laser components", Frances grumbled, her gaze wandering to the ceiling above: "And there's how he got in here, of course!"

"Of course", Jenniboni echoed, sighing, spotting likewise the open-air shaft. Situated near a tall rack laden with similar cargo all its own, reaching within a couple of short feet of that circular entrance high above, it provided easy access to the floor below—a convenient make-shift ladder for any would-be intruder:

"Rather heavy load, though, for such a young child… wouldn't you say?", Jenniboni observed even further: "Especially a boy".

"It would seem, Ma'am, that 'he', 'she', and/or 'it' appropriated a hover-dolly", Naomi offered, solving at least that little mystery: "There's one missing from its assigned space".

"So he must have taken the nearest ag-pod from here to 'Shuttle Maintenance'", Jenniboni reasoned out-loud for the benefit of all those within earshot: "And, with internal surveillance off-line, he got away Scott-free".

"Oh, goody", Naomi smiled, facetious: "Not only are these miserable creatures crazy, but they're also highly intelligent. Now there's one heck of a lethal combination!"

"Lethal indeed", Frances agreed with a stoic, solemn nod: "And there's only one thing I can think of they'd want both power cells and crystal refractors for in such quantities".

"Understood, Lt. Cmdr.", Jenniboni thought alike: "Somewhere on Bandros they must have more than at least one surface-to-air energy cannon. Somewhere no doubt in one or both of those Zelmorlite cities, planning to reactivate them now that we're on to their very existence".

"Taking into consideration the amount of parts they stole, not to mention the size of each stolen item, those cannons of theirs must be massive suckers", Naomi shook her head, uneasy just thinking about it.

"If they really have such defensive capabilities it'll make it all but impossible for us to likewise draw close enough in order to launch any legitimate attack of our own", Frances was quick to add: "None that is short of an all-inclusive global bombardment deployed from deep space; something beyond the ability of any one, single, starship".

"Which makes it doubly imperative we capture that shuttle, *at once!*, before that thing makes good its escape", Jenniboni vowed with every fiber of her being. Sounding determined, she addressed Naomi right thereafter in the same commanding tone:

"And I want you, Lt. Greensley, and the rest of your department to go over every square millimeter of this entire ship. Find out what exactly that blasted creature did to each and every one of our on-board systems paying special attention to Security, propulsion, and weapons!".

"Yes, Ma'am", Naomi obeyed, headed at once for parts unknown—Jenniboni likewise headed with equal dispatch for her bridge, Frances at her side.

****

"Status report, X.O.", Jenniboni called out crisp and clear the very moment she arrived on StarChild's active bridge, her step just as forceful.

"We're in pursuit of the target as per your instructions", Stasha gave her superior an immediate up-date: "It's approximately 800,000 kilometers directly ahead, maintaining at full speed on an exact course for Bandros. No further action has been taken pending further orders".

"Excellent, Commander", Jenniboni gave her complete approval, taking her rightful place smack-dab in the middle of that bustling command center all about her. Seated now in her majestic command chair she noted with equal satisfaction most all her senior officers likewise present—some, like Naomi Marlowe, unavoidably elsewhere.

Focusing her complete attention on the main viewer straight ahead Jenniboni ordered as well increased magnification, the runaway shuttle appearing now in the blink of an eye as if just a few hundred meters away:

"Time to reel him in", she announced, instructing the helmswoman in back of her to place a tractor beam on the small vessel, pulling it back into StarChild's waiting hangar bay. And doing so she likewise instructed Frances to send an armed detachment from Security after placing as well a quarantine shield around the captured shuttle.

If all went well that might contain the Emerog therein, allowing them some breathing space while they then determined the best way to liquidate it… *permanently*!!

However, giving the command to "reel him in", Jenniboni was soon informed, quite apologetically to be sure, that both their main tractor beam alongside all back-ups were off-line.

"Figures", she muttered, frustration mounting.

Thorough little creeps!

Took care of every possible contingency!!

Unless …?

"Ms. Straker, aim outer lasers on narrow beam, one-tenth full power, and take out both that shuttle's propulsion units".

Two pinpoint streaks of bright blue-white light leapt forth with blinding speed from the cannons located at the outer tip of each StarChild's broad wings, the neon lines making direct contact with their designated target.

"Very good, Ms. Marlowe", Jenniboni allowed herself a brief moment's celebration. Certain the Emerog would have tampered as well with all their on-line weapons she was just as sure why they were now all operational.

High spirits soon brought low however, Jenniboni took as well immediate

447

note of how their laser fire seemed to flatten out against some invisible barrier just behind the shuttle in question. Nor did she need Frances telling her its shields were all up-and-running to realize what just happened.

"Fine", she hissed in tart reply, mentally gnashing her teeth: "In that case increase power to fifty percent, continuous fire, until those shields are down. Then return to ten percent the moment they are, taking out right after that both propulsion units".

Although she knew it was crucial they re-take at all costs that small craft now defying them, Jenniboni had nevertheless fond hopes of sparing young Rodney his life.

It was still her dearest wish to grant him a chance at a happy future after all the misery he so far endured, wanting both shuttle and child retrieved intact. Given all the torment he suffered during his brief span he deserved better in Jenniboni's opinion than to die at so precious a young age, his life cut so short after knowing only bitter heartache.

However, even while expecting almost anything from these insanely brilliant horrors, what followed next still succeeded in taking Jenniboni's very breath away. Its sheer lunacy coming at her as it did out of complete left field maybe 'audacity' was a better word for it!

So audacious in fact that, when Jenniboni first saw the small shuttle veer at once to the right, she assumed quite naturally the creature aboard was trying to simply avoid their constant laser-fire.

It wasn't until the tiny vessel swung about, this time to the left, it finally occurred to her what that crazy parasite had in mind. Coming about in a wide arc, instead of firing Its own weapons at StarChild, It just came at them head-on. Full speed ahead their fugitive became now the aggressor!

"Forward shields at full strength", Jenniboni responded to this newest ploy: "Main viewer back to regular magnification!"

Appearing now in its flight path to jump back until nothing more on the distant horizon than a bright speck, an optical illusion resulting from the sudden decrease in magnification, the enemy craft maintained nonetheless its forward momentum.

"I knew they were crazy from the very get-go, but never suicidal", Frances almost laughed out-loud: "That little beggar's going to try and ram us!"

Given StarChild's superior size and shield strength there was little room for doubt who the winner would be in such an ultimate show-down, the tiny contender completely obliterated.

"No, Lt. Cmdr.; I don't think so", Jenniboni smiled, knowingly: "I think it's playing 'chicken' with us".

"Of course", Frances grinned, wondering why she hadn't seen it for herself...

So obvious!!

"'Chicken', Commodore?", Jenniboni heard her puzzled young helmswoman ask from behind, off to her left.

"Yes Ms. Smythe: It was a game popular among reckless young laddies back in the old patriarchates. They'd take their vehicles, usually cars, and race towards one-another at full speed. The first to flinch, pull out of the way of the other, was declared the 'Chicken'".

"I see, Ma'am. Yes. Thank you".

Able to note in the other woman's voice a subtle hint of disbelief, a certain dubious concern, Jenniboni was nevertheless confident in her reasoning, having no doubt whatsoever.

Having seen this exact same ploy during her days as a Protectorate Captain serving in their 'Air-Space Strategic Command' division Jenniboni recognized the very same maneuver here and now after pursuing in her one-woman patrol craft criminals using the same tactics to elude capture.

And as the swiftly approaching demon was soon to learn the 'hard way' Jenniboni never flinched, never the 'Chicken'! While true she wasn't dealing with a Human psyche this time around there were still three things she already knew about these creatures. Rodney's detailed description quite informative, one thing coming to mind was that they might be crazy, but definitely not stupid.

After all the trouble it went through in order to escape successfully with its ill-gotten booty Jenniboni couldn't see that mischievous creature just throwing it all away on some singular, futile, grandiose gesture.

Another Emerog trait convincing her this was likewise just a bluff was Its unerring instinct for survival, their strong sense of self-preservation. This lust for life precluded as well from her mind any thought of their risking annihilation unless confident of victory—something beyond all hope here.

More than that however it was their concept of Humanity that, when all was said and done, convinced Jenniboni most their adversary here was faking.

There was no doubt at all these monsters considered Womankind both weak and ineffectual just because her species could feel in abundance both pity, compassion, and even love. Despite her superior strength, Jenniboni's greater position, that heartless entity closing in on her anticipated only cowardice due to those very God-given virtues making Humanity greater.

Expecting her to turn tail and run at the very first sign of pending danger this more than anything else stuck in Jenniboni's craw, this arrogant assumption concerning both her and all Womankind. High time indeed to disabuse these loathsome individuals of such an erroneous conclusion. Her anger on a steady increase, this was one particular wake-up call she relished delivering:

"Ms. Smythe, set us on an immediate collision course with the approaching shuttle matching our speed with its: Ms. Straker, bring all lasers to full strength. Target the vessel and fire the very moment it swings about, tries to veer away".

"With all due respect, Ma'am, such fire-power at such close range will not only bring down its shields, but destroy also the shuttle itself ", Frances pointed out with no undue emotionalism. Projecting an assumed emotional detachment she hid well whatever she might have been feeling at that particular moment.

Whatever her personal feelings might be, they remained hidden behind a mask of practical stoicism.

"No it won't, Lt. Cmdr.", Jenniboni was just as quick: "Not if you aim for the very edge of either its port, or starboard shields the very moment it turns sideways", she explained with a cunning grin, Frances' new understanding accompanied as well by a smile all her own appearing at the corners of her thin, pale lips. Seeing this from the very corner of her eye it occurred right then and there to Jenniboni that her venerable Chief of Security did, *indeed*, look at times like a literal vampire.

No longer a dot now on the horizon the elusive shuttle drew ever closer. Its sleek curves and smart design readily visible now without magnification Jenniboni experienced a moment's doubt, wondering for a very brief moment if that putrid creature coming straight at her was crazy enough to ram them after all.

However, banking at incredible speeds, the shuttle in question altered quite suddenly its flight path, exposing its 'soft underbelly' to the larger vessel. Swerving as well to the right in an upward climb it continued to defy StarChild's superior might.

"NOW!", Jenniboni commanded, their fire-power striking where desired.

Sending that other vessel into an immediate sideways roll, spinning out of control in a dizzy blur away from StarChild himself, Jenniboni now had ample time to bring down its defenses—take its propulsion units off line—before the Emerog had similar time to regain control.

"Thank you Ms. Marlowe", she almost laughed aloud, about to give Frances the order to collapse its shields. Hearing also from Ms. Smythe tractor beams were back on-line Jenniboni turned about in her chair, glancing at the young ensign in question. Instructing her to lock onto the shuttle's position Jenniboni told her to bring it back onboard:

"Can't, Ma'am. The shuttle just disappeared!"

"Explain!!", Jenniboni demanded. Her head snapping about, she stared once more at the main viewer, wide-eyed.

"I don't know what happened", Ensign Penny Smythe stammered, perplexed: "One moment it was there, the next..."

"Confirm, Ms. Straker!"

"Confirmed, Commodore: It just vanished as though never there, both visually and on sensors. Frankly, I'm at a complete loss".

Opening at once a direct comm. link to Engineering Jenniboni reached out to the one person aboard ship most likely to explain what might have happened. If anyone could come up with a feasible, working hypothesis for what just took place it was her:

"Lt. Cmdr. Marlowe?"

"Yes, Ma'am: Marlowe here".

"Firstly, I want to thank you for your exceptional work getting both lasers, shields, and tractor beams all back on-line in such record short time".

"Thank you, Ma'am".

"However we seem to have yet another problem", Jenniboni added, detailing all which happened just moments ago.

Waiting for a possible explanation however Naomi's reply was delivered however in a reluctant voice resonant with guilty apprehension, a clear response forthcoming only after a rather hesitant pause. Recognizing that tone for what it was Jenniboni heard in her Chief Engineer the same apprehension when Andrei and/or her children confessed some wrong-doing guaranteed to vex her.

"Uhh, Commodore… would the shuttle that vanished be, by any chance, the 'Gene III'?"

"Yes, Ms. Marlowe. It was", Jenniboni affirmed, growing now more suspicious as well as concerned.

"Okay, then: In that case, Ma'am, may I suggest we discuss this matter further in the privacy of your office".

"Understood, Ms. Marlowe: On my way".

"And Ma'am…?"

"Yes, Lt. Cmdr.?"

"May I also suggest, Ma'am, you ask Commander Nikarov and Fra… Lt. Cmdr. Straker to join us? I think you'll want them there, too, for this".

"Yes, Lieutenant Commander! On my way!! Over".

Chapter 58

"CHOICES"

Arriving at Jenniboni's office with Gloria in tow Naomi found all three command officers she requested both present and accounted for, catching at first glance Jenniboni herself. Sitting across the room ahead she gave Naomi nothing but a studious frown, silent as the grave, the object of her severe notice looking elsewhere.

Doing so, catching right after that sight of both Stasha and Frances they sat gathered around a triangular table to Naomi's immediate left—they, too, saying not a word, giving the new arrivals similar looks.

None of this conducive to feelings of either inner peace, or tranquil wellbeing Naomi motioned Gloria towards a lone chair just to the immediate inside right of the doorway to Jenniboni's office.

Approaching immediately thereafter Jenniboni's desk Naomi felt more and more like some delinquent schoolgirl being called on the carpet by the entire senior faculty.

No…

Strike that…

On second thought it was more akin to some hasty court-martial, some ancient wartime 'drumhead', the befuddled but forbidding stare on the Commodore's face only adding to the trial-like atmosphere—Frances and Stasha, now in back of her, reminiscent of some dark jury straight out of some similar, arcane, star-chamber.

Everyone just staring at her from back and front, expectant eyes upon her from every side, Naomi could find no solace whatsoever from her increasing anxiety. Waiting until someone else than she chose to speak Naomi searched that very same room now closing in on her for some small distraction, no matter how trivial.

Grabbing in her mind onto anything at all she found at last some small comfort in the artwork arrayed with loving care on all four walls around her, hoping to take her immediate notice off all those silent eyes just watching her.

Clearly the work of young children, no doubt those of the Commodore herself, Naomi found them in fact quite good, having about them a sort of abstract, surrealist, appeal.

'Not bad for little kids', Naomi reflected: 'Very colourful'.

Glancing also at the family photo sitting on Jenniboni's desk she noticed as well both her Commanding Officer as well as, of course, Andrei... the three small children in the immediate foreground no doubt the little artists in question.

"Well, Lieutenant Commander?", Jenniboni broke at last the silent air, bringing Naomi's 'art appreciation' to an abrupt conclusion: "I understand you might be able to shed some light on how our quarry managed to elude capture?! Well ...?"

Waiting for an answer from the reluctant redhead across the way it was instead young Lt. Greensley who, leaping up from the chair in which she sat, arrived like some devoted servant at Naomi's side. Still in the dark as to why her youngest deputy chief was even there in the very first place Jenniboni was soon to learn, Lt. Greensley speaking up on Naomi's behalf before she herself had any similar chance:

"Actually, Ma'am, I was the one who came up with the idea to begin with", she declared in a hurried voice, coming at once to Naomi's defense.

"No Commodore", the other jumped in with both feet: "Lt. Greensley suggested it, but I was the one who gave her idea the final okay, helping her install the device. Therefore, all things considered, I'm the one here to blame".

Head lowered, elbows on her desk, Jenniboni began rubbing her temples with increasing pressure, employing the very tips of her fingers. Glimpsing the small family portrait to her immediate right she found herself wishing Andrei was likewise there; there to administer one of his tender, loving, and oh-so expert massages.

Quickly changing her mind Jenniboni decided better however of such wishes, glad in the long run her husband wasn't there. Given what they just discovered concerning the very nature of their immediate enemy, what each and every one of them was now up against, it was fortunate indeed for all concerned men were **not** allowed active duty aboard such extra-terrestrial craft as this:

"Look, Gentlewomen", Jenniboni sighed, her exasperation matched by feelings of intense frustration: "I'm not looking for a way to fix blame, or find fault here. I just want to know what the heck is going on here".

"Well, Ma'am: We started work on it in our spare time just before leaving the Commonwealth", Naomi hemmed and hawed, clearly uncomfortable with what she had to say: "We... Lt. Greensley and I... thought it might come in handy should we meet up with some alien fleet like originally anticipated.

"If it worked on the shuttle, which it obviously did", she added with a nervous titter; "then we planned to incorporate... install... a larger, more powerful version aboard StarChild himself".

"That's it!! No more procrastination", Jenniboni snapped, the start of a full-blown headache beginning to pound now at the base of her skull: "Just tell me what the darn heck it is we're dealing with here!!!"

"Well, we were experimenting with light infraction or, to be more precise, more accurate, the bending of light around any given object in order to render said object…"

"Stop-right-there!", Jenniboni held up her hand in weary protest: "Are you trying to tell me you installed on that shuttle an… a…"

"Yes, Ma'am", Naomi was so very kind enough to finish in her stead: "We installed aboard the 'Gene III' an invisibility screen".

"Oh, Dear Lord", the woman hearing all this for the very first time shook her head, leaning back yet again in her chair:

"Now the Emerog have in their possession a working invisibility device they can use now to their own purposes. Is that just about it?", Jenniboni stared in utter disbelief at both officers standing still before her.

"Yes, Ma'am", Naomi was first to confess: "Although I swear, Ma'am, that neither Lt. Greensley, nor myself ever completed the final hook-up of the darn thing into either the shuttle's drive systems, or shields! Right, Lieutenant?

"We didn't even file our preliminary research with Maccs, just the personal P.C.'s in our quarters, just in case the darn thing didn't work".

"Yes, Ma'am", Gloria offered as well, backing up her immediate superior:

"All I can assume is that the intruder must have infiltrated our personal, independent records along with the ship's general mistress blue-prints and database. Needless to say we both deeply regret all the trouble this has caused".

"Indeed, Ma'am", it was now Naomi's turn at bat: "You have our deepest apologies".

"Thank you, Gentlewomen", Jenniboni forgave, feeling a bit more charitable, having now the available facts at her immediate command: "Given the unique circumstances involved I'm willing to overlook for the moment the part each of you played in this situation. Neither of you had any foreseeable way of anticipating the final outcome of your little faux-pax and, under any other circumstances, your invention might have proven most useful.

"Most ingenious, in fact: All I ask is that, in the future, both of you come to me first, seek my approval, *before* conducting any future experiments of such a 'remarkable' nature aboard *my* ship".

"Yes, Ma'am", both engineering personnel agreed quite readily, sweet relief written all over their faces: "Thank you, Ma'am".

"If I may be so bold Commodore that still doesn't change the fact that the Emerog now possess a tactical advantage placing us at an even greater disadvantage than before", Frances announced without any preamble, whatsoever. Betraying as usual little-to-no emotion at all, seated at the little triangular table in the far corner of Jenniboni's private office, her voice remained as cool, as even, as always:

"Therefore, while I, too, hold neither Ms. Marlowe, or Ms. Greensley accountable the fact remains it's even more imperative now we find at once a viable means by which to neutralize these 'Emerog' the sooner the better".

"Even if we can't determine right away what killed them on either Earth, or Zelmorl we could still launch a pre-emptive counter-strike against the most likely site of whatever defenses they might possess", Stasha offered, speaking up from beside Frances: "Take out whatever technology they might try to resuscitate in the Zelmorlite ruins before they have equal chance to take us out with whatever theoretical arms they, too, might possess".

"Yes", Naomi jumped right on in, eager as can be: "If we take StarChild in closer to Bandros we could wipe out whatever strategic surface-to-space weapons they might have with both laser cannons and matter/anti-matter torpedoes!"

"Too risky", Frances differed, her demeanor phlegmatic, practical: "We have yet to determine where their defenses are and while we're taking pot-shots, willy-nilly, at wherever they might be that'll give them an even better chance of targeting us first.

"For all we know they may have already achieved their primary objective, the repair of their secret installations, allowing them to destroy us first.

"We don't know at all how long it might take them to get their defenses fully operational. For all we know they might have already done so and, if they've also added your invisibility screen to their capabilities that would make them only that much harder to target".

"Okay, okay", Naomi relented, desperate even so to keep hope alive: "If our close proximity is the problem why don't we just launch a few guided missiles from right here: Take them out at long range".

"Once again you have the problem of determining their exact location", Frances continued in that placid, analytical fashion Naomi found increasingly irksome as the other woman in question kept shooting down her every suggestion:

"Nor do we know the exact range of their theoretical defenses. Given what we've already seen of Zelmorlite technology it's not inconceivable their surface-to-space defenses could reach us even here at the outer limit of our own given resources".

Not yet ready to give up so easily in the face of such insurmountable logic Naomi still racked her brilliant mind for some feasible way with which to snatch victory out of the yawning mouth of looming defeat:

"I've got it!" she snapped her fingers in triumphant glee, an energetic spark dancing about in her emerald eyes: "A sonic cannon!! We could install another invisibility screen, this time in StarChild, and convert our sensor array into a sonic cannon. Then, taking us in even closer, we could shatter the surface of that entire planet before they could ever hope to retaliate.

"We don't even need to target their exact location, just set our cannon on a general sweep of the entire area".

'So help me', Naomi reflected immediately thereafter, fanning her smoldering frustration while waiting some possible feedback: 'If she shoots this one down, I'll scream'.

Not having to wait long she was still somewhat taken aback, Frances not the one to take her this time to task:

"No!", Jenniboni voice rose in sharp dissent: "Never!! There's a very good reason such weapons were banned the one-and-only time they were ever employed. Need I remind you what happened when the last men of the ancient patriarchates deployed them at the end of World War Three. The intensity of their discharge can't be regulated.

"The men back then thought they, too, could control such weapons to their own advantage and look what happened. Not only did they shatter each and every enemy city across the entire world, but shattered as well almost every tectonic plate under nearly every continent.

"And not only that, Ms. Marlowe, but …"

****

"When in the course of Human events it comes time to take a definitive stand, fighting for ones very beliefs against outrageous offense, it's likewise imperative we not compromise those very principals for which we now both stand and fight!!"

—St. Tammy E. Garfield
(2069 A.D.)

Crushing with their Lion's roar all who got in their way, their mighty bellow smashing about the poor Earth below, Sonic Cannons in their almost countless thousands blasted nearly all the planet below from synchronous orbital paths high above. And doing so in the late fall of 2038 A.D. they brought an old, decrepit and even perverse social order never meant to be to an apocalyptic, even ignoble, end.

Never deployed before in such great numbers until that one pivotal, tragic moment in all Human herstory they stepped far over the line, beyond their original purpose. Shattering asunder in their countless numbers not only every city across the world, they likewise collapsed every tectonic plate beneath nearly every major, global land mass.

Mighty walls of Bitter Ocean sweeping over nearly every land and inhabitant thereof, the entire world shaken about, continent after continent collapsed in on itself like so many fragile balloons succumbing to some malicious child's pinprick.

The very vibrations tearing all that old world apart, turning it as well on its side, north and south became back then the new east and west. Global regions once both Arctic and Antarctic becoming at the very same time the new equator, the whole wide world turned now on a completely new axis.

And as the dust of such wanton carnage began to once-and-for-all settle the dry surface of the entire world was reduced now to a mere pittance of its former self. A world of over seven billion souls finding itself reduced now to a single land mass of just over twelve million, only one land mass of any significant note survived the end of all patriarchal rule perverse to begin with…

****

Deemed from a military perspective back then too trivial to even bother with, left to its own devices, lowly Antarctica now found itself that only major land mass fortunate enough to survive both intact, and even unscathed.

Finding itself now resting at the new equator, the dramatic shift in the world's very poles left now this once-frozen wilderness a tropical paradise, the Sonic Cannons changing forever in just a few short hours the entire world! The entire world now turned on its side in but a single day a bitter, cold Antarctica was on its way now to becoming in a single generation another Garden of Eden.

Every other continental landmass across the planet reduced as well now to nothing, but a few scattered islands it was here in Antarctica the last remaining trace of all Womankind faced that awesome duty of rebuilding *all* Human civilization.

It was there that nothing, but a smattering of small colonies united themselves back then under the short-lived *"Ahnteekahn Matriarchate"*, changing as well the official name of their new homeland from "Antarctica" to "Ahnteekah".

Known only much later though as the "Ahnteekahn Matriarchate" each colony there was originally established by the recently deceased patriarchate nations now under miles of deepest ocean—this new provisional government formed only as a temporary measure to begin with.

Born as a result of the bio-engineered Yesinia-R Beta plague claiming nearly all the world's men the greater female populace surviving this deadly contagion found themselves forced out of simple necessity to take absolute control, hoping at the very same time to somehow establish a more harmonious balance between each gender.

Just one challenge among many it was nevertheless the most important they faced if hoping to ensure the very survival of all Womankind, the aforementioned plague having left the surviving male/female ratio at a mind-boggling count of only one man per every one thousand women. A pernicious bio-weapon employed during the last remaining months of 2035 it was this particular pandemic that, more than even war itself, had such a devastating effect on the entire male population.

And so it was those remote survivors scattered across all Ahnteekah had to determine now the most effective means by which to reestablish a fixed number of both male and female in order to avoid certain extinction. It was then that the act of 'cloning' was chosen after hasty debate as the most viable, cost effective means by which to guarantee Womankind's very future.

Caught between both a rock and hard-place it was a serious moral, ethical, and scientific choice requiring even so a speedy resolution before that present female populace found itself too old to bear such future generations—this decision leading to both the revival of perishing Womankind alongside the final demise of that first matriarchal order to begin with.

Brought about by the toxic influence of one 'Dr. Sybil Vojac' she was chosen at first Chief Administrator for their entire cloning operation. It was only later her superiors discovered what she really was; a vicious, psychotic androphobe with her own twisted agenda for all Womankind. Promoting the exclusive reproduction of women only she planned on even further the utter annihilation of every last male surviving the plague regardless of age.

Relieved of all her duties after learning this the leaders of the prevailing order way back then hoped that would be the end of all Sybil Vojac's pernicious plotting. Unfortunately that wasn't to be, Dr. Vojac managing to rally at her side other like-minded individuals. Vicious fanatics calling themselves *"Clonists"* they took their evil cause to the very streets below, each with her own particular axe to grind.

Making up in violent agitation what they lacked in genuine numbers Sybil and her followers did succeed at least in throwing that temporary, provisional order into complete disarray. Inexperienced, untried neophytes in the field of civil unrest that ad hoc government way back then proved itself in the end too ineffectual.

Brought to a complete standstill it was nothing but a polyglot body politic lacking that single, central personality strong enough to provide all Womankind superior, effective and determined leadership. Hands tied by both its bureaucratic policies, procedures and irresponsible approach to democratic order the old 'Ahnteekahn Matriarchate' both stumbled and fell—unable to determine among its own-rank-and-file that single individual possessing those independent, charismatic leadership skills so necessary in such times of crisis.

Coming apart in complete disarray, the political structure of all Ahnteekah unraveling at a steadily increasing rate, it seemed for a while Dr. Sybil Vojac might realize in just a few short years all her psychotic ambitions. In the end it was only one other, Reverend Tammy E. Garfield, who proved herself the only superior force in possession of both the noble dream and very real leadership ability needed to oppose both Clonist philosophy and violence.

A young clergywoman belonging not to the prevalent body politic Tammy lived at the time in a small British mining colony on the eastern shores of Ahnteekah, a rather insignificant hamlet known as only 'New Manchester'. Popular already for other philanthropic endeavors in service of the last reminents of Womankind, an already proven organizational leader and motivator of others, it was then and there this young priest first found herself bound by moral conviction to take action.

Urged on by popular demand to accept a role of ultimate leadership during times when no one else could or would, she gathered as well around her followers sharing in the end her own, unique version of a very special future including both male and female. It was a vision Mother Tammy recorded in her own rather lengthy manifesto called **The New Matriarchate**—an all-inclusive mistress blueprint for future Human civilization her supporters adopted as their very own.

Nor was it long before their natural opposition to both Clonist leadership and philosophy lead to an inevitable conflict between the followers of Dr. Sybil Vojac and those women backing the personable, even charismatic young priest born in bygone Liverpool, raised in once majestic London.

Women calling themselves 'The Sisterhood' the only thing both they and Mother Tammy shared in common with their Clonist opposition was a similar belief in the superiority of the Matriarchate system— the critical difference being that, unlike both the Clonists and their own murderous demagogue, both Tammy and her noble 'Sisterhood' cared deeply as well for the remaining male population, seeing the survival of both genders as vital for Womankind's future.

And promoting *The New Matriarchate* as that ultimate blueprint for future society theirs would be a perpetual matriarchate civilization dedicated to a voracious policy of both peace, charity, and justice for all Womankind regardless of race, creed, gender, and/or place of origin.

A proposition certain to elicit Clonist retaliation the final showdown between both Clonist and Sisterhood forces came about in the mid-summer months of 2065—a final, explosive, ultimate battle-royal between both these contradictory forces to decide the ultimate, eternal fate of all Womankind.

Known only later as the 'Ahnteekahn Civil War' it would last for seven years, ending with the defeat of Clonist forces and the banning of cloning itself once a more equitable balance between the sexes was achieved. Doing so to prevent the possible rise of future Sybil Vojac's it was then these noble women of days gone by established as well an everlasting peace...

The '*Tammyite Matriarchate*'.

Womankind crossing at long last the River Jordan, entering at long last the Promised Land, theirs would prove an eternal new order devoted forever-and-ever to both peace, charity, justice and the everlasting value of each and every Human soul![**]

****

"…And not only that Ms. Marlowe, but you're also forgetting another very important matter with each and every suggestion you've so far made", Jenniboni countered, sharply, in Naomi's very direction.

"Ma'am?"

"Simply put you run the very good risk of killing young Master Roderick with every single proposal you've so far put forth", the outraged mother of three added: "I refuse to let him die!!"

Ashamed to have forgotten already their recent 'houseguest' a hushed still descended over all those gathered about their C.O.'s private chambers, Frances nodding her solemn agreement as it did—no one ready to defy the silent pall all about until Stasha's hesitant voice pierced the surrounding quiet:

"I'm of course loathe to even suggest this, but it might be in fact impossible for us to save both his life as well as destroy the Emerog…"

The intense pain Stasha felt even raising the slightest hint of such a sad conclusion was written in oh-so-obvious view across her every feature, feeling it nevertheless her duty as ship's executive officer to do so:

"In the end it might just come down to a choice between the lesser of two evils, his life versus all those threatened by Emerog intent".

"In other words sacrifice his life for ours", Jenniboni smiled a sad smile,

---

[**] See "Jeremiah"; Chapter 31: Verse 22

shaking her head. The disappointed look she gave her oldest, dearest friend left Stasha feeling quite small indeed, her powerful physique notwithstanding.

"No, Cmdr. Nikarov: No! We can't allow ourselves the simple luxury of such baser rationale", Jenniboni continued in the same soft, sad, yet resolute voice: "There are always alternatives if you just look for them. Especially in the case of an innocent child. Fighting to the death against an enemy bent on your own destruction is one thing, but this would be a betrayal of all our civilization holds dear".

"Excuse me, but do you think I, in all honesty, enjoy making such a suggestion?!", Stasha shot back in her own defense, both hurt and even resentful: "The very idea of taking that poor boy's life sickens me to the core but I'm only doing my duty here as your second-in-command pointing out, no matter how disagreeable, every possible contingency!"

"Yes, Commander. Put that way I see your point", Jenniboni offered by way of apology, sympathetic: "But, be that as it may, the boy's life isn't an option here. We are going to save him!"

"The 'boy's' name here is 'Rodney'!", she heard as well Naomi mutter, angry, under her breath.

"Point taken, Ms. Marlowe. Quite right", Jenniboni smiled, turning then her attention towards her stoic Chief of Security:

"And you, Ms. Straker?" she asked: "You're the one in charge of security aboard StarChild, responsible as well for the safety of both this ship and his crew. What say you? Might as well have your opinion here since everyone else seems so ready with theirs".

With both her tone and expression betraying at last some bitter emotion, looking her commanding officer straight in the eye, Frances gave her answer from across the room—forthright—no wavering at all:

"My entire career, both here and as a Protector, has been without exception dedicated to the continual protection of Human life. Not its destruction!

"Therefore, all things considered, I think you should already have a pretty good idea my opinion".

Her opinion obvious in other ways than just her words it was there as well in her dark, expressive eyes; Jenniboni able to see in Frances a clear reflection of her own sensibilities.

Having already reached her final conclusion, her decision based on all the above, Jenniboni wasn't seeking the council of those under her command. Something of which Naomi was quite aware of herself when, fixed again with Jenniboni's steely gaze, it was now likewise her turn to render an opinion.

Nor did she feel put out in any way. Realizing no vote was being taken she planned nonetheless to be quite honest in her opinion. If her Commanding Officer was really interested in hearing what was on her mind it was Naomi's hope to be quite open and aboveboard even if her words, all said and done, counted for nothing:

"I'm afraid I have to agree with Cmdr. Nikarov. She might be right when she says we might have to sacrifice young Rodney in order to likewise take out the Emerog. Still though I don't think I could honestly live with myself were we not to explore every other possibility first before resorting to such an ultimate 'contingency'".

Hearing this, noticing as well from the corner of her eye Gloria's ready expression. Seeing there a look of serene confidence Jenniboni was interested to see her young Lieutenant so ready, come what may, to speak her mind.

'This should prove interesting', was Jenniboni's first immediate response, taken all the same by surprise, granting young Gloria the floor:

"Have you ever, by chance, read the Talmud; Ma'am?"

"No, Lieutenant: I can't in all honesty say I have", Jenniboni responded, slow and hesitant, confused by what seemed a sudden change in topic: "I've heard of it, but can't, to the very best of my recollection, remember ever reading it. Some sort of Jewish religious text, is it not?!"

"Yes, Ma'am", Gloria explained, smiling at the very same time: "You see, Ma'am; I have a young laddie friend who's Jewish so, in order to better understand his faith, I've been reading up on various..."

Frances, smiling when hearing this, was pretty sure who Gloria's young Laddie friend had to be. Frank clearly made one heck of a lasting impression!

"That's all very fine, Ms. Greensley", Jenniboni granted with a weary sigh, "but I fail to see how all this pertains to the immediate matter at hand".

"Well, Ma'am; there is a passage in the Talmud that says, 'Whosoever should save but one life, it is as though they had saved the world entire'. So by that very same philosophy it occurs to me that 'whosoever should sacrifice but one life, it is as though they sacrificed the world entire!'".

'Remarkable girl!', Jenniboni mused, leaning back in her chair. Eyebrows raised, full of admiration, it wasn't long after that she corrected herself:

'No', she reminded herself, a stern reprimand: 'I have to stop thinking of her in such terms. She's a woman, not a girl!'

Deeply impressed no matter which, it was still a brief moment after Gloria had her little say before Jenniboni addressed aloud the entire assembly gathered about her:

"As for me that just about says it all. Very good, Lieutenant! And on that note I think it high time to conclude this discussion, bring an end to debate, and begin at once a complete and thorough search for some viable means by which to destroy these 'Emerog' that, on the other hand, will spare young Master Roderick his life.

"Shouldn't be so difficult seeing as we already know from the boy's own testimony that whatever killed them on Earth nearly 7,000 years ago spared as well the rest of Womankind.

"Therefore, as of right now, Commander's Marlowe and Nikarov will begin together a most thorough search for their 'Achilles Heel' while, at the very same time, Lieutenant Greensley will continue the search for further Emerog sabotage aboard ship.

"I'm placing the rest of Engineering at her disposal while, at the same time, Lt. Cmdr. Straker shall begin to arrange a rescue party, putting together everything she'll need to recover young Master Roderick when the time comes.

"And while all of you are seeing to that I'll be on the bridge waiting for subsequent up-dates on all your final progress, all of which I expect soon!

"So, in conclusion", Jenniboni added, glancing at the timepiece embedded before her in the immediate surface of her desk; "I see it's now almost 23:00 Hours, time to break for a brief meal before getting on with each of your assigned duties: Thirty minutes, I think, should suffice.

"That's all, Gentlewomen: Dismissed!"

Chapter 59

"THEIR ACHILLES HEEL"
(Saturday, February 23rd, 2915AD)

Returning yet again to the 'Special Studies Lab' they occupied but several hours ago, both Naomi and Stasha sought this time around that one, fatal flaw their enemy suffered.

"I just don't know", Naomi groaned, rubbing hot, sore, tired eyes.

Staring over an hour at her screen, endless reams of comparative data, her vision beginning to blur, it was already the next day since she last slept. The wee, small hours of the morning and she was already finding it more and more difficult to concentrate.

Trying to remain focused on the immediate task at hand there was at least one plus, her companion not looking this time over her shoulder. Grinning, thinking about it further, Naomi wondered with similar affection how Stasha was likewise faring given such limitations, seated next to her at a neighbouring terminal:

"It's like you said yesterday evening in the conference room: This world seems to have everything going for it both Earth and Zelmorl do—if not more!"

"Maybe that's the key", Stasha granted, echoing Jenniboni's earlier conclusion: "Something essential to Emerog existence the other two lack".

"But what? Other than the fact Bandros has even more of the same the other two have. I can't see anything Earth and Zelmorl have that Bandros doesn't have going for it and more—no qualities unique to it other than the possible fact it has two suns, orbiting as well a gas giant".

"Well, we'd better find something. And soon! Time's running out for both us and the boy".

"Sure", Naomi granted with a weary scowl, studying yet another comparison chart detailing all three worlds in question:

"Oh, this isn't getting us anywhere", she muttered a few minutes later, shaking her head.

"Not necessarily", it was Stasha's turn to now observe: "I've been going over in my mind what you said earlier about Bandros orbiting a gas giant; the fact that it's not really a planet, but a moon. The answer must lie there".

"What answer?? Gas?", Naomi grumbled, facetious.

"I was thinking instead of what effect such a gas giant would have on such an Earth-like moon like Bandros", Stasha gave her companion a sour look: "For instance, the electro-magnetic discharge from that other, more Jovian world is directly responsible for Bandros having a greater magnetic field than either Earth, or Zelmorl.

"Now, if you'll likewise bear with me here for just a moment, what if the Emerog, being in fact energy-based life-forms, need that greater energy-field the same way we need more physical sustenance? What if what killed them on both Earth and Zelmorl was simple starvation, not enough energy?"

"Nooo, I don't think so", Naomi frowned after a mere moment's thought:

"Even though, as you say, Earth and Zelmorl don't possess magnetic fields as great as that surrounding Bandros, that wouldn't explain why they all died out... Some maybe, but not all.

"However, be that as it may, I think you might still be onto something", Naomi was at least fair enough to concede.

"Maybe Bandros' greater 'magnetism' is responsible for something else protecting the Emerog from whatever killed them on both Earth and Zelmorl. But what?", she added, almost as an afterthought, calling up yet another set of planetary comparisons.

Yes...!

It was there...!

Stasha could feel it!

Wriggling about in the back of her mind it seemed to remain forever elusive. Just beyond her immediate grasp it would squirm out of reach every single time she tried to get a more concrete hold on it.

Every time Stasha was confident it was hers for the asking, it just slipped away from between her mental fingers...

Something in fact Naomi herself referred to just moments ago.

If only she could remember...

Some sarcastic remark about...

"That's IT!!! Of course!", Stasha burst forth with such boisterous enthusiasm it almost made the woman next to her jump in her seat, her elusive prey now firmly in hand.

"Well; now that you've given me a veritable heart-attack would you care to explain why you're looking at me like the proverbial cat who ate the canary", Naomi managed at last, gasping for air, quite shook up.

"GAS!!" Stasha explained, ecstatic, giddy with delight: "You were right all along! The answer is gas!!"

"Yeah, right: Sure", Naomi countered, scornful: "Gas".

"Yes! Gas", her companion was quick to insist, undeterred. Stasha's broad grin even caused the vertical scar on the right side of her face to crinkle upwards a noticeable bit. This rather unnerving image, commingled with the gleeful twinkle in her remaining baby-blue, assured Naomi she was definitely on to something. Something big!

"Or, to be more precise, my dear colleague: OZONE!!", Stasha nearly giggled again, her excitement obvious.

"Ozone??"

"Yes!", StarChild's Chief Science Officer sped on, approaching at this point Seventh Heaven: "Bandros has an ozone level several times thicker than even the Prime Mother World, Earth itself: Earth's having grown three times thicker since the mid-21st century. And that's not even taking into consideration how there are no longer any holes in it!

"Due to the interaction of the electric discharges from the gas giant with the oxygen-rich atmosphere enveloping Bandros it has an abnormally high ozone count in its ozonosphere, measurably greater than even that on Earth produced since the end of World War Three—ours produced since then by the increase of planetary surface area covered now by water".

"All right: Granted", Naomi proceeded slowly, carefully, trying hard to determine what Stasha was trying to lead up to: "So Bandros is ozone-rich: Even more so than Earth, or Zelmorl. How does that help in any way the Emerog?"

"Radiation", Stasha smiled, patient, willing to play 'teacher' if need be.

Calling up another chart on both their screens, this one was a comparison of harmful rays reaching the surface of each celestial orb. Moving her chair closer to Naomi's she pointed out the individual display for each world likewise a part of their detailed analysis:

"Here's Earth, here's Zelmorl, and... finally... here's Bandros. Do you see it?"

"Yes, I see it: No harmful rays reach Bandros' surface: Especially ultra-violet. But I'm still unclear as to how this might, in fact, benefit the Emerog. In the case of Human Beings I can see the obvious advantage, but how can U.V. radiation have any detrimental effect whatsoever on pure energy life forms such as they".

"Ahhhh, but that's just it: They're *not* pure energy", Stasha grinned a sly little grin, calling upon yet another comparison of critical data assembled just yesterday: "Look here".

"Those are the readings Glor... Lt. Greensley... took of the Emerog both on Bandros as well as aboard ship. However, I don't recognize this set of... of...", Naomi pointed to a third diagram situated to the far right of her screen.

"That's a life-reading of Rodney Dr. Wei-Chang took after returning to StarChild. In all sincerity I don't blame her in the least missing it at first. Until just now I, too, didn't realize its true significance".

"I'm still not seeing it", Naomi confessed, a hint of grumpy frustration creeping into her voice.

"Fair enough. Basically it's like this: Our revered C.M.O. was right in her assumption concerning the Emerog being able to conceal themselves or, at least their energy patterns in the electrical impulses produced by the Human brain.

"However, by that very same token, they are just as unable to conceal—at least not in its entirety—their matter content. While it bears a strong resemblance to Human bio-matter, there are all the same definite tell-tale signs of both alien D.N.A. and R.N.A. to it. You'll notice the same alien bio-matter mix as well in the Emerog energy scanned by Lt. Greensley both in the androids as well as aboard ship".

"So they weren't completely converted into energy after all".

"Oh, yes, they were", another coy smile sprang to Stasha's lips.

"You're losing me again!" Naomi groaned.

"Sorry: What I mean to say is that, while the original matter content of their bodies was indeed converted into energy, the energy impulses also there were likewise converted into matter: Total matter/energy transference!!"

"Of course", Naomi shook her head. Embarrassed, she was surprised from the very get-go she could have missed something so basic. Having taken a college course on the various applications of micro-cyborg implants—how they were also powered by electrical impulses from the brain—it made sense that the original Emerog, like their later flesh and blood prey, would have been composed as well of such a balance when they were likewise physical entities.

"Furthermore, I consider it a just as reasonable hypothesis this is that part of them which now resembles swamp gas", Stasha carried on: "It's that part of the Emerog that glows now a putrid green, a gaseous substance which used to be energy when they had corporeal bodies like us:

"And on that note I consider it no less reasonable to assume that it's this specific physical matter still remaining in each and every one of them governing both their higher motor skills as well as their overall ability to interact as much as they do with the physical world".

"A safe assumption explaining no doubt why they require both host bodies and space craft to leave their present confinement on Bandros, as vulnerable to the cold vacuum of deep space as we".

"All right!", Naomi felt like celebrating: "Now we've got the little blighters right where we…"

High spirits soon dampened though by the frustrated look appearing on Stasha's face Naomi felt like screaming, barely able to contain her own dismay:

"What's wrong now?", she almost yelled.

"How are we going to deliver that very same U.V. needed to destroy them through that darned ozone layer protecting their very existence in the very first place? Even if by some chance we could punch a hole through that protective shield of theirs, focus a direct burst of ultraviolet radiation through it, it would saturate only one small area of the entire planet's surface.

"Radiation travels in a straight line: It doesn't curve! What we need is some sort of sure-fire method by which we can bombard the entire planet, every square centimeter, all at the very same time".

The solution coming to mind in one fell swoop, the dismay she felt at first now vanquished, a wicked grin spread at once across Naomi's otherwise cherubic face:

"No need to worry yourself over such minor concerns. Problem solved! Just leave that to your brilliant Chief Engineer".

"Well …?"

"I'll tell you on the way".

"On the way to where?"

"To seek audience with the 'great and tewwible Oz' of course", Naomi quipped, quite merry indeed: "I'm sure she, too, could use some good news right about now. Therefore I suggest you summon at once Commodore Saphira to your office while I transfer all the pertinent data to your private office P.C. there.

"And while you're at it, may I also suggest you ask Lt. Cmdr. Straker to join us there, too?"

"Only as long as you, Lt. Cmdr. Marlowe, keep in mind that nobody 'summons' Commodore Jenniboni Saphira anywhere aboard her ship. All you may do is request the honour of her presence"

"Well my dear Cmdr. Nikarov, will you in that case 'request the honour of her presence'… tout de suite… in your office".

Chapter 60

"PLAN OF ATTACK"

"Am I to understand you two gentlewomen have in fact some good news for me?", Jenniboni greeted each the very moment she saw both Naomi and Stasha step off a nearby ag-pod, waiting already in hopeful anticipation outside the door to Stasha's private office.

"Yes, Ma'am", Naomi was first to assure her. Thoroughly pleased to the point of looking radiant it was just then Frances likewise made herself known, appearing at the farthest end of that very same corridor. Last to arrive she rapidly approached them, quick as quick can be on long, graceful legs. Having the longest distance to travel she joined them at last.

"Very good, then", Jenniboni wasted little time at all, recommending they discuss the matter at hand in 'more private surroundings'.

"Yes, Ma'am", Stasha was just as ready, leading the way.

Except for the missing three-sided table, lacking also such homey touches as the work of small children on her walls, Stasha's neighbouring office was otherwise a mirror reflection of Jenniboni's in general appearance—same desk, a couple of chairs for visiting personnel and a small, rather utilitarian cabinet situated just right of their only way in.

Yet as the automatic door behind her slid shut with a gentle, mechanical hiss these new 'digs' struck the rather hedonistic Naomi Marlowe as lacking a certain hospitality. Too stark... even bleak... this Spartan chamber was, in her own humble opinion, the private domain of someone too occupied with the mere performance of duty... simple functionalism... to realize the just-as-simple importance of workplace aesthetics.

"Please be seated", Stasha invited her commanding officer. Offering Jenniboni her very own chair behind her own crescent-shaped desk, she called up as well on her personal P.C. all the relevant data Naomi transferred there from before.

Making herself to home at Stasha's private workstation Jenniboni listened as well with keen interest to their informative presentation. Watching the results of their thorough investigation on the broad screen before her, Naomi and Stasha standing to both her right and left, Jenniboni leaned forward for a closer examination of their many charts and diagrams—StarChild's Chief Science Officer talking her step-by-step through the complex process by which they discovered that one fatal flaw from which the Emerog suffered:

"Excellent work, Gentlewomen", Jenniboni complimented both her exceptional officers: "However, I fail to see how you plan to deploy this 'secret weapon' of yours against our common enemy".

"Well, Ma'am, since it was she who came up with it to begin with, I'll let Ms. Marlowe explain in greater detail the plan we have in mind".

"It's quite simple, really", Naomi took over: "Firstly, we take all the drone probes recently remodified, encasing each and every one in a series of heat-resistant light amplification lenses.

"Then, hooking up all these as well to radiation generation units installed in the nose cone of each and every probe, each and every lens will emit when employed a continuous burst of U.V. radiation controlled by remote control from StarChild's bridge.

"Once all the modifications to each and every probe are completed we will launch all said probes from the hangar bay, arranging them soon thereafter in synchronous orbit around Bandros just beneath the entire planet's ozone layer.

"Each probe will be programmed to orbit Bandros following parallel paths both longitudinal and latitudinal forming a grid pattern over the entire planet's surface. And since each and every lens covering each and every probe will be positioned at different angles from one-another this should guarantee complete saturation of the entire planet before the Emerog are even aware what's going on".

"Very creative indeed, Ms. Marlowe", Jenniboni gave her full approval. Staring up at her brilliant compatriot with all due admiration Naomi's enthusiasm proved contagious, infecting as well her superior: "The only problem I have with your proposal is the small problem of time necessary to destroy all the Emerog while, at the very same time, not harming the young laddie.

"Given his previous testimony I feel it safe to assume it took at least generations, if not centuries, for all the Emerog to perish on Earth. And as we are all painfully aware ultra-violet radiation is quite lethal as well for Human Beings. Especially given the large doses of said radiation you and Cmdr. Nikarov are suggesting".

"Don't worry, Commodore", Stasha was ready to guarantee, confident:

"We've also taken that into consideration while performing our many calculations. The only reason it took the Emerog so long to die on Earth was because the ultra-violet rays reaching them were still in the process of being filtered out to a considerable extent by the ozone layer even back then.

"Due to this they received only gradual doses of harmful radiation in smaller proportions than what we have in mind here. The effect back then was much like being slowly poisoned to death over an extended period rather than one, lethal dose of the exact same toxin administered to the very same victim, or victims all at once.

"Now while we confess this might pose a slight risk to young Rodney's similar well-being, we also believe it will kill the Emerog long before similar exposure results in any irreversible damage involving the young laddie. According to all our research the Emerog are much more susceptible to harmful doses of U.V. radiation, their vulnerable matter content less protected from its pernicious effects than we.

"Therefore, taking all the above into consideration, it shouldn't take us much more than a mere minute, or two to eliminate the entire Emerog population, leaving at the same time young Rodney a grace period of at least ten to twenty minutes before experiencing any lethal effects.

"The most he *might* suffer in the bargain is a treatable sunburn a wee bit painful at first. And to be sure all goes well, all according to plan, we likewise plan to monitor the entire procedure as it takes place by means of a series of onboard sensor arrays also built into each and every drone.

"Keeping a watchful eye on the elimination process this will likewise allow us continual up-dates on young Master Roderick, monitoring at the very same time his immediate condition during the entire progress of said operation".

Pursing her lips upon hearing such reassuring guarantees she sat back in Stasha's chair once all was said and done. Narrowing her luminous eyes in deep concentration all those gathered about her waited anxiously for Jenniboni's very next administrative decree:

"I would first like to test your assumptions in a practical trial-run of what you propose in order to determine the Emerog are as indeed vulnerable as you believe", Jenniboni reached a final conclusion after what seemed to everyone else a lengthy intermission:

"How long do you think it'll take you to ready first a test probe?"

"With all the modifications needed I think such a test scout might be ready in the next few hours", Naomi offered her professional opinion.

Jenniboni found herself beaten to the punch however, Frances requesting formal leave to make an observation of her very own. Standing on the opposite side of Stasha's desk Jenniboni's patient Chief of Security spoke up at long last from where she waited:

"Granted, Ms. Straker: You have the floor".

"Thank you, Ma'am. In my opinion there are two major drawbacks to launching such a test probe, the first being we can't be sure the probe might not malfunction during its preliminary test-run. That would give the enemy advance warning of our true intentions, allowing them ample time to launch a possible counter-strike of their very own.

"Secondly, and just as important, I also find the time needed to ready said probe worrisome. In my considered opinion we need quicker results, an alternative plan requiring less delay, during which the final outcome can be likewise observed up-close and personal".

Having already a pretty good idea what Frances had in mind, the kind of 'up-close-and-personal' test she was about to suggest, Jenniboni endured a rather unfortunate sinking sensation in the very pit of her stomach, asking nonetheless the other woman her alternative recommendation:

"I suggest we remodify several laser-rifles already in storage to fire a concentrated steam of U.V. radiation comparable to that Ms. Marlowe has in mind for the probes. All things considered it shouldn't take any more than an hour at most to remodify each and every rifle in question. Such modifications should require nothing more than a simple readjustment of the light spectrum channeled by, and through their internal refraction units.

"Then, once done, I could—with your permission, of course—lead an away team to Bandros composed of both myself, four members of my department, and Ensign Maytina Matthias. Once there we will seek out and target any available Emerog, making at the very same time both visual and scanner observations of the entire procedure.

"Knowing all we know already about Emerog psychology I have a pretty good idea we'll be 'warmly greeted' soon after our arrival by at least several representatives of their overall collective", Frances ended on a certain sarcastic note, a sly and dry wit: "No doubt they'll see us as being no threat. At least not at first".

Maybe so, maybe not…

Even so Jenniboni cared very little, *very little at all*, for this particular recommendation.

Unfortunately all her reasons for doing so were personal, private ones she couldn't allow to influence her final, overall decision-making process—excuses such as their developing friendship and Andrei's doubtless heartbreak were anything to happen to his *defender*.

Then again, on the other hand, Jenniboni could overrule quite easily Frances' proposal on such grounds as expendability. Should she choose to she'd be quite justified doing so. Taking into account what an invaluable asset Frances Straker was to both her and StarChild there was no possible way anyone could accuse Jenniboni of private interests denying Frances her request.

Sadly though there was no getting around the simple, cold yet practical logic behind her proposal now waiting Jenniboni's decision.

Delivered in that professional manner she was beginning to find now as irksome as Naomi before her, there was nevertheless no denying the simple truth that Ms. Straker's proposal was the best offered so far. And quite reasonable it also required the singular leadership of Jenniboni's best available tactician, her very best combat officer aboard ship, Frances herself:

"Permission granted, Lt. Cmdr.", Jenniboni gave her grudging consent: "You and Ms. Marlowe may begin at once remodifying whatever weapons you might need, selecting as well the members of your away team to the planet's surface".

Focusing then her attention on Naomi in particular Jenniboni instructed her to begin right after that the remodification of each and every probe required according to her own proposed plan of attack, a directive including as well the rest of Engineering. As it was Jenniboni wanted their 'secret weapon' ready for immediate deployment—A.S.A.P.!—pending the successful completion of Lt.

Cmdr. Straker's own fact-finding mission.

Dismissed right after that to go about their various duties both Naomi and Frances left Stasha's office, leaving to themselves StarChild's two highest-ranking officers. Leaning back in her X.O.'s chair, closing tired eyes, massaging her temples, StarChild's exhausted C.O. heard her second-in-command speak up through her weary haze:

"Jenniboni? As First Officer I, too, have a recommendation to make!".

Neither Stasha's serious tone nor informal address escaped her immediate superior's just-as-immediate notice, Jenniboni responding in kind:

"All right Stasha, let's have it. Needless to say you have something in mind you know I won't care for much. So let's just get it over with".

"All right! Fair enough. It'll be at least four hours before Lt. Cmdr. Straker returns with the results of her expedition so, until then, I suggest with all due respect you report at once to your personal quarters, get some meaningful rest!

"In the meantime I can handle the bridge while, likewise, I'm sure Ms. Marlowe can handle on her own the probes".

Gee Mommy, it's only 03:30 hours", Jenniboni teased in a little-girl falsetto: "I still got at least half-an-hour before my regular beddy-bye time".

"I'm not joking!!" Stasha vowed, sterner.

"If I'm not mistaken you've been up at least as long as I", Jenniboni was quick to counter, now rather annoyed.

"True enough", the other allowed: "And on that note I promise to also take a break once Lt. Cmdr. Straker gets back from Bandros.

"Don't forget that it was only the day before yesterday you yourself told me how you wanted at least one of us rested, at peak performance, at all times. So now I guess it's my turn to tell you the very same thing: *get some rest*!!

"However, if you continue in this obstinate behavior, I can always ask Dr. Wei-Chang's assistance, make it a more 'official' matter", Stasha threatened with good-natured reproach, a crafty little smile appearing at each corner of her mouth: "And don't think I won't where the safety of this ship is concerned".

"All right, all right"; Jenniboni laughed, hands held up in surrender: "You win, Commander: your wish is my command".

Accepting defeat with otherwise good humored grace Jenniboni was fully aware of her grumpy C.M.O.'s complete authority in all matters medical, fully in her rights as StarChild's Chief Medical Officer to veto even Jenniboni herself where the well-being of her entire ship's compliment was involved.

And likewise aware said '*compliment*' included her as well Jenniboni was confident, wearing now a lopsided grin, her curmudgeonly but efficient old crone of a C.M.O. would side with Stasha in this particular instance—Dr. Wei-Chang no doubt confining Jenniboni to her quarters should she protest the matter any further.

"Otherwise, all things considered, I must admit making the right choice making you my First Officer", Jenniboni added, getting at last out of Stasha's chair:

"Even if you are a wee bit pushy", she allowed herself a little giggle between dear old friends.

"About time you noticed", Stasha allowed herself a similar chuckle, wishing her oldest friend and C.O. 'Sweet Dreams' in a comedic little-girl voice all her own.

No sooner had she done so Stasha burst out laughing, Jenniboni giving her both a great big smile while flipping her off at the very same time—the door to Stasha's office sliding shut right thereafter between them.

Chapter 61

"TURKEY SHOOT"

Entering an evasive orbit around Bandros a little after 06:00 hours Frances was both pleased as well as a wee bit curious when, strangely enough, the Emerog took no provocative action against them.

Finding this more than just a little uncharacteristic given the nature of the enemy below Frances considered it more likely than not a positive indication they had yet to get their mystery weapon—or weapons—up-and-running in time for this impromptu little get-together.

From what she knew already knew concerning their quite arrogant constitution she couldn't imagine the Emerog just letting them violate at all 'enemy territory' without returning swift challenge.

Making little difference to her own natural inclinations Frances remained nonetheless alert, taking nothing for granted, at the ready as always. No telling for the moment just how close… exactly… their insidious foe was to being at last combat ready!

Nor did it fail to capture her immediate notice what a stunning world it was waiting their arrival below, bringing her away team's transport in on its final approach. No denying what a beautiful place it truly was, an exquisite prospect for further colonization once the Emerog themselves were dispatched to their final, just reward Frances was still unable to see herself living there.

The very thought of setting up permanent residence on Bandros left her cold. Too many bad memories down there infecting an otherwise bucolic setting that deplorable moon world below was to her way of thinking a graveyard.

HAUNTED!!

No different in that respect than Zelmorl: Inhabited by worse than those fanciful specters occupying Naomi's earlier imagination, this was likewise a world possessing an even more disturbing herstory of nothing but lost lives, lost loves, lost hopes, simple pain, and abject suffering needless beyond the obscene.

Inspecting now her onboard guidance system Frances observed as well that, given the period of rotation for that turquoise moon-world below, it was only an hour or so before sunrise over both Paradise as well as the neighbouring Zelmorlite ruins. While not relishing too much the singular idea of combat in the dark Frances was still loathe to delay their present assignment more than necessary.

Realizing everyone back on StarChild was waiting anxiously for the results of their current fact-finding mission as soon as Humanly possible it occurred as well to Frances that, given their 'luminous personalities', the Emerog should be easy targeting in any night sky.

"Good", she told herself with ruthless satisfaction. It was high time they gained the upper hand in the area of these loathsome monsters. No doubt about it, a world too tainted by past heartache, Bandros was simply too tragic a prospect for future colonization.

****

Locating the stolen shuttle not far from the collection of ruins Rodney referred to in his earlier testimony as 'the Northern City', Frances brought also their own vessel down less than forty, or so meters from the Gene III. Spotting at the same time no sign at all of physical activity she stepped out an open hatch not long after that, all still and quiet in the bright glow of her own shuttle's forward search lights.

Finding herself in the pre-dawn landscape of a still, quiet world she ordered as well two of her select team to stand close guard by their current transport, instructing everyone else to consider themselves likewise at full battle stations:

"Remember that, while the Emerog themselves can't hurt you, the androids they inhabit can", Frances cautioned: "So don't consider yourselves invulnerable just because you're wearing armor".

Mindful of Ensign Wilson… her pierced, violated body waiting now its final journey home in cold storage… Frances also made a point of warning all those present, no matter what, not to remove any item **whatsoever** of their current attire.

Asking if any further instruction was in fact needed, one of the guards Frances appointed sentry duty asked what to do if not encountering any androids but Rodney instead.

"Under no condition are you to approach the young laddie. Not until we've dealt once and for all with the Emerog. We can't risk taking him back aboard ship until sure the enemy isn't using him as some sort of proverbial Trojan horse.

"So should he indeed try and approach you, **armed or not**, your exact orders are to shoot him on sight, no hesitation!"

"Ma'am?" the very same sentry as before gave voice to a loud exclamation, horrified at the very thought of harming a mere child.

"Not with you laser gauntlets, Lt. Quint! With these!", Frances illustrated with equal force, indicating the recently converted U.V. rifles each member of

475

her landing party now carried at the ready:

"Hopefully it will drive out any enemy hostile in possible possession of his body. Keep in mind it's the Emerog inside him that's the enemy, not the actual boy himself: He's but a mere puppet, manipulated, under their control!"

Feeling no need to say anything further, no one having any further questions, Frances spun about. Leading the way over to what remained of the Gene III all those except the two sentries assigned guard duty followed her close behind. And growing even closer yet, Frances noted straightaway on further inspection that other shuttle before them endured anything but a smooth landing arriving on this hateful world.

Experiencing her own sudden rush of subtle dread, anticipating what might await them all inside, Frances observed at once the recognizable damage. The port side all crumpled in, dented, the small vessel looked like nothing more than so much tin-foil both spent and discarded after plenty of rigorous use.

Either the Emerog in control of young Rodney wasn't the skilled pilot it liked to believe itself, or the glancing shot StarChild delivered its active shields damaged the tiny transport's onboard guidance/landing systems more than they expected. Not even the lengthy shadows they cast on their approach proved able to obscure entirely the view of damage done.

Seemingly nestled in the center of a narrow oasis of bright light surrounded by a perpetual ocean of utter dark, a by-product of their own shuttle's operating lights shining now in back of them, this was however all they could see. Except for that nothing was visible now beyond the two Matriarchate craft but a star-studded sky dominated by that awesome gas giant Bandros orbited hanging just above the horizon.

The blackest of nocturnal landscapes not even the impressive glow from those rounded lamps a part of each crewwoman's armored helmet helped much penetrating that pre-dawn darkness all around them. Or at least not enough to suit Frances' own, exacting standards.

Nor did they receive much aid from the aforementioned world of which Bandros was just a moon. Not providing a significant source of light to reveal what lay all about them Frances found instead the very sight of that Jovian monster a continual distraction—a world that, while admittedly beautiful, posed as well a chilling sight in the night sky.

Reminding her a wee bit of Saturn high in the native sky of her own moon-world back on Titan it lacked however that cool, refreshing, blue/yellow glow back home. Looking instead molten hot given its burning, churning mass of compound gasses that Bandrosian monstrosity possessed in fact a fiery orange/red tint both ominous and compelling.

Even its brassy-gold rings, larger as well than those Frances remembered back home, looked like some sinister scythe stretched out to slice poor Bandros in half. The only hope of future illumination at all was a faint glimmer of approaching day appearing on the far horizon as Frances reached the Gene III's open hatch, peering through its yawning mouth.

Scanning with keen eyes the ruined shuttle's empty interior she breathed as well a deep sigh, relief flooding every single cell of her expectant being. Glad for what she didn't see, no sign whatsoever of Rodney's broken remains, she couldn't spy neither a single trace of ochre blood.

Not even the slightest, willow-the-wisp hint at all the young laddie was injured in this battered wreck Frances now climbed further into the now-derelict craft. Hope renewed she stood now just inside that open entry to whatever still might demand further inspection.

Investigating its barren interior once sure of her immediate balance the deck below was angled upwards at a steep incline towards the opposite bulkhead from where she stood. Making her way to the cramped cockpit, bracing herself as well inside its narrow doorway, she experienced yet again a certain rush of sweet relief.

Still unable to spot any sign young Rodney suffered injury during the imperfect landing evident all around her, it was proof enough he was at least capable of leaving the immediate vicinity on his own two feet. Hopefully he survived completely unscathed during his rough ordeal.

Having for the moment set her mind at rest where the young laddie was involved Frances began right after that a most thorough search for that same invisibility device both Naomi and Gloria installed much earlier. Looking straightaway for it right where they told her, kneeling before the pilot controls, she lay the riffle she still carried on the floor beside her, bending over even further.

Locating soon enough the emergency repair hatch Naomi told her about, situated floor-level directly below the shuttle's flight control panel, the small door handle stuck out in plain view from the tiny hatch. Grabbing the metal protrusion, giving it a firm yank, Frances discovered only then the small portal was jammed shut.

Pulling back even harder still on the tiny outlet, ripping the emergency repair hatch right off its hinges with a mighty tug, the wee little door came away in her waiting hand with an angry squeal of protest, metal-against-metal.

The troublesome device she looked for now quite visible she could see clearly as well it was ruined beyond all repair. No wonder the Emerog never bothered taking it with them, totaled no doubt in the same crash leaving its mark throughout the rest of the 'Gene III'.

Deciding all-the-same to play it safe Frances drew back her right forearm, blasting it as well into complete oblivion. Aiming her lethal gauntlet at the sanguinary contraption in question she totaled that entire mechanism both Naomi and her devoted junior spent likewise so many womanhours creating, doing so with just a single burst of brilliant laser-fire.

Leaving nothing useful of it in her wake she made sure there was nothing left now but a melted heap of steaming, smoldering slag destroyed beyond all hope of repair. Only then did Frances gather up again the converted riffle lying still at her side, getting once more to her feet.

One down and several more to go however, both the crystal refractors and power cells stolen earlier from StarChild's cargo deck all missing. Sure their enemy wouldn't have taken them if likewise rendered useless during the crash this could mean only one thing.

Much to their misfortune, the clock ticking away now even faster, it was all down now to a race between both Womankind and the Emerog—a mad dash to determine which in the greater scheme of things would deliver their enemy that final, ultimate, knock-out blow to their very existence.

And in the middle of cursing under her breath such bad luck Frances was interrupted soon enough by Maytina Matthias. Her voice possessing in fact a rather peculiar tone she called out to her from just outside the Gene III's open hatchway:

"Cmdr. Straker?! I think you should come see this at once!"

****

Poking her head straight away out the Gene III's open hatch Frances spied just as quickly an awestruck Maytina standing alongside the other two security personnel present. Shoulder-to-shoulder, their backs now to her, they stood erect and motionless some twelve meters away.

Staring towards the far horizon, rigid in deep wonder, it didn't take long at all to see what it was that had them so clearly bedazzled. Frances following as well the direction of their southward gaze she gaped likewise in mute fascination at *their* dramatic arrival. Having completely departed the Gene III's otherwise safe confines it seemed at first like a distant meteor shower of hitherto unheard of proportions, sickly green stars coming straight their way:

Not the androids Jenniboni made mention of during earlier conversations, but their masters themselves!

Pivoting about in a 360-degree turn, doing so in rather slow fashion, Frances watched them grow ever closer from every corner of that lousy, miserable moon-world they now stood on.

Streaking towards the small landing party now caught in their approaching crossfire, there must have been millions of them. Countless projectiles all a bilious green they traveled at high velocities, converging one-and-all in the night sky right above that small delegation representing all Womankind—the entire Human race.

And so they came in furious mass!

And came…

And came…

And just when it seemed they would all collide in their entirety, a spectacular air-borne disaster high above those Earth-bound, armor-clad crewwomen just below, each and every one of those hideous parasites in flight began swirling about.

Mingling all one with the other they formed in coordinated effort an angry, phosphorescent whirlpool blocking out the very stars beyond.

"Why are they showing themselves like this only now?", Frances heard someone ask, both confused and a wee bit fearful: "Why didn't they appear this way to Commodore Saphira's landing party??"

"Because they no longer see any reason to hide their true selves from us", Frances explained, her voice quite frosty indeed: "They know now we're onto them, knowing what they really are, and have decided to introduce themselves, nice and neat, out in the open!

"Isn't that *sweeeeet* of them", she added with a venomous drawl; sardonic, sarcastic.

Still, despite all that, she was nevertheless intrigued by the orchestrated simplicity of their highly organized activity, fluid moves as graceful as some choreographed dance.

Fascination turning just as quickly however into absolute rage, some of those airy performers high above dipped now towards the women below, pulling up at equal speed. Rejoining once more their compatriots in that strange, frantic air-borne ballet Frances clenched her teeth, realizing right then and there their pompous foe was in fact mocking them, taunting their flesh and blood audience watching all this from the ground below.

Trembling with absolute fury… incensed… angry… upset… enraged… it nevertheless occurred to her right about then these vile entities were themselves possessed of more than just one fatal flaw: Character flaws such as conceit, an unquenchable faith in their own invincibility, an unerring sense of racial superiority, and a chronic habit of always underestimating their enemy…

All continuous proof of Emerog weakness.

"All right, Gentlewomen", Frances decided right about then, full of grim resolve, her riffle raised to the very heavens above: "Time's come to bring these demons down a peg or two, show them for a change what harm Womankind can do!"

Taking aim at the enemy above, joining her shipmates in whatever came next, the unique personal irony of all this was not wasted at all on Maytina Matthias—her main reason for joining 'Project StarChild' being the dream both she and her sister, Phyllis, shared as one.

Speculating on many a long evening together what intelligent life might exist elsewhere beyond Womankind's own home System, what unknown form such sentient life might take, it was both their wish to be involved… first-hand… in that inevitable initial contact between both the Human race and such possible 'extra-stellar' life.

So much so that both she and Phyllis chose similar careers in communications, hoping by chance to be those actual individuals involved in that initial first "first contact" mission. Never did it occur to either that "first contact" would end up like this; a fight to the death with lethal, psychotic, will-o'-the-wisp's!

"All right", Frances commanded once confident everyone under her direction had taken careful aim:

"FIRE-AT-WILL!!!"

Although the discharge from each of those six weapons raised on high couldn't be seen by the naked eye, the effect it had on the enemy above was as both dramatic as it was likewise visible—U.V. wavelengths, although longer than X-rays, just a tad shorter than visible light.

Scattered at once on the existing breeze like so much dust the gaseous element making up each Emerog target fell away at once from their energized 'bodies'; the energy left behind, now lifeless, vanishing as well. And when several more air-borne '*targets*' were likewise '*dispossessed*' the rest of that awesome host froze also in their airborne tracks, motionless with shock at this most unanticipated turn of events.

Hovering there in their countless millions, suspended high above those puny mortals bold enough to attack them on familiar ground, each could feel those others in their mighty group removed forever from the collective Emerog consciousness.

Smiling up at this with icy pleasure, watching them just hang there like so many rabbits caught in the headlights of some oncoming vehicle, Frances didn't need at all their considerable telepathic abilities to know what frightened thoughts must be running through their many minds.

Thoughts like:

"This can't be happening…

"They can't destroy us…

"We're indestructible…

"How can this be …??

"Impossible …!!

"How dare they??!!"

"Payback's a bear", Frances muttered in sly reply to all their unspoken protests:

"And then you die!!!"

Continuing to pick them off one-by-one even as she spoke, targeting them in their stationary positions, the end result was nothing less than a good, old-fashioned "turkey-shoot". Requiring at first no effort whatsoever, everyone gathered about kept up her particular barrage of ultra-violet radiation. Maytina was the only one to set her weapon aside, monitoring instead for future analysis the entire process with scanner in hand.

Realizing at long last their very precarious situation, the immense jeopardy they were all now in, all those mortified Emerog just 'hanging about' recovered in all due time enough presence of mind to beat a hasty retreat—stunned for a moment into complete inaction, tasting death at the hands of 'mere others' for the first time in their too-long lives.

However, no longer paralyzed with fear, the spell they were under broken at last, they all scattered… every last one of them… to all four winds from whence they came. All alone now, their enemy's lightening retreat leaving them a trifle disoriented, the women from StarChild could but just gaze in wonder high above them. The Emerog all gone now all that remained in that dark, pre-dawn sky was 'AB-1', that churning red/orange/yellow gas giant Bandros orbited.

Its burnished gold rings girdling its mighty circumference, countless stars sparkling far off in the cosmic distance, it was only then everyone noticed as well another bright light beginning to take on both form and substance. This one in an easterly direction, each member of the landing party standing about watched in simple awe as dawn broke at last—the twin yellow/white suns both Bandros and its fearsome parent orbited together rising at long last in skies turning blue/green.

Reading into this a good omen full of hope, a sign of 'brighter fortune' on its way, the simple symbolism they all read into this filled each and every woman there with excellent cheer, each and every one rejoicing over their overall success—their apparent victory.

Everyone that is except Frances herself, choosing not to participate in that boisterous celebration going on all about her. Pleased all-the-same their mission was an evident success she still remained aware that, while triumphant here in obvious battle, their greater war with the Emerog collective was far from over.

Much more remaining to do, having further by far to go, there was also that 'unfortunate' matter concerning all those pilfered parts to deal with. Stolen right from under her very nose, taken during her particular watch aboard ship, that more than anything else left her feeling burned. Especially since there was still no telling what that slippery mass of alien crazies might be trying at that very moment to resurrect somewhere out there using those exact same parts.

In the process of explaining just that very same thing to all the others Frances was interrupted soon enough by the sound of heavy machinery approaching likewise from the north-east—twenty of those metal titans Jenniboni described just yesterday plodding their way into full view just a little ways off.

Approaching almost from the Gene III's opposite side, each colossal 'droid carried in its ponderous hands weapons identical to that Zelmorlite monster Lt. Greensley brought back with her from Paradise, a quite grievous contraption.

"Quick! On the double: Everybody back to the shuttle", Frances gave immediate orders to withdraw, the approaching juggernauts already aiming their bulky firearms in the landing party's very direction.

Firing at the retreating away team, white bolts of purest energy screaming their way through the air like a swarm of lunatic hornets, a couple of these burning cannonballs smashed their way into the nearby wreck in which Rodney… Emerog-possessed… fled StarChild with his/Its ill-gotten booty.

Now the turn of both Frances and her crew to beat a hasty retreat they almost reached the relative safety of their own nearby transport when one of those many energy pulses whizzed by, slamming without mercy Maytina Matthias in the back.

Lifting her high off her running feet it flung the hapless woman like a pathetic rag doll several meters through the air, the impressive weight of all that armor she wore making her return to solid ground all that much harder.

Remaining quite still as the rest of her sisters-in-arms did an abrupt about-face, they confronted at once those oncoming 'droids still in hot pursuit. Firing at once they didn't do so this time with the revamped rifles they still carried, but their armored gauntlets instead. Switching tactics their main hope was to deprive their enemy of its only immediate means of physical attack, the androids they employed, at least long enough to effect their immediate escape.

Unfortunately it was Frances and party who found themselves caught up now in a hopeless tactical disadvantage, the rising suns catching them full in the eye. Unable to destroy but six of the advancing horde the other two dozen mechanoids remained quite unharmed. Outnumbered, outgunned, StarChild's away team had no chance of taking down that spectral battalion before it reached that beleaguered group of women under now a constant barrage of enemy fire.

Hating with a passion the very thought of 'turning tail' in the face of such overwhelming odds Frances discovered right about then even more to stab at her very soul, gathering up Maytina's limp form from the stone-hard ground upon which it lay:

"Please, God, no!", she improvised in hasty prayer, fearing at first her fallen sister was dead: "Please don't let it be... *PLEASE*!!!"

Unable to bear tragic thoughts of yet another fatality under her command it seemed her quick petition to the Almighty was approved from on high, Ensign Matthias beginning right away to stir in her arms:

"What happened? Where am I??"

"Why do they always ask that after being knocked out flat?", Frances allowed herself to laugh, amused in spite of their precarious situation. Full of sweetest relief she wrapped a protective arm securely around Maytina's middle. Guiding her back to their waiting shuttle the other officer in question responded likewise, draping her right hand around the taller woman's shoulder.

Stumbling along in full withdrawal each one of them still kept shooting with their free arms at the nearing 'droids. Only when Frances began helping the dizzy woman into what was now their "get-away vehicle" did they call off their continual volley of return fire.

Breaking off her own personal attack to make sure instead everyone else was both safe and sound, Frances climbed right thereafter into the pilot seat. Activating their protective shields just in the nick of time she immediately noticed the enemy outside raise their cumbersome weapons in one, final parting shot.

Having already achieved lift-off by the time that fearsome discharge from all those active guns made contact their violent impact rocked about the tiny shuttle to-and-fro, knocking around with equal measure those inside:

"Those aren't energy rifles", Frances mused under her breath, ascending ever higher beyond their ultimate range of fire:

"They're energy bazooka's!!"

Chapter 62

"SECRET WEAPONS"

Effectively banished to her quarters, taking a quick shower in aid of further relaxation, Jenniboni changed soon after that into a fresh uniform.

Lying in bed, fully dressed, she planned to leap at once into action should any crisis at all occur. Caring little for sleeping in her clothes, preferring to sleep 'au-naturel', this probably explained best why she fell short of more meaningful slumber, managing little more than a drowsy state of semi-awareness.

Be that as it may she nevertheless felt more refreshed... rested... when Stasha informed her at a little after 09:00 hours Frances was back.

Still in the Hangar bay one level down from Jenniboni's own shipboard quarters, Jenniboni hurried in anxious hope of catching her there. Eager to hear the final outcome of her perilous mission into the heart of enemy territory Jenniboni's next move was—should her mission have proven successful—to proceed at once with 'Phase II' of '*Operation: Eradicate*'.

Arriving as the away team stepped down from their returning shuttle however, Jenniboni experienced a certain degree of approaching disaster seeing both Frances and yet another crewwoman supporting on either side Ensign Matthias.

Rushing as well to her side Jenniboni asked immediately how she was doing, Maytina stumbling along between those helping her:

"I'm quite all right, Ma'am", the young communications officer assured her ship's C.O., confident: "Just a little shaken up. Nothing serious".

"Why don't we just let Dr. Wei-Chang make that final determination", Jenniboni answered her, smiling kindly: "After all that's what she's here for".

"Yes, Ma'am".

Motioning someone else over to take her place at Maytina's side Frances removed the smart armor helmet she still wore, Ms. Matthias escorted right after that to sickbay.

"I trust your report is good, Lt. Cmdr.", Jenniboni got straight to the point once she and Frances were alone, that cavernous landing bay all about them otherwise empty… silent.

"Very good indeed, Ma'am", Frances beamed her a satisfied smile, handing her as well the survey scanner containing all the critical information Maytina captured therein.

Making a thorough study of all that precious data, calling it up on the mission recorder's tiny screen, Jenniboni listened as well to Frances Straker detailing all her many adventures planet-side. Also troubled to hear their missing cargo seemed to weather intact its arrival planet-side, Jenniboni was at least glad to hear little Rodney survived as well his rough ordeal.

Or so it would appear.

Looking up at long last from the scanning unit in hand Jenniboni stared at her companion in simple amazement, listening to how the Emerog gathered in their millions high above her survey team, taunting all those watching their airborne spectacle.

And laughing as well she was quite amused hearing how they all fled without exception the scene of their initial trouncing, tails as it were between their legs. Comforted to know these unholy terrors could at least feel fear, pleased also to remind them what it felt like, she expressed to Frances as well her heartfelt gratitude.

"Excellent, Lt. Cmdr.", Jenniboni continued in buoyant spirits: "Now let's hope Ms. Marlowe is having similar good fortune in the matter of her own current assignment. If so we should be all that much closer to a final reckoning with these arrogant, odious hobgoblins".

"Yes, Ma'am: However, be that as it may, I'm still a trifle worried concerning the missing parts stolen right from under our very noses. Seeing how they seem to have survived their tumultuous arrival planet-side, I'm afraid that means the Emerog also have a clear head-start on whatever they're likewise working on".

"Agreed", Jenniboni granted, frowning: "Maybe we should check in then with our worthy Ms. Marlowe, see how she's coming along. No doubt she'll also appreciate hearing all about your obvious success".

****

"NO", Naomi snapped, outright: "As I told you before, Ms. Derris, the lenses have to face *this* way in order to cover maximum territory without overlapping".

Removing straightaway from the other woman's hand the securing clamps reserved for such intricate procedures Naomi knelt at her side, readjusting herself one of those misaligned refractors needing further regulation:

"Get it now?", Naomi made no attempt hiding her lousy mood; frazzled, annoyed: "See what I mean?"

"Yes, Ma'am!"

484

"Very good, then"; Naomi added, no less pacified: "In that case you can re-calibrate those other three there, there, and there making sure as well to re-connect the guidance system from our original remodifications to the new U.V. transmit unit".

Glancing up just then from her current position she saw both Jenniboni and Frances step off a distant ag-pod, hearing as Naomi did the familiar sound of elevator doors swooshing open. Both senior officers heading her way they drew closer around the many personnel laboring now over the assorted probes between them.

Nor did it escape Jenniboni's keen notice how absolutely beat, even haggard Naomi looked, the weary redhead straight ahead getting now to her feet. Realizing right off the bat Naomi was no doubt awake since early yesterday morning it pained Jenniboni she couldn't tell the poor woman to take some well-earned down-time, regretting all the while she couldn't.

Racing now the literal clock they needed her technical expertise right where she was.

"How are you holding up, Lt. Cmdr.?"

"As well as can be expected, Ma'am", Naomi answered, a tired chuckle:

"I've even considered asking Dr. Wei-Chang to send us a round of Hype injections for the whole lot of us", she grinned, indicating with a weary wave all those gathered about.

"I can only imagine what our good ship's C.M.O. would have to say about that", Jenniboni smiled, sympathetic. Not only was Hype quite illegal, but addictive to boot.

"Yeah, so can I", Naomi giggled, a twinkle in her eyes, brushing from her face limp strands of dull, lifeless hair: "Be worth it though just to see the look on that old grump's face".

"Well... I'm sure it won't have the same dramatic effect as Hype, but Ms. Straker and I wanted to inform you, personally, her mission was a complete and thorough success. Thought hearing so might perk you up at least a little".

While not the particular substance Naomi made reference to but seconds ago Jenniboni's good news did elicit all-the-same a positive reaction, reviving quite visibly Naomi's flagging spirits. Knowing now for certain they weren't just wasting precious time, all their tiresome work justified now beyond any shadow of doubt, her voice grew stronger.

More animated she invited both Jenniboni and Frances to inspect even further all the steady progress her Department was making:

"... and Lt. Greensley is in the cargo deck below readying even more drone probes for final deployment, the rest of my people in Engineering there as well", Naomi added, explaining in technical jargon each intricate procedure they were introduced to during their grand tour of Naomi's very own, busy command:

"Hopefully all will be ready within the next three hours. Then, once done, we'll start loading the whole lot of them in the hangar bay above in preparation of final deployment".

"Excellent, Ms. Marlowe", Jenniboni expressed her honest appreciation, her sincere gratitude for a job well done: "With any luck, once we've put all this sordid business behind us, both you and your fine department can take a well-earned break".

"Thank you, Ma'am. Probably the first time in recorded herstory 'sun lamps' were ever used in combat as a lethal weapon", Naomi quipped, this followed at once by Stasha requesting Jenniboni's immediate presence on StarChild's distant bridge.

"Understood Commander":

Setting off even more warning bells inside her head, it was getting to the point now where it gave Jenniboni a moment's pause receiving in fact *any* communique from that particular area aboard ship. Knowing so well her dearest friend both inside and out, mistaking her forced calm for nothing else than trouble brewing, Jenniboni listened with mounting concern even further:

"Our long-distance sensor-sweeps of the immediate area are picking up something I think you might find interesting", Stasha added.

"On my way", Jenniboni rejoined. Employing the same false expression of complete indifference she apologized as well to Naomi for cutting short their little visit.

Watching however both Jenniboni and Frances hurry off like there was no tomorrow, Naomi Marlowe had no difficulty sensing some ugly commotion fermenting nearby. Fatigued as she was StarChild's weary Chief Engineer would need to be comatose not to pick up straight away on something amiss; the way Jenniboni leaned over, asking Frances if she'd care to 'tag-along', another tell-tale sign.

"If she'd like to", Naomi harrumphed, scornful: "Yeah, Right!!"

****

Hurrying onto her active bridge, pod-lift doors swooshing shut in back her, Jenniboni found at once both Stasha Nikarov and her erstwhile Chief Navigator, Lt. Miranda Netra, gathered about in deep conversation.

Arriving rather winded Jenniboni didn't pause any to catch her breath, approaching instead each senior bridge officer studying with keen interest the well-equipped sensor array a part of Miranda's duty station:

"Report, Gentlewomen", Jenniboni ordered. Suspicious, she and Frances joined them at once.

Speaking together in hushed whispers, Stasha looking over Ms. Netra's shoulder, both women examined with obvious concern the well-lit sensor display before them. Their grave expression gave Jenniboni little if any hope of good news:

"We picked up on sensor array only moments ago three rather large woman-made objects leaving now the Bandrosian surface", Stasha was first to announce, drawing herself up now to full height behind the chair in which Miranda still sat: "Too large it would seem to be missiles".

Glancing right then for herself at the circular panel around which they were all now gathered, Jenniboni noticed as well three hefty sensor blips clearing now Bandros's outer perimeter.

Ordering at once on the main viewer extreme magnification of that faraway moon she spotted at once three blue/grey silhouettes clearing now the rim of that distant orb. By now all three projectiles were well beyond the turquoise atmosphere enveloping that moon-world below:

"If I'm not mistaken I believe we're about to discover their secret weapon", Jenniboni offered, remaining calm.

"Surely not missiles", she added, taking now a seat in her impressive command chair center-stage of StarChild's anxious bridge. Leaning forward, pondering the main viewer occupying a full third of StarChild's oval command center, Jenniboni watched even further each curious phantom change course:

"Only one thing they could be, but how…"

Not finishing what she was starting to say, her eyes flashing instead wide open, it all came flooding back in one awful rush of sudden clarity. Even at this great distance there was no mistaking each alien menace for what it really was:

"Code Red!!", she wasted no time: "All hands to battle stations!!!"

Once again the emergency klaxon aboard ship rang out both loud and clear throughout every quarter of StarChild's grand interior, the three derelict spacecraft from outside the northern Zelmorlite city headed now straight their way!

Chapter 63

"BATTLE OVER BANDROS"

"Time of arrival, Ms. Straker?"

"At their current speed approximately twenty-three minutes, forty-five seconds".

Ordering a return to regular magnification Jenniboni turned then her immediate attention to Stasha, her first officer having returned now to her official post, her science station just left of the broad main viewer ahead.

"I don't know about you, Cmdr. Nikarov, but I'm getting pretty sick and tired of these miserable little horrors always having the last word with us. In my humble opinion it's high time we show them—once and for all—what we're really made of, take the initiative:

"Agreed?"

"Yes, Ma'am!"

"Very good, then", Jenniboni smiled, fierce: "Helm, lay in an intercept course matching our speed to theirs: Ms. Straker; bring all cannons to full power, preparing as well matter/anti-matter torpedoes for immediate launch on my command".

When soon assured all was ready for the battle ahead Jenniboni then ordered a thorough scan of all three ships closing in, a hesitant search for any trace **at all** of Human life aboard those exact same enemy craft now closing the gap between them. Reluctant to admit for even a second Stasha was right, suggesting before little Rodney might end up dying in order to achieve final victory, Jenniboni was compelled now to consider such a worst case scenario.

With her primary duty being the continued welfare of ship and crew she had no other choice now but to fight the 'good fight', their backs now against the wall, employing against the enemy ahead every considerable resource at her command:

"Oh, honey", she groaned, grieving already for that small boy somewhere else than her sheltering arms: "If you're aboard any of those wretched ships out there please, please forgive me. I'm so terribly, terribly sorry".

Grief turned to joy soon enough though, receiving word of no Human life aboard any of those three enemy vessels drawing ever closer. A wicked glint of savage delight smoldering now in Jenniboni's expression, it was the steely eyes and hardened smile of a seasoned warrior. At last her chance had come to pay these demons back their many crimes against Womankind, no longer hiding like the cowards they were behind a small child:

"Excellent!!", Jenniboni growled, ferocious.

****

Racing headlong into ultimate battle against those savage forces dead ahead, all three enemy hostiles beginning now to take on both form and substance on the main viewer before her, Jenniboni could make out at last both their straight, boxy lines and sturdy design even at regular magnification.

Like before, flying over them on Bandros on her way to Paradise, she could see in all three a definite resemblance to those 'tanks' employed by the ancient patriarchates back in the $20^{th}/21^{st}$ centuries. Although quite sure StarChild possessed both superior speed and maneuverability, Jenniboni had to admit as well the enemy ahead possessed more likely both superior durability and firepower.

Just to be space-worthy, still operational after seven thousand years of continued neglect, proved in itself these alien craft possessed some superior design quality. A durability still beyond Womankind's own current level of technical expertise it was a miracle indeed they were still operational.

That in itself truly amazed her.

Then again, given all they already knew of Zelmorlite technology, Jenniboni guessed it should come as no surprise they remained in such mint condition.

"Three-to-one, however?" she mused: "Not quite fair".

Not that Jenniboni imagined the Emerog as ever 'playing fair'.

No skin off her teeth though, she likewise having no desire to play fair with them.

Observing now the two outer vessels approaching side-by-side veer away from the center vessel Jenniboni recognized it at once for what it really was, a feeble bid to surround her on either side.

"Sorry, no way", she grinned yet again. Entering immediate firing range Jenniboni commanded Frances to target the middle craft with both StarChild's outer and inner cannons, raising after that all forward shields.

Giving the order to fire she had the very real pleasure watching the bow of that center ship splinter upon impact… fragmenting… jagged cracks forming along its front.

Increasing speed toward the injured hulk, the Emerog inside not having time to raise shields, StarChild veered upward as the other two Emerog ships observing all this seemed about to collide, a head-on encounter.

Passing over the enemy vessel wounded already on Jenniboni's command her own ship swung about in a wide, graceful arch traveling at nearly one eighth

489

light speed.

Slowing down right thereafter to target their initial prey from behind Jenniboni noticed the other two enemy vessels likewise turnabout. Moving in closer to their battered comrade they took up this time defensive positions, trying to protect the injured first.

Deciding who'd be next to feel the full onslaught of her burning wrath Jenniboni ordered Frances to target this time that enemy ship closest by, launching anti-matter torpedoes in serious hope of bringing down at least its forward shields. Deciding one should prove enough she figured this would allow her time to bring down the rest during their next pass.

"Lock, load, fire", she gave the order to attack, entering right after that the range of enemy weapons. Raising shields yet again Jenniboni watched as well their own projectile accelerate like a bullet flash from a gun.

Their torpedo detonating in a brilliant display of pyrotechnics against the outer edge of the other ship's starboard defenses the 'bulls-eye' in question swerved to the right in order to avoid Jenniboni's head-on attack. Having just raised shields StarChild was veering already past their second victim, the enemy vessel farthest away lowering its own defenses just long enough to open fire.

A series of bright orange energy pulses making swift contact against StarChild's similar portside defenses, violent tremors rocked now her entire ship to-and-fro:

"Damage report!", Jenniboni demanded, the enemy now behind them.

"Port shields down fifteen percent, Ma'am", Frances called out; remaining as always calm, cool, and collected under enemy fire.

"What just hit us?"

In many ways they reminded Jenniboni of the weapons discharge Frances described earlier during her hasty retreat from Bandros, the 'energy bazooka's' used against them during take-off.

"They appear to be some form of plasmatic-based energy pulses designed to drain both energy while, at the same time, inflicting physical damage".

Coming about yet again to face head-on their three antagonists Jenniboni observed this time around the other two enemy craft arranged now side-by-side.

Assuming a defensive posture between both StarChild and that original Emerog vessel she first attacked, the defender to the left was no doubt the very same ship Jenniboni just fired on soon after the first. An assumption confirmed soon after by a scan Frances ran on all three, Jenniboni learned even further that her last attack left their second victim's starboard shields at only half strength.

Just one more torpedo should do the trick!

Just one little problem though, the injured ship positioned so close now to its neighbour. Its vulnerable spot pressed up now against its ally it was protected quite well by the right-hand vessel, the right-hand ship's fully operational defenses.

Reducing speed during their next approach the answer came quick to Jenniboni's searching intellect what to do next. Ordering yet another torpedo launch she planned to detonate it midway between the two forward ships, the narrow passage between them. Driving a wedge between the two enemy vessels it should obliterate as well the flagging shields of one, compromising as well the others.

Watching with bated breath the bright trail left by the missile already on its way, closing in now on the Emerog ahead, the entire bridge observed a dazzling release of pure force drive apart each ship from the other. The two enemy craft protecting the one behind sent spinning, they tumbled away from one another in opposite directions.

Trapped for the moment in a sideways roll, rolling over-and-over again out of control, each squat vessel was now quite helpless indeed.

Smiling to herself a little smile Jenniboni couldn't help wondering how many of those blasted androids aboard each were now put out of commission. Sure above all else the Emerog were using them to pilot their 'secret weapons', she was just as confident a sizable number of those dread mechanoids were battered now beyond repair. Hopefully enough to hamper the Emerog in their continued attack.

With its compatriots spinning now in every which direction Jenniboni took aim now at the third warship within her sights, that original foe she injured first. Learning soon its shields were likewise inoperative thanks to that last crippling blow she delivered it, she decided it was time to finish once-and-for-all the job. Increasing speed, moving in now for the kill, she brought all cannons to full bear, wasting as well no time giving the order to fire.

Beginning to climb at a steady rate StarChild soared upward like an eagle over his beaten quarry, Jenniboni watching with ferocious pleasure the other ship's exterior shatter. Splintering apart in key areas of its outer hull, nothing left of its forward compartments but a jagged array of twisted metal, its own bridge was likewise exposed now to the harsh vacuum of deep space.

Debris flying about every which way she could even make out in the distance a few 'corpses'. Several 'droids reduced in the distance to nothing but specks on StarChild's main viewer, this too gave Jenniboni personal cause to smile:

"Time to finish them off ", she remarked aloud to no one in particular, her own ship completing yet another turn, ready for another go at their already mortally wounded antagonists.

Beyond her immediate target, its hapless rear now in her gun-sights, the other two ships from just before had already regained helm control. Sluggish, they moved in on her position in vain hope of impeding Jenniboni's forward momentum.

Not in too good a shape sensor sweeps revealed one ship leaking power at increasing speed, its shields all but inoperative while the other, although a wee bit better off, suffered extensive damage. Its structural integrity compromised it would be some time for sure before either could rejoin, if at all, the battle in progress.

Neither any immediate threat, having already decided to first take out her original target, Jenniboni was about to blow it out of the stars, stopped only by Stasha's urgent voice:

"Sensor readings of the target ahead show the energy flow to all systems has reversed direction, feeding back instead into its power core at a steady rate of acceleration, engines on overload."

"Confirm, Ms. Straker!"

"Confirmed, Ma'am: they're feeding power back in on itself: Cascade overload now in progress".

"All shields at full power. Helm, turn about: Hard to port", Jenniboni demanded, wasting no time.

Bringing StarChild hard about in desperate hope of avoiding that ticking time-bomb now before her Jenniboni watched with sick fascination the enemy ship begin already to glow an ugly, menacing red—the remaining area, still somewhat intact, venting highly compressed air through numerous fissures courtesy of the incredible atmospheric pressure building within.

Gushing every which way imaginable, solidifying into a fine, powdery mist upon contact with the frigid climes of deep space, the enemy hostile finished now glowing red—moving on to a shocking orange before the angle of StarChild's evasive course took it beyond Jenniboni's immediate range of visual observation.

Increasing speed once StarChild came about, headed away now from the desperate situation now in back of them, it wasn't long after that all hell broke loose, the incredible force of the explosion in back accompanied by a blinding light so intense they vanished momentarily inside its outer corona.

Facing the likelihood of her own sad demise, made only worse by the loss as well of all those under her command, she encountered no sense of self-pity whatsoever… no fear, or panic… only a swell of burning rage, feeling as though cheated.

"We're not going to make it", she mused, bordering on the stoic.

Spared destruction inside that tremendous release of volatile power the lucky starship was nonetheless treated rough, buffeted about like some wee child's plaything in the eye of some frightful storm. The metal fragments, all that was left of that other ship now gone, pummeled as well their protective shields.

Yet even that was nothing compared to the shock waves slamming them about without mercy, all those aboard StarChild likewise treated cruel.

Shaken harshly about it was nothing short of an actual miracle the entire bridge crew managed to remain each at her individual post. However, despite the G-force of that mighty forward thrust holding each and every one firmly in place, there were still others aboard ship who, rocked to-and-fro by those very same tremors, fared not so well.

****

Coming to rest in a more or less stationary position just beyond Bandros' upper atmosphere the injured starship came dangerously close to being caught, outright, in its gravitational pull. A perilous situation, the moon's bloated orb filled the ship's main viewer with its turquoise splendor almost to the utter exclusion of anything else:

'What happened to the lights?', was Jenniboni's first thought. The ceiling above now dark, emergency power kicked in soon thereafter.

Bathed now in only the ethereal glow of auxiliary back-up lights, their crimson hue lending her bridge an uneasy feel, her first thoughts were nonetheless those of joyful relief, another miracle they survived at all.

Be that as it may her initial sense of divine intervention was tempered on the heels of that by the further realization there remained out there two other operative Emerog hostiles. Didn't matter much each of those other ships were likewise hurt during the preceding battle, uncertain as she was to the damage done her own ship, the dramatic extent of his own combat-related injuries.

Inquiring however of her present bridge personnel how they were doing Jenniboni was at least glad to hear that they were all, to a single woman, quite well indeed—soon learning however from Dr. Wei-Chang there were others aboard ship doing less well.

Giving her commanding officer an impromptu status report from her current post in sick-bay StarChild's shaken C.M.O. sounded likewise irate. It were as though the cantankerous old gentlewoman held Jenniboni, herself, responsible for their all their current misfortunes.

Not holding it against her though Jenniboni was just grateful there were no fatalities anywhere at all among her wounded, taking little-to-no offense whatsoever at the older woman's rather testy attitude.

Unfortunately though she was about to learn StarChild himself fared not so well during their most recent ordeal.

Not at all!!

Chapter 64

"PAYBACK"

It wasn't the first time Naomi woke up on the floor, coming around face down in engineering, sprawled across the hard surface below after the violent explosion now behind them. Just the only time she did so without the 'usual' additional hangover, discovering herself at the very same time in some strange laddie's private domicile.

However, no time for such recollections, she got to her feet instead. Searching her dim surroundings for any indication of obvious damage the entire area, like the bridge itself, was lit only by back-up auxiliary generators.

Like some ethereal scene straight out of 'Dante's Inferno'… the dark, red emergency lights casting spectral shadows throughout the entire facility… the first clear image coming into immediate focus was that of Gloria, appearing now as though some ghostly figure hurrying about.

Already on the move, dashing back and forth now from one display board to another, she looked like some dark fairy, some little pixie, assigned some urgent mission in Hell itself:

"Like being hit by the Devil's own hammer!" Naomi muttered aloud, rueful, making her way already to Gloria's side.

Her progress brought up short however by some prostate form between them, Naomi stumbled right thereafter over some lost soul. A junior officer from her very own department, the poor woman's moan alerted her to at least three other personnel likewise injured:

"Jeepers Crispy!", she swore, ascertaining what was wrong with each unfortunate crewwoman quite helpless in the semi-dark:

"Darn them all to heck", she cursed this time the enemy responsible for all their current woes, contacting at the very same time Dr. Wei-Chang. Heaven only knew how many aboard ship likewise lay about in apparent agony, StarChild's overworked C.M.O. assuring Naomi she'd send at once a couple of medics the very moment they became available.

"Yes, Doctor: Understood. Thank you", Naomi signed off, feeling rather helpless herself. Making her injured personnel as comfortable as possible there still wasn't much she could do. Feeling quite small inside she apologized instead to those nearby wounded for which she couldn't do more, needing at the same time to move on, take care of that which she could.

"So, Glow-worm; how goes it?" she asked, reaching at last Gloria's side.

"Not so well", her frazzled assistant appeared quick to inform her: "Weapons are all off-line and, while sub-light propulsion is still available, it's operating at only fifty percent capacity. The same with shields: still functional, but at no more than thirty to forty percent full capacity, main generators all off-line.

"On the bright side however life-support, back-up generators, sensors, Maccs, all communications systems, and Ultra-Drive remain fully operational, operating at peak efficiency. Whatever the Emerog had in mind, it sure had its desired effect".

"Not quite, Lieutenant", Naomi was quick to correct her, frowning: "If it had we wouldn't be standing here right now. As it is we don't know what else they're capable of or, for that matter, what's going on out there. All I'm sure of is Commodore Saphira will no doubt be contacting us soon, letting us know.

"And on that note I suggest we assume the worst and start immediately on repairing weapons, propulsion, and shields: get them all up-and-running at peak efficiency before too late".

"Yes, Ma'am: Agreed. Therefore, with your permission, I'll take care of shields and propulsion while you take care of both main generators and weapons".

"Permission granted, Lieutenant".

Proceeding without delay Gloria ordered several crewwomen nearby to assist her, Naomi examining in the meantime the display board indicating the current status of all shipboard weapons—a detailed analysis transmitted from everywhere aboard poor StarChild, badly mauled as he was.

Not long after running a most thorough diagnostic of both weapons and main generators Naomi, as expected, received a direct communiqué from Jenniboni demanding a precise up-date on their current situation:

"According to your own profession estimation how long will it take before all key systems are up-and-running at peak efficiency?", Jenniboni demanded upon hearing Naomi's report.

Adding up the various figures, their many permutations, in her mind… factoring in likewise with rapid precision every possible variable… StarChild's venerable Chief Engineer rendered up her professional opinion with pinpoint accuracy.

"In that case concentrate on propulsion, shields, and main generators", Jenniboni instructed her: "Make those your primary concern".

Surprised to say the least Jenniboni made no mention at all of weapons, none whatsoever, Naomi questioned at once her ship's C.O.:

"By your own estimation repairs will take longer than we have. Don't worry, Ms. Marlowe; the situation is well in hand and will be dealt with by other means", Jenniboni assured her, sounding confident.

"Understood, Ma'am", Naomi lied outright, not understanding at all!

****

Severing at once her communications link with Engineering, having no wish to remain as is, Jenniboni ordered helm to bring them full about. Insisting she face any danger head-on she had no desire to remain as was, her rear flank exposed to the enemy. StarChild's engines responding however in sluggish reply a mighty shudder passed throughout the entire ship, labouring mightily to come full about.

'Come on now, my fine young laddie', Jenniboni beseeched in silence her crippled starship: 'Don't let us all down'.

For a short time it were as though the wounded vessel heard not his C.O., a sudden jolt vibrating soon after throughout every metal fiber of his synthetic form. Turning about despite his many injuries as if in answer to Jenniboni's silent plea he felt compelled as never before. Goaded into action by those who hurt him, StarChild wanted just as much as she to wreak havoc on that alien force still a threat to their very lives.

Both anger, hate, and even resentment being his primary feelings in the matter, furious as well on behalf of those aboard him, 'Master Young Maccs StarChild' wanted revenge on the Emerog as much as that dear crew dwelling within him. Never before had he known such dark emotions as he did at that very moment. His titanium hull both pitted and scarred he faced at last both enemy vessels now dead ahead.

Battered, seared, and scorched he relished the idea of vengeance satisfied. All that held him in check was waiting on Jenniboni's command to commence the attack. Watching the remaining two Emerog ships creep ever closer each brought to Jenniboni's mind the image of hungry hyenas stalking some wounded lion.

Regardless the fact they were as poorly off as StarChild himself Jenniboni realized they remained even so a definite danger, approaching her position wary but determined from either side:

"Helm; back off, maintaining optimal distance as long as you can before entering Bandros's gravitational pull". Another tremor passing yet again throughout StarChild's battered person, the injured starship obeyed nonetheless Jenniboni's current directive.

"Would I be correct in assuming neither of those enemy craft possess any Ultra-drive capabilities?", Jenniboni was soon to ask. From Rodney's earlier testimony she got the clear idea the Zelmorlites never achieved faster-than-light travel on a broader scale.

Or at least that would seem the case, Rodney telling her the Zelmorlite women discovered Earth only a brief time before their final demise, the Emerog-infested men hijacking their only faster-than-light vessel quick enough to make it there.

Nor was it long before Jenniboni had her answer, both Stasha and Frances confirming her initial assumption after independent scans:

"Excellent! Ms. Smythe; open a hyper-portal directly ahead".

"Yes, Ma'am", the current helmswoman on duty obeyed at once. Shocked, stunned quite rigid, this was a reaction shared as well by the rest of Jenniboni's senior personnel—their naked awe almost tangible.

Their sudden dismay thinly veiled, a palpable essence hanging about in the very air they breathed, Jenniboni noted right away each woman's similar consternation in the way Stasha likewise reacted. Seated at her post, the science station just left of the main viewer, Stasha's back visibly stiffened, remaining motionless and erect.

No doubt in Jenniboni's opinion what troubled her longtime friend so, having never known Jenniboni to turn tail, running away from any actual fight to the finish. Always sure of her convictions come Heck or high water, never backing down from a fight no matter the odds, Jenniboni was known by one and all to persevere—sticking to her guns—when sure of her cause.

'Worry not old friend', Jenniboni smiled within: 'Nothing's changed'.

Then, turning her attention back to helm control, she added with a crafty grin:

"Oh yes, Ms. Smythe: And while you're at it, open the portal as close as you can to those two Emerog ships."

It was a sly expression shared now by all those gathered about, each realizing now what their cunning C.O. had in mind:

"Let's see how those lousy 'girls-of-bears' handle a *real* 'hazard zone'!!"

"Yes, Ma'am!", Penny Smythe all but laughed. Gazing with expectant eyes across that great divide between them, each woman there watching the hyper-portal ahead take on both form and substance, they all took special note of its sudden appearance.

At first nothing but a jagged lightning bolt leaping at once into full view between both enemy warships still closing in, the hyper rift opened soon enough even wider than that. Its gaping maw taking on now it's more familiar form, ribbons of technicolour light steamed now into their own reality from that UltraSpace universe beyond.

Multi-hued tendrils rushing forth at the very same time, whipping about the immediate vicinity, fluttering about in their hungry search for anything at all to latch on to, they found it soon enough. Their image becoming distorted, appearing less solid, the Emerog ships on either side of this unearthly phenomena began to ripple, looking more fluid.

Simple, straight lines beginning now to warp and waver about, bending from their unprotected exposure to hyper-reality, this stunning display grew even more pronounced, each vessel in question beginning as well to shudder. Soft and malleable, elongating on StarChild's main viewer for all to see, both began stretching towards the hyper-rift between them.

Aware at long last what danger they were in, nevertheless doing so too late, each vessel tried hard to escape that now irresistible draw. A vain attempt it was doomed however to utter failure, that spatial anomaly holding each so very tight in its relentless grip. The multi-hued tendrils taking possession of them grew only tighter yet, lashing about in an even more frenzied manner.

Its time come at last to devour StarChild's ruthless foe that vengeful enemy realized only then they were lost. Spiteful to the very end, firing each in StarChild's direction another bright round of energy-based plasma, it was a parting blow of absolute defiance doing nothing at all to save them.

Hurtling towards her battered ship at high velocity, noting the very real threat careening towards them, Jenniboni leaned nevertheless forward in her regal command chair, watching with hungry eyes the outer hulls of each Emerog warship shatter into tiny pieces. An expression of savage joy plastered on her otherwise angelic face, she watched with mounting satisfaction the debris of each bulky ship sucked into UltraSpace.

All gone now in a wink of an eye, her ship now all on its own, she ordered helm only then to close down the hyper-rift still ahead—the spatial anomaly vanishing in a matter of micro-seconds the very same time that rapid volley of enemy discharge bombarded without mercy StarChild's weakened defenses:

"Shields now completely down", Frances announced, the intense shaking subsiding as she did: "It'll take approximately two hours, thirty-seven minutes to get them back on line".

"Understood, Ms. Straker", Jenniboni acknowledged, instructing Penny Smythe right after that to bring StarChild full-about once having put some distance between both them and Bandros. The injured starship trembling it struggled forward a fair distance before turning about right thereafter, confronting that moon-world's bluish-green disk:

"Yes, Gentlewomen", Jenniboni added for the benefit of all those present, her voice full of grim resolve: "This is it! Time at last to make sure those miserable demons below never harm again another living soul!"

Chapter 65

"JUSTICE"

The next three hours aboard ship were spent in busy preparation of all drone probes, each made ready for their deadly mission. And aware she wouldn't be able to get any meaningful rest until their ultimate deployment Jenniboni needed as well to take an active hand, close-up and personal, in the myriad preparations going on all around her.

Restless, fidgety, she too wanted to make a positive contribution, rolling up her sleeves as it were, pitching in with the actual work at hand—something more to do than just sit around on her 'bridge', waiting on status reports from Naomi. First telling Stasha to take a break, Jenniboni handed command of StarChild's bridge over to Frances right thereafter, wasting no time at all making her way to deck S-12.

Offering once there to assist Naomi in the preparation of the drones she assured Stasha as well she'd wake her up for the 'big event'. Promising her devoted X.O. she wouldn't be forgotten, it was Stasha's turn to be banished yet again to her quarters.

****

It was a little over an hour since her unexpected arrival on deck S-12 when Naomi, reluctant to be sure, approached Jenniboni hard at work, laboring over the remote guidance system for one particularly troublesome scout:

Assisting her staff in engineering wherever an extra pair of hands were needed, head down, she almost missed the look of apprehension clearly written all over Naomi's face, looking up at her subordinate only when hearing Naomi clear her throat.

"Yes, Ms. Marlowe?" Jenniboni enquired, getting as well to her feet: "How may I be of assistance?"

"Well, Ma'am; that's the thing of it", the other woman in question both

499

hemmed and hawed, hesitant: "Let me just say first off that we all appreciate your coming here, making time in your busy schedule to lend a hand. Yet, at the very same time, I was wondering if…"

"Come now, Lt. Cmdr.", Jenniboni smiled, mischievous: "No need to beat around the bush. Just spit it out. Are you trying to tell me in your own tactful way I'm getting under foot, that you'd like me to get out of your hair?"

"Well, sort of, but not exactly", Naomi sputtered, nervous: "To be perfectly honest, Ma'am, you are an excellent commanding officer in possession of exceptional leadership skills. However, in the field of engineering, how may I put this? …

"You… well… the thing of it is.…"

"I leave a lot to be desired? Is that it?", Jenniboni was at least merciful enough to put the anxious redhead out of her immediate misery, grinning all the while doing so:

"Don't worry, Ms. Marlowe. I can handle rejection with the best of them. I understand full well we can't all be experts in everything we do. Truth be told I appreciate very much your candor".

"Thank you, Ma'am: In fact, if you're still interested in helping out, there is somewhere we *really* do need help. Something I'm sure you could handle quite readily".

"Yes, Lt. Cmdr.?"

"Well… it's the hangar bay, Ma'am: We could really use an extra pair of hands up there, readying all the finished probes for eventual launch".

"Very good, then", Jenniboni accepted, cheerful, not put out in the very least: "The hangar bay it is".

* * * *

Riding another ag-pod to shuttle maintenance she rode as well the nearby 'small craft elevator' the rest of the way up to the Hangar bay one level above that. The entire area was bustling already with coordinated activity by the time Jenniboni likewise got there.

Constructing several neat rows of compartmentalized racks for the synchronous launch of the missiles below workwomen from all over the ship were all busy, going about their given tasks by the time Jenniboni made her appearance. The surrounding chamber, while intended for the deployment of such probes as those on deck S-12, wasn't designed for the simultaneous launch of quite so many as all those they planned to throw at Bandros.

Each set of honeycombed structures arranged one-behind-the-other they all faced together the landing bay doors already open to the vast expanse of deep space beyond. Their many slots arranged in such a way with such painstaking precision, the missiles in the rear racks would pass during launch through the slots in front once the missiles in front were launched first.

And reaching from floor to ceiling, stopping just a couple or so meters from either side of the grand expanse all around them, they reminded Jenniboni of the many racks once lining her late mother's carefully tended wine cellar. No denying the similarity between these particular shelves and those Elissa Saphira tended with such love, such affection, the resemblance to one-another was only enhanced further by the lethal probes already making their dramatic appearance.

Helping her people load each into its pre-assigned space their lens-coated surfaces evoked in Jenniboni's imagination images of gigantic wine bottles, this in turn conjuring up fond memories of her mother's collection of both fine Bordeaux and Beaujolais'.

Discussing with obvious devotion the personal herstory of each bottle with any guest fortunate enough to share them with her, Elissa referred to each in her fine collection as an 'old friend', treating each and every bottle as if it were some favored child.

Probably explains why, when just a little girl herself, it bothered Jenniboni more often than not when her mother ended by drinking her 'friends'. To the little girl Jenniboni was at the time this, to her way of thinking, smacked of vampirism:

"Well, Mother: I wonder what you'd made of *these* wine bottles'?", she reflected within... smiling... fond memories of her late mother coming to mind.

Nor could she forget her mother's simple delight learning Andrei shared as well her love of the grape, her interest in oenology. Jenniboni could recall most readily Elissa Saphira sharing with equal joy both her fine drink and stories with her new son-in-law, more often than not 'spoiling him rotten'.

It brought a warm smile to Jenniboni's lips, cherishing the memory of how her young husband enjoyed both her mother's wine and company so very much.

All-the-same though, pleasant recollections of times-gone-by gave way soon enough to more pressing matters—the last probe soon in place, secure in its designated niche, awaiting it's anticipated departure.

Getting down to the business at hand Jenniboni wasted no time waking Stasha up. Telling her the time had come at last to put 'Operation: Eradicate' into full swing, she requested as well her immediate presence on StarChild's bridge.

* * * *

Arriving on her bridge, finding both Stasha and Naomi at their respective posts, Jenniboni took as well her own place center-stage of StarChild's imposing command deck. Quite ready to begin she eased herself back into her command chair's padded surface. Crossing her legs she exuded an air of relaxed confidence, sure in the ability of her crew and their creative genius:

"Ms. Marlowe: Since you were the mistressmind here who came up with the idea how to deliver our little surprise, I leave to you the honour of sending our various packages—'C.O.D.'—on their way".

"Yes, Ma'am: Thank you", Naomi accepted. Enthusiastic, she activated from her console the launch sequence for each fearsome group of newly converted projectiles:

"First volley now on its way", she announced soon thereafter, everyone there watching that first set of glistening drones pass overhead. Increasing speed, they rushed headlong towards that scene of so much heartache both recent and long-ago.

"Second volley now on its way", Naomi added, following up where she left off only moments before, a swarm of identical missiles likewise on their way. Energized trails of white exhaust trailing behind each they left home as well with a purposeful 'stride', a mass of angry wasps ready to dispense final justice at any cost.

Listening to Naomi repeat this problem several more times Jenniboni watched all this from her supreme location aboard ship. However, the final group of oblong missiles having just left the 'nest', Jenniboni discovered all of a sudden feelings of both regret, and even profound disappointment.

Welling up in her heart it was a bitter spring not due to what they were about to do, but the actual situation itself. Feeling no remorse at all her melancholy stemmed not from feelings of either guilt, or pity. As far as she was concerned the Emerog ahead had this coming, she at the moment more merciful toward them than they ever were when dealing with their own sad victims.

It wasn't this that left her feeling so empty inside, so depressed, her bad feelings due instead to the simple twist of fate it was these diabolical horrors Womankind first encountered beyond their own home System. Of all the sentient life forms there **must** be out there why was it these repulsive horrors, the Emerog themselves, her people had to meet their very first time beyond the Tammyite Matriarchate…

Recalling right then and there all those mother/daughter talks she shared with J.J., gazing all-the-while from their apartment wall-windows at distant stars, speculating between them what might live out there, neither of them ever imagined anything like the Emerog.

Thinking about it further Jenniboni even prayed to the Good Lord above their next certain encounter with alien intelligences proved a friendlier one involving a more civilized, benevolent species such as themselves:

"Probes now in orbit, ready for activation", Naomi intruded upon Jenniboni's silent prayer. Turning instead her attention toward the moon-world ahead, so very close on StarChild's main viewer, she couldn't see the probes themselves—trails of bright exhaust telling her all-the-same where they were, forming as well a visible grid pattern crisscrossing Bandros's very surface:

"U.V. saturation beginning now", Naomi informed now everyone present, the drones performing now their lethal function.

"Thank you, Ms. Marlowe", Jenniboni answered her, ordering Stasha as well to monitor the planet's surface—telling her to keep tabs both on little Rodney while, at the very same time, tracking the ultimate effect of 'Operation: Eradicate' on the Emerog.

No sooner had she done so however, her last instructions having just passed her lips, she was immediately startled hearing Phyllis Matthias cry out. Slumped now foreword at her post, seated still at her station just right of the ship's main viewer, Jenniboni watched Phyllis grab as well her head. Face buried now in trembling hands she leaned forward with both elbows against that communications panel at which she still sat.

"What's the matter Lieutenant?" Jenniboni called out, rushing over to her the very moment all this took place. Full of concern, reaching her side, Jenniboni placed at once a comforting hand on her quaking shoulder.

"I can hear *them*, Commodore!!" she wept aloud, looking up this time straight at Jenniboni's worried face. Pale, shaking, she managed nonetheless to fix her commanding officer with a steady stare, conveying alongside all her words what she was enduring from one terrible moment to the next:

"I can hear their death screams, each and every one of them, in my head. Millions of them, billions, all going crazy inside of me!!"

Only then, with dawning horror, did Jenniboni understand what Phyllis meant; the Emerog registering somehow during their final death-throws on that telepathic link she shared with her twin.

"Would you like to leave the bridge?" Jenniboni asked immediately thereafter, her tone of voice one of gentle compassion: "Maybe you'd like to report to Sickbay, be with your sister?"

"No, Ma'am: Thank you", Phyllis closed her eyes, distraught. Swallowing, she tried hard to regain her former equilibrium: "Besides, Maytina is still unconscious; still sedated, asleep, after the explosion. She can't feel them. Thank God for small mercies!"

"Are you sure, Lieutenant?"

"Yes, Ma'am", Phyllis assured her caring C.O.. Her voice now more firm, steady, the colour in her cheeks began to return:

"I'm starting to feel better now. It was just a shock, suddenly hit from inside like that. They're starting to fade away. That's all. You can't imagine how horrid, how ugly, their very thoughts really are. Truly twisted beyond all measure. Even when they're afraid, dying, there's nothing about them worth saving…

"I'm glad they're dying!" she spat, feeling as violated as Jenniboni before her.

"They deserve whatever they get", she insisted, sitting up straight, pressing on: "They deserve to die!! All of them!!!"

"And I can think of at least one little boy down there who'd agree, who knows how you feel", Jenniboni verbalized her similar feelings, giving Phyllis' shoulder an approving, sympathetic squeeze.

Then, doing so, she turned as well to Stasha, requesting an immediate progress report concerning 'Operation: Eradicate':

"Emerog life-signs no longer exist: No trace to be found. Nevertheless, young Master Roderick appears both safe and sound. No sign whatsoever of U.V. poisoning", Stasha announced, everyone glad to hear this:

"And on a similar note he is, for the present, near the very center of the northern Zelmorlite colony; a more detailed reading on his exact whereabouts likewise available".

"Excellent, Cmdr. Nikarov", Jenniboni smiled, delighted: "Ms. Marlowe; terminate U.V. emissions. Bring the probes home. Then once they're all safely aboard, we'll retrieve young Master Roderick from his current location: Ms. Straker in charge of the rescue team".

"Drones now on a return trajectory for StarChild", Naomi soon informed her.

"Very good: Now we can get the young laddie in question, go home, and leave this hellish star-system once-and-for-all!"

****

The very last Emerog peered through the eyes of Its captive thrall beyond Its dark surroundings. The only one to survive the annihilation of all the rest, It took shelter inside young Rodney when all the others were likewise caught off-guard.

Remaining safe as well deep beneath the ground during the attack from above, It stared at the ruins beyond the dilapidated building in which It still hid. Its reaction, like the rest of Its unholy kind now dead, was one of complete disbelief... incomprehension... during that attack launched by Womankind above.

Listening to the telepathic shrieks of all those others now lost, not realizing It was already beyond all sense of normal, rational, thought that last Emerog left standing thought It would go crazy listening to the cries of all the rest.

So oblivious to the simple fact It was already quite insane, sure It would be driven mad by the tortured thoughts of all the rest of Its demonic kind, It swore vengeance in the name of all Its slaughtered compatriots on all those female Humans still up there, Its plan of retaliation already decided upon!!

Chapter 66

"LONE SURVIVOR"

Piloting the shuttle they all rode during its final approach Gloria could have lived the rest of her days happily-ever-after never seeing this wretched moon-world again. Bandros now right below her she slowed down in anticipation of somewhere to land.

While true the Emerog existed no more their legacy of pain and horror would nevertheless live on, immemorial, in every aspect of that tainted surface below. They'd remain forever a permanent stain scarring the very land they all now flew over.

Not even the smart armor uniform she wore, its golden fempacem emblazoned proud and noble on its polished white metal surface, could insulate her from that feeling of perpetual evil lingering about on that dead world below, seeping as it were under her very skin.

Decreasing both speed and altitude she watched the northern Zelmorlite city grow ever closer, the vast stretch of its crumbling remains reminding her of some endless graveyard.

"Onboard sensors show he's in the tower ahead, bearing north-by-north-east of our present position", Frances all-of-a-sudden addressed her, sitting off to her right:

"It should, for all intents and purposes, look like the one I described during our mission briefing back on StarChild. Every Zelmorlite community would seem to possess one", Frances elaborated, contemptuous: "So we'll need to find somewhere close-by to land".

"Yes, Ma'am".

Appearing to her immediate left soon enough, rising upward from the surrounding debris of ancient ruins spread out all around it, the cone-like edifice Frances referred to reached for the very heavens above like some alien 'Tower of Babel'.

Making even now a preliminary pass around and about their final destination, keeping her keen eye on both the scene ahead alongside the scanner to her immediate right, Gloria circled that imposing monster of alien design seeking out a suitable spot on which to land.

Somewhere nearby as possible both flat and, if she could manage it, rubble-free.

****

In silent procession Frances, Gloria, and the other six women in their rescue party walked down desolate streets, forsaken boulevards, where not even the toughest of native wildlife dared encroach—leaving the safe confines of their small shuttle for harsh, desolate surroundings shunned by even the simplest animal.

"Even they know this miserable place is cursed", Gloria muttered to herself in gloomy thought, Frances at her side.

Unable to either hear her, or read her mind Frances Straker would have agreed even so concerning their blighted surroundings, agreeing with Gloria they were walking indeed on unhallowed ground. Nor did this basic opinion of their immediate surroundings change any, re-enforced upon turning yet another rubble-laden street corner.

Observing dead ahead their ultimate goal, that fearsome tower's yawning entrance already wide open, it seemed to beckon them forth like some strange leviathan looking ready to devour whole all invaders.

However, looking on the bright side, at least that open entry to mysteries beyond supported young Rodney's earlier claim both he and his mother came and went unmolested, neither mother or son running into those same fearsome sentries as back on Zelmorl.

Troubled though by the very idea of something worse than hidden booby-traps Frances readjusted the shoulder strap sporting yet another U.V. rifle like before. Rearranging it even higher on her person she brought it along just in case her initial, private worries were justified. Suspicious long before leaving StarChild her fear Rodney was still in great danger appeared now even more justified than before.

Not out of the woods by any stretch of the imagination, hoping they weren't too late, this very place in which he sought shelter proved beyond any shadow of doubt something was truly amiss. Recalling quite well his very body language, his very tone of voice, when even talking about this very same place Frances likewise remembered young Rodney's naked fear, discussing this exact same location in terms of somewhere to avoid.

Under no circumstances whatsoever could she imagine that frightened young laddie coming here in hope of sanctuary, a place of refuge, in troubled times. Quite the contrary, remembering all he said back on StarChild, it was self-evident to anyone with half a brain this terrible tower held too many unpleasant memories for him to ever come here by choice.

506

So why was he here at all, Frances and her team crossing as well the waiting threshold to that dilapidated ruin. Making their way likewise to the belly of that still very active beast was he skulking about inside that dread colossus under the influence of someone, or *something* else altogether?

Quickening her pace, the rest of her rescue party following close behind, Frances was nevertheless certain… thank you oh-so very much… she'd find out soon enough the reason why "It" was here.

Making good time the internal layout of this grand complex was identical to that other back on Zelmorl right down to the ambivalent feelings it likewise evoked. The only difference Frances could observe here was that *this* ancient edifice remained open to the elements. A result no doubt of Rachael Roderick's earlier trespass here just five short years ago, closing **not** the way in after her.

Nor did the similarity between this tower and that other one end there, this one possessing as well a fully-operational power source—those exact same type of light fixtures as on Zelmorl providing a more than adequate glow guiding their way.

Strange how their initial survey of this pathetic moon failed to detect at all the still functional power-source supplying this tower all the remarkable energy it also seemed to need. A mystery explained no doubt by that very same magnetic interference playing havoc earlier with all their scanners, that naturally occurring electro-magnetic field surrounding Bandros.

Then again, interference aside, Dr. Wei-Change still managed by both chance and skill to determine young Rodney's exact whereabouts, informing Frances he was so very close. According to the medical scanner she monitored with such diligent care the young laddie in question lay at the end of the very next corridor, just around the bend, waiting their arrival at the very heart-and-soul of this awful edifice.

And there it was…

Beyond an open portal at the end of the next corridor…

The tower's core!

Approaching with extreme caution that wide threshold leading into the innermost chamber of their immediate surroundings, each woman there came to an immediate halt. Surveying with keen interest that broad expanse just beyond that grand opening, everything there was identical to what Frances observed as well back on Zelmorl.

The same cylindrical power matrix rising from the same ponderous pit below up to dizzying heights above…

The same churning, swirling mass of energy-based plasma inside that same transparent tube possessing a half-life approaching near infinity…

The same row-upon-row of computer access terminals arranged in endless procession around and about that cavernous chamber, its outer walls…

Everything identical right down to the grotesque majesty of that endless chamber, its grandiose design parameters…

Everything identical that is except for one very important feature sticking out almost right away. Looking to her left Frances caught sight of him sitting just a short distance away, perched atop of that same guardrail as back on Zelmorl, a fence as it were surrounding that almost bottomless pit beyond.

Sitting with his back to them all, his young face turned at a rather odd angle, it seemed as though young Rodney just sat there in deep meditation of that cylindrical power-matrix rising high above. Contemplating to the exclusion of everything else the fluid motion of all that blue/green energy deep within he seemed oblivious of their very existence, sitting as-still-as-still-can-be...

Leading the way slow and wary, concerned what might happen given his precarious situation, Frances crept up on him with all due caution, not wanting to startle him into any unfortunate mishap.

However, remaining quiet as humanly possible despite their already silent surroundings, it was Frances instead who was taken by surprise. Startled for a split second when the little boy in front of her spun around, his head snapped about with alarming speed. Staring right through her with a most malignant, hateful gaze he/It spoke right on up, a loud voice brimming with maniacal glee:

"Just one step closer and this... this... 'thing' you seem to care for so very much goes right-over-the-edge!"

Saying that the creature inside poor Rodney looked over and down the edge of that very deep pit alongside which he/It sat, adding dramatic emphasis to Its ugly threat. Quite unnecessary as far as Frances was concerned, stopping at once quite dead in her tracks. Believing right away that vile entity inside him would carry out Its murderous guarantee, she had no reason at all to doubt Its lunatic sincerity.

Nor did she need Dr. Wei-Chang telling her all about that alien bio-matter she picked up inside him, knowing right away to whom, or what she spoke. It only stood to reason one of them would in fact survive 'Operation: Eradicate', taking shelter inside their Human plaything during StarChild's attack.

That cruel voice full of spite, that expression of haughty arrogance... especially in the eyes!!... spoke volumes about that corrupt individual to which she now spoke. The good doctor's medical scan quite superfluous this wasn't any fair, innocent child full of grace sitting now before her but some ancient evil, the likes of which remained well beyond Womankind's very understanding:

"Gooooood", the Emerog inside him more sneered than smiled. Leaping off the railing ahead, It/He landed a short distance away from Frances herself:

"We like it best when your people are submissive... weak... obedient".

"I would've thought by now you'd have learned just how submissive, how weak, how 'obedient' we really are", Frances countered, wearing all the while a contemptuous sneer all her own.

"Ah, yes!" It shot back without any hesitation, whatsoever: "And yet you waste precious time coming all this way. And for what? Just to retrieve my little plaything instead of making good your escape?! Tisk, tisk, Ms. Chief of Security. Fatal tactical error, wouldn't you say? ...

"*Yes*!!", It added with a snicker, seeing through her visor the momentary surprise in Frances's eyes: "I know who each and every one of you are. Don't forget that everything this vessel knows I know".

"Well then: In that case you should know already what's coming next", Frances regained at once her casual demeanor. Slipping the rifle she still carried off of her shoulder the Emerog, catching sight of the weapon she now held, looked up at her, pretending a look of startled amusement:

"Sooo…. you were expecting me all along? I'm touched", It began to giggle—a crazy, maniacal sound: "I'm honoured. I guess your kind isn't all that ignorant after all. Then again we've never been able to use the female of your species, how shall I put it, as 'intimately' as the male. Maybe *your* gender isn't quite as stupid after all".

"Frankly, I wouldn't call *either gender* of my 'species' stupid!", Frances informed that mocking villain. Her vice quite frosty indeed she raised to her eyes at last the sighting mechanism for the rifle in hand.

Yet looking down the barrel of that deadly gun, Frances taking sure, careful aim at both poor Rodney and that vile creature inside him, the parasite using him showed no fear at all. Just gazing up instead at the armor-clad woman standing before It, It watched with scornful eyes her expression through her transparent visor:

"Still though you plan to destroy me before learning what it is I've already done, what I already have in store for you. Come now, Lieutenant Commander 'High-And-Mighty' Straker. I'd call *that* stupid….

"Or, at the very least, very short-sighted".

"Fine: So what is it you've done?" Frances granted the thing before her a moment's reprieve, giving It a wary, guarded look:

"Just spit it out!" she snapped, annoyed, slowly lowering her U.V. rifle.

The Emerog inside young Rodney just stared at her as if contemplating some meager bug beneath contempt, grinning up at her, head cocked to one side:

"That's for me to know and for you to find out", It answered her at last, taunting one-and-all, giving the power-matrix to her right a furtive glance.

Following Its sly gaze Frances gave the monstrous tube a closer look-see, giving it for the very first time more than just a moment's pause. Giving that ancient power-base greater scrutiny she noticed within the colossal cylinder towering high above them a clearly marked difference; an obvious dissimilarity between the almost liquid substance inside this grand apparatus versus its identical twin back on Zelmorl.

The plasma-based energy-form here less languid… less relaxed… more antic… the blue versus green elements comprising this energy matrix were clearly behaving in a more frantic… agitated… manner.

Appearing not satisfied with the slow, graceful dance they did around-and-about each other back on that other world the different components of this particular power-source seemed to do battle with one-another in jerky, violent patterns:

"As your people would say 'an eye for an eye and a tooth for a tooth'", It now cackled a shrill, crazy sound. The very tone and timbre of it sending a chill up her very spine, Frances raised again… quick this time… the U.V. rifle clutched in angry hands:

"Wellll… in that case I'd say our little conversation here has come to an end", she took aim once more at the creature/boy in front of her, lining It/him up in her sights.

"So who are the monsters now?", the Emerog inside that little boy snapped, contemptuous: "At least **WE** never murdered ***your*** entire race!!"

"I refuse to either lower, or demean myself discussing morality with the likes of you!" Frances countered, disdainful.

"So that's it?!", that demonic entity she addressed raged on: "You killed all my kind and now you're here to finish that job you began??"

"Exactly!!", she pronounced sentence on the very last of Its kind, her steady voice devoid of all pity, all compassion whatsoever.

Squinting now through her U.V. rifle's tapered scope she took careful aim, squeezing with deliberate ease the touch-sensitive trigger pressed up against her steady finger. Looking through her clear titanium visor at those cold, hard obsidian eyes burning with justice outraged, realizing at long last Frances was in deadly earnest, the foul thing inside poor Rodney threw his head back at a quite unnatural angle.

Almost snapping in Its awesome rage the poor boy's neck, It streamed upwards out of both the little boys nose and wide-open mouth like so much bilious green smoke. Bellowing as It departed like some mad bull It formed Itself once more into a sickly green orb, a glowing sphere just above Rodney's very head.

"Just like flushing quail", Frances muttered now under her breath. An evil grimace plastered on her thin, pale lips she watched that dispossessed entity soar away with all-due haste.

Unsure at first if her bluff would work, unsure at all she could reach It inside the safe confines of Its Human thrall, she nevertheless hoped that wicked life-force now flying away didn't know where Its safety lay. Abandoning It's safe-haven It didn't realize that, when It hid indoors from StarChild's attack, Rodney's body provided It almost as much shelter as the ruins in which it hid.

Choosing instead to flee that scene of utter defeat it left Itself no future at all. Swift but not swift enough Frances tracked Its heaven-bound flight path with unerring precision, catching the frantic Emerog dead center. The lifeless matter making up that now dead entity falling into the pit below like so much pale, green talc the energy left behind likewise vanished once and for all into utter oblivion, fading away in the air above:

"So much for the last Emerog" she sniffed, scornful. Discarding at last the weapon she held between clenched fingers, Frances switched now her attention to the small boy crumpled up before her on bended knee.

Head hung low, face touching almost the very ground beneath him, she could hear him weeping soft and low.

"Come, now, Rodney", she smiled, gentle, approaching him where he remained kneeling: "It's time now to be going".

"What's the point?" he muttered, mumbling: "There's no place to go".

"Of course there is", Frances assured him, her smile now uncertain: "We'll go back now to StarChild and, after that, back to Earth".

"No we won't", Rodney moaned through tears now running down his cheeks.

"Why not?"

"I didn't want to!" he began to wail, inconsolable: "It made me do it!!"

"Do what??" Frances felt all of a sudden a certain stab of worry, a knot forming in the pit of her stomach.

"Made me make that computer over there send all that energy back into the middle of the planet where it comes from", the young laddie groaned in obvious despair, pointing now at the blue/green power matrix off to their right:

"Make the planet blow up real soon... I don't know when... and take your ship with it just like a big bomb—BOOM!!!"

That very last word, "boom", exploded from between his lips. His arms likewise flying out to either side of him it was a childish, yet fair illustration of some major cataclysm well on its way. Rodney's meaning both loud and clear despite his limited vocabulary, it was an explosive power Frances could only imagine—some sort of chain reaction employing like before some colossal, highly charged energy feedback overload.

Only now, instead of employing some ruined spacecraft set on self-destruct in order to take them out, the Emerog were now willing to throw at them an entire planet programmed as it were for Armageddon—their final, lunatic gesture of ultimate defiance!

"Come, Rodney", Frances held out to him her hand, her voice taking on now a more urgent tone: "It's time we get going".

"Why bother?" he breathed a despondent little sigh: "We got no hope. They always win in the end".

"NO-THEY-DON'T!!!" she snapped, hands on hips, both angry and even frustrated at this rather unexpected turn. Gazing down at the thoroughly demoralized child still kneeling before her, the almost animal vehemence appearing at once in her sharp, strident voice elicited at long last a definite response other than self-pity.

Staring up at her both wide-eyed, even confused, never had Frances seen someone look so forlorn, so incredibly lost, as this young child now so helpless before her... head hung low:

"Now you listen to me, young laddie", she continued; angry, stern: "I realize you've been to Hell and back several times over, but we risked our very lives coming back here just for you. And as far as hope is concerned there's always hope for the future.

"But at the very same time you have to take a positive stand when that chance for a better life comes along, do your part. You can't just sit around on your sorry little butt, moaning your life away, expecting things to get better by giving up. Now come with me if you want to live!!"

One could tell from his very expression, the very look in his eyes, young

Rodney wanted nothing more in life than to reach out. Wanting to grab hold of that hand she now offered him, live in a brand-new world where hope was at least possible, he found himself nevertheless unable to do so.

So thoroughly broken by those who made most all of his young life so very miserable, the last thing Rodney could do anymore was hope, giving up at long last even though so close to the finish line. And of all those watching this sad spectacle of spiritual degradation, emotional defeat, the most affected was none other than Lt. Gloria Greensley.

The closest to tears, her overwhelming sense of both great pity and deep sorrow commingled as well now with a keen sense of absolute shame, a profound sense of personal regret. Only now, after bemoaning all the hardships she endured growing up, the way she was treated so rough… rebuffed by others… did she come face-to-face with someone else in life who suffered much worse than she could ever imagine.

Ashamed of all the bellyaching she'd done over the years, wallowing in her own special brand of self-pity, never did she endure such overwhelming circumstance it left her so barren inside she'd rather die. Never in her own short life did she ever come close to all this poor boy suffered, choosing certain death over salvation itself.

Looking down at him from her superior position young Gloria came right then so very close to weeping anew both for him as well as her own stupid waste, the time she spent so very blind to all those many good things in life.

"All right! Fine", Frances addressed that little boy still on his knees, intruding as well on Gloria's inner torment with a firm, no-nonsense voice commanding absolute attention: "If that's the way it has to be, so be it!!"

No less moved by the tragic state in which young Rodney now found himself, no less moved to the very core by his broken psyche dehumanized for so very long, Frances found herself likewise too pressed for time to try coaxing him along any further.

Precious moments ticking away, choosing instead a more direct approach more in keeping with her own way of doing things, Frances grabbed him under his arms. Leaning over, grabbing him on either side, she lifted him high above the ground upon which he sat, the young laddie now held between strong hands making no protest either physical or verbal.

Hanging there instead like some limp, lifeless little ragdoll forgotten for so long, chin resting on his chest, his continued breathing was literally the only sign of life.

"Here my good Doctor", Frances offered up now her 'precious cargo' to Dr. Wei-Chang: "You have a new charge".

"Thank you, Lt. Cmdr.", she accepted. Gathering up Rodney in her own arms as though holding a newborn she herself just delivered, she arranged him with tender-loving-care over her armor-plated shoulder.

"Good", Frances added with a mighty huff: "Now that that's taken care of let's get off this freakin', gull-darn planet once-and-for-all!!"

"Excuse me, Ma'am", it was now Gloria's turn to be heard, "but I believe we have yet *another* problem".

Nor did it take long for her to explain, pointing as she did the way they came before. Looking behind them in the direction Gloria indicated, Frances saw as well a group of unexpected visitors crowd their way through the chamber entrance in back of them:

Visitors as unwanted as they were unanticipated!

Chapter 67

"GLORIA'S GRENADE"

Blocking from side-to-side their only apparent escape, the way into that spacious chamber in which they now found themselves trapped, Frances Straker and the rest of her boxed-in rescue party faced now a grotesque number of lumbering mechanoids advancing upon one-and-all…

A solid wall of walking metal making its way towards them, slow but sure.

"But how?", Frances hissed, furious, grinding her teeth: "There's no one left here to inhabit them!"

"All I can assume is that they've been controlled now by Emerog for so long… each and every one of them… their original core program has been so corrupted by Emerog influence they now act like Emerog even when left to their own devices", Gloria offered by way of explanation, ending with a nervous smile: "No pun intended".

"I'm getting sick and tired of androids!" Frances ripped loose with a throaty growl, a menacing expression coming to light in her dark, fiery eyes.

Wasting no time at all she thrust forward her right arm, firing at the approaching hoard a barrage of laser-fire. Gloria and the five other security women present following suit the intricate weaponry built into their smart-armor gauntlets likewise emitted lethal beams, rivers of hot blue light cutting down some of the mindless enemy ahead.

Although taking out a few of that approaching mass, a synthetic army composed now of nothing but dark automatons void of all reason, it was nevertheless too few to really count. One of those injured 'droid's, ripped to pieces above its broad shoulders, still marched towards them, nothing left now of its massive head but a few wires sticking up from inside its tank-like torso.

"*REALLY* sick and tired", Frances roared, fanning now that mounting rage burning inside her. Possessed now by an ever-increasing need to vent her inner contempt in more physical terms she marched up to that headless specter still in the lead. Executing that same flawless martial-arts maneuver she taught Gloria the week before, spinning about to face her relentless foe sideways, she delivered it a powerful kick.

Her right leg thrust out likewise to the right, her booted foot connected with that headless giant right above its helpless groin. The sheer force of her attack propelling it backwards, it spiraled back into the rest with a sharp, metallic clank—none of those other metal behemoths following close behind possessing either the speed, or agility to get out its way.

Tumbling instead backwards to the ground below like a set of pins struck by a bowling ball they fell on their broad, flat backs with a most resounding crash and clatter like metal thunder ripping loose, filling the very air all about them.

Ineffectual, rolling both around and about in vain hope of getting once more to their feet, they made now quite easy prey. Their solid bulks ripped apart with swift dispatch, Frances took out now her considerable frustration on each and every one.

The brief sense of immediate gratification she enjoyed not lasting long however it was now her turn to retreat, more of them approaching in the wake of their fallen comrades. Regrouping with the rest of her team Frances fired now at this new battalion with even greater fury.

"Always outnumbered, always outgunned", she observed more to herself than the rest. Ordering everyone there to withdraw further back into the chamber behind them, aware she could take down those monsters closing in on them if only given the time, that's what bothered her most—the time it would take to clear a safe path through that approaching wall of metal giants.

Having no clue how long any of them had before Bandros decided at last to 'blow its top', Frances hoped to be as far away as Humanly possible before it did.

****

From the outer wall and its endless row upon row of computer technology to the guardrail encircling the pit itself the mechanoids marching toward them formed an impenetrable blockade, Frances racking her brain for a quick answer when remembering something she'd almost forgotten.

If this tower was as identical to the one on Zelmorl as it appeared to be then this chamber should likewise possess at least two other exits. It was something that took a moment to recall given her previous desire to completely forget those sentry robots back on Zelmorl, what they did to the late Ensign Wilson.

Wishing to forget that scene where her fallen subordinate lost her very life, Frances almost forgot as well those other two mechanoids made their dramatic arrival back on Zelmorl through two additional gateways on either side of that other chamber now so far away.

Therefore, all things being equal, maybe...

Turning about, performing a quick 'about-face', her suspicions were confirmed, able to see in the distance yet another exit way. There it was, another opening a quarter of the way around that circular chamber from which they needed to retreat.

YES!!!

However, instead of pleasure, Frances felt right away a renewed surge of animal rage, boxed in now between two battalions of those mindless yet menacing entities. Another battalion of zombie-like automatons coming straight for them, there was little hope at all of making good their escape before that lousy little moon-world decided to likewise split asunder.

Nor was there any way to inform StarChild what was likewise in store for them if they also remained in the immediate vicinity—Frances swearing out-loud, a fit of pique, over their worsening situation.

Hearing this Gloria likewise spun about, hearing as well the tech-scanner hanging over her shoulder slap against those bright, white scales comprising her smart-armor uniform. Emitting as it did a dull clank of hard metal-against-metal, feeling it was getting in her way, she removed it at once from her person. About to toss it into the nearby pit, she nevertheless stopped herself from doing so.

Seeing as well that second army of approaching mechanoids another idea came instead, a wicked grin spreading from ear-to-ear:

Maybe, just maybe …?

But could she …?

Yes!

But was it …?

Oh, to Heck with legalities!!!

"Cmdr. Straker?"

"Yes, Lieutenant?"

"Keep the second group of androids busy. I'll take care of the first!"

Looking about in Gloria's direction the moment she said that, Frances couldn't believe her eyes—the young woman now on her knees getting out her auxiliary tool kit from around her belt, taking as well her scanner in hand.

Watching Gloria begin to take it apart, removing its back, Frances chose at once to trust whatever it was Gloria had in mind, disbelief notwithstanding.

Doing as requested she ordered those security personnel with her to open fire on the second set of new arrivals, commanding them as well to arrange themselves around both Dr. Wei-Chang and the young laddie still in her arms.

Firing at will at the second set of mechanized invaders growing ever closer, Frances couldn't help but sneak a curious peek at whatever it was Gloria was up to. Setting out before her in a calm, orderly fashion the tools she carried with her at all times it were as though she planned a leisurely session of tinkering about.

Nothing leisurely however about the way her fingers danced with agile genius across the inner components of the scanner she now took apart. Appearing on her knees as though oblivious to everything else going on around her a cunning gleam set fire to her brilliant eyes. All Frances could really tell for sure was that Gloria seemed to be in the process of converting her scanning unit into something else altogether; something necessitating a remodification of both the machine's power cells, external sensors, and primary broadcast system:

"Would you mind, Lieutenant, telling me what it is you're up to?" Frances couldn't at last refrain from asking.

"All standard scanners whether portable, or not… medical, engineering, and/or science… utilize the focused deployment of amplified sound-waves bouncing off the item they're programmed to analyze just like the main sensor arrays aboard StarChild", Gloria informed her superior as though that took care of that—thank you oh-so very much—not looking up at all from whatever it was she was doing.

"Once again please, for us simple laywomen who are *not* engineering wiz-kids with I.Q.'s over 200"?

"Well, to put it more simply, I'm making a 'sonic grenade'"".

"Never heard of such a thing": If it ever existed… past or present… Frances Straker would have certainly heard of it, the expert that she was in all manner of military combat both armed as well as hand-to-hand.

"That's because I just invented it", Gloria informed her, sounding quite chipper indeed given their grave situation: "Should have the same general effect as a sonic cannon, but with a shorter-range set on a more general dispersal pattern".

"So when will it be ready?"

"*Right now!*", Gloria wasted no more time, a triumphant proclamation.

Crouching forward, creation in hand, she tossed it underhand like a discus low to the ground. Sliding across the chamber floor with an angry little squeal, coming to a full stop right in the direct path of that first army of mindless mechanoids, the wee sonic device let loose right after that with a high-pitched whistle.

Almost beyond the range of Human detection Frances was certain she felt something go straight through her head, the overall effect it had on their mindless enemy even more dramatic. Freezing in their tracks as though stunned beyond all belief, their dark grey bodies began to shiver as though chilled to the very bone.

Their shivers turning soon after that into violent quakes, their insectoid faceplates disintegrated as well into nothing but so many tiny shards of jagged metal. One could see now the countless wires and other such intricate circuitry making up each and every synthetic entity.

Each enduring now its own gross version of some grand mall seizure what remained of the rest of their outer shells went the same way, their metal torso's and bulky extremities shattering also all outward. No longer possessing the sturdy support of any sort of outer chassis whatsoever all those many internal components exposed, naked, and utterly defenseless toppled at once to the ground below.

And also a twisted lump of smoking, smoldering wires and sparking circuit boards Gloria's grenade exploded as well with a loud pop nary a second later.

"Good work, Lt. Greensley", Frances expressed at once her sincere, heartfelt gratitude:

"Very good indeed!", she added, wasting as well no time ordering the rest of her party to retreat.

Fleeing at once that second company of approaching automatons almost right on top of them, making good their final escape, Frances had to confess a certain sense of twisted pleasure hearing the 'crispy crunch' of what remained of those first mechanoids beneath her heavy, white, armor-plated boots.

Chapter 68

"... THE LAST WORD ..."

Drumming impatient fingers against the armrest of her imperious command chair Jenniboni waited, anxious for the return of Lt. Cmdr. Straker's rescue shuttle.

Contacting Jenniboni after leaving Bandros with the truly good news of both Rodney's safe retrieval and the death of the very last Emerog, Frances also told her how that atrocious moon-world was nothing less now than some ticking time-bomb ready to exit all reality in some fiery swansong.

Ready to take StarChild with it the worst part was not even knowing when that unstable mass might go up at last in an absolute blaze of unholy glory, its short fuse smoldering away, both planet and nearby starship torn apart beyond all recognition.

Reduced now to a nerve-wracking cycle of anxious waiting... tense, worried, growing more and more impatient... Jenniboni stared with a quite stony expression at StarChild's main viewer before her.

Hoping to catch sight of that returning shuttle now on its way, unable to leave until both it and crew were all back aboard safe-and-sound, she hated with a purple passion feeling so ineffectual—so incredibly helpless—unable until then to give the blessed command to 'get the sanguinary heck outta here'.

Bad news after bad, fueling further her already burning rage, it was then Stasha's turn to likewise inform her Bandros was starting to show already signs of its impending demise.

Having just conducted a most thorough scan of that cursed moon-world just hovering there in plain sight, her X.O. added its innermost core was already showing definite signs of some sort of increased energy—a massive buildup of excess energy akin to a nuclear reactor approaching now critical mass.

Occupying now most of StarChild's main viewer, almost taunting her with its gentle turquoise surface looking so peaceful and serene, her frustration increased when hearing from Naomi all sub-light engines were running now at only sixty percent maximum efficiency, experiencing unstable energy fluctuations.

Contacting Jenniboni from Engineering Naomi's list continued: power for aft shields up now to ninety percent, power for the rest however at just forty to fifty percent of peak efficiency.

Listening to her Chief Engineer express grave doubt concerning StarChild's now battered shields, Jenniboni hated even further not being able to do anything more than just stare at that blue-green moon set against both the double-backdrop of deep space and that angry red/orange planet it orbited.

Could they withstand the calamity awaiting them should Bandros self-destruct before able to open yet again another hyper-rift?

Needing however to put enough meaningful distance between both them and Bandros before doing so, Naomi wasn't too hopeful concerning their meager chance of escaping Emerog vengeance. Or at least not long enough to make good any escape into that other reality beyond normal space.

This little news flash helping likewise to worsen Jenniboni's already foul mood she did at least find some small comfort seeing the shuttle from Bandros pass overhead, trepidation eased at least somewhat by a new sense of relief.

Free at last to leap into full swing, taking charge at once of the situation brewing all about her, she leapt into action like a coiled spring finding release. Ordering first all hangar bay doors closed once the shuttle was safely aboard ship, she followed that with the immediate command to get the heck out of there.

Removing themselves from the immediate vicinity as quick as possible she could feel a sudden vibration reverberate throughout the entire bridge, reaching her through the heavy command chair she sat in. Able to detect as well a lingering trace of their previous sluggishness, their reluctant sub-light engines appearing rather hesitant, at least they behaved a wee bit better than before.

StarChild no longer shaking like a cold Chihuahua she all-the-same found herself biting her tongue, reigning in her sudden desire to scream 'Come on darn it, get a move on!!'. Her poor battered ship seeming to hobble away from where he'd been so grievously injured, it was a sensation not unlike some slow-motion nightmare where, no matter how fast you run, you can never escape that nocturnal phantom out to take your very life:

No significant distance put between either you, or that monster in hot pursuit Jenniboni found herself begging like before her sadly done starship to 'shake his booty' and get on with it.

Distracted soon enough however by the rather intrusive sound of those ag-pod doors opening in back of her Jenniboni was met almost straightaway by Frances Straker, the new arrival removing first her helmet before pausing just a brief moment at Jenniboni's side:

"Yes, Lt. Cmdr.?"

"Just wanted to inform you, Ma'am, that young Master Roderick is back both safe and sound in Sickbay. Dr. Wei-Chang is giving him at this moment a most thorough examination. So far she sees no evidence of any U.V. poisoning, whatsoever".

"Very good, Ms. Straker: Well done".

"Thank you, Ma'am", Frances accepted her commanding officer's sincere congratulations. Replacing right after that Lt. Baynes at her Security post on StarChild's rather tense bridge, nearly all of Jenniboni's command staff were now present and accounted for.

Nor did it escape Jenniboni's keen notice Frances hadn't removed the rest of her smart armor. Taking her rightful place off to Jenniboni's forward left it's almost luminous white scales glistened under the lights above. Added protection that struck Jenniboni right about then a wise precaution, wishing for the briefest moment she thought of that very same thing.

Just as quick to rebuke herself though for such clear pessimism in the face of overwhelming danger, she corrected herself harshly for not having greater faith in their all-the-same slim chances:

"Helm; how long before we reach a safe minimum distance at which to open a portal to UltraSpace?".

"Fifteen minutes, Ma'am, at current speed".

"Good. In that case…."

"Commodore; I think you should see this", Stasha cut in.

Interrupting Jenniboni mid-sentence she punched up on the main viewer before her a clear image of that perilous moon-world now in back of them. Not quite sure at first what to look for, peering through squinting eyes, it became apparent soon enough.

A vicious red "scar" flashing all of a sudden across Bandros' very surface it was a rough, diagonal rip running along an entire fifth of that moon-world's very surface.

No: Strike that!

Not a scar, but a gaping wound.

The incredible rise in the growing internal temperature causing a steady increase in pressure from within, pushing outward against Bandros' outer crust, both mantle and outer surface approached now that final, explosive moment before violent release.

Watching in horror along with the rest of her senior staff Jenniboni could see yet more cracks begin as well, magma spewing up from one such canyon stretching around the edge of that planetary disk now in back of them—a bright, molten orange/red geyser shooting upwards well over a hundred miles, reaching far above into its very upper atmosphere.

A mind-numbing sight conjuring images of some severed artery gushing alien blood this was no less than the hot, boiling life-force of an entire world going now through its own, very unique death-throws.

Both StarChild and his crew watching from their perilous viewpoint an already cursed celestial entity doomed now to some painful, tortured end what worried Jenniboni most was the sad lack of any significant distance they seemed to be putting between both themselves and that terminal moon-world about ready to "blow its top".

Growing smaller on the screen before her it was nevertheless not far enough away to suit her own, particular needs—poisonous gasses from its very interior turning it soon a murky, noxious, charcoal grey.

Unaware how anxious she really was she realized soon enough when hearing right about then the sudden 'click-click-clicking' sound coming from the very surface of her right armrest—the clear, sharp, rat-a-tat-tat sound of fingernails against metal putting Jenniboni to utter shame the very same moment she realized what it was:

"Helm!! How long before we can open that hyper-portal??" Jenniboni demanded, abrupt. Clenching tight both fists she drew actual blood.

"Now, Ma'am".

"Excellent!!", she felt like laughing, uproarious: "Put viewer on fore-aft split-screen and activate Ultra-drive".

Anticipation mounting, counting the very seconds one-by-one, she watched with bated breath the main viewer divide into two separate, but equal sides—the star-studded expanse of deep space to the left, the frightful visage of Bandros approaching critical mass to the right.

Having by now turned a grayish-black... toxic clouds glowing here and there a dull, angry red... that once-beautiful moon-world was now quite ugly indeed. Heaven or Hell only knew what fiery landscape of utter damnation existed now on that suffering sphere dying in back of her retreating starship.

Be that as it may however intense joy was also to be had, watching ahead of StarChild that familiar lightning bolt flash at once into glorious being, appearing as it did off their port bow. Thoughts of home and hearth came at once to mind at mere sight of that blessed gateway starting to form, their passport to that alternate reality known also as 'UltraSpace'.

Feelings of blessed relief that were yet again squelched, banished instead by a sudden rush of crushing defeat, a wall of absolute despair watching that very same portal home vanish as quickly as it appeared.

Everyone present stunned... mortified... staring in absolute disbelief, it was then Jenniboni heard as well a loud, nearby pop and sizzle—disbelief turning into a sudden, definite sense of moral outrage.

Feeling cheated... outright... by such outrageous misfortune Jenniboni felt her ship come as well to a complete stop, dead in his tracks, soon after that sudden pop and sizzle of something technical:

"What happened?", she all but yelled; addressing in a sharp, angry voice the young helmswoman in back of her. Swinging about in her agile command chair to face that other bridge officer in question, noting as well hazy tendrils of light grey smoke drifting up from Helm control, the smell of burnt wiring was likewise unmistakable—a cloying, acrid stench stinging as well her nasal passages.

Serving at helm this time around was a young ensign, Ms. Jayne Fielding, who seemed not to hear her Commanding Officer. Staring instead with utter dismay at her damaged control panel, stunned by this sudden reversal of once-good fortune, it was a few seconds before she ventured any sort of reply:

"Some kind of power surge, or reverse-energy flow just took out my entire board!", she answered at last Jenniboni's harsh demand for further information.

Turning back yet again to the main viewer before her Jenniboni received soon after an even more detailed analysis of their current situation, Naomi contacting her almost straight away from Engineering:

"It was those power fluctuations I told you about. When we engaged all the Ultra-drive engines all at once they were hit by a massive energy buildup, overloading each and every power coupling: Both sub-light and Ultra-drive engines are now inoperative, connector relays all off-line".

Jenniboni's tone of voice hearing this reflected the same note of disgust present in Naomi's, giving her following reply through clenched teeth:

"Understood, Ms. Marlowe. In that case forget sub-light. Concentrate instead on all UltraDrive systems. Get them back on-line at once".

"Yes, Ma'am: Ms. Greensley's right on top of it right now as we speak. She'll be contacting you as soon as possible with a complete up-date on all work in progress".

Naomi's reassurances now falling on deaf ears Jenniboni's complete, undivided attention was focused instead on the rather spectacular sight of Bandros flying apart in its own sudden release of pent-up energy. Watching it fly apart in every which direction, her heart now lodged firmly in her throat, innumerable pieces of that former moon hurdled now towards them.

Propelled every which way in a wide assortment of both shapes and sizes—some the size of mere pebbles, some the size of large asteroids—it seemed a good portion of that former moon-world was headed likewise their way, solid matter mixed together with burning magma from its very core.

"By the way Ms. Marlowe; I recommend you also get each and every available shield fully operational, back on-line, as soon as possible."

All things considered Jenniboni did an amazing job keeping her tone quite casual; sounding quite calm, cool and collected given their current situation:

"Consider that an order Ms. Marlowe".

****

Arriving in Engineering as soon as she returned to StarChild Gloria, like Frances before her, bothered not removing her smart-armor attire, leaving even her heavy-duty helmet firmly in place. Nor was it long after getting there Naomi grabbed hold of her, instructing her to inspect all those relay systems and power couplings for both sub-light and Ultra-drive engines.

Although the 'Systems Analysis Board' in Engineering told Naomi all was in perfect working order she wanted visual confirmation nevertheless. What with all those recent energy fluctuations running throughout every part of StarChild his persnickety Chief Engineer didn't completely trust the readings she monitored on her S.A.B.'s colourful display panel.

Doing as ordered Gloria scurried along down the long, narrow corridor connecting both "Main Engineering" with that smaller chamber devoted exclusively to ship's propulsion, met soon enough at the other end by three other crewwomen also monitoring similar S.A.B.'s.

Ignoring however each and every one, leaving all three to each their assigned duties, she made instead her way across the room ahead to a small access hatch embedded in the far wall. Behind it was a narrow maintenance tube, a cramped passage just wide enough for one, single woman pulling herself along its narrow confines.

Doing so on her back, employing a series of hand grips embedded right above her, the weight of her heavy armor posed no problem once inside. Having to bend over backwards to gain entry Gloria was sure for a brief moment climbing in she'd fall flat on her back but, luckily for her, that wasn't the case.

Each and every maintenance shaft replete with its very own rolling platform Gloria surveyed with keen eye each and every relay circuit, each and every conduit, each and every power coupling running throughout the entire crawl-way all about her—locating at the very same time no sign whatsoever of any mechanical error, or malfunction currently in progress.

Sure all was running smooth as clockwork, everything in perfect operating order measuring up to her own, exacting standards of excellence it was then—and only then—she breathed a sigh of utter relief, rolling herself back to where she began after checking the very last energy conduit visible.

Nor was it long after extracting herself from inside the tube now behind her, steady once more on her own two feet, Gloria heard one of those three young tech officers from before relay from across the way direct orders from StarChild's distant bridge:

"Engage all Ultra-drive Engines!!"

"No problem", Gloria assured all three women also present with a confident smile: "Everything is in perfect working order. I can foresee no…"

"*Energy surge coming down the line*!!!", the same tech officer from before cut in, her voice full of loud alarm: "*We have a power spike headed straight our…*"

Interrupted however before she could finish, a muffled explosion traveled down that very same work-shaft from which Gloria just came; thick, white smoke billowing as well all around her, drifting up between Gloria's legs from that open hatch in back of her.

"*Sanguinary darn feakin' heck*!!!!", she ripped loose with a mighty stream of angry cuss words, her passionate swearing cut-off even so by the low, grumble/rumble sound of a nearby emergency containment seal rolling into firm place.

"*Get outta here*!!", Gloria ordered right then all three junior officers still gathered about, the small room all around them in the process of immediate quarantine—an automatic safety measure protecting the rest of Engineering from the quite lethal fumes now filling the entire area.

"But what about you, Ma'am??", the nearest to her asked, concern for Gloria written all over her worried face.

"I'll be fine enough in this suit", she promised, their only way out almost halfway blocked: "It has ample air filtration units. Now get out of here and tell Lt. Cmdr. Marlowe I'll affect immediate repairs from here and keep Commodore Saphira updated on my progress myself: GO!!"

For one heart-pounding moment Gloria feared they might not make it out before the quarantine barrier was firmly in place, one of her underlings still hesitant to leave with the others.

However, instead of trying to coax her along with mere words alone, Gloria took a more direct approach. Rushing forward towards to the reluctant N.C.O. she shoved her with both hands out the narrow way still left, the other woman barely making it through the shrinking exit.

Once taking care of that she turned her attention back to other, more pressing matters. All alone in the sealed-off chamber she ordered Maccs to alleviate the obstruction to her vision, unable to see through all that poisonous, smoke-laden air. Maybe he could filter out at least some of the deadly toxins surrounding her, the air around her already a little bit less murky once having asked.

Not so thick with such viscous fumes, she could at least see some of what she was doing by the time she found again the small crawlway hatch from before. Not taking long to discover the object of her frantic search once back inside that cramped service tube scorched, melted, and blown circuitry fried beyond recognition stood out like a sore thumb halfway down the narrow passage.

"Maccs, link the comm. unit in my helmet into Commodore Saphira's command console. Priority: Alpha-One!"

"Yes, Ma'am", came his dutiful reply, Jenniboni's sharp-edged voice requesting soon enough a complete, thorough report:

"Power-couplings to both sub-light and Ultra-drive systems have all been shorted out", Gloria wasted no time; her voice remaining quite calm, cool, and collected: "And since I didn't have time to bring with me replacement parts before containment seals were activated I'll need to effect all major repairs right here, cannibalizing what I can from one drive system to repair the other.

"Therefore, with your permission Ma'am, I suggest I concentrate all my efforts on the damaged components for Ultra-drive".

"Permission granted, Lieutenant. Keep me posted on your continued progress. I'll leave this comm. channel open".

Performing with lightning proficiency a complete diagnostic on all the technical hardware requiring her immediate attention, lying on her back, Gloria positioned as well her tool-kit atop of her armor-plated bosom.

Doing so in such a way its contents were easy enough to find when needed she removed right after that both good wires and ample circuitry from the remaining sub-light relays still intact. Carefully removing anything even suspect from them she then installed them straightaway into the Ultra-drive power-couplings.

Eyes darting from left to right from where she took jury-rigged parts to where she replaced damaged ones, glancing as she did back and forth, she bypassed both the ruined relay boards and original power-couplings still to her right. Hurried fingers working with furious precision she realized the need for all-due haste. Even if that darned-to-heck moon-world now behind them hadn't already "blown its lid" she had no doubt it would soon enough.

Working already under strenuous conditions maybe it was better she didn't know what Jenniboni already knew from her superior vantage point on

StarChild's anxious bridge—ignorance indeed bliss—as Gloria went about her own critical business at hand. All things considered, taking great pains not to make any possible mistakes whatsoever, it wouldn't have helped much knowing their situation had already gone from bad to worse.

Affording as much time as she thought she could, her hands still almost a blur in the performance of their assigned duty, she checked and rechecked her work-in-progress for any possible error—no matter how slight—stopping at long last only when she knew she could do no more.

"Commodore, I'm finished", Gloria informed her distant C.O.: "I've done all I can at this end, but there still remain a few problems".

"Problems, Lieutenant?"

"Yes, Ma'am", Gloria explained in patient detail, careful not to leave out any relevant information: "I wasn't able to re-establish automatic control so you'll have to activate the portal ahead by hand. I couldn't re-establish a direct connection between the main power auto-flow relay system, Maccs, and the actual Ultra-drive propulsion units.

"Instead, I had to jury-rig both the power-flow regulation units and the standard Ultra-drive power-couplings through redundant systems built already into helm control".

"Lieutenant???"

"Sorry, Ma'am: What I mean is that you'll have to press down on both the 'Ultra-drive Activation Sequence' pad on the right side of the Helm control panel while, at the very same time, pressing down on the 'Power Flow Relay' pad to the left of the panel.

"And you'll have to keep both hands firmly on each until enough power builds inside the 'Ultra-drive Activation Matrix' to carry us through the Hyper-portal into UltraSpace. Only when safely inside UltraSpace can you release manual pressure! Understood??"

"Yes, Lieutenant: Very good: Excellent work, Ms. Greensley!!"

"Thank you, Ma'am".

****

The beatific smile of sweet relief she wore plastered all over her face did nothing at all to hide Jenniboni's true inner feelings, her utter joy.

Nor in her absolute ecstasy did she really care!!

"Well, Ms. Fielding: You heard our good Ms. Greensley. Time to get out of here".

"Yes, Ma'am", Jayne was happy to oblige, just as cheerful hearing all this as everyone else, sharing right then the same buoyant spirits.

"Ms. Straker, how long until the debris from Bandros reaches our current position?"

"A little under ten minutes, Ma'am", came her immediate reply, a sudden gasp interrupting right then the otherwise merry mood all about them—a shocked intake of tortured breath off to Jenniboni's immediate left, just in back of her stately command post.

526

"What's wrong Ms. Fielding?", she demanded at once, fear stabbing yet again at her deepest heart.

"It's my console", Jayne came back at her in utter dismay, stunned.

Standing now in front of her chair at Helm Control she held her just-burnt hands under her armpits, arms crossed, staring dejectedly at the defective control panel before her:

"It's burning hot! Scalding!! The internal coolant systems must all be off-line, shorted-out during that last power-surge!!"

"NOOOO!!!", Jenniboni roared all her pent-up anger, a wounded lioness enraged: *"THEY WILL NOT HAVE THE LAST WORD HERE!!!"*

Leaping from her majestic perch, rushing for the Helm, she pushed poor Ms. Fielding roughly aside. Shoving her with brute force out of the way when it seemed the frightened Ensign was either unable, or unwilling to move on her own there was no time to consider what she was about to do.

No time at all for second thoughts Jenniboni thrust both hands—palms down—against the very controls Gloria instructed her to just moments ago.

Placing her full weight against the panel now before her, Jenniboni's first inclination was to wonder what the 'sanguinary heck' Jayne was gibbering on about.

"What's she talking about?", she muttered aloud: "It's freezing!!"

Not taking long to find out though, her brain recovering quick enough from the sudden jolt to her entire nervous system, waves of hot agony came crashing down on her like an avalanche of burning coals. Rising from her very hands the searing pain consumed soon enough every fiber of her being, registering now throughout her entire body like some unquenchable fire.

A burning lake welling up from deep inside, eating her up from the inside out, she bit down on her tongue, almost severing it in half. Trying to stifle the tortured scream seeking final release Jenniboni settled instead for a loud groan through clenched teeth.

Keeping her sights focused instead on the main viewer directly ahead, its left-hand side relayed to her tear-filled eyes what lay before them all. Already she could see through her consummate agony the comforting image of yet another white lightning-bolt appearing off their port bow, their safe-passage home beginning to take on both form and substance

Meanwhile the battered remains of ruined Bandros showed up just as clear on the main viewer's split screen image to the right. Rushing in on their stationary position they grew still closer-and-closer yet. The jagged missiles appearing now almost on top of her motionless starship, fiery debris of various shapes and sizes chased him down like some hapless prey caught otherwise in some fiendish trap.

"Just a little more time: That's all I ask", Jenniboni pleaded in earnest prayer, struck right then by a sickly-sweet odor she couldn't for a moment recognize. It wasn't until looking for a brief second down at from where the smell originated, smoke rising from between her own fingers, did she realize what it actually was.

Understanding now that the hellish scent attacking her olfactory senses was the actual smell of her very own flesh roasting alive as if on some hot plate turned on high, she fought like never before to keep her gorge from rising. Doing her very best to keep down her churning stomach, it was all Jenniboni could do to ignore that grievous injury she was doing to her very own body.

Making a concentrated effort to keep her mind focused on other matters instead she focused all her attention on the hyper-portal forming before her.

And in doing so she remained as well quite oblivious to the looks of both horror, and even pity granted her by the rest of her bridge crew. Realizing they couldn't ease any her considerable suffering each and every member of her command staff just stared instead at her tortured face with the same feelings of helpless impotence.

Gazing instead through dimming eyes at the portal ahead taking on its familiar, triangular shape Jenniboni watched its infinite range of rainbow colours cascading all towards them. Filling the entire bridge with their radiant, multi-hued light the frightful image of what lay in back of them likewise disappeared from sight.

Energy from the portal ahead interfering now with the split-screen mode requested what seemed like years ago Jenniboni cared not, having no more desire to watch the Hell chasing them from behind with Heaven now *so very close.*

Even her body felt nothing more now of the injury being done to her tortured hands, the Hell she was going through in order to save all their lives. An overload of incredible pain beyond Human belief it was a complete shutdown of her entire nervous system. A blessing in deep disguise, she even felt a brief moment of relief.

Not lasting long however Jenniboni discovered yet another cause for immediate alarm; starting to feel both dizzy, faint, and even light-headed. Even as the rainbow-hued tendrils forming now at the hyper-portal's every edge made ready to draw them soon into UltraSpace Jenniboni's head tilted back.

Eyes rolling up now in their sockets it was all she could do to cry out; a desperate, strangled scream for help at the very moment she needed it most:

"DON'T LET ME FAAAA…"

Watching along with the rest of StarChild's sickened bridge this gruesome spectacle Frances leapt up at once from her own duty station. Already on her feet as Jenniboni cried out her very first word, she rushed with all due haste over to her side.

Grabbing her by the upper left arm Frances knew already what was unfolding the very moment she saw Jenniboni arch her back, eyes beginning to flutter, taking charge at once of the situation developing:

"Get the sanguinary Heck over here and help me hold her up!!", she snapped right away at nearby Ensign Fielding, the sheer force of her irate voice waking with a jolt the young Helmswoman from her own state of emotional paralysis.

Both women bolstering now their flagging C.O. between them, the sight of Jenniboni's perpetual torment tore at Frances both heart and soul. Driven herself almost to tears she would have quite readily, even cheerfully, traded places: No hesitation whatsoever!!

With those insulated, armor-plated gloves she still wore Frances would have remained quite safe, immune to the same injurious pain and suffering Jenniboni now endured on behalf of her entire ship and crew.

Doing so however she would nullify as well all that Jenniboni already achieved—the removal of her burning flesh from Helm control ending also that vital power-flow needed to activate each and every Ultra-drive system aboard ship.

Were Frances to interfere at this perilous time with all Jenniboni succeeded in doing so far they'd have to start all over again, an option none of them had given the precious little time left now each and every soul aboard ship.

Precious little time indeed!

StarChild now shaken to the very core of his being, the very first bits and pieces of that former moon reached now their stationary position, violent tremors reverberating all throughout every quarter aboard ship. Slamming into their every active port, starboard, and aft force-shield other fragments likewise followed in quick procession, rocking the now fragile vessel back and forth.

Nor was it long after this everyone there could likewise hear as well Naomi's urgent voice. A call from Engineering coming through loud and clear from the comm. unit in Jenniboni's nearby command chair, it was a persistent sound coming from the right armrest of her now-vacant command post:

"Commodore, shields are all down to just thirty percent maximum efficiency. At this rate they won't survive much longer. Aft shields are already beginning to fluctuate, hull breaches on both decks S-10 and S-8.

"Both breaches are now contained but, even if we divert all available power from every other system, shields won't remain intact much longer!"

Receiving of course no answer from StarChild's tortured C.O., Naomi's very tone grew even more insistent each and every time she demanded some sort of reply.

Making her way over to Jenniboni's empty command seat, Stasha acknowledged instead Naomi's impromptu up-date:

"Ms. Marlowe: This is Cmdr. Nikarov. Please be informed Commodore Saphira has indeed received your report."

There was no mistaking the pronounced irritation in both Stasha's voice and very demeanor, sitting now in Jenniboni's chair:

"But as of this very moment the Commodore has more pressing matters on her hands. So please just use your best judgment in the matter: Over and out!"

Grinning in reply when hearing Stasha's unintentional pun, Jenniboni's smile translated however into a quite rictus grimace. Sending a chill throughout anyone unfortunate enough to see it, StarChild's suffering C.O. slipped now both in and out of conscious awareness.

Before passing out for good however Jenniboni watched at last their coming deliverance take hold, brilliant feelers reaching out for them. Rainbow tentacles from the hyper-rift ahead latching on at last to their sorry hull, they drew StarChild once-and-for-all into that other reality just beyond both normal time and space.

"Just like children gathered up in a parent's arms", Jenniboni muttered aloud. Allowing herself the luxury of utter collapse only when sure both ship and crew were truly safe, it was then—and only then—she fell back into the safe embrace of Frances' waiting arms.

EPILOGUE

"TEARS OF JOY"
(Monday, March 4th, 2915AD)

Waking up a full forty-eight hours after her arduous ordeal on StarChild's bridge, finding herself in the same Recovery Ward as little Rodney, Jenniboni found herself in full possession of both a throbbing headache and a complete syntha-skin graft on both hands.

The second courtesy of Dr. Wei-Chang herself they consisted not only of a new epidermal layer but also new flesh and muscle underneath. Her original hands burned all the way to the very bone she left behind charred remains of her former flesh on the very console upon which she held them. Torn away from the rest of her when she fell back her hands were quite literally rebuilt from the inside out, Eartha injecting her with micro-bee's after applying to both Jenniboni's hands their synthetic exterior.

Using both her own cellular structure alongside the more synthetic material added, the tiny macrobiotic "surgeons" still inside her went about their specific program. Repairing Jenniboni's wounded person while she herself slept through the entire process, creating new flesh and muscle to replace the old, no visual evidence remained at all that she ever suffered any injury whatsoever.

Disposing of previous tissue damaged beyond repair they helped adhere even further to the rest of her body the synthetic skin applied before. Doing without question excellent work, the terrible injury done to her was almost healed nearly eleven days later. All that was left to remind her of the experience was a slight tingling sensation in Jenniboni's 'new' palms, something Eartha assured her would disappear after just a few more days.

Thinking such good progress would gain her immediate release from medical confinement however, Jenniboni had another thing coming. Insisting she stay put in the neighbouring bed next to young Rodney himself, one reason cited for Jenniboni's prolonged stay in Recovery was the very micro-bee's responsible for her remarkable progress. Her curmudgeonly C.M.O. the only member of her entire crew who could give Jenniboni orders aboard her very own ship, Eartha insisted they be flushed out thoroughly from within before letting her go.

While feeling somewhat put out by all this the other reason cited for her prolonged stay was a more personal one, one that bristled mightily as far as Jenniboni was concerned. Told it was due to the general shock endured both physically and psychologically during the event which landed her there in the very first place what really wounded Jenniboni's pride was the 'required treatment' her tireless C.M.O. insisted on.

Scheduling regular sessions for Jenniboni with Dr. Janelle Higgins on the basis of the 'emotional stress' she was sure occurred, StarChild's resident psychologist aboard ship treated more often than not both Jenniboni and Rodney at the very same time!

All the same though there was nevertheless one issue on which Jenniboni would neither compromise, nor relent. One on which she insisted having her own way! Having to do with the actual wearing of one of those all-too-revealing hospital gowns issued to everyone in her similar situation, something medical science had still to remedy after almost a thousand years, she refused to parade around her present location leaving nothing to the imagination.

Not that is when sharing accommodations with such a young laddie of Rodney's tender years, compromising both his innocence and modesty, exposing herself without shame before his very eyes! And seeing her point Eartha supplied Jenniboni instead with both a couple of new uniforms alongside two pull-over night-gowns consisting of a soft-yet-thick durable material. Both quite modest and feminine, she'd change from one outfit to another in the adjacent bathroom both she and Master Roderick shared on rotation.

Even so, inconvenience aside, Rodney was in fact the one-and-only good thing about her prolonged stay in Recovery, making it not only bearable but even enjoyable. The two of them making quite excellent roommates, Jenniboni even proved as good for him as he was for her.

Not that she didn't have initial doubts first waking up in the bed next to his, his traumatized condition quite apparent. Rather listless, even zombie-like, after his immediate arrival back on ship it wasn't until a few days after that he began acting more like a normal child. And recovering from his emotional lethargy in record time Jenniboni played a large part in drawing him out of his self-imposed shell, her continued presence and continued encouragement.

Yet while Dr. Higgins remained pleased with how he was doing she still had to confess her young patient had a long way to go before achieving full recovery. Especially after his own prolonged ordeal on that miserable moon-world behind him—a world on which he spent most of his young life both abused and beaten, deprived for so very long of any Human love whatsoever.

Understandably there were times even now during which he'd withdraw into brief bouts of chronic depression even though, during the rest of his waking hours, he proved himself a most entertaining, convivial young laddie quite cheerful, humorous, outgoing, and even highly intelligent by nature.

Much of their time alone spent playing various games Jenniboni discovered in him the one bright spot in an otherwise ponderous confinement, both she and the rest of her crew restricted as well to StarChild. Unable to disembark until further debriefing by S.E.A. higher-ups ever since their return to the Tammyite Matriarchate, both she and young Rodney spent much of their time either playing games, talking, or going together over status reports courtesy of Stasha Nikarov.

Always presented on ei-pad, delivered in person by Stasha herself, these rather routine up-dates seemed to fascinate him almost as much as the very manner of their presentation. Seemingly interested in learning all about that very ship all around him, Jenniboni's 'little playmate' he seemed intrigued as well by the 'teeny-tiny' bio-computer pads on which that information appeared.

Nevertheless Jenniboni still limited his viewing material to general matters only, those shipboard activities deemed unclassified, teaching him most of the time childhood games popular now amongst children his own age—board games often played on a portable table set up between their respective beds, hand-held computer games also on ei-pad, or even word games popular among young people throughout the entire Commonwealth.

Nor was all this learning so one-sided, Rodney teaching her as well a few innocent pastimes still remembered from earlier times-gone-by. Games he still managed to remember playing as well with both his father and mother what seemed like an eternity ago.

"Got any three's?". It was one of these Jenniboni learned now, she and her 'teacher' sitting now across a small card table from one another.

"Go fish", Rodney grinned in impish reply.

"So that's how this game's played", Jenniboni sighed, good-natured, reaching for yet another card atop of the deck between them—both looking up at the sudden interruption of yet another new arrival, each sitting on the edge of their respective beds.

"Have a couple of visitors here to see the both of you", Eartha informed both woman and child, wasting no time, stepping through the Recovery room door.

'Oh, no', Jenniboni groaned inside, her apparent disapproval a direct contrast to the expression of obvious delight plastered all over young Rodney's expectant features.

Starved for so very long of simple Human companionship the young laddie in the bed next to her was eating up quite readily all the attention he could get, Jenniboni at the very same time sick-and-tired of all the many V.I.P.'s passing through—a constant blur of anonymous individuals coming and going since their dramatic return to the Commonwealth just last Friday eve.

Fortunately Admiral Sellers had managed to at least keep away all the many press hounds from within her domain, barring all members whosoever of the "Fourth Estate" from StarChild, the dry dock facility above, and the nearby

'Project StarChild Base' back on Demeter below. Keeping them at bay instead she fobbed them all off with a simple, dry-as-dust, readymade press release composed already for immediate dissemination by the masses.

No doubt a security measure thought up in advance, in anticipation of StarChild's 'sure' return, by both she and the Prime Arch Matri.

God Bless Them!!!

And as far as those other, more official representatives were concerned Jenniboni had to likewise admit her crusty, crabby old C.M.O. was quite adept shooing away, too, any unwanted visitors. No government/S.E.A. V.I.P. proved herself so big, so powerful, or so influential as to intimidate Dr. Eartha Wei-Chang where the welfare of her patients was concerned—turning away one-and-all in no uncertain terms whenever Jenniboni and/or Rodney seemed fatigued in the least by their unwelcome attentions.

"Sure; send them in", Jenniboni granted… reluctant… feeling much better at immediate sight both of Frances and Gloria rather than some well-wishing stranger:

"Well, Gentlewomen", she greeted both with genuine warmth, Eartha scanning her by now for any micro-bee's still in her system: "What can we do for you?"

"Actually, Commodore, we've come across a wee bit of good news for and about our young guest here", Frances was first to speak, nodding with a friendly smile in young Rodney's direction, Rodney staring up at her in wide-eyed curiosity. Silent, suspicious, the young laddie in question found in StarChild's venerable Chief of Security a continuing source of both deep awe and simple bewilderment.

However, as far as Jenniboni herself was concerned, it was the much shorter, younger woman to Frances' immediate right who captured both her increased interest and abiding respect.

Far from giving Lt. Gloria Greensley the original three options Jenniboni feared she might have to at the beginning of their voyage, she planned instead to include in Gloria's personal 'S.E.A. Service File' a glowing report—including an official commendation as Gloria's commanding officer regarding the outstanding manner in which she performed both above-and-beyond the very call of duty itself!

"So what is it ya got fer me?", Rodney asked at long last in that peculiar, ancient way of his, displaying at the very same time that special brand of unbridled enthusiasm reserved for the very young.

"Well, since an on-duty starship is no place for a young laddie of your delicate years, we've all been racking our brains for a more suitable home in which you can live".

Knowing what Frances meant by "…a more suitable home…" Jenniboni also realized that, given young Rodney's special case, being shipped around from one foster home to another just wouldn't do. Not after all he endured both physically and emotionally during his own sad past.

No…

After all he'd been through young Rodney needed most of all a permanent, fixed family environment in which he'd receive both constant love and supervision—somewhere he could heal at last surrounded by caring, supportive people he could both trust and grow close to.

"And I gather from both your smiling faces Gentlewomen you've managed to locate such a lucky situation for our young 'houseguest' here?", Jenniboni questioned both Frances and Gloria at the very same time, looking from one to the other.

"Yes indeed, Ma'am", Frances assured her: "And since it was Lt. Greensley who came up with the solution going through the data she likewise downloaded from the colony ship, I'll let her explain in her own words".

"Well Commodore, as Lt. Cmdr. Straker said I was re-examining the information retrieved from Bandros, from the computer files left behind in Paradise, during our first away mission.

"And in doing so I re-read a series of personal correspondences sent to the colonists aboard their ship during the first couple of years after leaving Earth, including among them a couple of personal communiqués to young Rodney's mother, Raechal Roderick, I missed my first time around".

Turning then her immediate attention from Jenniboni to Rodney Gloria continued, asking young Rodney some rather pointed questions, addressing him in a rather playful voice:

"Is it not true, young Master Roderick, you had a maternal Uncle by the name of 'Mr. Stanley Garfield'— a lorry driver in London, England who had also a young daughter at that time by the name of 'Ms. Tammy E. Garfield'?"

"Yeah, I guess so?", Rodney answered her… slowly… taking his time, unsure where all this was leading:

"I know Mom said I had an uncle in England, a truck driver, and he had a girl older than me called 'Tammy' going to a cemetery to become a preacher".

"Well, young laddie, the term is 'Seminary'; Trinity College, Dublin to be exact", Gloria corrected him with a wee giggle: "And your cousin Tammy ended up much more than just some noteworthy cleric…"

Regaling him right after that with a brief herstory lesson concerning his most illustrious relative, she covered that time from when his people left Earth to the time St. Tammy likewise passed on at the ripe old age of ninety-six.

Listening spellbound to every single word Rodney paid rapt attention to all that Gloria said, Jenniboni likewise impressed hearing of her young roomie's obvious pedigree. And having all the same a faint inkling where all this was headed Jenniboni, like Rodney before her, was nevertheless not so sure, waiting until Gloria finished her brief narrative before asking.

"When Lt. Greensley first learned of young Rodney's family background she thought it might be best in the long run for him to live with actual relatives in order to complete that necessary sense of family", Frances offered further clarification, speaking in Gloria's stead:

"So with that in mind she came to me asking further assistance tracking down Saint Tammy's current descendants, the most suitable candidate of which is a 'Dr. Leslie Garfield' living now in Soupol City.

"What makes her an especially qualified choice is the fact she just so happens to be a child psychologist, her husband likewise a school teacher before they got married. Both even have a young son Rodney's very same age.

"I just got through talking to them on Earth and, once all the necessary 'paperwork' is seen to, they're all looking forward to taking in such a prestigious member of the family. Each and every one of them are looking forward to giving young Master Roderick a warm 'welcome home'".

"Isn't that just wonderful, Honey??", Jenniboni beamed the young laddie sitting opposite her a great big smile, delighted, full of heartfelt encouragement.

"Yeah, I guess so", he mumbled in reply… uncertain… overwhelmed as he was by all the recent changes going on all around him, all the many things happening to him in recent days. Understanding at once what the matter was, the reason for his hesitant behavior, his apparent lack of genuine enthusiasm, Jenniboni spoke to him further in tender tones full of equal compassion:

"Don't fear, Sweetie. I'm sure they'll all love you very much, take very good care of you. And you'll be as well with other children your own age. You'll even have a brand-new brother just your age to show you the ropes, help you get used to being a regular little boy again: A whole new family I'm sure will love you very, very much".

"Yeah, sure, but they won't be my real parents: They're both dead!"

"Maybe so, but I'm sure they'll love you as much as your real parents, care for you just as much. Besides, it's a whole new chance for a whole new life for you: Hope for a better future".

"Yeah; hope", Rodney muttered yet again. Repeating to himself over and over that one word he never allowed himself to truly believe in "…hope…" his voice began at last to hitch, catch in his very throat, tears forming now in the corners of each eye:

Not content to remain there they began trickling as well down newly flushed cheeks, young Rodney crying now quite freely.

"What's wrong??", Gloria exclaimed, both concerned and even confounded by such a reaction. Getting up from the edge of her own bed, sitting next to him on the edge of his, Jenniboni knew very well what 'troubled' the young laddie so.

Putting her arms around him she drew him close. His head resting now on her shoulder, his arms slipped likewise around her:

"Why, Lt. Greensley?" she looked up now at Gloria herself, smiling now a soft, gentle smile: "Have you never seen tears of joy before??"

****

It was later that day, early evening, the crew aboard StarChild was granted at last final release from their shipboard confinement. And deciding to spend the rest of that very same day just relaxing on the Base below Gloria was greeted as well by the concierge; entering the bright, sparkling, crystal/chrome lobby of the very same Base apartment complex she just so happened to live in:

"Ahhh, Lt. Greensley", the elderly receptionist called out from across the wide lobby, cheerful as ever behind his impressive desk: "It's a pleasure indeed to see you safe, back home again! All of us here throughout the Matriarchate have been praying earnestly for your safe return".

"Why, thank you Elliot", she returned his sincere welcome, just as upbeat, just as cheerful: "Great to be back and see you again, of course".

Amazed by the apparent transformation in the young Gentlewoman before him, evident in both her outgoing rejoinder and the care-free, jaunty way she sashayed her way over to the apartment lift units, Elliot had always seen in Gloria a rather quiet, mousey, and even sad sort of person he more-often-than-not felt sorry for:

Even pitied.

Until now that is.

Whatever happened to her during her prolonged absence from Womankind's home System must have been a quite positive experience to bring about such a remarkable change... recovering from his initial surprise just long enough to hastily inform her he had something waiting for her behind his desk.

"What is it?", she approached the pepper-haired man still at his post, about to step into an open lift had he not called her over.

"It came for you 'Special Delivery' several days ago", he explained even further, retrieving it from a secure shelf under his desktop:

"It required an authorized signature, so I signed for it myself. Hope you don't mind, Lieutenant", he added, handing her a medium-sized rectangular package sealed in a protective green/white cover.

"Not at all", Gloria reassured him, smiling, appreciative: "Very kind of you, I must say".

"Thank you, Ma'am".

If Gloria's transformation for the better amazed already the elderly man behind the desk what came next left him truly speechless beyond words, Gloria finding at once the return address listed in an upper-right-hand corner:

"NO!!! Thank you, Elliot", she cried out loud. Ecstatic, her eyes sprung open in absolute delight. Stunned beyond all belief the pepper-haired attendant replete in his crisp, dignified silver/blue server's uniform submitted in meek surprise when the young woman in question—overcome in her obvious joy—lunged across the broad, narrow desk between them, grabbing the older man in a firm embrace.

Left quite helpless in her somewhat powerful grip Elliot offered no resistance when Gloria drew him swiftly closer, bestowing upon him a quite ardent kiss full of exceeding gratitude.

Nor did he know what to say when, finally let go, he watched now the young Lieutenant dash away in a merry scramble for the nearest lift, the clear sensation of her lips pressed to his lingering well after the fact.

****

Tempted as she was to open her surprise package right there on the lift ride all the way up to her private living unit she all-the-same reigned in her curiosity, noticing the word **'FRAGILE'** stamped all over it in large… even threatening… letters, afraid in her trembling excitement she might drop it.

Cursing instead her slow progress to the very floor on which she lived, quite impatient to open that precious parcel secure in both hands, Gloria was out of there like a shot the very moment both elevator doors slid wide open.

Slamming shut the door to her apartment behind her, tossing her standard issue S.E.A. purse across the room, it landed near the very far wall of her living room area. Both abandoned and forgotten in the general direction of her distant sofa, its owner not even looking where it fell, all her attention was focused instead on the new arrival.

Placing with gentle care the green/white insulated container on her dining-room table Gloria was about to retrieve from the nearby kitchen something with which to cut it open, hesitating however in her trepidation least she might damage whatever was inside. Nervous indeed she breathed all-the-same a deep sigh of utter relief, taking note immediately thereafter it was one of those heavy-duty mailers replete with its very own self-opening tab.

Pulling back in eager anticipation on the indicated tab sticking out from the rest, she watched with mounting desire the parcel lid flip wide open. Burrowing inside with frantic fingers through a flurry of thick packing material, little foam pellets flew about every which way.

Unsure at first what it was so carefully sent, wrapped as it was in a heavy piece of lined writing paper, she handled it even so with diligent care. Lifting it ever so gingerly from the box it came in, placing it with careful ease on the hardwood table below, she unwrapped from around it that piece of paper hiding it from full view.

Overcome as she was at the very sight of two exquisitely wrought plaster hands, their golden wedding bands glistening in the artificial light streaming down from above, a sudden gasp of utter delight filled the entire room around her—the gold/white sculpture sitting before her a direct contrast to the dark brown syntha-wood table upon which it now sat.

Unable to believe her very eyes a feeling of utter warmth spread even so throughout her entire being. A sense of unearthly happiness filling her very soul it was then she noticed as well a short, hand-written note on that lined piece of paper she set to the side but seconds ago.

Holding it in now trembling hands… shaky fingers… she read over-and-over again every sweet word until burned in her memory; a brief missive written in an equally neat, precise, masculine hand.

Short, sweet, and to the point it was the most beautiful thing she ever read, her lower lip beginning to quiver, gentle tears glistening now in the corners of each eye:

"My Dearest Gloria.

"As I told you before I could never give
*this to anyone, but someone **I truly** care*
*for: Someone **I truly love** ...*

*"—With **ALL** my love,*

"Frank"

Scrambling soon enough for the V-phone number he'd given her what seemed like an eternity ago it was now Gloria's turn to wipe away from misty eyes tears of joy, calling right away that special new man in her life, the future "Mister Frank Greensley".

****

Several levels above, and a couple of hours later, Jenniboni was no less joyful to likewise be home... home again after what seemed like forever... receiving at long last a clean bill of health from Dr. Wei-Chang. However, unlike Gloria before her, Jenniboni chose not to rush through their front door full of noisy excitement.

Deciding instead to take great care, remaining as quiet as she knew how, Jenniboni was sure Andrei had by that late hour put all three children to bed, himself likewise turning in. Not wanting to disturb any of them during their slumber she planned instead with a mischievous little smile to surprise them in the morning.

At least that was her original intent, noticing right off-the-bat however a major, glaring oddity the very moment she crossed that familiar threshold to their penthouse apartment. The sound of their 3-DV unit blaring away off to the far right Andrei always insisted in no uncertain terms it be kept low when both J.J. and the twins were all asleep, going even so far as to insist both he and Jenniboni use their wireless earbuds when watching it late at night.

There was no way in heck he'd let it remain at such a volume during this time of night, the "boob-cube" as he called it situated right next to J.J.'s private quarters.

Determined to solve this little mystery at once Jenniboni found her answer soon enough in that shrouded corner of the same living/dining room complex, her entire family gathered together on their large sitting room couch. Sound asleep right next to that rather intrusive 'idiot-box' mentioned above she took note as well of a holographic news broadcast, quite ignored by one-and-all, inside its transparent exterior.

Mystery solved a loving smile sprang at once to Jenniboni's full lips, greeted as she was by such a homey little scene of domestic bliss. Turning off that noisome device with the nearby remote control sitting on the coffee table she placed it back down again, just standing there in the new-found quiet gathered now all about her.

Contemplating at first that tender image arrayed before her she gazed down with travel-weary, homesick eyes at those four very special people in her own very special life. Having fallen asleep together, each propped up against the other, little Tammy's weary head rested against young Tommy's slender shoulder, the little four-year-old boy sleeping as well all scrunched-up at his father's side.

Meanwhile Andrei's right arm was draped around both twins at the very same time, his other arm gathering as well young J.J to his side. Her head nestled up against her father's chest, cheek pressed firmly to his side in sweet repose, her legs were likewise tucked up beneath her. Hidden under the hem of a light-yellow nightie there lay as well on her lap a forgotten homework assignment Andrei was no doubt helping her with when they, each and every one of them, fell asleep.

Although the glowing, bright image on the small ei-pad's screen remained from Jenniboni's viewpoint upside-down she could still make out with relative ease a simple math problem both father and daughter were working on, drifting-off mid-lesson. Deriving great pleasure from the tranquil scene before her Jenniboni felt all the same a definite twinge of remorse commingling with her love, the immense affection, already swelling in her very heart.

Gazing down at their restful faces in sweet repose, feeling bad inside she wasn't around more, involved more in their daily lives, she vowed right then and there to remedy that unfortunate situation. Nor could she foresee any great difficulty doing so, keeping in mind Naomi's professional estimate StarChild would require extensive repairs. A massive overhaul to all his major operational systems he'd remain in dry dock for at least two months to come.

No doubt both she and her senior staff in Engineering could manage quite nicely on their own, sending Jenniboni when necessary status reports requiring from time-to-time her personal authorization. Otherwise Jenniboni planned to devote the greater majority of that time to those four individuals asleep now in front of her, the most important people in her entire life, deciding to do so first thing in the morning.

Turning however in the direction of the mistress bedroom in hopes of a good night's rest, planning to surprise one-and-all the very next day with her 'triumphant' return, Jenniboni nonetheless hesitated mid-stride. Catching sight of something else from the corner of her eye, something going unnoticed until that very moment she almost turned away, it never occurred to her until then how Andrei slept.

Chin touching his chest, facial features obscured, it wasn't until that very moment Jenniboni caught out of the corner of her eye a partial view of his actual expression. Drawing even closer, crouching down in front of him, the troubled look etched into every line and feature of her husband's worried face spoke volumes even as he slept of what he surely suffered when awake.

Sad, troubled herself at what she saw there, never before had she seen in Andrei such a tired, weary, and even haggard expression as that which he wore right now. The expression not of a man at peace but a man possessed still by waking demons even in his slumber. It was surely a tortured rest, a haunted sleep, from which one could not escape by the simple act of waking up.

No wonder he never stirred—not once!—since her arrival home, looking more as though he passed out from simple exhaustion, driven to the point where he could no longer continue on his own. Nor did it take Jenniboni long to understand his present condition, aware as she was how he must have suffered; no doubt getting no meaningful, decent sleep since StarChild's return nearly four days ago.

Even now she could see in her poor husband his continual torment, his prolonged agony, unendurable anxiety allowing him no rest; her entire ship and crew kept under a total, absolute, communications blackout all that time…

No escape even in the deepest sleep possible!

Not any longer, though! Enough was enough!! Telling herself right then and there the time had come to free him at last from such emotional bondage, no further delay permissible, Jenniboni stood up straight yet again:

"Well, well, well… a fine welcome home if I do say so myself!!", she announced, hands on hips in a jovial parody of stern disapproval.

****

Cutting through those disturbing images haunting troubled dreams Andrei heard Jenniboni's angelic voice reach out to him like some Heavenly benediction from on high. Believing at first he was still asleep, opening weary eyes, glimpsing her divine countenance was nevertheless preferable by far to other spectral entities bedeviling previous dreams.

Looking up into her eyes full of sweetest love it wasn't until hearing the children calling out to their mother such childish exclamations like "…Mommy, mommy, you're home again…" he realized despite his initial confusion he was actually awake.

All three rushing into their mother's embrace even J.J. forwent her self-imposed reserve, leaping up from Andrei's side, ecstatic. Running as well into her mother's waiting arms she hugged Jenniboni tightly about the waist, wearing on her little-girl face a look of consummate bliss, unbridled joy.

As for their father he found himself reduced though to nothing but watching in helpless uncertainty, his beloved wife lifting in the meantime both twins in her arms. Tommy and Tammy showering her with eager, repetitive kisses on both her cheeks only then did Andrei realize his painful ordeal was at long last over and done with. With a tremendous rush of happy relief flooding his entire being he knew at last his nightmare was over, a tremendous emotional burden Andrei handled until the last few days quite well indeed.

While true he worried for her personal safety all the time she was gone, Andrei acquitted himself even so with flying colours during those first two weeks. Not knowing how she was doing he managed even so to carry on. Never parted from her for such a long time he bore up nonetheless in superb form under the natural strain of her continued absence.

Doing all that time an expert job running the home, keeping their family together, Andrei did an excellent job to the very best of his own considerable abilities. Filling in the void Jenniboni left in their lives all that time the only embarrassing moment came when, during those first three mornings she was away, he caught himself making her breakfast—a force of habit ceasing not long thereafter.

Then there came just last Friday that initial taste of sweetest joy, Jenniboni's starship reappearing in a flash of brilliant, technicolour light right on the edge of Womankind's very own home System. Whooping with delight at the very sight of it coalescing inside their very cube, 3-DV news broadcasts televised StarChild's dramatic return across the entire Tammyite Matriarchate.

An infectious delight to say the least the entire Commonwealth broke out in spontaneous celebration. Commemorating alongside the Saphira family that most auspicious moment in Womankind's recent herstory raucous parties and impromptu rallies broke out on every single planet, inhabited moon and populated asteroid across the entire System.

A mass demonstration of both public support and deepest enthusiasm every single, solitary citizen welcomed home in their own special way, in their deepest heart and soul, Womankind's first starship back now from its bachelor voyage.

For Andrei himself though exceeding joy soon turned to consummate dread, watching as he did S.E.A. tugs drag poor StarChild back to dry-dock. His sub-light engines quite inoperable the sad, weary starship looked as though he passed through all the inner circles of Hell itself rather than some simple jaunt to some other, close-by System.

Battered... beaten... cruelly used!

Nor ending there Andrei's anxiety doubled when the entire ship and crew found themselves sequestered from all the rest of Womankind, no messages from loved ones allowed to pass beyond his metal confines.

Wrapped up nice and tight in an all-pervasive blanket of utter secrecy, the only news smuggled off-ship served to aggravate even moreso Andrei's already frayed nerves—media sources informing the outside System there were indeed one *or* more onboard fatalities; name(s) and identity(ies) withheld from the general populace.

By this time desperate for answers, not knowing if it was Jenniboni herself lying in some cold, sterile morgue Andrei made his way with all due haste to

Melissa Sellers. Storming his way into the Admiral's office, demanding immediate answers, he almost screamed a stream of ugly epitaphs right in her face when she also refused to identify the deceased individual in question.

After all the years they'd known each other how dare she not tell him if the very light of his life lay extinguished now inside some pale, sealed-tight body-bag never to return to either him, or their three children—the woman he loved more than his very own life never to hold him again in her arms, never to love him ever again so long as he lived.

Assuring him she'd tell him all were she not under orders the only thing that kept him from tearing Melissa apart, giving her a good and thorough piece of his mind, was the look of abject misery she also wore. Almost in a state of tears herself seeing him so distraught, Andrei chose in the end not to press with her the matter any further.

Seeing in the Admiral's eyes only the bleakest remorse, pleading as she did for his simple understanding based on their already long association—a friendship shared through their common bond with Jenniboni herself—it was then Andrei just gave up pushing her for more, leaving her office, returning home yet again.

And so it was, keeping up his usual daily routine for the next three days, Andrei suffered in silent anguish. Keeping his inner turmoil hidden for the sake of both J.J. and the twins, only for the children's sake did he even bother keeping up a brave exterior, dying inside over and over again not knowing at all if Jenniboni was even alive.

Carrying on in the face of such unbearable adversity he didn't want to contribute even further to their own increasing sense of utter confusion, the natural fear they were likewise enduring, instinctively aware something was wrong.

Persevering in fact for them alone it was through such single-minded devotion to their specific needs Andrei found at least some small modicum of relief. Rendering comfort to his three small children, easing their own troubled hearts, helped him at the very same time to cope with his own keen sense of increasing trepidation.

So now that Jenniboni was once more safe at home, having come back to all four of them at long, long last all Andrei wanted at that very moment was to run to her with open arms, hold on to her with all his might, never letting go.

However, even after recovering from his initial shock seeing her standing now before him, recovering enough presence of mind to get up from the sitting-room couch upon which he was just sleeping, Andrei was now horrified to find himself rooted instead to that very spot upon which he now stood.

Overwhelmed, trembling from head to toe, unable in budge a single inch towards her, he was shaken to the very core by an intense longing just to hold her once more in wanting arms. Paralyzed in fact by his all-inclusive delight just having her back, desiring no more in life than to feel once more the warmth of her body next to his, never before did Andrei feel so helpless, so lost.

Wearing an expression of utter dismay, looking up at Jenniboni full of silent entreaty, he begged her in mute desperation for some small solution, eyes wide with desperate alarm. Understanding straight away his inner dilemma, recognizing right off the bat what the matter was, Jenniboni disengaged herself with gentle ease from all three children still holding on.

Sympathetic to his inner plight she reached now for her suffering husband, gathering him up at once in her sure, strong arms. Her face now angled down towards his, his ever so slightly towards her, she parted right then full, soft lips, bestowing upon him a tender kiss expressing in its simple beauty all her heartfelt joy returning home, him back at her side.

Resting his head once again upon her shoulder, giving way at last to all those pent-up tears held in check for so very long now, the children likewise watched with reverent eyes all that took place, understanding in their simple, childish wisdom these were tears of joy their father now shed.

Returning as well her ardent embrace with one of his own, slipping his arms around her waist, Andrei took comfort also in her whispered assurance everything was again all right. Brushing with a most tender touch stray hairs from his tear-soaked face Jenniboni gave him as well her undying word she'd always return to his waiting side…

Her most solemn oath offered in the most soothing of voices not unlike a silken caress.

And having everlasting faith in her precious guarantee given with all her heartfelt love it was right then and there, even while he'd truly miss her next time they were parted, Andrei was now sure deep in his innermost heart that, come what may, she'd always find her way back to him again.